THE UNSTOPPABLE WASP

G.I.R.L. POWER

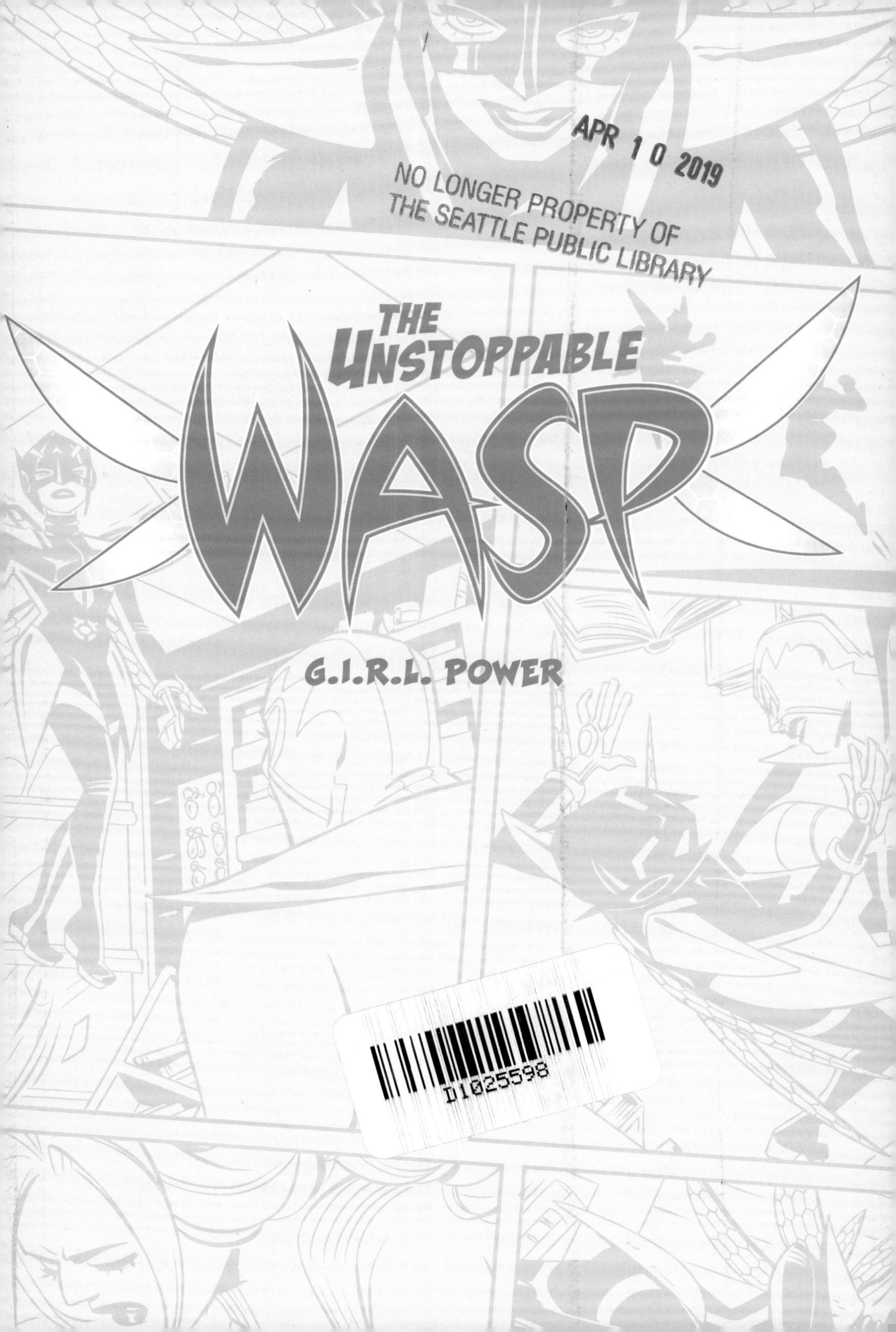

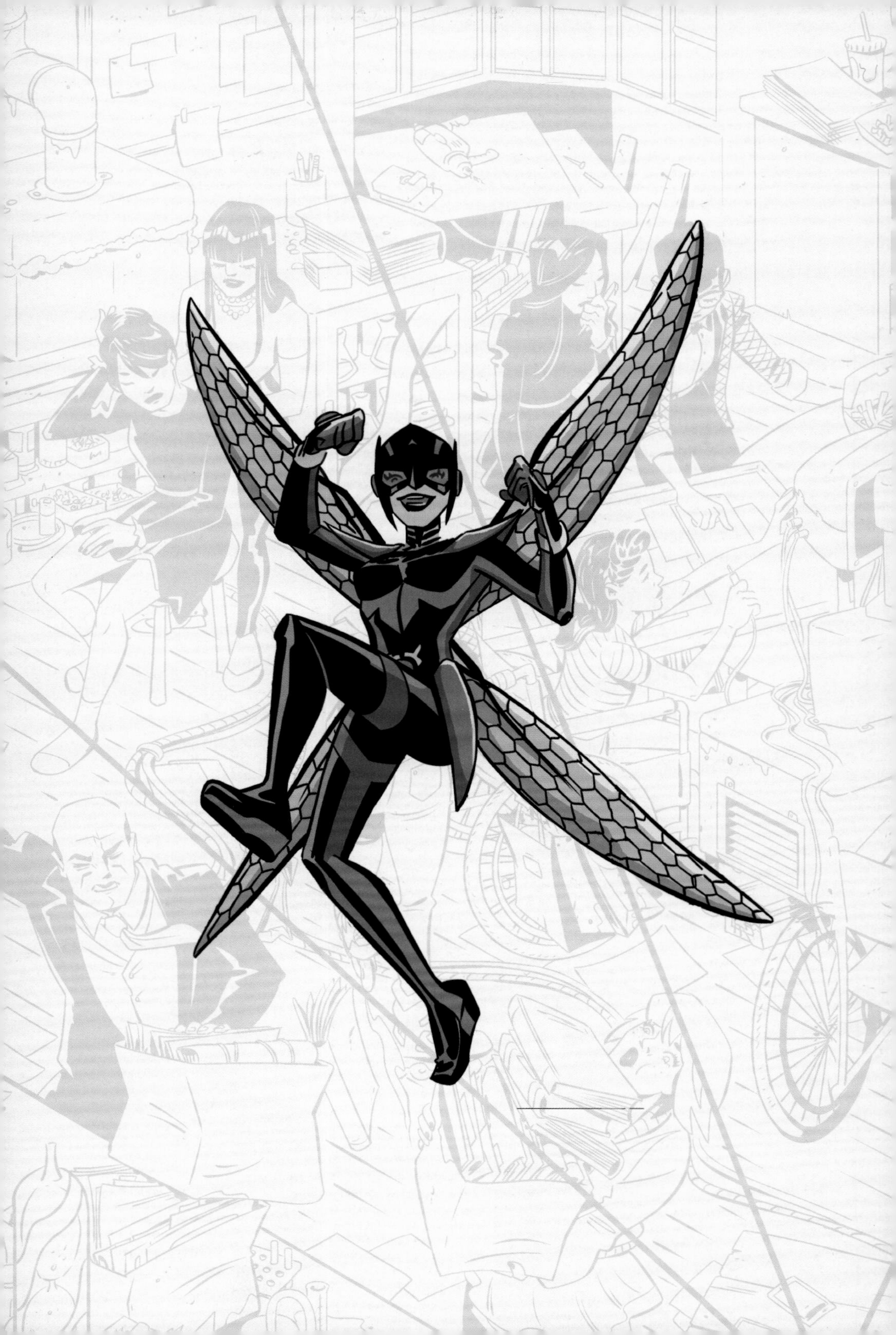

THE UNSTOPPABLE WASP

G.I.R.L. POWER

WRITER
JEREMY WHITLEY

ARTISTS
ELSA CHARRETIER (#1-6), VERONICA FISH (#7)
AND RO STEIN & TED BRANDT (#8)

COLOR ARTIST
MEGAN WILSON

LETTERER
VC's JOE CARAMAGNA

COVER ART
ELSA CHARRETIER & NICOLAS BANNISTER

EDITOR
ALANNA SMITH

EXECUTIVE EDITOR
TOM BREVOORT

SPECIAL THANKS TO
PREETI CHHIBBER, MARK WAID & ALEX ROSS

COLLECTION COVER
ELSA CHARRETIER

WASP CREATED BY STAN LEE, ERNIE HART & JACK KIRBY

collection editor JENNIFER GRÜNWALD
assistant editor CAITLIN O'CONNELL • associate managing editor KATERI WOODY
editor, special projects MARK D. BEAZLEY • vp production & special projects JEFF YOUNGQUIST
svp print, sales & marketing DAVID GABRIEL

editor in chief C.B. CEBULSKI • chief creative officer JOE QUESADA
president DAN BUCKLEY • executive producer ALAN FINE

THE UNSTOPPABLE WASP: G.I.R.L. POWER. Contains material originally published in magazine form as THE UNSTOPPABLE WASP #1-8. First printing 2019. ISBN 978-1-302-91656-5. Published by MARVEL WORLDWIDE, INC., a subsidiary of MARVEL ENTERTAINMENT, LLC. OFFICE OF PUBLICATION: 135 West 50th Street, New York, NY 10020. Copyright © 2019 MARVEL No similarity between any of the names, characters, persons, and/or institutions in this magazine with those of any living or dead person or institution is intended, and any such similarity which may exist is purely coincidental. Printed in Canada. DAN BUCKLEY, President, Marvel Entertainment; JOHN NEE, Publisher; JOE QUESADA, Chief Creative Officer; TOM BREVOORT, SVP of Publishing; DAVID BOGART, SVP of Business Affairs & Operations, Publishing & Partnership; DAVID GABRIEL, SVP of Sales & Marketing, Publishing; JEFF YOUNGQUIST, VP of Production & Special Projects; DAN CARR, Executive Director of Publishing Technology; ALEX MORALES, Director of Publishing Operations; DAN EDINGTON, Managing Editor; SUSAN CRESPI, Production Manager; STAN LEE, Chairman Emeritus. For information regarding advertising in Marvel Comics or on Marvel.com, please contact Vit DeBellis, Custom Solutions & Integrated Advertising Manager, at vdebellis@marvel.com. For Marvel subscription inquiries, please call 888-511-5480. Manufactured between 1/25/2019 and 2/26/2019 by SOLISCO PRINTERS, SCOTT, QC, CANADA.

10 9 8 7 6 5 4 3 2 1

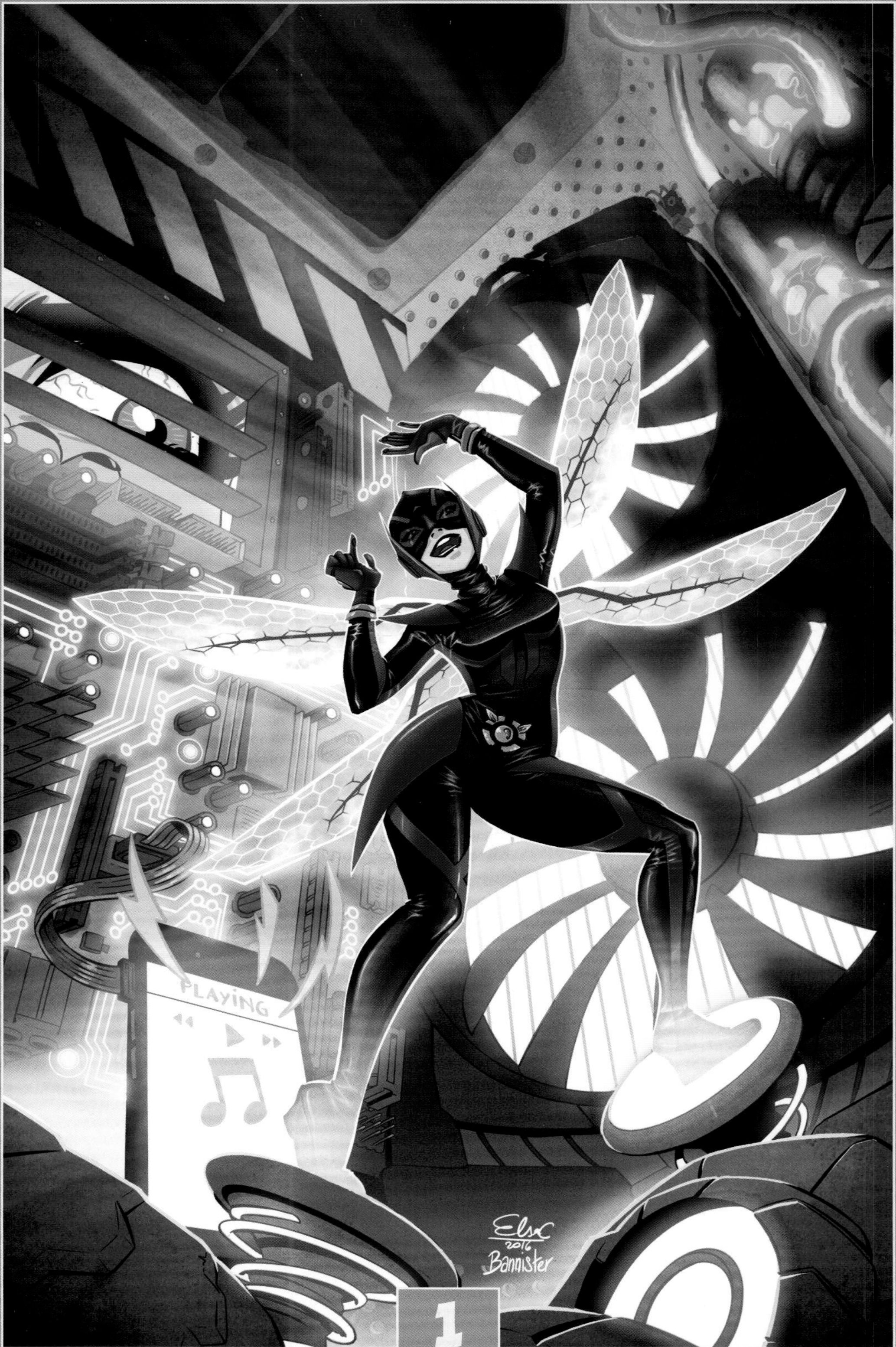
PLAYING
Elsa 2016
Bannister
1

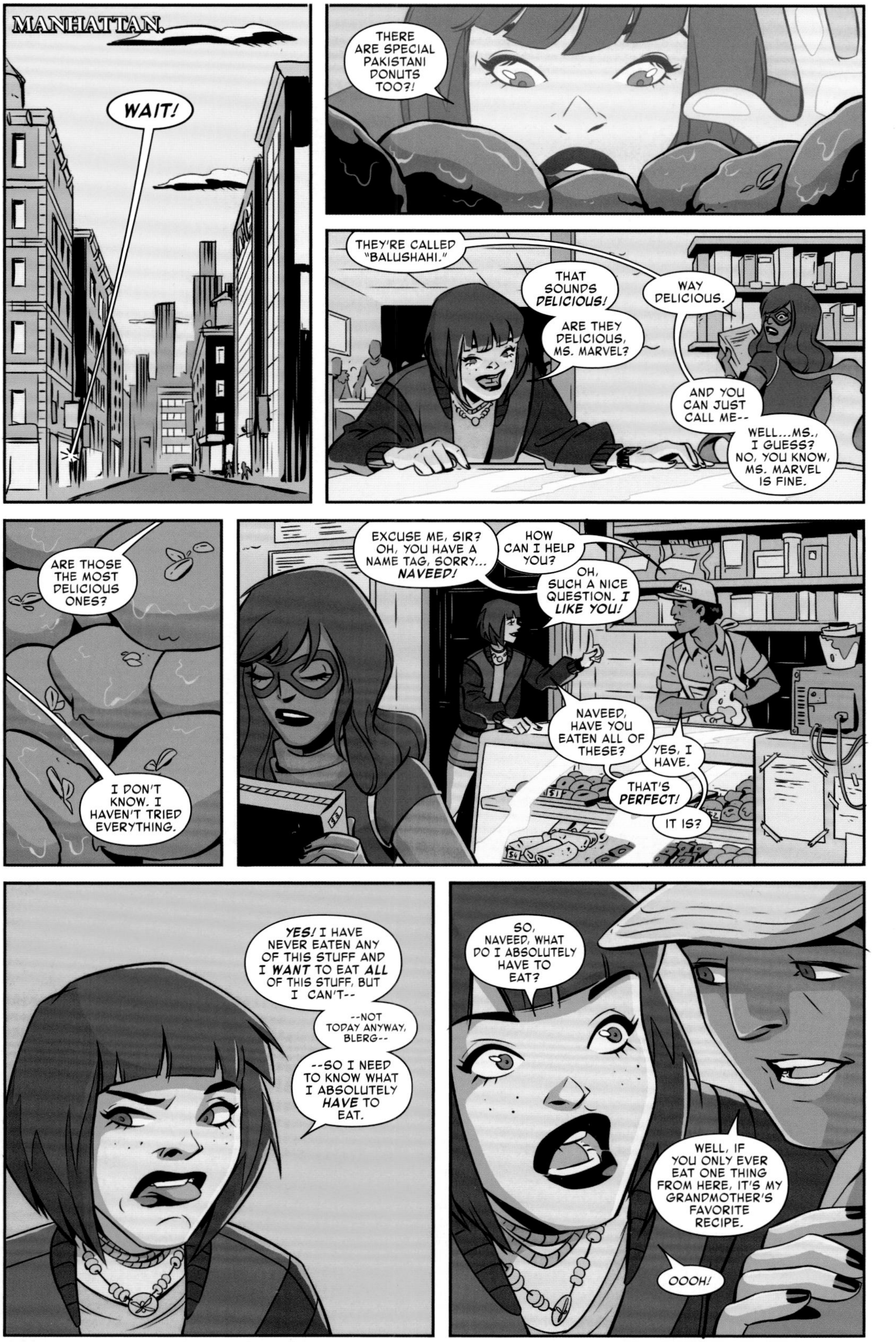
MANHATTAN.
WAIT!
THERE ARE SPECIAL PAKISTANI DONUTS TOO?!
THEY'RE CALLED "BALUSHAHI."
THAT SOUNDS DELICIOUS!
ARE THEY DELICIOUS, MS. MARVEL?
WAY DELICIOUS.
AND YOU CAN JUST CALL ME--
WELL...MS., I GUESS? NO, YOU KNOW, MS. MARVEL IS FINE.
ARE THOSE THE MOST DELICIOUS ONES?
I DON'T KNOW. I HAVEN'T TRIED EVERYTHING.
EXCUSE ME, SIR? OH, YOU HAVE A NAME TAG, SORRY... NAVEED!
HOW CAN I HELP YOU?
OH, SUCH A NICE QUESTION. I LIKE YOU!
NAVEED, HAVE YOU EATEN ALL OF THESE?
YES, I HAVE.
THAT'S PERFECT!
IT IS?
YES! I HAVE NEVER EATEN ANY OF THIS STUFF AND I WANT TO EAT ALL OF THIS STUFF, BUT I CAN'T--
--NOT TODAY ANYWAY, BLERG--
--SO I NEED TO KNOW WHAT I ABSOLUTELY HAVE TO EAT.
SO, NAVEED, WHAT DO I ABSOLUTELY HAVE TO EAT?
WELL, IF YOU ONLY EVER EAT ONE THING FROM HERE, IT'S MY GRANDMOTHER'S FAVORITE RECIPE.
OOOH!

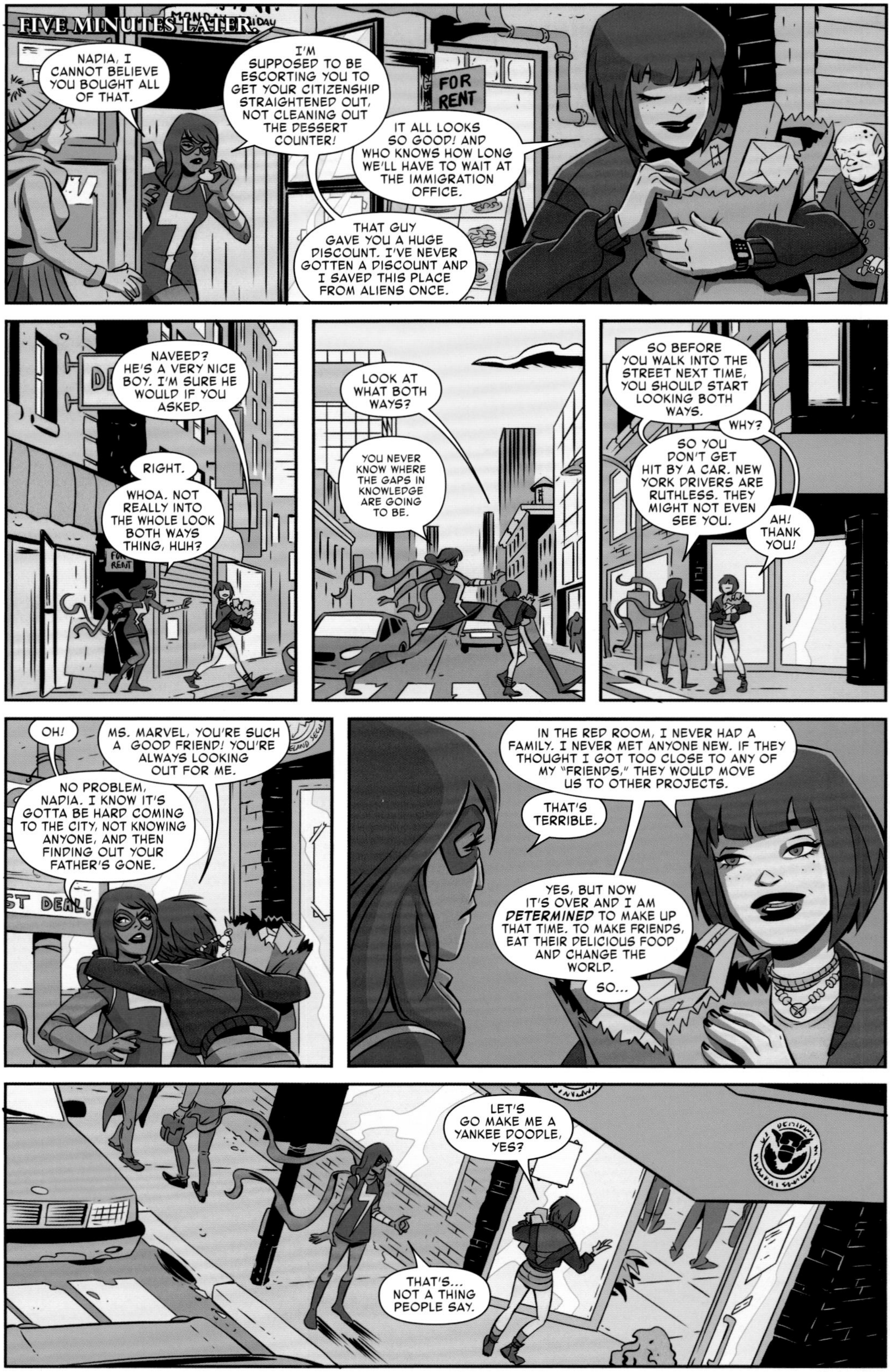
FIVE MINUTES LATER.
NADIA, I CANNOT BELIEVE YOU BOUGHT ALL OF THAT.
I'M SUPPOSED TO BE ESCORTING YOU TO GET YOUR CITIZENSHIP STRAIGHTENED OUT, NOT CLEANING OUT THE DESSERT COUNTER!
FOR RENT
IT ALL LOOKS SO GOOD! AND WHO KNOWS HOW LONG WE'LL HAVE TO WAIT AT THE IMMIGRATION OFFICE.
THAT GUY GAVE YOU A HUGE DISCOUNT. I'VE NEVER GOTTEN A DISCOUNT AND I SAVED THIS PLACE FROM ALIENS ONCE.
NAVEED? HE'S A VERY NICE BOY. I'M SURE HE WOULD IF YOU ASKED.
RIGHT.
WHOA. NOT REALLY INTO THE WHOLE LOOK BOTH WAYS THING, HUH?
LOOK AT WHAT BOTH WAYS?
YOU NEVER KNOW WHERE THE GAPS IN KNOWLEDGE ARE GOING TO BE.
SO BEFORE YOU WALK INTO THE STREET NEXT TIME, YOU SHOULD START LOOKING BOTH WAYS.
WHY?
SO YOU DON'T GET HIT BY A CAR. NEW YORK DRIVERS ARE RUTHLESS. THEY MIGHT NOT EVEN SEE YOU.
AH! THANK YOU!
OH!
MS. MARVEL, YOU'RE SUCH A GOOD FRIEND! YOU'RE ALWAYS LOOKING OUT FOR ME.
NO PROBLEM, NADIA. I KNOW IT'S GOTTA BE HARD COMING TO THE CITY, NOT KNOWING ANYONE, AND THEN FINDING OUT YOUR FATHER'S GONE.
ST DEAL!
IN THE RED ROOM, I NEVER HAD A FAMILY. I NEVER MET ANYONE NEW. IF THEY THOUGHT I GOT TOO CLOSE TO ANY OF MY "FRIENDS," THEY WOULD MOVE US TO OTHER PROJECTS.
THAT'S TERRIBLE.
YES, BUT NOW IT'S OVER AND I AM DETERMINED TO MAKE UP THAT TIME. TO MAKE FRIENDS, EAT THEIR DELICIOUS FOOD AND CHANGE THE WORLD.
SO...
LET'S GO MAKE ME A YANKEE DOODLE, YES?
THAT'S... NOT A THING PEOPLE SAY.

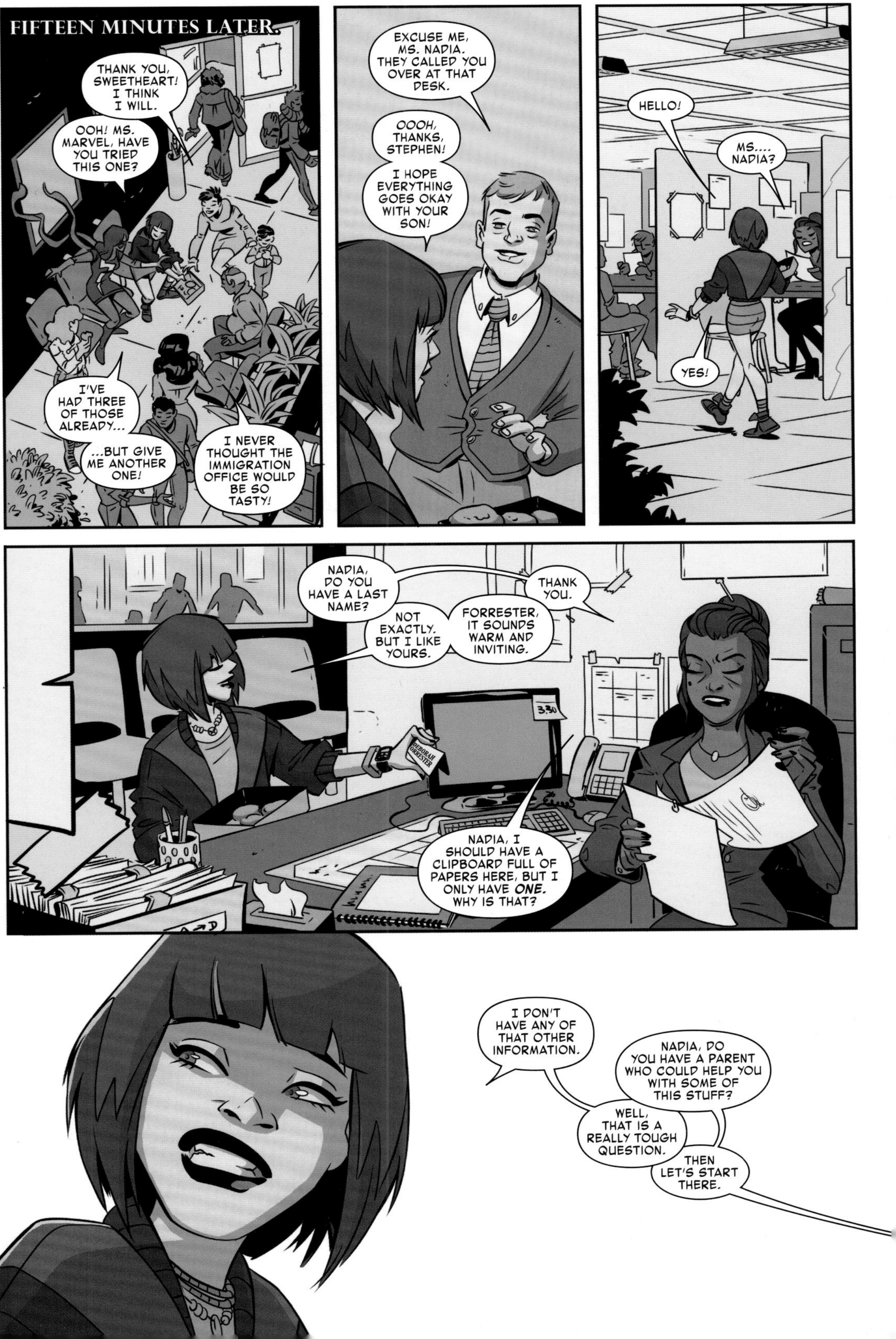
FIFTEEN MINUTES LATER.
THANK YOU, SWEETHEART! I THINK I WILL.
OOH! MS. MARVEL, HAVE YOU TRIED THIS ONE?
I'VE HAD THREE OF THOSE ALREADY...
...BUT GIVE ME ANOTHER ONE!
I NEVER THOUGHT THE IMMIGRATION OFFICE WOULD BE SO TASTY!
EXCUSE ME, MS. NADIA. THEY CALLED YOU OVER AT THAT DESK.
OOOH, THANKS, STEPHEN!
I HOPE EVERYTHING GOES OKAY WITH YOUR SON!
HELLO!
MS.... NADIA?
YES!
NADIA, DO YOU HAVE A LAST NAME?
NOT EXACTLY. BUT I LIKE YOURS.
FORRESTER, IT SOUNDS WARM AND INVITING.
THANK YOU.
DEBORAH FORRESTER
330
NADIA, I SHOULD HAVE A CLIPBOARD FULL OF PAPERS HERE, BUT I ONLY HAVE *ONE.* WHY IS THAT?
I DON'T HAVE ANY OF THAT OTHER INFORMATION.
NADIA, DO YOU HAVE A PARENT WHO COULD HELP YOU WITH SOME OF THIS STUFF?
WELL, THAT IS A REALLY TOUGH QUESTION.
THEN LET'S START THERE.

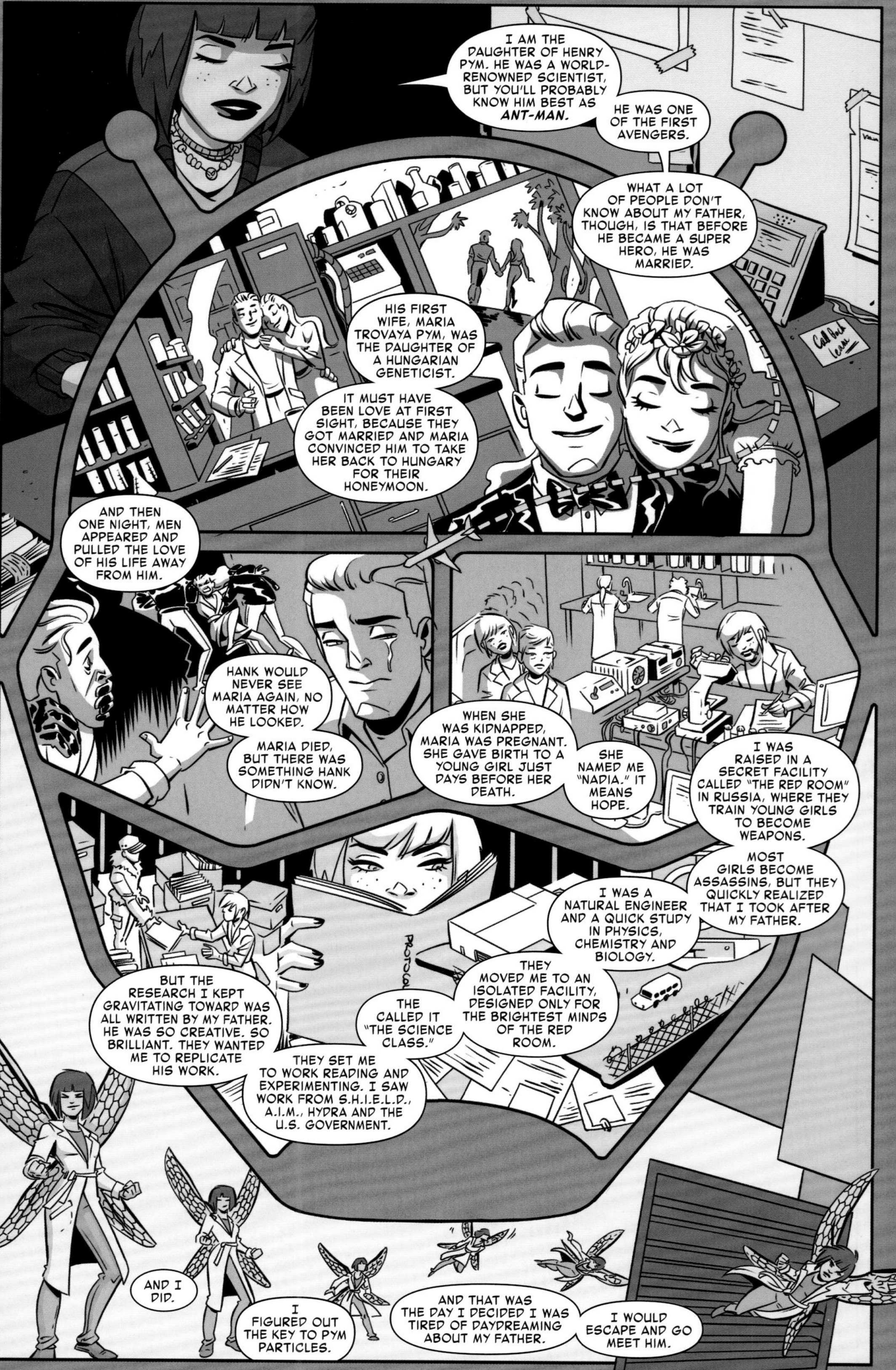
I AM THE DAUGHTER OF HENRY PYM. HE WAS A WORLD-RENOWNED SCIENTIST, BUT YOU'LL PROBABLY KNOW HIM BEST AS ***ANT-MAN.***
HE WAS ONE OF THE FIRST AVENGERS.
WHAT A LOT OF PEOPLE DON'T KNOW ABOUT MY FATHER, THOUGH, IS THAT BEFORE HE BECAME A SUPER HERO, HE WAS MARRIED.
HIS FIRST WIFE, MARIA TROVAYA PYM, WAS THE DAUGHTER OF A HUNGARIAN GENETICIST.
IT MUST HAVE BEEN LOVE AT FIRST SIGHT, BECAUSE THEY GOT MARRIED AND MARIA CONVINCED HIM TO TAKE HER BACK TO HUNGARY FOR THEIR HONEYMOON.
AND THEN ONE NIGHT, MEN APPEARED AND PULLED THE LOVE OF HIS LIFE AWAY FROM HIM.
HANK WOULD NEVER SEE MARIA AGAIN, NO MATTER HOW HE LOOKED.
BUT MARIA DIED, BUT THERE WAS SOMETHING HANK DIDN'T KNOW.
WHEN SHE WAS KIDNAPPED, MARIA WAS PREGNANT. SHE GAVE BIRTH TO A YOUNG GIRL JUST DAYS BEFORE HER DEATH.
SHE NAMED ME "NADIA." IT MEANS HOPE.
I WAS RAISED IN A SECRET FACILITY CALLED "THE RED ROOM" IN RUSSIA, WHERE THEY TRAIN YOUNG GIRLS TO BECOME WEAPONS.
MOST GIRLS BECOME ASSASSINS, BUT THEY QUICKLY REALIZED THAT I TOOK AFTER MY FATHER.
I WAS A NATURAL ENGINEER AND A QUICK STUDY IN PHYSICS, CHEMISTRY AND BIOLOGY.
THEY MOVED ME TO AN ISOLATED FACILITY, DESIGNED ONLY FOR THE BRIGHTEST MINDS OF THE RED ROOM.
THE CALLED IT "THE SCIENCE CLASS."
BUT THE RESEARCH I KEPT GRAVITATING TOWARD WAS ALL WRITTEN BY MY FATHER. HE WAS SO CREATIVE. SO BRILLIANT. THEY WANTED ME TO REPLICATE HIS WORK.
THEY SET ME TO WORK READING AND EXPERIMENTING. I SAW WORK FROM S.H.I.E.L.D., A.I.M., HYDRA AND THE U.S. GOVERNMENT.
AND I DID.
I FIGURED OUT THE KEY TO PYM PARTICLES.
AND THAT WAS THE DAY I DECIDED I WAS TIRED OF DAYDREAMING ABOUT MY FATHER.
I WOULD ESCAPE AND GO MEET HIM.

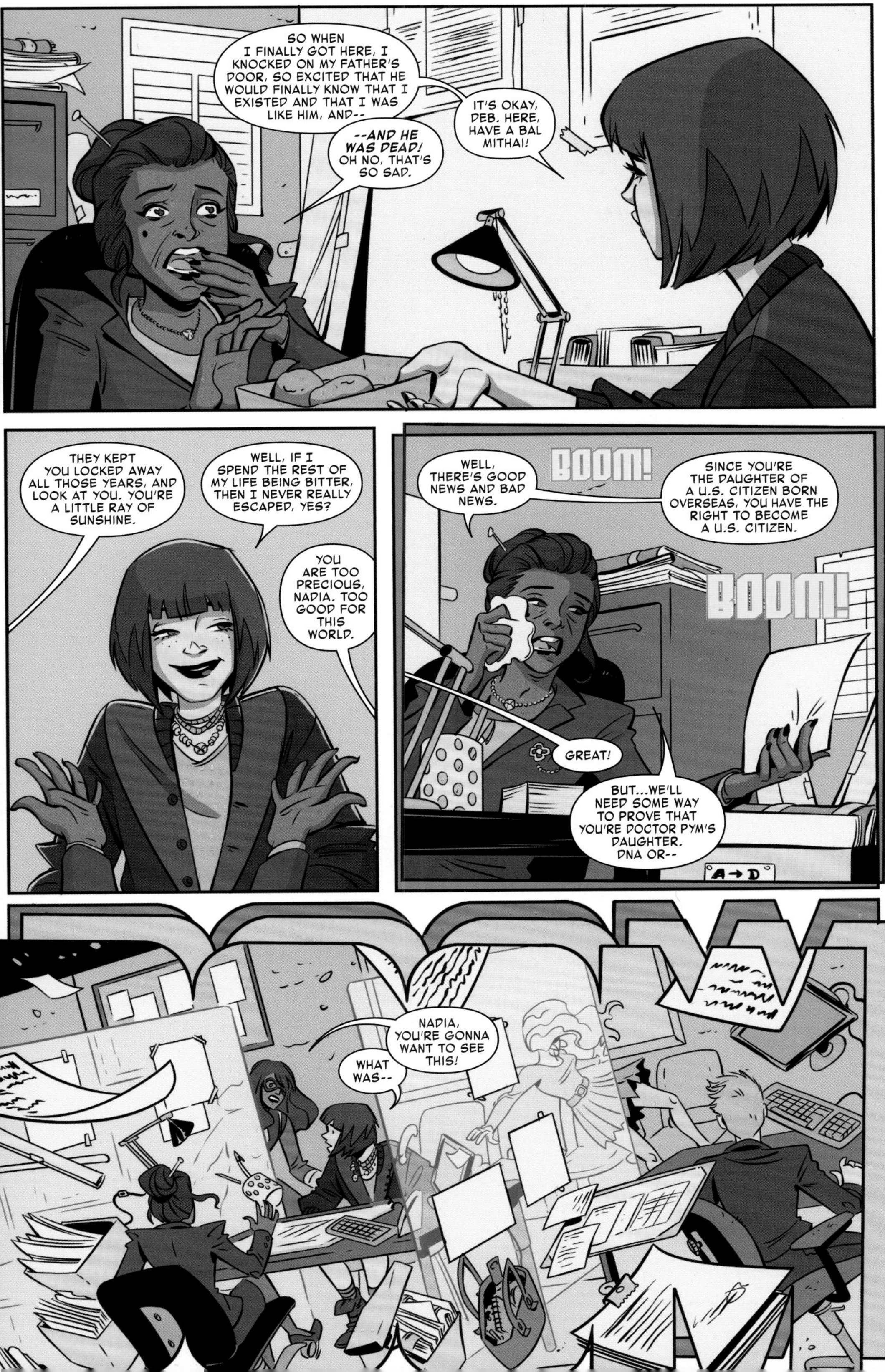
SO WHEN I FINALLY GOT HERE, I KNOCKED ON MY FATHER'S DOOR, SO EXCITED THAT HE WOULD FINALLY KNOW THAT I EXISTED AND THAT I WAS LIKE HIM, AND--
--AND HE WAS DEAD! OH NO, THAT'S SO SAD.
IT'S OKAY, DEB. HERE, HAVE A BAL MITHAI!
THEY KEPT YOU LOCKED AWAY ALL THOSE YEARS, AND LOOK AT YOU. YOU'RE A LITTLE RAY OF SUNSHINE.
WELL, IF I SPEND THE REST OF MY LIFE BEING BITTER, THEN I NEVER REALLY ESCAPED, YES?
YOU ARE TOO PRECIOUS, NADIA. TOO GOOD FOR THIS WORLD.
BOOM!
WELL, THERE'S GOOD NEWS AND BAD NEWS.
SINCE YOU'RE THE DAUGHTER OF A U.S. CITIZEN BORN OVERSEAS, YOU HAVE THE RIGHT TO BECOME A U.S. CITIZEN.
BOOM!
GREAT!
BUT...WE'LL NEED SOME WAY TO PROVE THAT YOU'RE DOCTOR PYM'S DAUGHTER. DNA OR--
A → D
NADIA, YOU'RE GONNA WANT TO SEE THIS!
WHAT WAS--

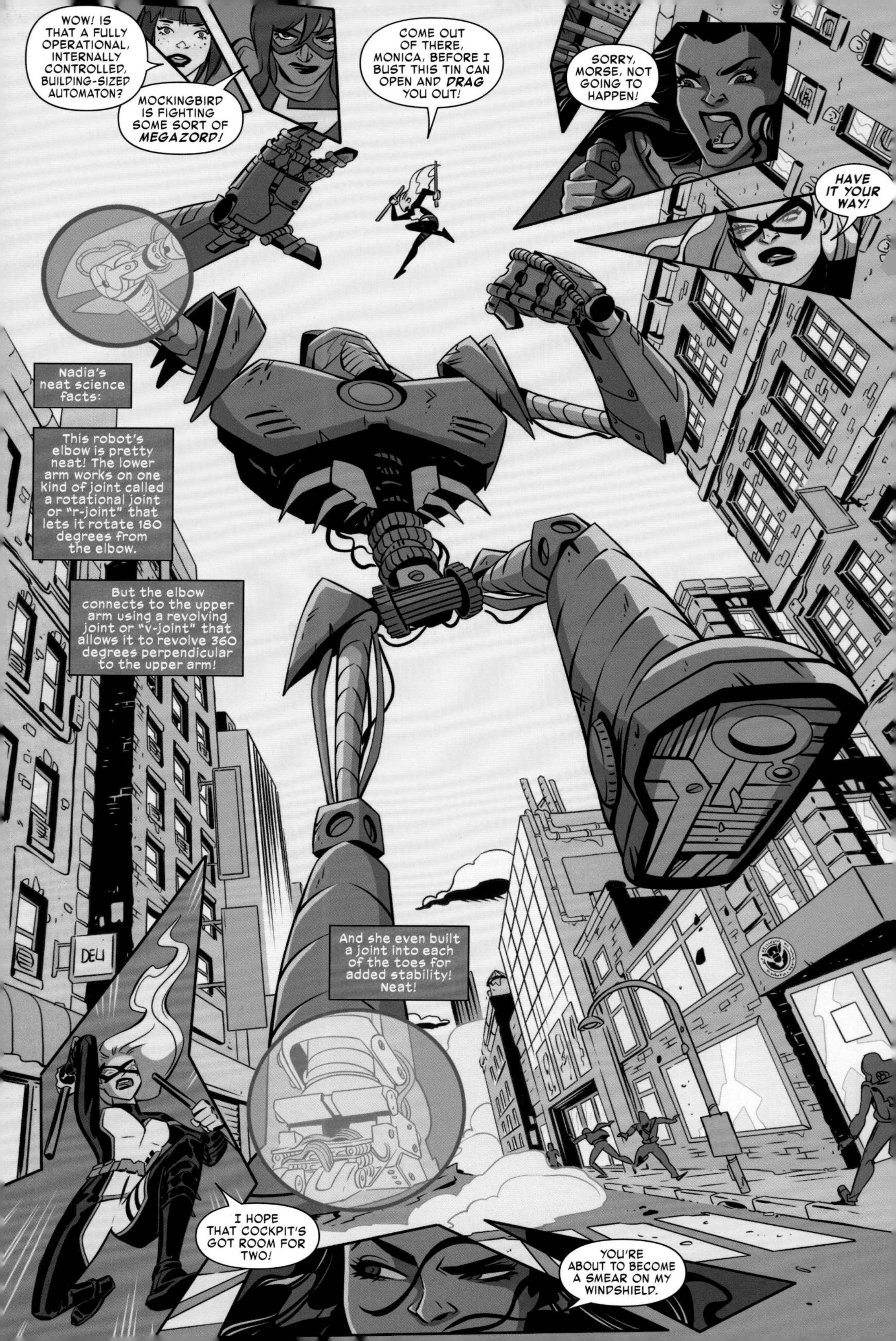

WOW! IS THAT A FULLY OPERATIONAL, INTERNALLY CONTROLLED, BUILDING-SIZED AUTOMATON?
MOCKINGBIRD IS FIGHTING SOME SORT OF MEGAZORD!
COME OUT OF THERE, MONICA, BEFORE I BUST THIS TIN CAN OPEN AND DRAG YOU OUT!
SORRY, MORSE, NOT GOING TO HAPPEN!
HAVE IT YOUR WAY!
Nadia's neat science facts:
This robot's elbow is pretty neat! The lower arm works on one kind of joint called a rotational joint or "r-joint" that lets it rotate 180 degrees from the elbow.
But the elbow connects to the upper arm using a revolving joint or "v-joint" that allows it to revolve 360 degrees perpendicular to the upper arm!
And she even built a joint into each of the toes for added stability! Neat!
DELI
I HOPE THAT COCKPIT'S GOT ROOM FOR TWO!
YOU'RE ABOUT TO BECOME A SMEAR ON MY WINDSHIELD.

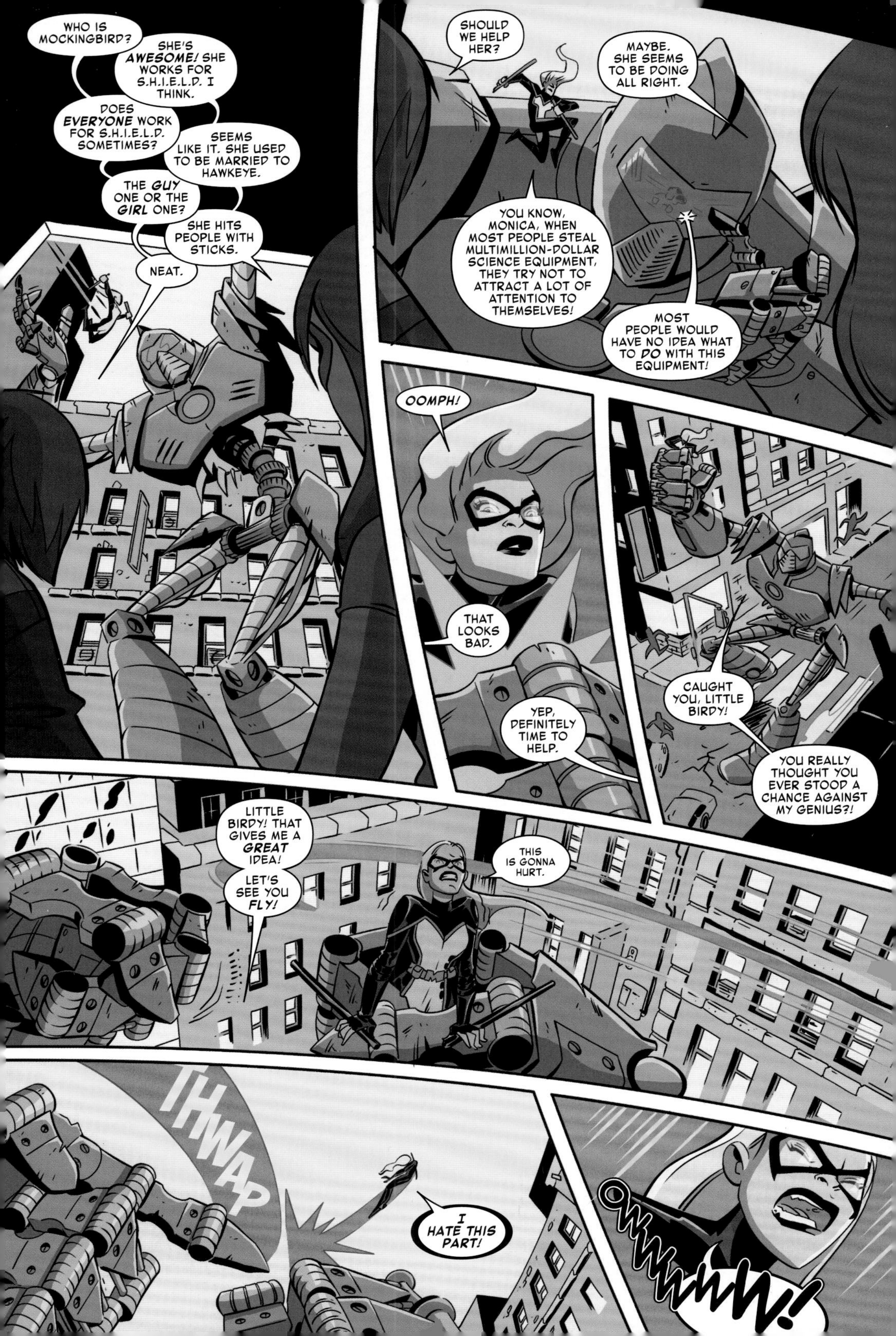
WHO IS MOCKINGBIRD?
SHE'S AWESOME! SHE WORKS FOR S.H.I.E.L.D. I THINK.
DOES EVERYONE WORK FOR S.H.I.E.L.D. SOMETIMES?
SEEMS LIKE IT. SHE USED TO BE MARRIED TO HAWKEYE.
THE GUY ONE OR THE GIRL ONE?
SHE HITS PEOPLE WITH STICKS.
NEAT.
SHOULD WE HELP HER?
MAYBE. SHE SEEMS TO BE DOING ALL RIGHT.
YOU KNOW, MONICA, WHEN MOST PEOPLE STEAL MULTIMILLION-DOLLAR SCIENCE EQUIPMENT, THEY TRY NOT TO ATTRACT A LOT OF ATTENTION TO THEMSELVES!
MOST PEOPLE WOULD HAVE NO IDEA WHAT TO DO WITH THIS EQUIPMENT!
OOMPH!
THAT LOOKS BAD.
YEP, DEFINITELY TIME TO HELP.
CAUGHT YOU, LITTLE BIRDY!
YOU REALLY THOUGHT YOU EVER STOOD A CHANCE AGAINST MY GENIUS?!
LITTLE BIRDY! THAT GIVES ME A GREAT IDEA!
LET'S SEE YOU FLY!
THIS IS GONNA HURT.
THWAP
I HATE THIS PART!
OWWWWW!

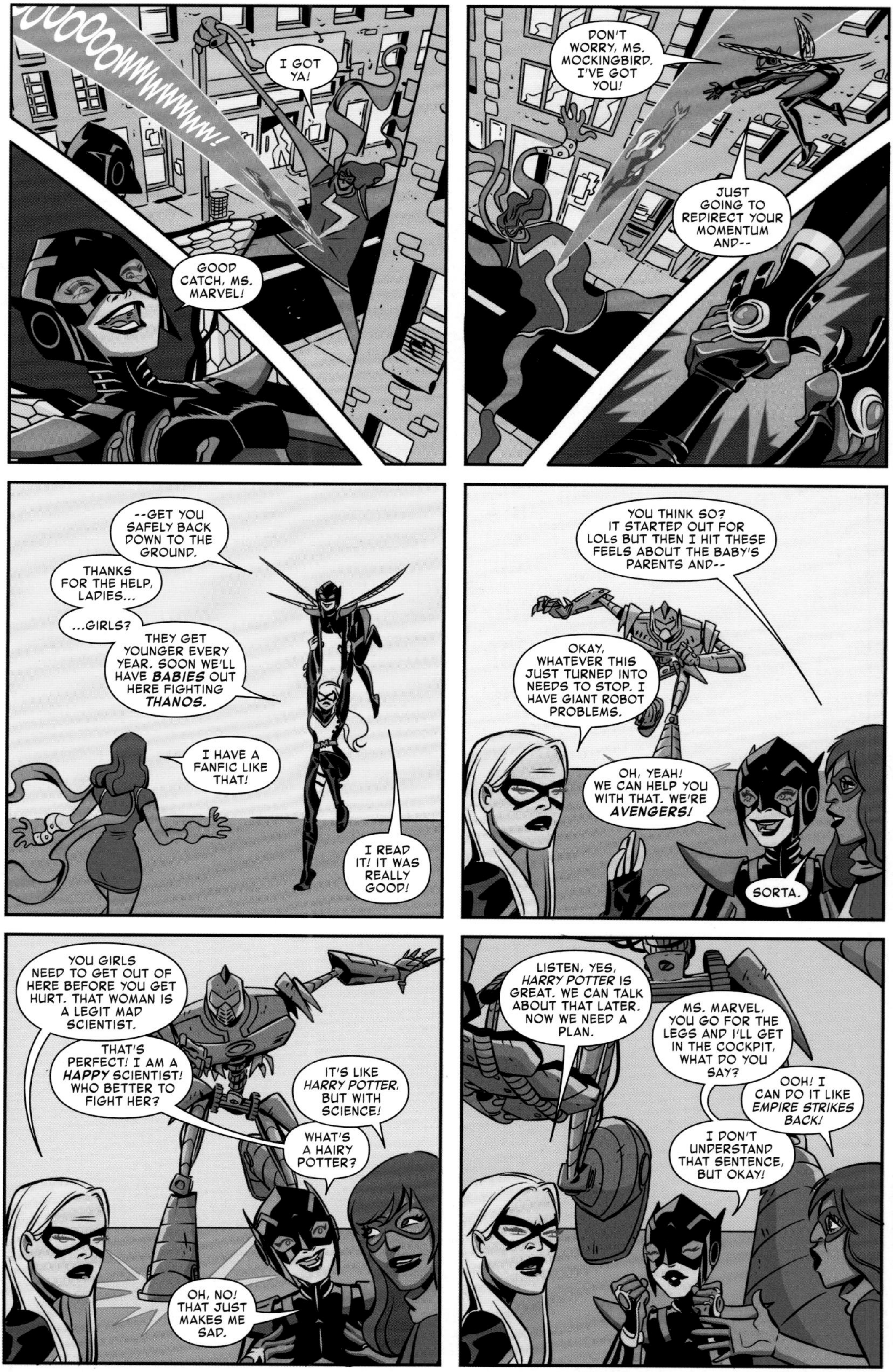
OOOOOOWWWWWWW!
I GOT YA!
GOOD CATCH, MS. MARVEL!
DON'T WORRY, MS. MOCKINGBIRD. I'VE GOT YOU!
JUST GOING TO REDIRECT YOUR MOMENTUM AND--
--GET YOU SAFELY BACK DOWN TO THE GROUND.
THANKS FOR THE HELP, LADIES...
...GIRLS?
THEY GET YOUNGER EVERY YEAR. SOON WE'LL HAVE BABIES OUT HERE FIGHTING THANOS.
I HAVE A FANFIC LIKE THAT!
I READ IT! IT WAS REALLY GOOD!
YOU THINK SO? IT STARTED OUT FOR LOLS BUT THEN I HIT THESE FEELS ABOUT THE BABY'S PARENTS AND--
OKAY, WHATEVER THIS JUST TURNED INTO NEEDS TO STOP. I HAVE GIANT ROBOT PROBLEMS.
OH, YEAH! WE CAN HELP YOU WITH THAT. WE'RE AVENGERS!
SORTA.
YOU GIRLS NEED TO GET OUT OF HERE BEFORE YOU GET HURT. THAT WOMAN IS A LEGIT MAD SCIENTIST.
THAT'S PERFECT! I AM A HAPPY SCIENTIST! WHO BETTER TO FIGHT HER?
OH, NO! THAT JUST MAKES ME SAD.
IT'S LIKE HARRY POTTER, BUT WITH SCIENCE!
WHAT'S A HAIRY POTTER?
LISTEN, YES, HARRY POTTER IS GREAT. WE CAN TALK ABOUT THAT LATER. NOW WE NEED A PLAN.
MS. MARVEL, YOU GO FOR THE LEGS AND I'LL GET IN THE COCKPIT, WHAT DO YOU SAY?
OOH! I CAN DO IT LIKE EMPIRE STRIKES BACK!
I DON'T UNDERSTAND THAT SENTENCE, BUT OKAY!

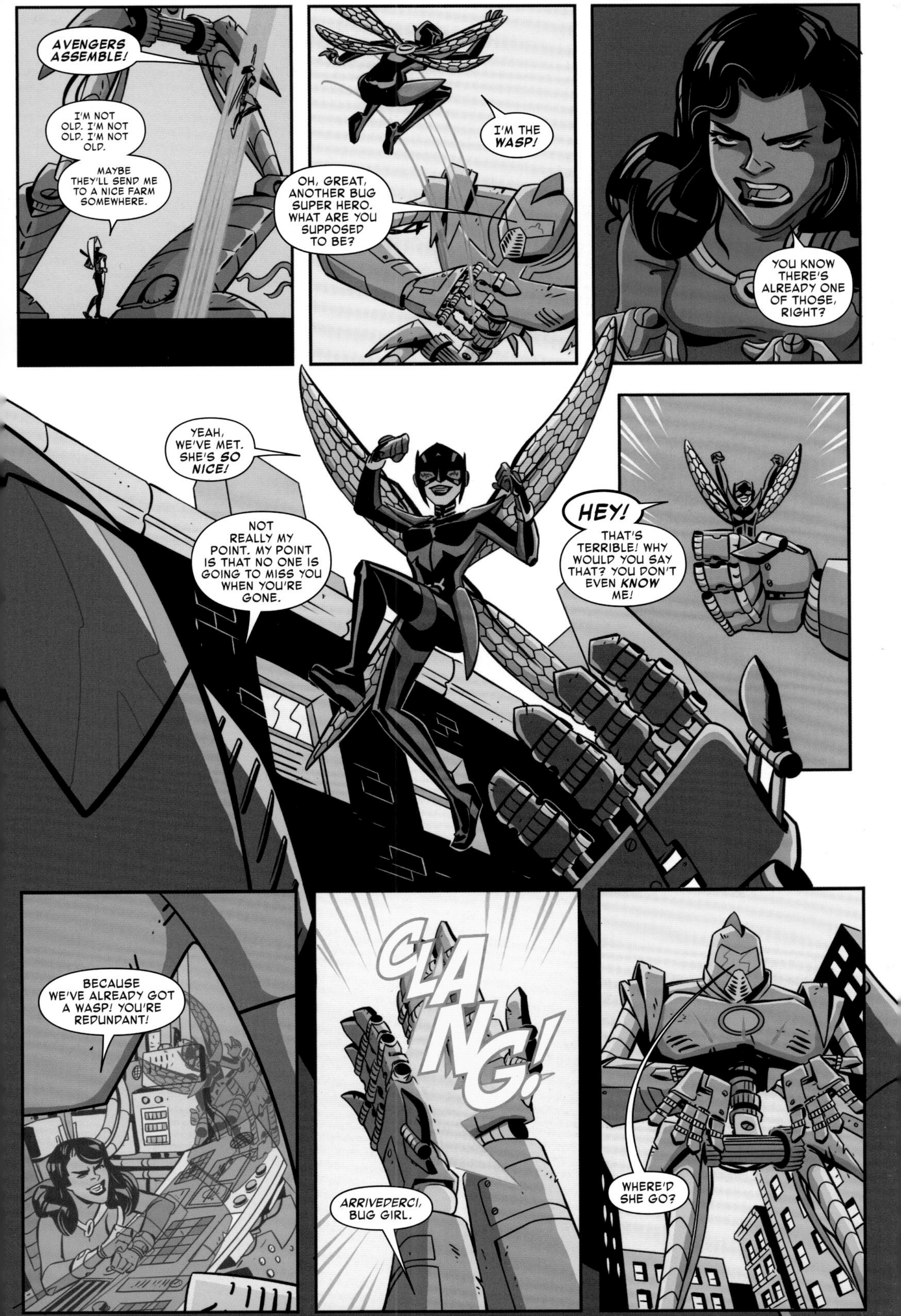
AVENGERS ASSEMBLE!
I'M NOT OLD. I'M NOT OLD. I'M NOT OLD.
MAYBE THEY'LL SEND ME TO A NICE FARM SOMEWHERE.
I'M THE WASP!
OH, GREAT, ANOTHER BUG SUPER HERO. WHAT ARE YOU SUPPOSED TO BE?
YOU KNOW THERE'S ALREADY ONE OF THOSE, RIGHT?
YEAH, WE'VE MET. SHE'S SO NICE!
NOT REALLY MY POINT. MY POINT IS THAT NO ONE IS GOING TO MISS YOU WHEN YOU'RE GONE.
HEY!
THAT'S TERRIBLE! WHY WOULD YOU SAY THAT? YOU DON'T EVEN KNOW ME!
BECAUSE WE'VE ALREADY GOT A WASP! YOU'RE REDUNDANT!
CLANG!
ARRIVEDERCI, BUG GIRL.
WHERE'D SHE GO?

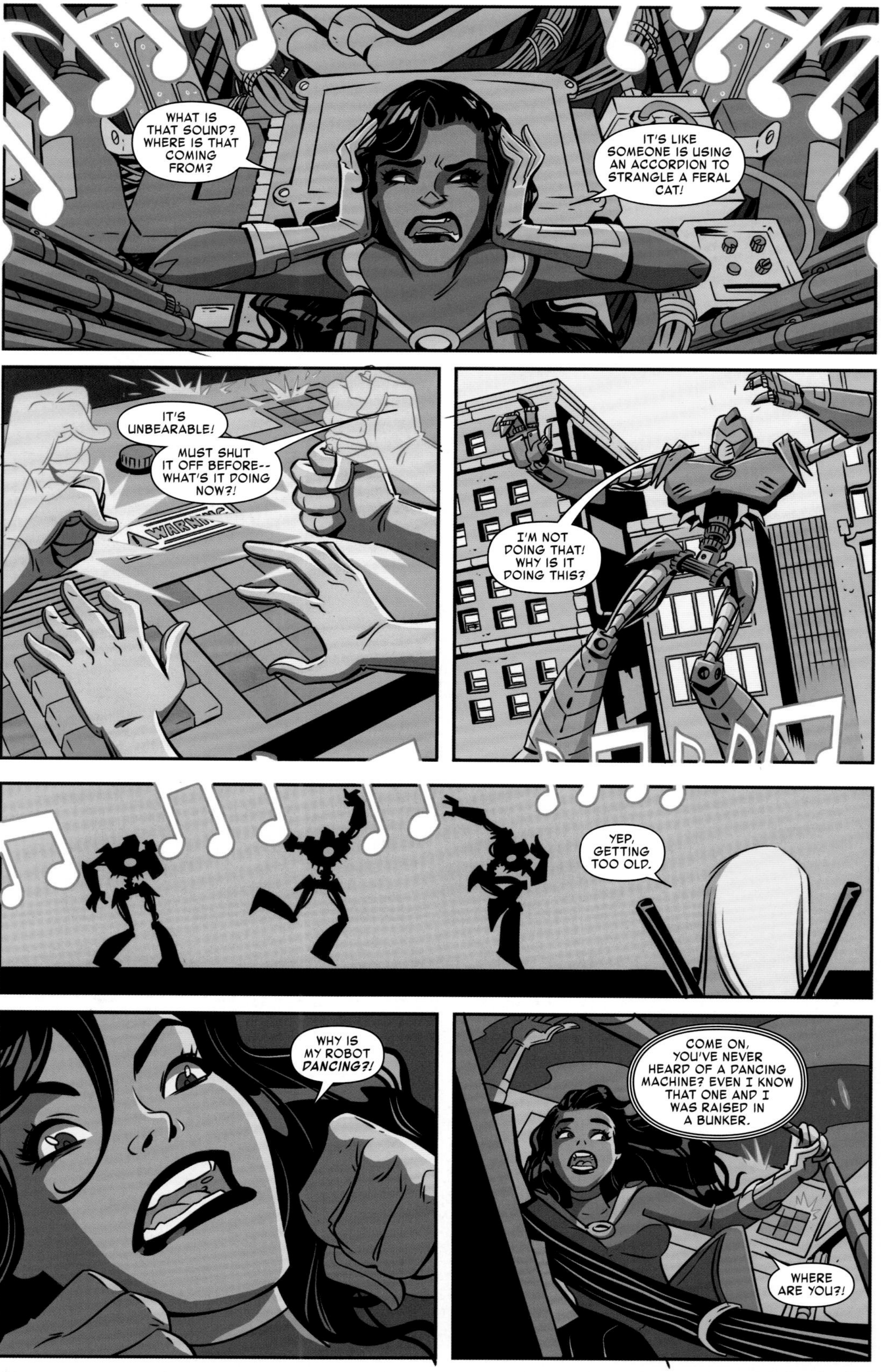
WHAT IS THAT SOUND? WHERE IS THAT COMING FROM?
IT'S LIKE SOMEONE IS USING AN ACCORDION TO STRANGLE A FERAL CAT!
WARNING
IT'S UNBEARABLE!
MUST SHUT IT OFF BEFORE-- WHAT'S IT DOING NOW?!
I'M NOT DOING THAT! WHY IS IT DOING THIS?
YEP, GETTING TOO OLD.
WHY IS MY ROBOT DANCING?!
COME ON, YOU'VE NEVER HEARD OF A DANCING MACHINE? EVEN I KNOW THAT ONE AND I WAS RAISED IN A BUNKER.
WHERE ARE YOU?!

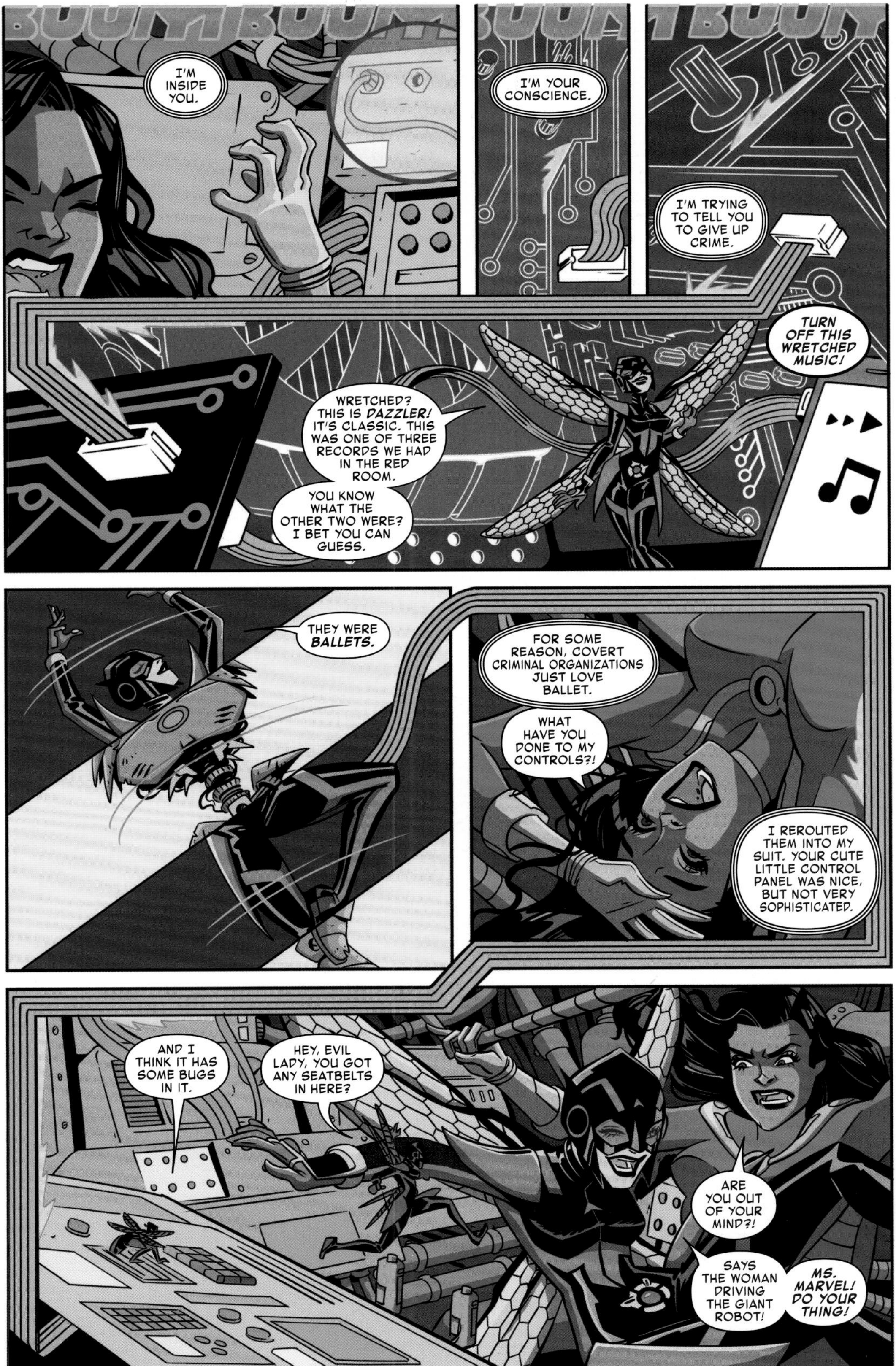

I'M INSIDE YOU.
I'M YOUR CONSCIENCE.
I'M TRYING TO TELL YOU TO GIVE UP CRIME.
TURN OFF THIS WRETCHED MUSIC!
WRETCHED? THIS IS DAZZLER! IT'S CLASSIC. THIS WAS ONE OF THREE RECORDS WE HAD IN THE RED ROOM.
YOU KNOW WHAT THE OTHER TWO WERE? I BET YOU CAN GUESS.
THEY WERE BALLETS.
FOR SOME REASON, COVERT CRIMINAL ORGANIZATIONS JUST LOVE BALLET.
WHAT HAVE YOU DONE TO MY CONTROLS?!
I REROUTED THEM INTO MY SUIT. YOUR CUTE LITTLE CONTROL PANEL WAS NICE, BUT NOT VERY SOPHISTICATED.
AND I THINK IT HAS SOME BUGS IN IT.
HEY, EVIL LADY, YOU GOT ANY SEATBELTS IN HERE?
ARE YOU OUT OF YOUR MIND?!
SAYS THE WOMAN DRIVING THE GIANT ROBOT!
MS. MARVEL! DO YOUR THING!

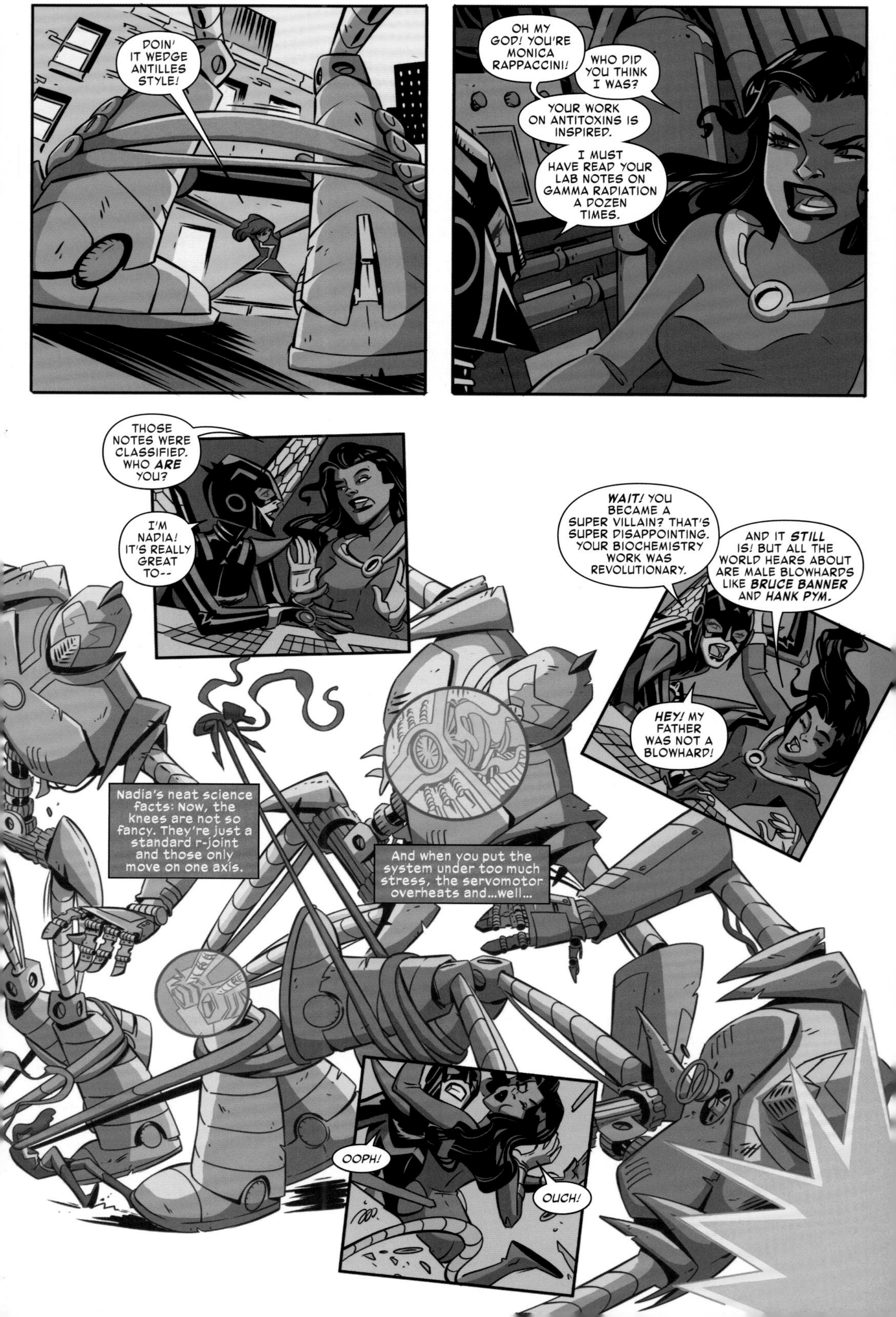
DOIN' IT WEDGE ANTILLES STYLE!
OH MY GOD! YOU'RE MONICA RAPPACCINI!
WHO DID YOU THINK I WAS?
YOUR WORK ON ANTITOXINS IS INSPIRED.
I MUST HAVE READ YOUR LAB NOTES ON GAMMA RADIATION A DOZEN TIMES.
THOSE NOTES WERE CLASSIFIED. WHO ARE YOU?
I'M NADIA! IT'S REALLY GREAT TO--
WAIT! YOU BECAME A SUPER VILLAIN? THAT'S SUPER DISAPPOINTING. YOUR BIOCHEMISTRY WORK WAS REVOLUTIONARY.
AND IT STILL IS! BUT ALL THE WORLD HEARS ABOUT ARE MALE BLOWHARDS LIKE BRUCE BANNER AND HANK PYM.
HEY! MY FATHER WAS NOT A BLOWHARD!
Nadia's neat science facts: Now, the knees are not so fancy. They're just a standard r-joint and those only move on one axis.
And when you put the system under too much stress, the servomotor overheats and...well...
OOPH!
OUCH!

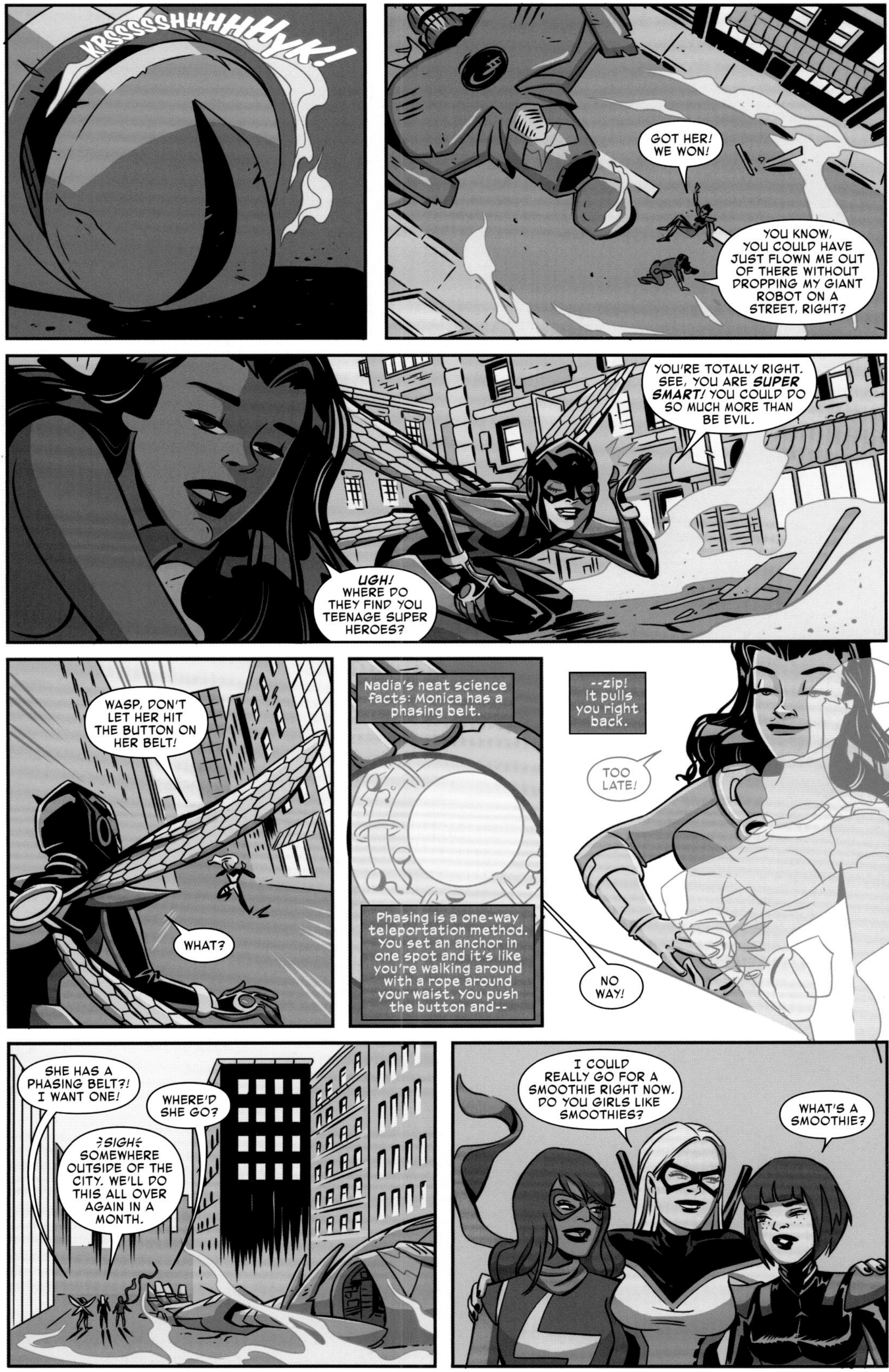
KRSSSSSHHHHHYK!
GOT HER! WE WON!
YOU KNOW, YOU COULD HAVE JUST FLOWN ME OUT OF THERE WITHOUT DROPPING MY GIANT ROBOT ON A STREET, RIGHT?
YOU'RE TOTALLY RIGHT. SEE, YOU ARE SUPER SMART! YOU COULD DO SO MUCH MORE THAN BE EVIL.
UGH! WHERE DO THEY FIND YOU TEENAGE SUPER HEROES?
WASP, DON'T LET HER HIT THE BUTTON ON HER BELT!
WHAT?
Nadia's neat science facts: Monica has a phasing belt.
Phasing is a one-way teleportation method. You set an anchor in one spot and it's like you're walking around with a rope around your waist. You push the button and--
--zip! It pulls you right back.
TOO LATE!
NO WAY!
SHE HAS A PHASING BELT?! I WANT ONE!
WHERE'D SHE GO?
SIGH SOMEWHERE OUTSIDE OF THE CITY. WE'LL DO THIS ALL OVER AGAIN IN A MONTH.
I COULD REALLY GO FOR A SMOOTHIE RIGHT NOW. DO YOU GIRLS LIKE SMOOTHIES?
WHAT'S A SMOOTHIE?

SMOOTHIES ARE AMAZING!

THERE'S FIVE KINDS OF BERRIES IN HERE!

YOU'RE AN EXCITABLE ONE.

SHE SPENT HER WHOLE LIFE LOCKED IN THE RED ROOM DOING MANDATORY SCIENCE.

WAIT...DO PEOPLE JUST KNOW WHAT THE RED ROOM IS NOW? IS THAT COMMON KNOWLEDGE?

I MEAN, I DO, BUT THEN I DON'T KNOW ABOUT "HAIRY POTTERS" OR "EMPIRES TRIKESBACK."

IT HURTS MY HEAD WHEN YOU SAY IT LIKE THAT.

BLACK WIDOW USED TO HAVE TO EXPLAIN THAT TO EVERYBODY. SHE'D SAY IT LIKE SHE WAS SAYING "HYDRA" BUT PEOPLE WOULD JUST STARE AT HER.

WELL, IT'S NOT A GREAT PLACE. ONCE I FIGURED OUT HOW TO REPLICATE MY DAD'S PYM PARTICLES, I GOT OUT.

WAIT, YOU'RE HANK'S KID? WITH WHO?

MY MOTHER WAS MARIA PYM.

MARIA? OH MY GOD. I ONLY MET MARIA A FEW TIMES, BUT I'VE KNOWN YOUR DAD SINCE...BEFORE SUPER HERO STUFF EVEN. WE WORKED ON A GOVERNMENT PROJECT TOGETHER.

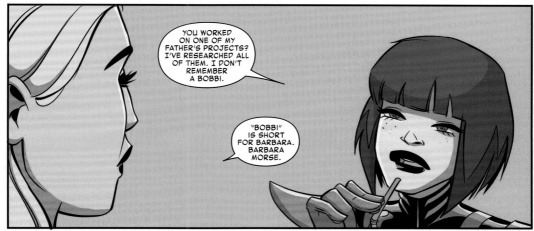

YOU WORKED ON ONE OF MY FATHER'S PROJECTS? I'VE RESEARCHED ALL OF THEM. I DON'T REMEMBER A BOBBI.

"BOBBI" IS SHORT FOR BARBARA. BARBARA MORSE.

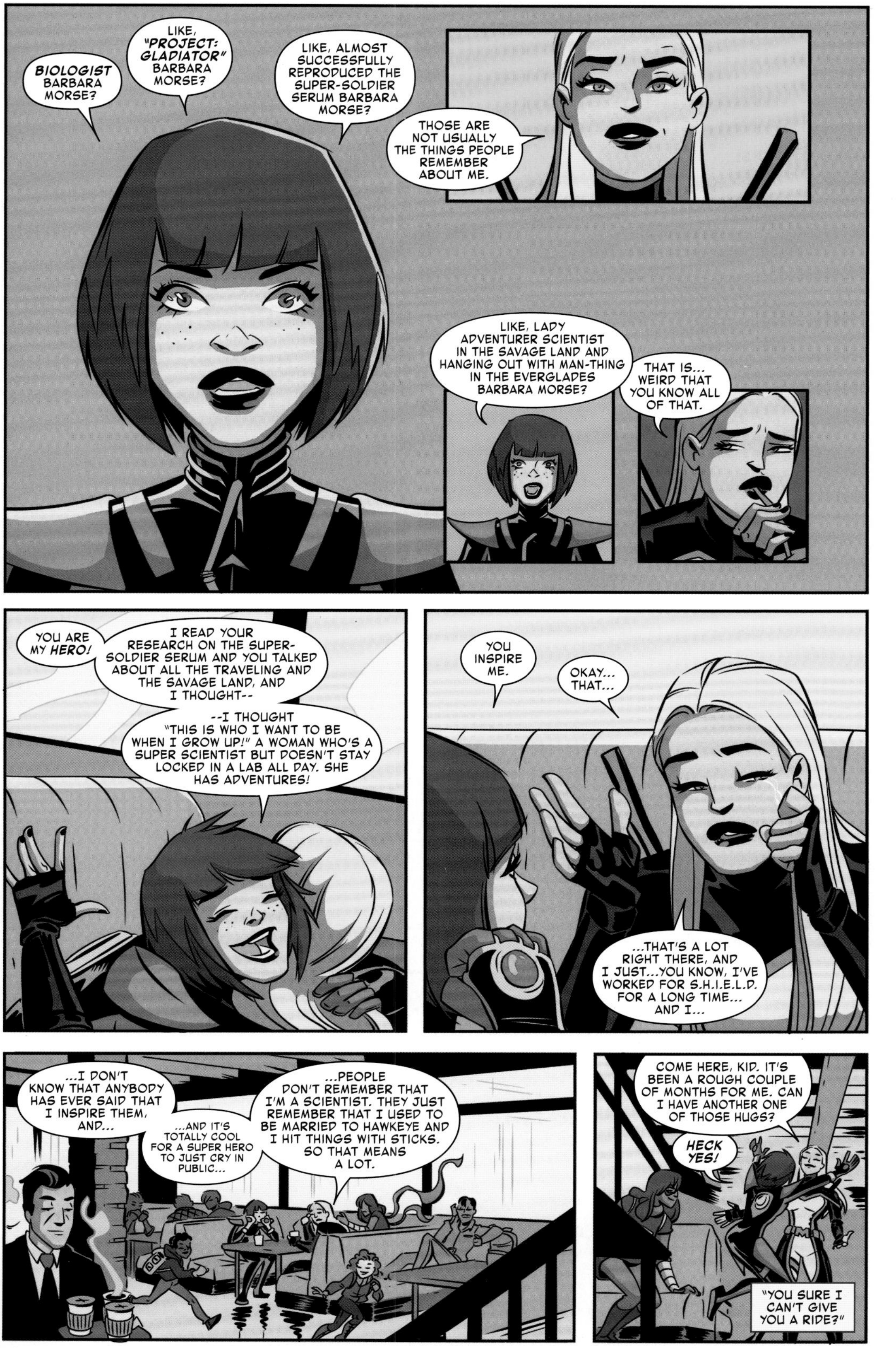
BIOLOGIST BARBARA MORSE?
LIKE, "PROJECT: GLADIATOR" BARBARA MORSE?
LIKE, ALMOST SUCCESSFULLY REPRODUCED THE SUPER-SOLDIER SERUM BARBARA MORSE?
THOSE ARE NOT USUALLY THE THINGS PEOPLE REMEMBER ABOUT ME.
LIKE, LADY ADVENTURER SCIENTIST IN THE SAVAGE LAND AND HANGING OUT WITH MAN-THING IN THE EVERGLADES BARBARA MORSE?
THAT IS... WEIRD THAT YOU KNOW ALL OF THAT.
YOU ARE MY HERO!
I READ YOUR RESEARCH ON THE SUPER-SOLDIER SERUM AND YOU TALKED ABOUT ALL THE TRAVELING AND THE SAVAGE LAND, AND I THOUGHT--
--I THOUGHT "THIS IS WHO I WANT TO BE WHEN I GROW UP!" A WOMAN WHO'S A SUPER SCIENTIST BUT DOESN'T STAY LOCKED IN A LAB ALL DAY. SHE HAS ADVENTURES!
YOU INSPIRE ME.
OKAY... THAT...
...THAT'S A LOT RIGHT THERE, AND I JUST...YOU KNOW, I'VE WORKED FOR S.H.I.E.L.D. FOR A LONG TIME... AND I...
...I DON'T KNOW THAT ANYBODY HAS EVER SAID THAT I INSPIRE THEM, AND...
...AND IT'S TOTALLY COOL FOR A SUPER HERO TO JUST CRY IN PUBLIC...
...PEOPLE DON'T REMEMBER THAT I'M A SCIENTIST. THEY JUST REMEMBER THAT I USED TO BE MARRIED TO HAWKEYE AND I HIT THINGS WITH STICKS. SO THAT MEANS A LOT.
COME HERE, KID. IT'S BEEN A ROUGH COUPLE OF MONTHS FOR ME. CAN I HAVE ANOTHER ONE OF THOSE HUGS?
HECK YES!
"YOU SURE I CAN'T GIVE YOU A RIDE?"

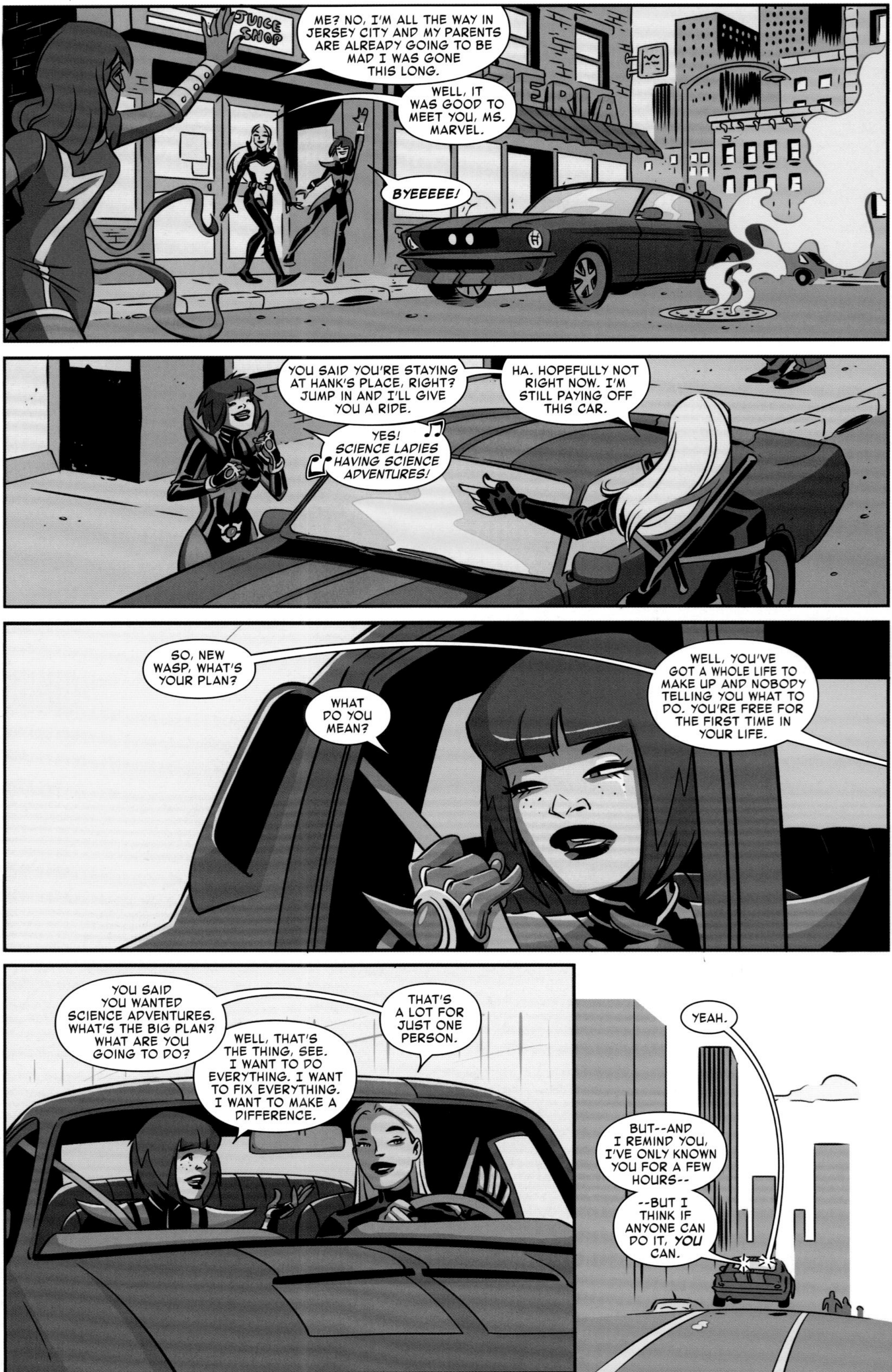
JUICE SHOP
ME? NO, I'M ALL THE WAY IN JERSEY CITY AND MY PARENTS ARE ALREADY GOING TO BE MAD I WAS GONE THIS LONG.
WELL, IT WAS GOOD TO MEET YOU, MS. MARVEL.
BYEEEEE!
YOU SAID YOU'RE STAYING AT HANK'S PLACE, RIGHT? JUMP IN AND I'LL GIVE YOU A RIDE.
HA. HOPEFULLY NOT RIGHT NOW. I'M STILL PAYING OFF THIS CAR.
YES! SCIENCE LADIES HAVING SCIENCE ADVENTURES!
SO, NEW WASP, WHAT'S YOUR PLAN?
WHAT DO YOU MEAN?
WELL, YOU'VE GOT A WHOLE LIFE TO MAKE UP AND NOBODY TELLING YOU WHAT TO DO. YOU'RE FREE FOR THE FIRST TIME IN YOUR LIFE.
YOU SAID YOU WANTED SCIENCE ADVENTURES. WHAT'S THE BIG PLAN? WHAT ARE YOU GOING TO DO?
WELL, THAT'S THE THING, SEE. I WANT TO DO EVERYTHING. I WANT TO FIX EVERYTHING. I WANT TO MAKE A DIFFERENCE.
THAT'S A LOT FOR JUST ONE PERSON.
YEAH.
BUT--AND I REMIND YOU, I'VE ONLY KNOWN YOU FOR A FEW HOURS--
--BUT I THINK IF ANYONE CAN DO IT, *YOU* CAN.

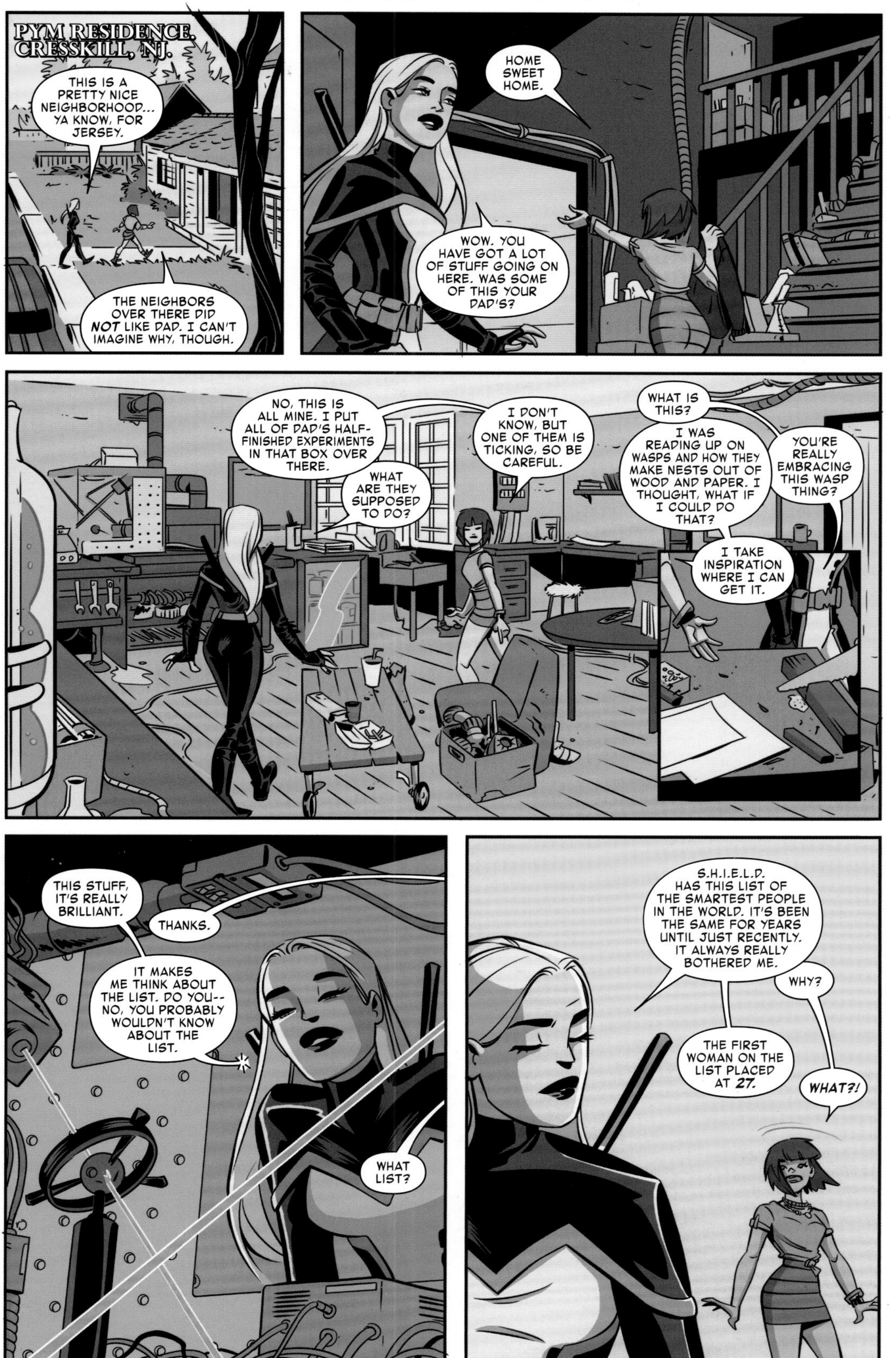
PYM RESIDENCE, CRESSKILL, NJ.
THIS IS A PRETTY NICE NEIGHBORHOOD... YA KNOW, FOR JERSEY.
THE NEIGHBORS OVER THERE DID NOT LIKE DAD. I CAN'T IMAGINE WHY, THOUGH.
HOME SWEET HOME.
WOW. YOU HAVE GOT A LOT OF STUFF GOING ON HERE. WAS SOME OF THIS YOUR DAD'S?
NO, THIS IS ALL MINE. I PUT ALL OF DAD'S HALF-FINISHED EXPERIMENTS IN THAT BOX OVER THERE.
WHAT ARE THEY SUPPOSED TO DO?
I DON'T KNOW, BUT ONE OF THEM IS TICKING, SO BE CAREFUL.
WHAT IS THIS?
I WAS READING UP ON WASPS AND HOW THEY MAKE NESTS OUT OF WOOD AND PAPER. I THOUGHT, WHAT IF I COULD DO THAT?
YOU'RE REALLY EMBRACING THIS WASP THING?
I TAKE INSPIRATION WHERE I CAN GET IT.
THIS STUFF, IT'S REALLY BRILLIANT.
THANKS.
IT MAKES ME THINK ABOUT THE LIST. DO YOU-- NO, YOU PROBABLY WOULDN'T KNOW ABOUT THE LIST.
WHAT LIST?
S.H.I.E.L.D. HAS THIS LIST OF THE SMARTEST PEOPLE IN THE WORLD. IT'S BEEN THE SAME FOR YEARS UNTIL JUST RECENTLY. IT ALWAYS REALLY BOTHERED ME.
WHY?
THE FIRST WOMAN ON THE LIST PLACED AT 27.
WHAT?!

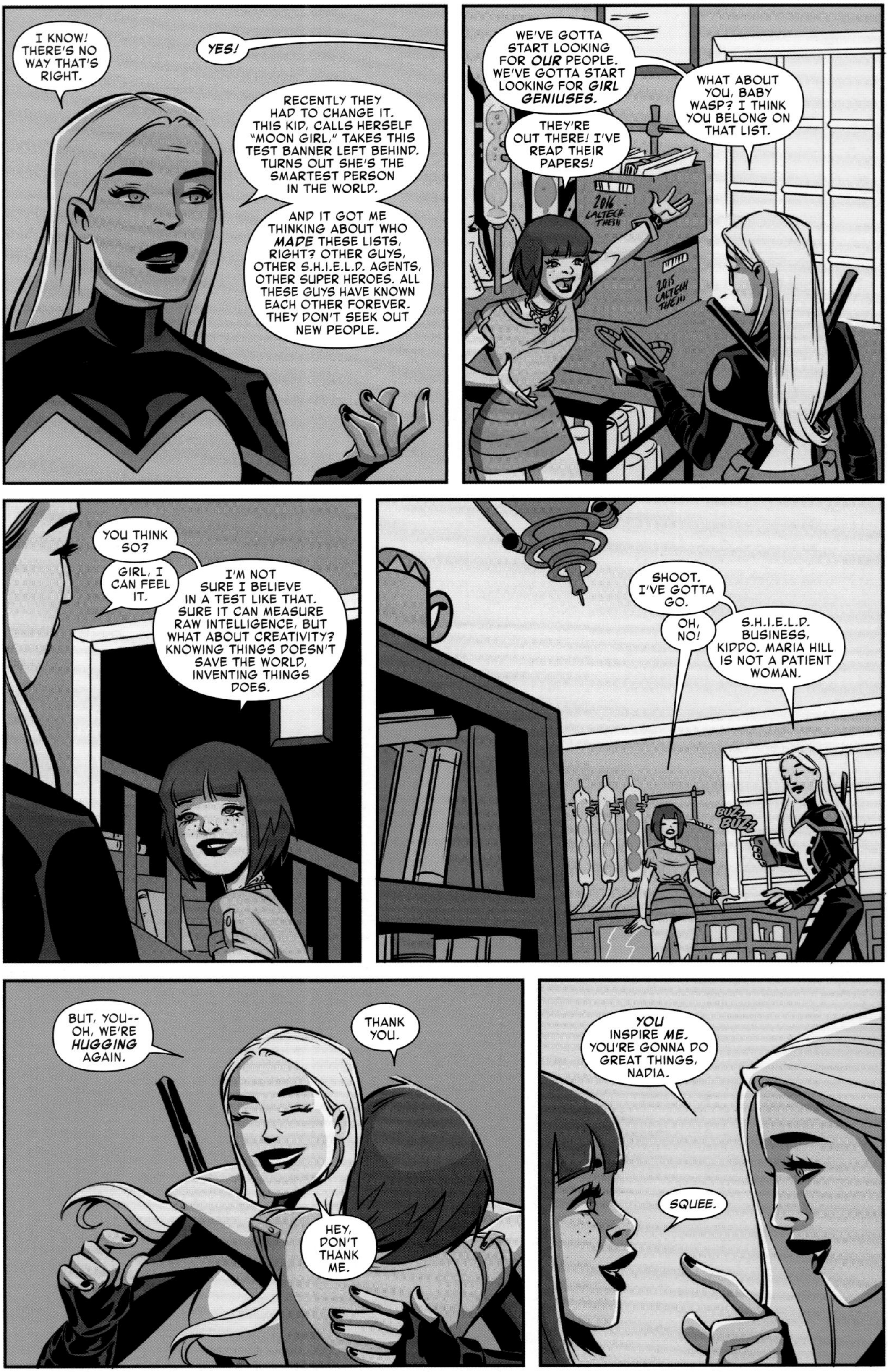
I KNOW! THERE'S NO WAY THAT'S RIGHT.
YES!
RECENTLY THEY HAD TO CHANGE IT. THIS KID, CALLS HERSELF "MOON GIRL," TAKES THIS TEST BANNER LEFT BEHIND. TURNS OUT SHE'S THE SMARTEST PERSON IN THE WORLD.
AND IT GOT ME THINKING ABOUT WHO MADE THESE LISTS, RIGHT? OTHER GUYS, OTHER S.H.I.E.L.D. AGENTS, OTHER SUPER HEROES. ALL THESE GUYS HAVE KNOWN EACH OTHER FOREVER. THEY DON'T SEEK OUT NEW PEOPLE.
WE'VE GOTTA START LOOKING FOR OUR PEOPLE. WE'VE GOTTA START LOOKING FOR GIRL GENIUSES.
THEY'RE OUT THERE! I'VE READ THEIR PAPERS!
WHAT ABOUT YOU, BABY WASP? I THINK YOU BELONG ON THAT LIST.
2016 CALTECH THESIS
2015 CALTECH THESIS
YOU THINK SO?
GIRL, I CAN FEEL IT.
I'M NOT SURE I BELIEVE IN A TEST LIKE THAT. SURE IT CAN MEASURE RAW INTELLIGENCE, BUT WHAT ABOUT CREATIVITY? KNOWING THINGS DOESN'T SAVE THE WORLD, INVENTING THINGS DOES.
SHOOT. I'VE GOTTA GO.
OH, NO!
S.H.I.E.L.D. BUSINESS, KIDDO. MARIA HILL IS NOT A PATIENT WOMAN.
BUZZ BUZZ
BUT, YOU-- OH, WE'RE HUGGING AGAIN.
THANK YOU.
HEY, DON'T THANK ME.
YOU INSPIRE ME. YOU'RE GONNA DO GREAT THINGS, NADIA.
SQUEE.

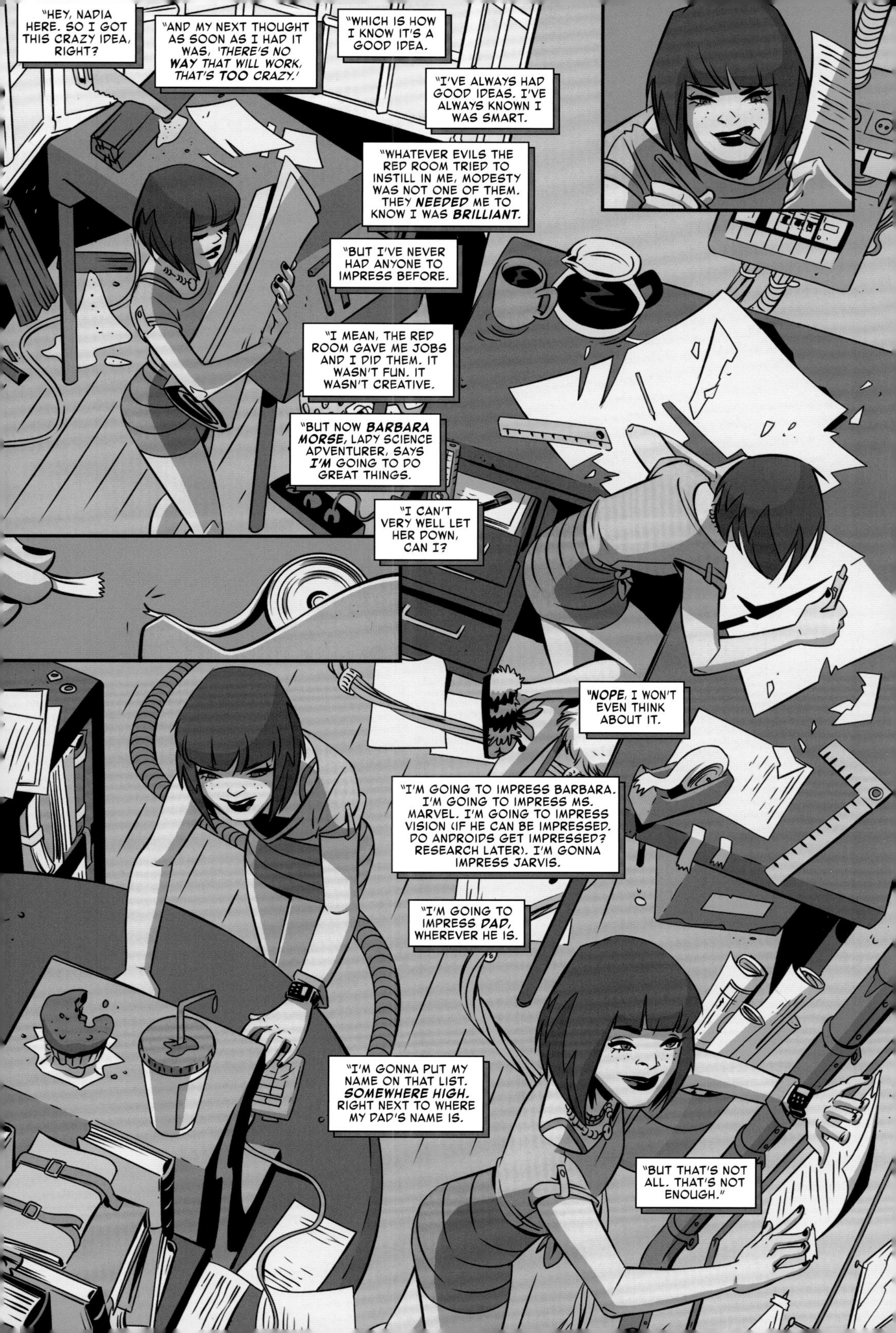
"HEY, NADIA HERE. SO I GOT THIS CRAZY IDEA, RIGHT?
"AND MY NEXT THOUGHT AS SOON AS I HAD IT WAS, 'THERE'S NO WAY THAT WILL WORK, THAT'S TOO CRAZY.'
"WHICH IS HOW I KNOW IT'S A GOOD IDEA.
"I'VE ALWAYS HAD GOOD IDEAS. I'VE ALWAYS KNOWN I WAS SMART.
"WHATEVER EVILS THE RED ROOM TRIED TO INSTILL IN ME, MODESTY WAS NOT ONE OF THEM. THEY NEEDED ME TO KNOW I WAS BRILLIANT.
"BUT I'VE NEVER HAD ANYONE TO IMPRESS BEFORE.
"I MEAN, THE RED ROOM GAVE ME JOBS AND I DID THEM. IT WASN'T FUN. IT WASN'T CREATIVE.
"BUT NOW BARBARA MORSE, LADY SCIENCE ADVENTURER, SAYS I'M GOING TO DO GREAT THINGS.
"I CAN'T VERY WELL LET HER DOWN, CAN I?
"NOPE, I WON'T EVEN THINK ABOUT IT.
"I'M GOING TO IMPRESS BARBARA. I'M GOING TO IMPRESS MS. MARVEL. I'M GOING TO IMPRESS VISION (IF HE CAN BE IMPRESSED. DO ANDROIDS GET IMPRESSED? RESEARCH LATER). I'M GONNA IMPRESS JARVIS.
"I'M GOING TO IMPRESS DAD, WHEREVER HE IS.
"I'M GONNA PUT MY NAME ON THAT LIST. SOMEWHERE HIGH. RIGHT NEXT TO WHERE MY DAD'S NAME IS.
"BUT THAT'S NOT ALL. THAT'S NOT ENOUGH."

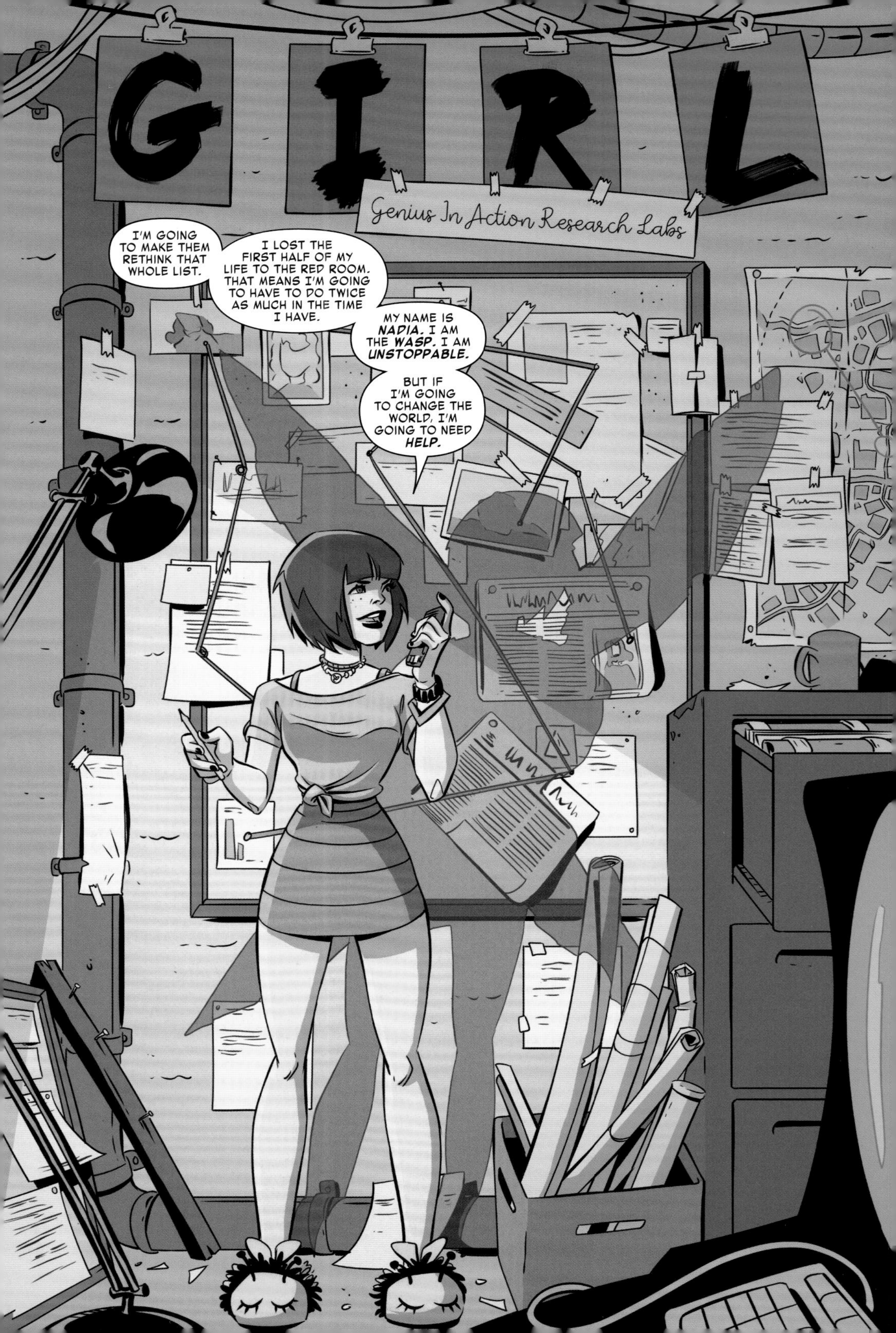
GIRL
Genius In Action Research Labs
I'M GOING TO MAKE THEM RETHINK THAT WHOLE LIST.
I LOST THE FIRST HALF OF MY LIFE TO THE RED ROOM. THAT MEANS I'M GOING TO HAVE TO DO TWICE AS MUCH IN THE TIME I HAVE.
MY NAME IS NADIA. I AM THE WASP. I AM UNSTOPPABLE.
BUT IF I'M GOING TO CHANGE THE WORLD, I'M GOING TO NEED HELP.

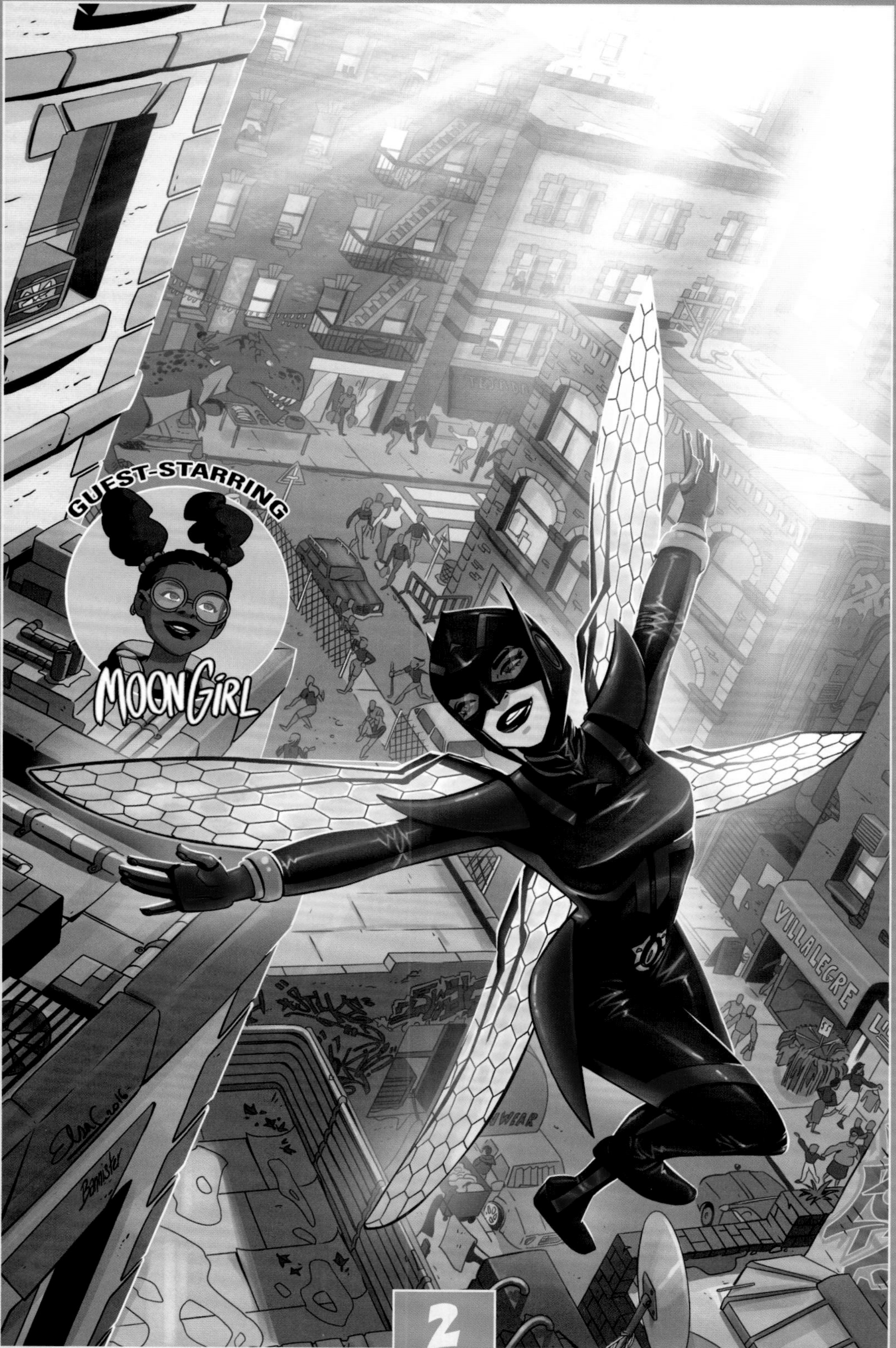
GUEST-STARRING
MOON GIRL
VILLALEGRE
2

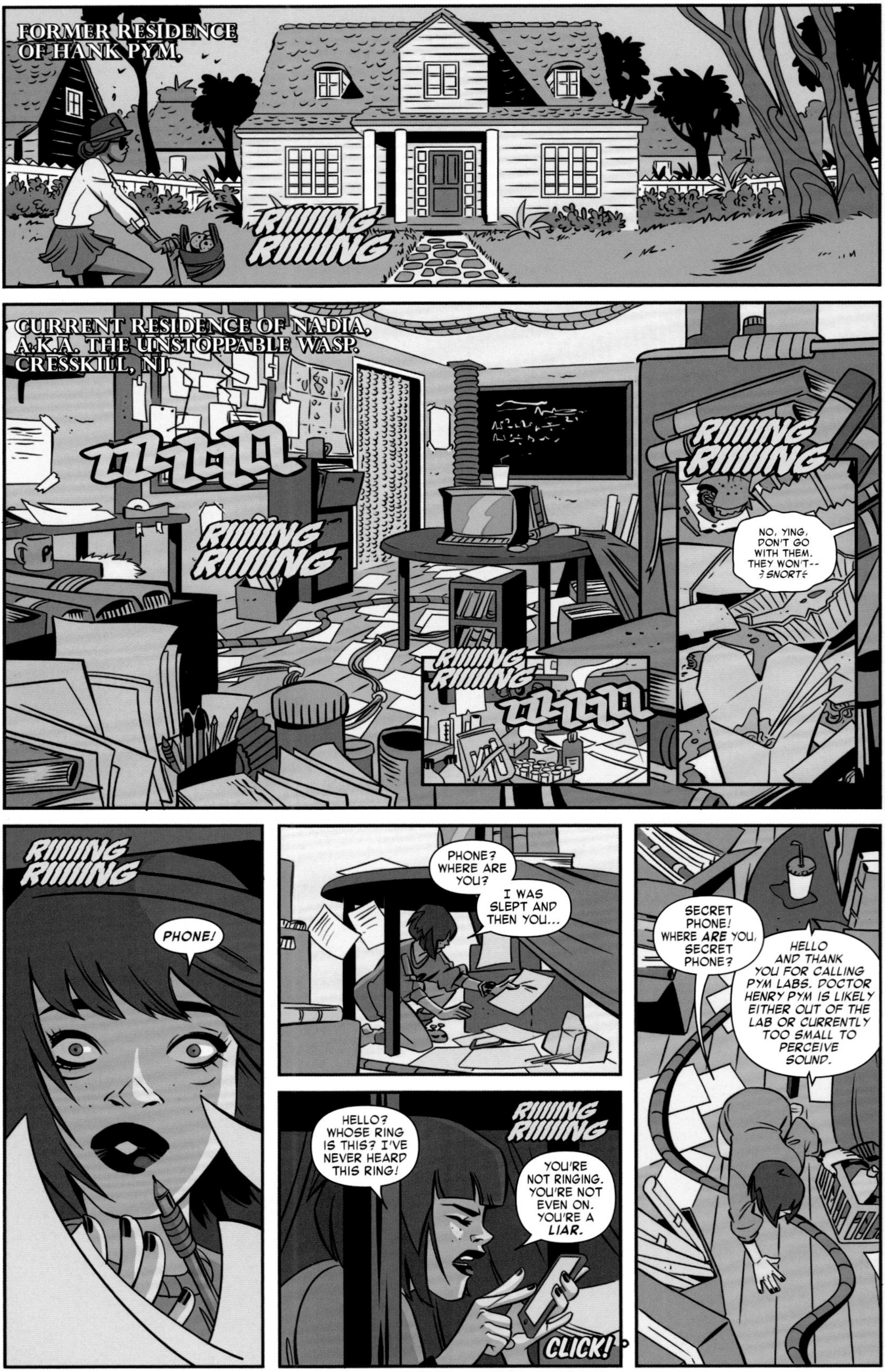
FORMER RESIDENCE OF HANK PYM.
RIIIING RIIIING
CURRENT RESIDENCE OF NADIA, A.K.A. THE UNSTOPPABLE WASP. CRESSKILL, NJ.
ZZZZZZ
RIIIING RIIIING
RIIIING RIIIING
NO, YING, DON'T GO WITH THEM. THEY WON'T-- ⸗SNORT⸗
RIIIING RIIIING
ZZZZZ
RIIIING RIIIING
PHONE!
PHONE? WHERE ARE YOU?
I WAS SLEPT AND THEN YOU...
HELLO? WHOSE RING IS THIS? I'VE NEVER HEARD THIS RING!
RIIIING RIIIING
YOU'RE NOT RINGING. YOU'RE NOT EVEN ON. YOU'RE A LIAR.
CLICK!
SECRET PHONE! WHERE ARE YOU, SECRET PHONE?
HELLO AND THANK YOU FOR CALLING PYM LABS. DOCTOR HENRY PYM IS LIKELY EITHER OUT OF THE LAB OR CURRENTLY TOO SMALL TO PERCEIVE SOUND.

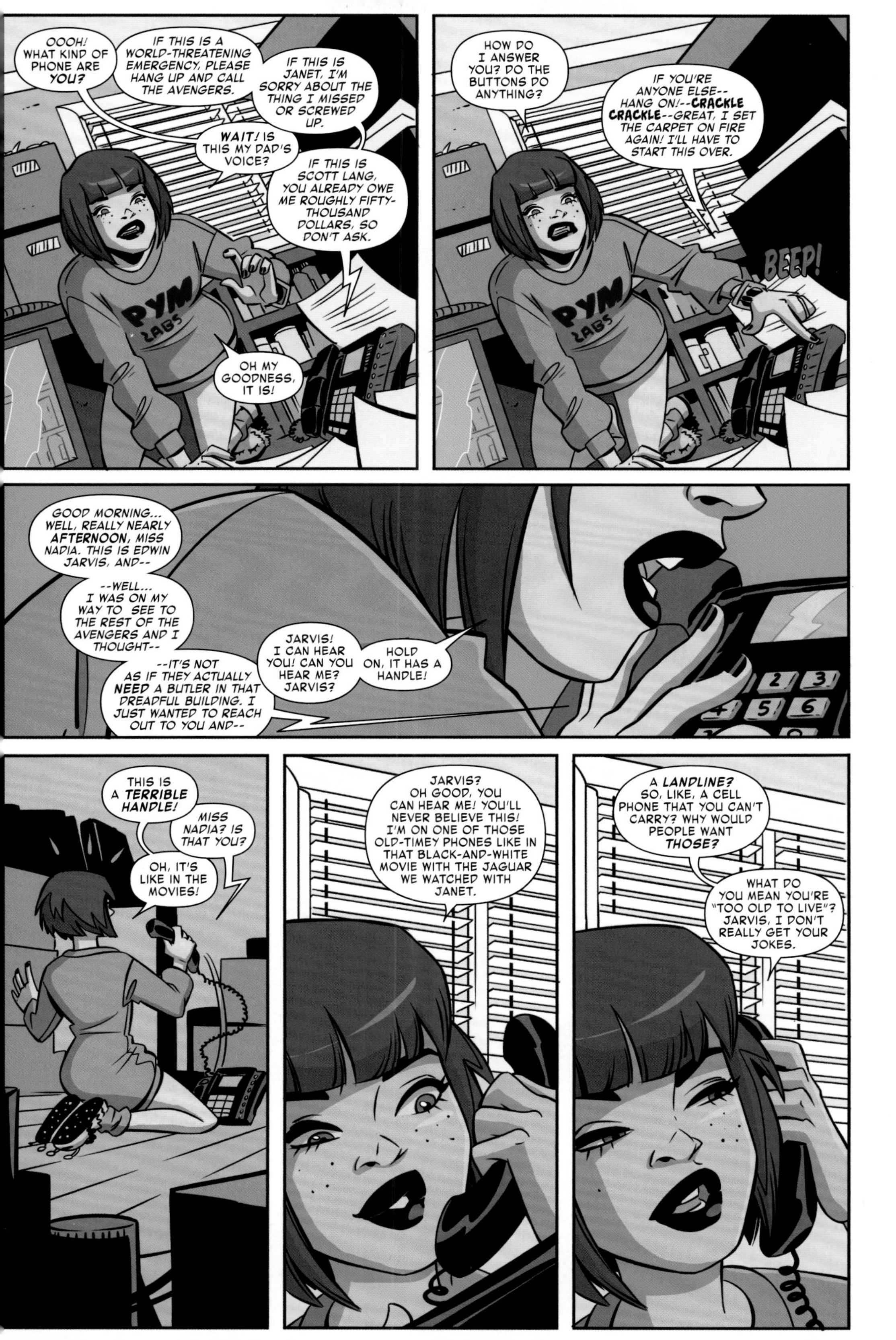
OOOH! WHAT KIND OF PHONE ARE YOU?
IF THIS IS A WORLD-THREATENING EMERGENCY, PLEASE HANG UP AND CALL THE AVENGERS.
IF THIS IS JANET, I'M SORRY ABOUT THE THING I MISSED OR SCREWED UP.
WAIT! IS THIS MY DAD'S VOICE?
IF THIS IS SCOTT LANG, YOU ALREADY OWE ME ROUGHLY FIFTY-THOUSAND DOLLARS, SO DON'T ASK.
OH MY GOODNESS, IT IS!
PYM LABS
HOW DO I ANSWER YOU? DO THE BUTTONS DO ANYTHING?
IF YOU'RE ANYONE ELSE-- HANG ON!--CRACKLE CRACKLE--GREAT, I SET THE CARPET ON FIRE AGAIN! I'LL HAVE TO START THIS OVER.
BEEP!
PYM LABS
GOOD MORNING... WELL, REALLY NEARLY AFTERNOON, MISS NADIA. THIS IS EDWIN JARVIS, AND--
--WELL... I WAS ON MY WAY TO SEE TO THE REST OF THE AVENGERS AND I THOUGHT--
--IT'S NOT AS IF THEY ACTUALLY NEED A BUTLER IN THAT DREADFUL BUILDING. I JUST WANTED TO REACH OUT TO YOU AND--
JARVIS! I CAN HEAR YOU! CAN YOU HEAR ME? JARVIS?
HOLD ON, IT HAS A HANDLE!
THIS IS A TERRIBLE HANDLE!
MISS NADIA? IS THAT YOU?
OH, IT'S LIKE IN THE MOVIES!
JARVIS? OH GOOD, YOU CAN HEAR ME! YOU'LL NEVER BELIEVE THIS! I'M ON ONE OF THOSE OLD-TIMEY PHONES LIKE IN THAT BLACK-AND-WHITE MOVIE WITH THE JAGUAR WE WATCHED WITH JANET.
A LANDLINE? SO, LIKE, A CELL PHONE THAT YOU CAN'T CARRY? WHY WOULD PEOPLE WANT THOSE?
WHAT DO YOU MEAN YOU'RE "TOO OLD TO LIVE"? JARVIS, I DON'T REALLY GET YOUR JOKES.

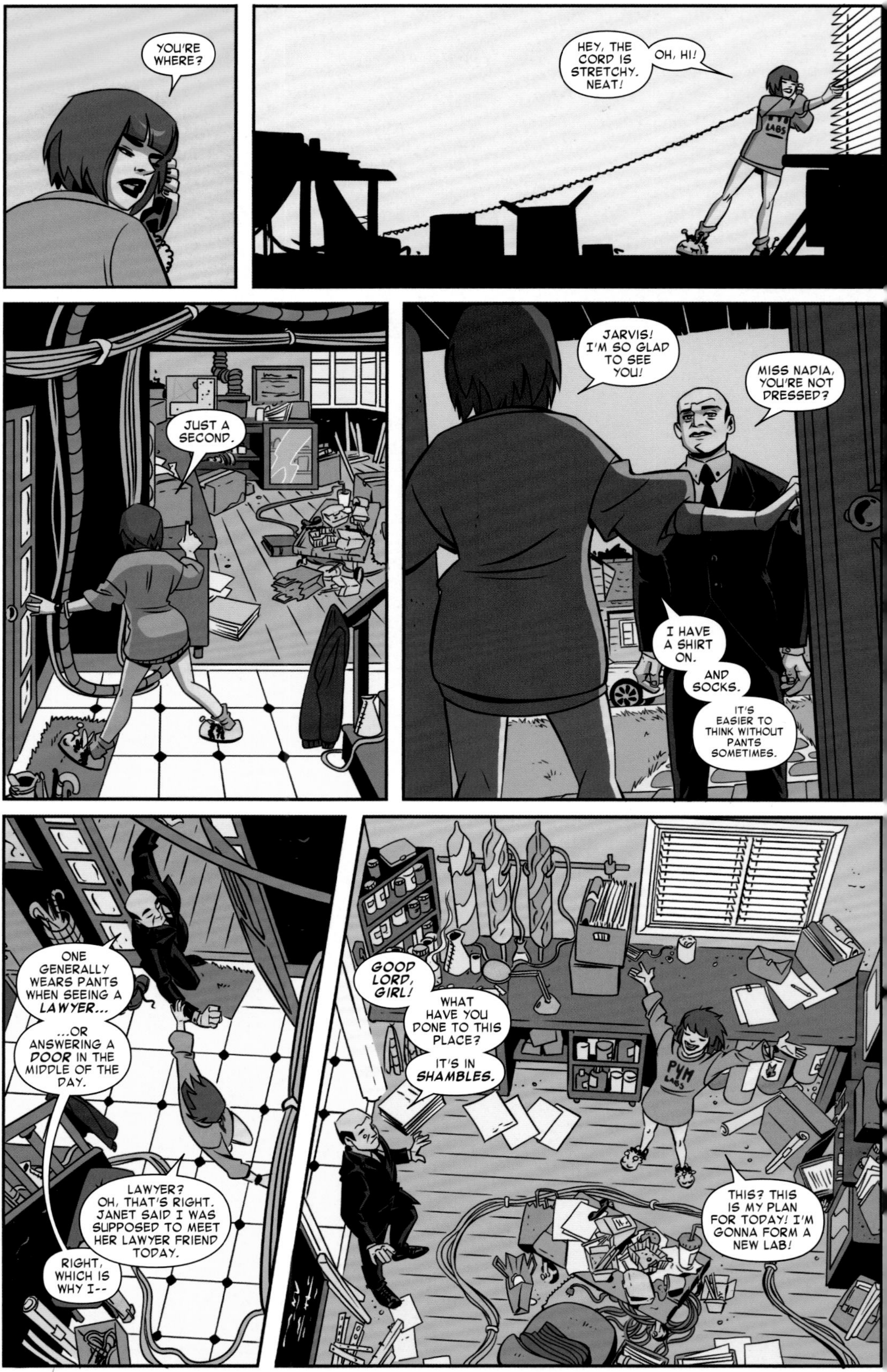
YOU'RE WHERE?
HEY, THE CORD IS STRETCHY. NEAT!
OH, HI!
JUST A SECOND.
JARVIS! I'M SO GLAD TO SEE YOU!
MISS NADIA, YOU'RE NOT DRESSED?
I HAVE A SHIRT ON.
AND SOCKS.
IT'S EASIER TO THINK WITHOUT PANTS SOMETIMES.
ONE GENERALLY WEARS PANTS WHEN SEEING A LAWYER...
...OR ANSWERING A DOOR IN THE MIDDLE OF THE DAY.
LAWYER? OH, THAT'S RIGHT. JANET SAID I WAS SUPPOSED TO MEET HER LAWYER FRIEND TODAY.
RIGHT, WHICH IS WHY I--
GOOD LORD, GIRL!
WHAT HAVE YOU DONE TO THIS PLACE?
IT'S IN SHAMBLES.
THIS? THIS IS MY PLAN FOR TODAY! I'M GONNA FORM A NEW LAB!

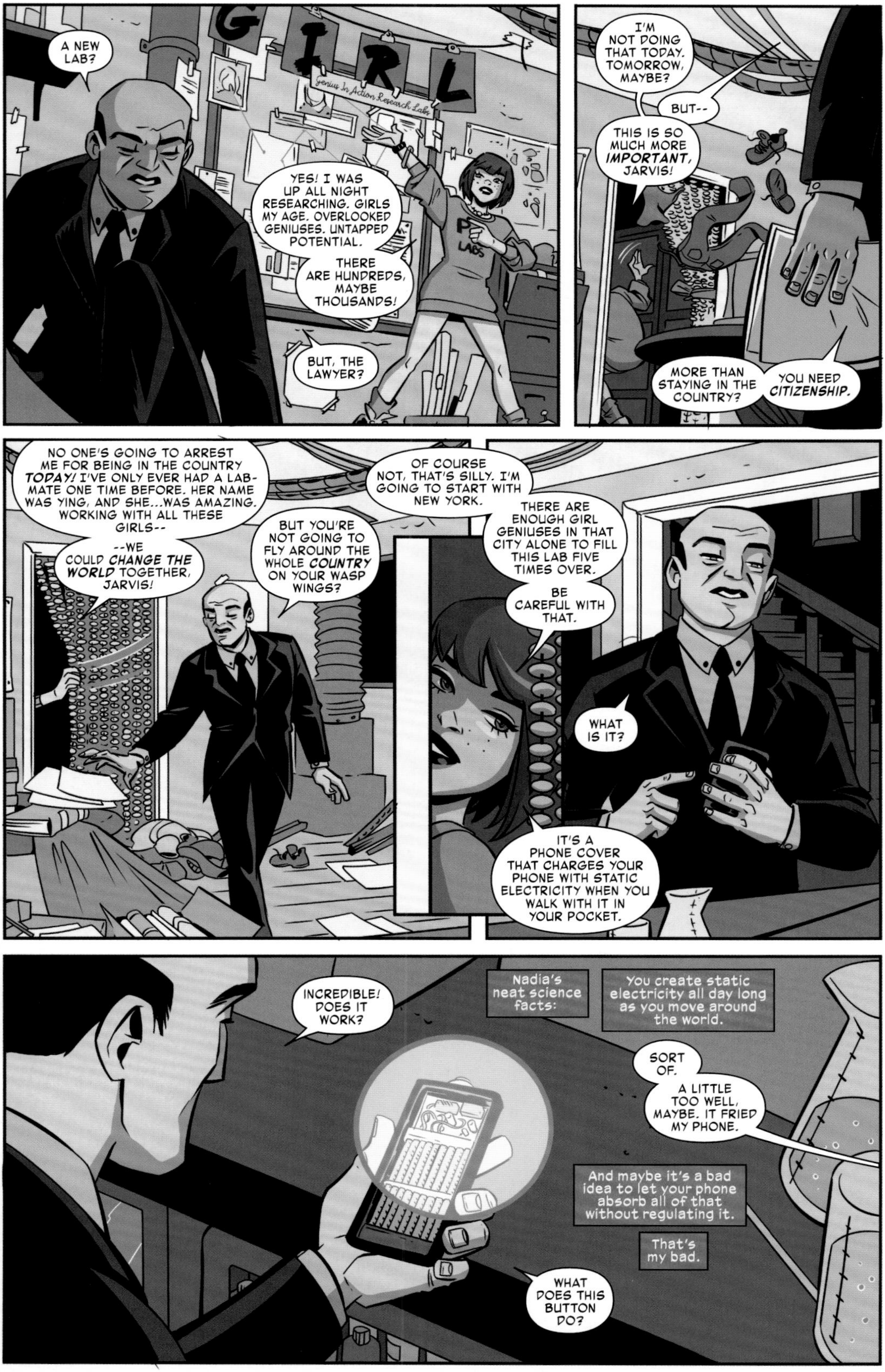
A NEW LAB?
GIRL
Genius In Action Research Labs
YES! I WAS UP ALL NIGHT RESEARCHING. GIRLS MY AGE. OVERLOOKED GENIUSES. UNTAPPED POTENTIAL.
THERE ARE HUNDREDS, MAYBE THOUSANDS!
BUT, THE LAWYER?
I'M NOT DOING THAT TODAY. TOMORROW, MAYBE?
BUT--
THIS IS SO MUCH MORE IMPORTANT, JARVIS!
MORE THAN STAYING IN THE COUNTRY?
YOU NEED CITIZENSHIP.
NO ONE'S GOING TO ARREST ME FOR BEING IN THE COUNTRY TODAY! I'VE ONLY EVER HAD A LAB-MATE ONE TIME BEFORE. HER NAME WAS YING, AND SHE...WAS AMAZING. WORKING WITH ALL THESE GIRLS--
--WE COULD CHANGE THE WORLD TOGETHER, JARVIS!
BUT YOU'RE NOT GOING TO FLY AROUND THE WHOLE COUNTRY ON YOUR WASP WINGS?
OF COURSE NOT, THAT'S SILLY. I'M GOING TO START WITH NEW YORK.
THERE ARE ENOUGH GIRL GENIUSES IN THAT CITY ALONE TO FILL THIS LAB FIVE TIMES OVER.
BE CAREFUL WITH THAT.
WHAT IS IT?
IT'S A PHONE COVER THAT CHARGES YOUR PHONE WITH STATIC ELECTRICITY WHEN YOU WALK WITH IT IN YOUR POCKET.
INCREDIBLE! DOES IT WORK?
Nadia's neat science facts:
You create static electricity all day long as you move around the world.
SORT OF.
A LITTLE TOO WELL, MAYBE. IT FRIED MY PHONE.
And maybe it's a bad idea to let your phone absorb all of that without regulating it.
That's my bad.
WHAT DOES THIS BUTTON DO?

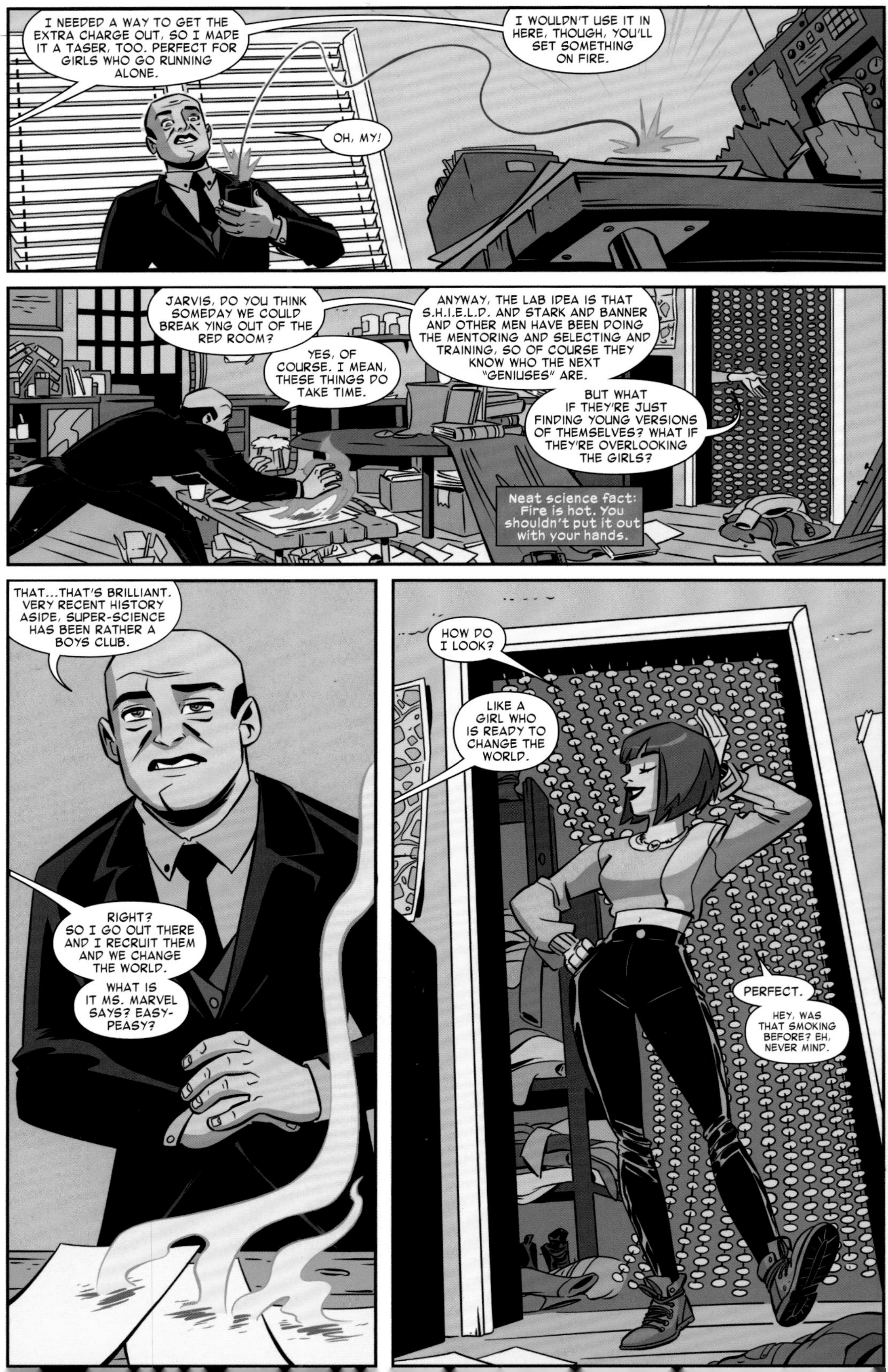

I NEEDED A WAY TO GET THE EXTRA CHARGE OUT, SO I MADE IT A TASER, TOO. PERFECT FOR GIRLS WHO GO RUNNING ALONE.
I WOULDN'T USE IT IN HERE, THOUGH, YOU'LL SET SOMETHING ON FIRE.
OH, MY!
JARVIS, DO YOU THINK SOMEDAY WE COULD BREAK YING OUT OF THE RED ROOM?
YES, OF COURSE. I MEAN, THESE THINGS DO TAKE TIME.
ANYWAY, THE LAB IDEA IS THAT S.H.I.E.L.D. AND STARK AND BANNER AND OTHER MEN HAVE BEEN DOING THE MENTORING AND SELECTING AND TRAINING, SO OF COURSE THEY KNOW WHO THE NEXT "GENIUSES" ARE.
BUT WHAT IF THEY'RE JUST FINDING YOUNG VERSIONS OF THEMSELVES? WHAT IF THEY'RE OVERLOOKING THE GIRLS?
Neat science fact: Fire is hot. You shouldn't put it out with your hands.
THAT...THAT'S BRILLIANT. VERY RECENT HISTORY ASIDE, SUPER-SCIENCE HAS BEEN RATHER A BOYS CLUB.
RIGHT? SO I GO OUT THERE AND I RECRUIT THEM AND WE CHANGE THE WORLD.
WHAT IS IT MS. MARVEL SAYS? EASY-PEASY?
HOW DO I LOOK?
LIKE A GIRL WHO IS READY TO CHANGE THE WORLD.
PERFECT.
HEY, WAS THAT SMOKING BEFORE? EH, NEVER MIND.

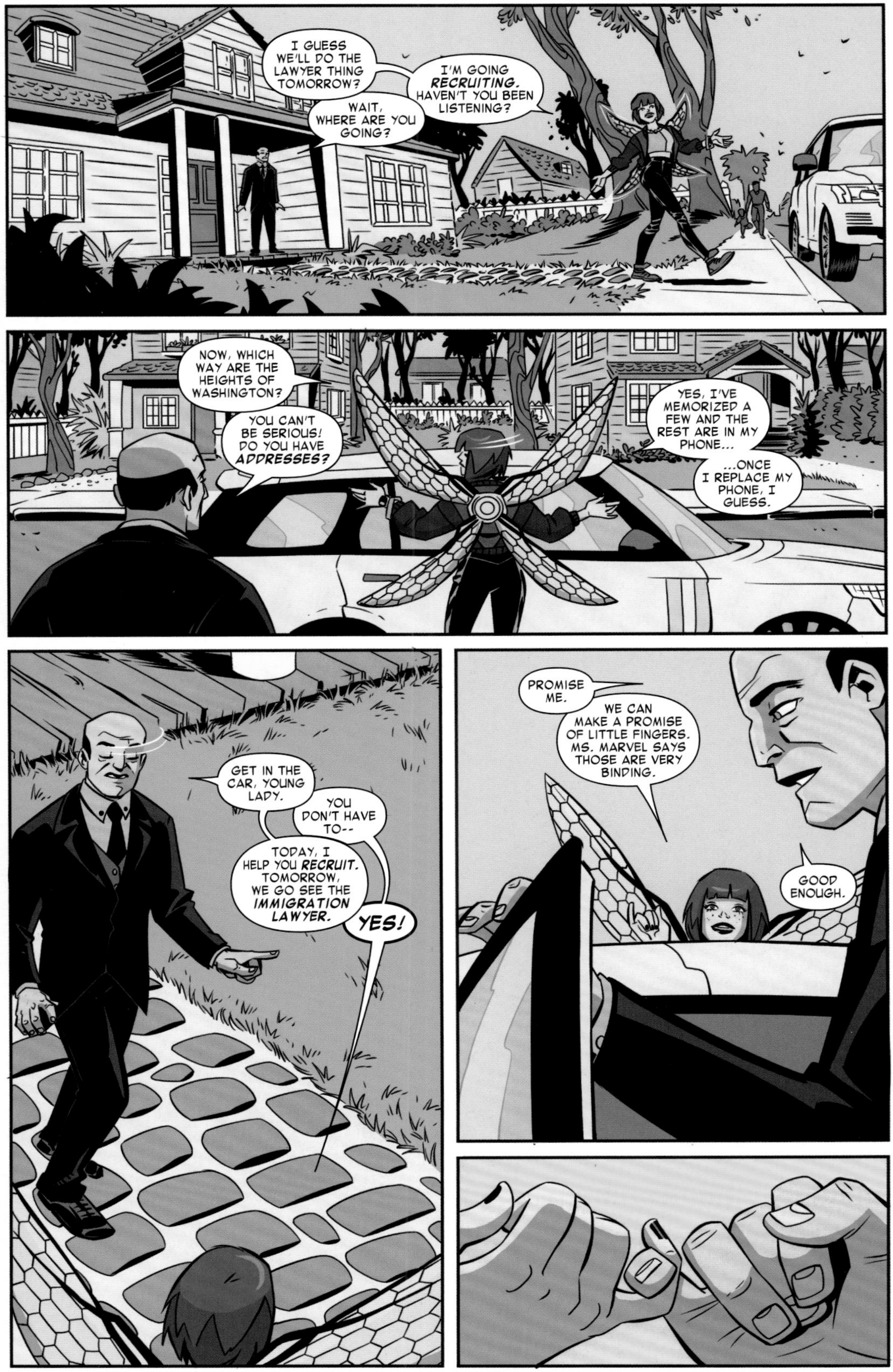
I GUESS WE'LL DO THE LAWYER THING TOMORROW?
I'M GOING RECRUITING. HAVEN'T YOU BEEN LISTENING?
WAIT, WHERE ARE YOU GOING?
NOW, WHICH WAY ARE THE HEIGHTS OF WASHINGTON?
YOU CAN'T BE SERIOUS! DO YOU HAVE ADDRESSES?
YES, I'VE MEMORIZED A FEW AND THE REST ARE IN MY PHONE...
...ONCE I REPLACE MY PHONE, I GUESS.
GET IN THE CAR, YOUNG LADY.
YOU DON'T HAVE TO--
TODAY, I HELP YOU RECRUIT. TOMORROW, WE GO SEE THE IMMIGRATION LAWYER.
YES!
PROMISE ME.
WE CAN MAKE A PROMISE OF LITTLE FINGERS. MS. MARVEL SAYS THOSE ARE VERY BINDING.
GOOD ENOUGH.

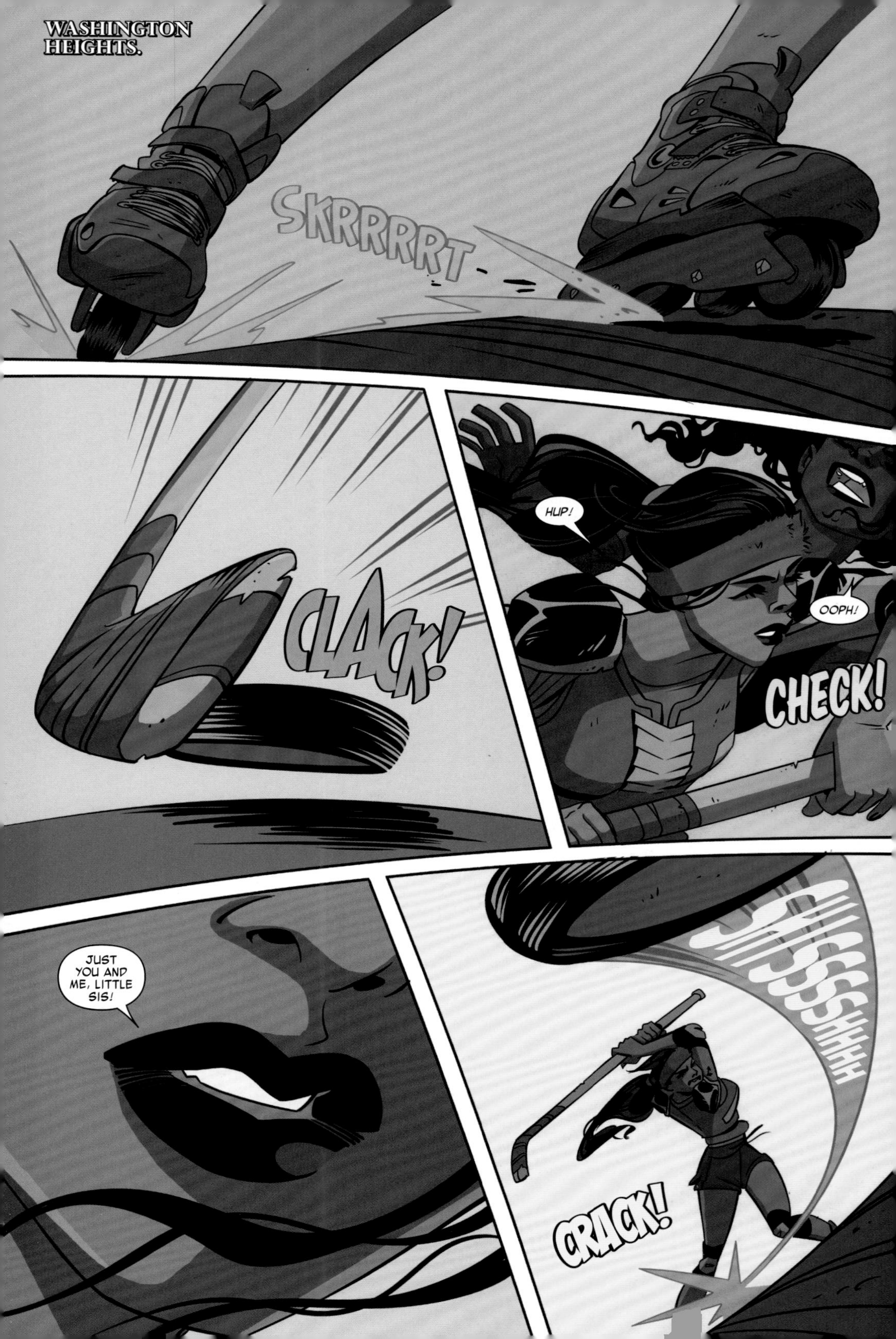
WASHINGTON HEIGHTS.
SKRRRRT
CLACK!
HUP!
OOPH!
CHECK!
JUST YOU AND ME, LITTLE SIS!
SHHSSSSHHHH
CRACK!

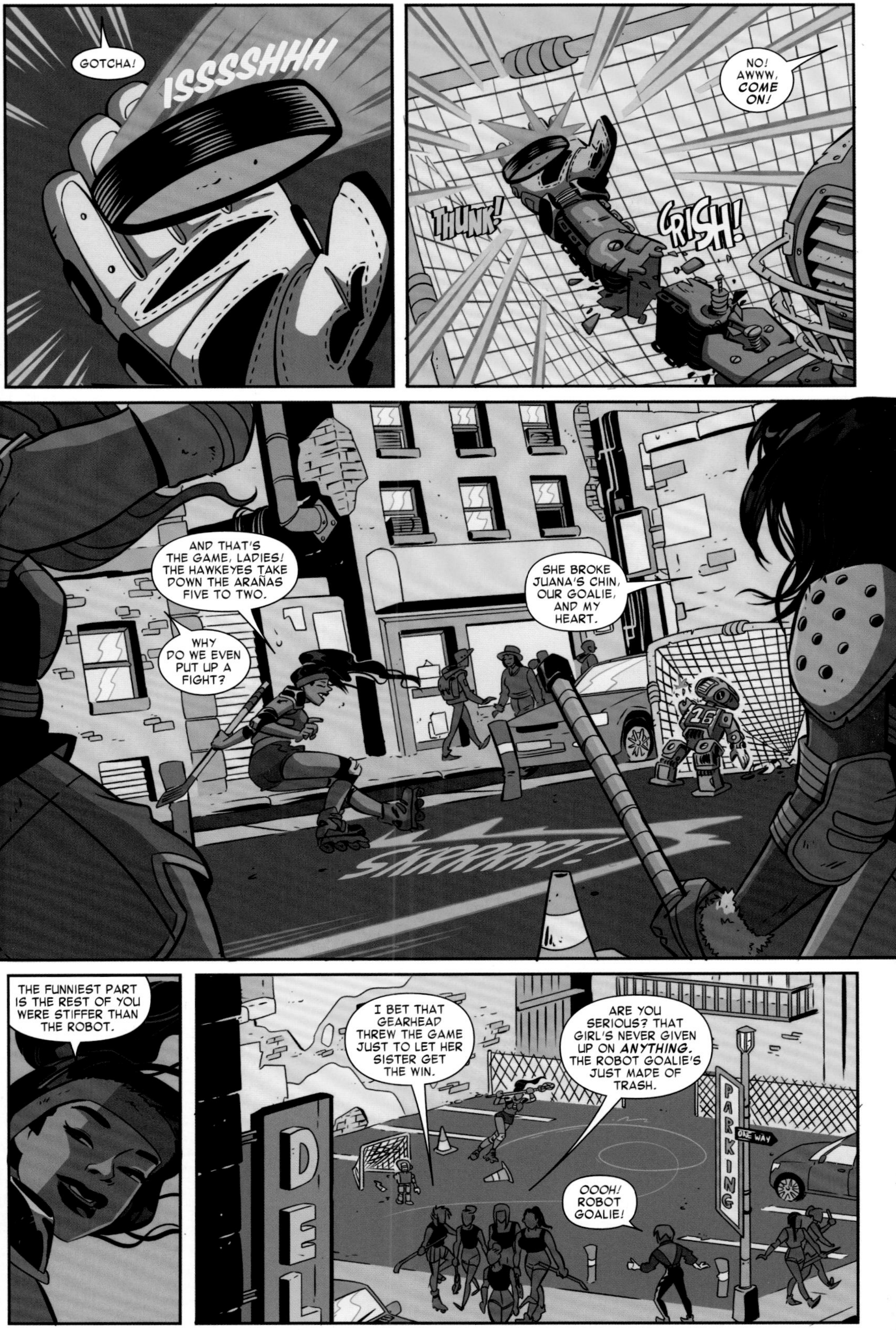
GOTCHA!
ISSSSHHH
NO! AWWW, COME ON!
THUNK!
CRISH!
AND THAT'S THE GAME, LADIES! THE HAWKEYES TAKE DOWN THE ARAÑAS FIVE TO TWO.
WHY DO WE EVEN PUT UP A FIGHT?
SHE BROKE JUANA'S CHIN, OUR GOALIE, AND MY HEART.
SKRRRRT!
THE FUNNIEST PART IS THE REST OF YOU WERE STIFFER THAN THE ROBOT.
I BET THAT GEARHEAD THREW THE GAME JUST TO LET HER SISTER GET THE WIN.
ARE YOU SERIOUS? THAT GIRL'S NEVER GIVEN UP ON ANYTHING. THE ROBOT GOALIE'S JUST MADE OF TRASH.
OOOH! ROBOT GOALIE!
DELI
PARKING
ONE WAY

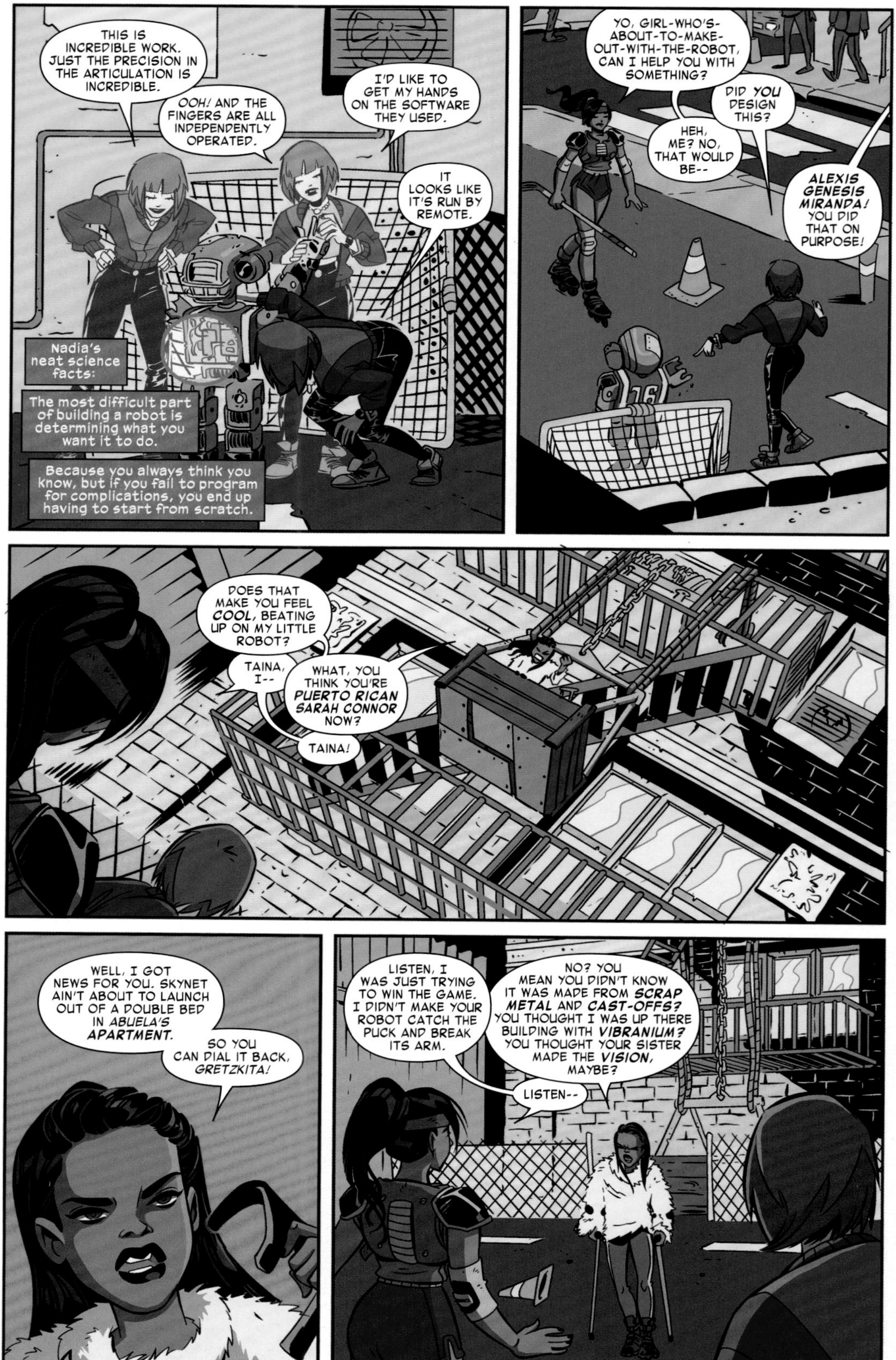

THIS IS INCREDIBLE WORK. JUST THE PRECISION IN THE ARTICULATION IS INCREDIBLE.
OOH! AND THE FINGERS ARE ALL INDEPENDENTLY OPERATED.
I'D LIKE TO GET MY HANDS ON THE SOFTWARE THEY USED.
IT LOOKS LIKE IT'S RUN BY REMOTE.
Nadia's neat science facts:
The most difficult part of building a robot is determining what you want it to do.
Because you always think you know, but if you fail to program for complications, you end up having to start from scratch.
YO, GIRL-WHO'S-ABOUT-TO-MAKE-OUT-WITH-THE-ROBOT, CAN I HELP YOU WITH SOMETHING?
DID YOU DESIGN THIS?
HEH, ME? NO, THAT WOULD BE--
ALEXIS GENESIS MIRANDA! YOU DID THAT ON PURPOSE!
DOES THAT MAKE YOU FEEL COOL, BEATING UP ON MY LITTLE ROBOT?
TAINA, I--
WHAT, YOU THINK YOU'RE PUERTO RICAN SARAH CONNOR NOW?
TAINA!
WELL, I GOT NEWS FOR YOU. SKYNET AIN'T ABOUT TO LAUNCH OUT OF A DOUBLE BED IN ABUELA'S APARTMENT.
SO YOU CAN DIAL IT BACK, GRETZKITA!
LISTEN, I WAS JUST TRYING TO WIN THE GAME. I DIDN'T MAKE YOUR ROBOT CATCH THE PUCK AND BREAK ITS ARM.
NO? YOU MEAN YOU DIDN'T KNOW IT WAS MADE FROM SCRAP METAL AND CAST-OFFS? YOU THOUGHT I WAS UP THERE BUILDING WITH VIBRANIUM? YOU THOUGHT YOUR SISTER MADE THE VISION, MAYBE?
LISTEN--

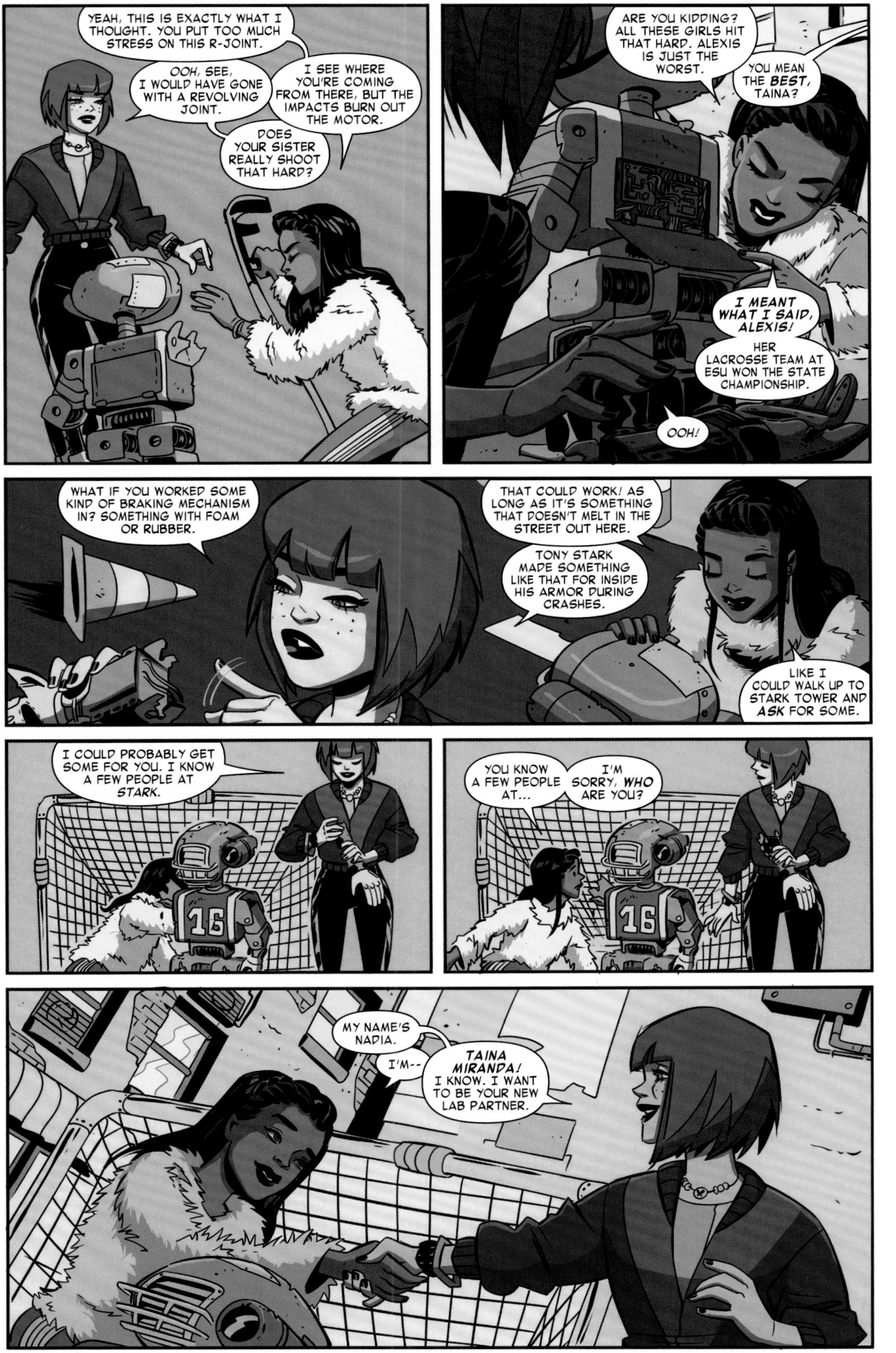
YEAH, THIS IS EXACTLY WHAT I THOUGHT. YOU PUT TOO MUCH STRESS ON THIS R-JOINT.
OOH, SEE, I WOULD HAVE GONE WITH A REVOLVING JOINT.
I SEE WHERE YOU'RE COMING FROM THERE, BUT THE IMPACTS BURN OUT THE MOTOR.
DOES YOUR SISTER REALLY SHOOT THAT HARD?
ARE YOU KIDDING? ALL THESE GIRLS HIT THAT HARD. ALEXIS IS JUST THE WORST.
YOU MEAN THE BEST, TAINA?
I MEANT WHAT I SAID, ALEXIS!
HER LACROSSE TEAM AT ESU WON THE STATE CHAMPIONSHIP.
OOH!
WHAT IF YOU WORKED SOME KIND OF BRAKING MECHANISM IN? SOMETHING WITH FOAM OR RUBBER.
THAT COULD WORK! AS LONG AS IT'S SOMETHING THAT DOESN'T MELT IN THE STREET OUT HERE.
TONY STARK MADE SOMETHING LIKE THAT FOR INSIDE HIS ARMOR DURING CRASHES.
LIKE I COULD WALK UP TO STARK TOWER AND ASK FOR SOME.
I COULD PROBABLY GET SOME FOR YOU. I KNOW A FEW PEOPLE AT STARK.
YOU KNOW A FEW PEOPLE AT...
I'M SORRY, WHO ARE YOU?
MY NAME'S NADIA.
I'M--
TAINA MIRANDA! I KNOW. I WANT TO BE YOUR NEW LAB PARTNER.

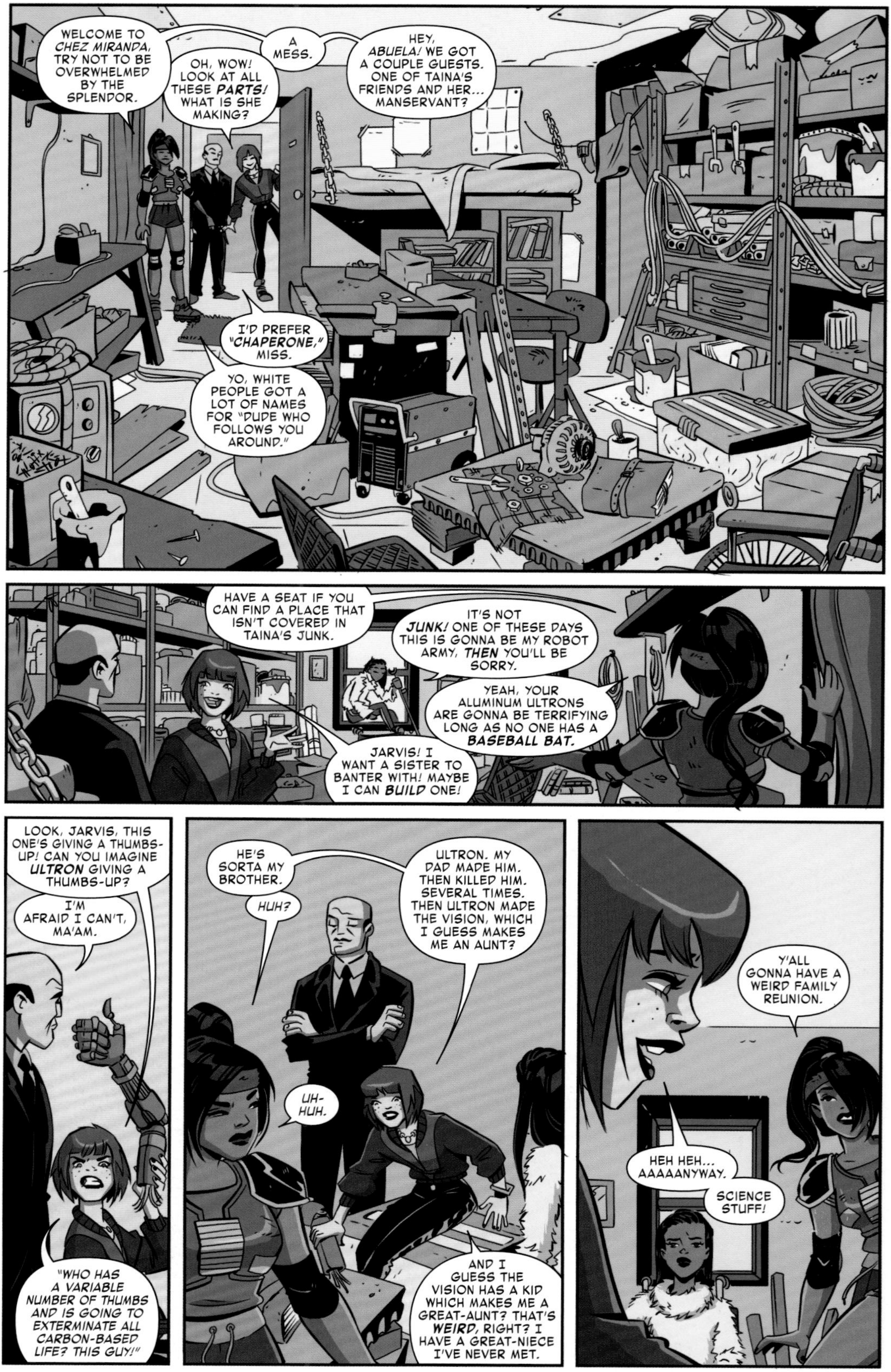

WELCOME TO CHEZ MIRANDA. TRY NOT TO BE OVERWHELMED BY THE SPLENDOR.
A MESS.
OH, WOW! LOOK AT ALL THESE PARTS! WHAT IS SHE MAKING?
HEY, ABUELA! WE GOT A COUPLE GUESTS. ONE OF TAINA'S FRIENDS AND HER... MANSERVANT?
I'D PREFER "CHAPERONE," MISS.
YO, WHITE PEOPLE GOT A LOT OF NAMES FOR "DUDE WHO FOLLOWS YOU AROUND."
HAVE A SEAT IF YOU CAN FIND A PLACE THAT ISN'T COVERED IN TAINA'S JUNK.
IT'S NOT JUNK! ONE OF THESE DAYS THIS IS GONNA BE MY ROBOT ARMY, THEN YOU'LL BE SORRY.
YEAH, YOUR ALUMINUM ULTRONS ARE GONNA BE TERRIFYING LONG AS NO ONE HAS A BASEBALL BAT.
JARVIS! I WANT A SISTER TO BANTER WITH! MAYBE I CAN BUILD ONE!
LOOK, JARVIS, THIS ONE'S GIVING A THUMBS-UP! CAN YOU IMAGINE ULTRON GIVING A THUMBS-UP?
I'M AFRAID I CAN'T, MA'AM.
"WHO HAS A VARIABLE NUMBER OF THUMBS AND IS GOING TO EXTERMINATE ALL CARBON-BASED LIFE? THIS GUY!"
HE'S SORTA MY BROTHER.
HUH?
ULTRON. MY DAD MADE HIM. THEN KILLED HIM. SEVERAL TIMES. THEN ULTRON MADE THE VISION, WHICH I GUESS MAKES ME AN AUNT?
UH-HUH.
AND I GUESS THE VISION HAS A KID WHICH MAKES ME A GREAT-AUNT? THAT'S WEIRD, RIGHT? I HAVE A GREAT-NIECE I'VE NEVER MET.
Y'ALL GONNA HAVE A WEIRD FAMILY REUNION.
HEH HEH... AAAAANYWAY.
SCIENCE STUFF!

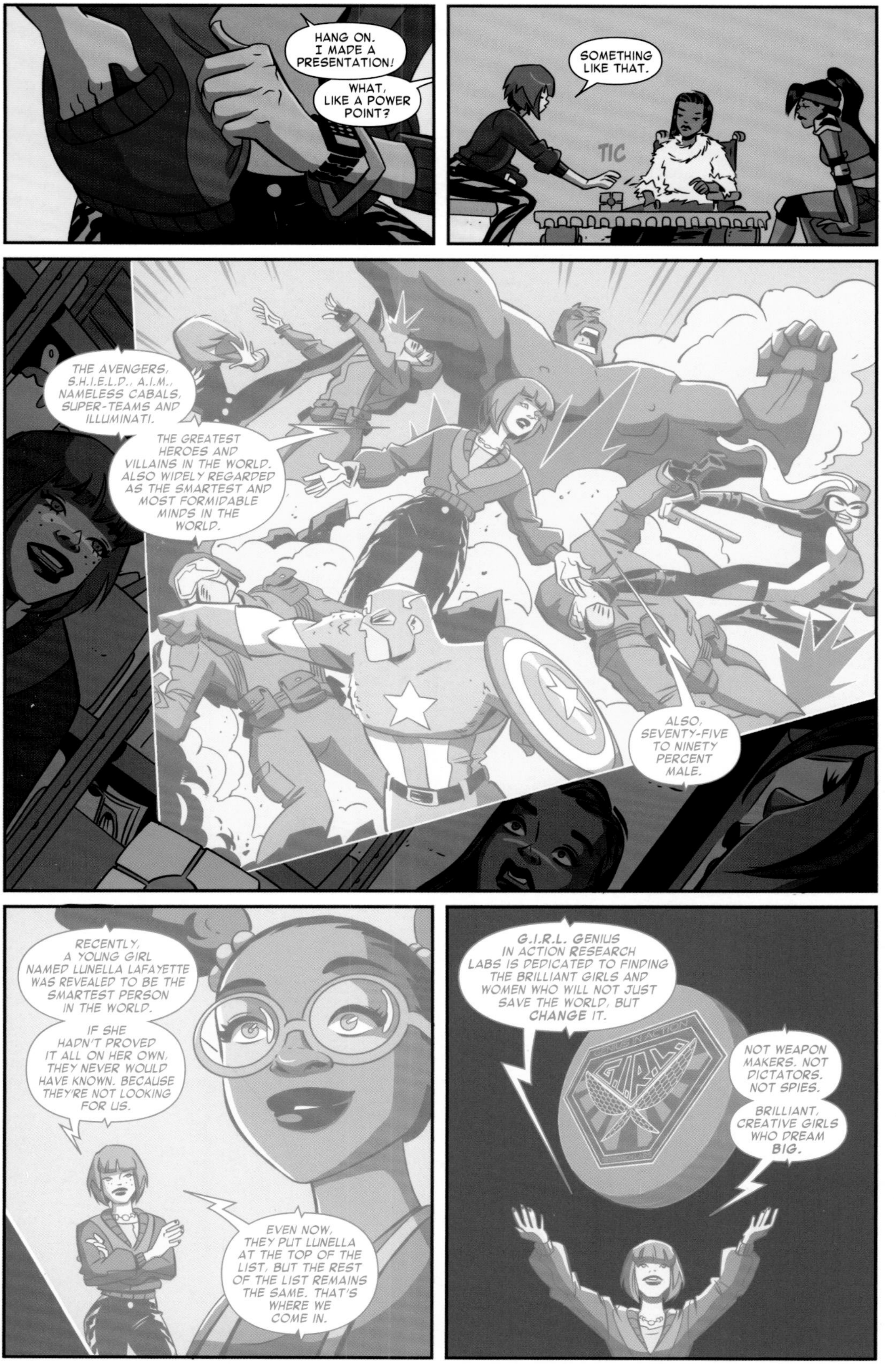
HANG ON. I MADE A PRESENTATION!
WHAT, LIKE A POWER POINT?
SOMETHING LIKE THAT.
TIC
THE AVENGERS, S.H.I.E.L.D., A.I.M., NAMELESS CABALS, SUPER-TEAMS AND ILLUMINATI.
THE GREATEST HEROES AND VILLAINS IN THE WORLD. ALSO WIDELY REGARDED AS THE SMARTEST AND MOST FORMIDABLE MINDS IN THE WORLD.
ALSO, SEVENTY-FIVE TO NINETY PERCENT MALE.
RECENTLY, A YOUNG GIRL NAMED LUNELLA LAFAYETTE WAS REVEALED TO BE THE SMARTEST PERSON IN THE WORLD.
IF SHE HADN'T PROVED IT ALL ON HER OWN, THEY NEVER WOULD HAVE KNOWN. BECAUSE THEY'RE NOT LOOKING FOR US.
EVEN NOW, THEY PUT LUNELLA AT THE TOP OF THE LIST, BUT THE REST OF THE LIST REMAINS THE SAME. THAT'S WHERE WE COME IN.
G.I.R.L. GENIUS IN ACTION RESEARCH LABS IS DEDICATED TO FINDING THE BRILLIANT GIRLS AND WOMEN WHO WILL NOT JUST SAVE THE WORLD, BUT CHANGE IT.
NOT WEAPON MAKERS. NOT DICTATORS. NOT SPIES.
BRILLIANT, CREATIVE GIRLS WHO DREAM BIG.

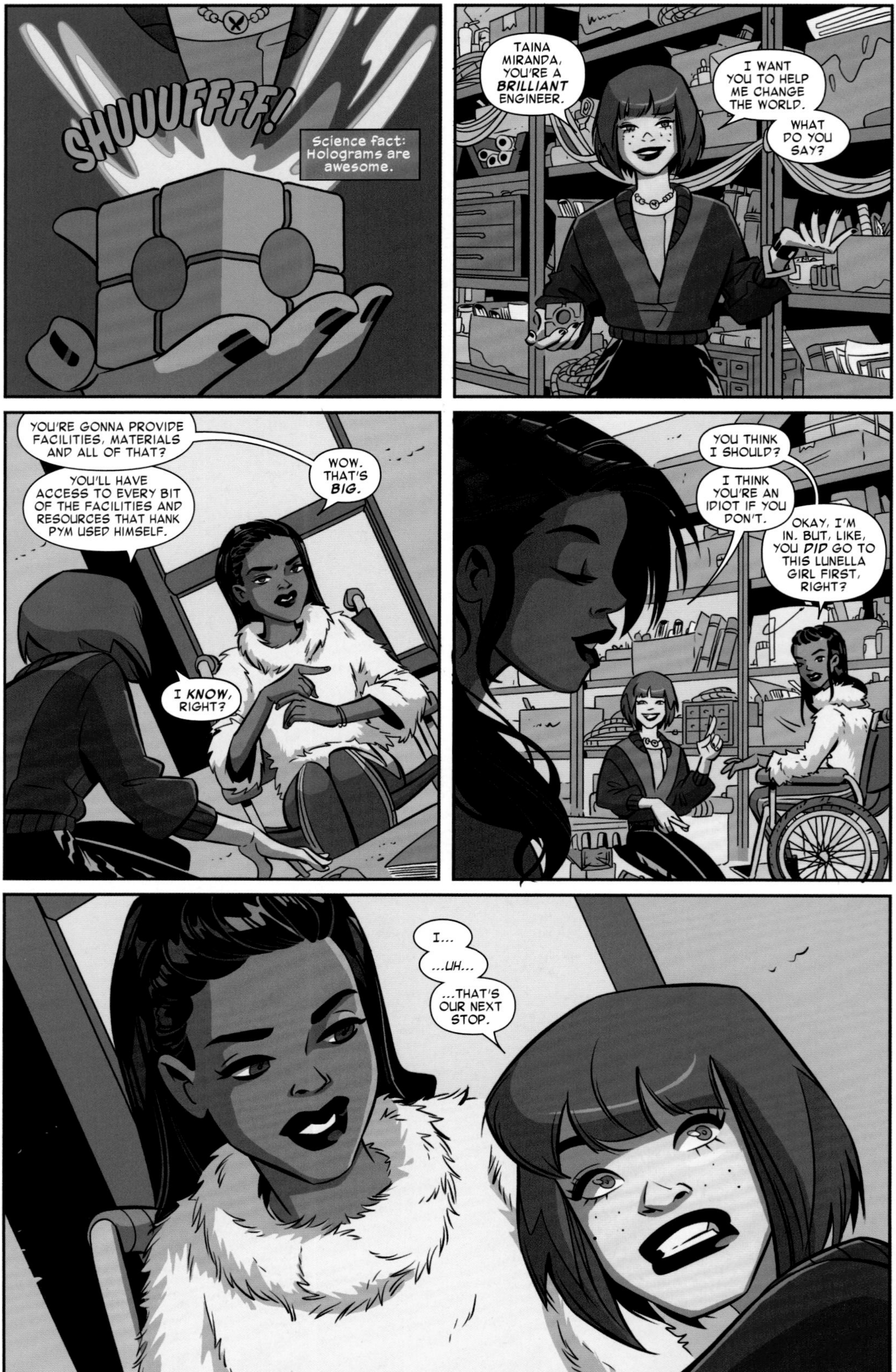
SHUUUFFFF!
Science fact: Holograms are awesome.
TAINA MIRANDA, YOU'RE A BRILLIANT ENGINEER.
I WANT YOU TO HELP ME CHANGE THE WORLD.
WHAT DO YOU SAY?
YOU'RE GONNA PROVIDE FACILITIES, MATERIALS AND ALL OF THAT?
YOU'LL HAVE ACCESS TO EVERY BIT OF THE FACILITIES AND RESOURCES THAT HANK PYM USED HIMSELF.
WOW. THAT'S BIG.
I KNOW, RIGHT?
YOU THINK I SHOULD?
I THINK YOU'RE AN IDIOT IF YOU DON'T.
OKAY, I'M IN. BUT, LIKE, YOU DID GO TO THIS LUNELLA GIRL FIRST, RIGHT?
I...
...UH...
...THAT'S OUR NEXT STOP.

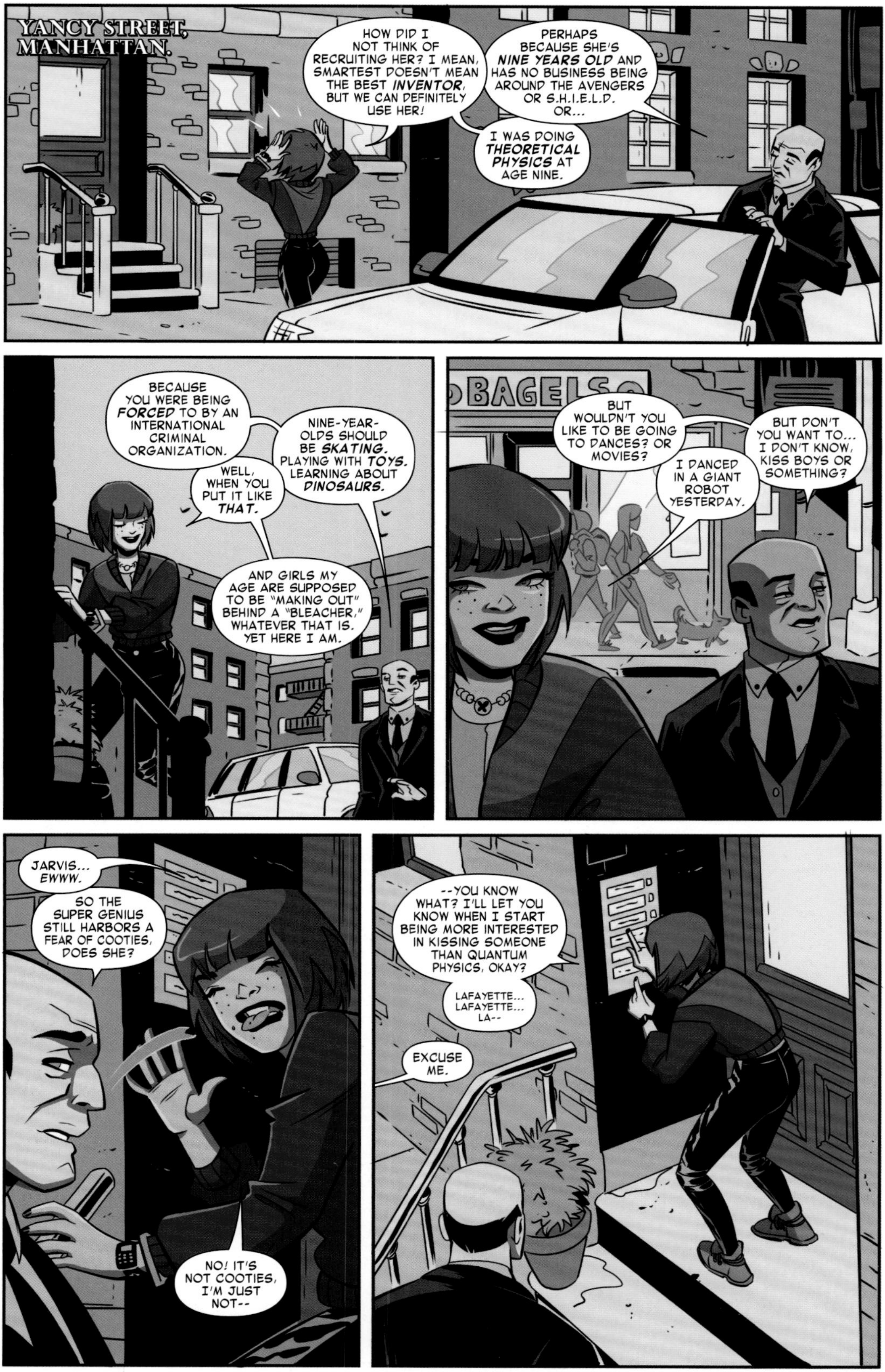
YANCY STREET, MANHATTAN.
HOW DID I NOT THINK OF RECRUITING HER? I MEAN, SMARTEST DOESN'T MEAN THE BEST INVENTOR, BUT WE CAN DEFINITELY USE HER!
PERHAPS BECAUSE SHE'S NINE YEARS OLD AND HAS NO BUSINESS BEING AROUND THE AVENGERS OR S.H.I.E.L.D. OR...
I WAS DOING THEORETICAL PHYSICS AT AGE NINE.
BECAUSE YOU WERE BEING FORCED TO BY AN INTERNATIONAL CRIMINAL ORGANIZATION.
WELL, WHEN YOU PUT IT LIKE THAT.
NINE-YEAR-OLDS SHOULD BE SKATING. PLAYING WITH TOYS. LEARNING ABOUT DINOSAURS.
AND GIRLS MY AGE ARE SUPPOSED TO BE "MAKING OUT" BEHIND A "BLEACHER," WHATEVER THAT IS. YET HERE I AM.
BAGELS
BUT WOULDN'T YOU LIKE TO BE GOING TO DANCES? OR MOVIES?
I DANCED IN A GIANT ROBOT YESTERDAY.
BUT DON'T YOU WANT TO... I DON'T KNOW, KISS BOYS OR SOMETHING?
JARVIS... EWWW.
SO THE SUPER GENIUS STILL HARBORS A FEAR OF COOTIES, DOES SHE?
NO! IT'S NOT COOTIES, I'M JUST NOT--
--YOU KNOW WHAT? I'LL LET YOU KNOW WHEN I START BEING MORE INTERESTED IN KISSING SOMEONE THAN QUANTUM PHYSICS, OKAY?
LAFAYETTE... LAFAYETTE... LA--
EXCUSE ME.

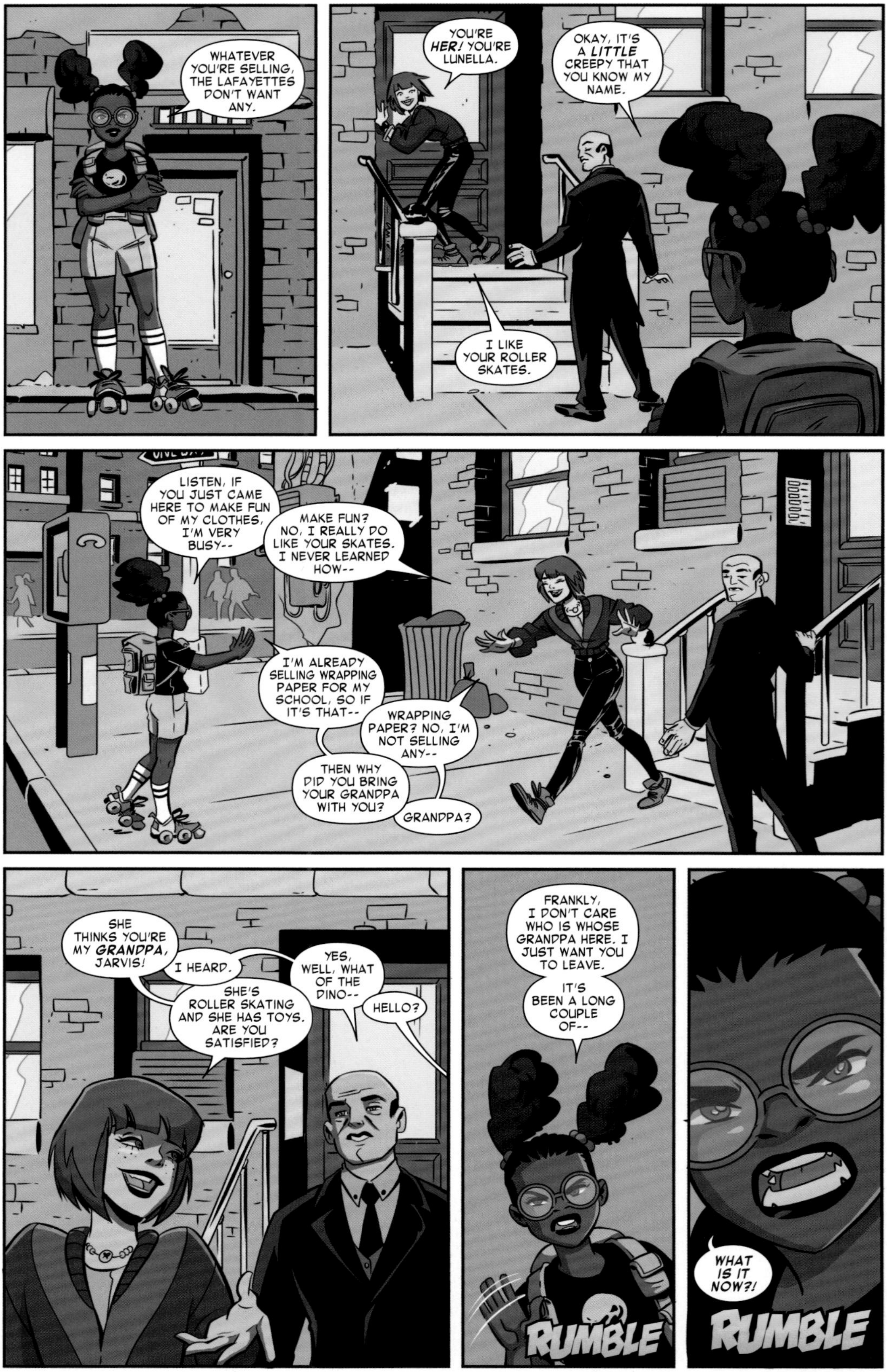
WHATEVER YOU'RE SELLING, THE LAFAYETTES DON'T WANT ANY.
YOU'RE HER! YOU'RE LUNELLA.
OKAY, IT'S A LITTLE CREEPY THAT YOU KNOW MY NAME.
I LIKE YOUR ROLLER SKATES.
LISTEN, IF YOU JUST CAME HERE TO MAKE FUN OF MY CLOTHES, I'M VERY BUSY--
MAKE FUN? NO, I REALLY DO LIKE YOUR SKATES. I NEVER LEARNED HOW--
I'M ALREADY SELLING WRAPPING PAPER FOR MY SCHOOL, SO IF IT'S THAT--
WRAPPING PAPER? NO, I'M NOT SELLING ANY--
THEN WHY DID YOU BRING YOUR GRANDPA WITH YOU?
GRANDPA?
SHE THINKS YOU'RE MY GRANDPA, JARVIS!
I HEARD.
SHE'S ROLLER SKATING AND SHE HAS TOYS. ARE YOU SATISFIED?
YES, WELL, WHAT OF THE DINO--
HELLO?
FRANKLY, I DON'T CARE WHO IS WHOSE GRANDPA HERE. I JUST WANT YOU TO LEAVE.
IT'S BEEN A LONG COUPLE OF--
RUMBLE
WHAT IS IT NOW?!
RUMBLE

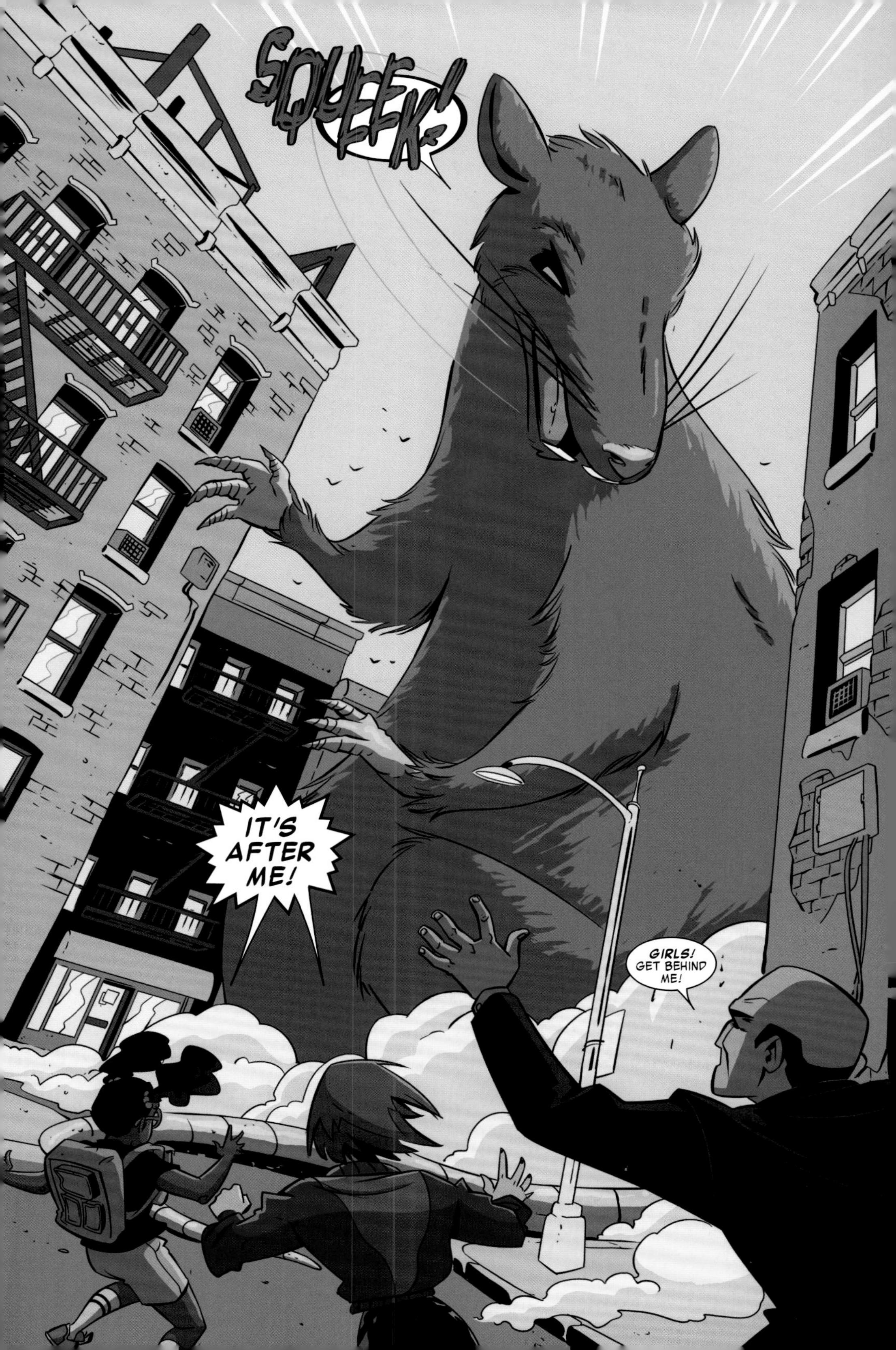
SQUEEK!
IT'S AFTER ME!
GIRLS! GET BEHIND ME!

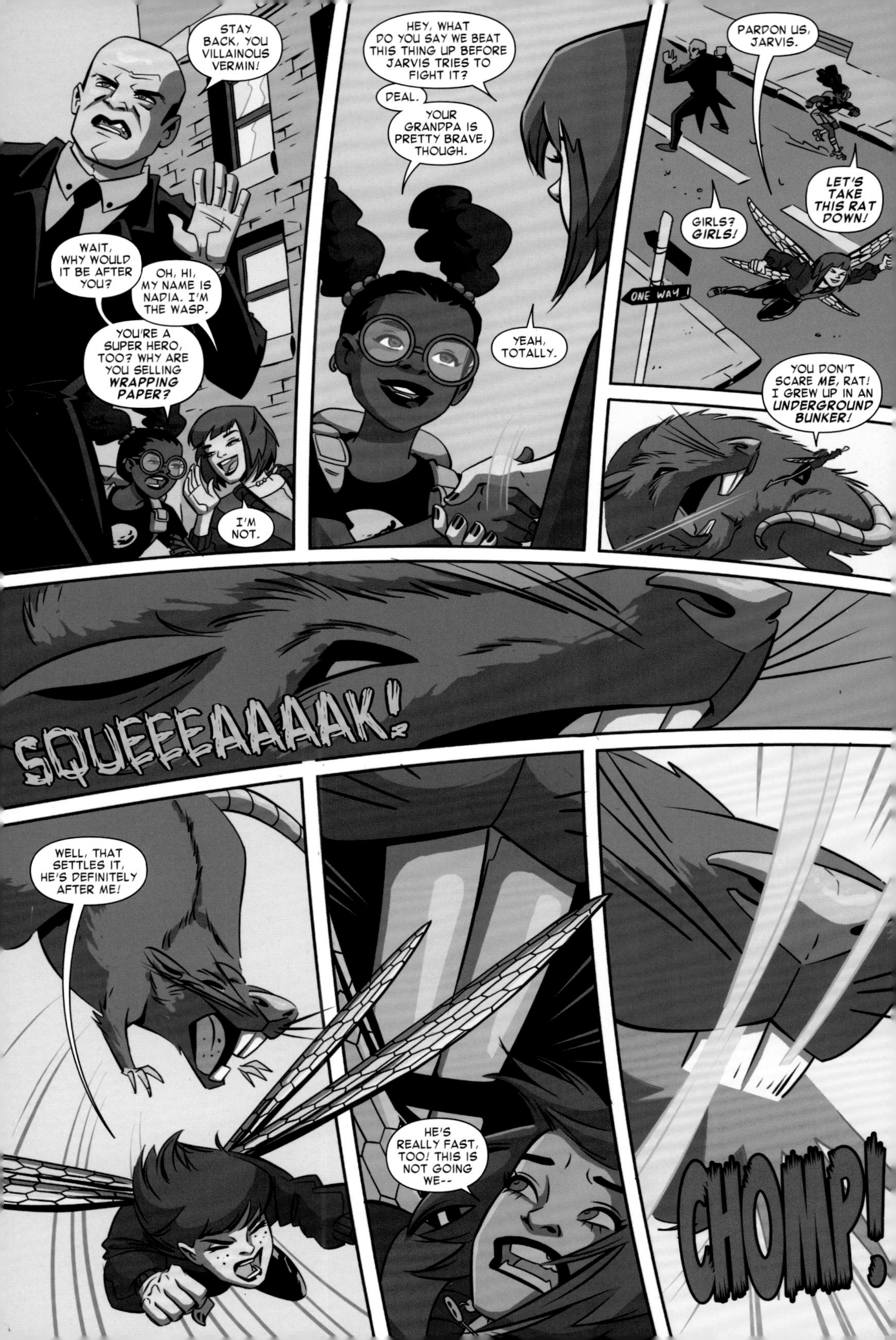

STAY BACK, YOU VILLAINOUS VERMIN!
WAIT, WHY WOULD IT BE AFTER YOU?
OH, HI, MY NAME IS NADIA. I'M THE WASP.
YOU'RE A SUPER HERO, TOO? WHY ARE YOU SELLING WRAPPING PAPER?
I'M NOT.
HEY, WHAT DO YOU SAY WE BEAT THIS THING UP BEFORE JARVIS TRIES TO FIGHT IT?
DEAL.
YOUR GRANDPA IS PRETTY BRAVE, THOUGH.
YEAH, TOTALLY.
PARDON US, JARVIS.
ONE WAY
GIRLS? GIRLS!
LET'S TAKE THIS RAT DOWN!
YOU DON'T SCARE ME, RAT! I GREW UP IN AN UNDERGROUND BUNKER!
SQUEEEAAAAK!
WELL, THAT SETTLES IT, HE'S DEFINITELY AFTER ME!
HE'S REALLY FAST, TOO! THIS IS NOT GOING WE--
CHOMP!

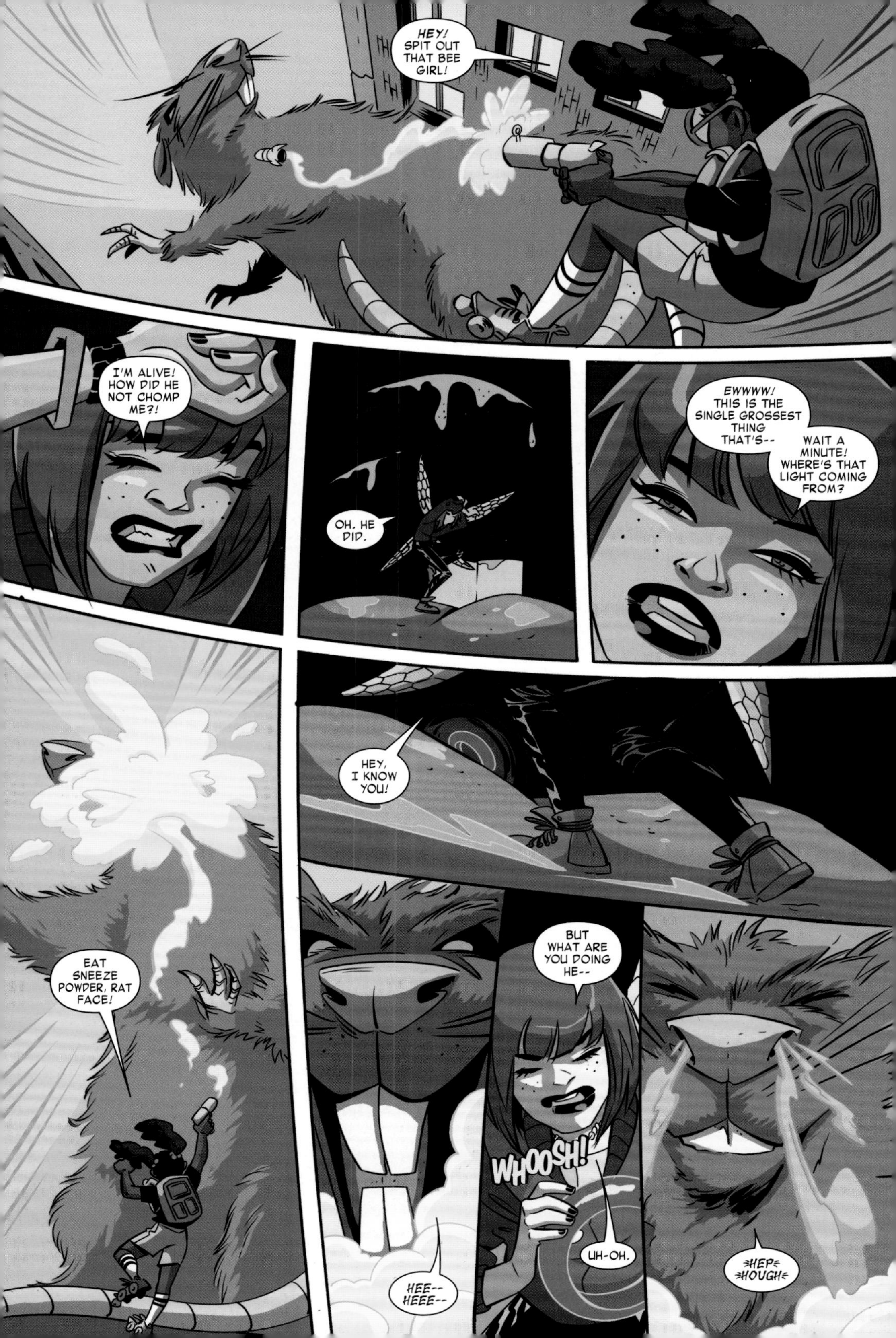

HEY! SPIT OUT THAT BEE GIRL!
I'M ALIVE! HOW DID HE NOT CHOMP ME?!
OH. HE DID.
EWWWW! THIS IS THE SINGLE GROSSEST THING THAT'S--
WAIT A MINUTE! WHERE'S THAT LIGHT COMING FROM?
EAT SNEEZE POWDER, RAT FACE!
HEY, I KNOW YOU!
BUT WHAT ARE YOU DOING HE--
WHOOSH!
HEE-- HEEE--
UH-OH.
HEP HOUGH

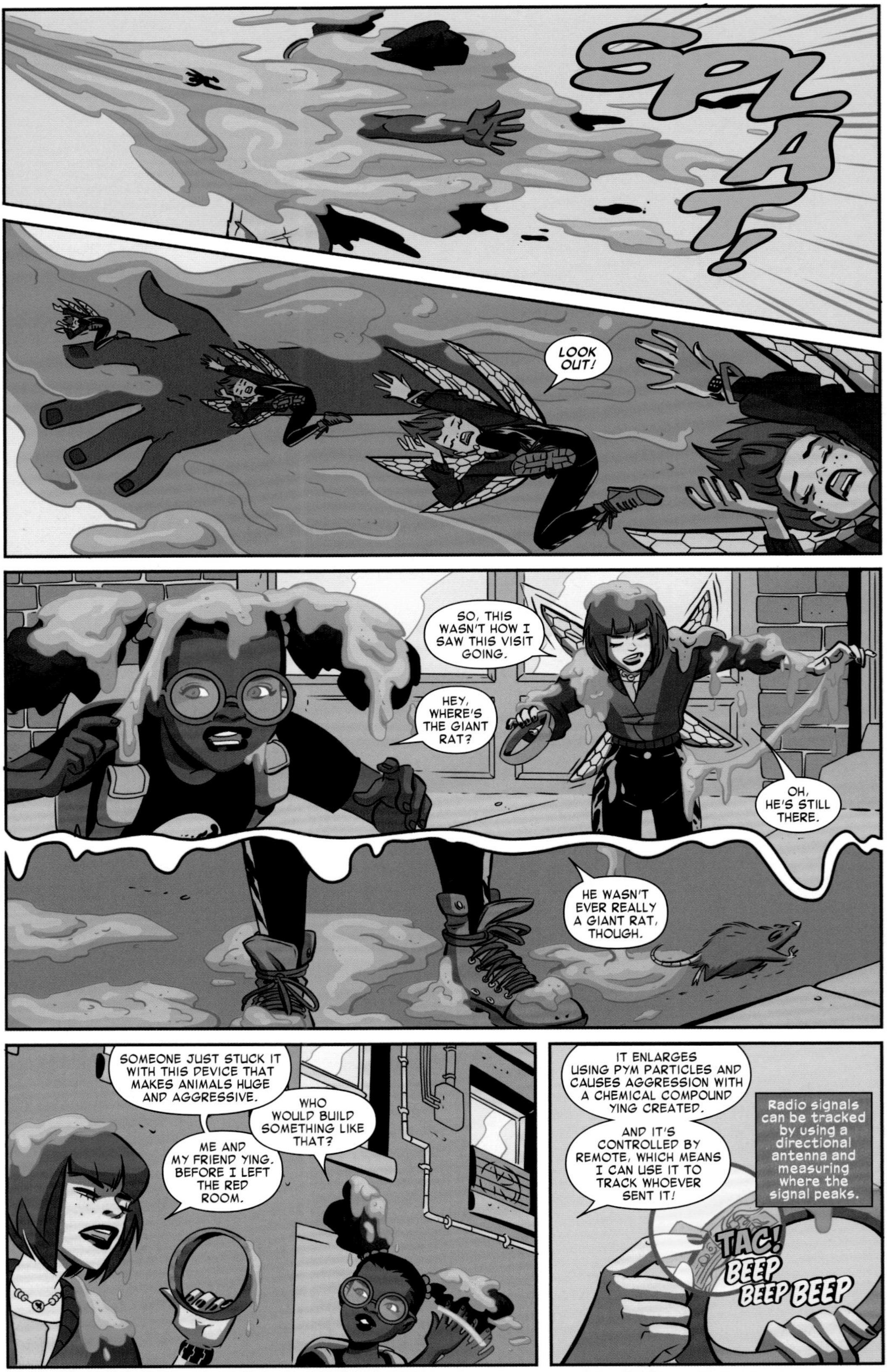
SPLAT!
LOOK OUT!
SO, THIS WASN'T HOW I SAW THIS VISIT GOING.
HEY, WHERE'S THE GIANT RAT?
OH, HE'S STILL THERE.
HE WASN'T EVER REALLY A GIANT RAT, THOUGH.
SOMEONE JUST STUCK IT WITH THIS DEVICE THAT MAKES ANIMALS HUGE AND AGGRESSIVE.
WHO WOULD BUILD SOMETHING LIKE THAT?
ME AND MY FRIEND YING. BEFORE I LEFT THE RED ROOM.
IT ENLARGES USING PYM PARTICLES AND CAUSES AGGRESSION WITH A CHEMICAL COMPOUND YING CREATED.
AND IT'S CONTROLLED BY REMOTE, WHICH MEANS I CAN USE IT TO TRACK WHOEVER SENT IT!
Radio signals can be tracked by using a directional antenna and measuring where the signal peaks.
TAC!
BEEP
BEEP BEEP

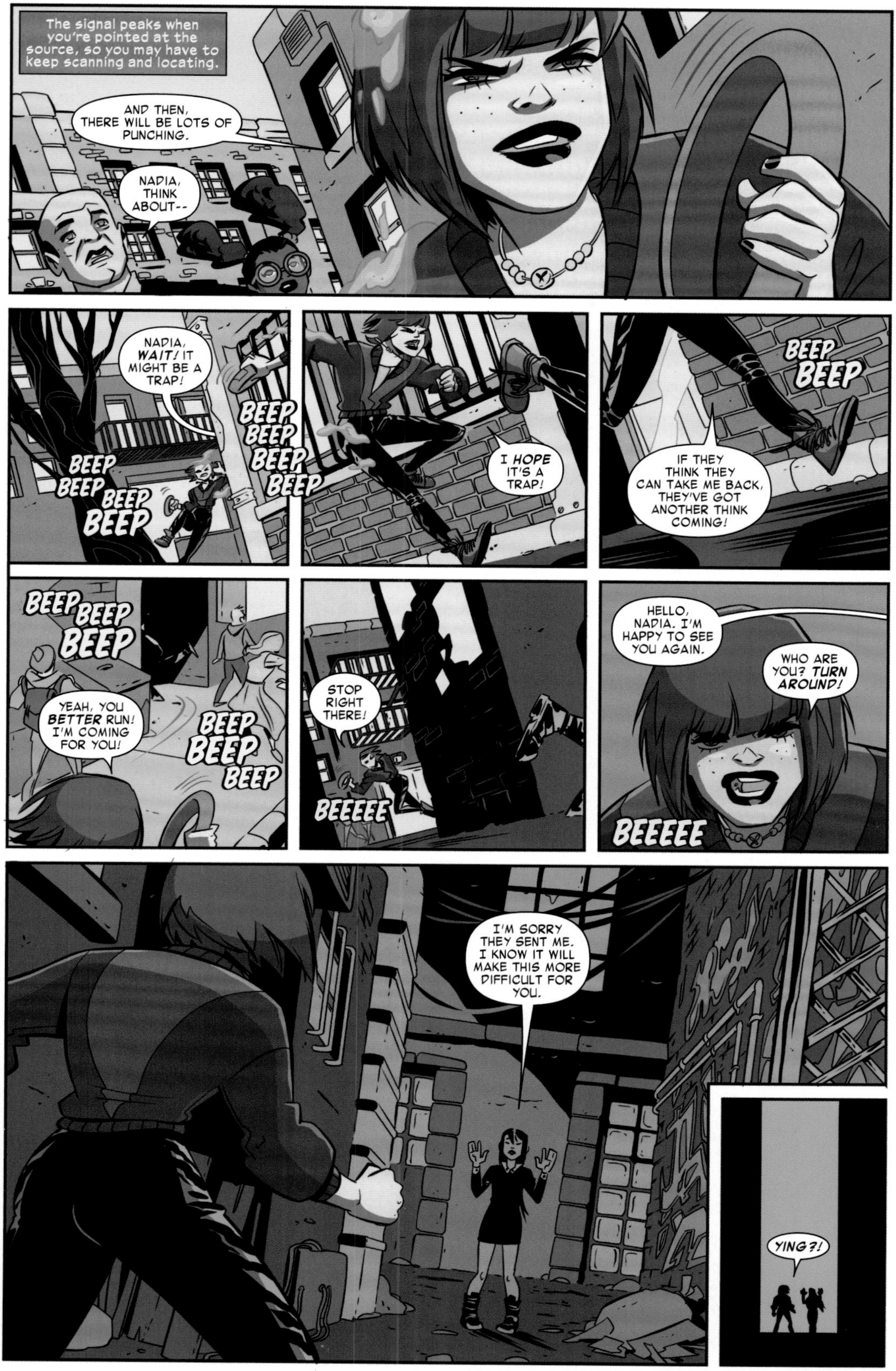
The signal peaks when you're pointed at the source, so you may have to keep scanning and locating.
AND THEN, THERE WILL BE LOTS OF PUNCHING.
NADIA, THINK ABOUT--
NADIA, WAIT! IT MIGHT BE A TRAP!
BEEP BEEP BEEP BEEP
BEEP BEEP BEEP BEEP
I HOPE IT'S A TRAP!
BEEP BEEP
IF THEY THINK THEY CAN TAKE ME BACK, THEY'VE GOT ANOTHER THINK COMING!
BEEP BEEP BEEP
YEAH, YOU BETTER RUN! I'M COMING FOR YOU!
BEEP BEEP BEEP
STOP RIGHT THERE!
BEEEEE
HELLO, NADIA. I'M HAPPY TO SEE YOU AGAIN.
WHO ARE YOU? TURN AROUND!
BEEEEE
I'M SORRY THEY SENT ME. I KNOW IT WILL MAKE THIS MORE DIFFICULT FOR YOU.
YING?!

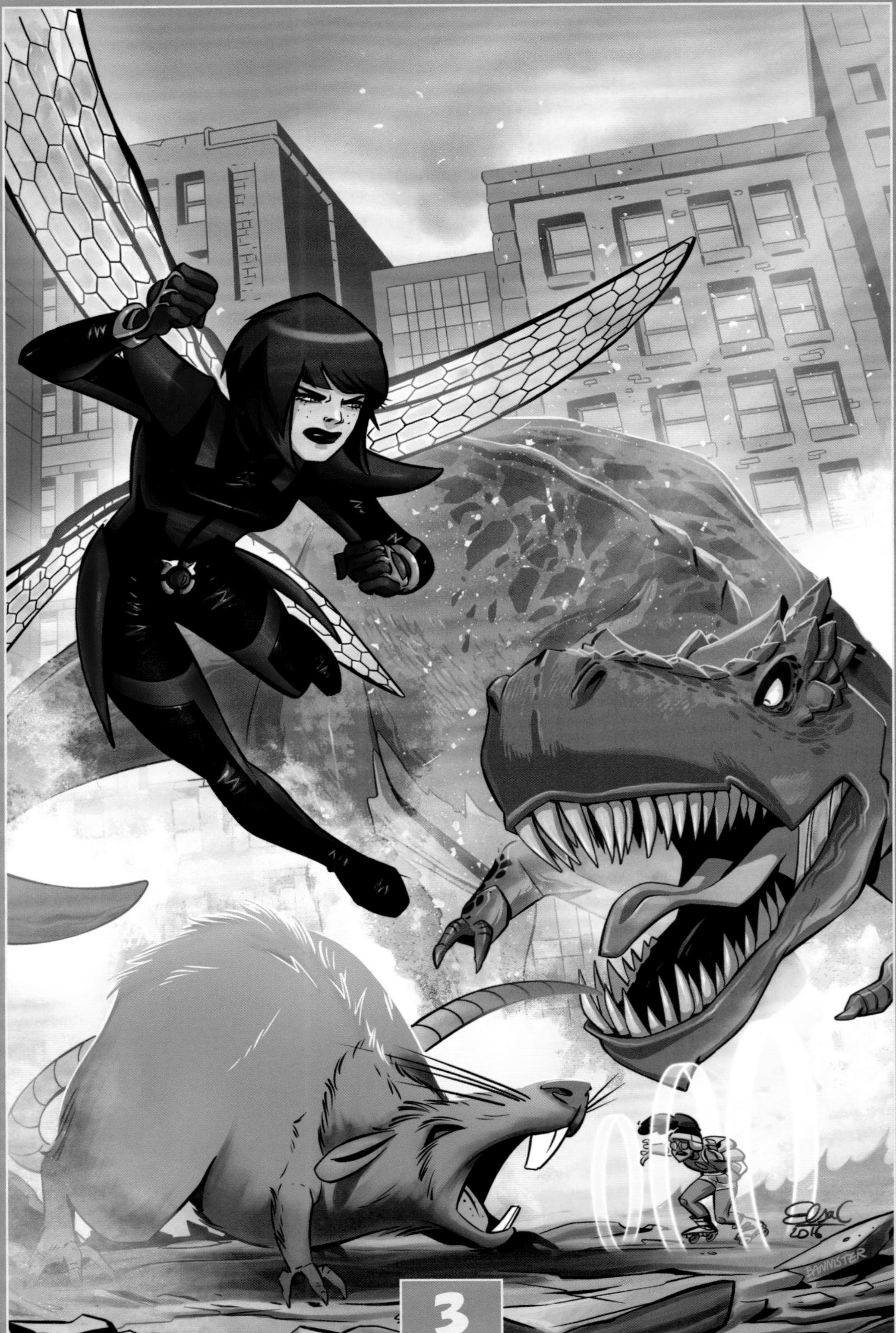
BANNISTER

3

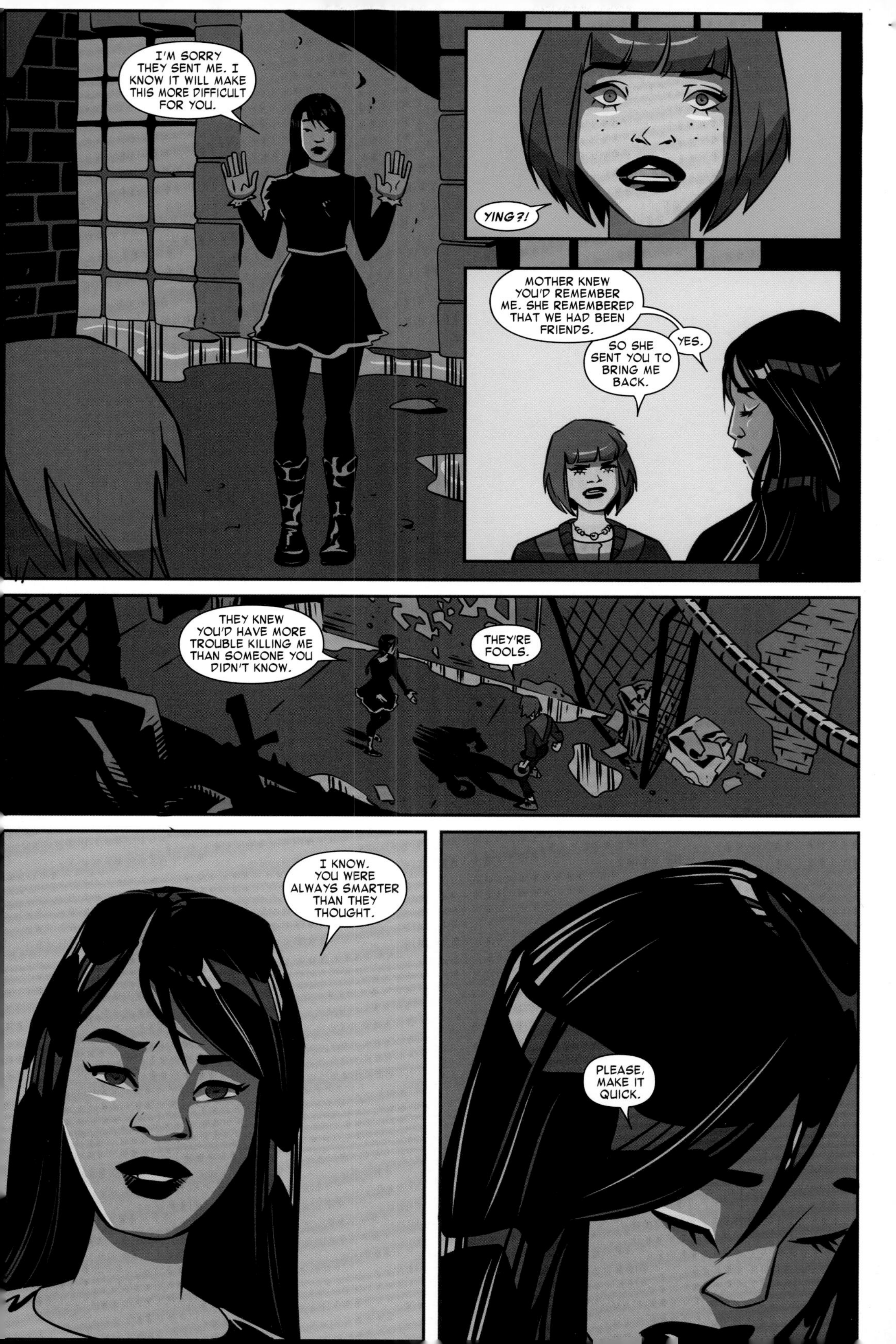
I'M SORRY THEY SENT ME. I KNOW IT WILL MAKE THIS MORE DIFFICULT FOR YOU.
YING?!
MOTHER KNEW YOU'D REMEMBER ME. SHE REMEMBERED THAT WE HAD BEEN FRIENDS.
YES.
SO SHE SENT YOU TO BRING ME BACK.
THEY KNEW YOU'D HAVE MORE TROUBLE KILLING ME THAN SOMEONE YOU DIDN'T KNOW.
THEY'RE FOOLS.
I KNOW. YOU WERE ALWAYS SMARTER THAN THEY THOUGHT.
PLEASE, MAKE IT QUICK.

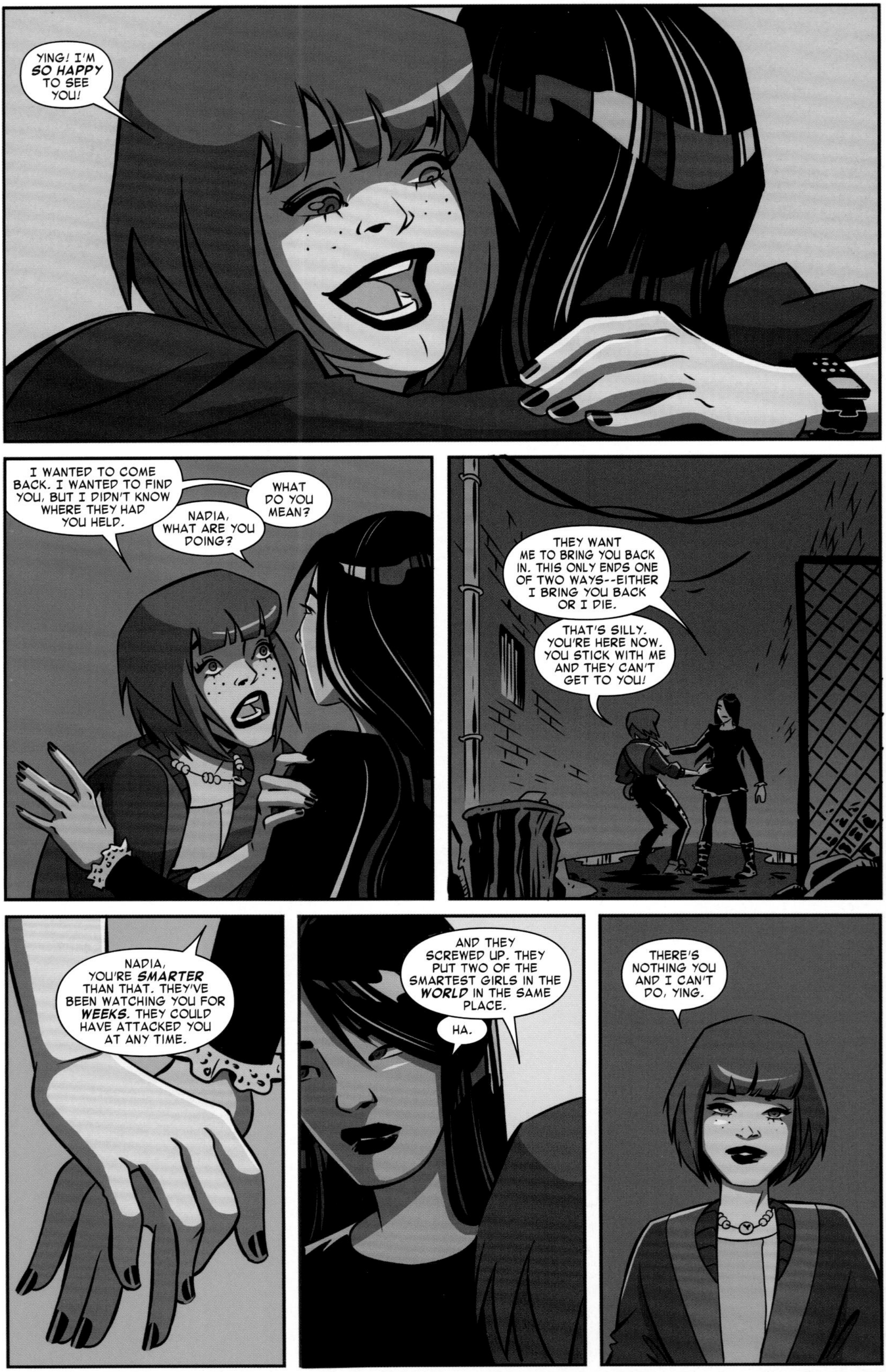
YING! I'M SO HAPPY TO SEE YOU!
I WANTED TO COME BACK. I WANTED TO FIND YOU, BUT I DIDN'T KNOW WHERE THEY HAD YOU HELD.
NADIA, WHAT ARE YOU DOING?
WHAT DO YOU MEAN?
THEY WANT ME TO BRING YOU BACK IN. THIS ONLY ENDS ONE OF TWO WAYS--EITHER I BRING YOU BACK OR I DIE.
THAT'S SILLY. YOU'RE HERE NOW. YOU STICK WITH ME AND THEY CAN'T GET TO YOU!
NADIA, YOU'RE SMARTER THAN THAT. THEY'VE BEEN WATCHING YOU FOR WEEKS. THEY COULD HAVE ATTACKED YOU AT ANY TIME.
AND THEY SCREWED UP. THEY PUT TWO OF THE SMARTEST GIRLS IN THE WORLD IN THE SAME PLACE.
HA.
THERE'S NOTHING YOU AND I CAN'T DO, YING.

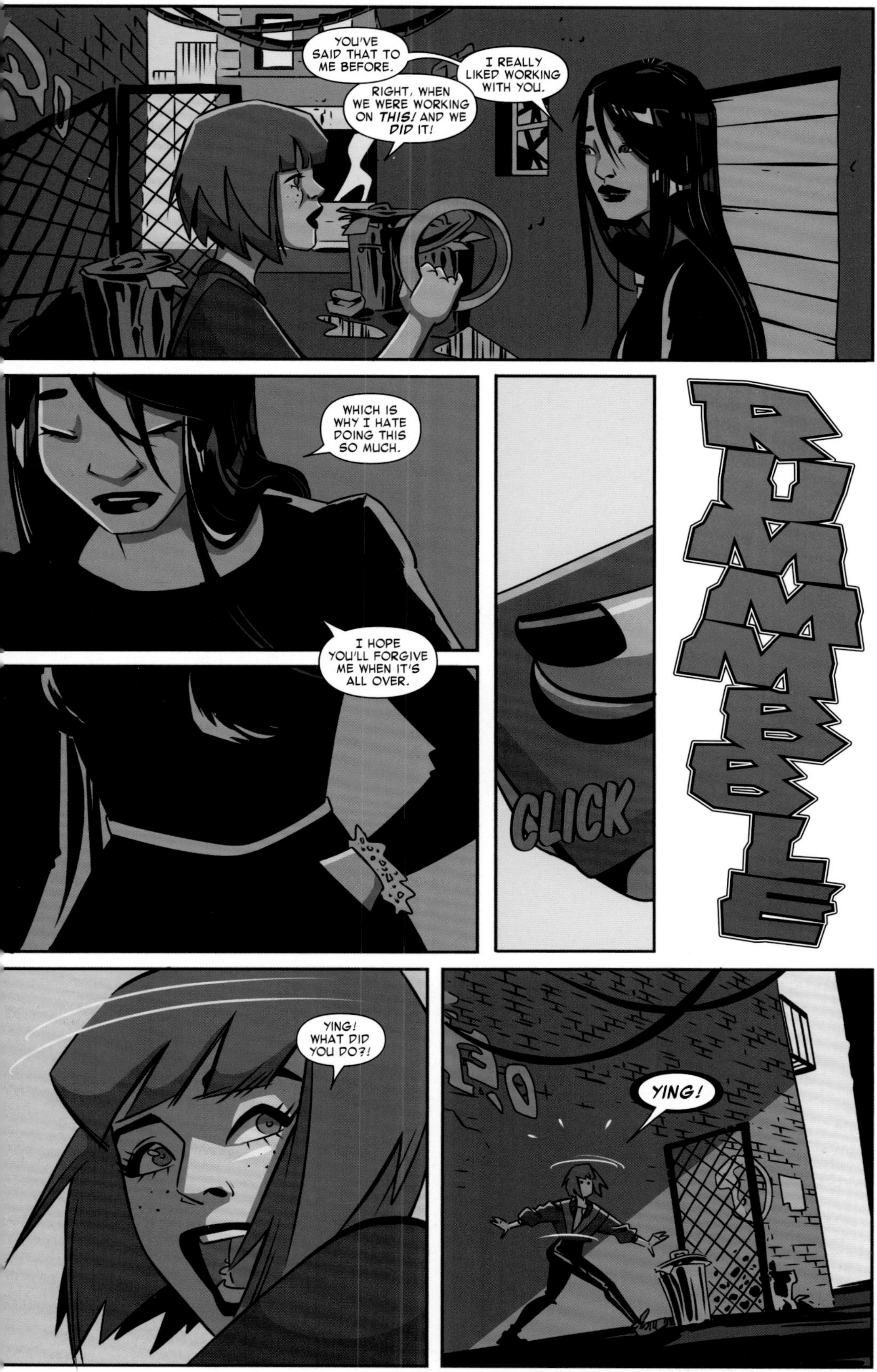
YOU'VE SAID THAT TO ME BEFORE.
I REALLY LIKED WORKING WITH YOU.
RIGHT, WHEN WE WERE WORKING ON THIS! AND WE DID IT!
WHICH IS WHY I HATE DOING THIS SO MUCH.
I HOPE YOU'LL FORGIVE ME WHEN IT'S ALL OVER.
CLICK
RUMMMBBLE
YING! WHAT DID YOU DO?!
YING!

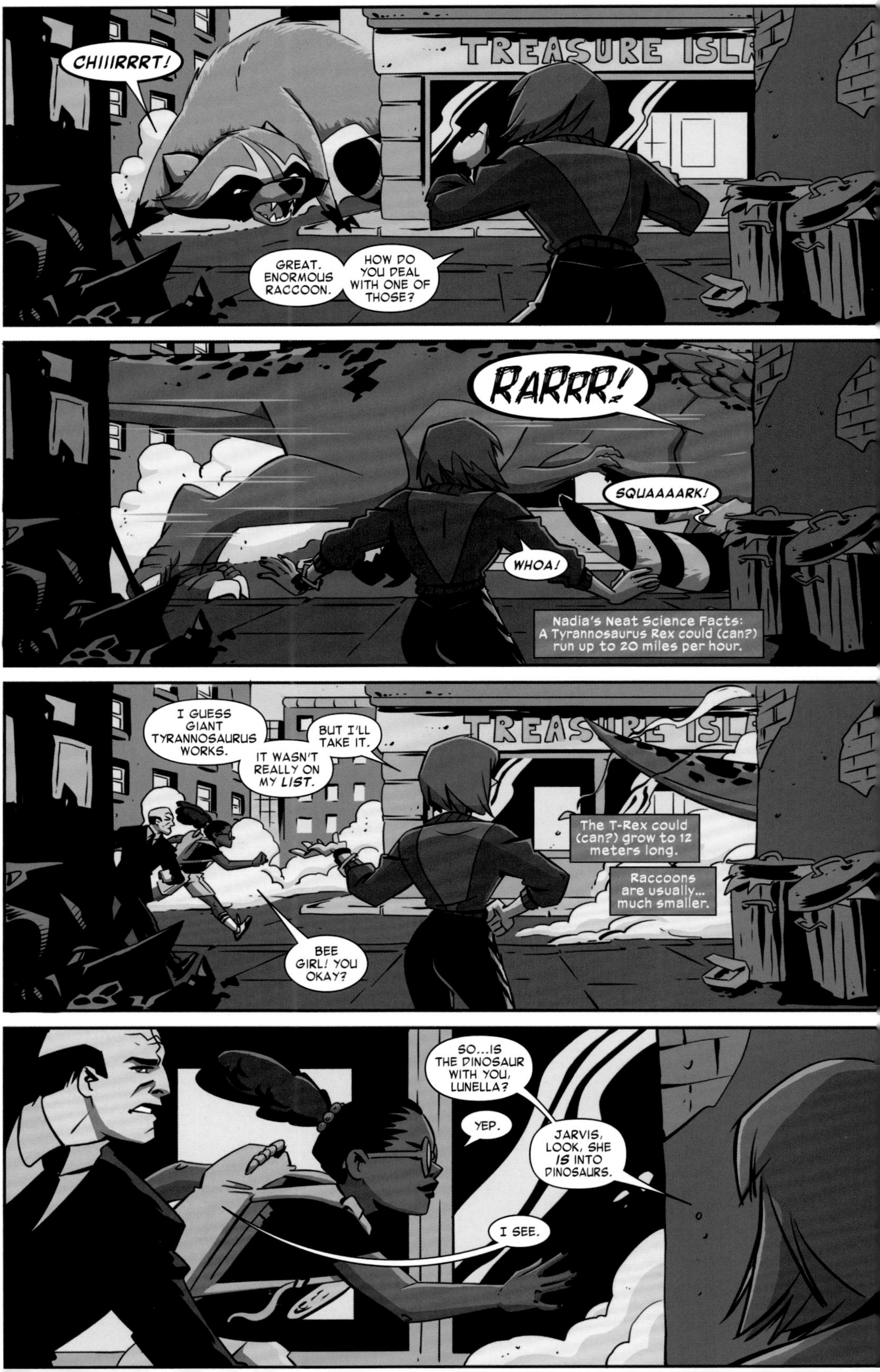
CHIIIRRRT!
TREASURE ISLA
GREAT. ENORMOUS RACCOON.
HOW DO YOU DEAL WITH ONE OF THOSE?
RARRR!
SQUAAAARK!
WHOA!
Nadia's Neat Science Facts: A Tyrannosaurus Rex could (can?) run up to 20 miles per hour.
I GUESS GIANT TYRANNOSAURUS WORKS.
IT WASN'T REALLY ON MY LIST.
BUT I'LL TAKE IT.
TREASURE ISLA
The T-Rex could (can?) grow to 12 meters long.
Raccoons are usually... much smaller.
BEE GIRL! YOU OKAY?
SO...IS THE DINOSAUR WITH YOU, LUNELLA?
YEP.
JARVIS, LOOK, SHE IS INTO DINOSAURS.
I SEE.

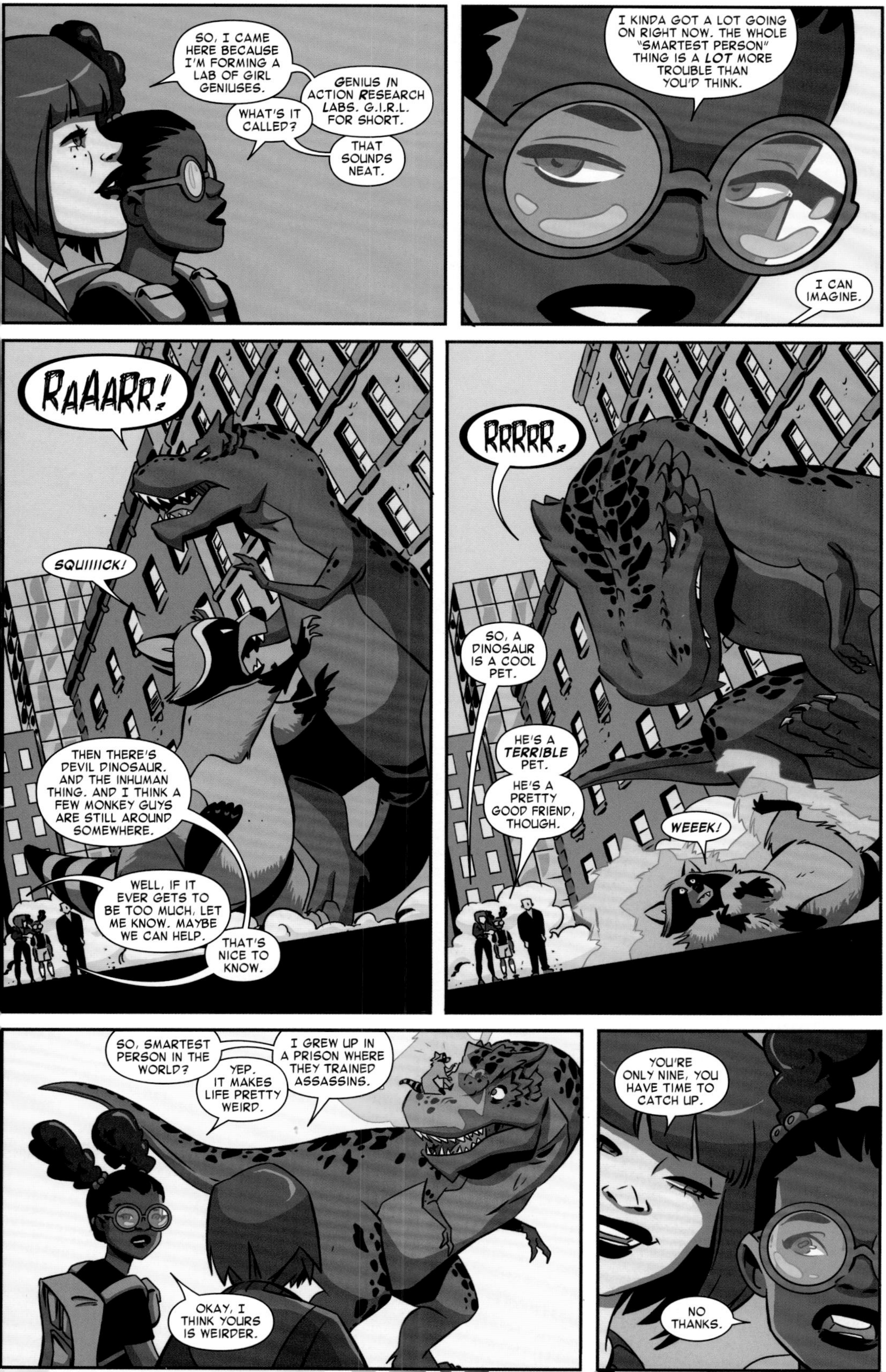

SO, I CAME HERE BECAUSE I'M FORMING A LAB OF GIRL GENIUSES.
WHAT'S IT CALLED?
GENIUS IN ACTION RESEARCH LABS. G.I.R.L. FOR SHORT.
THAT SOUNDS NEAT.
I KINDA GOT A LOT GOING ON RIGHT NOW. THE WHOLE "SMARTEST PERSON" THING IS A LOT MORE TROUBLE THAN YOU'D THINK.
I CAN IMAGINE.
RAAARR!
SQUIIIICK!
THEN THERE'S DEVIL DINOSAUR. AND THE INHUMAN THING. AND I THINK A FEW MONKEY GUYS ARE STILL AROUND SOMEWHERE.
WELL, IF IT EVER GETS TO BE TOO MUCH, LET ME KNOW. MAYBE WE CAN HELP.
THAT'S NICE TO KNOW.
RRRRR.
SO, A DINOSAUR IS A COOL PET.
HE'S A TERRIBLE PET.
HE'S A PRETTY GOOD FRIEND, THOUGH.
WEEEK!
SO, SMARTEST PERSON IN THE WORLD?
YEP. IT MAKES LIFE PRETTY WEIRD.
I GREW UP IN A PRISON WHERE THEY TRAINED ASSASSINS.
OKAY, I THINK YOURS IS WEIRDER.
YOU'RE ONLY NINE, YOU HAVE TIME TO CATCH UP.
NO THANKS.

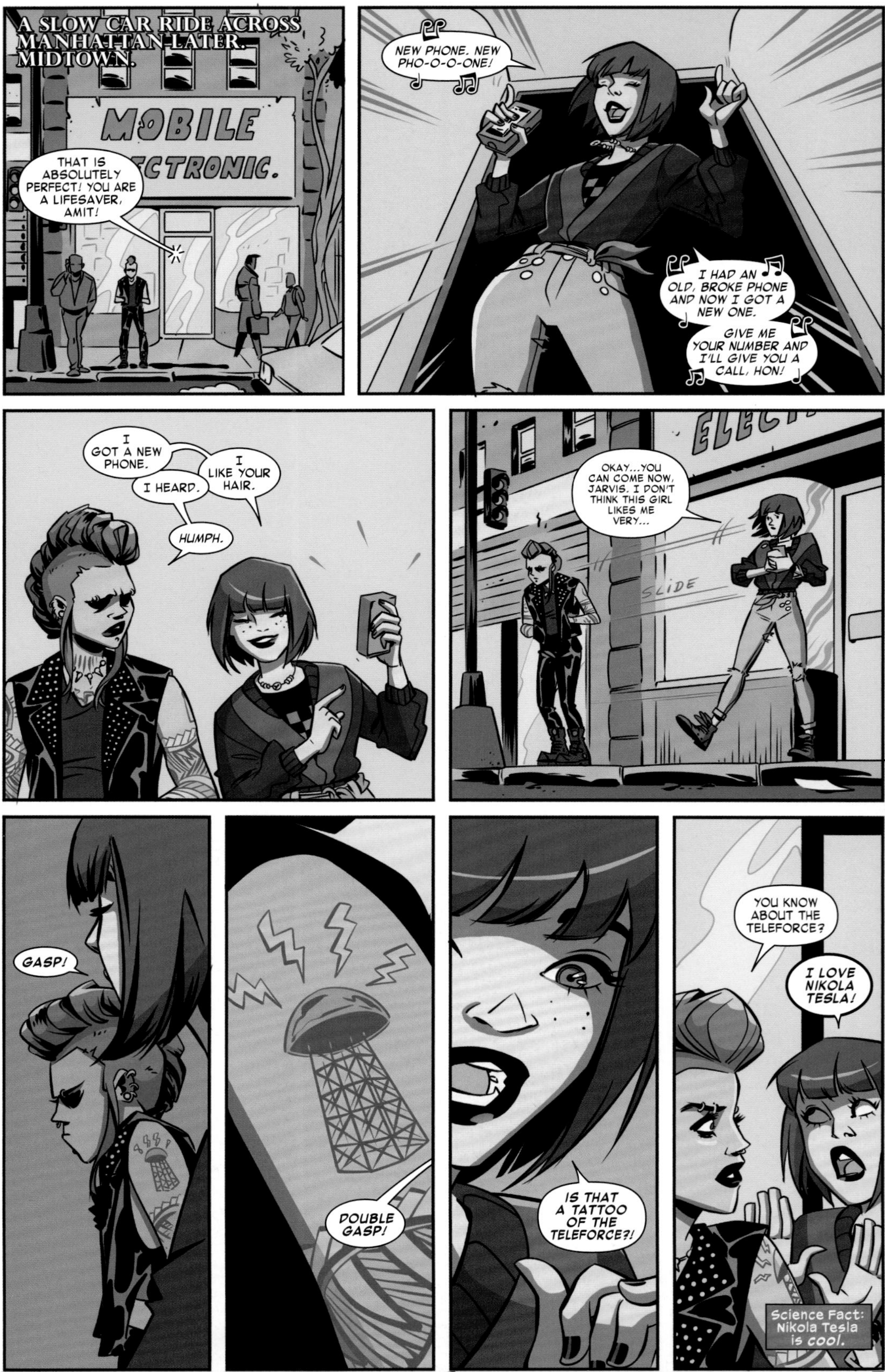
A SLOW CAR RIDE ACROSS MANHATTAN LATER. MIDTOWN.
MOBILE ...CTRONIC.
THAT IS ABSOLUTELY PERFECT! YOU ARE A LIFESAVER, AMIT!
NEW PHONE. NEW PHO-O-O-ONE!
I HAD AN OLD, BROKE PHONE AND NOW I GOT A NEW ONE.
GIVE ME YOUR NUMBER AND I'LL GIVE YOU A CALL, HON!
I GOT A NEW PHONE.
I HEARD.
I LIKE YOUR HAIR.
HUMPH.
OKAY...YOU CAN COME NOW, JARVIS. I DON'T THINK THIS GIRL LIKES ME VERY...
SLIDE
GASP!
DOUBLE GASP!
IS THAT A TATTOO OF THE TELEFORCE?!
YOU KNOW ABOUT THE TELEFORCE?
I LOVE NIKOLA TESLA!
Science Fact: Nikola Tesla is cool.

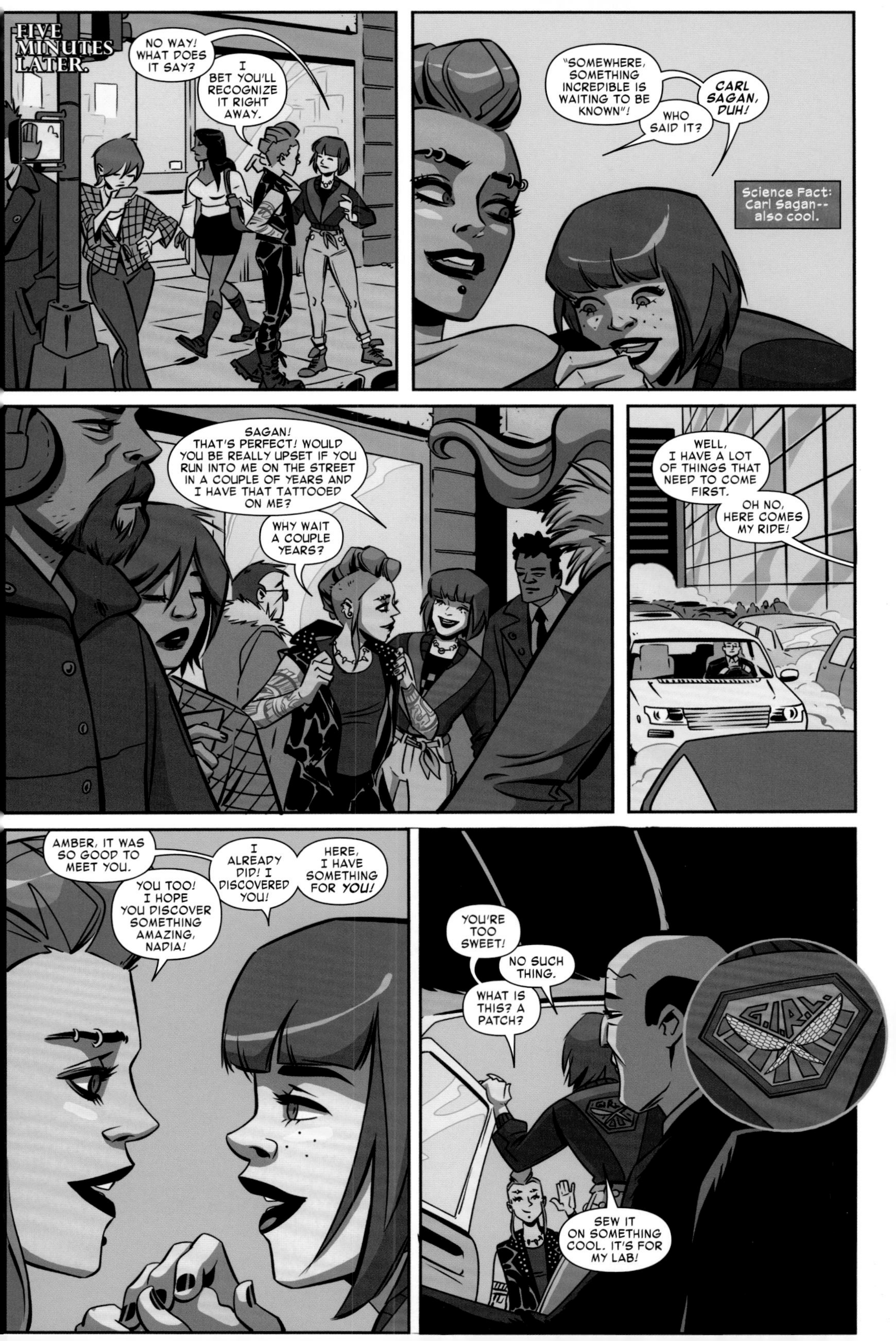
FIVE MINUTES LATER.
NO WAY! WHAT DOES IT SAY?
I BET YOU'LL RECOGNIZE IT RIGHT AWAY.
"SOMEWHERE, SOMETHING INCREDIBLE IS WAITING TO BE KNOWN"!
WHO SAID IT?
CARL SAGAN, DUH!
Science Fact: Carl Sagan-- also cool.
SAGAN! THAT'S PERFECT! WOULD YOU BE REALLY UPSET IF YOU RUN INTO ME ON THE STREET IN A COUPLE OF YEARS AND I HAVE THAT TATTOOED ON ME?
WHY WAIT A COUPLE YEARS?
WELL, I HAVE A LOT OF THINGS THAT NEED TO COME FIRST.
OH NO, HERE COMES MY RIDE!
AMBER, IT WAS SO GOOD TO MEET YOU.
YOU TOO! I HOPE YOU DISCOVER SOMETHING AMAZING, NADIA!
I ALREADY DID! I DISCOVERED YOU!
HERE, I HAVE SOMETHING FOR YOU!
YOU'RE TOO SWEET!
NO SUCH THING.
WHAT IS THIS? A PATCH?
SEW IT ON SOMETHING COOL. IT'S FOR MY LAB!

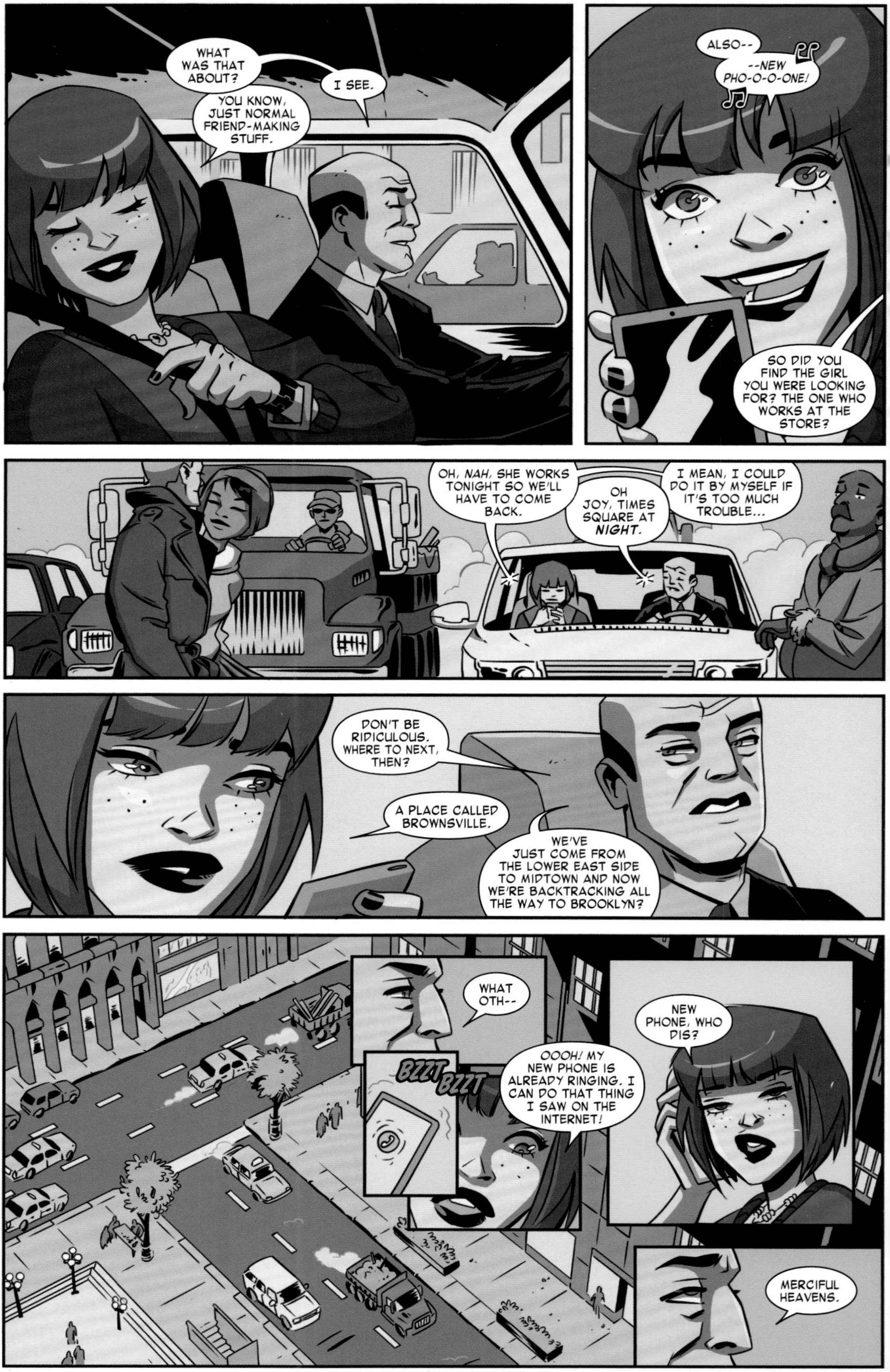
WHAT WAS THAT ABOUT?
YOU KNOW, JUST NORMAL FRIEND-MAKING STUFF.
I SEE.
ALSO--
--NEW PHO-O-O-ONE!
SO DID YOU FIND THE GIRL YOU WERE LOOKING FOR? THE ONE WHO WORKS AT THE STORE?
OH, NAH, SHE WORKS TONIGHT SO WE'LL HAVE TO COME BACK.
OH JOY, TIMES SQUARE AT NIGHT.
I MEAN, I COULD DO IT BY MYSELF IF IT'S TOO MUCH TROUBLE...
DON'T BE RIDICULOUS. WHERE TO NEXT, THEN?
A PLACE CALLED BROWNSVILLE.
WE'VE JUST COME FROM THE LOWER EAST SIDE TO MIDTOWN AND NOW WE'RE BACKTRACKING ALL THE WAY TO BROOKLYN?
WHAT OTH--
BZZT BZZT
OOOH! MY NEW PHONE IS ALREADY RINGING. I CAN DO THAT THING I SAW ON THE INTERNET!
NEW PHONE, WHO DIS?
MERCIFUL HEAVENS.

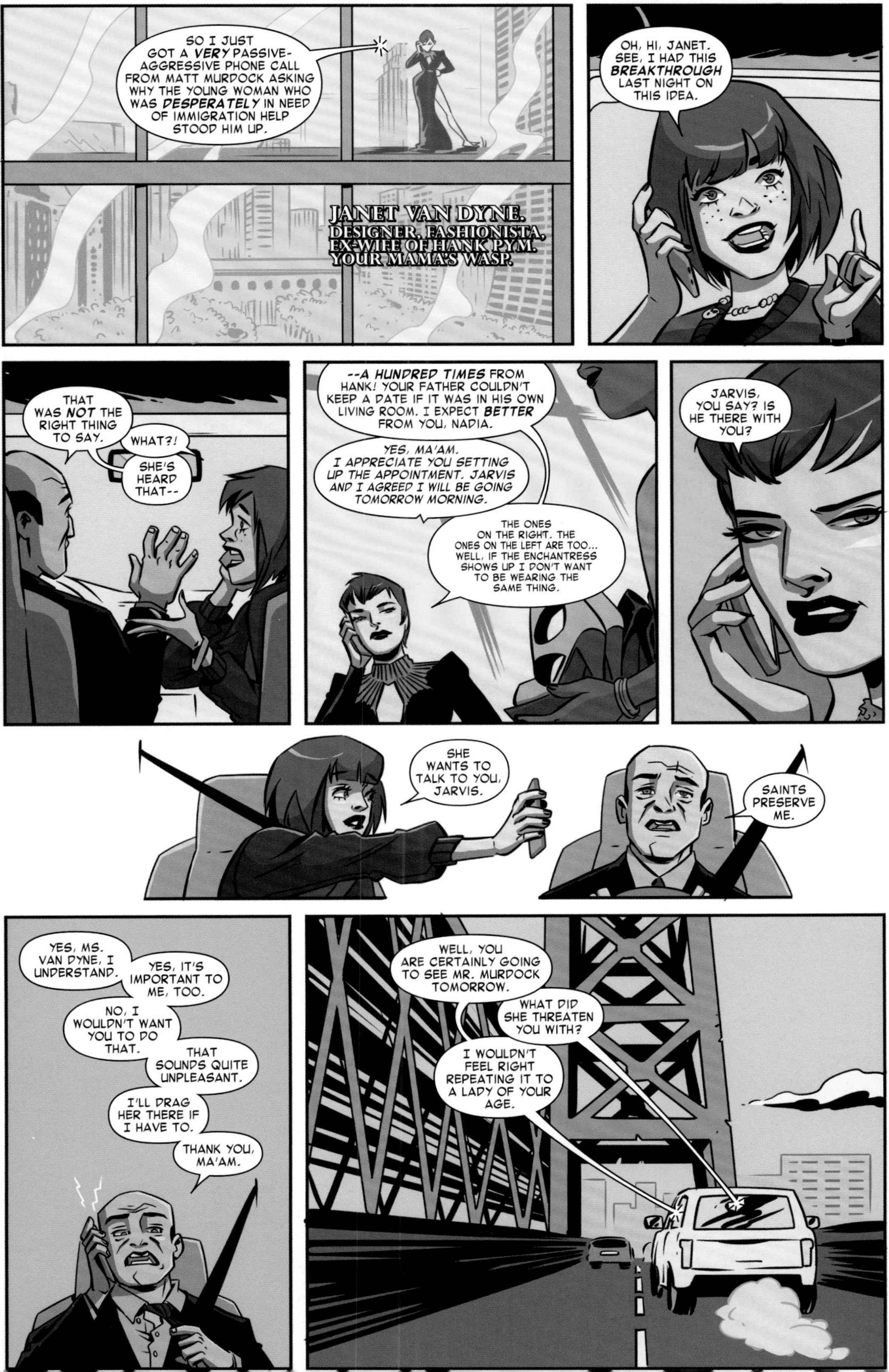

SO I JUST GOT A VERY PASSIVE-AGGRESSIVE PHONE CALL FROM MATT MURDOCK ASKING WHY THE YOUNG WOMAN WHO WAS DESPERATELY IN NEED OF IMMIGRATION HELP STOOD HIM UP.
JANET VAN DYNE. DESIGNER, FASHIONISTA, EX-WIFE OF HANK PYM. YOUR MAMA'S WASP.
OH, HI, JANET. SEE, I HAD THIS BREAKTHROUGH LAST NIGHT ON THIS IDEA.
THAT WAS NOT THE RIGHT THING TO SAY.
WHAT?!
SHE'S HEARD THAT--
--A HUNDRED TIMES FROM HANK! YOUR FATHER COULDN'T KEEP A DATE IF IT WAS IN HIS OWN LIVING ROOM. I EXPECT BETTER FROM YOU, NADIA.
YES, MA'AM. I APPRECIATE YOU SETTING UP THE APPOINTMENT. JARVIS AND I AGREED I WILL BE GOING TOMORROW MORNING.
THE ONES ON THE RIGHT. THE ONES ON THE LEFT ARE TOO... WELL, IF THE ENCHANTRESS SHOWS UP I DON'T WANT TO BE WEARING THE SAME THING.
JARVIS, YOU SAY? IS HE THERE WITH YOU?
SHE WANTS TO TALK TO YOU, JARVIS.
SAINTS PRESERVE ME.
YES, MS. VAN DYNE, I UNDERSTAND.
YES, IT'S IMPORTANT TO ME, TOO.
NO, I WOULDN'T WANT YOU TO DO THAT.
THAT SOUNDS QUITE UNPLEASANT.
I'LL DRAG HER THERE IF I HAVE TO.
THANK YOU, MA'AM.
WELL, YOU ARE CERTAINLY GOING TO SEE MR. MURDOCK TOMORROW.
WHAT DID SHE THREATEN YOU WITH?
I WOULDN'T FEEL RIGHT REPEATING IT TO A LADY OF YOUR AGE.

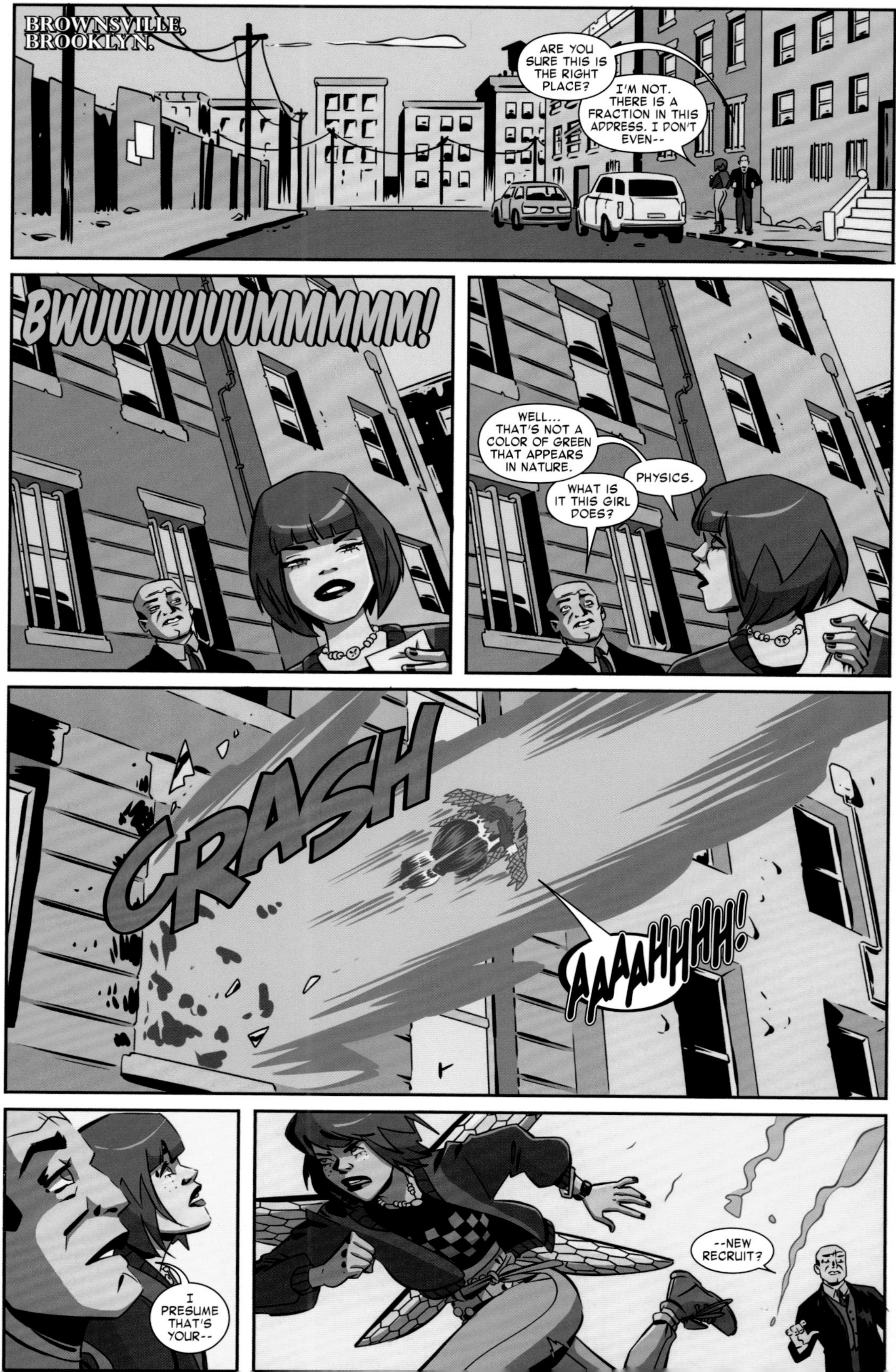
BROWNSVILLE, BROOKLYN.
ARE YOU SURE THIS IS THE RIGHT PLACE?
I'M NOT. THERE IS A FRACTION IN THIS ADDRESS. I DON'T EVEN--
BWUUUUUUUMMMMM!
WELL... THAT'S NOT A COLOR OF GREEN THAT APPEARS IN NATURE.
PHYSICS.
WHAT IS IT THIS GIRL DOES?
CRASH
AAAAHHHH!
I PRESUME THAT'S YOUR--
--NEW RECRUIT?

PLEASE DON'T BREAK YOUR TAILBONE AGAIN.

PLEASE DON'T BREAK YOUR TAILBONE AGAIN.

PLEASE DON'T--

EXCUSE ME?

OH, HELLO.

HI, I CAUGHT YOU.

I SEE.

I HAVE TO SAY, I CONSIDERED A LOT OF DIFFERENT OUTCOMES FOR THIS EXPERIMENT, HENCE THE HELMET.

BUT BEING SNATCHED OUT OF THE AIR BY TINKERBELL WAS NOT ONE OF THEM.

WELL, LET'S JUST CALL THAT THE FIRST OF MANY GOOD SURPRISES. I GOT SAVED BY A DINOSAUR EARLIER.

NOW, I RETURN YOU TO THE EARTH WITH NO BROKEN TAILBONE.

THAT'S A RELIEF. YOU EVER BROKE YOUR TAILBONE? I COULDN'T SIT DOWN COMFORTABLY FOR LIKE TWO MONTHS.

WAS THAT ANOTHER EXPERIMENT THAT LAUNCHED YOU FROM A WINDOW?

YEAH, SORTA... MOSTLY... OKAY, WAIT.

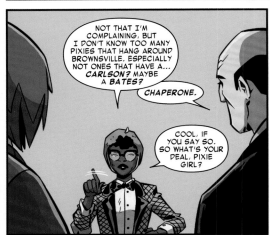

NOT THAT I'M COMPLAINING, BUT I DON'T KNOW TOO MANY PIXIES THAT HANG AROUND BROWNSVILLE. ESPECIALLY NOT ONES THAT HAVE A... CARLSON? MAYBE A BATES?

CHAPERONE.

COOL, IF YOU SAY SO. SO WHAT'S YOUR DEAL, PIXIE GIRL?

LASHAYLA SMITH, I HAVE AN OFFER FOR YOU.

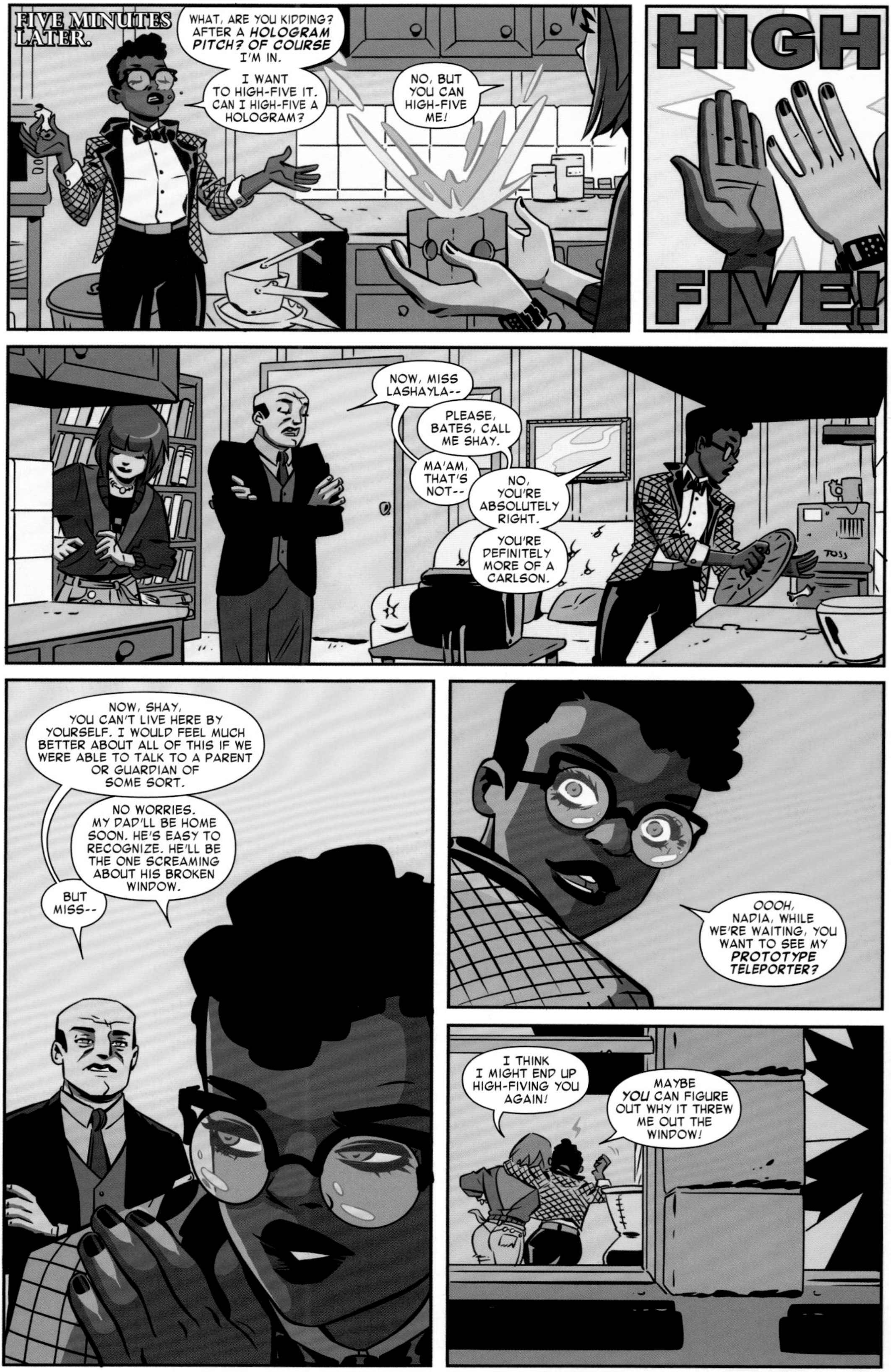
FIVE MINUTES LATER.
WHAT, ARE YOU KIDDING? AFTER A *HOLOGRAM PITCH? OF COURSE* I'M IN.
I WANT TO HIGH-FIVE IT. CAN I HIGH-FIVE A HOLOGRAM?
NO, BUT YOU CAN HIGH-FIVE ME!
HIGH FIVE!
NOW, MISS LASHAYLA--
PLEASE, BATES, CALL ME SHAY.
MA'AM, THAT'S NOT--
NO, YOU'RE ABSOLUTELY RIGHT.
YOU'RE DEFINITELY MORE OF A CARLSON.
TOSS
NOW, SHAY, YOU CAN'T LIVE HERE BY YOURSELF. I WOULD FEEL MUCH BETTER ABOUT ALL OF THIS IF WE WERE ABLE TO TALK TO A PARENT OR GUARDIAN OF SOME SORT.
NO WORRIES. MY DAD'LL BE HOME SOON. HE'S EASY TO RECOGNIZE. HE'LL BE THE ONE SCREAMING ABOUT HIS BROKEN WINDOW.
BUT MISS--
OOOH, NADIA, WHILE WE'RE WAITING, YOU WANT TO SEE MY *PROTOTYPE TELEPORTER?*
I THINK I MIGHT END UP HIGH-FIVING YOU AGAIN!
MAYBE *YOU* CAN FIGURE OUT WHY IT THREW ME OUT THE WINDOW!

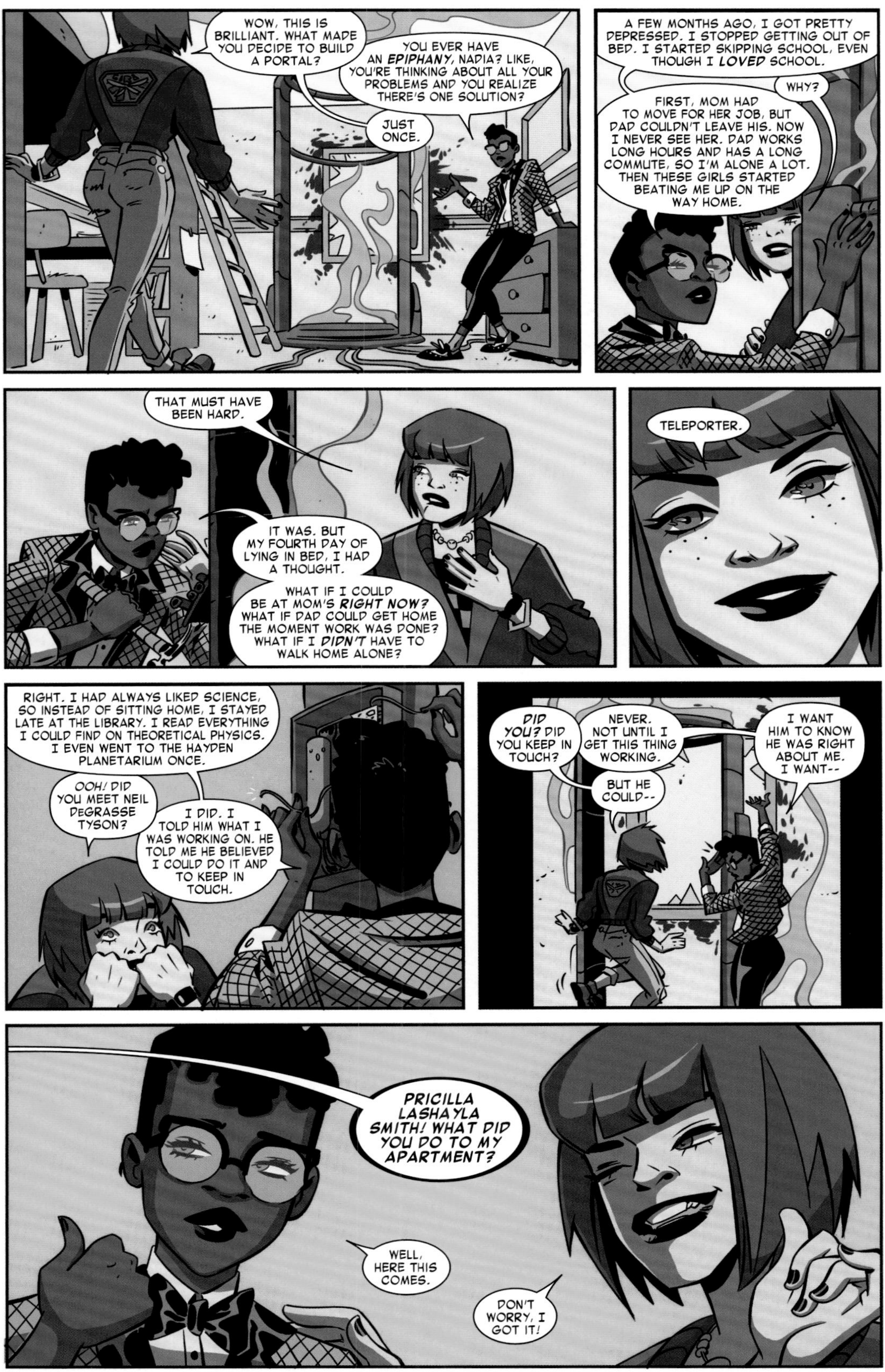
WOW, THIS IS BRILLIANT. WHAT MADE YOU DECIDE TO BUILD A PORTAL?
YOU EVER HAVE AN *EPIPHANY*, NADIA? LIKE, YOU'RE THINKING ABOUT ALL YOUR PROBLEMS AND YOU REALIZE THERE'S ONE SOLUTION?
JUST ONCE.
A FEW MONTHS AGO, I GOT PRETTY DEPRESSED. I STOPPED GETTING OUT OF BED. I STARTED SKIPPING SCHOOL, EVEN THOUGH I *LOVED* SCHOOL.
WHY?
FIRST, MOM HAD TO MOVE FOR HER JOB, BUT DAD COULDN'T LEAVE HIS. NOW I NEVER SEE HER. DAD WORKS LONG HOURS AND HAS A LONG COMMUTE, SO I'M ALONE A LOT. THEN THESE GIRLS STARTED BEATING ME UP ON THE WAY HOME.
THAT MUST HAVE BEEN HARD.
IT WAS. BUT MY FOURTH DAY OF LYING IN BED, I HAD A THOUGHT.
WHAT IF I COULD BE AT MOM'S *RIGHT NOW?* WHAT IF DAD COULD GET HOME THE MOMENT WORK WAS DONE? WHAT IF I *DIDN'T* HAVE TO WALK HOME ALONE?
TELEPORTER.
RIGHT. I HAD ALWAYS LIKED SCIENCE, SO INSTEAD OF SITTING HOME, I STAYED LATE AT THE LIBRARY. I READ EVERYTHING I COULD FIND ON THEORETICAL PHYSICS. I EVEN WENT TO THE HAYDEN PLANETARIUM ONCE.
OOH! DID YOU MEET NEIL DEGRASSE TYSON?
I DID. I TOLD HIM WHAT I WAS WORKING ON. HE TOLD ME HE BELIEVED I COULD DO IT AND TO KEEP IN TOUCH.
DID YOU? DID YOU KEEP IN TOUCH?
NEVER. NOT UNTIL I GET THIS THING WORKING.
BUT HE COULD--
I WANT HIM TO KNOW HE WAS RIGHT ABOUT ME. I WANT--
PRICILLA LASHAYLA SMITH! WHAT DID YOU DO TO MY APARTMENT?
WELL, HERE THIS COMES.
DON'T WORRY, I GOT IT!

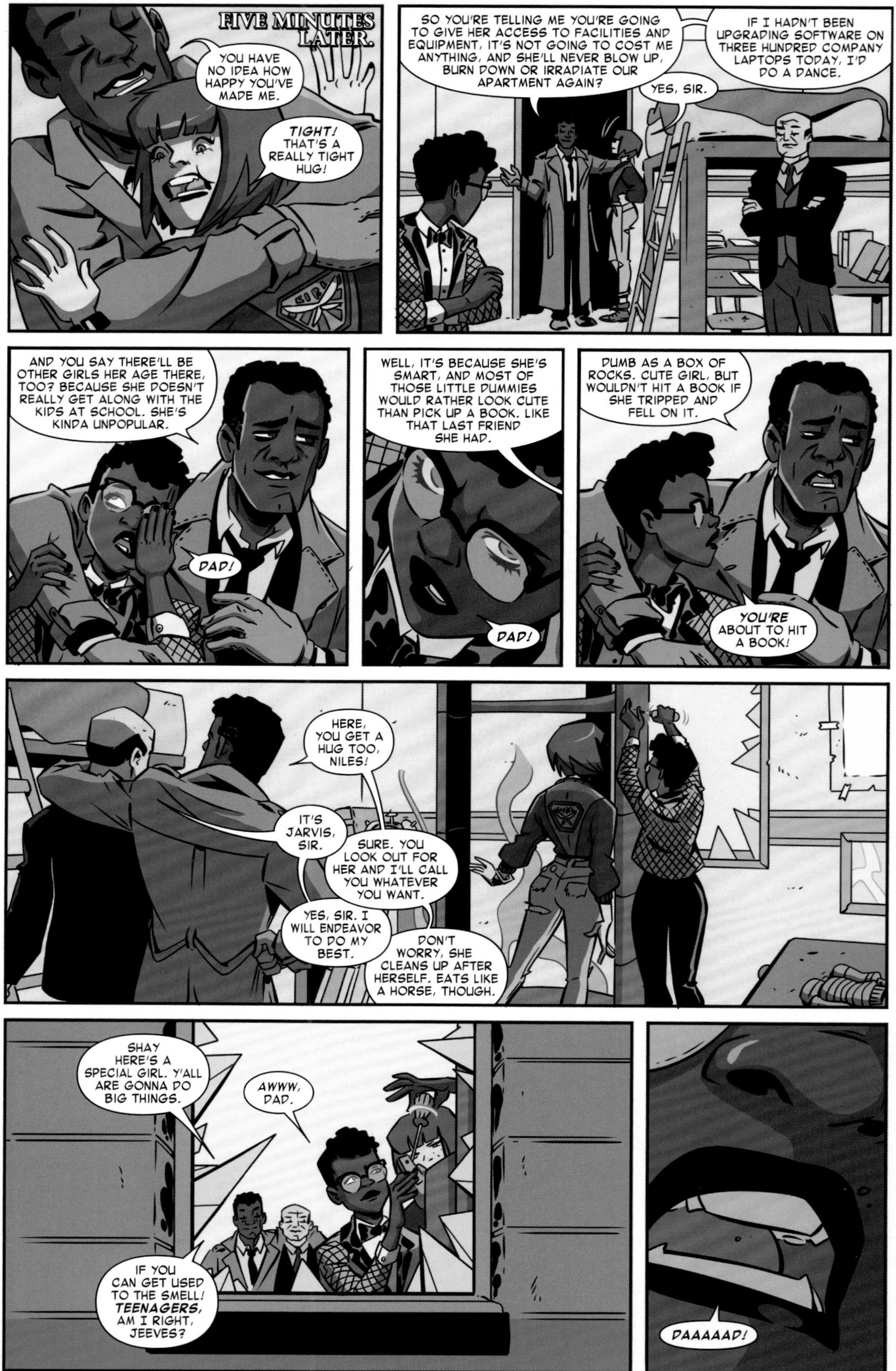
FIVE MINUTES LATER.
YOU HAVE NO IDEA HOW HAPPY YOU'VE MADE ME.
TIGHT! THAT'S A REALLY TIGHT HUG!
SO YOU'RE TELLING ME YOU'RE GOING TO GIVE HER ACCESS TO FACILITIES AND EQUIPMENT, IT'S NOT GOING TO COST ME ANYTHING, AND SHE'LL NEVER BLOW UP, BURN DOWN OR IRRADIATE OUR APARTMENT AGAIN?
YES, SIR.
IF I HADN'T BEEN UPGRADING SOFTWARE ON THREE HUNDRED COMPANY LAPTOPS TODAY, I'D DO A DANCE.
AND YOU SAY THERE'LL BE OTHER GIRLS HER AGE THERE, TOO? BECAUSE SHE DOESN'T REALLY GET ALONG WITH THE KIDS AT SCHOOL. SHE'S KINDA UNPOPULAR.
DAD!
WELL, IT'S BECAUSE SHE'S SMART, AND MOST OF THOSE LITTLE DUMMIES WOULD RATHER LOOK CUTE THAN PICK UP A BOOK. LIKE THAT LAST FRIEND SHE HAD.
DAD!
DUMB AS A BOX OF ROCKS. CUTE GIRL, BUT WOULDN'T HIT A BOOK IF SHE TRIPPED AND FELL ON IT.
YOU'RE ABOUT TO HIT A BOOK!
HERE, YOU GET A HUG TOO, NILES!
IT'S JARVIS, SIR.
SURE. YOU LOOK OUT FOR HER AND I'LL CALL YOU WHATEVER YOU WANT.
YES, SIR. I WILL ENDEAVOR TO DO MY BEST.
DON'T WORRY, SHE CLEANS UP AFTER HERSELF. EATS LIKE A HORSE, THOUGH.
SHAY HERE'S A SPECIAL GIRL. Y'ALL ARE GONNA DO BIG THINGS.
AWWW, DAD.
IF YOU CAN GET USED TO THE SMELL! TEENAGERS, AM I RIGHT, JEEVES?
DAAAAAD!

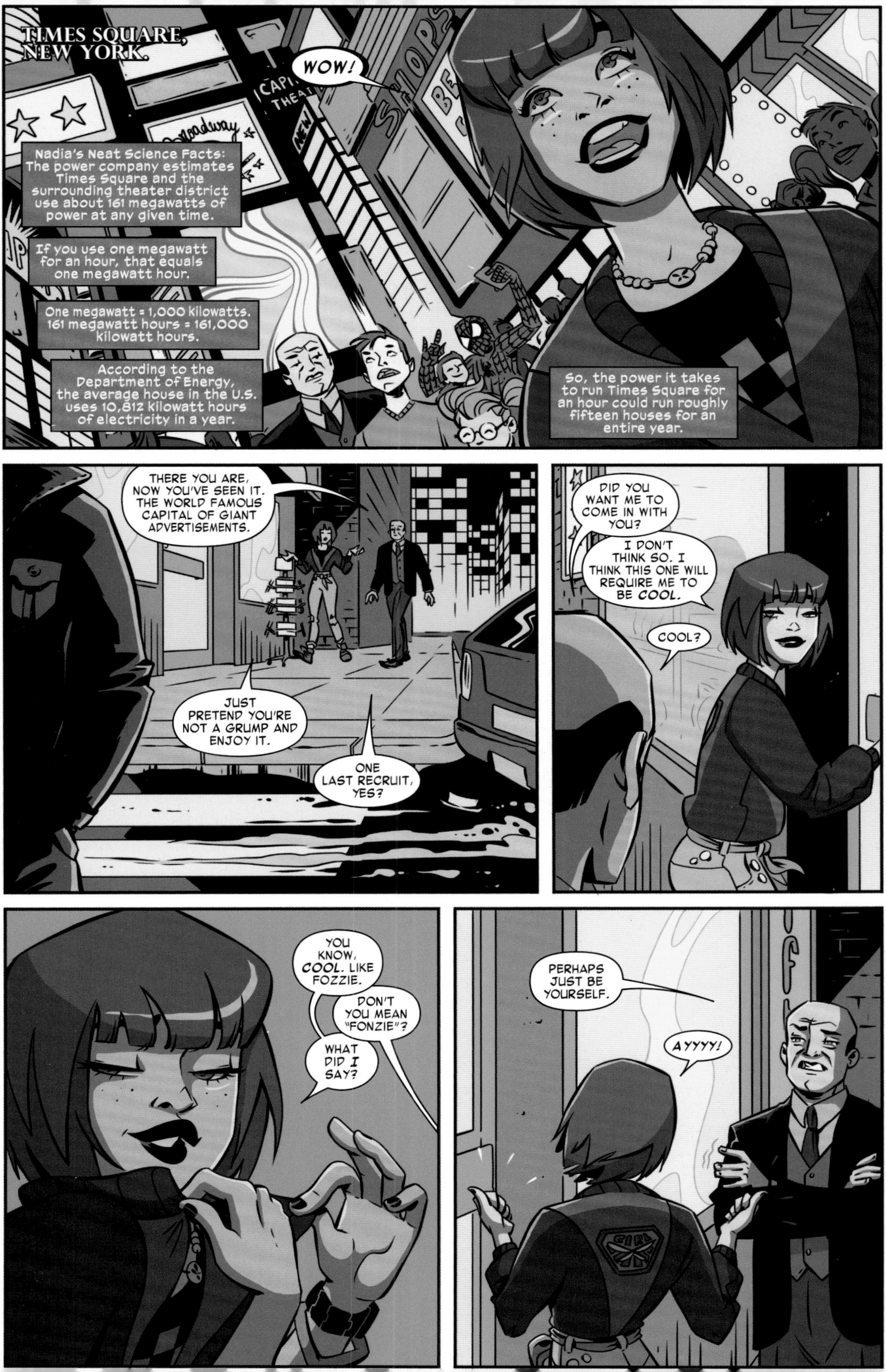

TIMES SQUARE, NEW YORK.
WOW!
Nadia's Neat Science Facts: The power company estimates Times Square and the surrounding theater district use about 161 megawatts of power at any given time.
If you use one megawatt for an hour, that equals one megawatt hour.
One megawatt = 1,000 kilowatts. 161 megawatt hours = 161,000 kilowatt hours.
According to the Department of Energy, the average house in the U.S. uses 10,812 kilowatt hours of electricity in a year.
So, the power it takes to run Times Square for an hour could run roughly fifteen houses for an entire year.
THERE YOU ARE, NOW YOU'VE SEEN IT. THE WORLD FAMOUS CAPITAL OF GIANT ADVERTISEMENTS.
JUST PRETEND YOU'RE NOT A GRUMP AND ENJOY IT.
ONE LAST RECRUIT, YES?
DID YOU WANT ME TO COME IN WITH YOU?
I DON'T THINK SO. I THINK THIS ONE WILL REQUIRE ME TO BE COOL.
COOL?
YOU KNOW, COOL. LIKE FOZZIE.
DON'T YOU MEAN "FONZIE"?
WHAT DID I SAY?
PERHAPS JUST BE YOURSELF.
AYYYY!

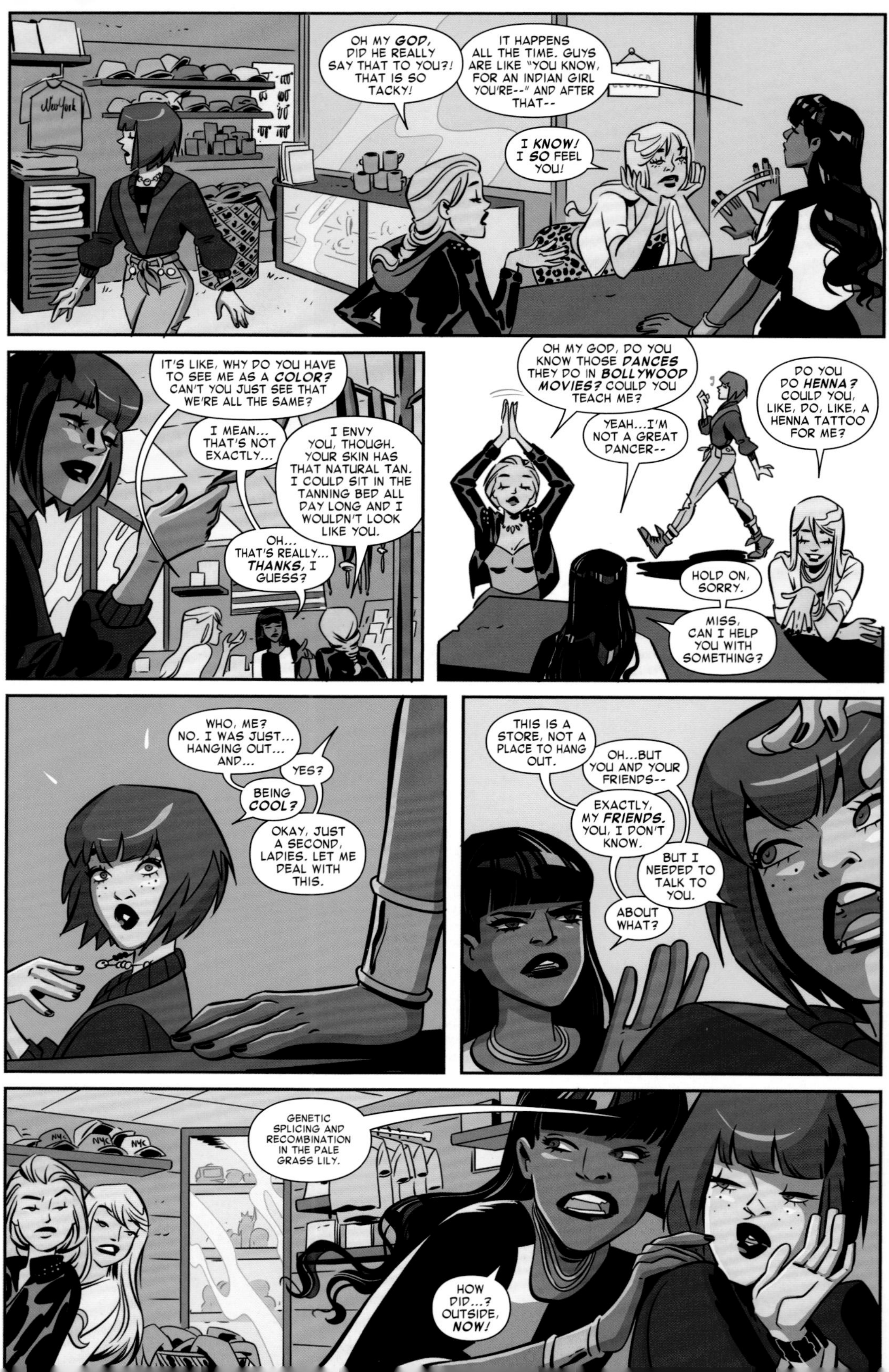

OH MY GOD, DID HE REALLY SAY THAT TO YOU?! THAT IS SO TACKY!
IT HAPPENS ALL THE TIME. GUYS ARE LIKE "YOU KNOW, FOR AN INDIAN GIRL YOU'RE--" AND AFTER THAT--
I KNOW! I SO FEEL YOU!
New York
IT'S LIKE, WHY DO YOU HAVE TO SEE ME AS A COLOR? CAN'T YOU JUST SEE THAT WE'RE ALL THE SAME?
I MEAN... THAT'S NOT EXACTLY...
I ENVY YOU, THOUGH. YOUR SKIN HAS THAT NATURAL TAN. I COULD SIT IN THE TANNING BED ALL DAY LONG AND I WOULDN'T LOOK LIKE YOU.
OH... THAT'S REALLY... THANKS, I GUESS?
OH MY GOD, DO YOU KNOW THOSE DANCES THEY DO IN BOLLYWOOD MOVIES? COULD YOU TEACH ME?
YEAH...I'M NOT A GREAT DANCER--
DO YOU DO HENNA? COULD YOU, LIKE, DO, LIKE, A HENNA TATTOO FOR ME?
HOLD ON, SORRY.
MISS, CAN I HELP YOU WITH SOMETHING?
WHO, ME? NO. I WAS JUST... HANGING OUT... AND...
YES?
BEING COOL?
OKAY, JUST A SECOND, LADIES. LET ME DEAL WITH THIS.
THIS IS A STORE, NOT A PLACE TO HANG OUT.
OH...BUT YOU AND YOUR FRIENDS--
EXACTLY, MY FRIENDS. YOU, I DON'T KNOW.
BUT I NEEDED TO TALK TO YOU.
ABOUT WHAT?
NYC
GENETIC SPLICING AND RECOMBINATION IN THE PALE GRASS LILY.
HOW DID...? OUTSIDE, NOW!

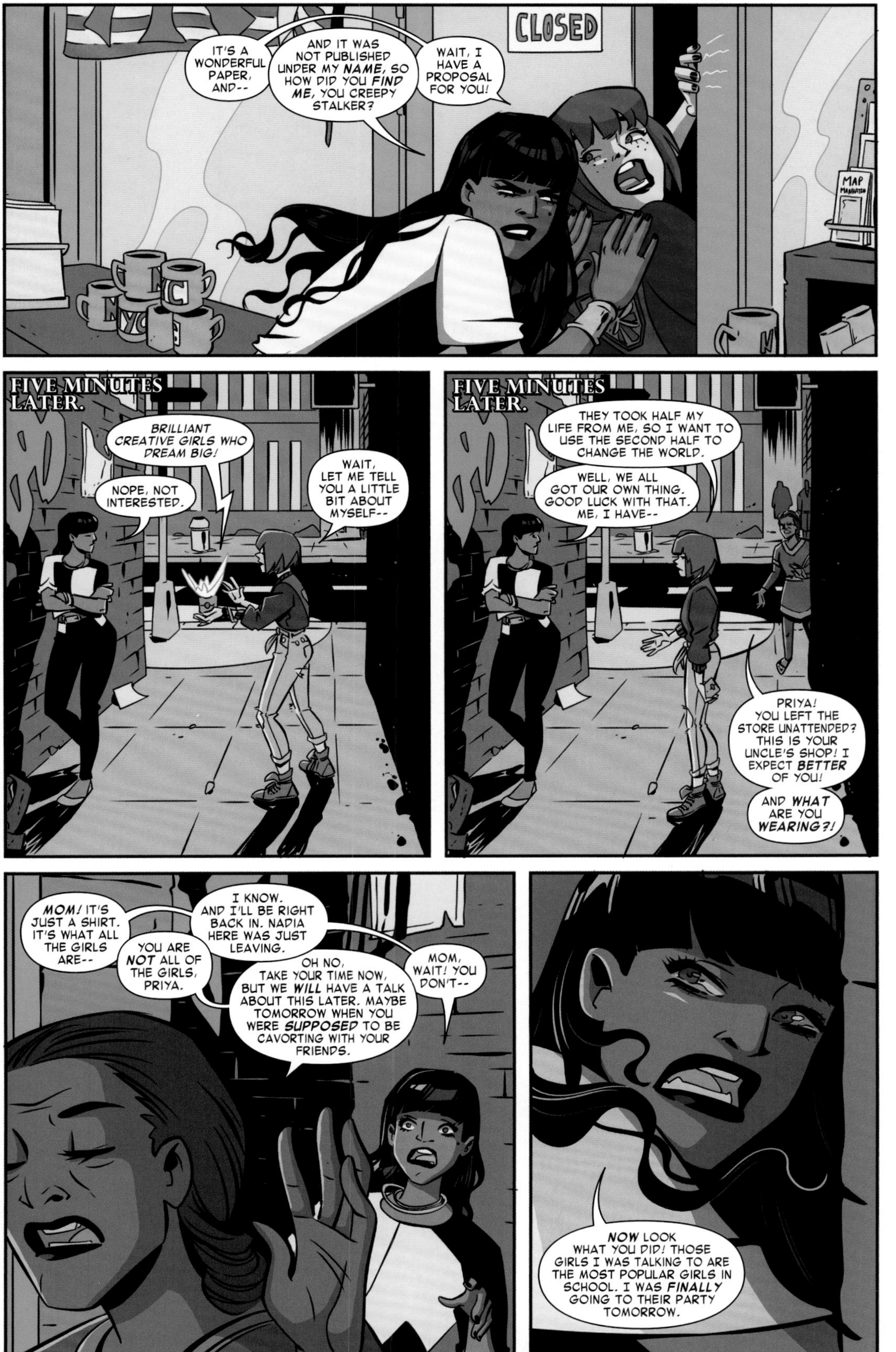
CLOSED
IT'S A WONDERFUL PAPER, AND--
AND IT WAS NOT PUBLISHED UNDER MY NAME, SO HOW DID YOU FIND ME, YOU CREEPY STALKER?
WAIT, I HAVE A PROPOSAL FOR YOU!
MAP
FIVE MINUTES LATER.
BRILLIANT CREATIVE GIRLS WHO DREAM BIG!
NOPE, NOT INTERESTED.
WAIT, LET ME TELL YOU A LITTLE BIT ABOUT MYSELF--
FIVE MINUTES LATER.
THEY TOOK HALF MY LIFE FROM ME, SO I WANT TO USE THE SECOND HALF TO CHANGE THE WORLD.
WELL, WE ALL GOT OUR OWN THING. GOOD LUCK WITH THAT. ME, I HAVE--
PRIYA! YOU LEFT THE STORE UNATTENDED? THIS IS YOUR UNCLE'S SHOP! I EXPECT BETTER OF YOU!
AND WHAT ARE YOU WEARING?!
MOM! IT'S JUST A SHIRT. IT'S WHAT ALL THE GIRLS ARE--
YOU ARE NOT ALL OF THE GIRLS, PRIYA.
I KNOW. AND I'LL BE RIGHT BACK IN. NADIA HERE WAS JUST LEAVING.
OH NO, TAKE YOUR TIME NOW, BUT WE WILL HAVE A TALK ABOUT THIS LATER. MAYBE TOMORROW WHEN YOU WERE SUPPOSED TO BE CAVORTING WITH YOUR FRIENDS.
MOM, WAIT! YOU DON'T--
NOW LOOK WHAT YOU DID! THOSE GIRLS I WAS TALKING TO ARE THE MOST POPULAR GIRLS IN SCHOOL. I WAS FINALLY GOING TO THEIR PARTY TOMORROW.

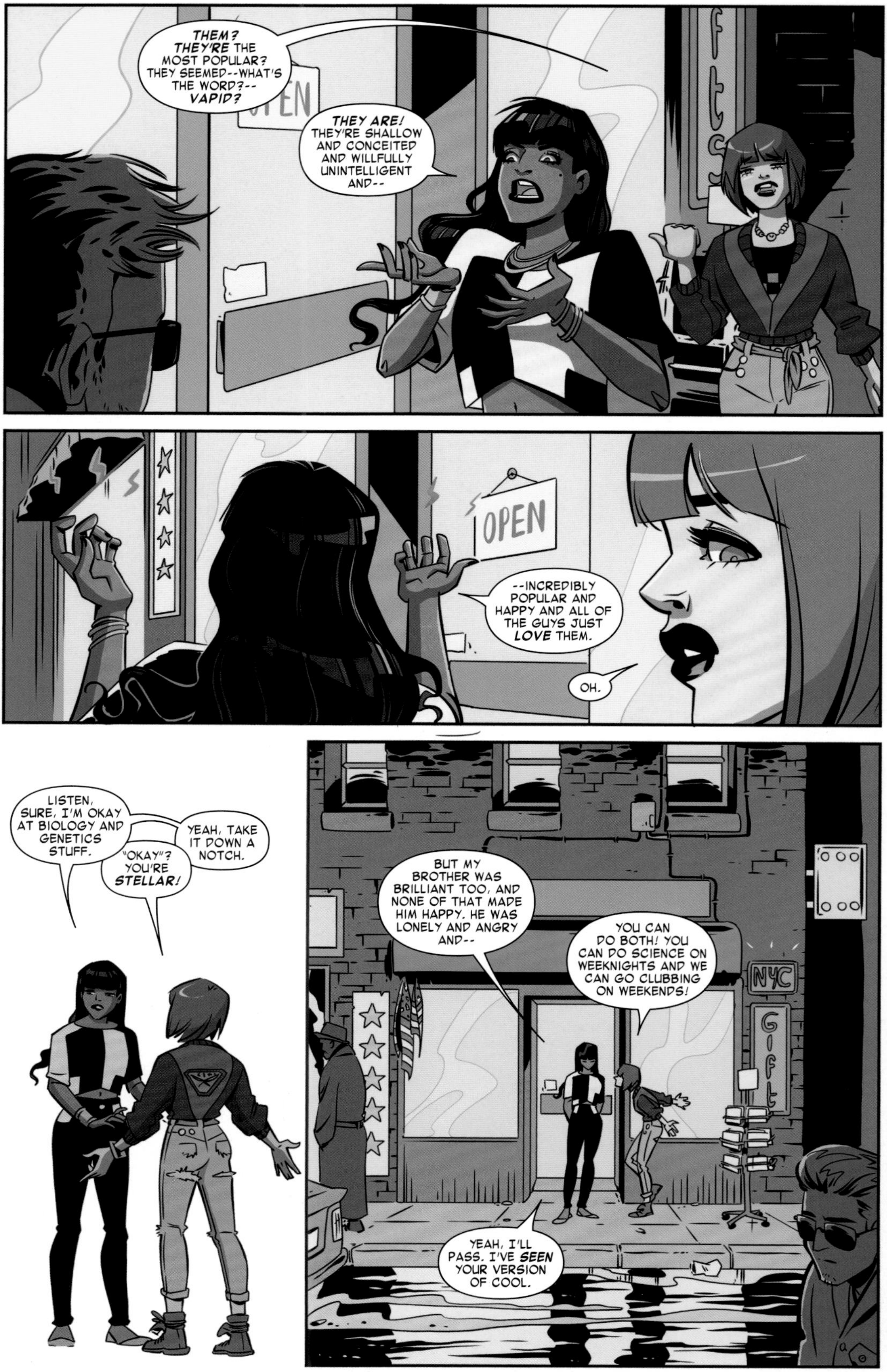
THEM? THEY'RE THE MOST POPULAR? THEY SEEMED--WHAT'S THE WORD?-- VAPID?
THEY ARE! THEY'RE SHALLOW AND CONCEITED AND WILLFULLY UNINTELLIGENT AND--
OPEN
--INCREDIBLY POPULAR AND HAPPY AND ALL OF THE GUYS JUST LOVE THEM.
OH.
LISTEN, SURE, I'M OKAY AT BIOLOGY AND GENETICS STUFF.
YEAH, TAKE IT DOWN A NOTCH.
"OKAY"? YOU'RE STELLAR!
BUT MY BROTHER WAS BRILLIANT TOO, AND NONE OF THAT MADE HIM HAPPY. HE WAS LONELY AND ANGRY AND--
YOU CAN DO BOTH! YOU CAN DO SCIENCE ON WEEKNIGHTS AND WE CAN GO CLUBBING ON WEEKENDS!
NYC
GIFT
YEAH, I'LL PASS. I'VE SEEN YOUR VERSION OF COOL.

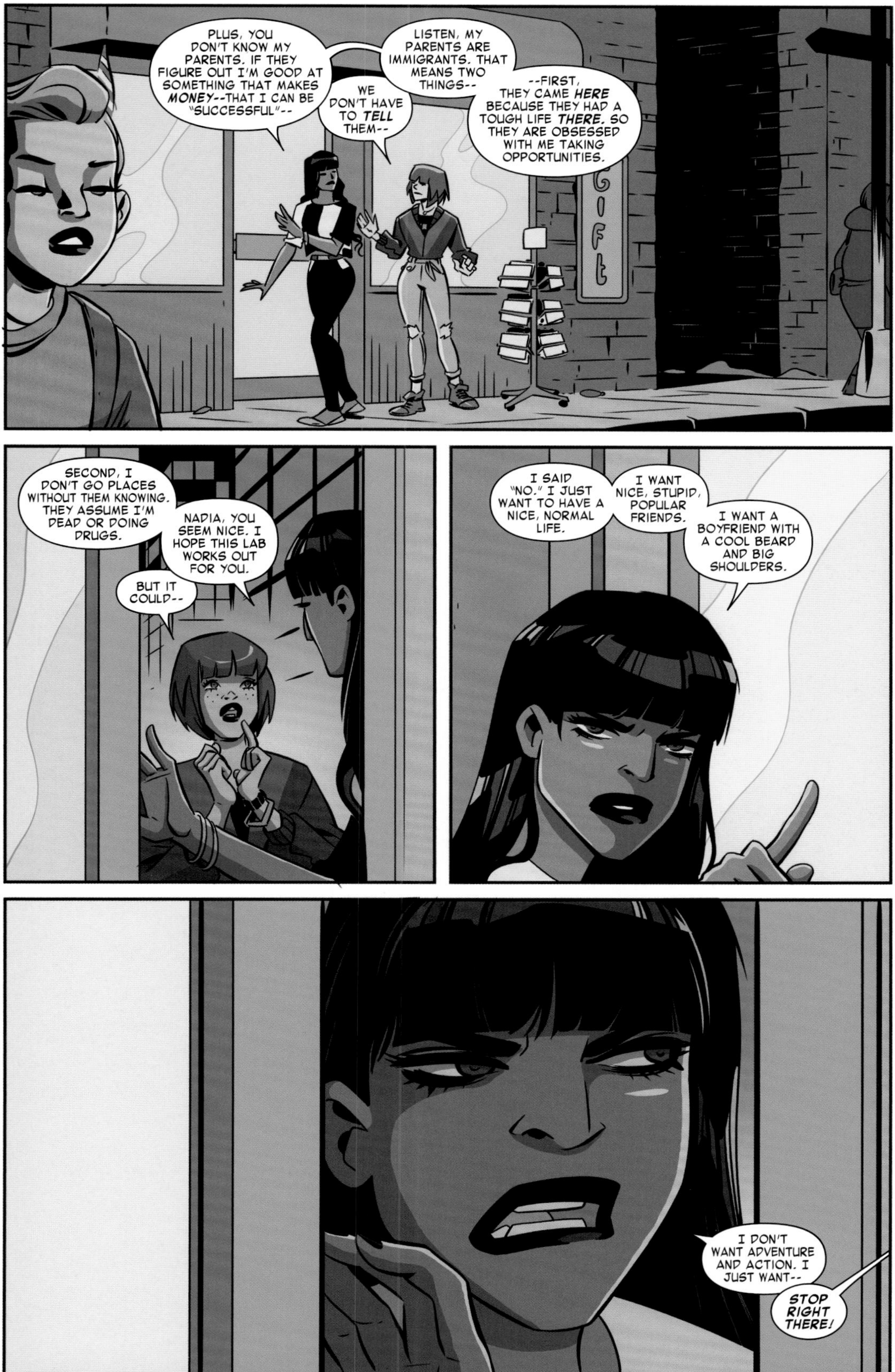
PLUS, YOU DON'T KNOW MY PARENTS. IF THEY FIGURE OUT I'M GOOD AT SOMETHING THAT MAKES MONEY--THAT I CAN BE "SUCCESSFUL"--
WE DON'T HAVE TO TELL THEM--
LISTEN, MY PARENTS ARE IMMIGRANTS. THAT MEANS TWO THINGS--
--FIRST, THEY CAME HERE BECAUSE THEY HAD A TOUGH LIFE THERE. SO THEY ARE OBSESSED WITH ME TAKING OPPORTUNITIES.
GIFT
SECOND, I DON'T GO PLACES WITHOUT THEM KNOWING. THEY ASSUME I'M DEAD OR DOING DRUGS.
NADIA, YOU SEEM NICE. I HOPE THIS LAB WORKS OUT FOR YOU.
BUT IT COULD--
I SAID "NO." I JUST WANT TO HAVE A NICE, NORMAL LIFE.
I WANT NICE, STUPID, POPULAR FRIENDS.
I WANT A BOYFRIEND WITH A COOL BEARD AND BIG SHOULDERS.
I DON'T WANT ADVENTURE AND ACTION. I JUST WANT--
STOP RIGHT THERE!

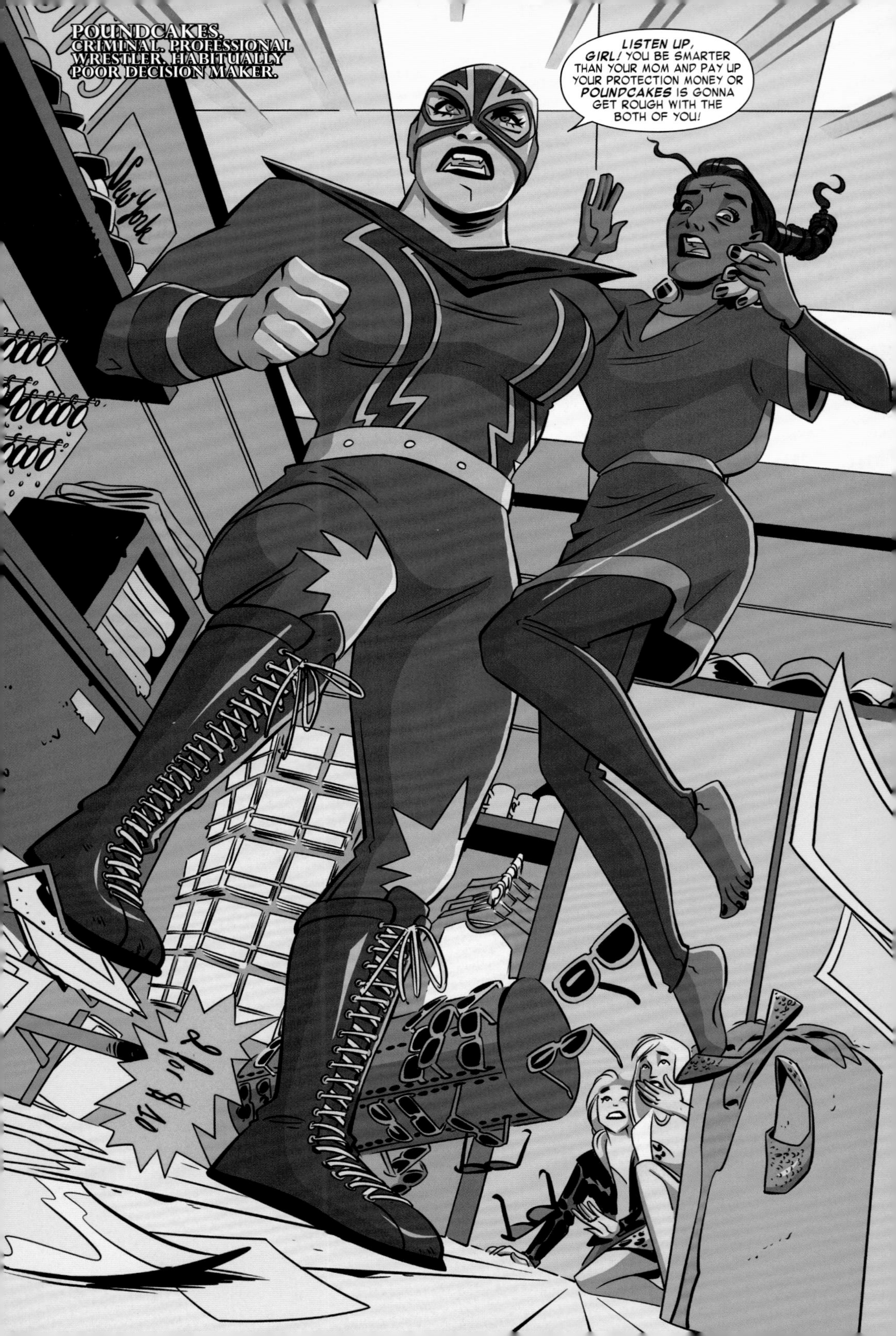
POUNDCAKES. CRIMINAL. PROFESSIONAL WRESTLER. HABITUALLY POOR DECISION MAKER.
LISTEN UP, GIRL! YOU BE SMARTER THAN YOUR MOM AND PAY UP YOUR PROTECTION MONEY OR POUNDCAKES IS GONNA GET ROUGH WITH THE BOTH OF YOU!
New York

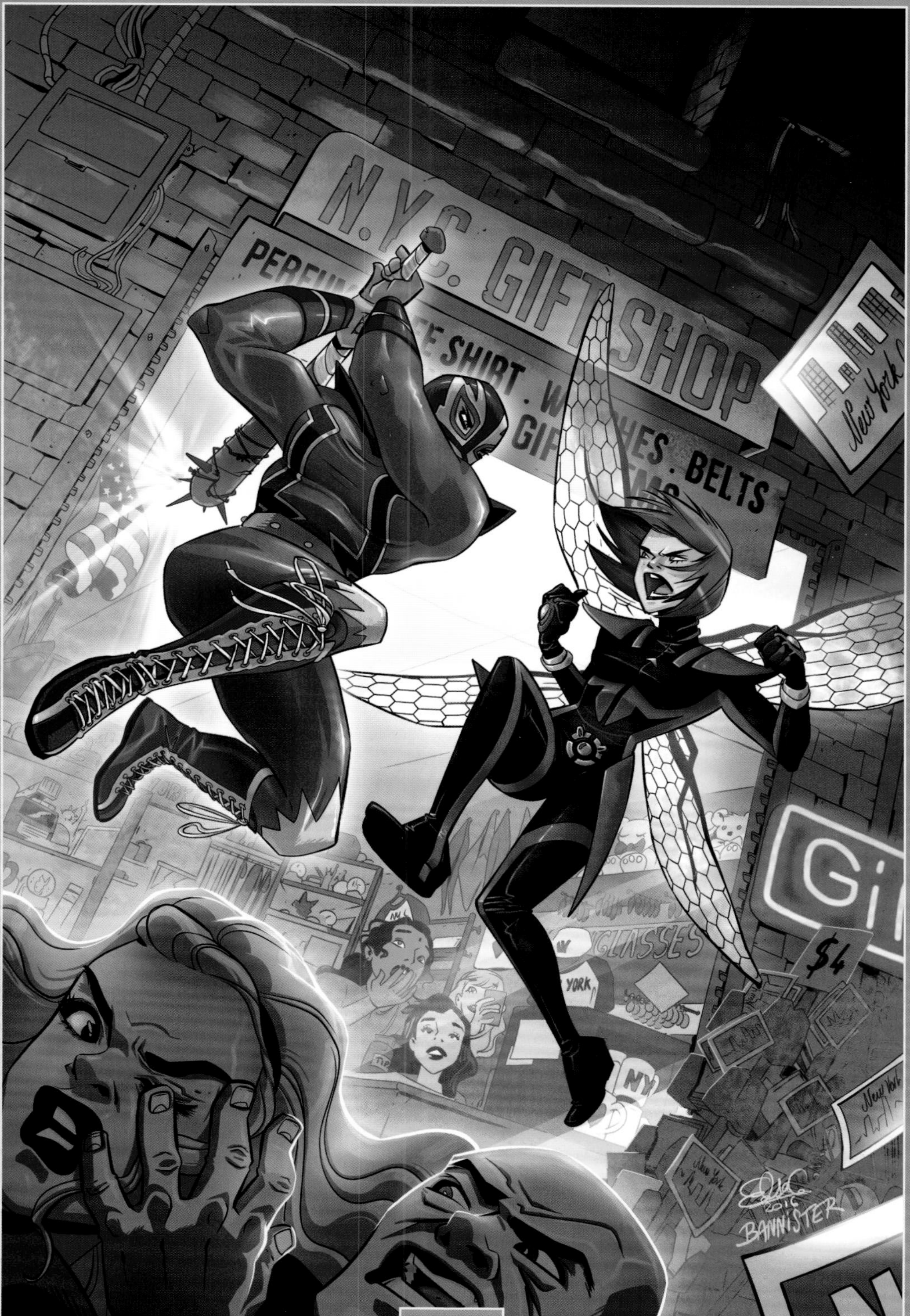
N.Y.C. GIFT SHOP
BELTS
New York
GLASSES
YORK
$4
BANNISTER
4

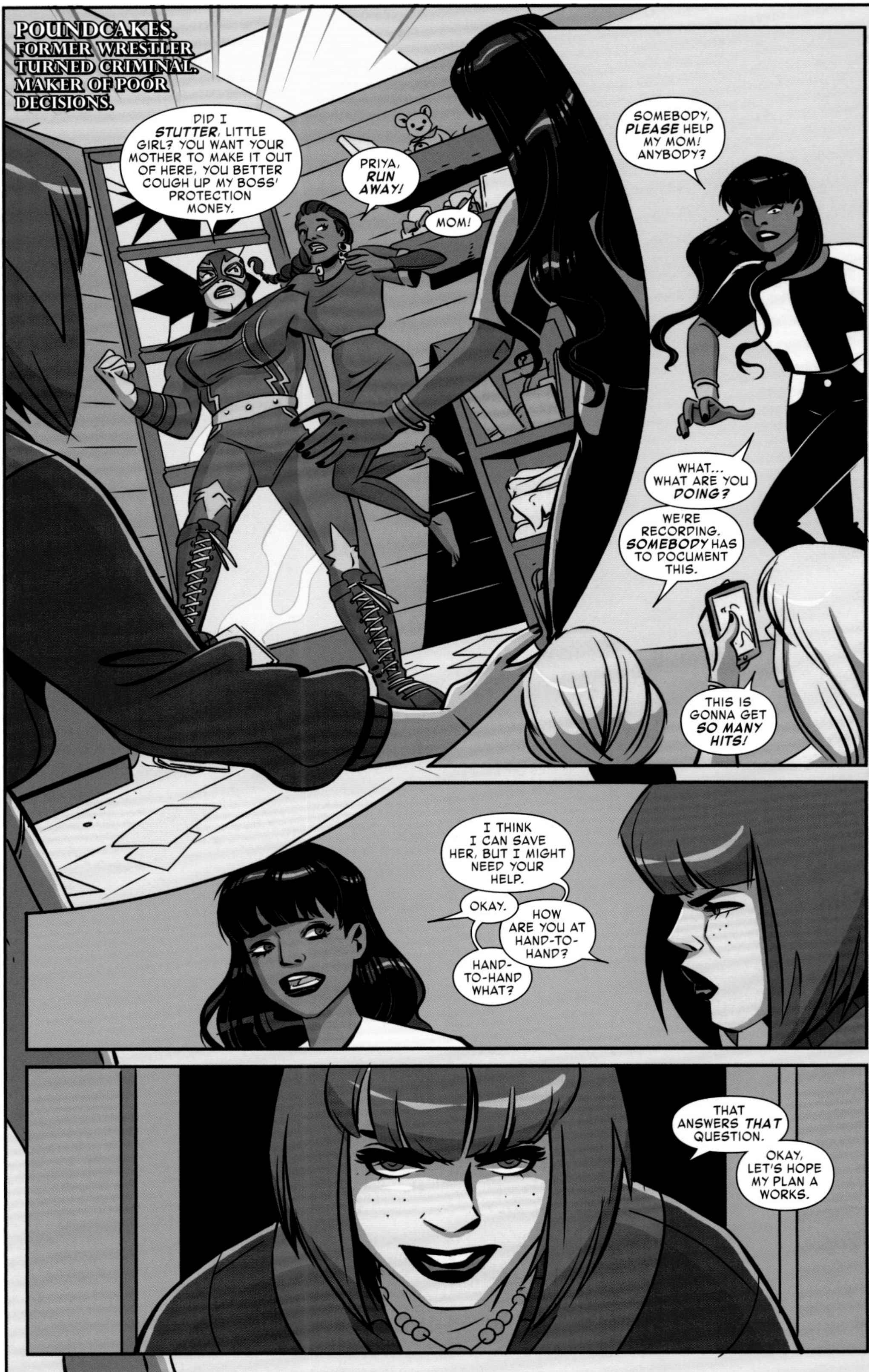
POUNDCAKES. FORMER WRESTLER TURNED CRIMINAL. MAKER OF POOR DECISIONS.
DID I STUTTER, LITTLE GIRL? YOU WANT YOUR MOTHER TO MAKE IT OUT OF HERE, YOU BETTER COUGH UP MY BOSS' PROTECTION MONEY.
PRIYA, RUN AWAY!
MOM!
SOMEBODY, PLEASE HELP MY MOM! ANYBODY?
WHAT... WHAT ARE YOU DOING?
WE'RE RECORDING. SOMEBODY HAS TO DOCUMENT THIS.
THIS IS GONNA GET SO MANY HITS!
I THINK I CAN SAVE HER, BUT I MIGHT NEED YOUR HELP.
OKAY.
HOW ARE YOU AT HAND-TO-HAND?
HAND-TO-HAND WHAT?
THAT ANSWERS THAT QUESTION.
OKAY, LET'S HOPE MY PLAN A WORKS.

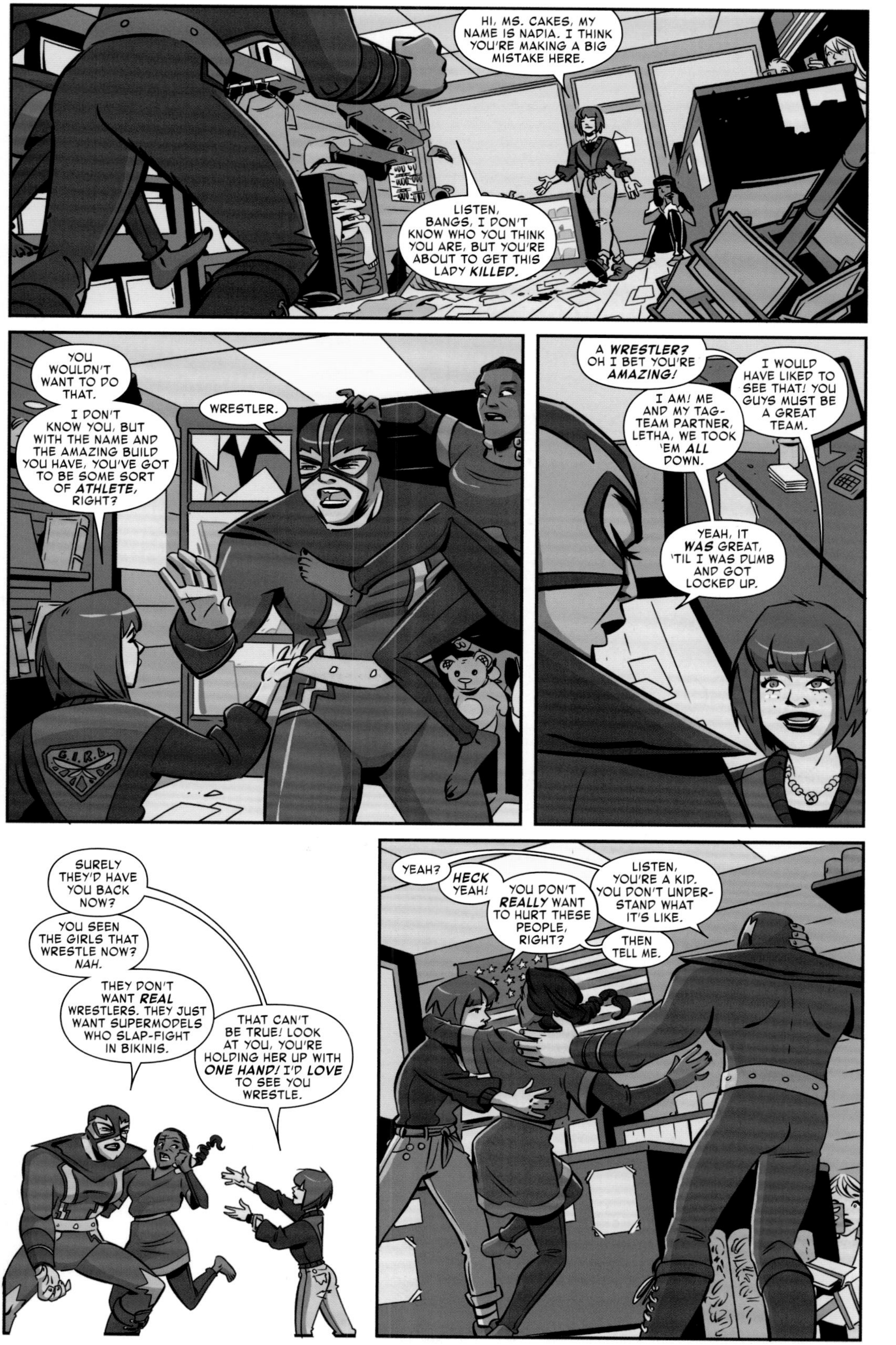

HI, MS. CAKES, MY NAME IS NADIA. I THINK YOU'RE MAKING A BIG MISTAKE HERE.
LISTEN, BANGS, I DON'T KNOW WHO YOU THINK YOU ARE, BUT YOU'RE ABOUT TO GET THIS LADY KILLED.
YOU WOULDN'T WANT TO DO THAT.
I DON'T KNOW YOU, BUT WITH THE NAME AND THE AMAZING BUILD YOU HAVE, YOU'VE GOT TO BE SOME SORT OF ATHLETE, RIGHT?
WRESTLER.
G.I.R.L.
A WRESTLER? OH I BET YOU'RE AMAZING!
I AM! ME AND MY TAG-TEAM PARTNER, LETHA, WE TOOK 'EM ALL DOWN.
I WOULD HAVE LIKED TO SEE THAT! YOU GUYS MUST BE A GREAT TEAM.
YEAH, IT WAS GREAT, 'TIL I WAS DUMB AND GOT LOCKED UP.
SURELY THEY'D HAVE YOU BACK NOW?
YOU SEEN THE GIRLS THAT WRESTLE NOW? NAH.
THEY DON'T WANT REAL WRESTLERS. THEY JUST WANT SUPERMODELS WHO SLAP-FIGHT IN BIKINIS.
THAT CAN'T BE TRUE! LOOK AT YOU, YOU'RE HOLDING HER UP WITH ONE HAND! I'D LOVE TO SEE YOU WRESTLE.
YEAH?
HECK YEAH!
YOU DON'T REALLY WANT TO HURT THESE PEOPLE, RIGHT?
LISTEN, YOU'RE A KID. YOU DON'T UNDERSTAND WHAT IT'S LIKE.
THEN TELL ME.

HEALTHY BAR
100% ORGANIC PRODUCTS
SEVEN DOLLARS FOR A CUP OF TEA? WHAT'S THIS CITY COME TO?
IT'S A DISGRACE. I'VE PAID LESS FOR A MONTH'S SUPPLY.
LAST TIME SOMEONE CHARGED THAT MUCH FOR TEA, WE THREW IT IN A HARBOR.
BLOODY RIGHT! SOMEBODY OUGHT TO PITCH A LOAD OF THIS IN THE HUDSON.
OPEN
OPEN
HEY, YOU MIND IF I ASK WHAT TIME IT IS?
NOT AT ALL. IT'S HALF PAST.
THIS IS TAKING A LOT LONGER THAN I THOUGHT.
WAITING ON SOMEONE?
MY PARTNER. SHE'S, UH...PICKING UP SOME THINGS.
PARDON ME, BUT... DON'T I KNOW YOU?

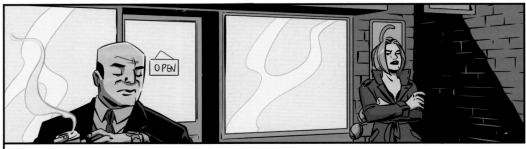

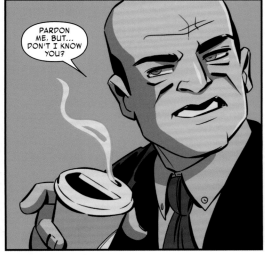

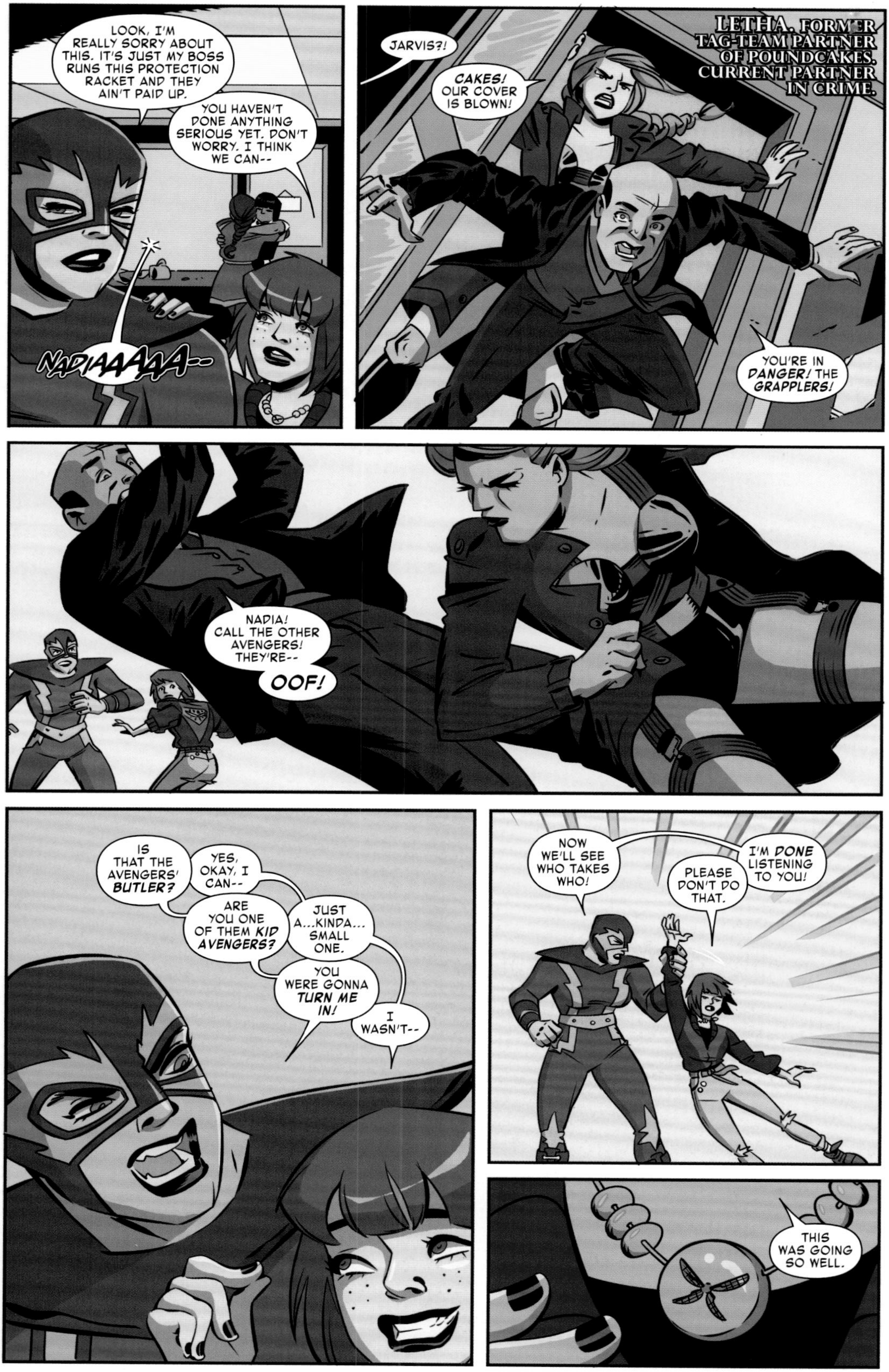
LOOK, I'M REALLY SORRY ABOUT THIS. IT'S JUST MY BOSS RUNS THIS PROTECTION RACKET AND THEY AIN'T PAID UP.
YOU HAVEN'T DONE ANYTHING SERIOUS YET. DON'T WORRY. I THINK WE CAN--
NADIAAAAAA--
JARVIS?!
LETHA. FORMER TAG-TEAM PARTNER OF POUNDCAKES. CURRENT PARTNER IN CRIME.
CAKES! OUR COVER IS BLOWN!
YOU'RE IN DANGER! THE GRAPPLERS!
NADIA! CALL THE OTHER AVENGERS! THEY'RE--
OOF!
IS THAT THE AVENGERS' BUTLER?
YES, OKAY, I CAN--
ARE YOU ONE OF THEM KID AVENGERS?
JUST A...KINDA... SMALL ONE.
YOU WERE GONNA TURN ME IN!
I WASN'T--
NOW WE'LL SEE WHO TAKES WHO!
I'M DONE LISTENING TO YOU!
PLEASE DON'T DO THAT.
THIS WAS GOING SO WELL.

WHAT'S THAT?!

FOR ME? A NECKLACE.

AND A WHOLE LOT MORE.

FOR YOU?

IT'S BAD NEWS.

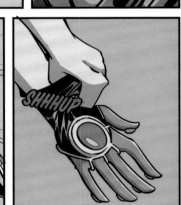

SHHHUP

ZZZZIP!

SHUNK

FLUTTER!

TIP

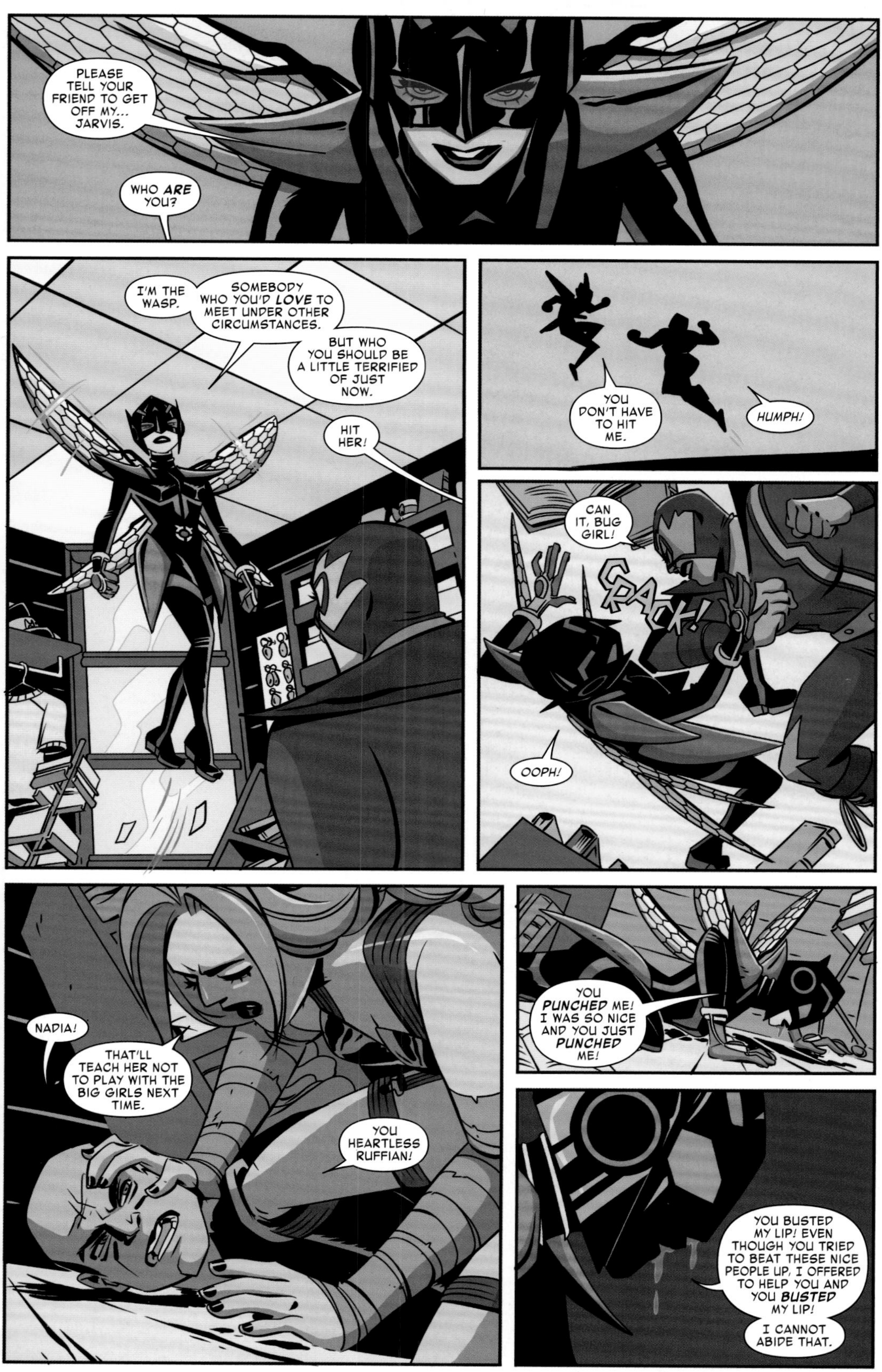
PLEASE TELL YOUR FRIEND TO GET OFF MY... JARVIS.
WHO *ARE* YOU?
I'M THE WASP.
SOMEBODY WHO YOU'D *LOVE* TO MEET UNDER OTHER CIRCUMSTANCES.
BUT WHO YOU SHOULD BE A LITTLE TERRIFIED OF JUST NOW.
HIT HER!
YOU DON'T HAVE TO HIT ME.
HUMPH!
CAN IT, BUG GIRL!
CRACK!
OOPH!
NADIA!
THAT'LL TEACH HER NOT TO PLAY WITH THE BIG GIRLS NEXT TIME.
YOU HEARTLESS RUFFIAN!
YOU *PUNCHED* ME! I WAS SO NICE AND YOU JUST *PUNCHED* ME!
YOU BUSTED MY LIP! EVEN THOUGH YOU TRIED TO BEAT THESE NICE PEOPLE UP, I OFFERED TO HELP YOU AND YOU *BUSTED* MY LIP!
I CANNOT ABIDE THAT.

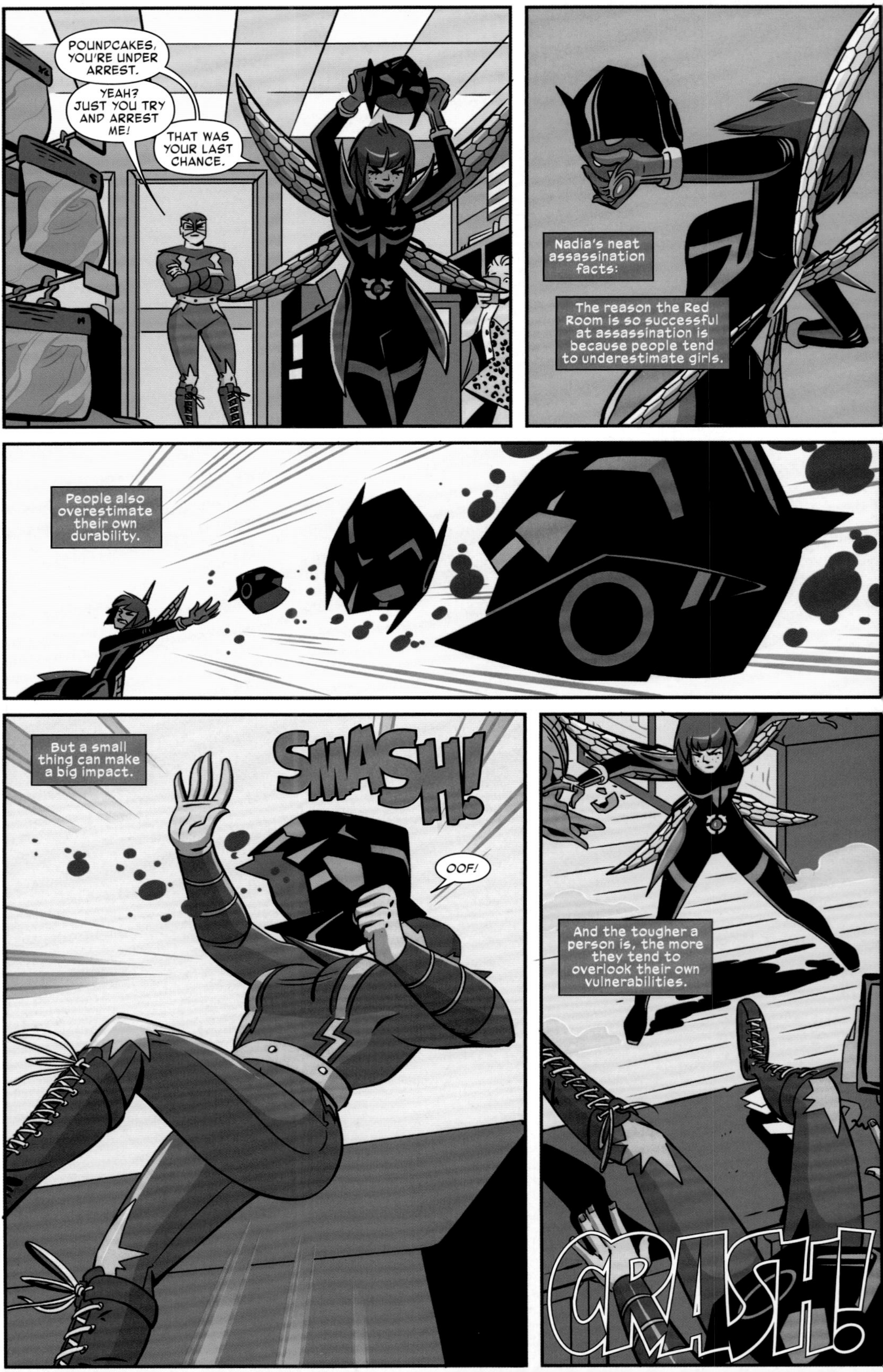
POUNDCAKES, YOU'RE UNDER ARREST.
YEAH? JUST YOU TRY AND ARREST ME!
THAT WAS YOUR LAST CHANCE.
Nadia's neat assassination facts:
The reason the Red Room is so successful at assassination is because people tend to underestimate girls.
People also overestimate their own durability.
But a small thing can make a big impact.
SMASH!
OOF!
And the tougher a person is, the more they tend to overlook their own vulnerabilities.
CRASH!

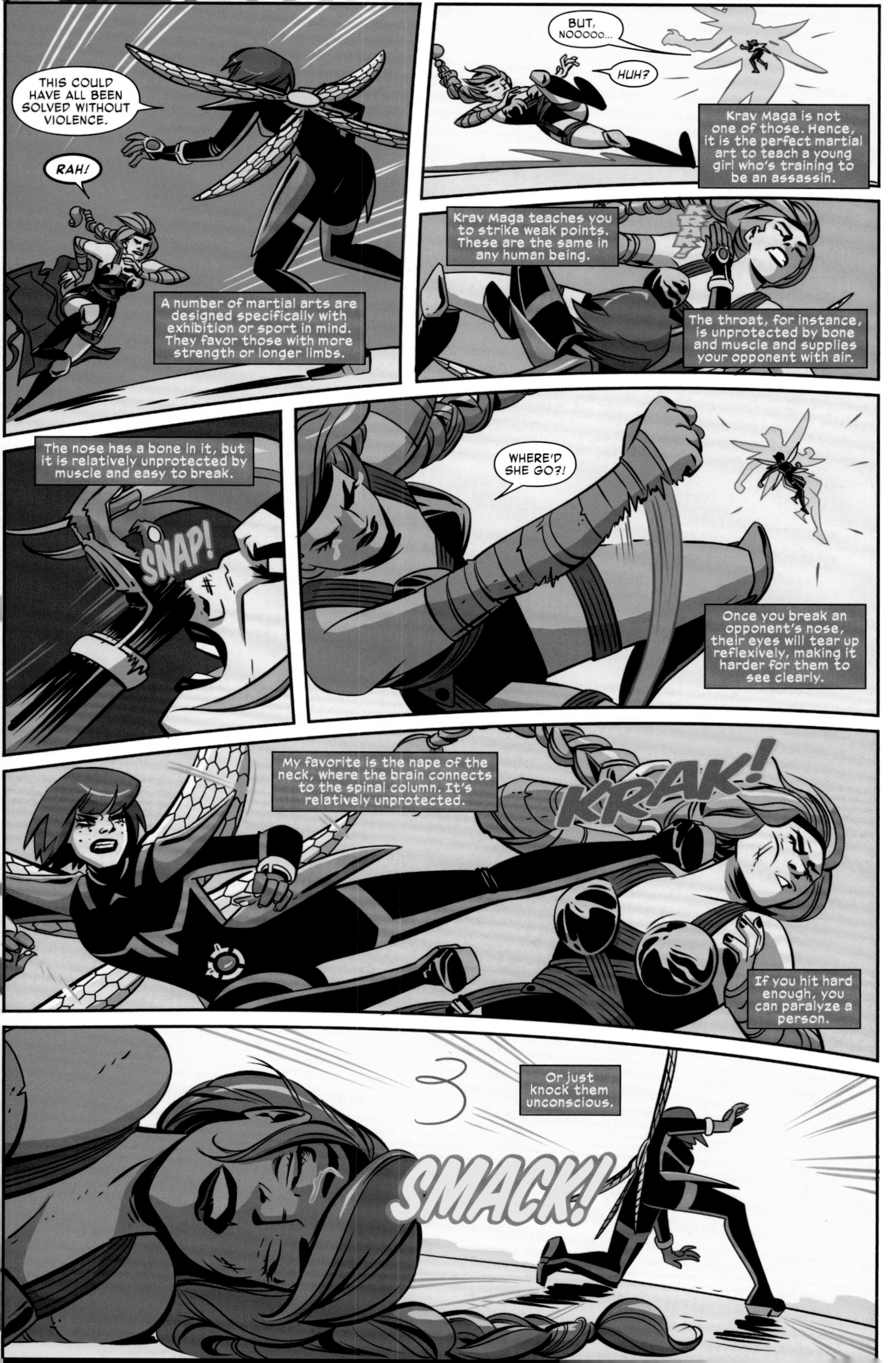
THIS COULD HAVE ALL BEEN SOLVED WITHOUT VIOLENCE.
RAH!
A number of martial arts are designed specifically with exhibition or sport in mind. They favor those with more strength or longer limbs.
BUT, NOOOOO...
HUH?
Krav Maga is not one of those. Hence, it is the perfect martial art to teach a young girl who's training to be an assassin.
Krav Maga teaches you to strike weak points. These are the same in any human being.
KRAK!
The throat, for instance, is unprotected by bone and muscle and supplies your opponent with air.
The nose has a bone in it, but it is relatively unprotected by muscle and easy to break.
SNAP!
WHERE'D SHE GO?!
Once you break an opponent's nose, their eyes will tear up reflexively, making it harder for them to see clearly.
My favorite is the nape of the neck, where the brain connects to the spinal column. It's relatively unprotected.
KRAK!
If you hit hard enough, you can paralyze a person.
Or just knock them unconscious.
SMACK!

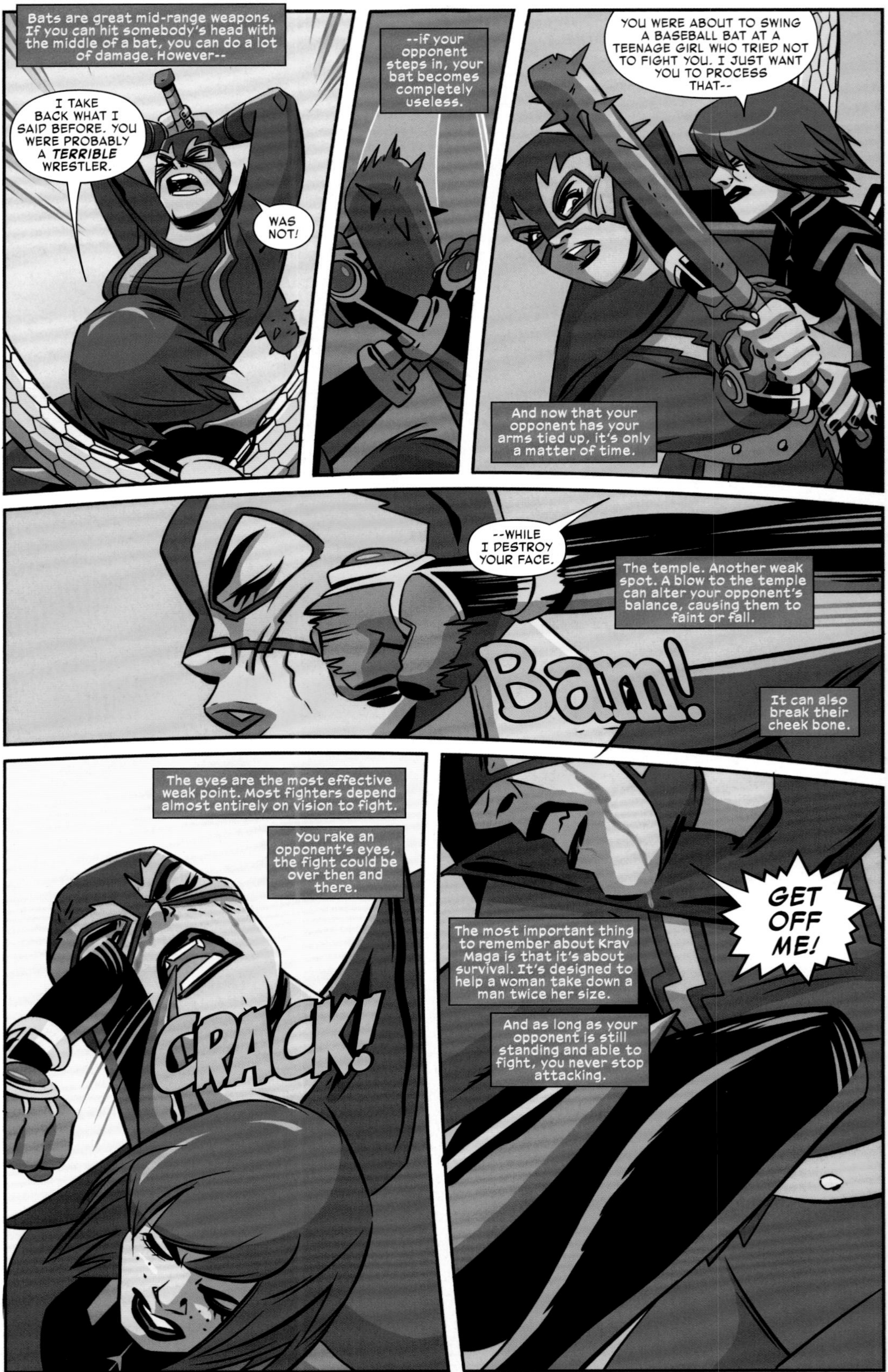
Bats are great mid-range weapons. If you can hit somebody's head with the middle of a bat, you can do a lot of damage. However--
I TAKE BACK WHAT I SAID BEFORE. YOU WERE PROBABLY A *TERRIBLE* WRESTLER.
WAS NOT!
--if your opponent steps in, your bat becomes completely useless.
YOU WERE ABOUT TO SWING A BASEBALL BAT AT A TEENAGE GIRL WHO TRIED NOT TO FIGHT YOU. I JUST WANT YOU TO PROCESS THAT--
And now that your opponent has your arms tied up, it's only a matter of time.
--WHILE I DESTROY YOUR FACE.
The temple. Another weak spot. A blow to the temple can alter your opponent's balance, causing them to faint or fall.
Bam!
It can also break their cheek bone.
The eyes are the most effective weak point. Most fighters depend almost entirely on vision to fight.
You rake an opponent's eyes, the fight could be over then and there.
CRACK!
GET OFF ME!
The most important thing to remember about Krav Maga is that it's about survival. It's designed to help a woman take down a man twice her size.
And as long as your opponent is still standing and able to fight, you never stop attacking.

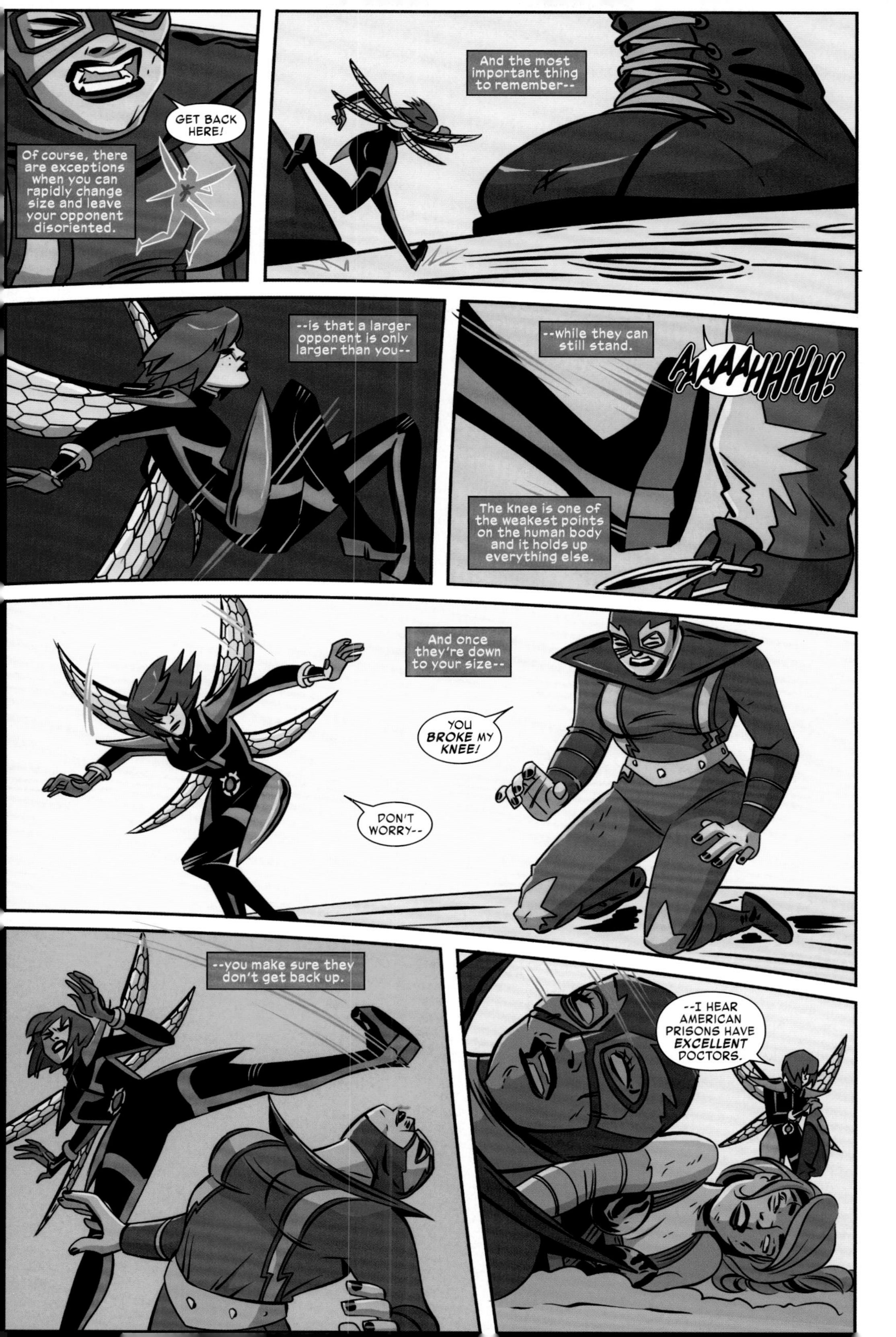
Of course, there are exceptions when you can rapidly change size and leave your opponent disoriented.
GET BACK HERE!
And the most important thing to remember--
--is that a larger opponent is only larger than you--
--while they can still stand.
AAAAAHHHH!
The knee is one of the weakest points on the human body and it holds up everything else.
And once they're down to your size--
YOU BROKE MY KNEE!
DON'T WORRY--
--you make sure they don't get back up.
--I HEAR AMERICAN PRISONS HAVE EXCELLENT DOCTORS.

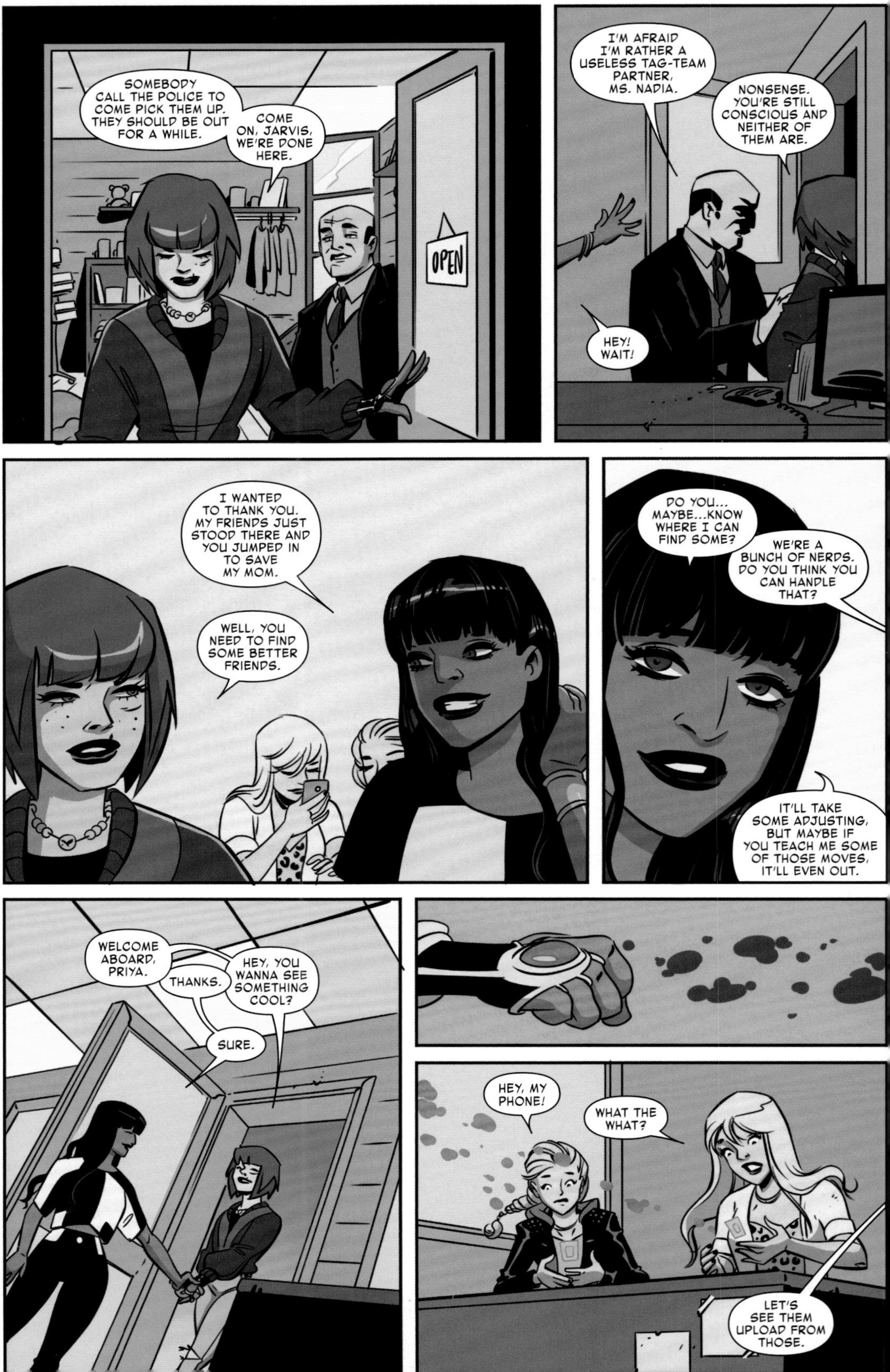
SOMEBODY CALL THE POLICE TO COME PICK THEM UP. THEY SHOULD BE OUT FOR A WHILE.
COME ON, JARVIS, WE'RE DONE HERE.
OPEN
I'M AFRAID I'M RATHER A USELESS TAG-TEAM PARTNER, MS. NADIA.
NONSENSE. YOU'RE STILL CONSCIOUS AND NEITHER OF THEM ARE.
HEY! WAIT!
I WANTED TO THANK YOU. MY FRIENDS JUST STOOD THERE AND YOU JUMPED IN TO SAVE MY MOM.
WELL, YOU NEED TO FIND SOME BETTER FRIENDS.
DO YOU... MAYBE...KNOW WHERE I CAN FIND SOME?
WE'RE A BUNCH OF NERDS. DO YOU THINK YOU CAN HANDLE THAT?
IT'LL TAKE SOME ADJUSTING, BUT MAYBE IF YOU TEACH ME SOME OF THOSE MOVES, IT'LL EVEN OUT.
WELCOME ABOARD, PRIYA.
THANKS.
HEY, YOU WANNA SEE SOMETHING COOL?
SURE.
HEY, MY PHONE!
WHAT THE WHAT?
LET'S SEE THEM UPLOAD FROM THOSE.

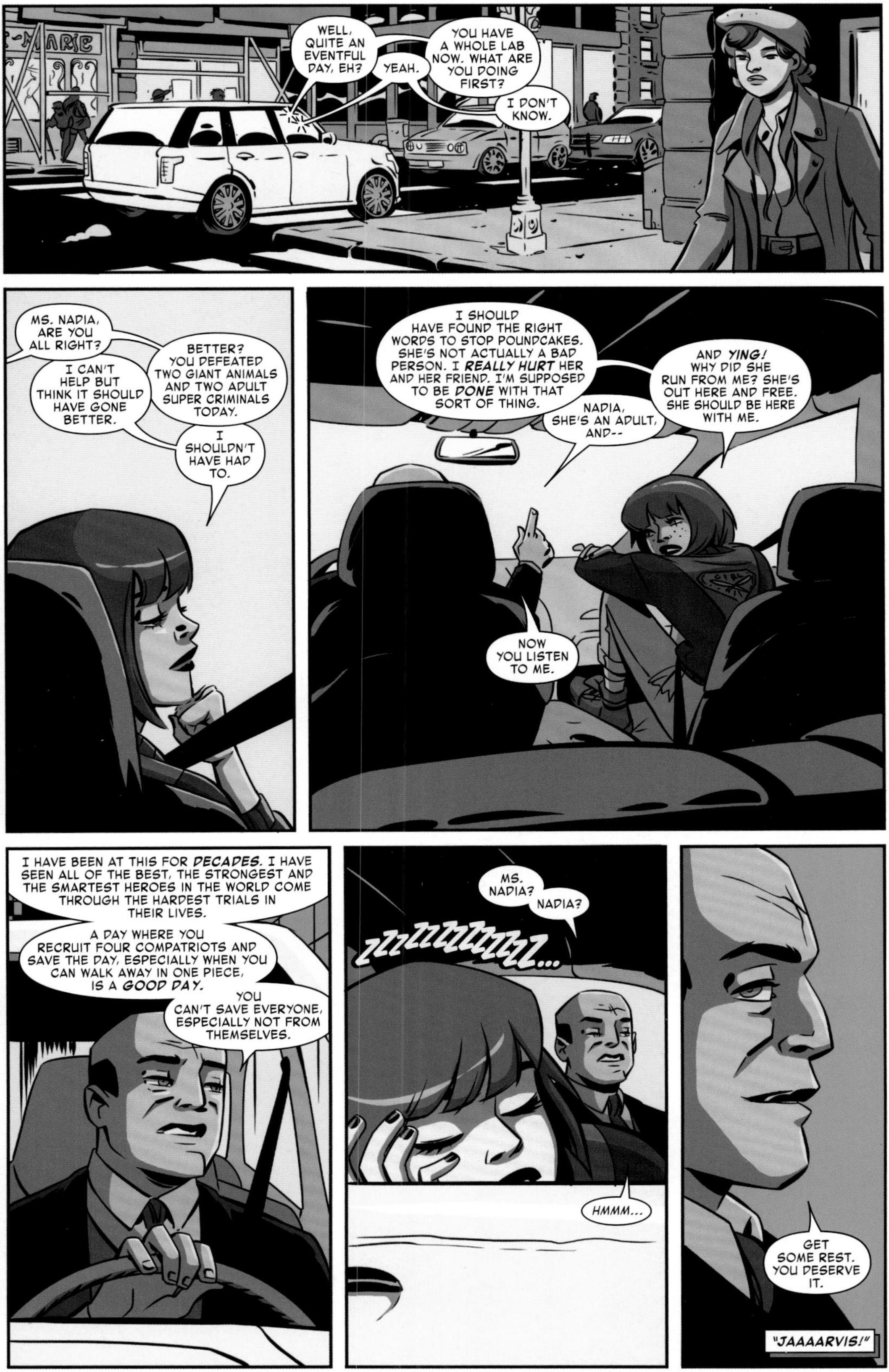
MARIE
WELL, QUITE AN EVENTFUL DAY, EH?
YEAH.
YOU HAVE A WHOLE LAB NOW. WHAT ARE YOU DOING FIRST?
I DON'T KNOW.
MS. NADIA, ARE YOU ALL RIGHT?
I CAN'T HELP BUT THINK IT SHOULD HAVE GONE BETTER.
BETTER? YOU DEFEATED TWO GIANT ANIMALS AND TWO ADULT SUPER CRIMINALS TODAY.
I SHOULDN'T HAVE HAD TO.
I SHOULD HAVE FOUND THE RIGHT WORDS TO STOP POUNDCAKES. SHE'S NOT ACTUALLY A BAD PERSON. I REALLY HURT HER AND HER FRIEND. I'M SUPPOSED TO BE DONE WITH THAT SORT OF THING.
AND YING! WHY DID SHE RUN FROM ME? SHE'S OUT HERE AND FREE. SHE SHOULD BE HERE WITH ME.
NADIA, SHE'S AN ADULT, AND--
NOW YOU LISTEN TO ME.
I HAVE BEEN AT THIS FOR DECADES. I HAVE SEEN ALL OF THE BEST, THE STRONGEST AND THE SMARTEST HEROES IN THE WORLD COME THROUGH THE HARDEST TRIALS IN THEIR LIVES.
A DAY WHERE YOU RECRUIT FOUR COMPATRIOTS AND SAVE THE DAY, ESPECIALLY WHEN YOU CAN WALK AWAY IN ONE PIECE, IS A GOOD DAY.
YOU CAN'T SAVE EVERYONE, ESPECIALLY NOT FROM THEMSELVES.
MS. NADIA?
NADIA?
ZZZZZZZZZZZZZZZ...
HMMM...
GET SOME REST. YOU DESERVE IT.
"JAAAARVIS!"

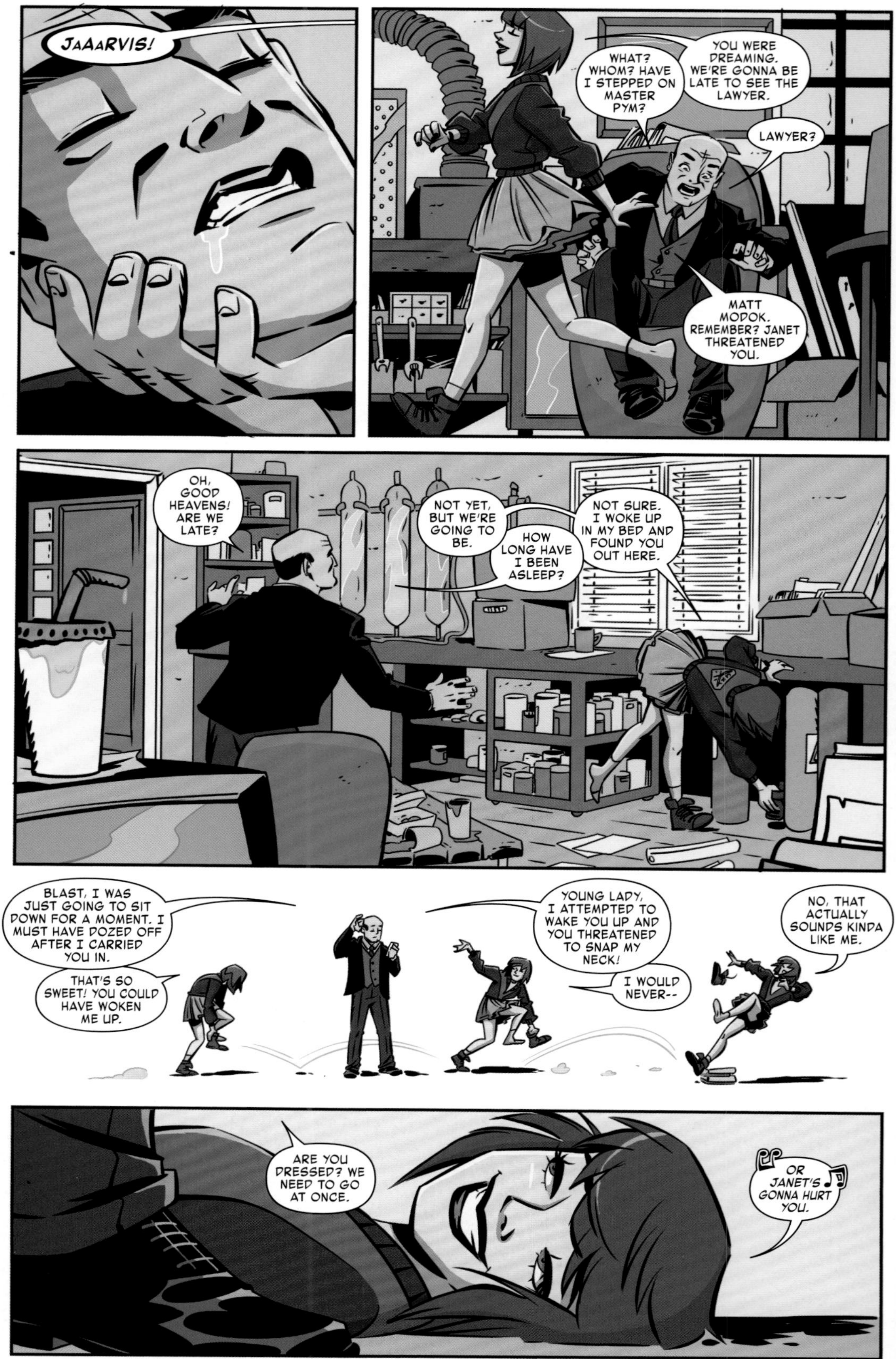
JAAARVIS!
YOU WERE DREAMING. WE'RE GONNA BE LATE TO SEE THE LAWYER.
WHAT? WHOM? HAVE I STEPPED ON MASTER PYM?
LAWYER?
MATT MODOK. REMEMBER? JANET THREATENED YOU.
OH, GOOD HEAVENS! ARE WE LATE?
NOT YET, BUT WE'RE GOING TO BE.
NOT SURE. I WOKE UP IN MY BED AND FOUND YOU OUT HERE.
HOW LONG HAVE I BEEN ASLEEP?
BLAST, I WAS JUST GOING TO SIT DOWN FOR A MOMENT. I MUST HAVE DOZED OFF AFTER I CARRIED YOU IN.
THAT'S SO SWEET! YOU COULD HAVE WOKEN ME UP.
YOUNG LADY, I ATTEMPTED TO WAKE YOU UP AND YOU THREATENED TO SNAP MY NECK!
I WOULD NEVER--
NO, THAT ACTUALLY SOUNDS KINDA LIKE ME.
ARE YOU DRESSED? WE NEED TO GO AT ONCE.
OR JANET'S GONNA HURT YOU.

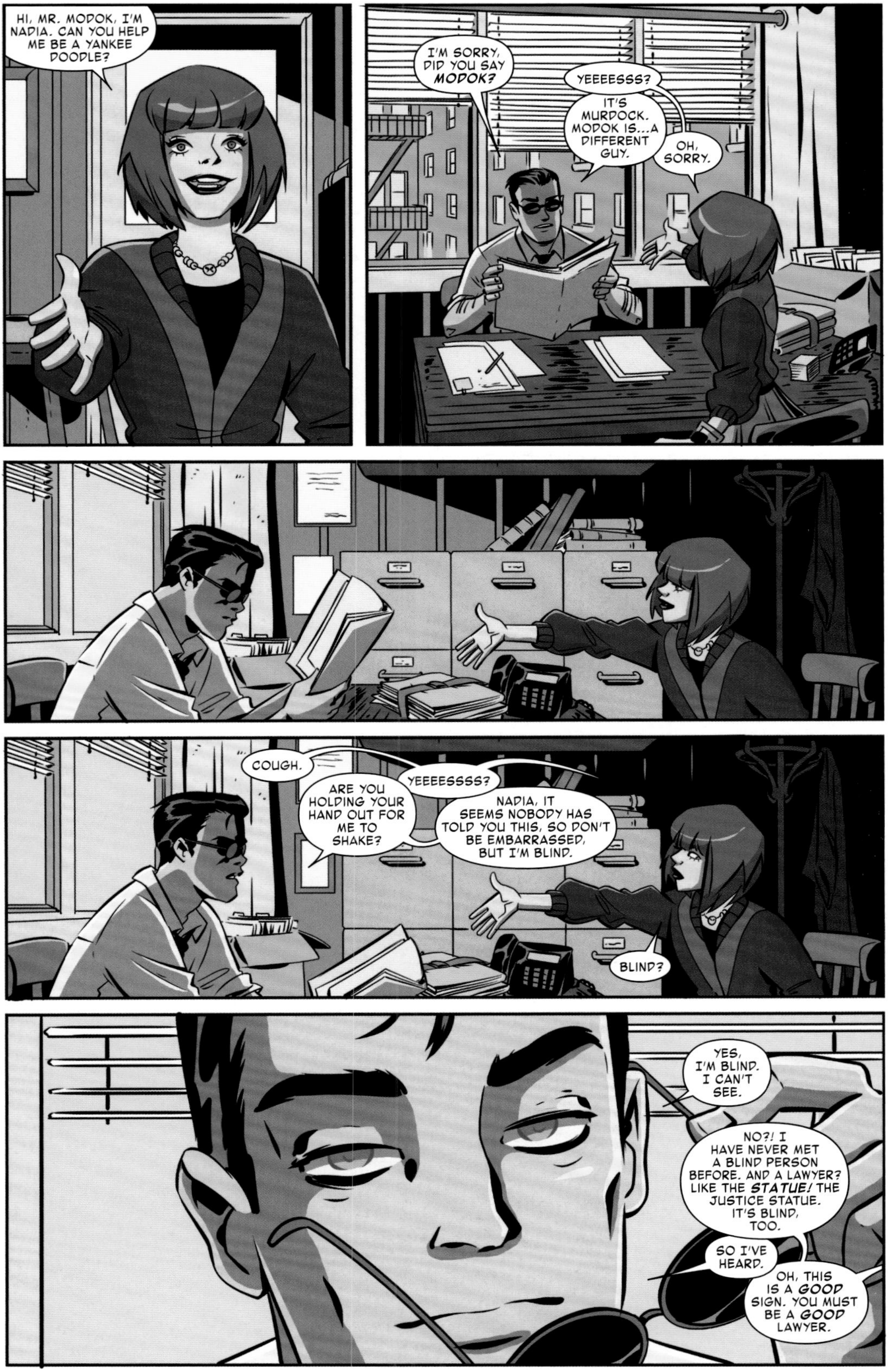
HI, MR. MODOK, I'M NADIA. CAN YOU HELP ME BE A YANKEE DOODLE?
I'M SORRY, DID YOU SAY *MODOK?*
YEEEESSS?
IT'S MURDOCK. MODOK IS...A DIFFERENT GUY.
OH, SORRY.
COUGH.
ARE YOU HOLDING YOUR HAND OUT FOR ME TO SHAKE?
YEEEESSSS?
NADIA, IT SEEMS NOBODY HAS TOLD YOU THIS, SO DON'T BE EMBARRASSED, BUT I'M BLIND.
BLIND?
YES, I'M BLIND. I CAN'T SEE.
NO?! I HAVE NEVER MET A BLIND PERSON BEFORE. AND A LAWYER? LIKE THE *STATUE!* THE JUSTICE STATUE. IT'S BLIND, TOO.
SO I'VE HEARD.
OH, THIS IS A *GOOD* SIGN. YOU MUST BE A *GOOD* LAWYER.

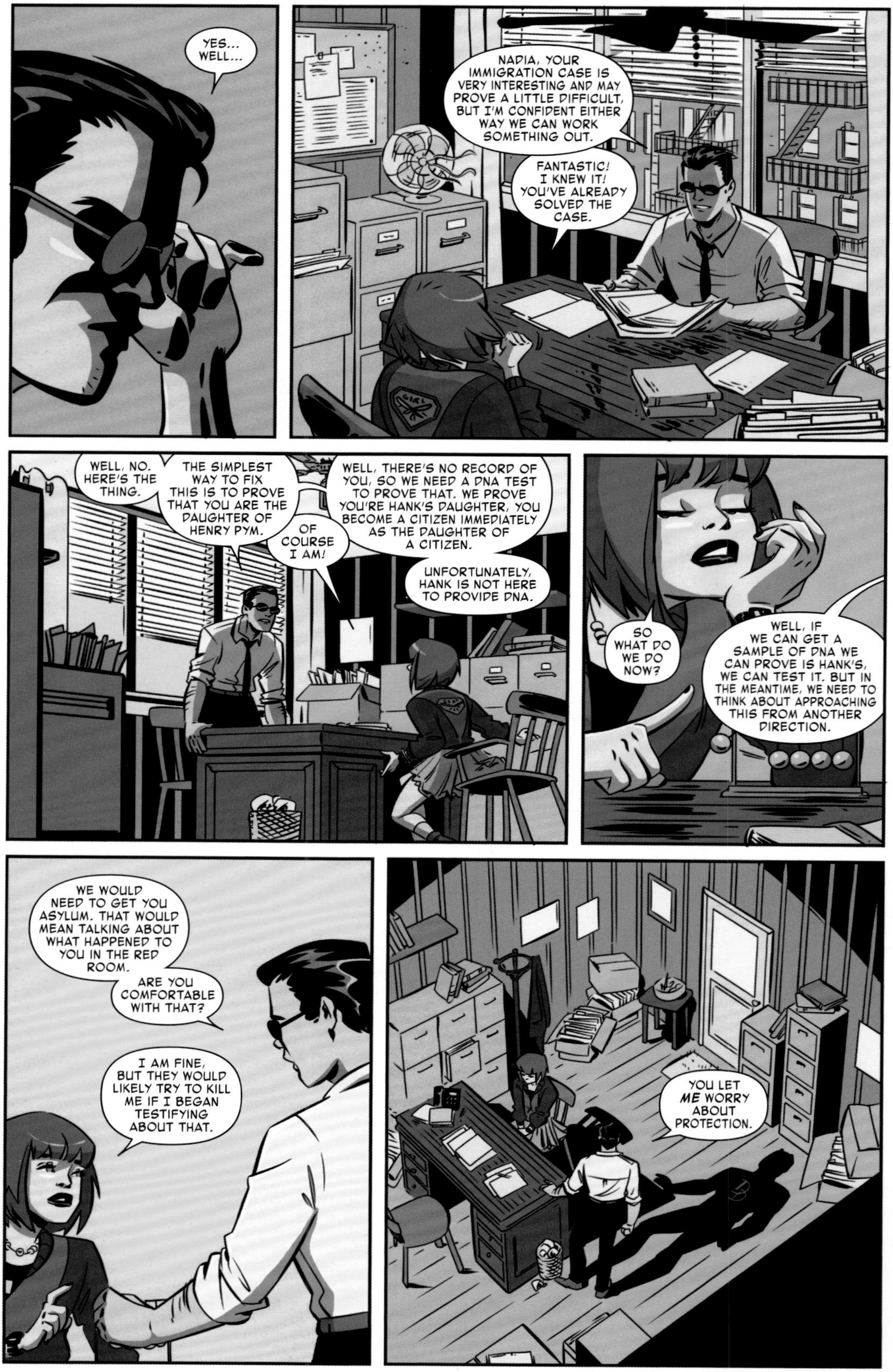
YES... WELL...
NADIA, YOUR IMMIGRATION CASE IS VERY INTERESTING AND MAY PROVE A LITTLE DIFFICULT, BUT I'M CONFIDENT EITHER WAY WE CAN WORK SOMETHING OUT.
FANTASTIC! I KNEW IT! YOU'VE ALREADY SOLVED THE CASE.
WELL, NO. HERE'S THE THING.
THE SIMPLEST WAY TO FIX THIS IS TO PROVE THAT YOU ARE THE DAUGHTER OF HENRY PYM.
OF COURSE I AM!
WELL, THERE'S NO RECORD OF YOU, SO WE NEED A DNA TEST TO PROVE THAT. WE PROVE YOU'RE HANK'S DAUGHTER, YOU BECOME A CITIZEN IMMEDIATELY AS THE DAUGHTER OF A CITIZEN.
UNFORTUNATELY, HANK IS NOT HERE TO PROVIDE DNA.
SO WHAT DO WE DO NOW?
WELL, IF WE CAN GET A SAMPLE OF DNA WE CAN PROVE IS HANK'S, WE CAN TEST IT. BUT IN THE MEANTIME, WE NEED TO THINK ABOUT APPROACHING THIS FROM ANOTHER DIRECTION.
WE WOULD NEED TO GET YOU ASYLUM. THAT WOULD MEAN TALKING ABOUT WHAT HAPPENED TO YOU IN THE RED ROOM.
ARE YOU COMFORTABLE WITH THAT?
I AM FINE, BUT THEY WOULD LIKELY TRY TO KILL ME IF I BEGAN TESTIFYING ABOUT THAT.
YOU LET ME WORRY ABOUT PROTECTION.

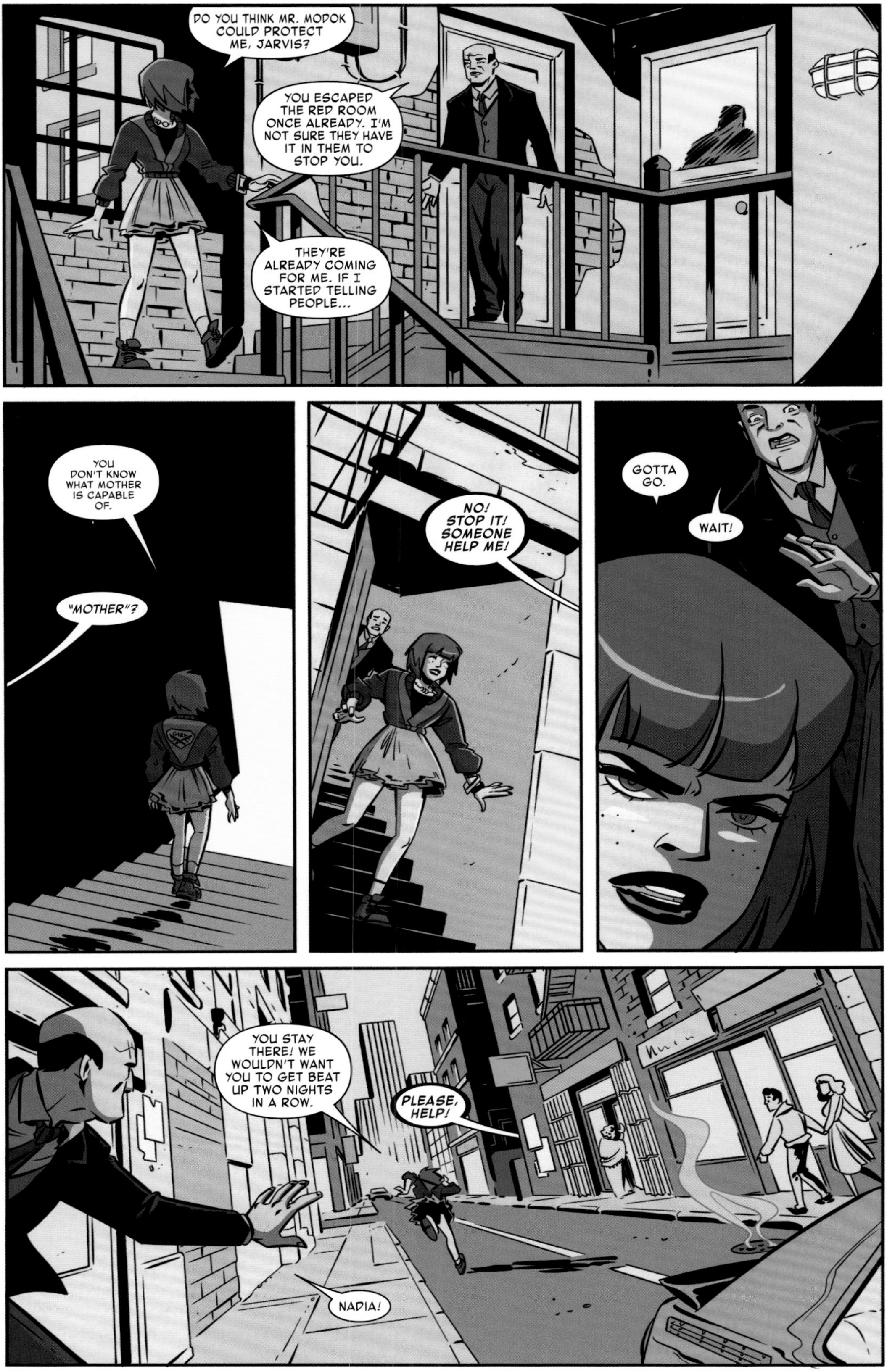
DO YOU THINK MR. MODOK COULD PROTECT ME, JARVIS?
YOU ESCAPED THE RED ROOM ONCE ALREADY. I'M NOT SURE THEY HAVE IT IN THEM TO STOP YOU.
THEY'RE ALREADY COMING FOR ME. IF I STARTED TELLING PEOPLE...
YOU DON'T KNOW WHAT MOTHER IS CAPABLE OF.
"MOTHER"?
NO! STOP IT! SOMEONE HELP ME!
GOTTA GO.
WAIT!
YOU STAY THERE! WE WOULDN'T WANT YOU TO GET BEAT UP TWO NIGHTS IN A ROW.
PLEASE, HELP!
NADIA!

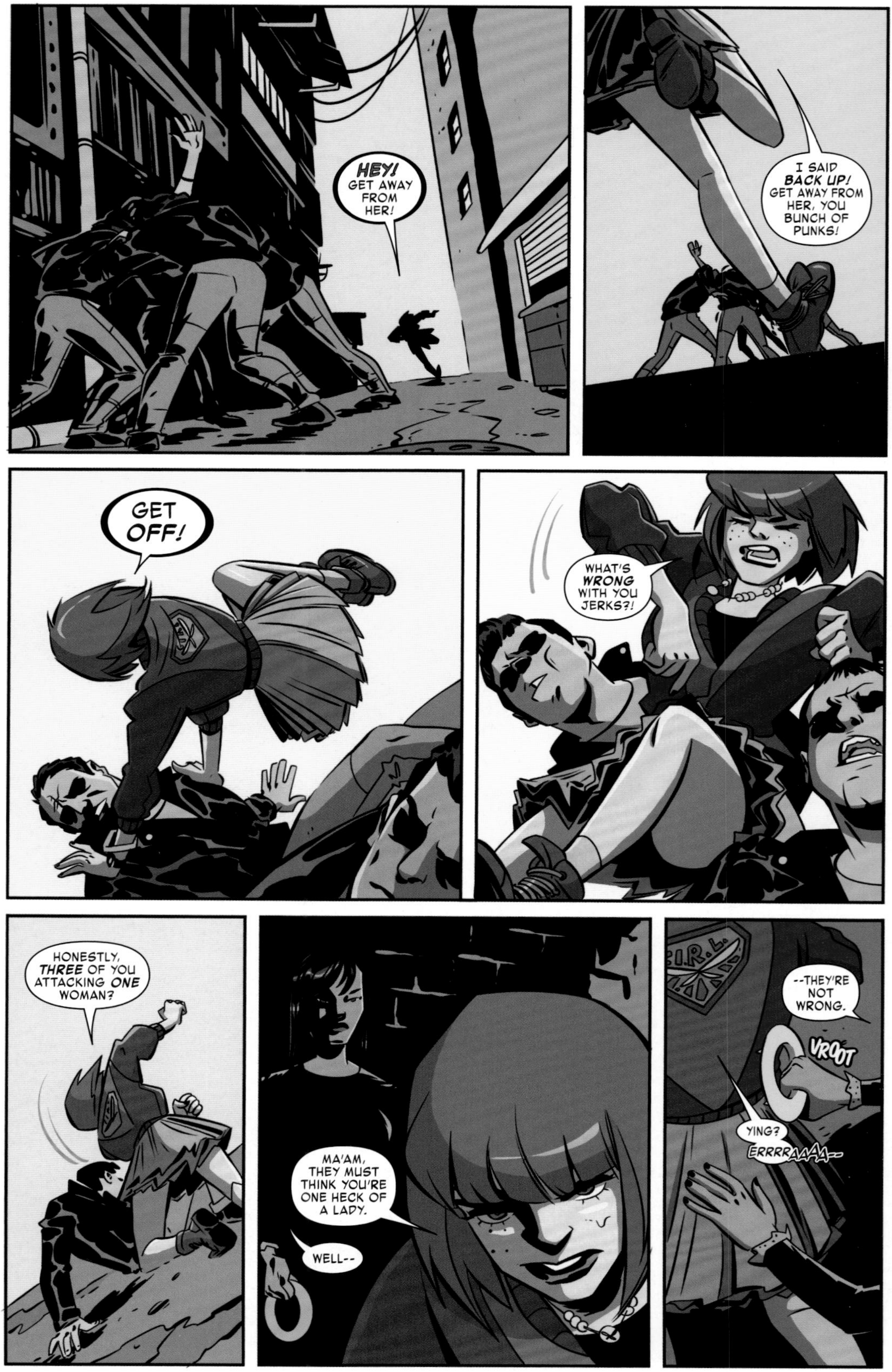
HEY! GET AWAY FROM HER!
I SAID BACK UP! GET AWAY FROM HER, YOU BUNCH OF PUNKS!
GET OFF!
WHAT'S WRONG WITH YOU JERKS?!
HONESTLY, THREE OF YOU ATTACKING ONE WOMAN?
MA'AM, THEY MUST THINK YOU'RE ONE HECK OF A LADY.
WELL--
--THEY'RE NOT WRONG.
VROOT
YING?
ERRRRAAAA--

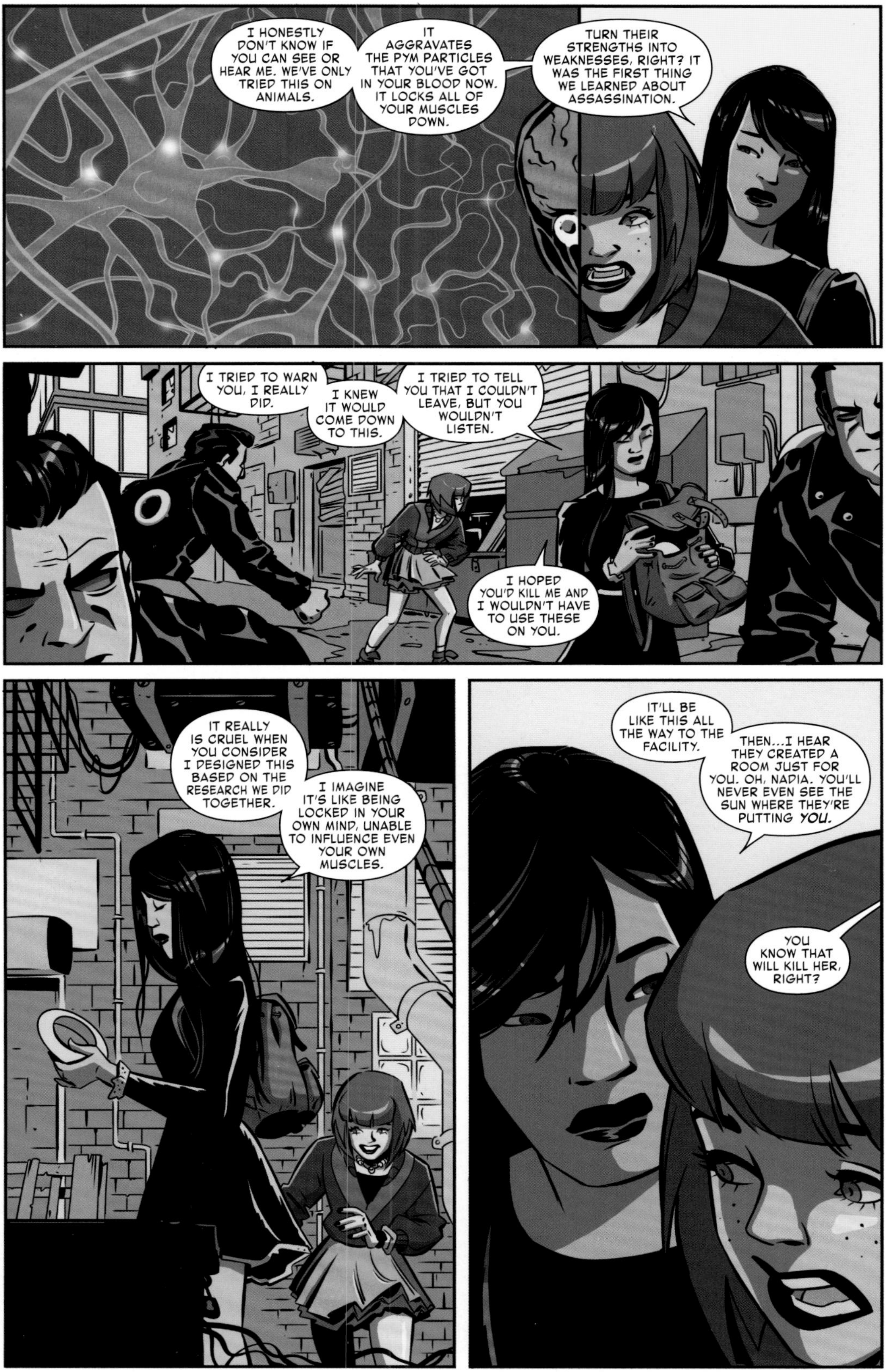
I HONESTLY DON'T KNOW IF YOU CAN SEE OR HEAR ME. WE'VE ONLY TRIED THIS ON ANIMALS.
IT AGGRAVATES THE PYM PARTICLES THAT YOU'VE GOT IN YOUR BLOOD NOW. IT LOCKS ALL OF YOUR MUSCLES DOWN.
TURN THEIR STRENGTHS INTO WEAKNESSES, RIGHT? IT WAS THE FIRST THING WE LEARNED ABOUT ASSASSINATION.
I TRIED TO WARN YOU, I REALLY DID.
I KNEW IT WOULD COME DOWN TO THIS.
I TRIED TO TELL YOU THAT I COULDN'T LEAVE, BUT YOU WOULDN'T LISTEN.
I HOPED YOU'D KILL ME AND I WOULDN'T HAVE TO USE THESE ON YOU.
IT REALLY IS CRUEL WHEN YOU CONSIDER I DESIGNED THIS BASED ON THE RESEARCH WE DID TOGETHER.
I IMAGINE IT'S LIKE BEING LOCKED IN YOUR OWN MIND, UNABLE TO INFLUENCE EVEN YOUR OWN MUSCLES.
IT'LL BE LIKE THIS ALL THE WAY TO THE FACILITY.
THEN...I HEAR THEY CREATED A ROOM JUST FOR YOU. OH, NADIA. YOU'LL NEVER EVEN SEE THE SUN WHERE THEY'RE PUTTING *YOU.*
YOU KNOW THAT WILL KILL HER, RIGHT?

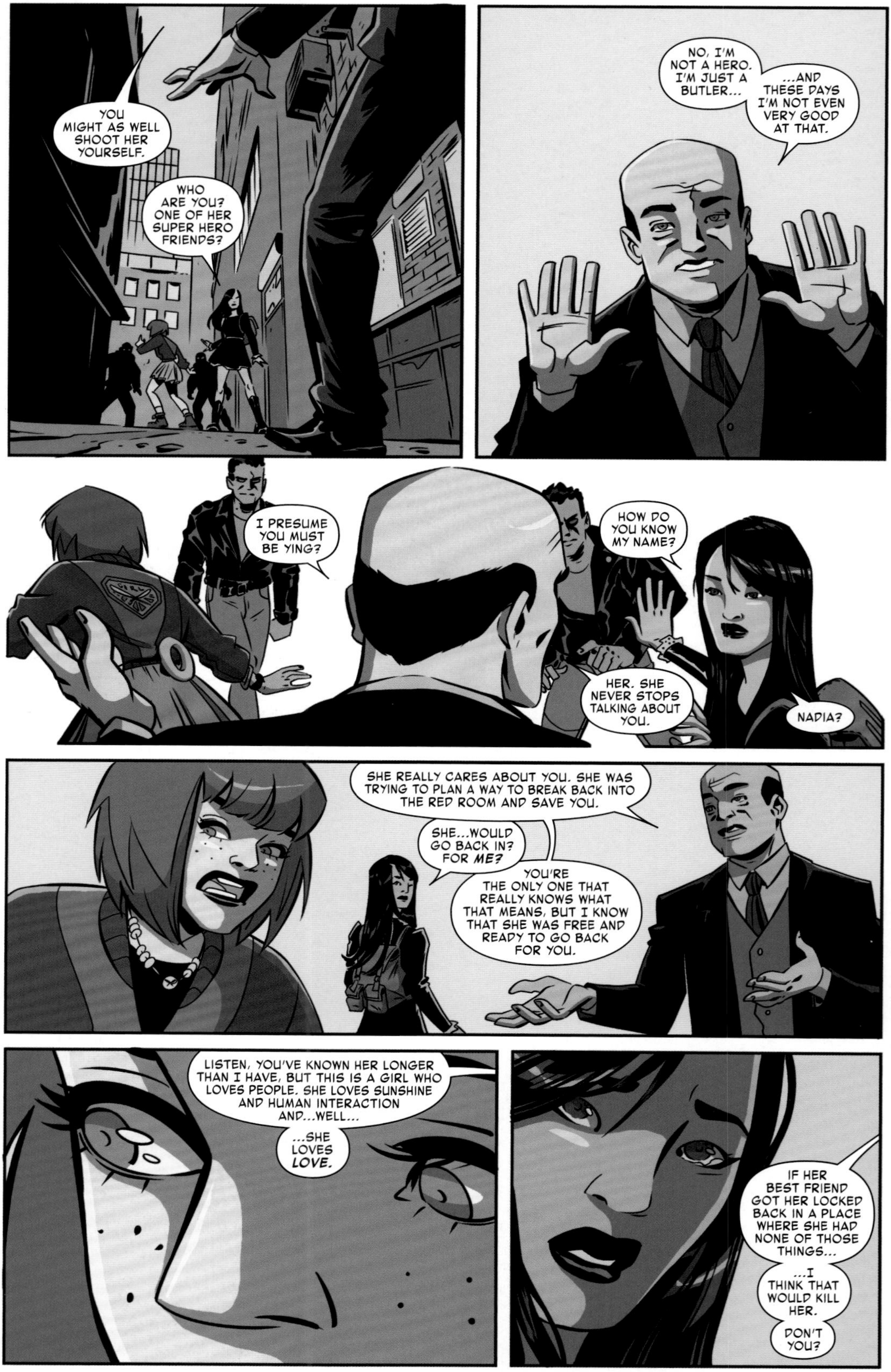
YOU MIGHT AS WELL SHOOT HER YOURSELF.
WHO ARE YOU? ONE OF HER SUPER HERO FRIENDS?
NO, I'M NOT A HERO. I'M JUST A BUTLER...
...AND THESE DAYS I'M NOT EVEN VERY GOOD AT THAT.
I PRESUME YOU MUST BE YING?
HOW DO YOU KNOW MY NAME?
HER. SHE NEVER STOPS TALKING ABOUT YOU.
NADIA?
SHE REALLY CARES ABOUT YOU. SHE WAS TRYING TO PLAN A WAY TO BREAK BACK INTO THE RED ROOM AND SAVE YOU.
SHE...WOULD GO BACK IN? FOR *ME?*
YOU'RE THE ONLY ONE THAT REALLY KNOWS WHAT THAT MEANS, BUT I KNOW THAT SHE WAS FREE AND READY TO GO BACK FOR YOU.
LISTEN, YOU'VE KNOWN HER LONGER THAN I HAVE, BUT THIS IS A GIRL WHO LOVES PEOPLE. SHE LOVES SUNSHINE AND HUMAN INTERACTION AND...WELL...
...SHE LOVES *LOVE.*
IF HER BEST FRIEND GOT HER LOCKED BACK IN A PLACE WHERE SHE HAD NONE OF THOSE THINGS...
...I THINK THAT WOULD KILL HER.
DON'T YOU?

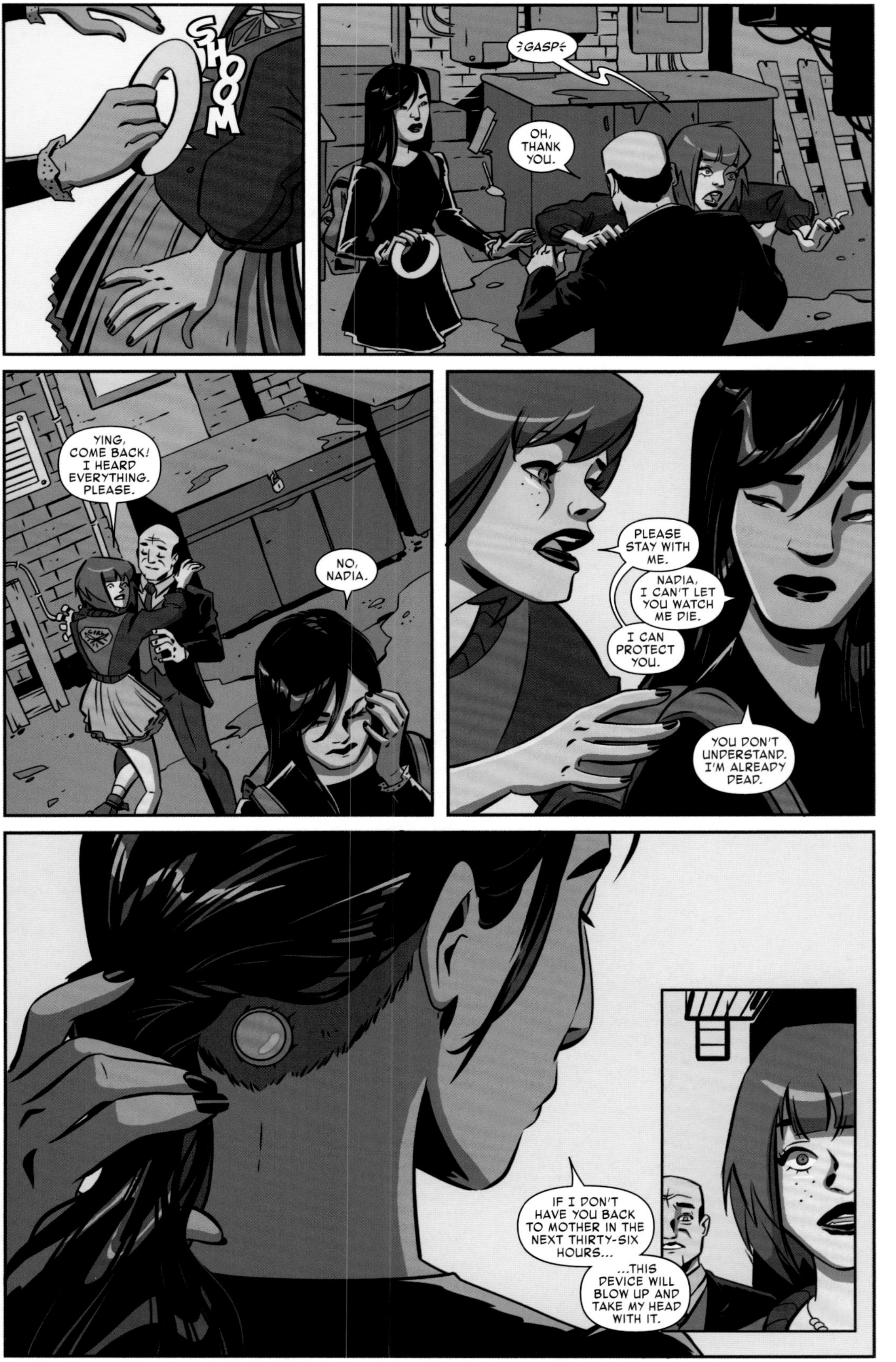
SHOOM
GASP
OH, THANK YOU.
YING, COME BACK! I HEARD EVERYTHING. PLEASE.
NO, NADIA.
PLEASE STAY WITH ME.
NADIA, I CAN'T LET YOU WATCH ME DIE.
I CAN PROTECT YOU.
YOU DON'T UNDERSTAND. I'M ALREADY DEAD.
IF I DON'T HAVE YOU BACK TO MOTHER IN THE NEXT THIRTY-SIX HOURS...
...THIS DEVICE WILL BLOW UP AND TAKE MY HEAD WITH IT.

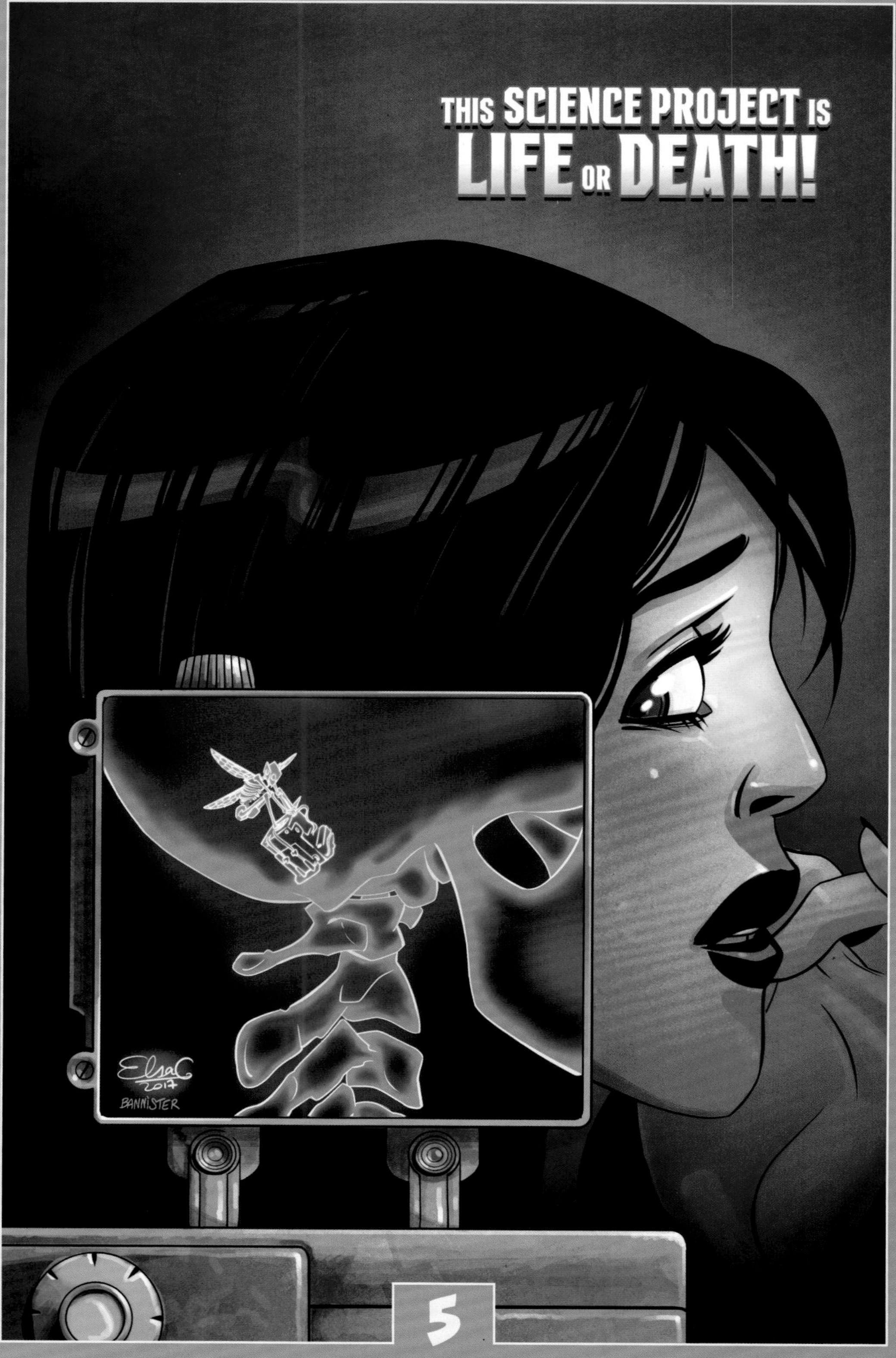
THIS SCIENCE PROJECT IS
LIFE OR DEATH!
BANNISTER
5

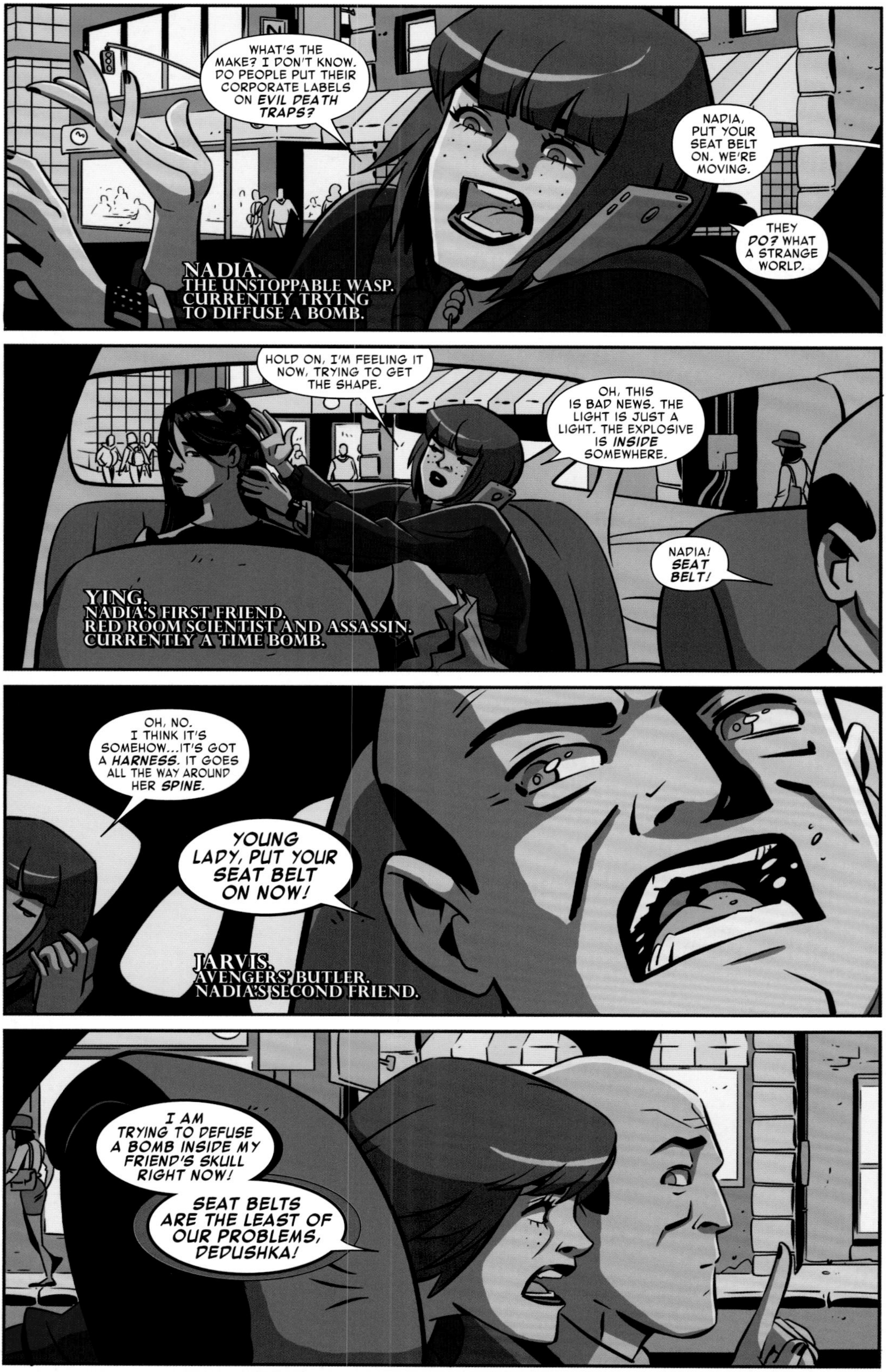
WHAT'S THE MAKE? I DON'T KNOW. DO PEOPLE PUT THEIR CORPORATE LABELS ON EVIL DEATH TRAPS?
NADIA, PUT YOUR SEAT BELT ON. WE'RE MOVING.
THEY DO? WHAT A STRANGE WORLD.
NADIA. THE UNSTOPPABLE WASP. CURRENTLY TRYING TO DIFFUSE A BOMB.
HOLD ON, I'M FEELING IT NOW, TRYING TO GET THE SHAPE.
OH, THIS IS BAD NEWS. THE LIGHT IS JUST A LIGHT. THE EXPLOSIVE IS INSIDE SOMEWHERE.
NADIA! SEAT BELT!
YING. NADIA'S FIRST FRIEND. RED ROOM SCIENTIST AND ASSASSIN. CURRENTLY A TIME BOMB.
OH, NO. I THINK IT'S SOMEHOW...IT'S GOT A HARNESS. IT GOES ALL THE WAY AROUND HER SPINE.
YOUNG LADY, PUT YOUR SEAT BELT ON NOW!
JARVIS. AVENGERS' BUTLER. NADIA'S SECOND FRIEND.
I AM TRYING TO DEFUSE A BOMB INSIDE MY FRIEND'S SKULL RIGHT NOW!
SEAT BELTS ARE THE LEAST OF OUR PROBLEMS, DEDUSHKA!

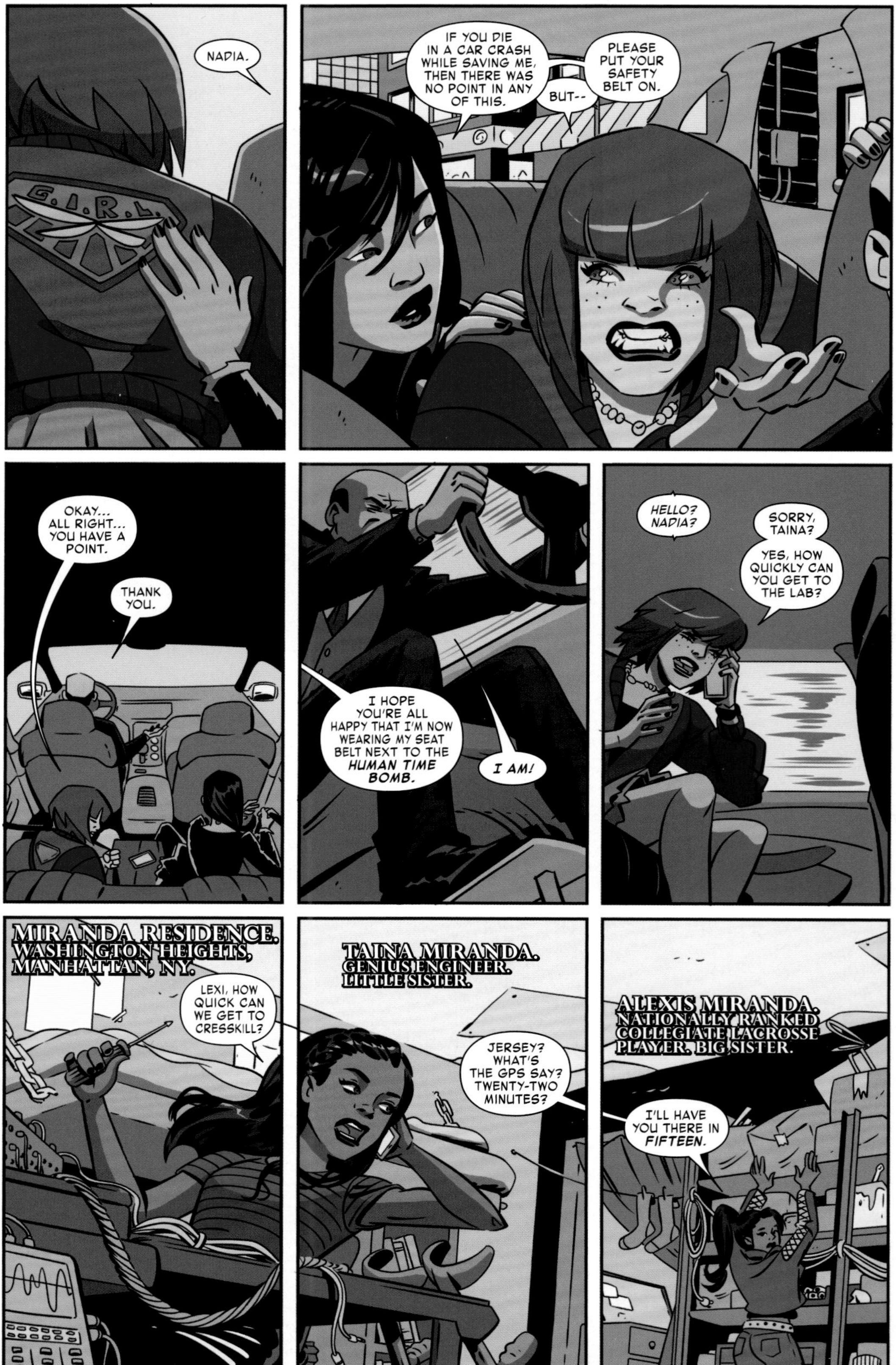
NADIA.
IF YOU DIE IN A CAR CRASH WHILE SAVING ME, THEN THERE WAS NO POINT IN ANY OF THIS.
BUT--
PLEASE PUT YOUR SAFETY BELT ON.
OKAY... ALL RIGHT... YOU HAVE A POINT.
THANK YOU.
I HOPE YOU'RE ALL HAPPY THAT I'M NOW WEARING MY SEAT BELT NEXT TO THE HUMAN TIME BOMB.
I AM!
HELLO? NADIA?
SORRY, TAINA?
YES, HOW QUICKLY CAN YOU GET TO THE LAB?
MIRANDA RESIDENCE. WASHINGTON HEIGHTS, MANHATTAN, NY.
LEXI, HOW QUICK CAN WE GET TO CRESSKILL?
TAINA MIRANDA. GENIUS ENGINEER. LITTLE SISTER.
JERSEY? WHAT'S THE GPS SAY? TWENTY-TWO MINUTES?
ALEXIS MIRANDA. NATIONALLY RANKED COLLEGIATE LACROSSE PLAYER. BIG SISTER.
I'LL HAVE YOU THERE IN FIFTEEN.

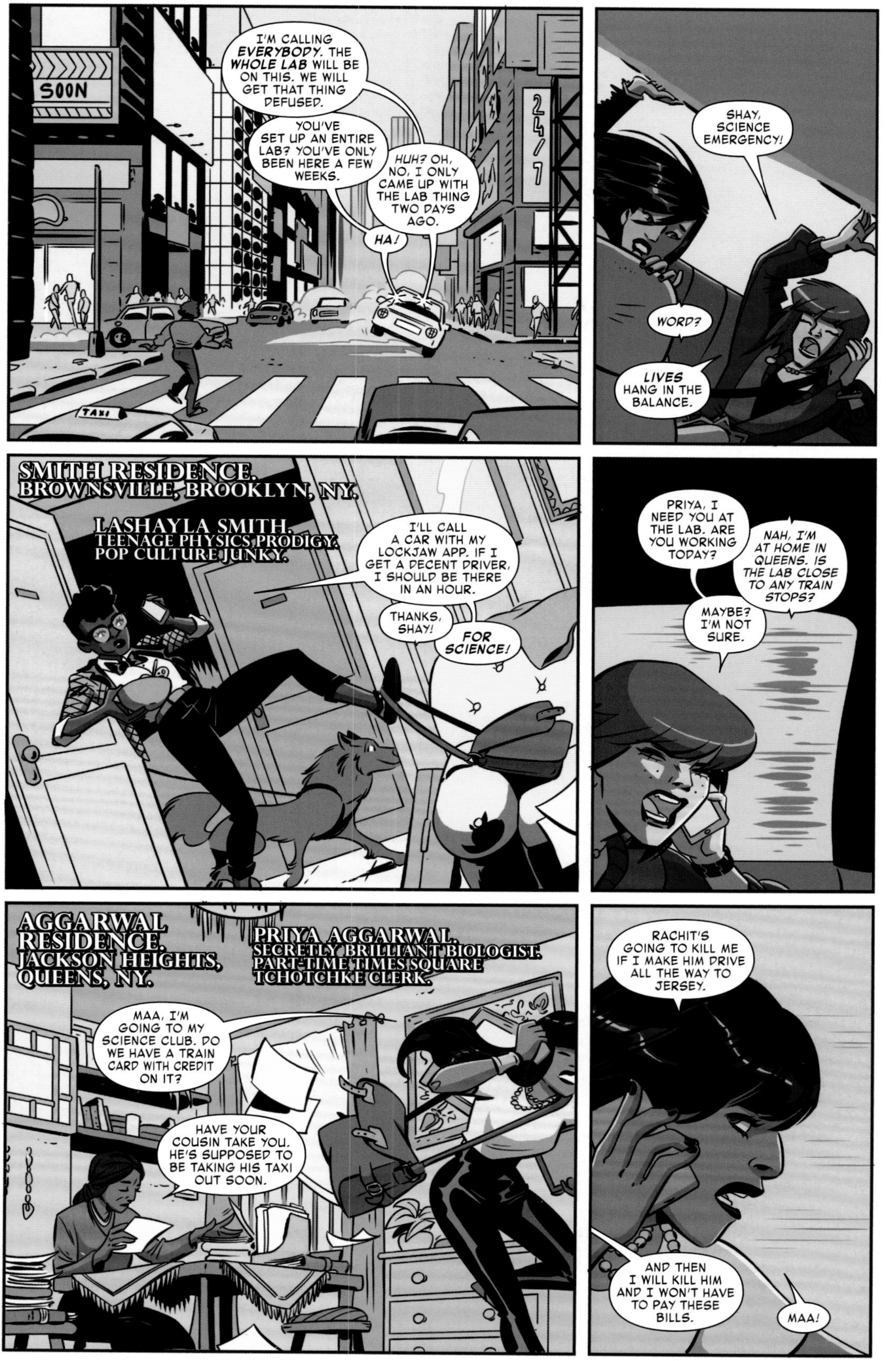
SOON
I'M CALLING EVERYBODY. THE WHOLE LAB WILL BE ON THIS. WE WILL GET THAT THING DEFUSED.
YOU'VE SET UP AN ENTIRE LAB? YOU'VE ONLY BEEN HERE A FEW WEEKS.
HUH? OH, NO, I ONLY CAME UP WITH THE LAB THING TWO DAYS AGO.
HA!
24/7
TAXI
SHAY, SCIENCE EMERGENCY!
WORD?
LIVES HANG IN THE BALANCE.
SMITH RESIDENCE. BROWNSVILLE, BROOKLYN, NY.
LASHAYLA SMITH. TEENAGE PHYSICS PRODIGY. POP CULTURE JUNKY.
I'LL CALL A CAR WITH MY LOCKJAW APP. IF I GET A DECENT DRIVER, I SHOULD BE THERE IN AN HOUR.
THANKS, SHAY!
FOR SCIENCE!
PRIYA, I NEED YOU AT THE LAB. ARE YOU WORKING TODAY?
NAH, I'M AT HOME IN QUEENS. IS THE LAB CLOSE TO ANY TRAIN STOPS?
MAYBE? I'M NOT SURE.
AGGARWAL RESIDENCE. JACKSON HEIGHTS, QUEENS, NY.
PRIYA AGGARWAL. SECRETLY BRILLIANT BIOLOGIST. PART-TIME TIMES SQUARE TCHOTCHKE CLERK.
MAA, I'M GOING TO MY SCIENCE CLUB. DO WE HAVE A TRAIN CARD WITH CREDIT ON IT?
HAVE YOUR COUSIN TAKE YOU. HE'S SUPPOSED TO BE TAKING HIS TAXI OUT SOON.
RACHIT'S GOING TO KILL ME IF I MAKE HIM DRIVE ALL THE WAY TO JERSEY.
AND THEN I WILL KILL HIM AND I WON'T HAVE TO PAY THESE BILLS.
MAA!

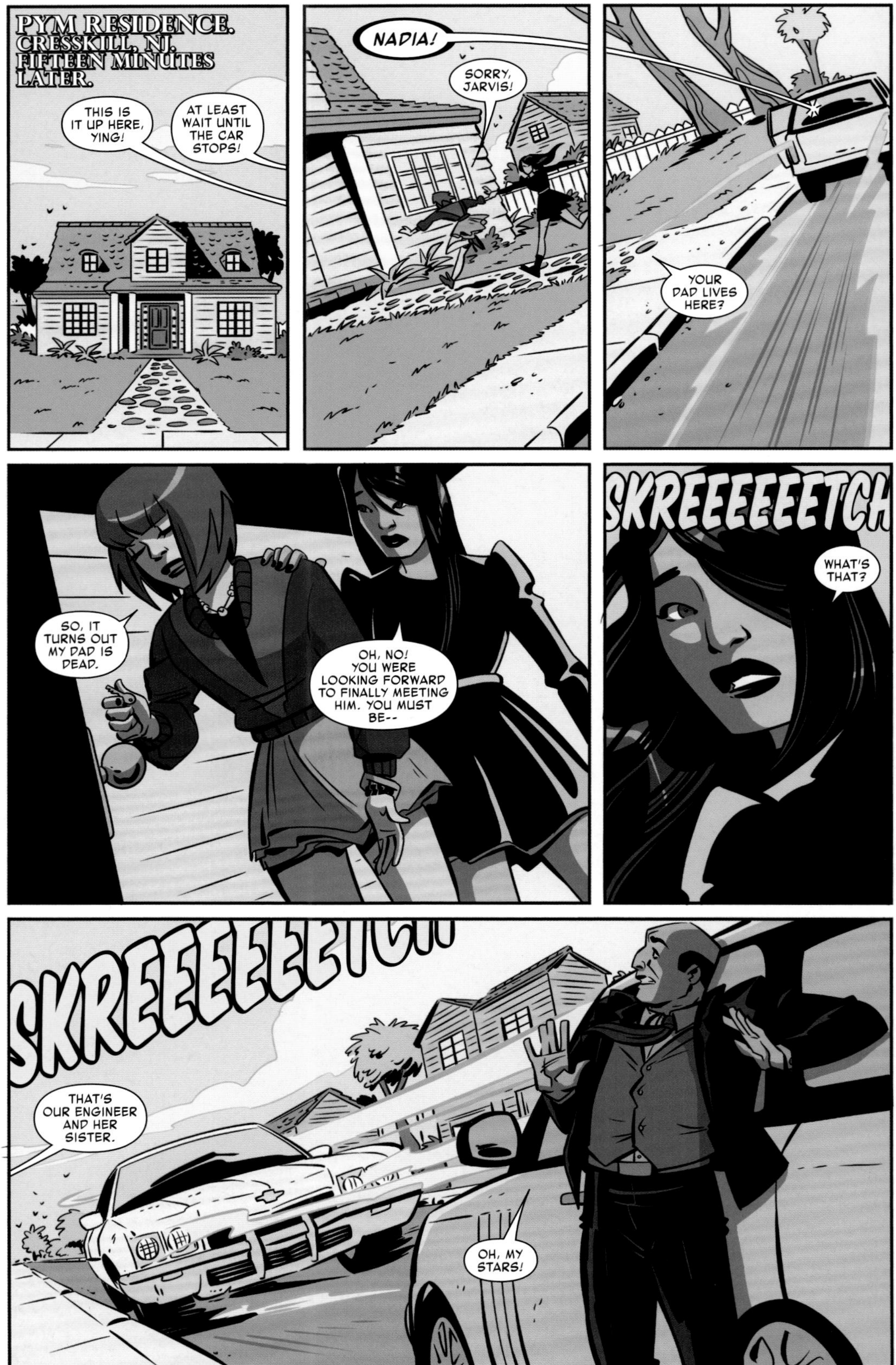
PYM RESIDENCE. CRESSKILL, NJ. FIFTEEN MINUTES LATER.
THIS IS IT UP HERE, YING!
AT LEAST WAIT UNTIL THE CAR STOPS!
NADIA!
SORRY, JARVIS!
YOUR DAD LIVES HERE?
SO, IT TURNS OUT MY DAD IS DEAD.
OH, NO! YOU WERE LOOKING FORWARD TO FINALLY MEETING HIM. YOU MUST BE--
SKREEEEEEETCH
WHAT'S THAT?
SKREEEEEETCH
THAT'S OUR ENGINEER AND HER SISTER.
OH, MY STARS!

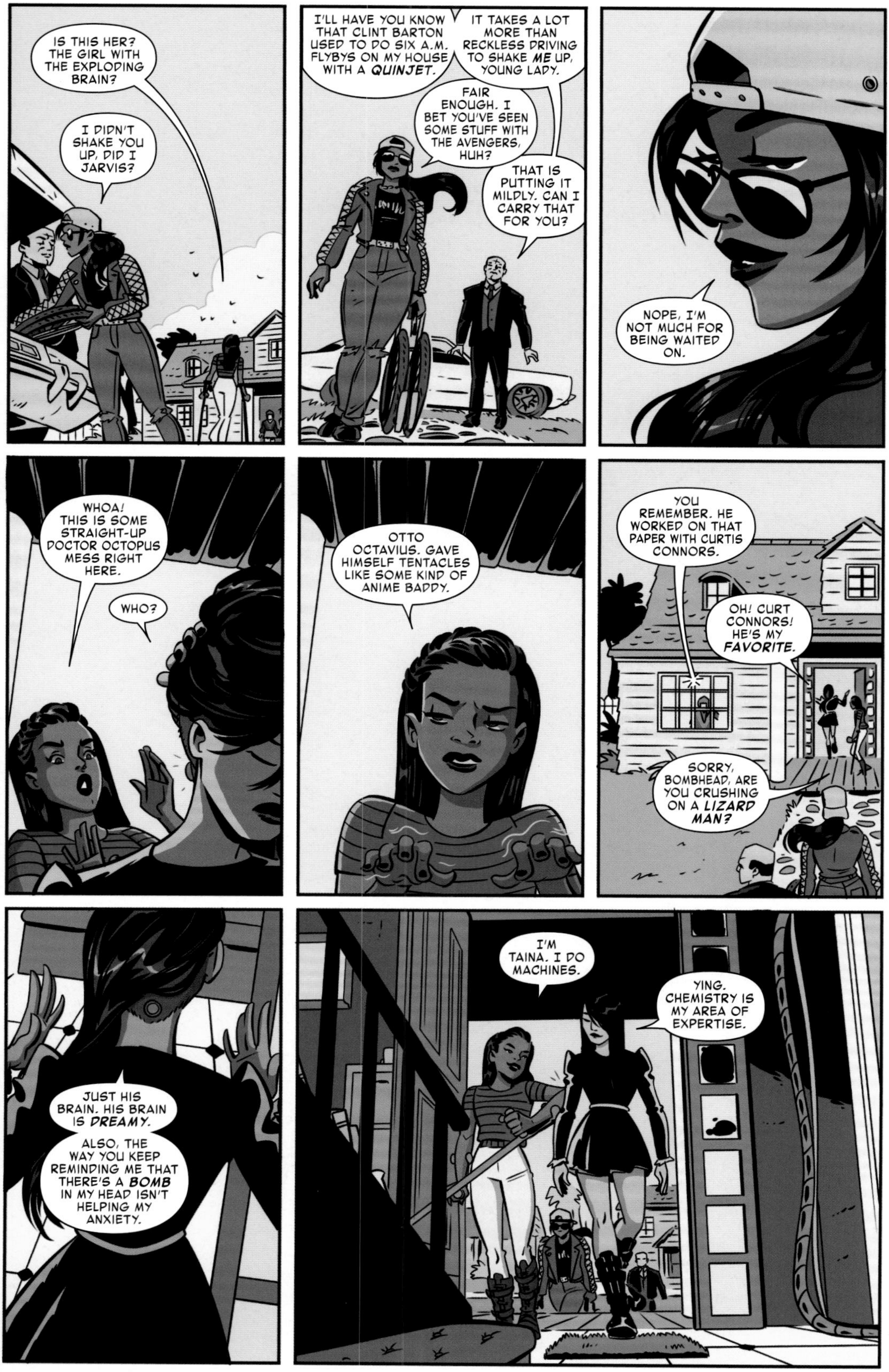
IS THIS HER? THE GIRL WITH THE EXPLODING BRAIN?
I DIDN'T SHAKE YOU UP, DID I JARVIS?
I'LL HAVE YOU KNOW THAT CLINT BARTON USED TO DO SIX A.M. FLYBYS ON MY HOUSE WITH A *QUINJET*.
IT TAKES A LOT MORE THAN RECKLESS DRIVING TO SHAKE *ME* UP, YOUNG LADY.
FAIR ENOUGH. I BET YOU'VE SEEN SOME STUFF WITH THE AVENGERS, HUH?
THAT IS PUTTING IT MILDLY. CAN I CARRY THAT FOR YOU?
NOPE, I'M NOT MUCH FOR BEING WAITED ON.
WHOA! THIS IS SOME STRAIGHT-UP DOCTOR OCTOPUS MESS RIGHT HERE.
WHO?
OTTO OCTAVIUS. GAVE HIMSELF TENTACLES LIKE SOME KIND OF ANIME BADDY.
YOU REMEMBER. HE WORKED ON THAT PAPER WITH CURTIS CONNORS.
OH! CURT CONNORS! HE'S MY *FAVORITE.*
SORRY, BOMBHEAD, ARE YOU CRUSHING ON A *LIZARD MAN?*
JUST HIS BRAIN. HIS BRAIN IS *DREAMY.*
ALSO, THE WAY YOU KEEP REMINDING ME THAT THERE'S A *BOMB* IN MY HEAD ISN'T HELPING MY ANXIETY.
I'M TAINA. I DO MACHINES.
YING. CHEMISTRY IS MY AREA OF EXPERTISE.

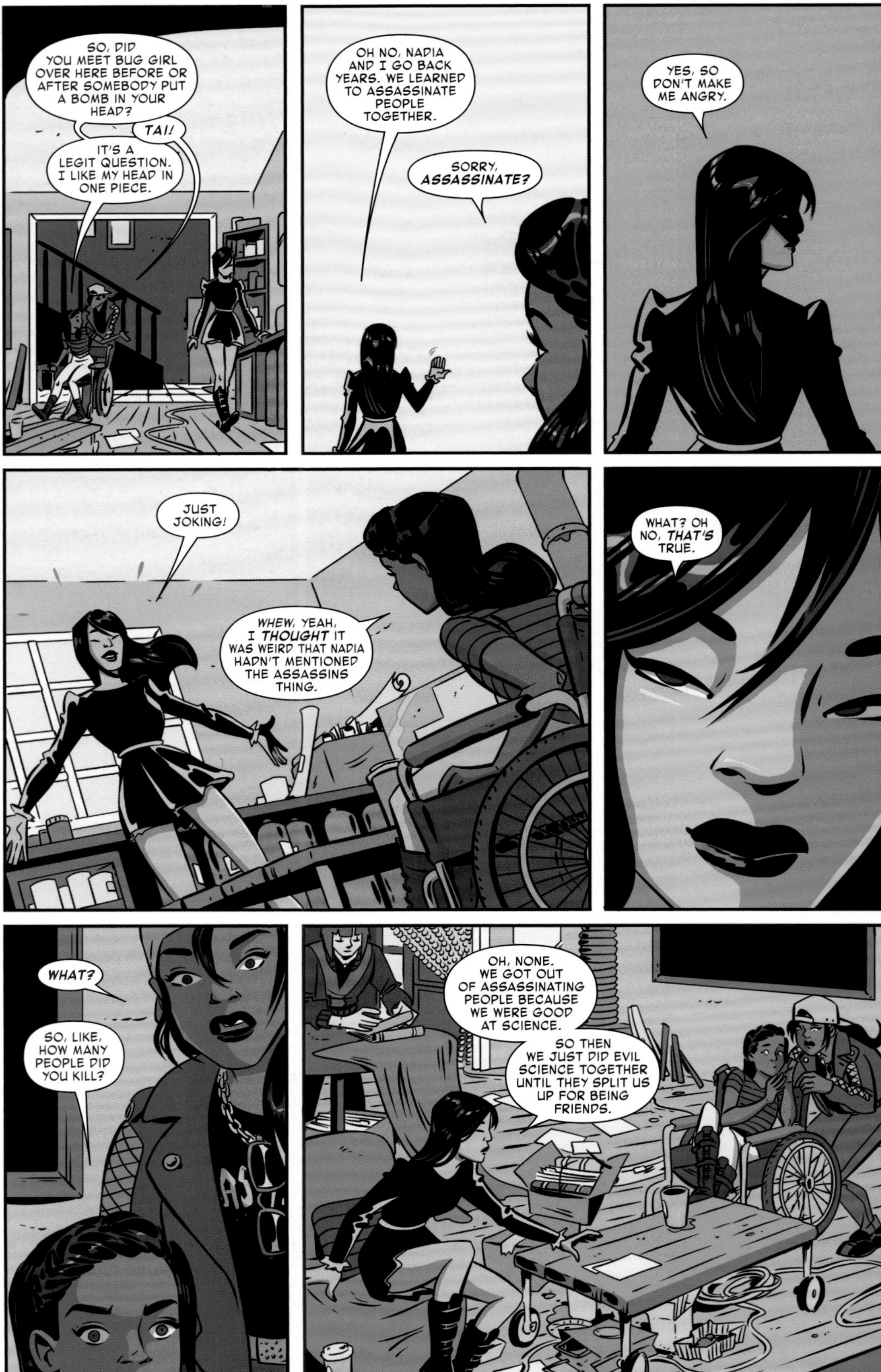
SO, DID YOU MEET BUG GIRL OVER HERE BEFORE OR AFTER SOMEBODY PUT A BOMB IN YOUR HEAD?
TAI!
IT'S A LEGIT QUESTION. I LIKE MY HEAD IN ONE PIECE.
OH NO, NADIA AND I GO BACK YEARS. WE LEARNED TO ASSASSINATE PEOPLE TOGETHER.
SORRY, ASSASSINATE?
YES, SO DON'T MAKE ME ANGRY.
JUST JOKING!
WHEW, YEAH, I THOUGHT IT WAS WEIRD THAT NADIA HADN'T MENTIONED THE ASSASSINS THING.
WHAT? OH NO, THAT'S TRUE.
WHAT?
SO, LIKE, HOW MANY PEOPLE DID YOU KILL?
OH, NONE. WE GOT OUT OF ASSASSINATING PEOPLE BECAUSE WE WERE GOOD AT SCIENCE.
SO THEN WE JUST DID EVIL SCIENCE TOGETHER UNTIL THEY SPLIT US UP FOR BEING FRIENDS.

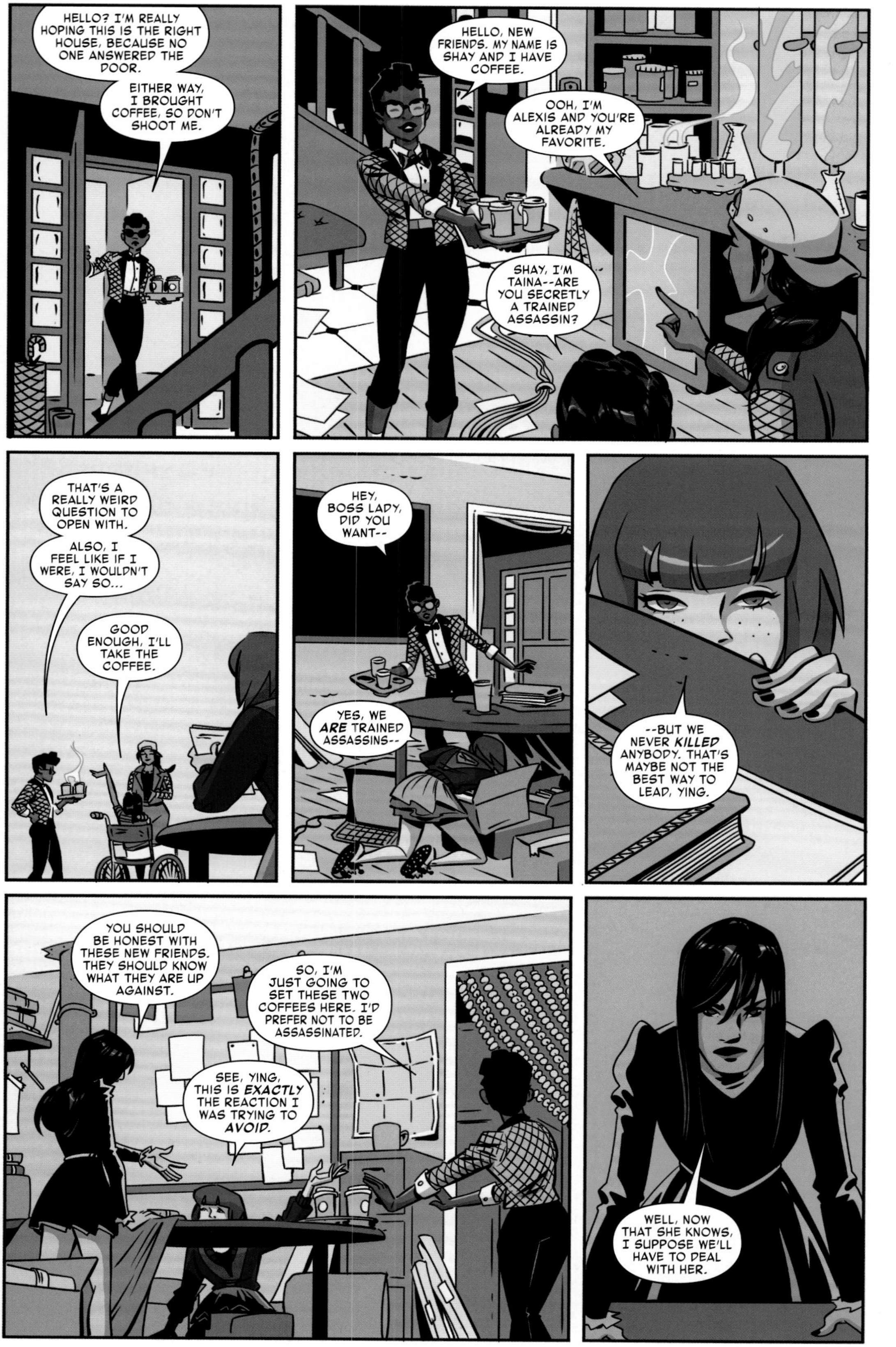
HELLO? I'M REALLY HOPING THIS IS THE RIGHT HOUSE, BECAUSE NO ONE ANSWERED THE DOOR.
EITHER WAY, I BROUGHT COFFEE, SO DON'T SHOOT ME.
HELLO, NEW FRIENDS. MY NAME IS SHAY AND I HAVE COFFEE.
OOH, I'M ALEXIS AND YOU'RE ALREADY MY FAVORITE.
SHAY, I'M TAINA--ARE YOU SECRETLY A TRAINED ASSASSIN?
THAT'S A REALLY WEIRD QUESTION TO OPEN WITH.
ALSO, I FEEL LIKE IF I WERE, I WOULDN'T SAY SO...
GOOD ENOUGH, I'LL TAKE THE COFFEE.
HEY, BOSS LADY, DID YOU WANT--
YES, WE ARE TRAINED ASSASSINS--
--BUT WE NEVER KILLED ANYBODY. THAT'S MAYBE NOT THE BEST WAY TO LEAD, YING.
YOU SHOULD BE HONEST WITH THESE NEW FRIENDS. THEY SHOULD KNOW WHAT THEY ARE UP AGAINST.
SO, I'M JUST GOING TO SET THESE TWO COFFEES HERE. I'D PREFER NOT TO BE ASSASSINATED.
SEE, YING, THIS IS EXACTLY THE REACTION I WAS TRYING TO AVOID.
WELL, NOW THAT SHE KNOWS, I SUPPOSE WE'LL HAVE TO DEAL WITH HER.

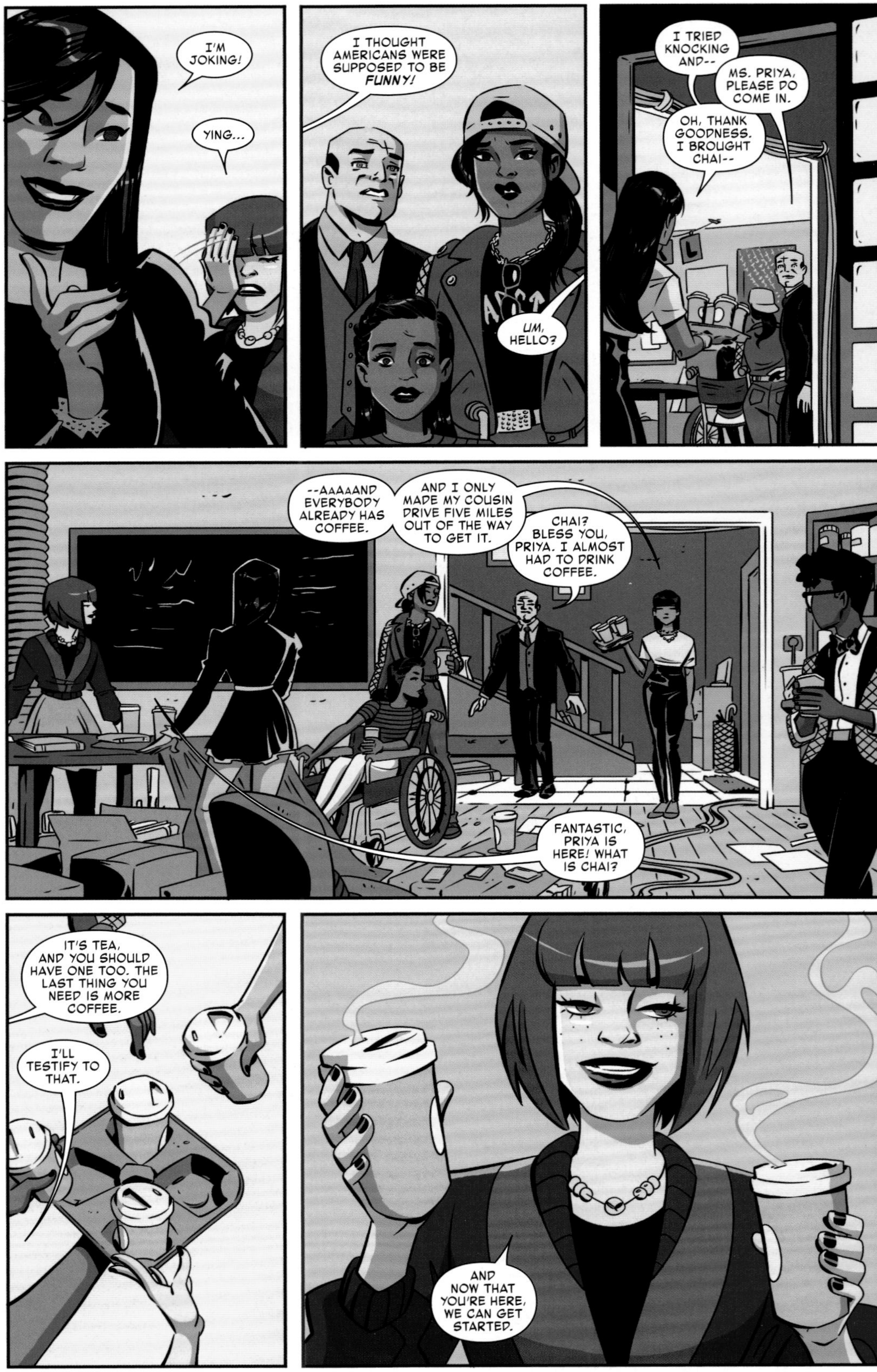
I'M JOKING!
YING...
I THOUGHT AMERICANS WERE SUPPOSED TO BE FUNNY!
UM, HELLO?
I TRIED KNOCKING AND--
MS. PRIYA, PLEASE DO COME IN.
OH, THANK GOODNESS. I BROUGHT CHAI--
--AAAAAND EVERYBODY ALREADY HAS COFFEE.
AND I ONLY MADE MY COUSIN DRIVE FIVE MILES OUT OF THE WAY TO GET IT.
CHAI? BLESS YOU, PRIYA. I ALMOST HAD TO DRINK COFFEE.
FANTASTIC, PRIYA IS HERE! WHAT IS CHAI?
IT'S TEA, AND YOU SHOULD HAVE ONE TOO. THE LAST THING YOU NEED IS MORE COFFEE.
I'LL TESTIFY TO THAT.
AND NOW THAT YOU'RE HERE, WE CAN GET STARTED.

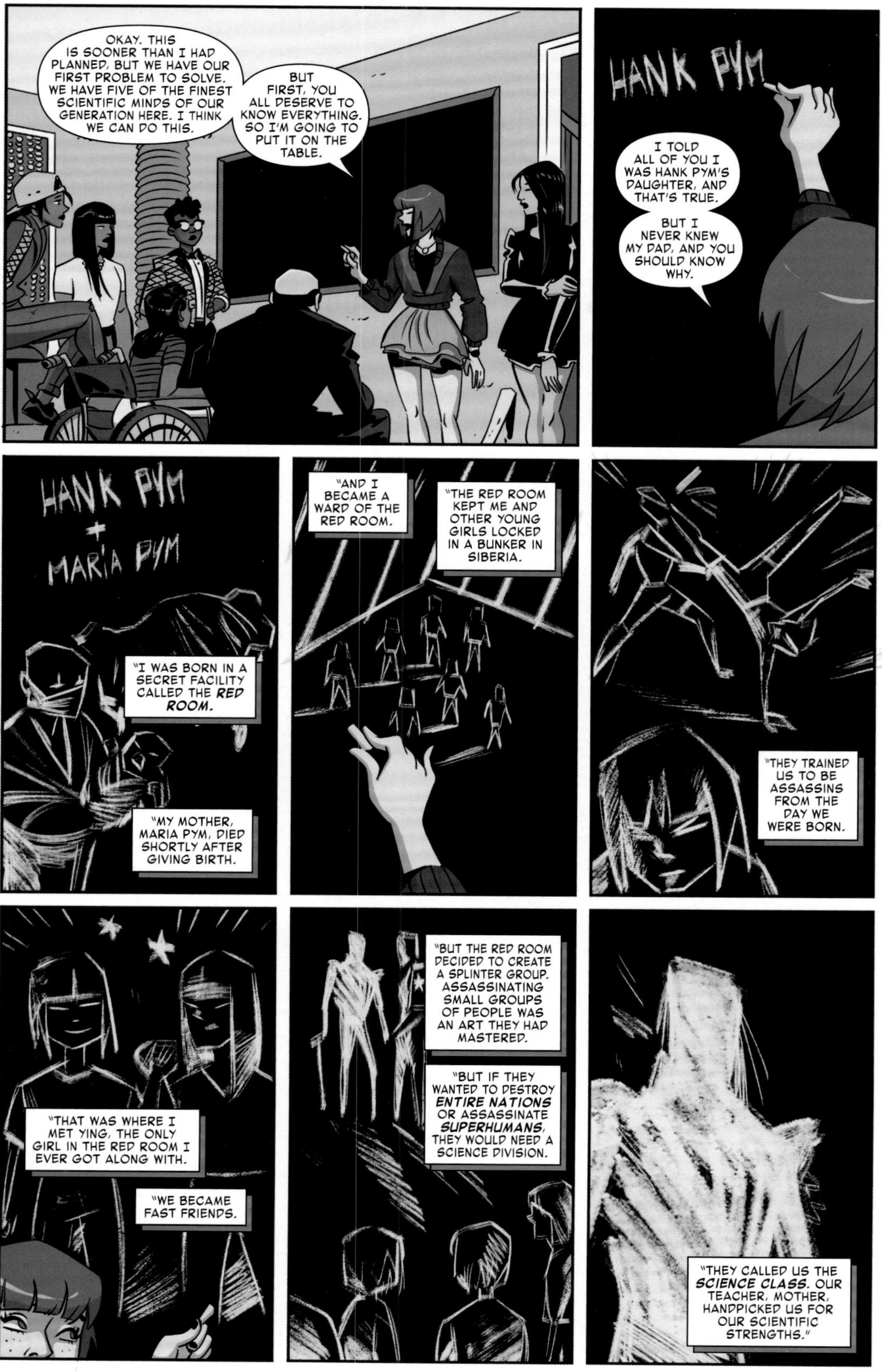
OKAY. THIS IS SOONER THAN I HAD PLANNED, BUT WE HAVE OUR FIRST PROBLEM TO SOLVE. WE HAVE FIVE OF THE FINEST SCIENTIFIC MINDS OF OUR GENERATION HERE. I THINK WE CAN DO THIS.
BUT FIRST, YOU ALL DESERVE TO KNOW EVERYTHING. SO I'M GOING TO PUT IT ON THE TABLE.
HANK PYM
I TOLD ALL OF YOU I WAS HANK PYM'S DAUGHTER, AND THAT'S TRUE.
BUT I NEVER KNEW MY DAD, AND YOU SHOULD KNOW WHY.
HANK PYM + MARIA PYM
"I WAS BORN IN A SECRET FACILITY CALLED THE *RED ROOM.*
"MY MOTHER, MARIA PYM, DIED SHORTLY AFTER GIVING BIRTH.
"AND I BECAME A WARD OF THE RED ROOM.
"THE RED ROOM KEPT ME AND OTHER YOUNG GIRLS LOCKED IN A BUNKER IN SIBERIA.
"THEY TRAINED US TO BE ASSASSINS FROM THE DAY WE WERE BORN.
"THAT WAS WHERE I MET YING, THE ONLY GIRL IN THE RED ROOM I EVER GOT ALONG WITH.
"WE BECAME FAST FRIENDS.
"BUT THE RED ROOM DECIDED TO CREATE A SPLINTER GROUP. ASSASSINATING SMALL GROUPS OF PEOPLE WAS AN ART THEY HAD MASTERED.
"BUT IF THEY WANTED TO DESTROY *ENTIRE NATIONS* OR ASSASSINATE *SUPERHUMANS*, THEY WOULD NEED A SCIENCE DIVISION.
"THEY CALLED US THE *SCIENCE CLASS.* OUR TEACHER, MOTHER, HANDPICKED US FOR OUR SCIENTIFIC STRENGTHS."

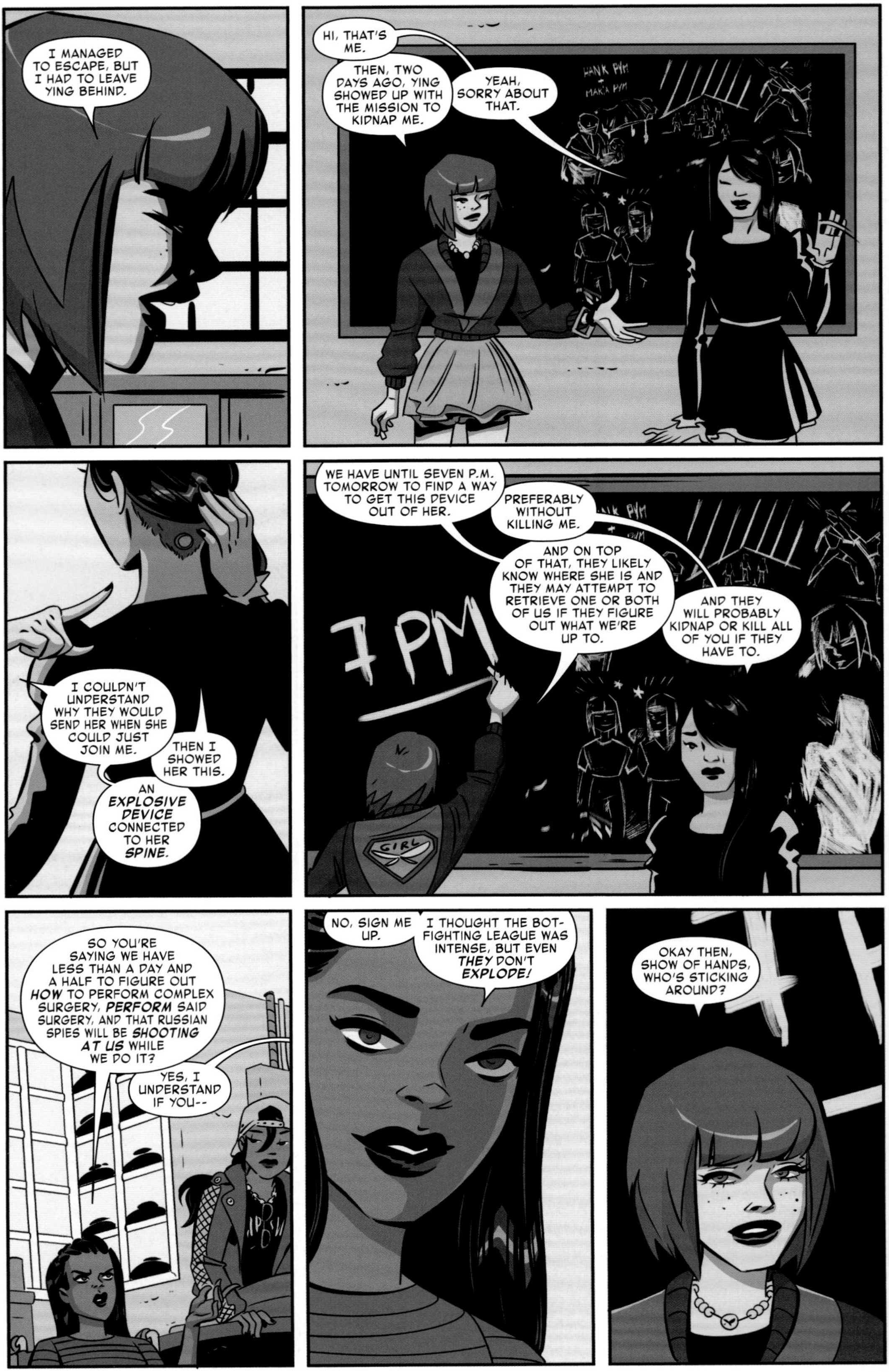
I MANAGED TO ESCAPE, BUT I HAD TO LEAVE YING BEHIND.
HI, THAT'S ME.
THEN, TWO DAYS AGO, YING SHOWED UP WITH THE MISSION TO KIDNAP ME.
YEAH, SORRY ABOUT THAT.
HANK PYM
I COULDN'T UNDERSTAND WHY THEY WOULD SEND HER WHEN SHE COULD JUST JOIN ME.
THEN I SHOWED HER THIS.
AN EXPLOSIVE DEVICE CONNECTED TO HER SPINE.
WE HAVE UNTIL SEVEN P.M. TOMORROW TO FIND A WAY TO GET THIS DEVICE OUT OF HER.
PREFERABLY WITHOUT KILLING ME.
AND ON TOP OF THAT, THEY LIKELY KNOW WHERE SHE IS AND THEY MAY ATTEMPT TO RETRIEVE ONE OR BOTH OF US IF THEY FIGURE OUT WHAT WE'RE UP TO.
AND THEY WILL PROBABLY KIDNAP OR KILL ALL OF YOU IF THEY HAVE TO.
7 PM
GIRL
SO YOU'RE SAYING WE HAVE LESS THAN A DAY AND A HALF TO FIGURE OUT HOW TO PERFORM COMPLEX SURGERY, PERFORM SAID SURGERY, AND THAT RUSSIAN SPIES WILL BE SHOOTING AT US WHILE WE DO IT?
YES, I UNDERSTAND IF YOU--
NO, SIGN ME UP.
I THOUGHT THE BOT-FIGHTING LEAGUE WAS INTENSE, BUT EVEN THEY DON'T EXPLODE!
OKAY THEN, SHOW OF HANDS, WHO'S STICKING AROUND?

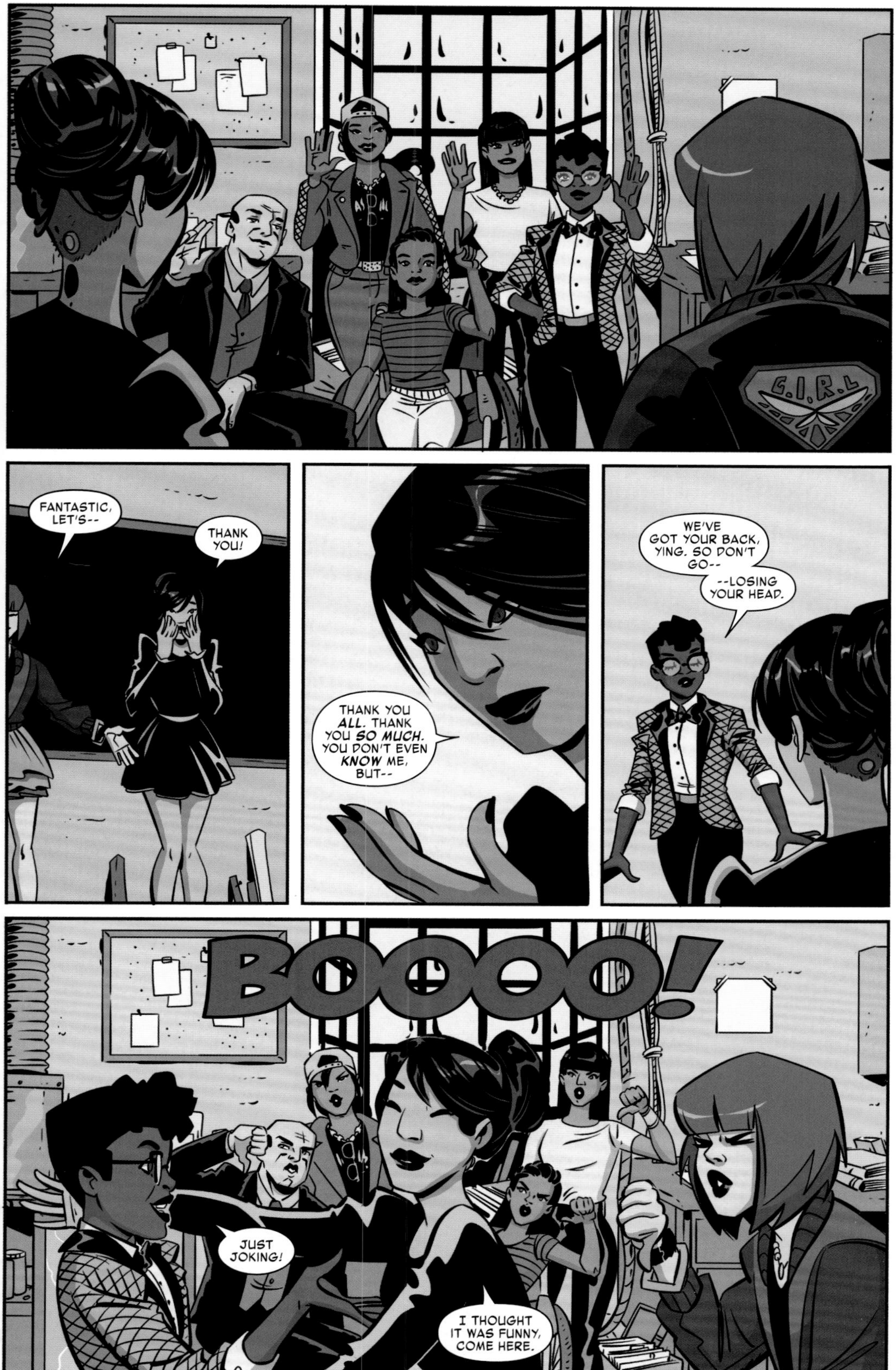
FANTASTIC, LET'S--
THANK YOU!
THANK YOU ALL. THANK YOU SO MUCH. YOU DON'T EVEN KNOW ME, BUT--
WE'VE GOT YOUR BACK, YING. SO DON'T GO--
--LOSING YOUR HEAD.
BOOOO!
JUST JOKING!
I THOUGHT IT WAS FUNNY, COME HERE.

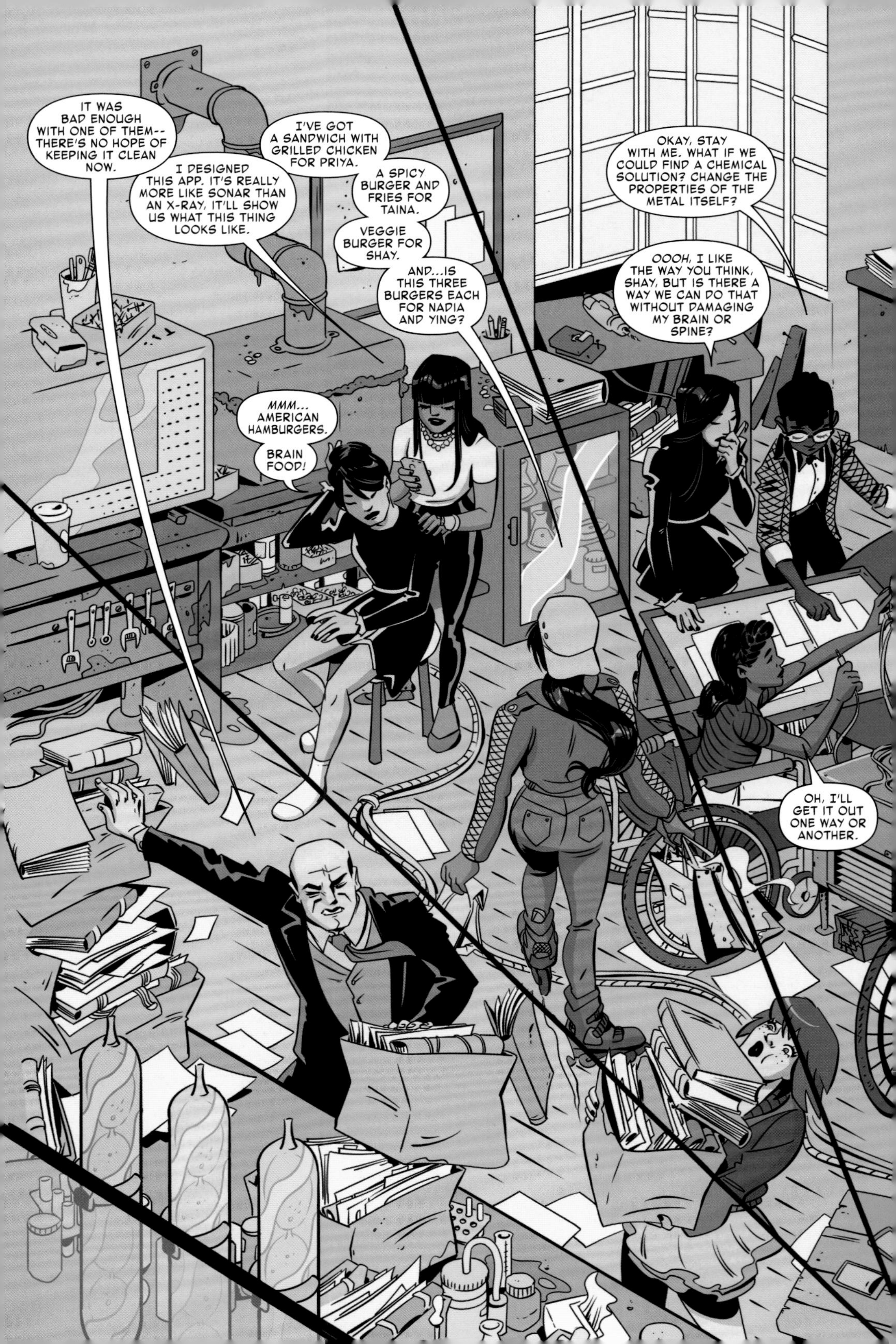
IT WAS BAD ENOUGH WITH ONE OF THEM-- THERE'S NO HOPE OF KEEPING IT CLEAN NOW.
I DESIGNED THIS APP. IT'S REALLY MORE LIKE SONAR THAN AN X-RAY, IT'LL SHOW US WHAT THIS THING LOOKS LIKE.
I'VE GOT A SANDWICH WITH GRILLED CHICKEN FOR PRIYA.
A SPICY BURGER AND FRIES FOR TAINA.
VEGGIE BURGER FOR SHAY.
AND...IS THIS THREE BURGERS EACH FOR NADIA AND YING?
MMM... AMERICAN HAMBURGERS.
BRAIN FOOD!
OKAY, STAY WITH ME. WHAT IF WE COULD FIND A CHEMICAL SOLUTION? CHANGE THE PROPERTIES OF THE METAL ITSELF?
OOOH, I LIKE THE WAY YOU THINK, SHAY, BUT IS THERE A WAY WE CAN DO THAT WITHOUT DAMAGING MY BRAIN OR SPINE?
OH, I'LL GET IT OUT ONE WAY OR ANOTHER.

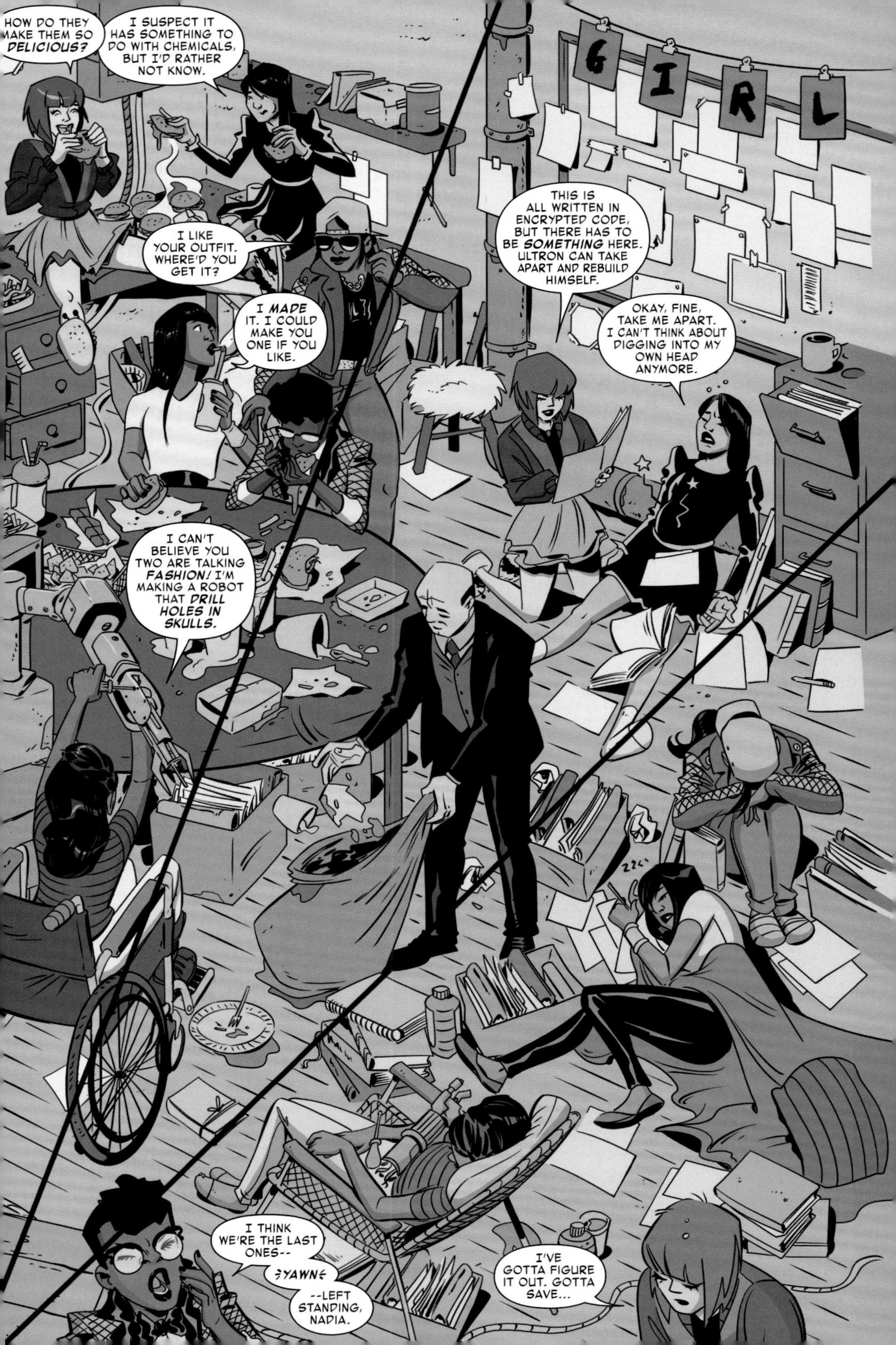
HOW DO THEY MAKE THEM SO DELICIOUS?
I SUSPECT IT HAS SOMETHING TO DO WITH CHEMICALS, BUT I'D RATHER NOT KNOW.
I LIKE YOUR OUTFIT. WHERE'D YOU GET IT?
I MADE IT. I COULD MAKE YOU ONE IF YOU LIKE.
I CAN'T BELIEVE YOU TWO ARE TALKING FASHION! I'M MAKING A ROBOT THAT DRILL HOLES IN SKULLS.
THIS IS ALL WRITTEN IN ENCRYPTED CODE, BUT THERE HAS TO BE SOMETHING HERE. ULTRON CAN TAKE APART AND REBUILD HIMSELF.
OKAY, FINE, TAKE ME APART. I CAN'T THINK ABOUT DIGGING INTO MY OWN HEAD ANYMORE.
GIRL
I THINK WE'RE THE LAST ONES--
YAWN
--LEFT STANDING, NADIA.
I'VE GOTTA FIGURE IT OUT. GOTTA SAVE...

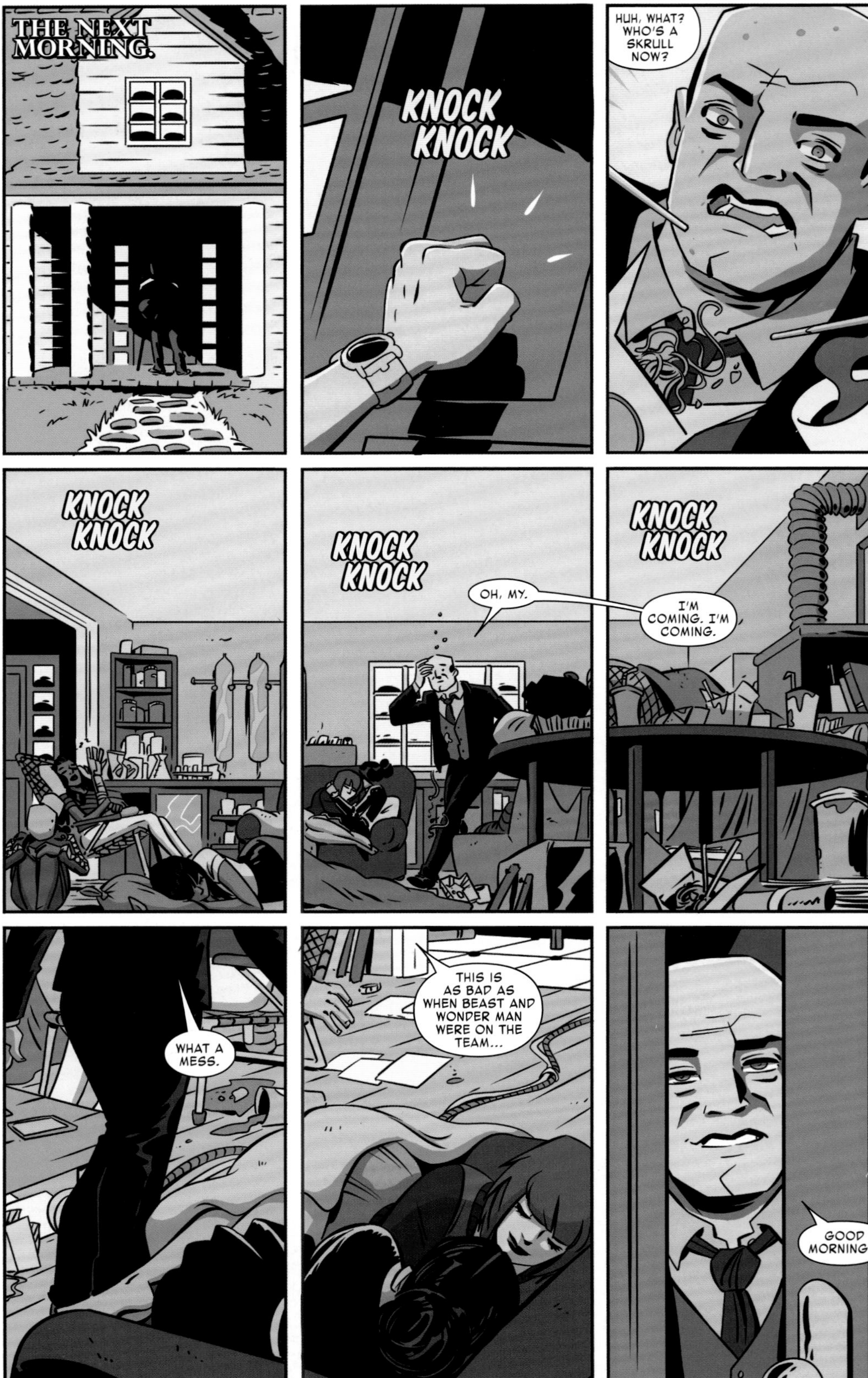
THE NEXT MORNING.
KNOCK KNOCK
HUH, WHAT? WHO'S A SKRULL NOW?
KNOCK KNOCK
KNOCK KNOCK
OH, MY.
KNOCK KNOCK
I'M COMING. I'M COMING.
WHAT A MESS.
THIS IS AS BAD AS WHEN BEAST AND WONDER MAN WERE ON THE TEAM...
GOOD MORNING?

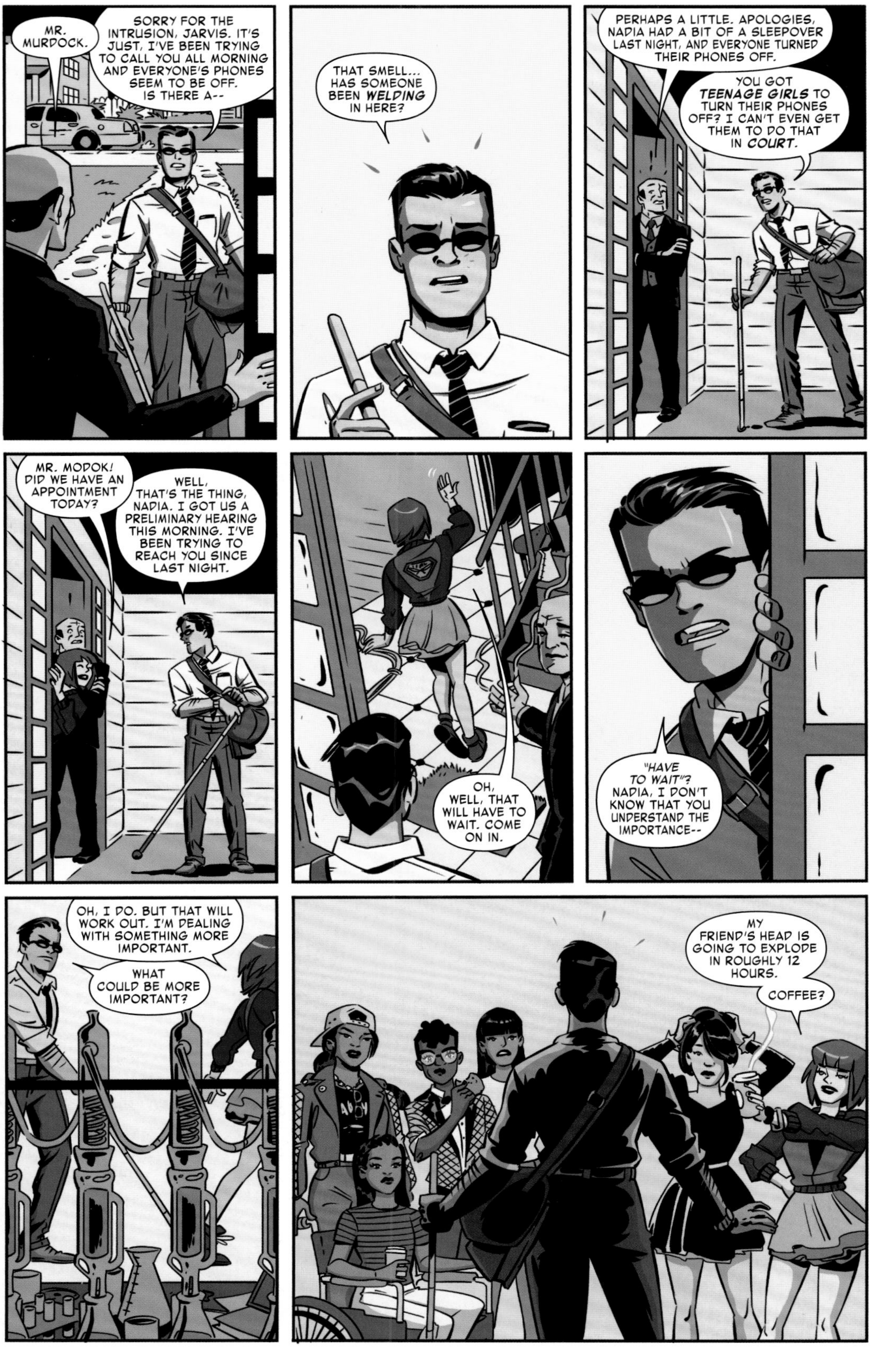
MR. MURDOCK.
SORRY FOR THE INTRUSION, JARVIS. IT'S JUST, I'VE BEEN TRYING TO CALL YOU ALL MORNING AND EVERYONE'S PHONES SEEM TO BE OFF. IS THERE A--
THAT SMELL... HAS SOMEONE BEEN WELDING IN HERE?
PERHAPS A LITTLE. APOLOGIES, NADIA HAD A BIT OF A SLEEPOVER LAST NIGHT, AND EVERYONE TURNED THEIR PHONES OFF.
YOU GOT TEENAGE GIRLS TO TURN THEIR PHONES OFF? I CAN'T EVEN GET THEM TO DO THAT IN COURT.
MR. MODOK! DID WE HAVE AN APPOINTMENT TODAY?
WELL, THAT'S THE THING, NADIA. I GOT US A PRELIMINARY HEARING THIS MORNING. I'VE BEEN TRYING TO REACH YOU SINCE LAST NIGHT.
OH, WELL, THAT WILL HAVE TO WAIT. COME ON IN.
"HAVE TO WAIT"? NADIA, I DON'T KNOW THAT YOU UNDERSTAND THE IMPORTANCE--
OH, I DO. BUT THAT WILL WORK OUT. I'M DEALING WITH SOMETHING MORE IMPORTANT.
WHAT COULD BE MORE IMPORTANT?
MY FRIEND'S HEAD IS GOING TO EXPLODE IN ROUGHLY 12 HOURS.
COFFEE?

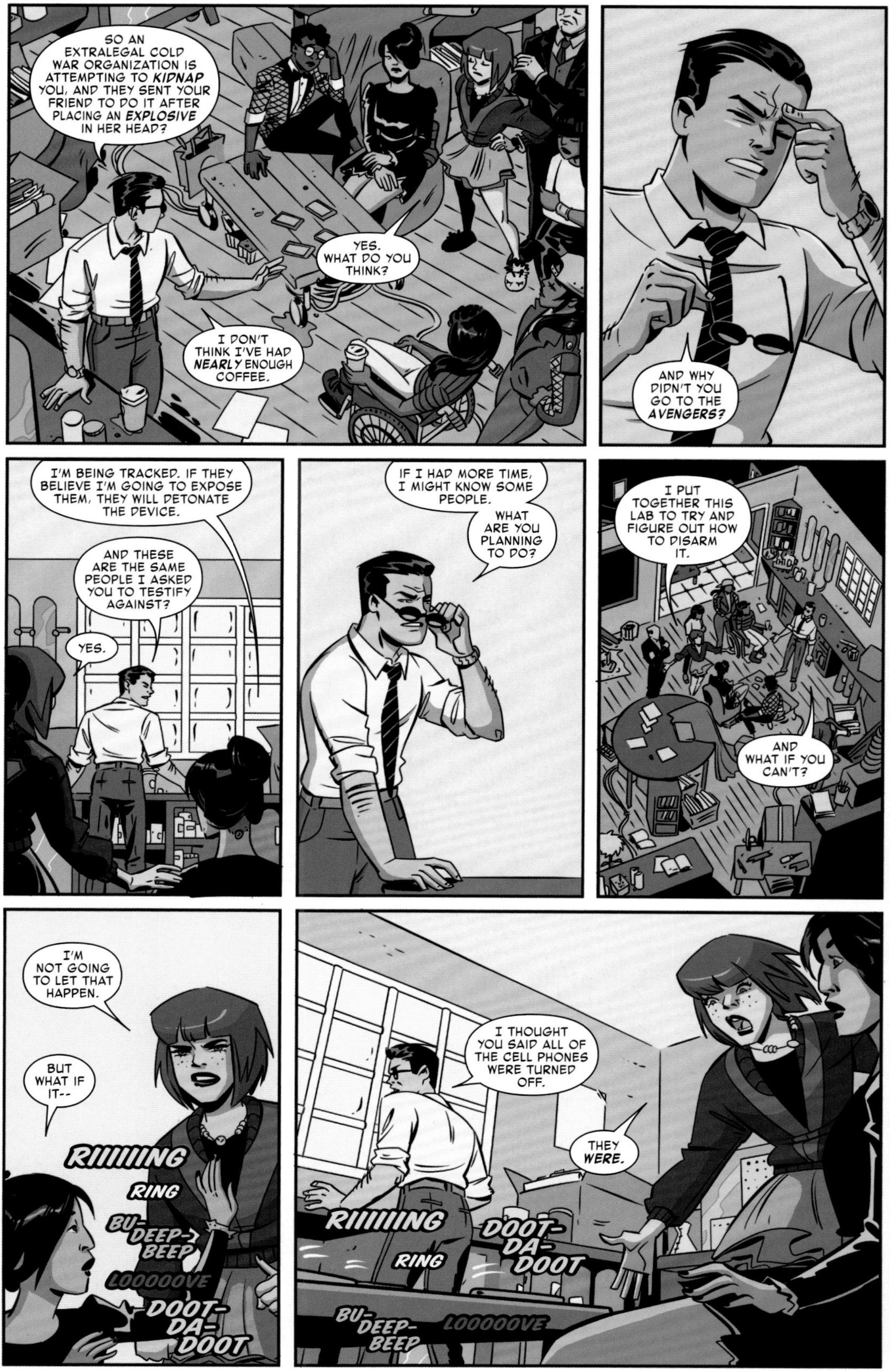
SO AN EXTRALEGAL COLD WAR ORGANIZATION IS ATTEMPTING TO KIDNAP YOU, AND THEY SENT YOUR FRIEND TO DO IT AFTER PLACING AN EXPLOSIVE IN HER HEAD?
YES. WHAT DO YOU THINK?
I DON'T THINK I'VE HAD NEARLY ENOUGH COFFEE.
AND WHY DIDN'T YOU GO TO THE AVENGERS?
I'M BEING TRACKED. IF THEY BELIEVE I'M GOING TO EXPOSE THEM, THEY WILL DETONATE THE DEVICE.
AND THESE ARE THE SAME PEOPLE I ASKED YOU TO TESTIFY AGAINST?
YES.
IF I HAD MORE TIME, I MIGHT KNOW SOME PEOPLE.
WHAT ARE YOU PLANNING TO DO?
I PUT TOGETHER THIS LAB TO TRY AND FIGURE OUT HOW TO DISARM IT.
AND WHAT IF YOU CAN'T?
I'M NOT GOING TO LET THAT HAPPEN.
BUT WHAT IF IT--
RIIIIIING
RING
BU-DEEP-BEEP
LOOOOOVE
DOOT-DA-DOOT
I THOUGHT YOU SAID ALL OF THE CELL PHONES WERE TURNED OFF.
THEY WERE.
RIIIIIING
RING
DOOT-DA-DOOT
BU-DEEP-BEEP
LOOOOOVE

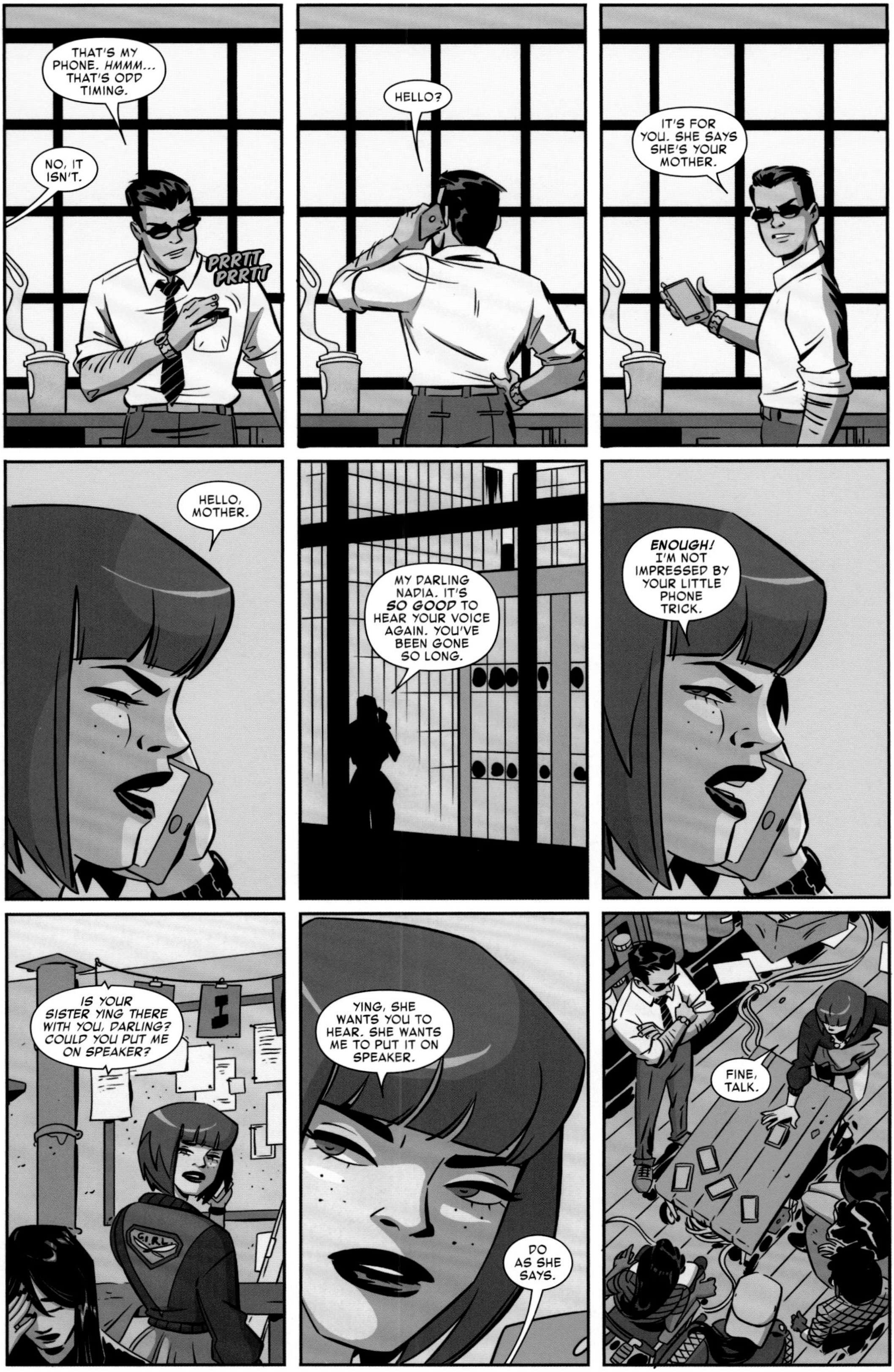
THAT'S MY PHONE. *HMMM...* THAT'S ODD TIMING.
NO, IT ISN'T.
PRRTT PRRTT
HELLO?
IT'S FOR YOU. SHE SAYS SHE'S YOUR MOTHER.
HELLO, MOTHER.
MY DARLING NADIA. IT'S **SO GOOD** TO HEAR YOUR VOICE AGAIN. YOU'VE BEEN GONE SO LONG.
ENOUGH! I'M NOT IMPRESSED BY YOUR LITTLE PHONE TRICK.
IS YOUR SISTER YING THERE WITH YOU, DARLING? COULD YOU PUT ME ON SPEAKER?
YING, SHE WANTS YOU TO HEAR. SHE WANTS ME TO PUT IT ON SPEAKER.
DO AS SHE SAYS.
FINE, TALK.

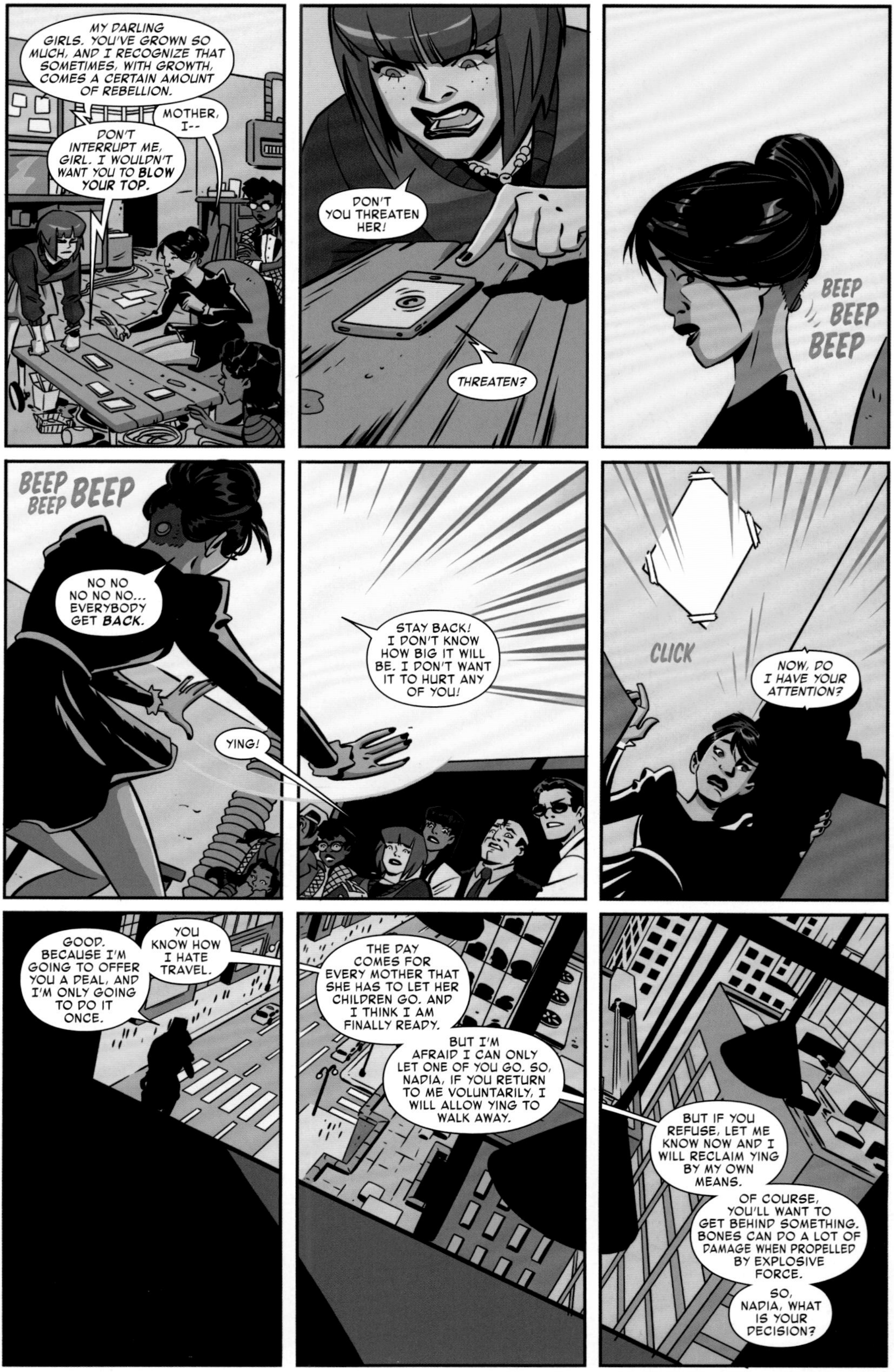
MY DARLING GIRLS. YOU'VE GROWN SO MUCH, AND I RECOGNIZE THAT SOMETIMES, WITH GROWTH, COMES A CERTAIN AMOUNT OF REBELLION.
MOTHER, I--
DON'T INTERRUPT ME, GIRL. I WOULDN'T WANT YOU TO **BLOW YOUR TOP.**
DON'T YOU THREATEN HER!
THREATEN?
BEEP BEEP BEEP
BEEP BEEP BEEP
NO NO NO NO NO... EVERYBODY GET **BACK.**
YING!
STAY BACK! I DON'T KNOW HOW BIG IT WILL BE. I DON'T WANT IT TO HURT ANY OF YOU!
CLICK
NOW, DO I HAVE YOUR ATTENTION?
GOOD. BECAUSE I'M GOING TO OFFER YOU A DEAL, AND I'M ONLY GOING TO DO IT ONCE.
YOU KNOW HOW I HATE TRAVEL.
THE DAY COMES FOR EVERY MOTHER THAT SHE HAS TO LET HER CHILDREN GO. AND I THINK I AM FINALLY READY.
BUT I'M AFRAID I CAN ONLY LET ONE OF YOU GO. SO, NADIA, IF YOU RETURN TO ME VOLUNTARILY, I WILL ALLOW YING TO WALK AWAY.
BUT IF YOU REFUSE, LET ME KNOW NOW AND I WILL RECLAIM YING BY MY OWN MEANS.
OF COURSE, YOU'LL WANT TO GET BEHIND SOMETHING. BONES CAN DO A LOT OF DAMAGE WHEN PROPELLED BY EXPLOSIVE FORCE.
SO, NADIA, WHAT IS YOUR DECISION?

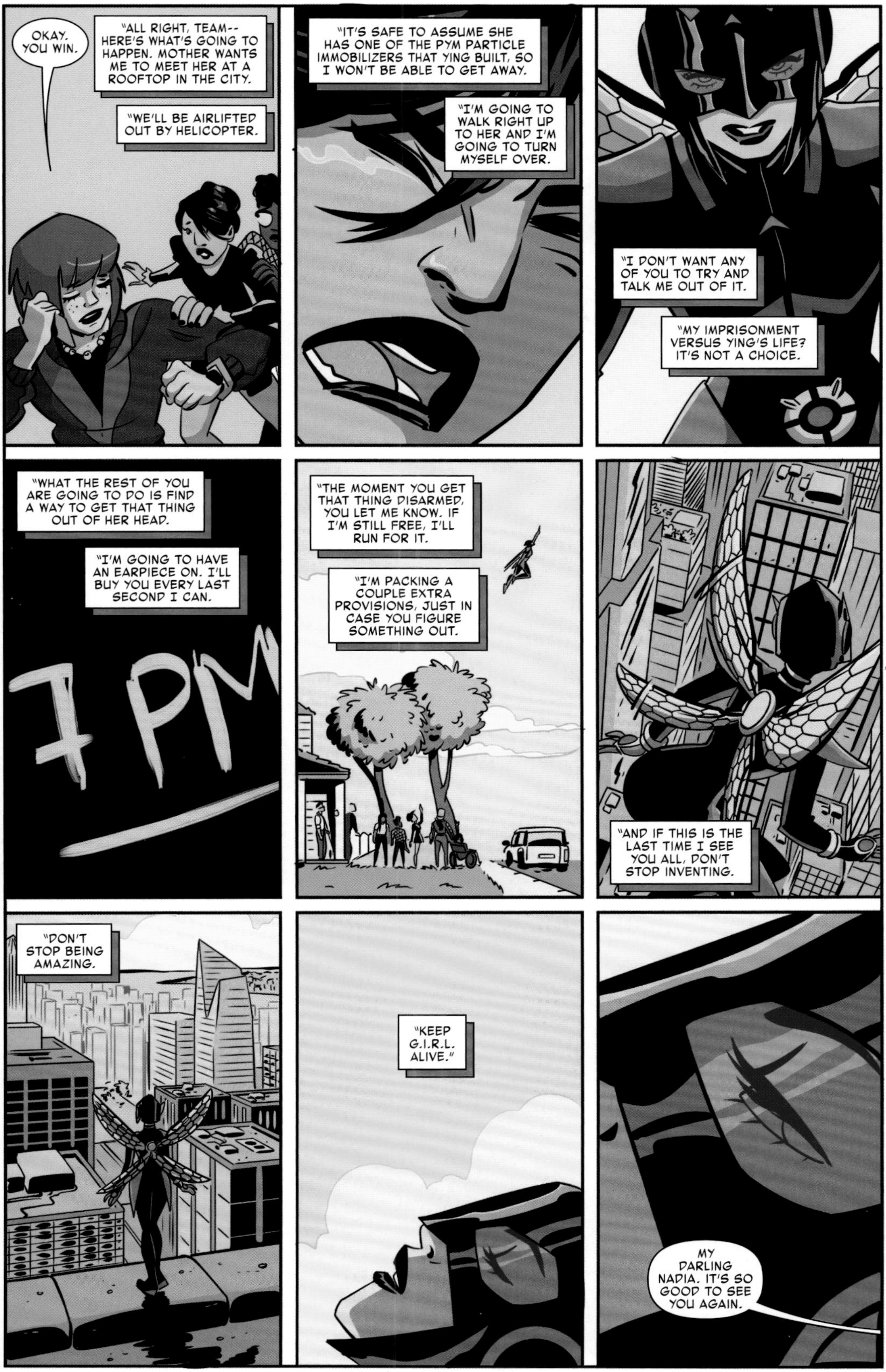
OKAY. YOU WIN.
"ALL RIGHT, TEAM--HERE'S WHAT'S GOING TO HAPPEN. MOTHER WANTS ME TO MEET HER AT A ROOFTOP IN THE CITY.
"WE'LL BE AIRLIFTED OUT BY HELICOPTER.
"IT'S SAFE TO ASSUME SHE HAS ONE OF THE PYM PARTICLE IMMOBILIZERS THAT YING BUILT, SO I WON'T BE ABLE TO GET AWAY.
"I'M GOING TO WALK RIGHT UP TO HER AND I'M GOING TO TURN MYSELF OVER.
"I DON'T WANT ANY OF YOU TO TRY AND TALK ME OUT OF IT.
"MY IMPRISONMENT VERSUS YING'S LIFE? IT'S NOT A CHOICE.
"WHAT THE REST OF YOU ARE GOING TO DO IS FIND A WAY TO GET THAT THING OUT OF HER HEAD.
"I'M GOING TO HAVE AN EARPIECE ON. I'LL BUY YOU EVERY LAST SECOND I CAN.
7 PM
"THE MOMENT YOU GET THAT THING DISARMED, YOU LET ME KNOW. IF I'M STILL FREE, I'LL RUN FOR IT.
"I'M PACKING A COUPLE EXTRA PROVISIONS, JUST IN CASE YOU FIGURE SOMETHING OUT.
"AND IF THIS IS THE LAST TIME I SEE YOU ALL, DON'T STOP INVENTING.
"DON'T STOP BEING AMAZING.
"KEEP G.I.R.L. ALIVE."
MY DARLING NADIA. IT'S SO GOOD TO SEE YOU AGAIN.

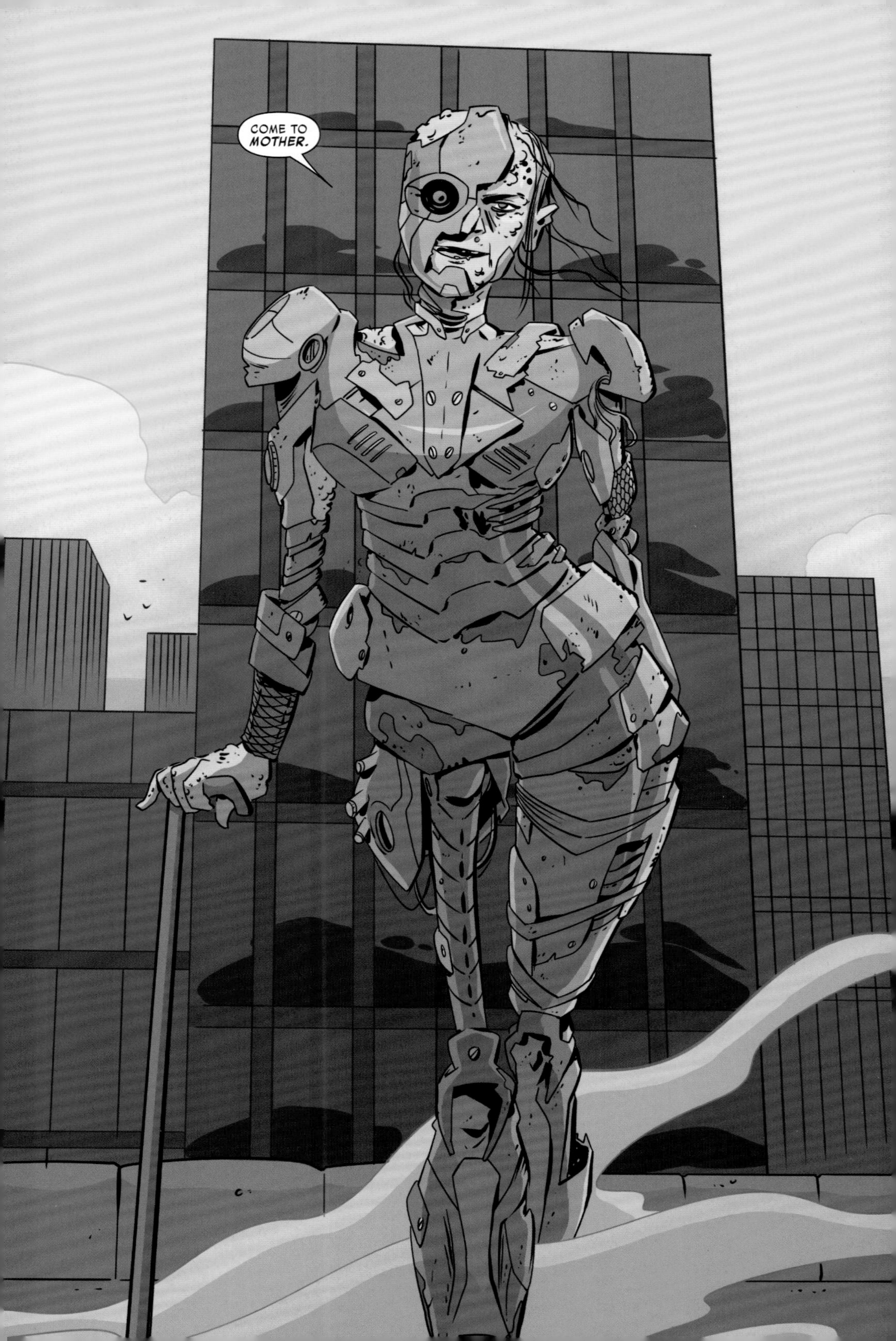
COME TO MOTHER.

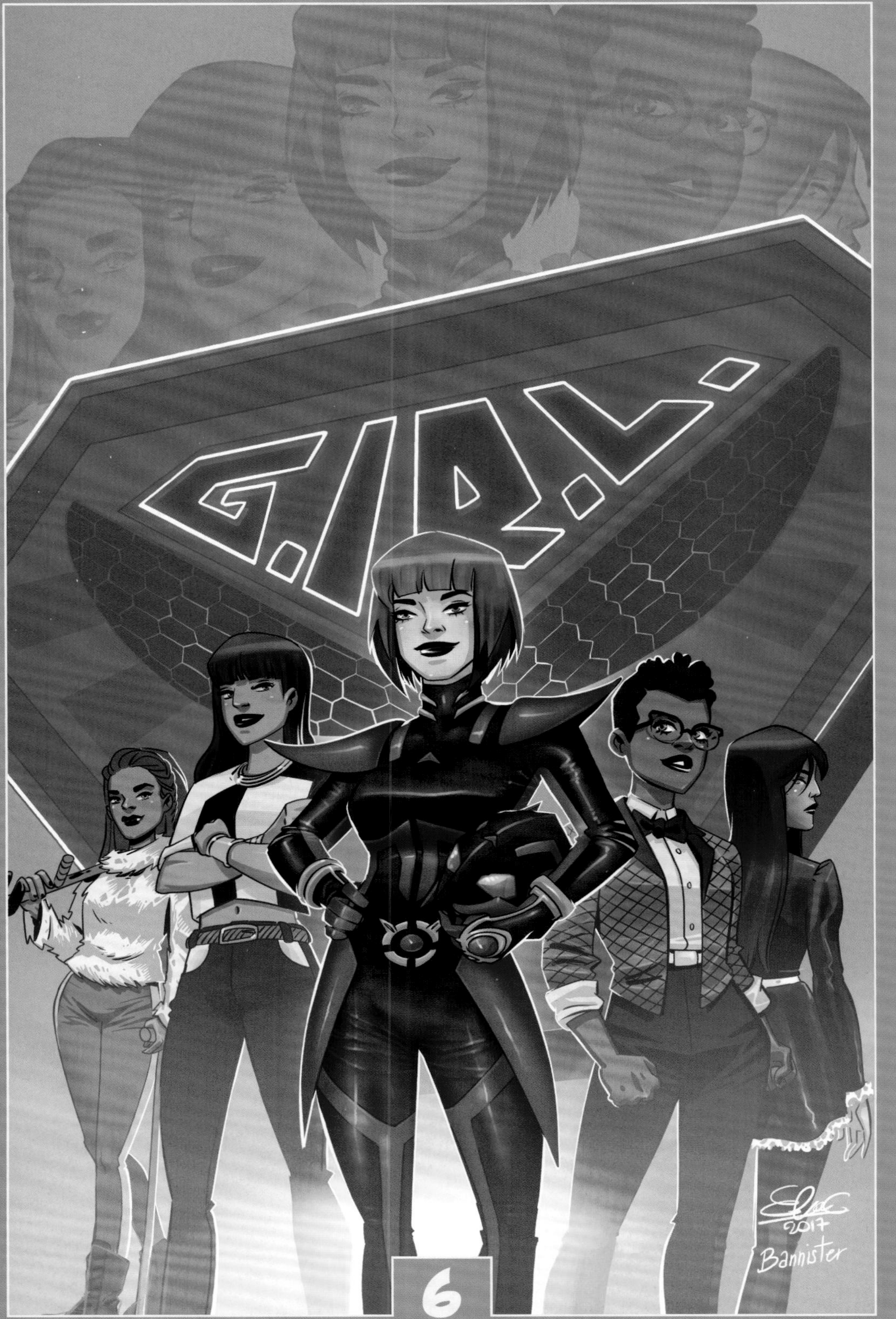
G.I.R.L.
2017
Bannister
6

15 MINUTES AGO.

NADIA, THE UNSTOPPABLE WASP, RUNNING OUT OF OPTIONS TO SAVE HER FRIEND.

AND IF THIS IS THE LAST TIME I SEE YOU ALL, DON'T STOP INVENTING. DON'T STOP BEING AMAZING. KEEP G.I.R.L. ALIVE.

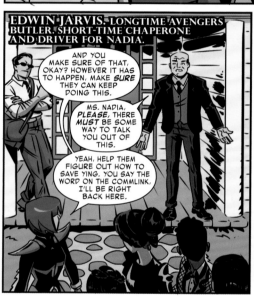

EDWIN JARVIS. LONGTIME AVENGERS BUTLER. SHORT-TIME CHAPERONE AND DRIVER FOR NADIA.

AND YOU MAKE SURE OF THAT, OKAY? HOWEVER IT HAS TO HAPPEN, MAKE **SURE** THEY CAN KEEP DOING THIS.

MS. NADIA, *PLEASE*, THERE **MUST** BE SOME WAY TO TALK YOU OUT OF THIS.

YEAH, HELP THEM FIGURE OUT HOW TO SAVE YING. YOU SAY THE WORD ON THE COMMLINK, I'LL BE RIGHT BACK HERE.

MR. MODOK, I'M SORRY I WASTED YOUR TIME.

I'M...NOT SO CONVINCED THIS IS GOODBYE. IF YOU DON'T MIND, I THINK I'LL WAIT HERE FOR YOU.

WELL, I HOPE WE GET TO DO MORE BORING PAPERWORK TOGETHER.

MATT MURDOCK. NADIA'S IMMIGRATION LAWYER. OTHERWISE A NORMAL GUY-- WHY, WHAT HAVE YOU HEARD?

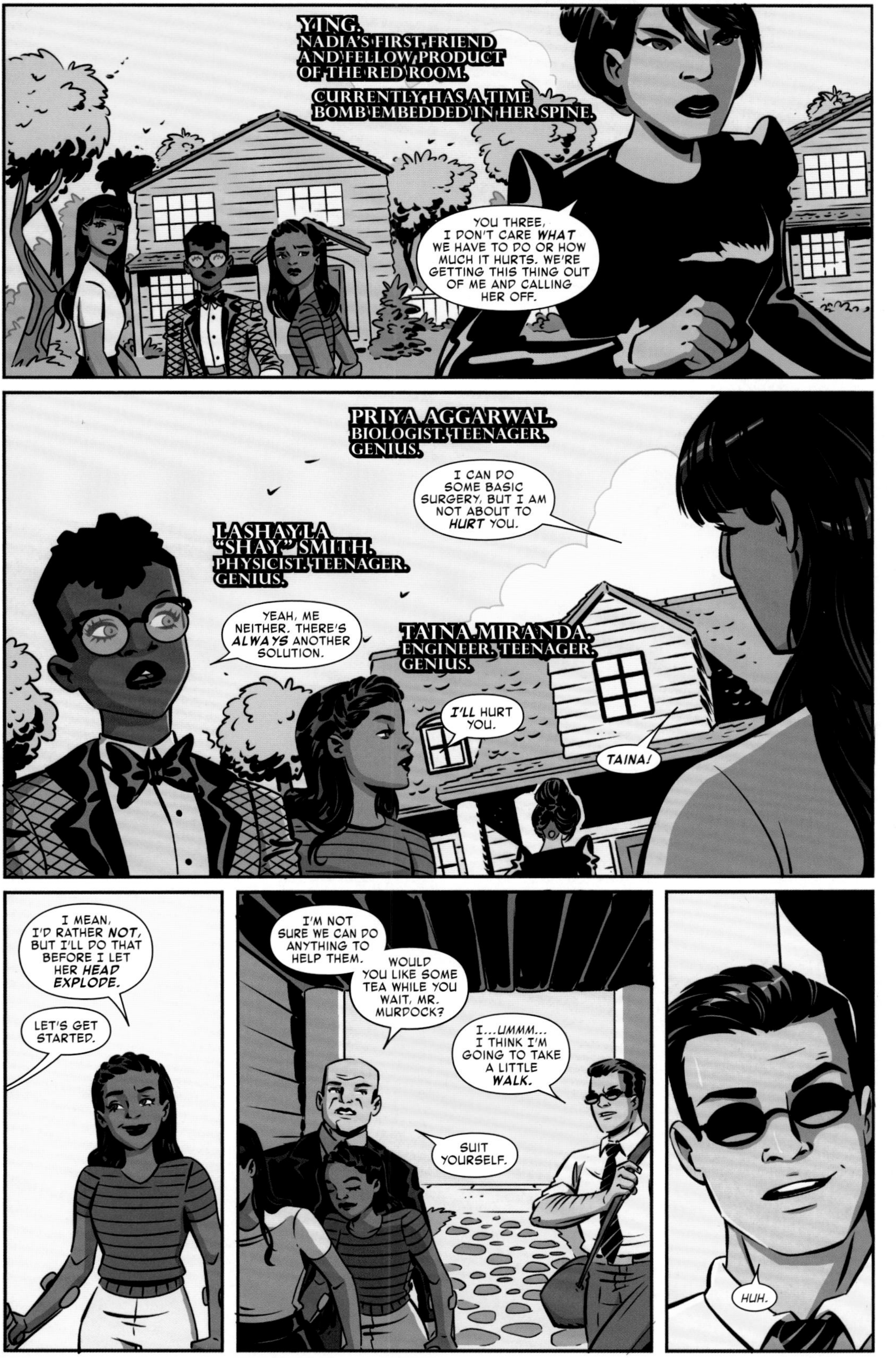
YING.
NADIA'S FIRST FRIEND AND FELLOW PRODUCT OF THE RED ROOM.
CURRENTLY HAS A TIME BOMB EMBEDDED IN HER SPINE.
YOU THREE, I DON'T CARE WHAT WE HAVE TO DO OR HOW MUCH IT HURTS. WE'RE GETTING THIS THING OUT OF ME AND CALLING HER OFF.
PRIYA AGGARWAL.
BIOLOGIST. TEENAGER. GENIUS.
I CAN DO SOME BASIC SURGERY, BUT I AM NOT ABOUT TO HURT YOU.
LASHAYLA "SHAY" SMITH.
PHYSICIST. TEENAGER. GENIUS.
YEAH, ME NEITHER. THERE'S ALWAYS ANOTHER SOLUTION.
TAINA MIRANDA.
ENGINEER. TEENAGER. GENIUS.
I'LL HURT YOU.
TAINA!
I MEAN, I'D RATHER NOT, BUT I'LL DO THAT BEFORE I LET HER HEAD EXPLODE.
LET'S GET STARTED.
I'M NOT SURE WE CAN DO ANYTHING TO HELP THEM.
WOULD YOU LIKE SOME TEA WHILE YOU WAIT, MR. MURDOCK?
I...UMMM... I THINK I'M GOING TO TAKE A LITTLE WALK.
SUIT YOURSELF.
HUH.

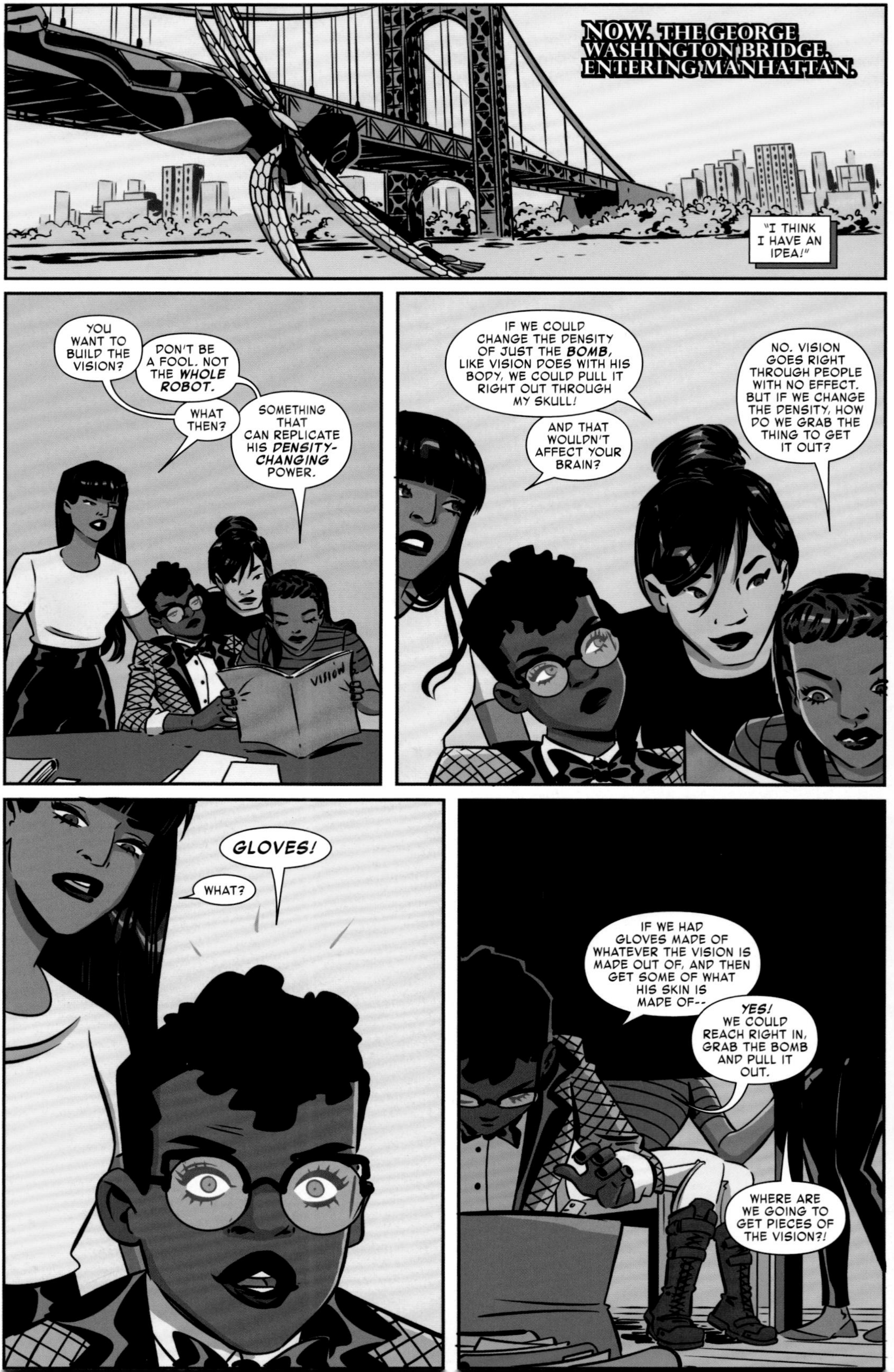
NOW. THE GEORGE WASHINGTON BRIDGE. ENTERING MANHATTAN.
"I THINK I HAVE AN IDEA!"
YOU WANT TO BUILD THE VISION?
DON'T BE A FOOL. NOT THE WHOLE ROBOT.
WHAT THEN?
SOMETHING THAT CAN REPLICATE HIS DENSITY-CHANGING POWER.
VISION
IF WE COULD CHANGE THE DENSITY OF JUST THE BOMB, LIKE VISION DOES WITH HIS BODY, WE COULD PULL IT RIGHT OUT THROUGH MY SKULL!
AND THAT WOULDN'T AFFECT YOUR BRAIN?
NO. VISION GOES RIGHT THROUGH PEOPLE WITH NO EFFECT. BUT IF WE CHANGE THE DENSITY, HOW DO WE GRAB THE THING TO GET IT OUT?
GLOVES!
WHAT?
IF WE HAD GLOVES MADE OF WHATEVER THE VISION IS MADE OUT OF, AND THEN GET SOME OF WHAT HIS SKIN IS MADE OF--
YES! WE COULD REACH RIGHT IN, GRAB THE BOMB AND PULL IT OUT.
WHERE ARE WE GOING TO GET PIECES OF THE VISION?!

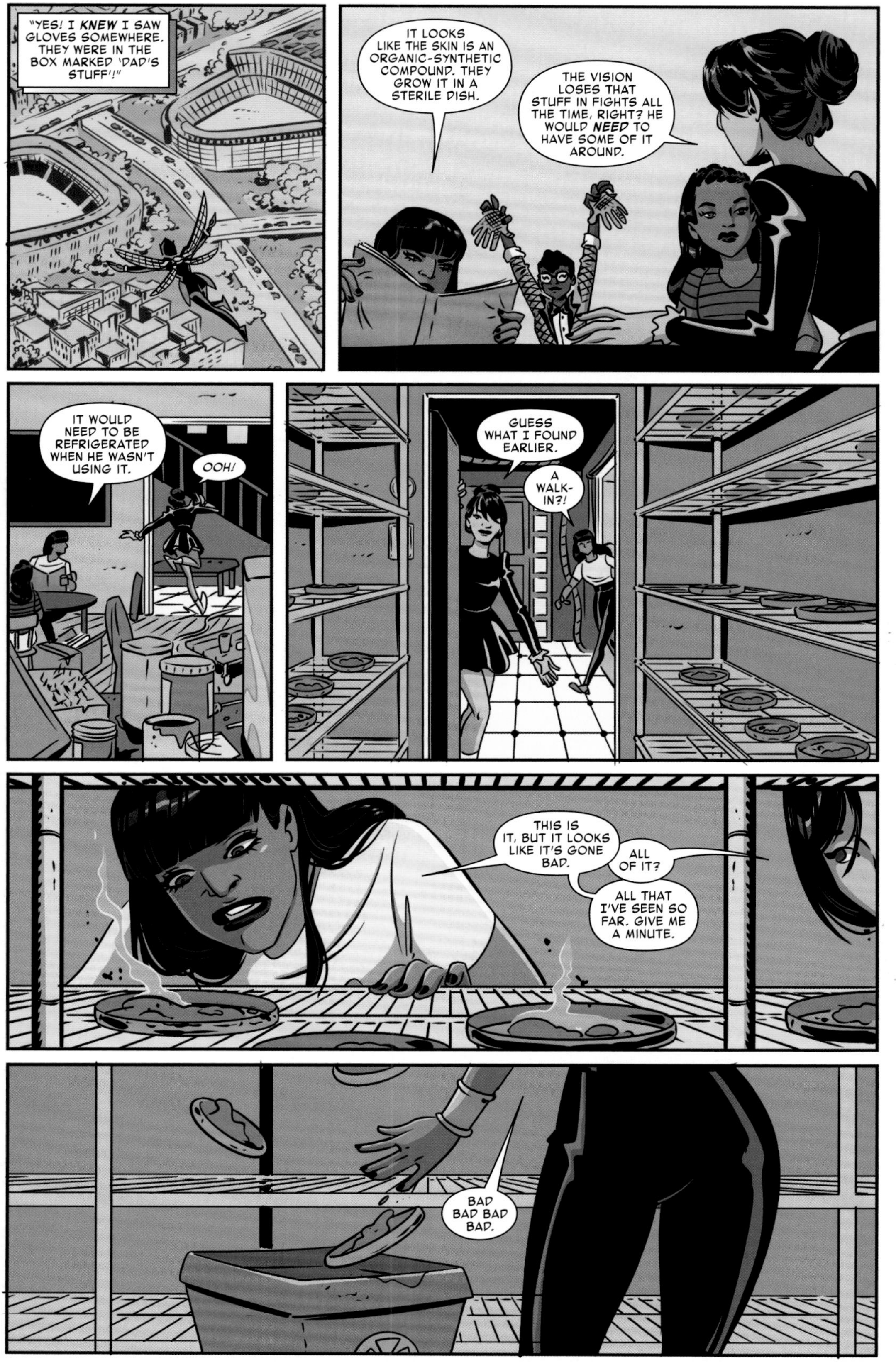
"YES! I *KNEW* I SAW GLOVES SOMEWHERE. THEY WERE IN THE BOX MARKED 'DAD'S STUFF'!"
IT LOOKS LIKE THE SKIN IS AN ORGANIC-SYNTHETIC COMPOUND. THEY GROW IT IN A STERILE DISH.
THE VISION LOSES THAT STUFF IN FIGHTS ALL THE TIME, RIGHT? HE WOULD *NEED* TO HAVE SOME OF IT AROUND.
IT WOULD NEED TO BE REFRIGERATED WHEN HE WASN'T USING IT.
OOH!
GUESS WHAT I FOUND EARLIER.
A WALK-IN?!
THIS IS IT, BUT IT LOOKS LIKE IT'S GONE BAD.
ALL OF IT?
ALL THAT I'VE SEEN SO FAR. GIVE ME A MINUTE.
BAD BAD BAD BAD.

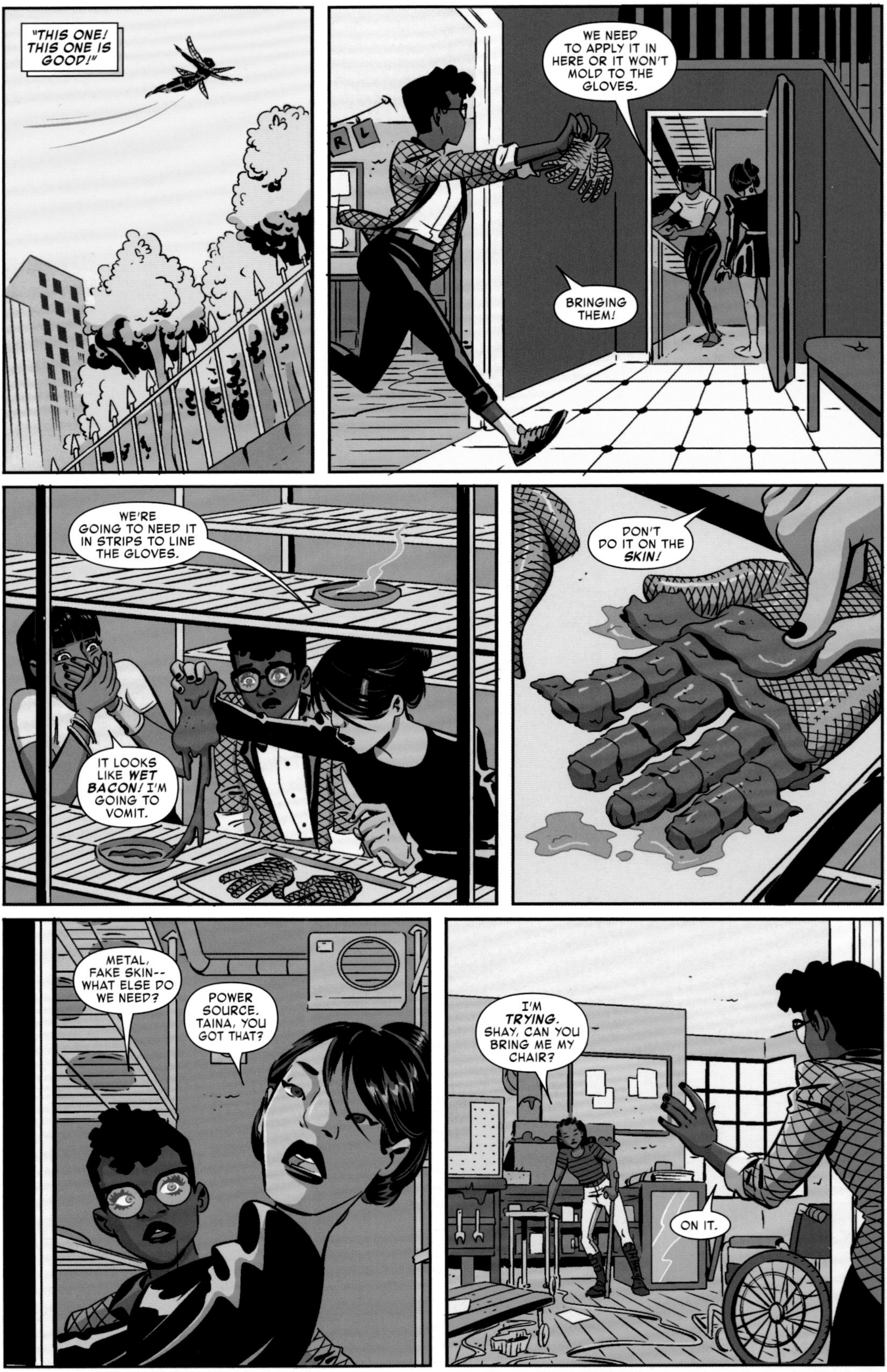
"THIS ONE! THIS ONE IS GOOD!"
WE NEED TO APPLY IT IN HERE OR IT WON'T MOLD TO THE GLOVES.
BRINGING THEM!
WE'RE GOING TO NEED IT IN STRIPS TO LINE THE GLOVES.
IT LOOKS LIKE WET BACON! I'M GOING TO VOMIT.
DON'T DO IT ON THE SKIN!
METAL, FAKE SKIN-- WHAT ELSE DO WE NEED?
POWER SOURCE. TAINA, YOU GOT THAT?
I'M TRYING. SHAY, CAN YOU BRING ME MY CHAIR?
ON IT.

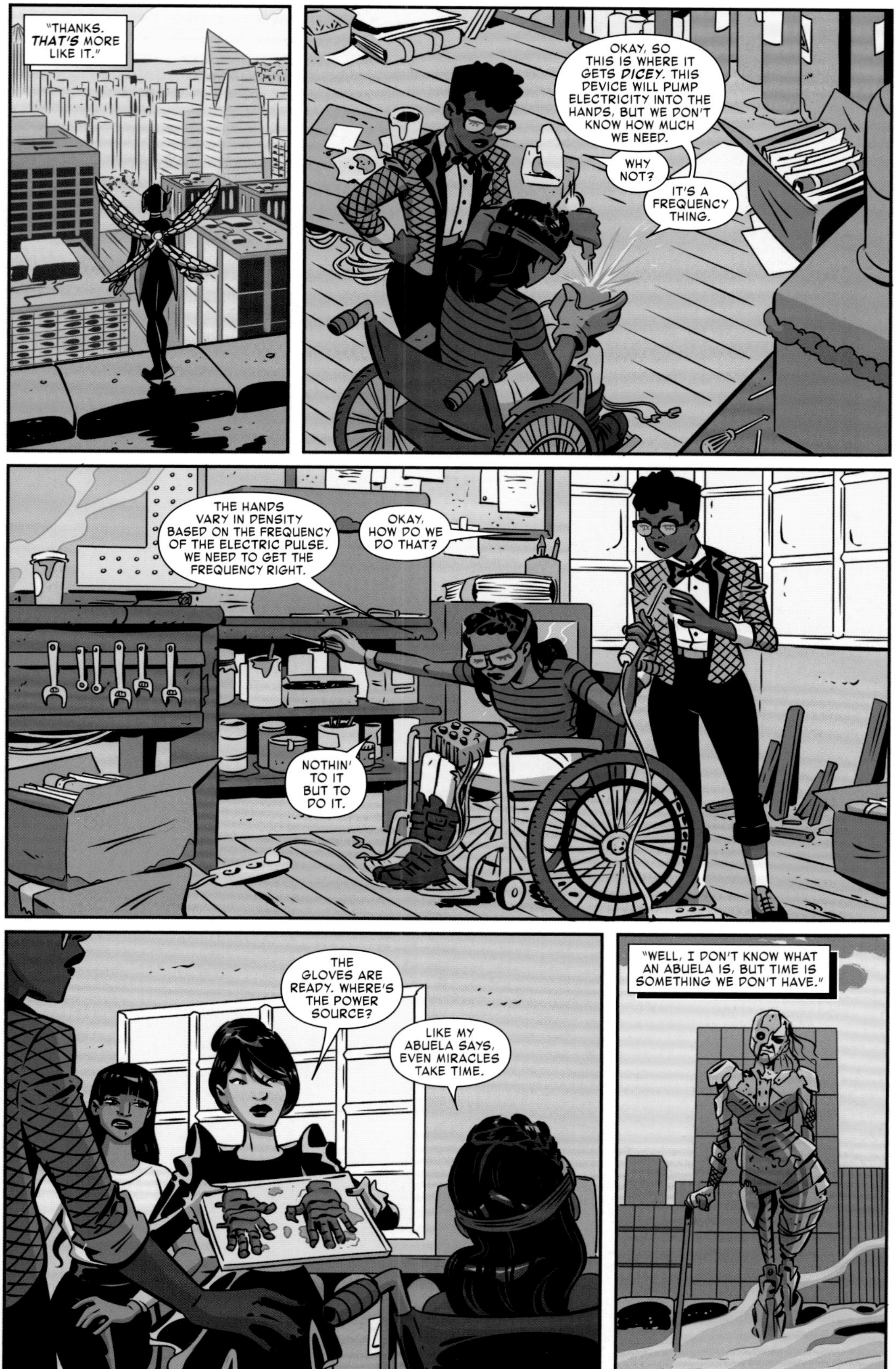
"THANKS. THAT'S MORE LIKE IT."
OKAY, SO THIS IS WHERE IT GETS DICEY. THIS DEVICE WILL PUMP ELECTRICITY INTO THE HANDS, BUT WE DON'T KNOW HOW MUCH WE NEED.
WHY NOT?
IT'S A FREQUENCY THING.
THE HANDS VARY IN DENSITY BASED ON THE FREQUENCY OF THE ELECTRIC PULSE. WE NEED TO GET THE FREQUENCY RIGHT.
OKAY, HOW DO WE DO THAT?
NOTHIN' TO IT BUT TO DO IT.
THE GLOVES ARE READY. WHERE'S THE POWER SOURCE?
LIKE MY ABUELA SAYS, EVEN MIRACLES TAKE TIME.
"WELL, I DON'T KNOW WHAT AN ABUELA IS, BUT TIME IS SOMETHING WE DON'T HAVE."

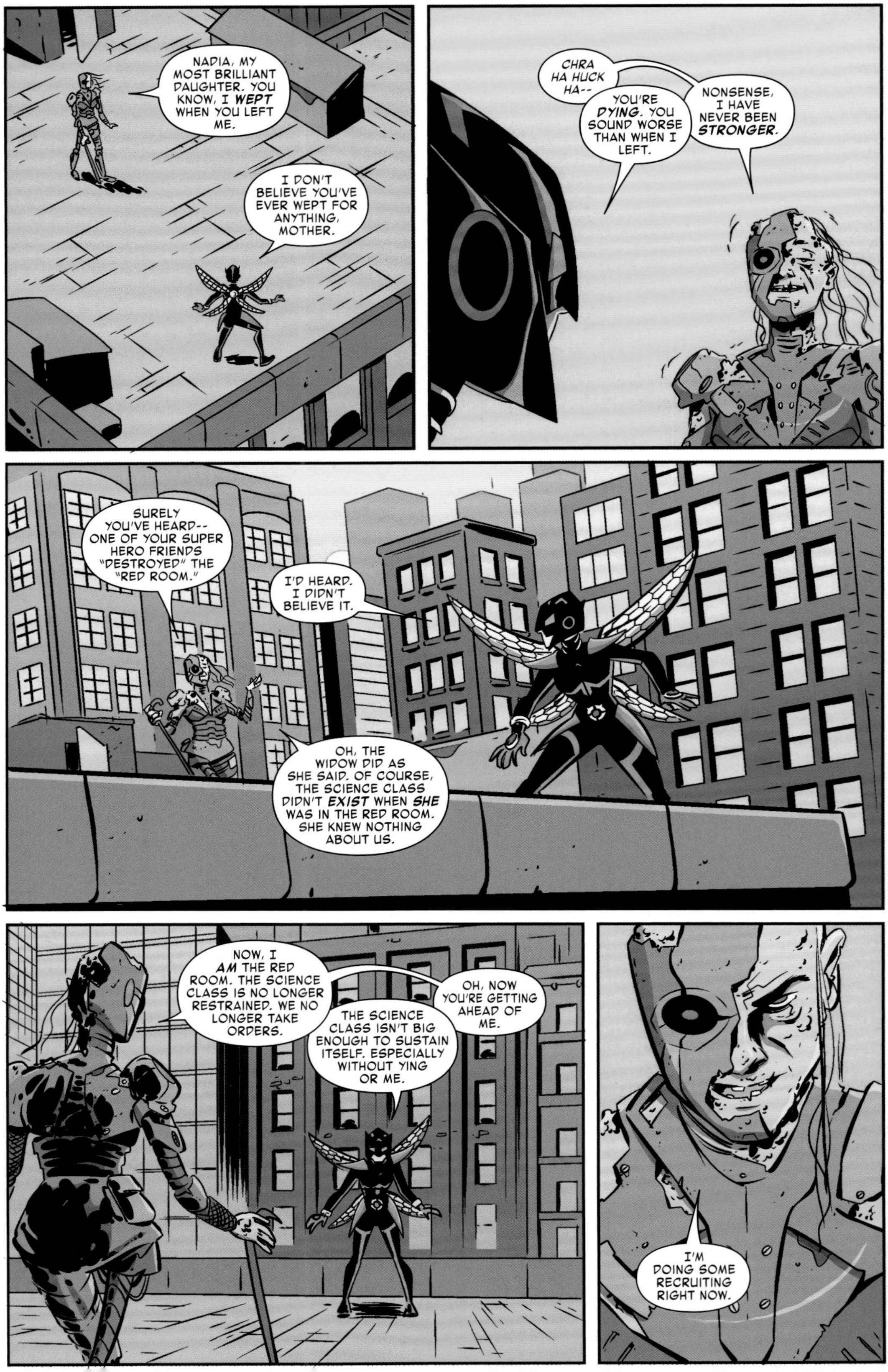
NADIA, MY MOST BRILLIANT DAUGHTER. YOU KNOW, I WEPT WHEN YOU LEFT ME.
I DON'T BELIEVE YOU'VE EVER WEPT FOR ANYTHING, MOTHER.
CHRA HA HUCK HA--
NONSENSE, I HAVE NEVER BEEN STRONGER.
YOU'RE DYING. YOU SOUND WORSE THAN WHEN I LEFT.
SURELY YOU'VE HEARD-- ONE OF YOUR SUPER HERO FRIENDS "DESTROYED" THE "RED ROOM."
I'D HEARD. I DIDN'T BELIEVE IT.
OH, THE WIDOW DID AS SHE SAID. OF COURSE, THE SCIENCE CLASS DIDN'T EXIST WHEN SHE WAS IN THE RED ROOM. SHE KNEW NOTHING ABOUT US.
NOW, I AM THE RED ROOM. THE SCIENCE CLASS IS NO LONGER RESTRAINED. WE NO LONGER TAKE ORDERS.
THE SCIENCE CLASS ISN'T BIG ENOUGH TO SUSTAIN ITSELF. ESPECIALLY WITHOUT YING OR ME.
OH, NOW YOU'RE GETTING AHEAD OF ME.
I'M DOING SOME RECRUITING RIGHT NOW.

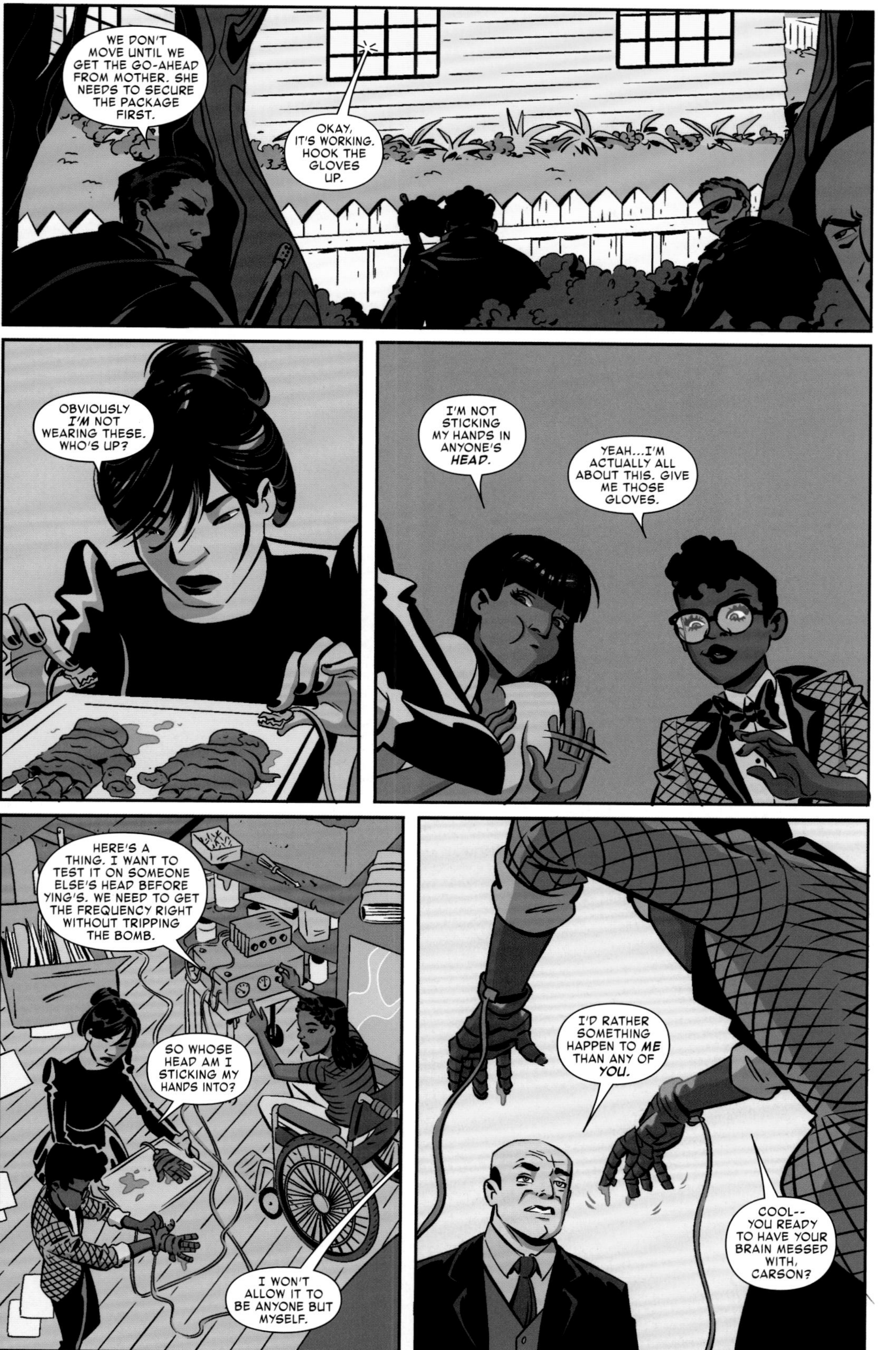
WE DON'T MOVE UNTIL WE GET THE GO-AHEAD FROM MOTHER. SHE NEEDS TO SECURE THE PACKAGE FIRST.
OKAY, IT'S WORKING. HOOK THE GLOVES UP.
OBVIOUSLY *I'M* NOT WEARING THESE. WHO'S UP?
I'M NOT STICKING MY HANDS IN ANYONE'S *HEAD.*
YEAH...I'M ACTUALLY ALL ABOUT THIS. GIVE ME THOSE GLOVES.
HERE'S A THING. I WANT TO TEST IT ON SOMEONE ELSE'S HEAD BEFORE YING'S. WE NEED TO GET THE FREQUENCY RIGHT WITHOUT TRIPPING THE BOMB.
SO WHOSE HEAD AM I STICKING MY HANDS INTO?
I WON'T ALLOW IT TO BE ANYONE BUT MYSELF.
I'D RATHER SOMETHING HAPPEN TO *ME* THAN ANY OF *YOU.*
COOL-- YOU READY TO HAVE YOUR BRAIN MESSED WITH, CARSON?

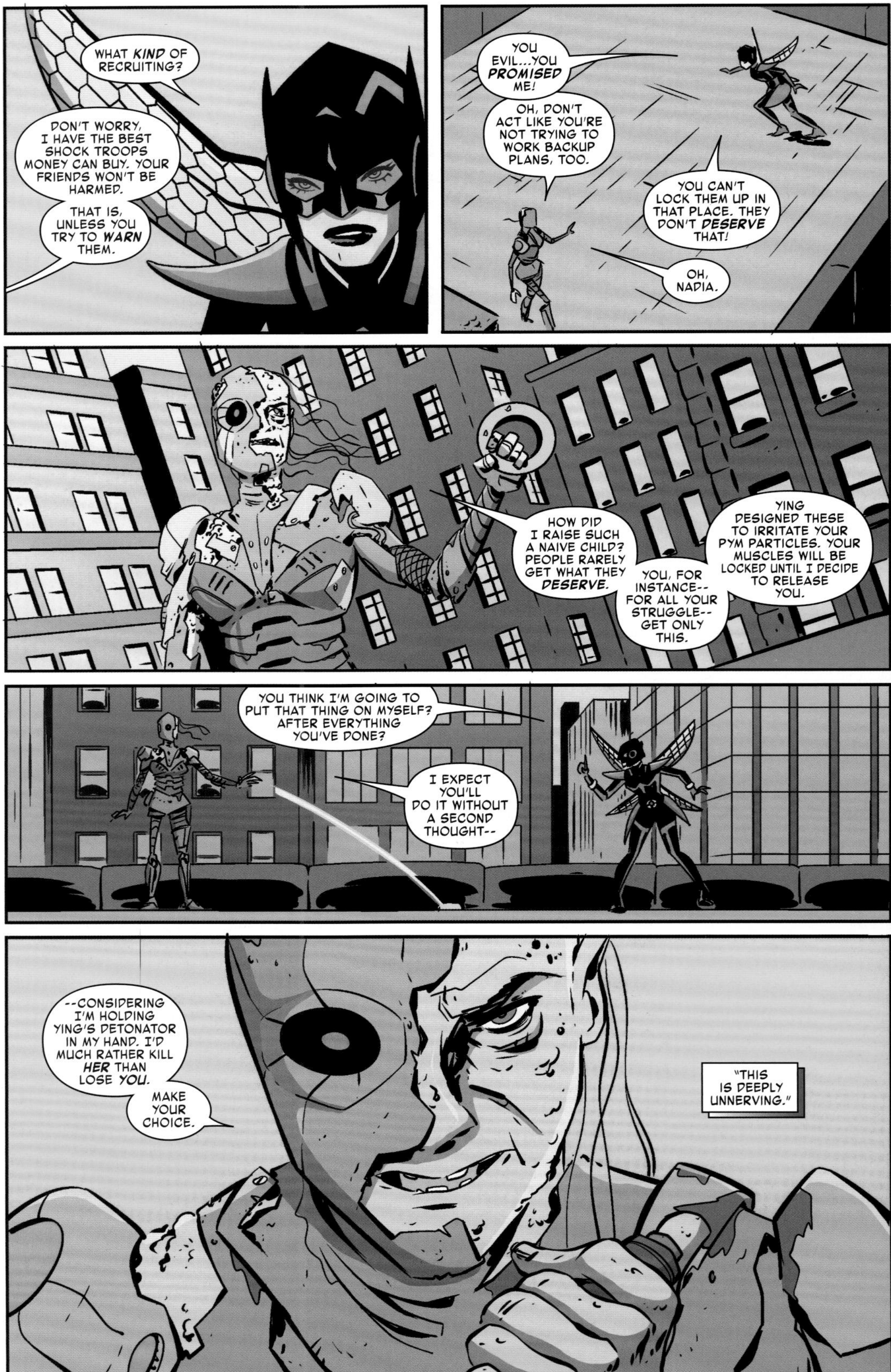
WHAT *KIND* OF RECRUITING?
DON'T WORRY, I HAVE THE BEST SHOCK TROOPS MONEY CAN BUY. YOUR FRIENDS WON'T BE HARMED.
THAT IS, UNLESS YOU TRY TO *WARN* THEM.
YOU EVIL...YOU *PROMISED* ME!
OH, DON'T ACT LIKE YOU'RE NOT TRYING TO WORK BACKUP PLANS, TOO.
YOU CAN'T LOCK THEM UP IN THAT PLACE. THEY DON'T *DESERVE* THAT!
OH, NADIA.
HOW DID I RAISE SUCH A NAIVE CHILD? PEOPLE RARELY GET WHAT THEY *DESERVE.*
YOU, FOR INSTANCE-- FOR ALL YOUR STRUGGLE-- GET ONLY THIS.
YING DESIGNED THESE TO IRRITATE YOUR PYM PARTICLES. YOUR MUSCLES WILL BE LOCKED UNTIL I DECIDE TO RELEASE YOU.
YOU THINK I'M GOING TO PUT THAT THING ON MYSELF? AFTER EVERYTHING YOU'VE DONE?
I EXPECT YOU'LL DO IT WITHOUT A SECOND THOUGHT--
--CONSIDERING I'M HOLDING YING'S DETONATOR IN MY HAND. I'D MUCH RATHER KILL *HER* THAN LOSE *YOU*.
MAKE YOUR CHOICE.
"THIS IS DEEPLY UNNERVING."

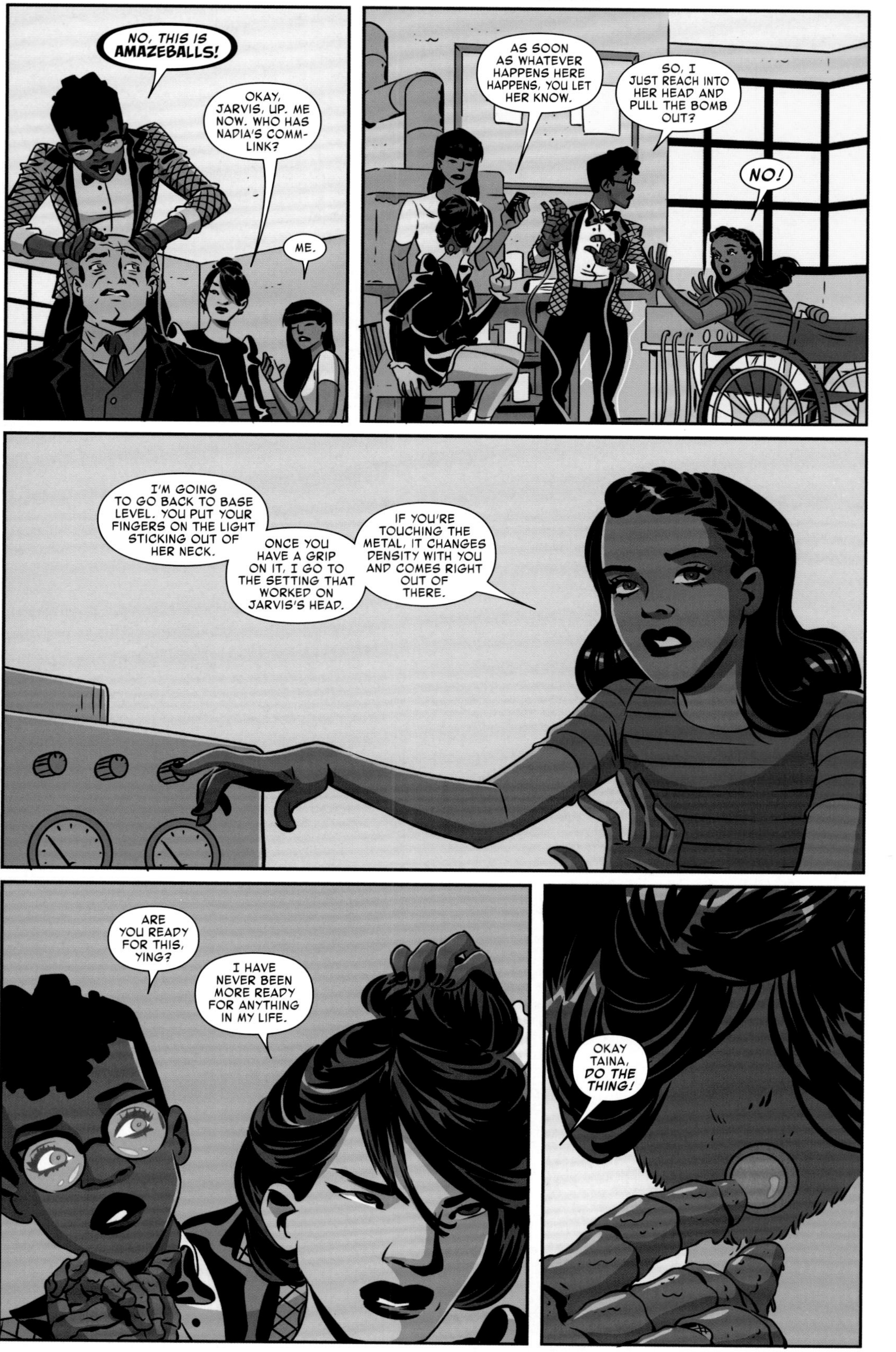
NO, THIS IS AMAZEBALLS!
OKAY, JARVIS, UP. ME NOW. WHO HAS NADIA'S COMM-LINK?
ME.
AS SOON AS WHATEVER HAPPENS HERE HAPPENS, YOU LET HER KNOW.
SO, I JUST REACH INTO HER HEAD AND PULL THE BOMB OUT?
NO!
I'M GOING TO GO BACK TO BASE LEVEL. YOU PUT YOUR FINGERS ON THE LIGHT STICKING OUT OF HER NECK.
ONCE YOU HAVE A GRIP ON IT, I GO TO THE SETTING THAT WORKED ON JARVIS'S HEAD.
IF YOU'RE TOUCHING THE METAL, IT CHANGES DENSITY WITH YOU AND COMES RIGHT OUT OF THERE.
ARE YOU READY FOR THIS, YING?
I HAVE NEVER BEEN MORE READY FOR ANYTHING IN MY LIFE.
OKAY TAINA, DO THE THING!

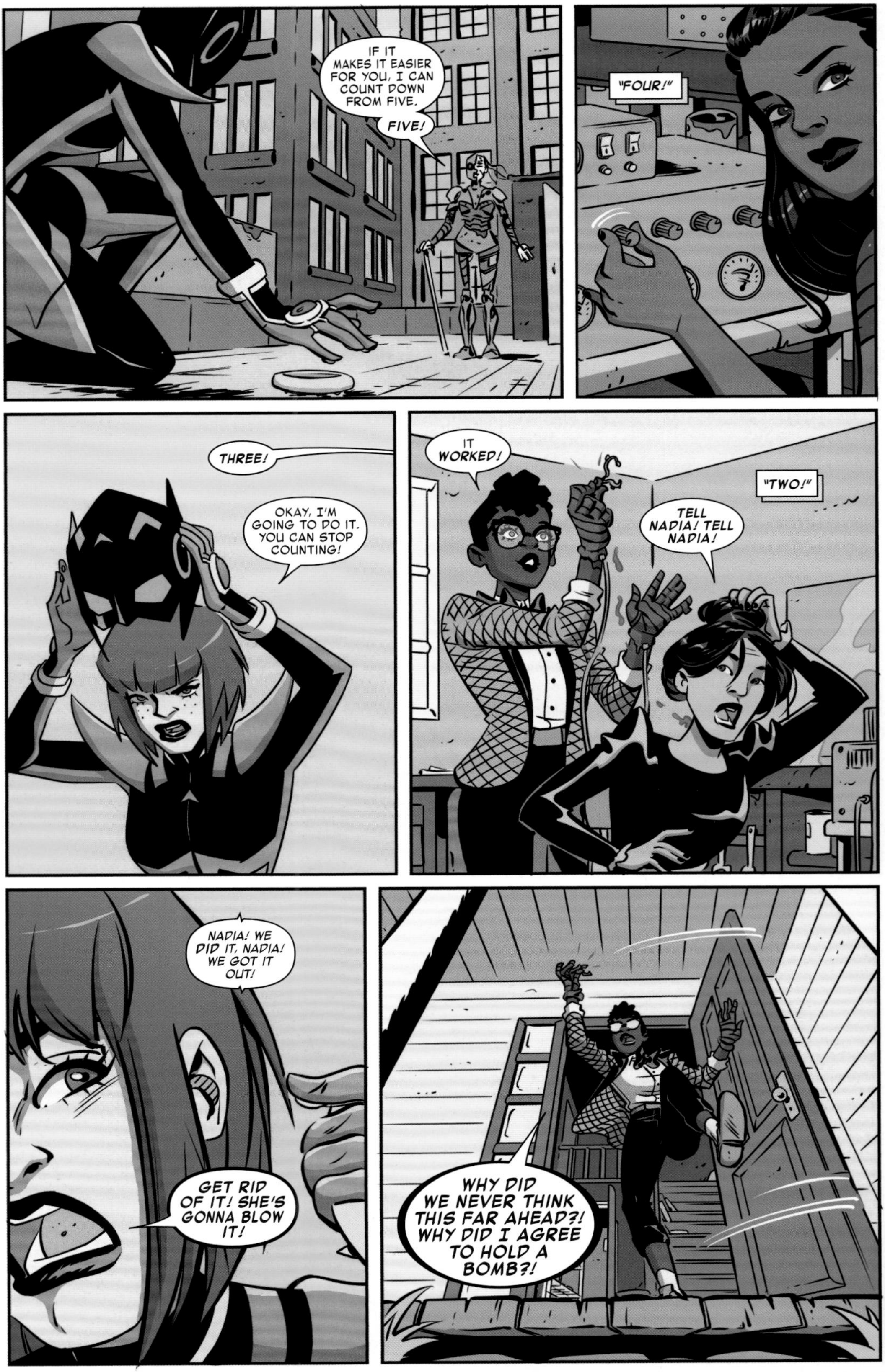
IF IT MAKES IT EASIER FOR YOU, I CAN COUNT DOWN FROM FIVE.
FIVE!
"FOUR!"
THREE!
OKAY, I'M GOING TO DO IT. YOU CAN STOP COUNTING!
IT WORKED!
"TWO!"
TELL NADIA! TELL NADIA!
NADIA! WE DID IT, NADIA! WE GOT IT OUT!
GET RID OF IT! SHE'S GONNA BLOW IT!
WHY DID WE NEVER THINK THIS FAR AHEAD?! WHY DID I AGREE TO HOLD A BOMB?!

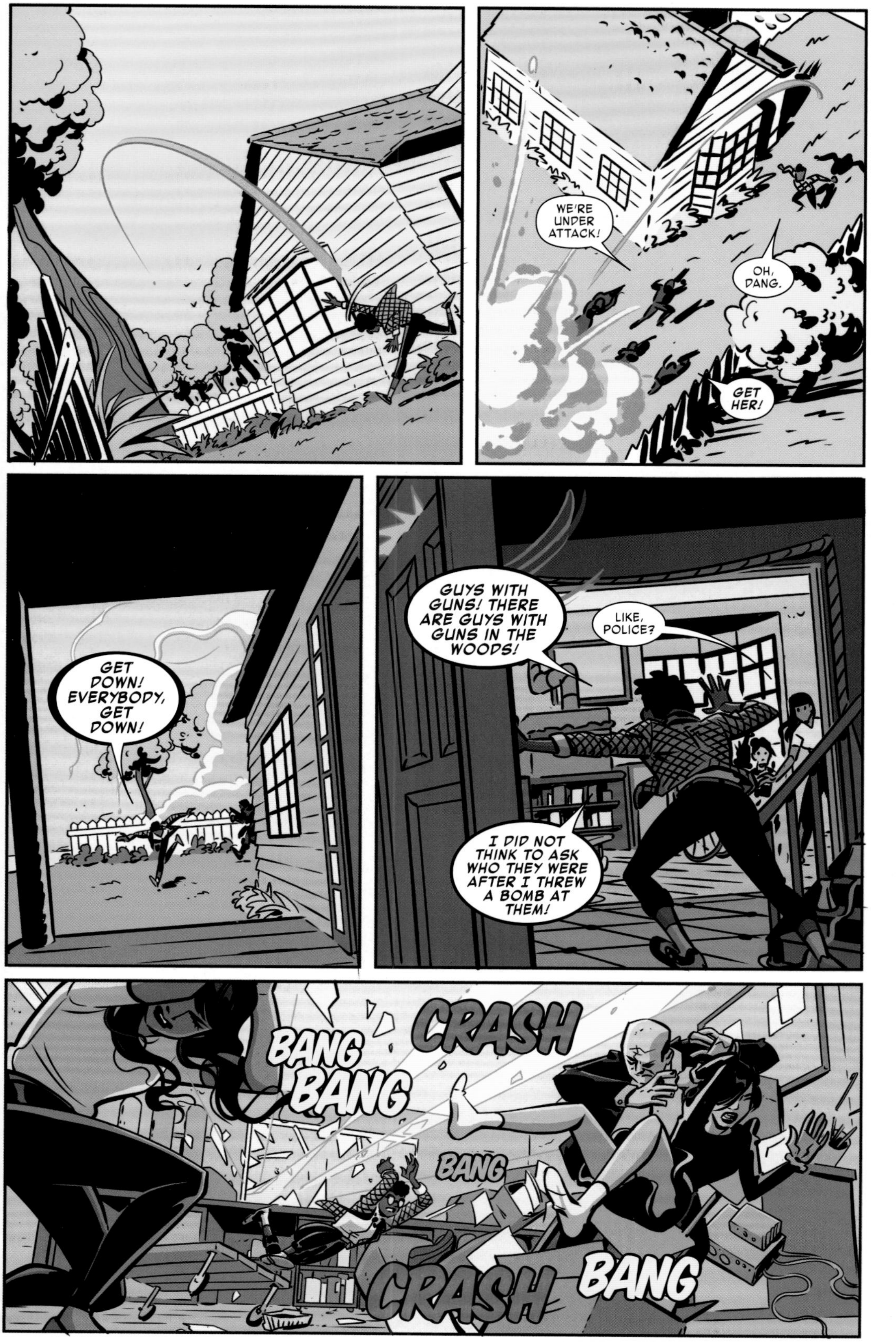
WE'RE UNDER ATTACK!
OH, DANG.
GET HER!
GET DOWN! EVERYBODY, GET DOWN!
GUYS WITH GUNS! THERE ARE GUYS WITH GUNS IN THE WOODS!
LIKE, POLICE?
I DID NOT THINK TO ASK WHO THEY WERE AFTER I THREW A BOMB AT THEM!
BANG
BANG
CRASH
BANG
CRASH
BANG

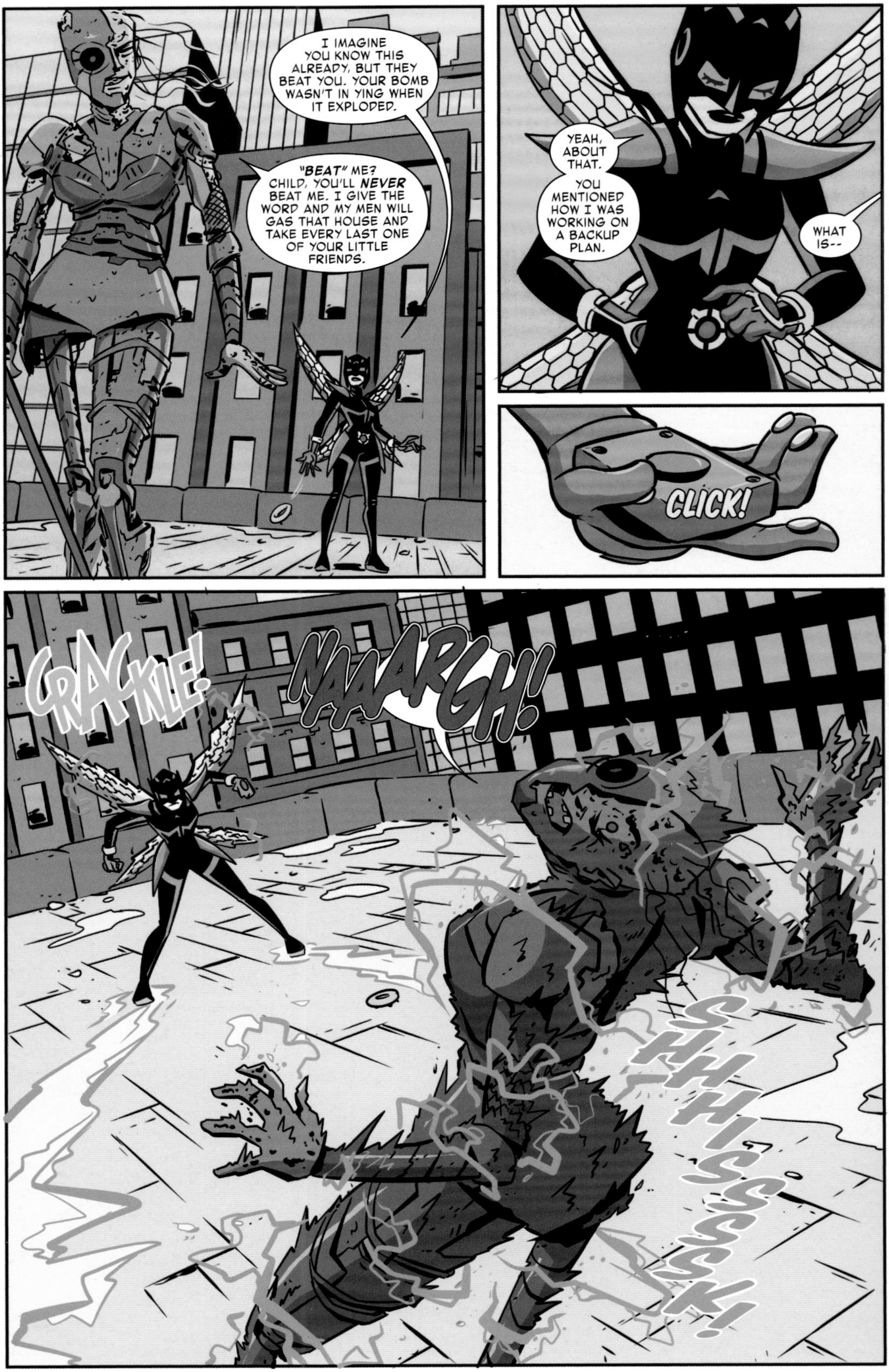
I IMAGINE YOU KNOW THIS ALREADY, BUT THEY BEAT YOU. YOUR BOMB WASN'T IN YING WHEN IT EXPLODED.
"BEAT" ME? CHILD, YOU'LL NEVER BEAT ME. I GIVE THE WORD AND MY MEN WILL GAS THAT HOUSE AND TAKE EVERY LAST ONE OF YOUR LITTLE FRIENDS.
YEAH, ABOUT THAT.
YOU MENTIONED HOW I WAS WORKING ON A BACKUP PLAN.
WHAT IS--
CLICK!
CRACKLE!
NAAARGH!
SHHHISSSSK!

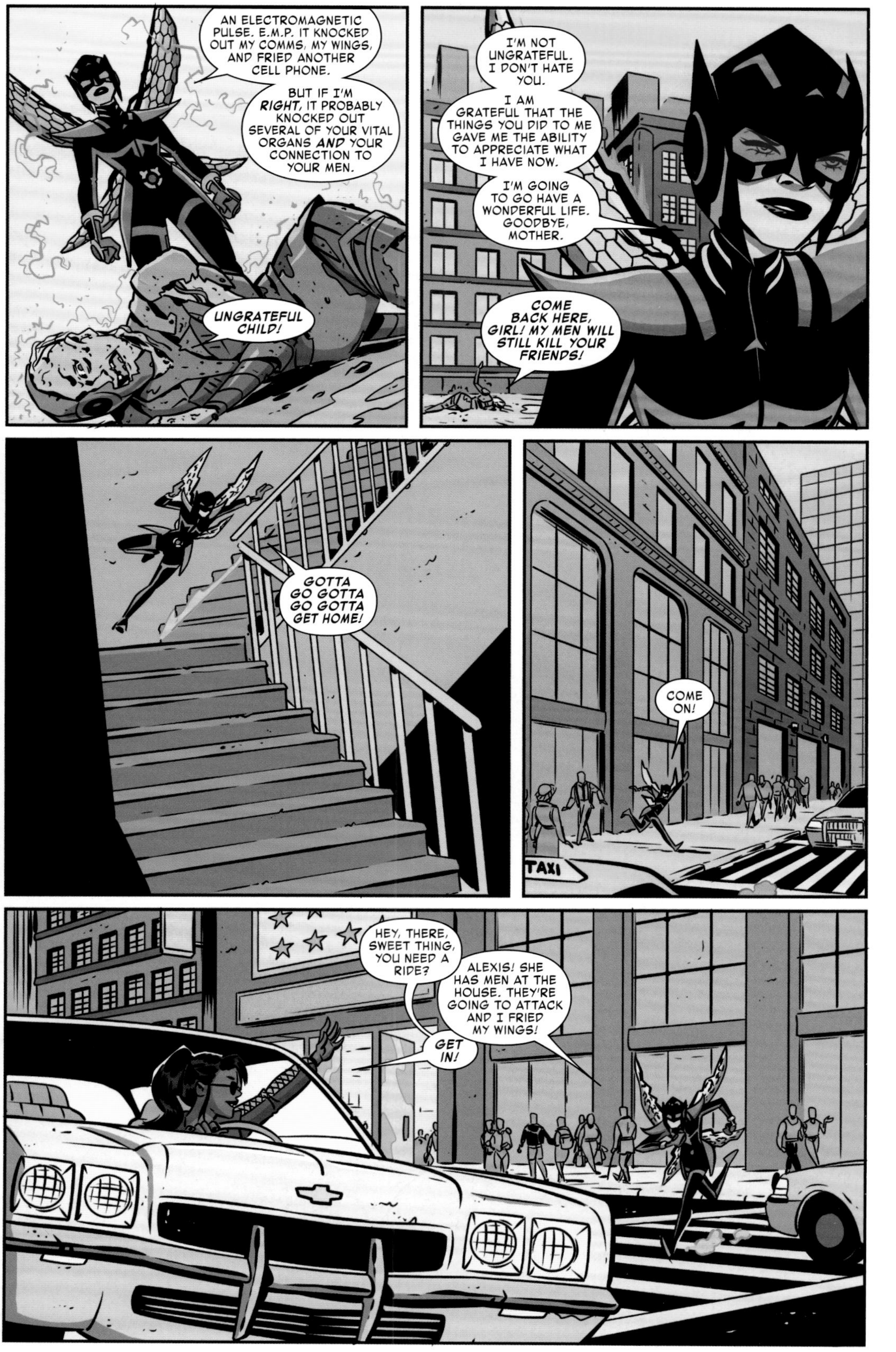
AN ELECTROMAGNETIC PULSE. E.M.P. IT KNOCKED OUT MY COMMS, MY WINGS, AND FRIED ANOTHER CELL PHONE.
BUT IF I'M RIGHT, IT PROBABLY KNOCKED OUT SEVERAL OF YOUR VITAL ORGANS AND YOUR CONNECTION TO YOUR MEN.
UNGRATEFUL CHILD!
I'M NOT UNGRATEFUL. I DON'T HATE YOU.
I AM GRATEFUL THAT THE THINGS YOU DID TO ME GAVE ME THE ABILITY TO APPRECIATE WHAT I HAVE NOW.
I'M GOING TO GO HAVE A WONDERFUL LIFE. GOODBYE, MOTHER.
COME BACK HERE, GIRL! MY MEN WILL STILL KILL YOUR FRIENDS!
GOTTA GO GOTTA GO GOTTA GET HOME!
COME ON!
TAXI
HEY, THERE, SWEET THING, YOU NEED A RIDE?
ALEXIS! SHE HAS MEN AT THE HOUSE. THEY'RE GOING TO ATTACK AND I FRIED MY WINGS!
GET IN!

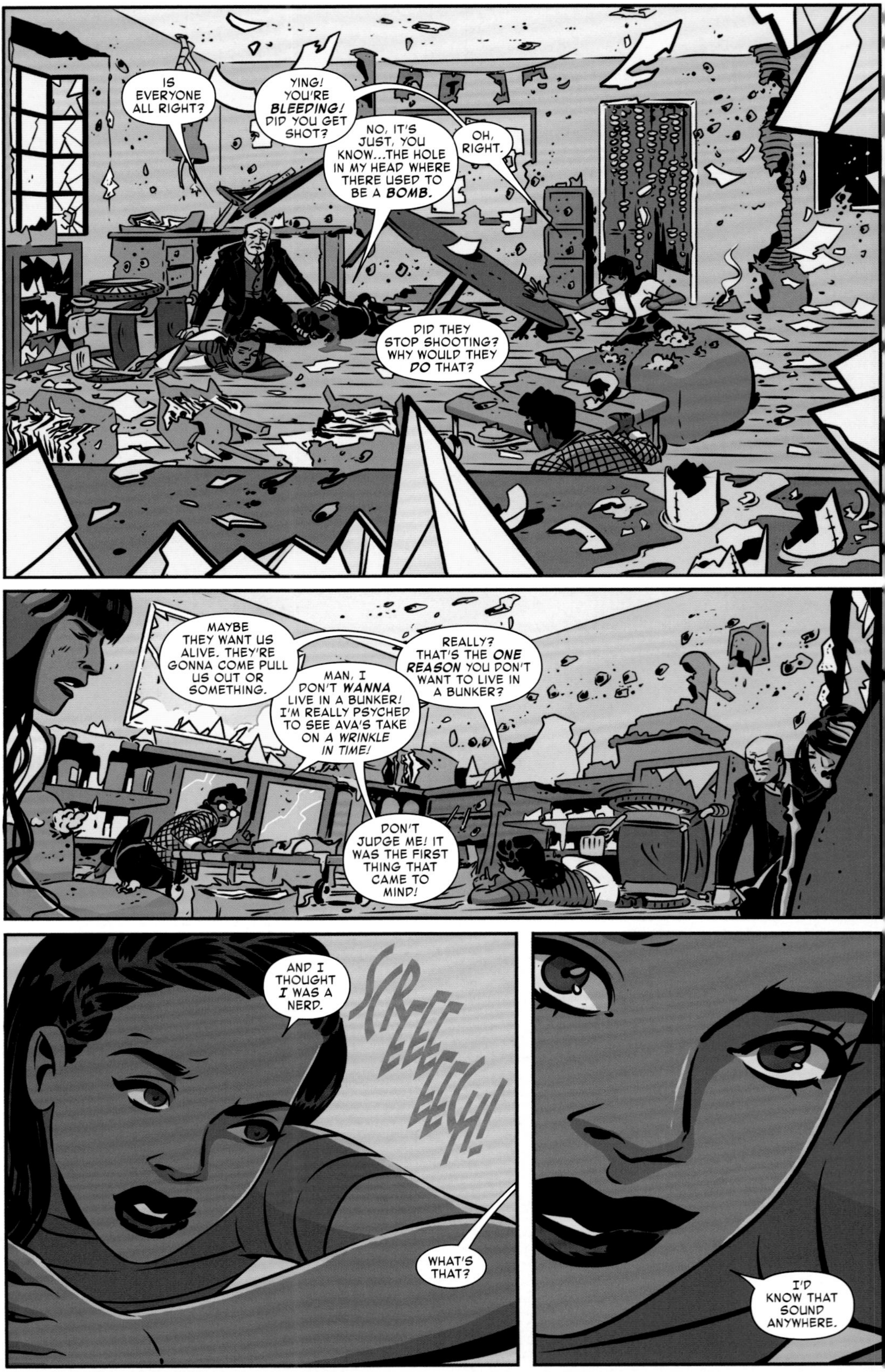
IS EVERYONE ALL RIGHT?
YING! YOU'RE BLEEDING! DID YOU GET SHOT?
NO, IT'S JUST, YOU KNOW...THE HOLE IN MY HEAD WHERE THERE USED TO BE A BOMB.
OH, RIGHT.
DID THEY STOP SHOOTING? WHY WOULD THEY DO THAT?
MAYBE THEY WANT US ALIVE. THEY'RE GONNA COME PULL US OUT OR SOMETHING.
MAN, I DON'T WANNA LIVE IN A BUNKER! I'M REALLY PSYCHED TO SEE AVA'S TAKE ON A WRINKLE IN TIME!
REALLY? THAT'S THE ONE REASON YOU DON'T WANT TO LIVE IN A BUNKER?
DON'T JUDGE ME! IT WAS THE FIRST THING THAT CAME TO MIND!
AND I THOUGHT I WAS A NERD.
SCREEEEECH!
WHAT'S THAT?
I'D KNOW THAT SOUND ANYWHERE.

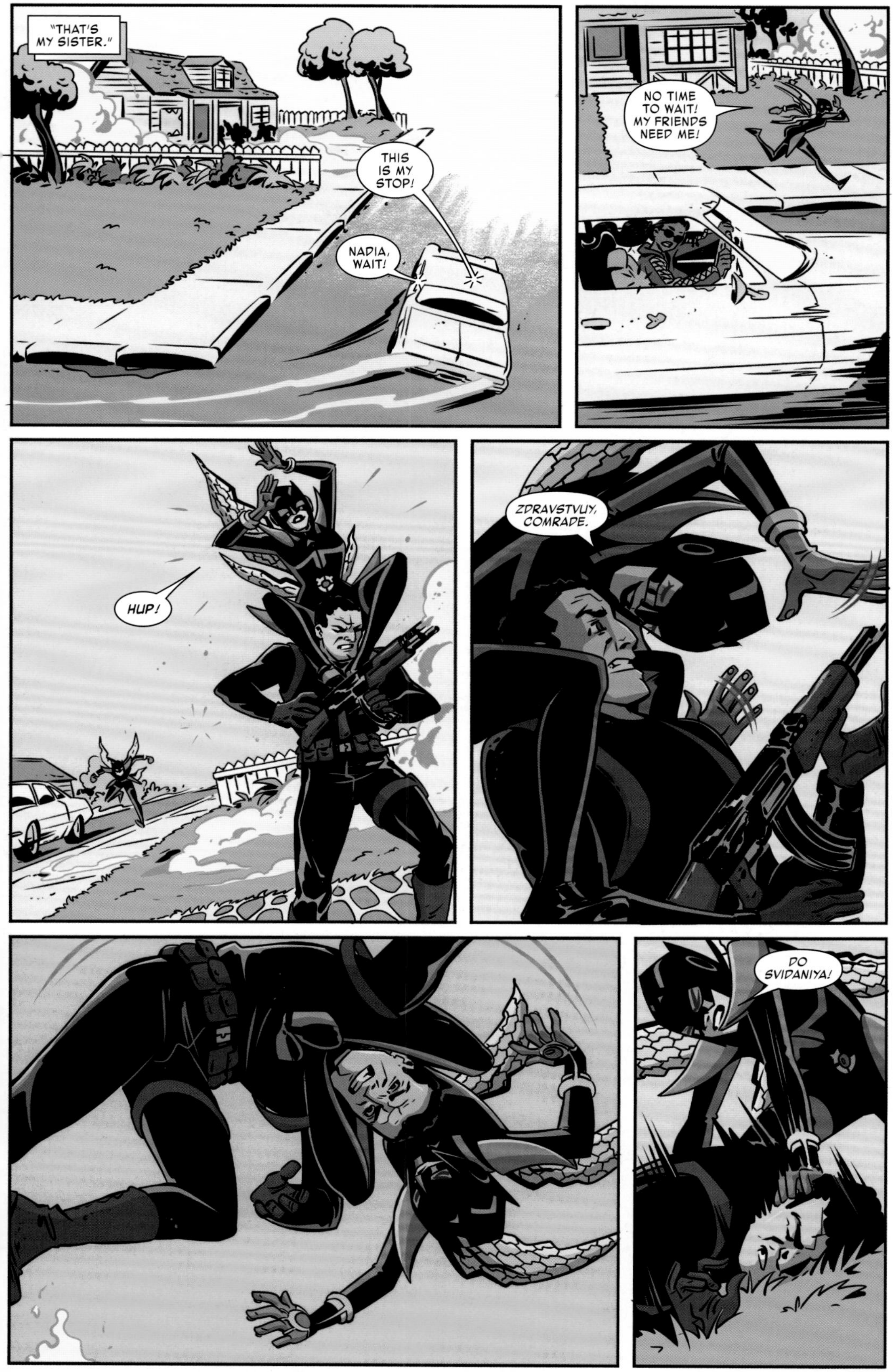
"THAT'S MY SISTER."
THIS IS MY STOP!
NADIA, WAIT!
NO TIME TO WAIT! MY FRIENDS NEED ME!
HUP!
ZDRAVSTVUY, COMRADE.
DO SVIDANIYA!

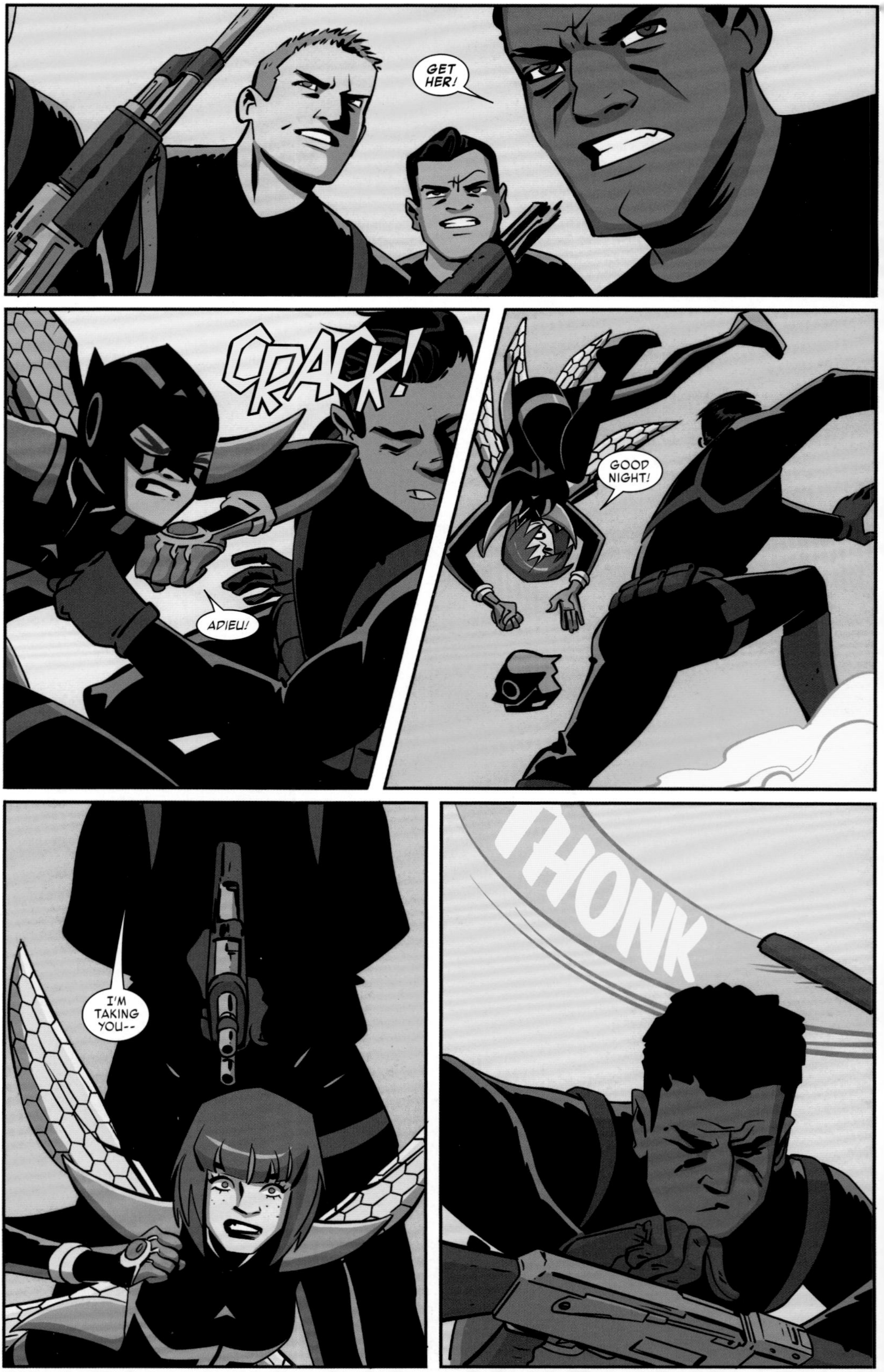
GET HER!
CRACK!
ADIEU!
GOOD NIGHT!
I'M TAKING YOU--
THONK

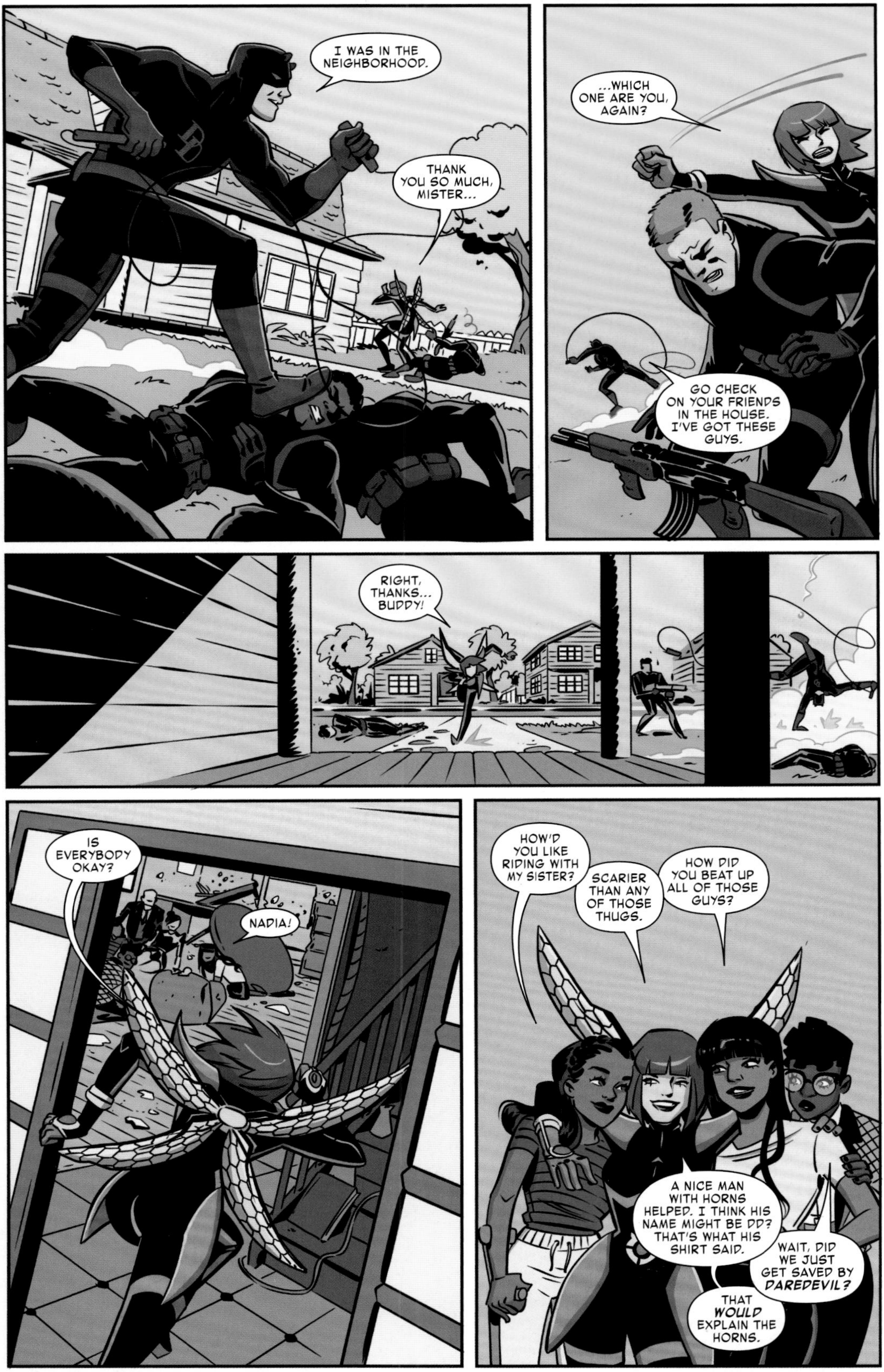
I WAS IN THE NEIGHBORHOOD.
THANK YOU SO MUCH, MISTER...
...WHICH ONE ARE YOU, AGAIN?
GO CHECK ON YOUR FRIENDS IN THE HOUSE. I'VE GOT THESE GUYS.
RIGHT, THANKS... BUDDY!
IS EVERYBODY OKAY?
NADIA!
HOW'D YOU LIKE RIDING WITH MY SISTER?
SCARIER THAN ANY OF THOSE THUGS.
HOW DID YOU BEAT UP ALL OF THOSE GUYS?
A NICE MAN WITH HORNS HELPED. I THINK HIS NAME MIGHT BE DD? THAT'S WHAT HIS SHIRT SAID.
WAIT, DID WE JUST GET SAVED BY DAREDEVIL?
THAT WOULD EXPLAIN THE HORNS.

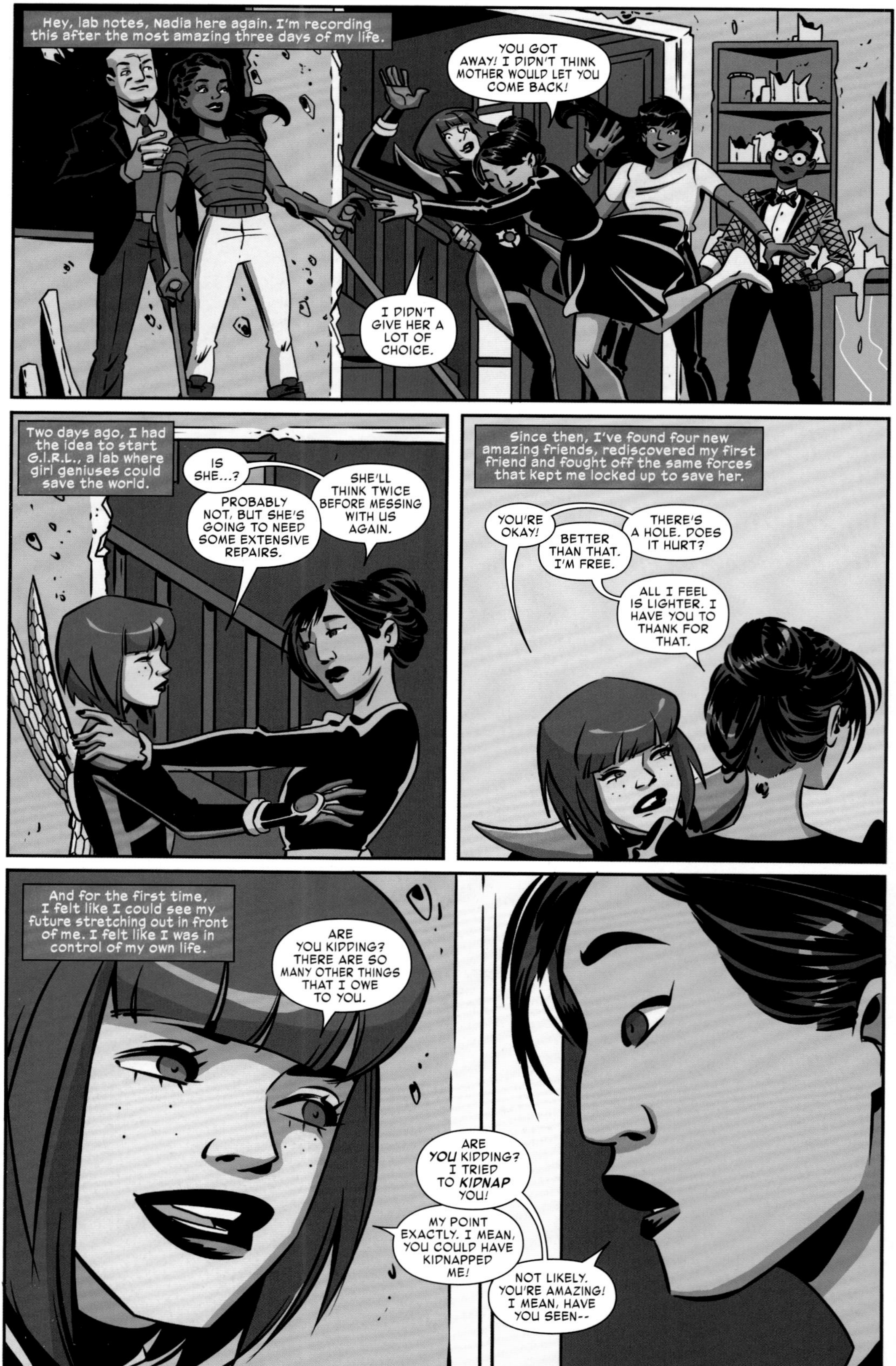

Hey, lab notes, Nadia here again. I'm recording this after the most amazing three days of my life.
YOU GOT AWAY! I DIDN'T THINK MOTHER WOULD LET YOU COME BACK!
I DIDN'T GIVE HER A LOT OF CHOICE.
Two days ago, I had the idea to start G.I.R.L., a lab where girl geniuses could save the world.
IS SHE...?
PROBABLY NOT, BUT SHE'S GOING TO NEED SOME EXTENSIVE REPAIRS.
SHE'LL THINK TWICE BEFORE MESSING WITH US AGAIN.
Since then, I've found four new amazing friends, rediscovered my first friend and fought off the same forces that kept me locked up to save her.
YOU'RE OKAY!
BETTER THAN THAT. I'M FREE.
THERE'S A HOLE. DOES IT HURT?
ALL I FEEL IS LIGHTER. I HAVE YOU TO THANK FOR THAT.
And for the first time, I felt like I could see my future stretching out in front of me. I felt like I was in control of my own life.
ARE YOU KIDDING? THERE ARE SO MANY OTHER THINGS THAT I OWE TO YOU.
ARE *YOU* KIDDING? I TRIED TO *KIDNAP* YOU!
MY POINT EXACTLY. I MEAN, YOU COULD HAVE KIDNAPPED ME!
NOT LIKELY. YOU'RE AMAZING! I MEAN, HAVE YOU SEEN--

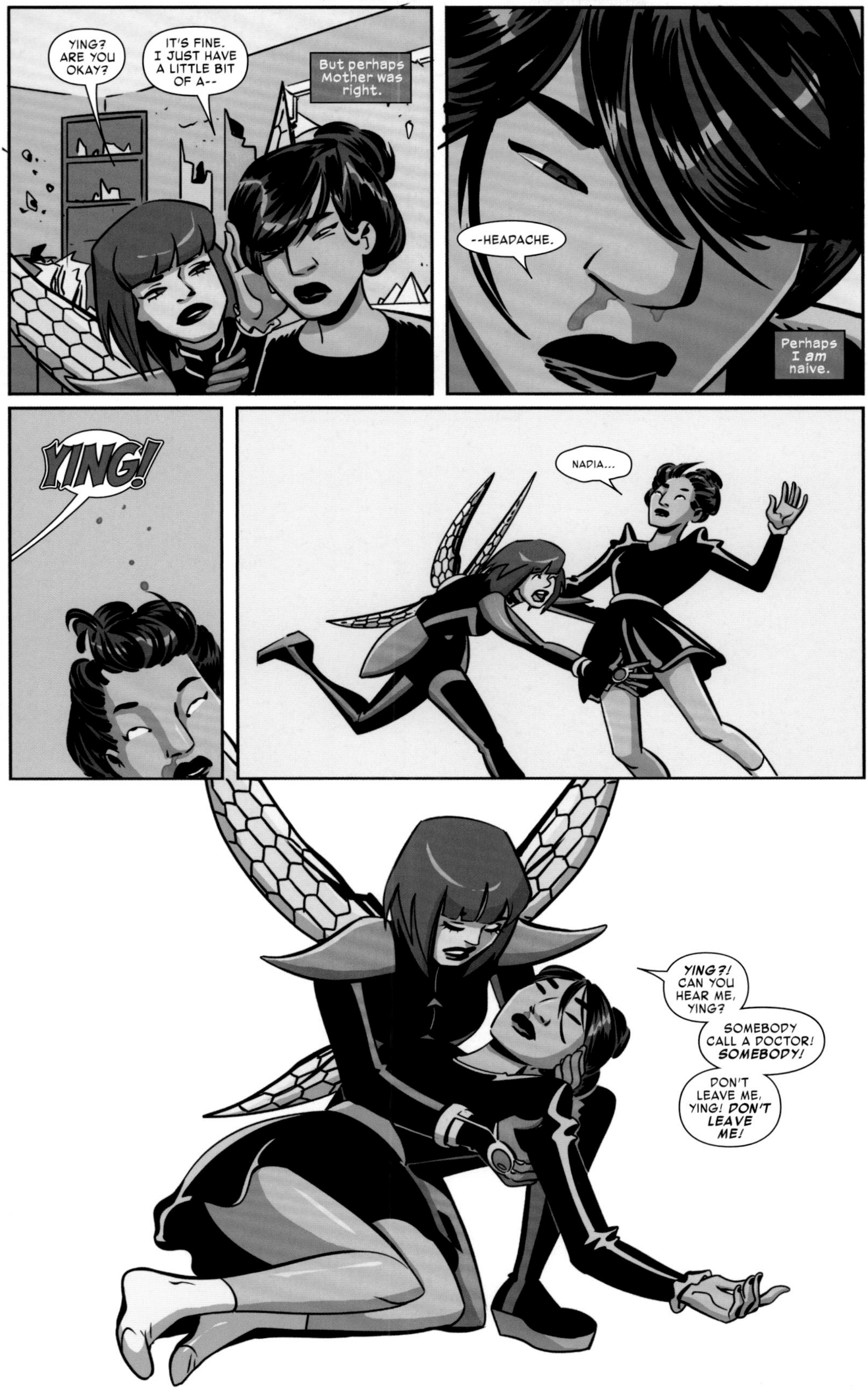

YING? ARE YOU OKAY?
IT'S FINE. I JUST HAVE A LITTLE BIT OF A--
But perhaps Mother was right.
--HEADACHE.
Perhaps I *am* naive.
YING!
NADIA...
YING?! CAN YOU HEAR ME, YING?
SOMEBODY CALL A DOCTOR! ***SOMEBODY!***
DON'T LEAVE ME, YING! ***DON'T LEAVE ME!***

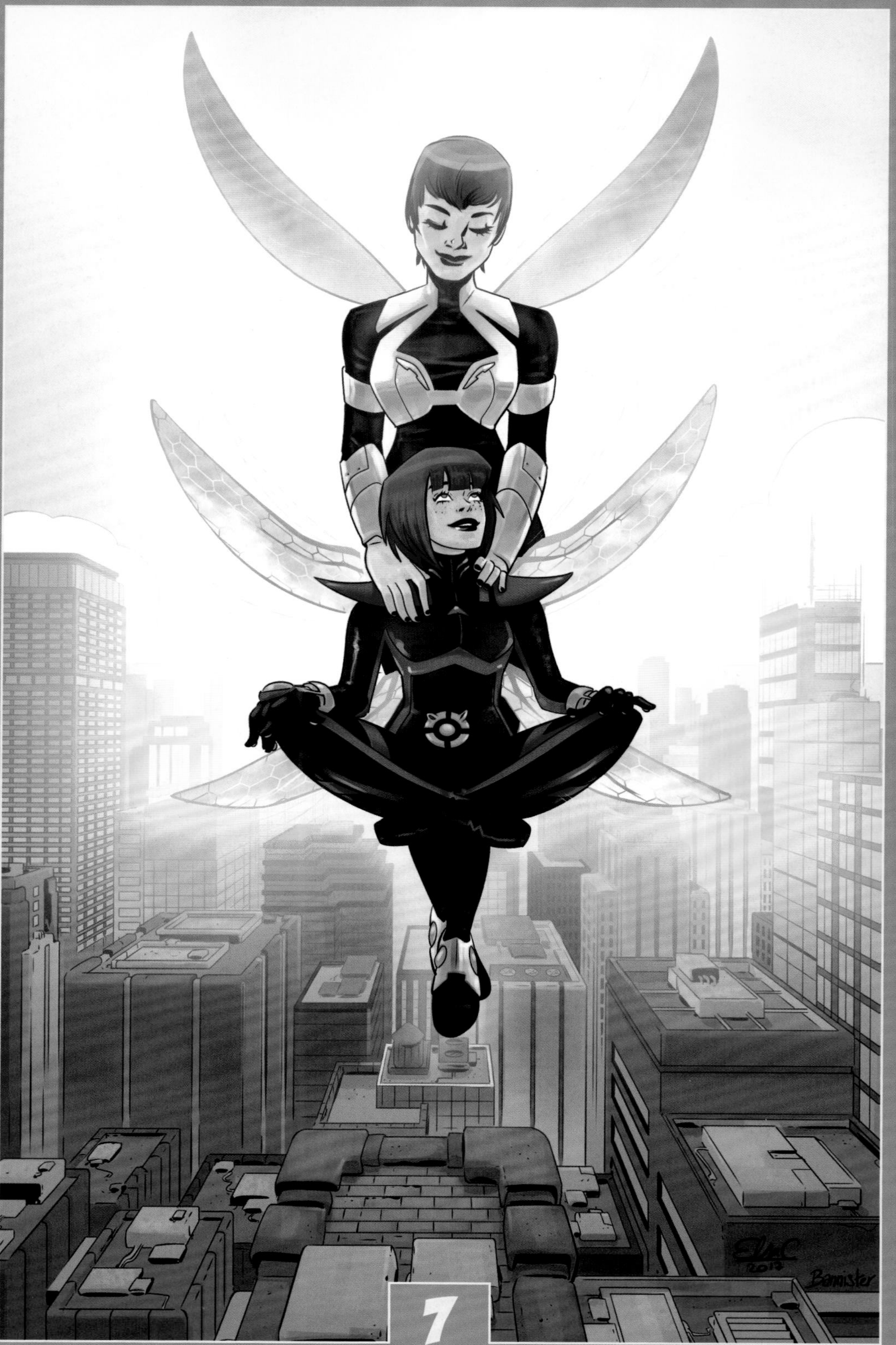
7

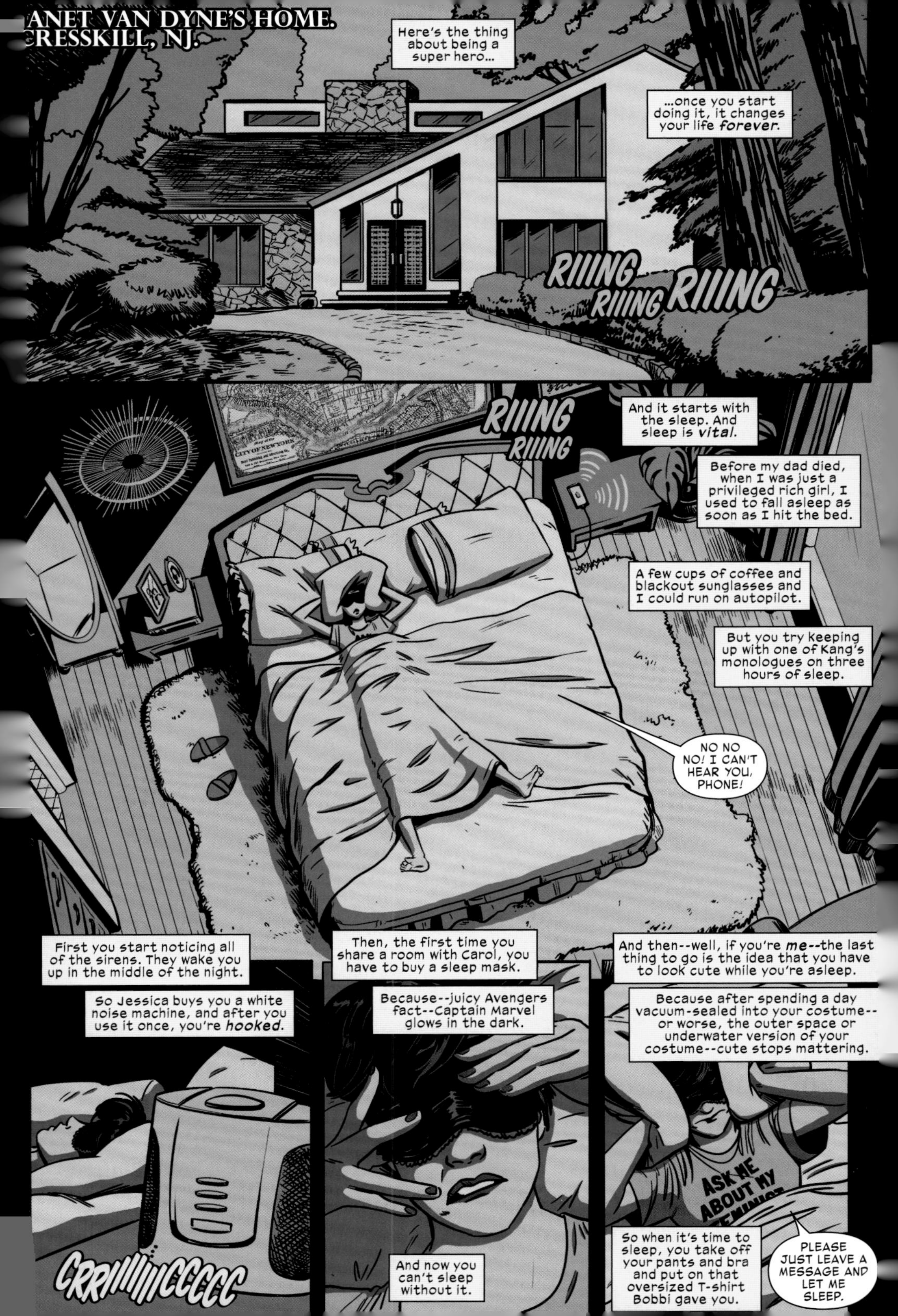

ANET VAN DYNE'S HOME.
CRESSKILL, NJ.
Here's the thing about being a super hero...
...once you start doing it, it changes your life forever.
RIIING RIIING RIIING
RIIING RIIING
And it starts with the sleep. And sleep is vital.
Before my dad died, when I was just a privileged rich girl, I used to fall asleep as soon as I hit the bed.
A few cups of coffee and blackout sunglasses and I could run on autopilot.
But you try keeping up with one of Kang's monologues on three hours of sleep.
NO NO NO! I CAN'T HEAR YOU, PHONE!
First you start noticing all of the sirens. They wake you up in the middle of the night.
So Jessica buys you a white noise machine, and after you use it once, you're hooked.
CRRIIIIIICCCCC
Then, the first time you share a room with Carol, you have to buy a sleep mask.
Because--juicy Avengers fact--Captain Marvel glows in the dark.
And now you can't sleep without it.
And then--well, if you're me--the last thing to go is the idea that you have to look cute while you're asleep.
Because after spending a day vacuum-sealed into your costume--or worse, the outer space or underwater version of your costume--cute stops mattering.
ASK ME ABOUT MY
So when it's time to sleep, you take off your pants and bra and put on that oversized T-shirt Bobbi gave you.
PLEASE JUST LEAVE A MESSAGE AND LET ME SLEEP.

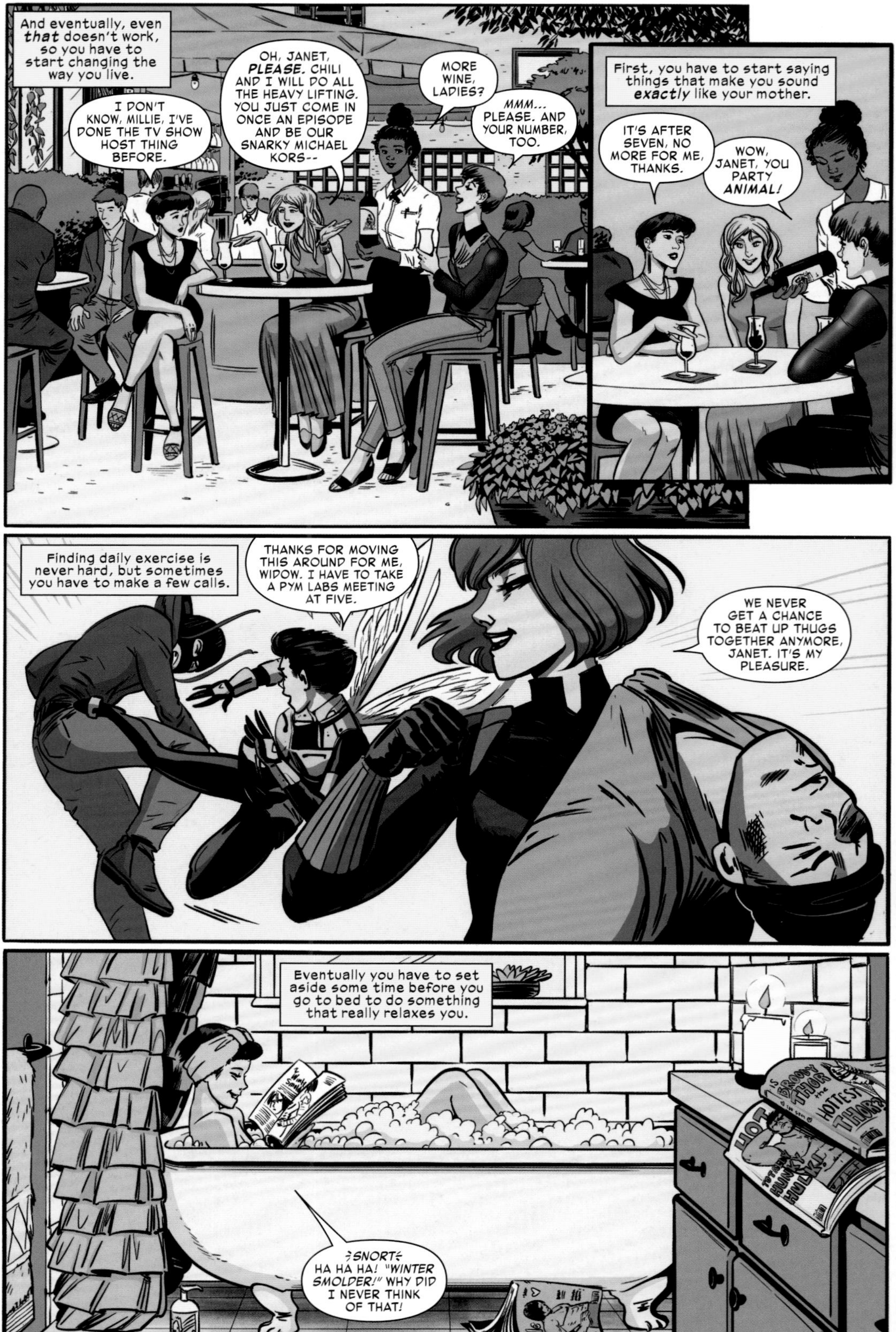

And eventually, even *that* doesn't work, so you have to start changing the way you live.
I DON'T KNOW, MILLIE, I'VE DONE THE TV SHOW HOST THING BEFORE.
OH, JANET, *PLEASE.* CHILI AND I WILL DO ALL THE HEAVY LIFTING. YOU JUST COME IN ONCE AN EPISODE AND BE OUR SNARKY MICHAEL KORS--
MORE WINE, LADIES?
MMM... PLEASE. AND YOUR NUMBER, TOO.
First, you have to start saying things that make you sound *exactly* like your mother.
IT'S AFTER SEVEN, NO MORE FOR ME, THANKS.
WOW, JANET, YOU PARTY *ANIMAL!*
Finding daily exercise is never hard, but sometimes you have to make a few calls.
THANKS FOR MOVING THIS AROUND FOR ME, WIDOW. I HAVE TO TAKE A PYM LABS MEETING AT FIVE.
WE NEVER GET A CHANCE TO BEAT UP THUGS TOGETHER ANYMORE, JANET. IT'S MY PLEASURE.
Eventually you have to set aside some time before you go to bed to do something that really relaxes you.
SNORT
HA HA HA! *"WINTER SMOLDER!"* WHY DID I NEVER THINK OF THAT!

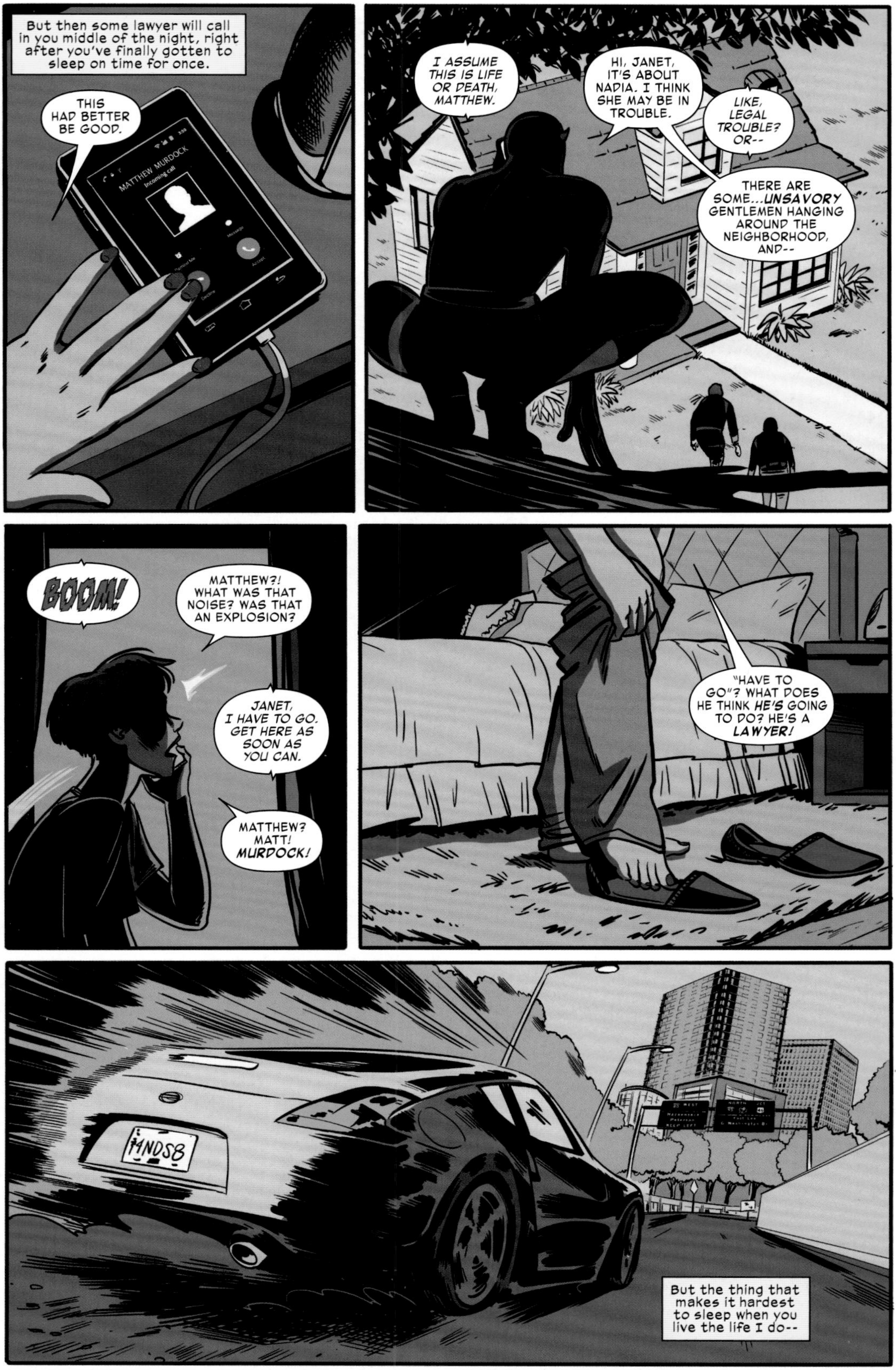

But then some lawyer will call in you middle of the night, right after you've finally gotten to sleep on time for once.
THIS HAD BETTER BE GOOD.
MATTHEW MURDOCK
Incoming call
I ASSUME THIS IS LIFE OR DEATH, MATTHEW.
HI, JANET, IT'S ABOUT NADIA. I THINK SHE MAY BE IN TROUBLE.
LIKE, LEGAL TROUBLE? OR--
THERE ARE SOME...UNSAVORY GENTLEMEN HANGING AROUND THE NEIGHBORHOOD, AND--
BOOM!
MATTHEW?! WHAT WAS THAT NOISE? WAS THAT AN EXPLOSION?
JANET, I HAVE TO GO. GET HERE AS SOON AS YOU CAN.
MATTHEW? MATT! MURDOCK!
"HAVE TO GO"? WHAT DOES HE THINK HE'S GOING TO DO? HE'S A LAWYER!
14NDS8
But the thing that makes it hardest to sleep when you live the life I do--

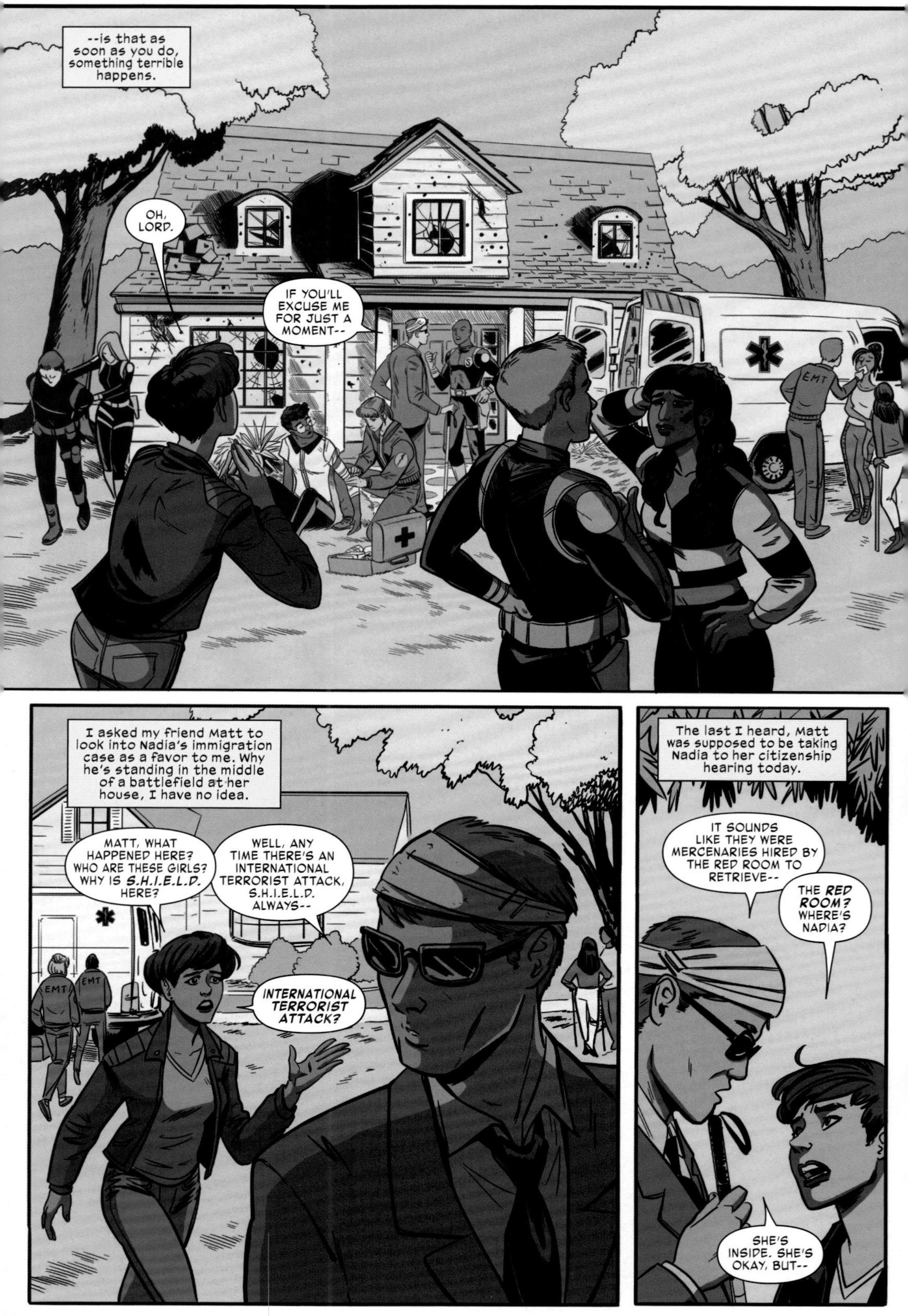
--is that as soon as you do, something terrible happens.
OH, LORD.
IF YOU'LL EXCUSE ME FOR JUST A MOMENT--
EMT
I asked my friend Matt to look into Nadia's immigration case as a favor to me. Why he's standing in the middle of a battlefield at her house, I have no idea.
MATT, WHAT HAPPENED HERE? WHO ARE THESE GIRLS? WHY IS S.H.I.E.L.D. HERE?
WELL, ANY TIME THERE'S AN INTERNATIONAL TERRORIST ATTACK, S.H.I.E.L.D. ALWAYS--
INTERNATIONAL TERRORIST ATTACK?
EMT
EMT
The last I heard, Matt was supposed to be taking Nadia to her citizenship hearing today.
IT SOUNDS LIKE THEY WERE MERCENARIES HIRED BY THE RED ROOM TO RETRIEVE--
THE RED ROOM? WHERE'S NADIA?
SHE'S INSIDE. SHE'S OKAY, BUT--

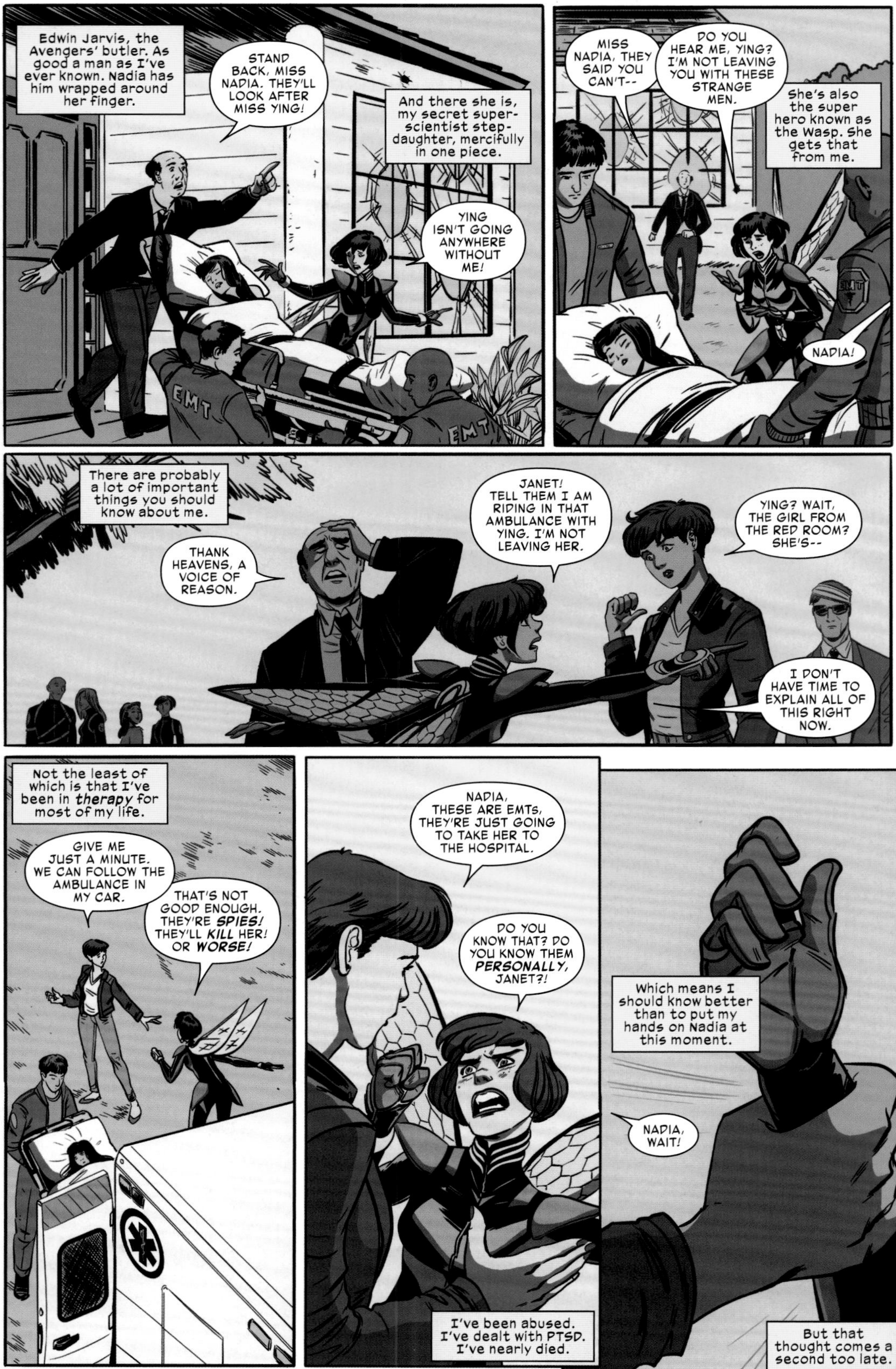
Edwin Jarvis, the Avengers' butler. As good a man as I've ever known. Nadia has him wrapped around her finger.
STAND BACK, MISS NADIA. THEY'LL LOOK AFTER MISS YING!
And there she is, my secret super-scientist step-daughter, mercifully in one piece.
YING ISN'T GOING ANYWHERE WITHOUT ME!
EMT
EMT
MISS NADIA, THEY SAID YOU CAN'T--
DO YOU HEAR ME, YING? I'M NOT LEAVING YOU WITH THESE STRANGE MEN.
She's also the super hero known as the Wasp. She gets that from me.
NADIA!
There are probably a lot of important things you should know about me.
THANK HEAVENS, A VOICE OF REASON.
JANET! TELL THEM I AM RIDING IN THAT AMBULANCE WITH YING. I'M NOT LEAVING HER.
YING? WAIT, THE GIRL FROM THE RED ROOM? SHE'S--
I DON'T HAVE TIME TO EXPLAIN ALL OF THIS RIGHT NOW.
Not the least of which is that I've been in *therapy* for most of my life.
GIVE ME JUST A MINUTE. WE CAN FOLLOW THE AMBULANCE IN MY CAR.
THAT'S NOT GOOD ENOUGH. THEY'RE ***SPIES!*** THEY'LL ***KILL*** HER! OR ***WORSE!***
NADIA, THESE ARE EMTS, THEY'RE JUST GOING TO TAKE HER TO THE HOSPITAL.
DO YOU KNOW THAT? DO YOU KNOW THEM ***PERSONALLY,*** JANET?!
I've been abused. I've dealt with PTSD. I've nearly died.
Which means I should know better than to put my hands on Nadia at this moment.
NADIA, WAIT!
But that thought comes a second too late.

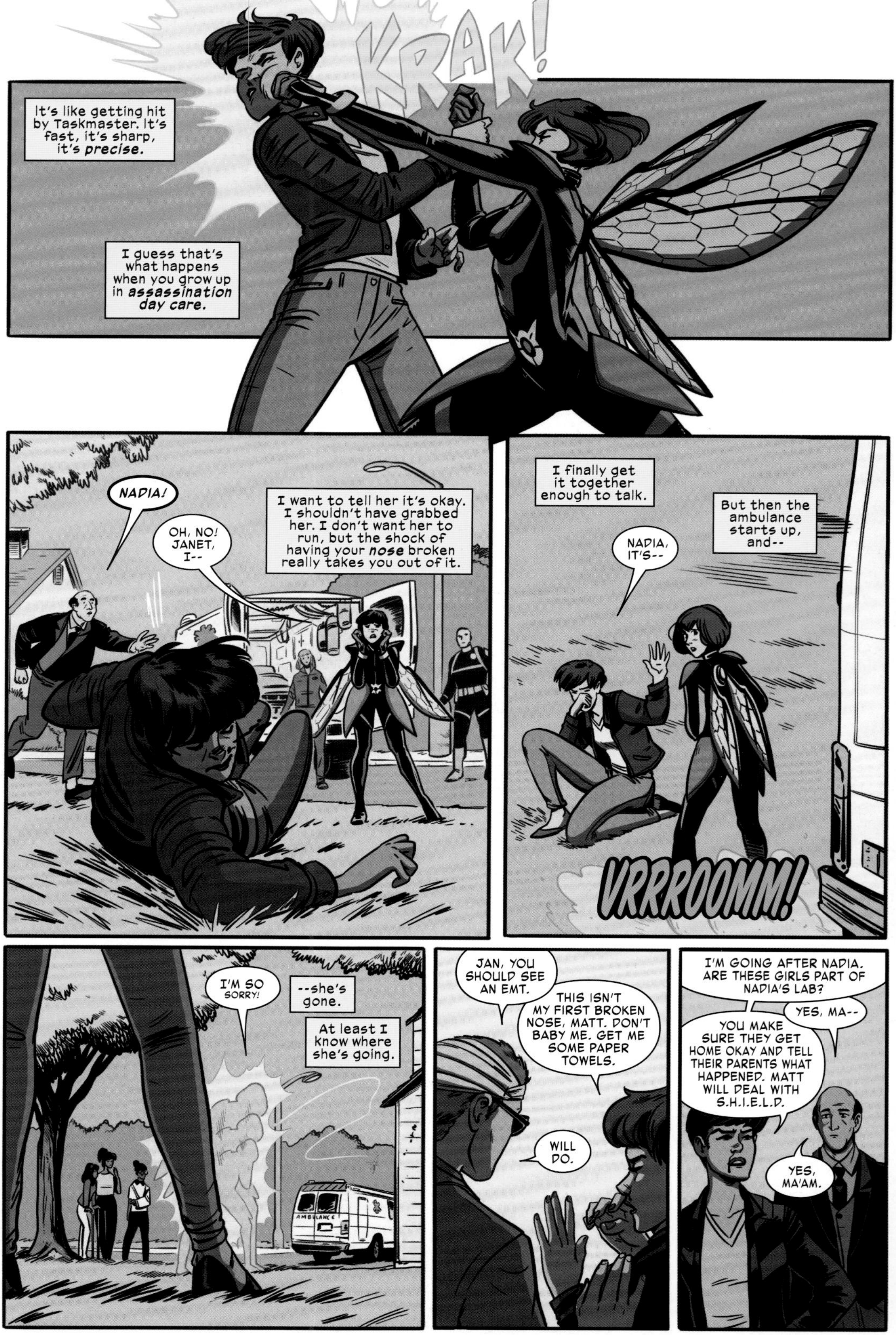
KRAK!
It's like getting hit by Taskmaster. It's fast, it's sharp, it's precise.
I guess that's what happens when you grow up in assassination day care.
NADIA!
OH, NO! JANET, I--
I want to tell her it's okay. I shouldn't have grabbed her. I don't want her to run, but the shock of having your nose broken really takes you out of it.
I finally get it together enough to talk.
NADIA, IT'S--
But then the ambulance starts up, and--
VRRROOMM!
I'M SO SORRY!
--she's gone.
At least I know where she's going.
AMBULANCE
JAN, YOU SHOULD SEE AN EMT.
THIS ISN'T MY FIRST BROKEN NOSE, MATT. DON'T BABY ME. GET ME SOME PAPER TOWELS.
WILL DO.
I'M GOING AFTER NADIA. ARE THESE GIRLS PART OF NADIA'S LAB?
YES, MA--
YOU MAKE SURE THEY GET HOME OKAY AND TELL THEIR PARENTS WHAT HAPPENED. MATT WILL DEAL WITH S.H.I.E.L.D.
YES, MA'AM.

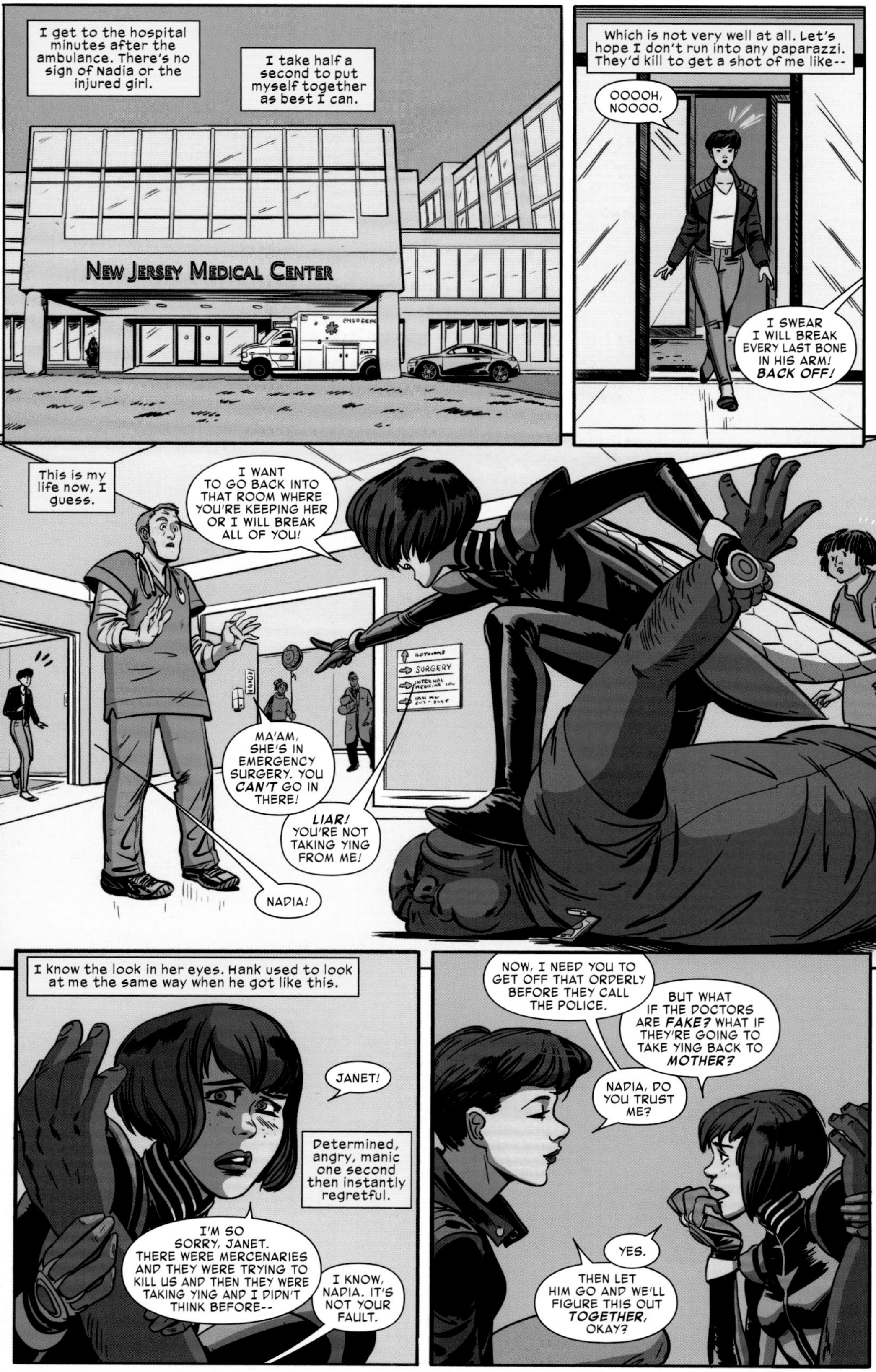
I get to the hospital minutes after the ambulance. There's no sign of Nadia or the injured girl.
I take half a second to put myself together as best I can.
NEW JERSEY MEDICAL CENTER
Which is not very well at all. Let's hope I don't run into any paparazzi. They'd kill to get a shot of me like--
OOOOH, NOOOO.
I SWEAR I WILL BREAK EVERY LAST BONE IN HIS ARM! BACK OFF!
This is my life now, I guess.
I WANT TO GO BACK INTO THAT ROOM WHERE YOU'RE KEEPING HER OR I WILL BREAK ALL OF YOU!
SURGERY
MA'AM, SHE'S IN EMERGENCY SURGERY. YOU CAN'T GO IN THERE!
LIAR! YOU'RE NOT TAKING YING FROM ME!
NADIA!
I know the look in her eyes. Hank used to look at me the same way when he got like this.
JANET!
Determined, angry, manic one second then instantly regretful.
I'M SO SORRY, JANET. THERE WERE MERCENARIES AND THEY WERE TRYING TO KILL US AND THEN THEY WERE TAKING YING AND I DIDN'T THINK BEFORE--
I KNOW, NADIA. IT'S NOT YOUR FAULT.
NOW, I NEED YOU TO GET OFF THAT ORDERLY BEFORE THEY CALL THE POLICE.
BUT WHAT IF THE DOCTORS ARE FAKE? WHAT IF THEY'RE GOING TO TAKE YING BACK TO MOTHER?
NADIA, DO YOU TRUST ME?
YES.
THEN LET HIM GO AND WE'LL FIGURE THIS OUT TOGETHER, OKAY?

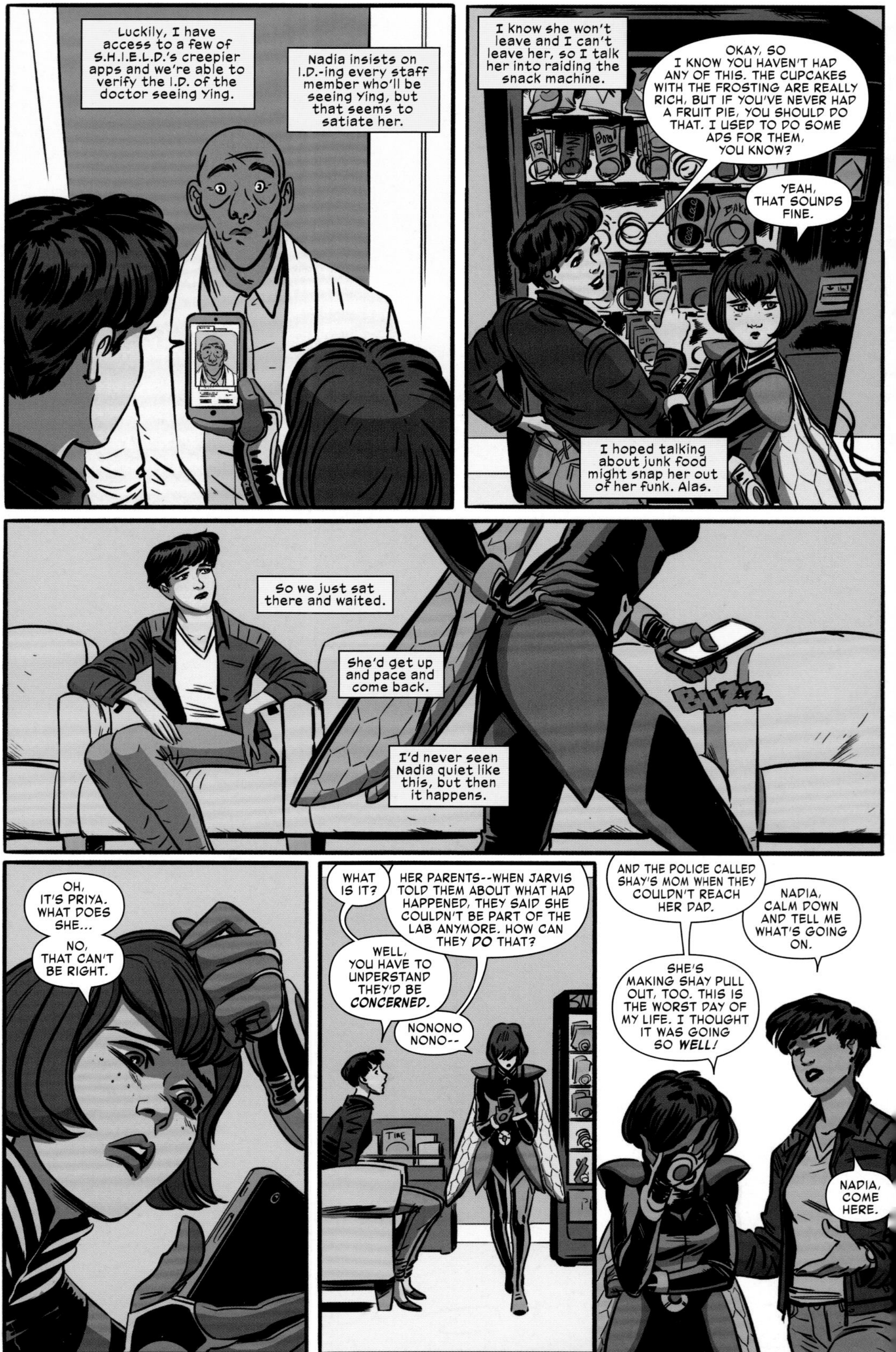

Luckily, I have access to a few of S.H.I.E.L.D.'s creepier apps and we're able to verify the I.D. of the doctor seeing Ying.
Nadia insists on I.D.-ing every staff member who'll be seeing Ying, but that seems to satiate her.
I know she won't leave and I can't leave her, so I talk her into raiding the snack machine.
OKAY, SO I KNOW YOU HAVEN'T HAD ANY OF THIS. THE CUPCAKES WITH THE FROSTING ARE REALLY RICH, BUT IF YOU'VE NEVER HAD A FRUIT PIE, YOU SHOULD DO THAT. I USED TO DO SOME ADS FOR THEM, YOU KNOW?
YEAH, THAT SOUNDS FINE.
I hoped talking about junk food might snap her out of her funk. Alas.
So we just sat there and waited.
She'd get up and pace and come back.
I'd never seen Nadia quiet like this, but then it happens.
BUZZ
OH, IT'S PRIYA. WHAT DOES SHE...
NO, THAT CAN'T BE RIGHT.
WHAT IS IT?
HER PARENTS--WHEN JARVIS TOLD THEM ABOUT WHAT HAD HAPPENED, THEY SAID SHE COULDN'T BE PART OF THE LAB ANYMORE. HOW CAN THEY DO THAT?
WELL, YOU HAVE TO UNDERSTAND THEY'D BE CONCERNED.
NONONO NONO--
AND THE POLICE CALLED SHAY'S MOM WHEN THEY COULDN'T REACH HER DAD.
NADIA, CALM DOWN AND TELL ME WHAT'S GOING ON.
SHE'S MAKING SHAY PULL OUT, TOO. THIS IS THE WORST DAY OF MY LIFE. I THOUGHT IT WAS GOING SO WELL!
NADIA, COME HERE.

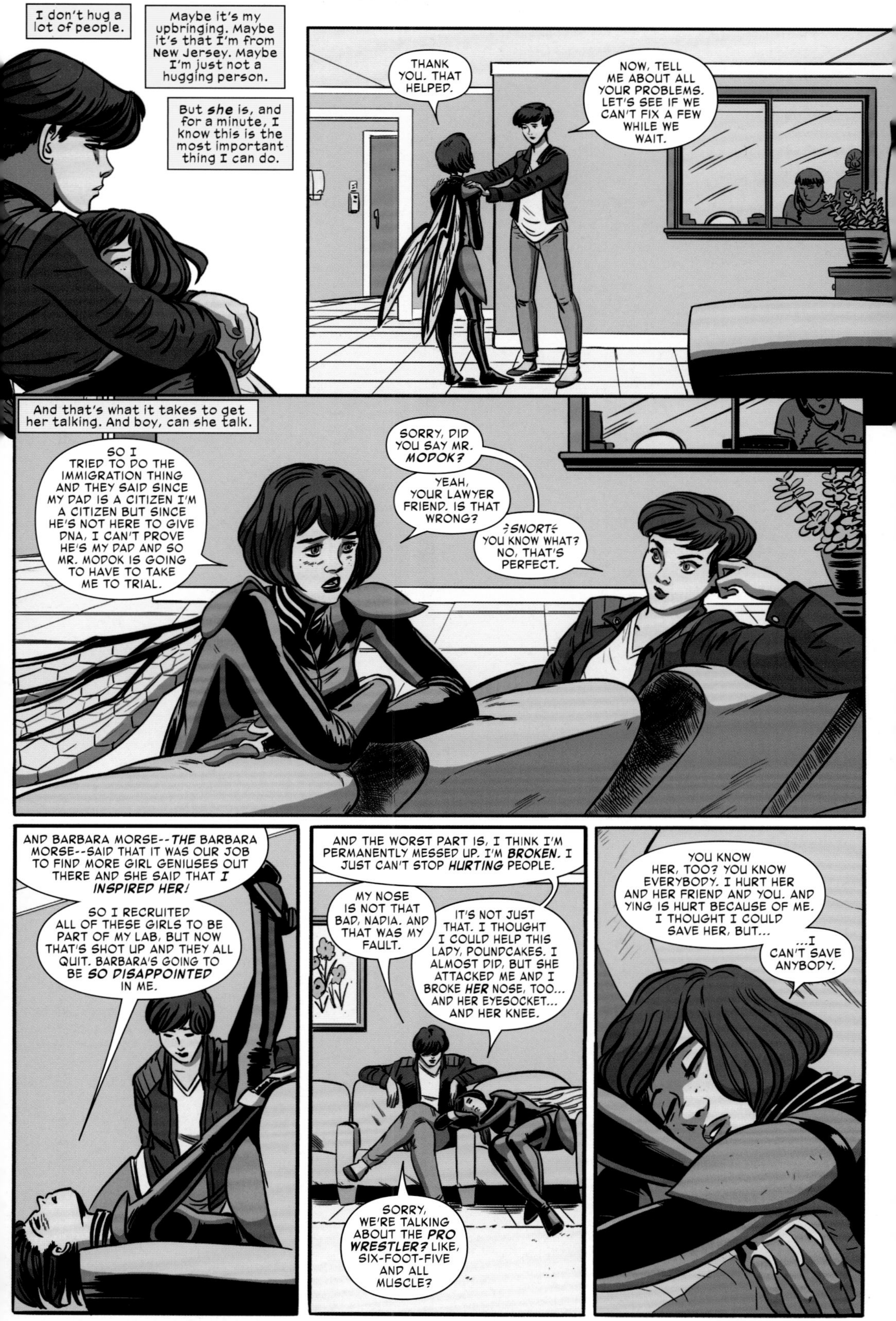

I don't hug a lot of people.
Maybe it's my upbringing. Maybe it's that I'm from New Jersey. Maybe I'm just not a hugging person.
But *she* is, and for a minute, I know this is the most important thing I can do.
THANK YOU. THAT HELPED.
NOW, TELL ME ABOUT ALL YOUR PROBLEMS. LET'S SEE IF WE CAN'T FIX A FEW WHILE WE WAIT.
And that's what it takes to get her talking. And boy, can she talk.
SO I TRIED TO DO THE IMMIGRATION THING AND THEY SAID SINCE MY DAD IS A CITIZEN I'M A CITIZEN BUT SINCE HE'S NOT HERE TO GIVE DNA, I CAN'T PROVE HE'S MY DAD AND SO MR. MODOK IS GOING TO HAVE TO TAKE ME TO TRIAL.
SORRY, DID YOU SAY MR. *MODOK?*
YEAH, YOUR LAWYER FRIEND. IS THAT WRONG?
SNORT YOU KNOW WHAT? NO, THAT'S PERFECT.
AND BARBARA MORSE--*THE* BARBARA MORSE--SAID THAT IT WAS OUR JOB TO FIND MORE GIRL GENIUSES OUT THERE AND SHE SAID THAT *I INSPIRED HER!*
SO I RECRUITED ALL OF THESE GIRLS TO BE PART OF MY LAB, BUT NOW THAT'S SHOT UP AND THEY ALL QUIT. BARBARA'S GOING TO BE *SO DISAPPOINTED* IN ME.
AND THE WORST PART IS, I THINK I'M PERMANENTLY MESSED UP. I'M *BROKEN.* I JUST CAN'T STOP *HURTING* PEOPLE.
MY NOSE IS NOT THAT BAD, NADIA, AND THAT WAS MY FAULT.
IT'S NOT JUST THAT. I THOUGHT I COULD HELP THIS LADY, POUNDCAKES. I ALMOST DID, BUT SHE ATTACKED ME AND I BROKE *HER* NOSE, TOO... AND HER EYESOCKET... AND HER KNEE.
SORRY, WE'RE TALKING ABOUT THE *PRO WRESTLER?* LIKE, SIX-FOOT-FIVE AND ALL MUSCLE?
YOU KNOW HER, TOO? YOU KNOW EVERYBODY. I HURT HER AND HER FRIEND AND YOU. AND YING IS HURT BECAUSE OF ME. I THOUGHT I COULD SAVE HER, BUT...
...I CAN'T SAVE ANYBODY.

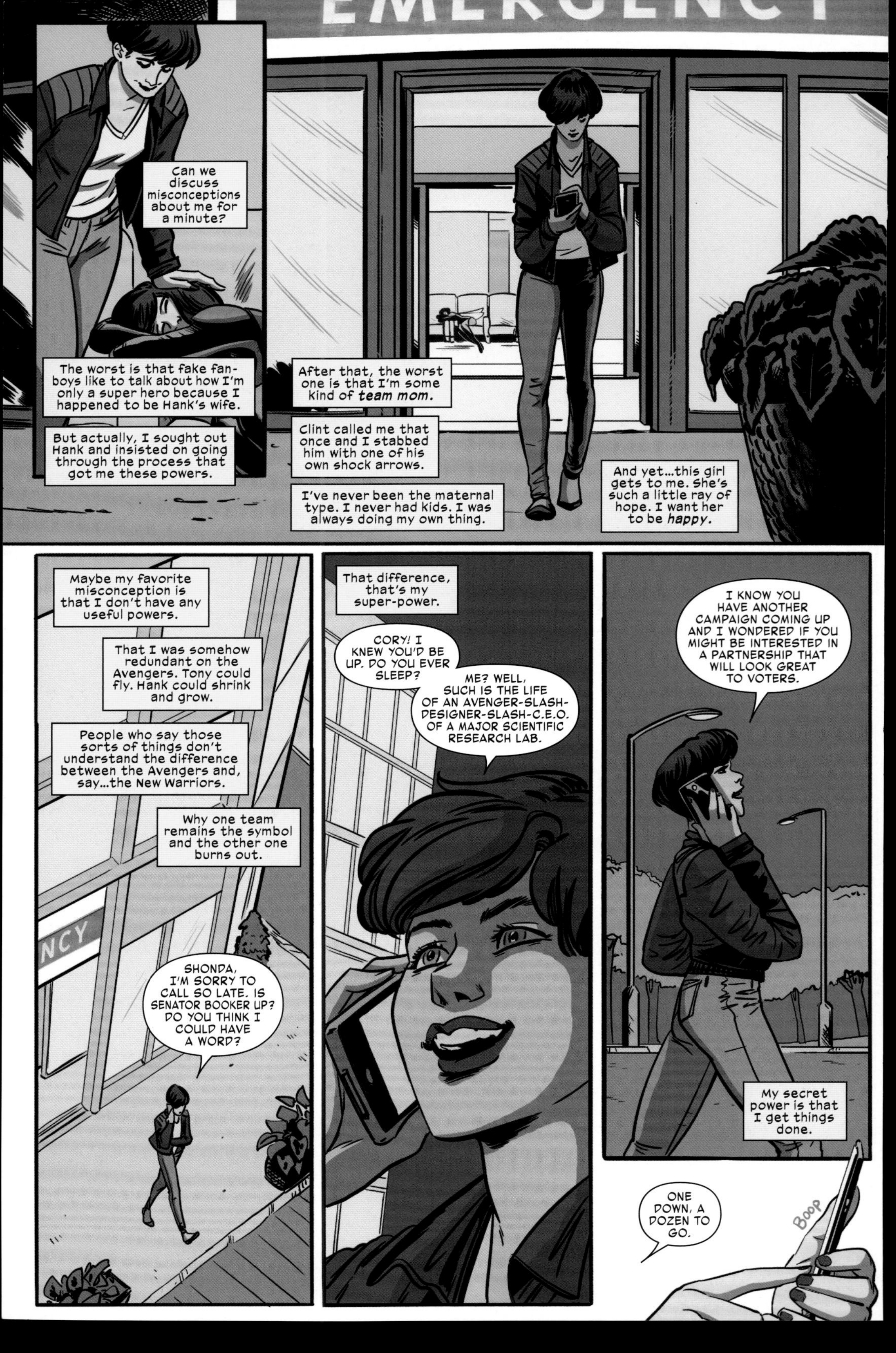
EMERGENCY
Can we discuss misconceptions about me for a minute?
The worst is that fake fanboys like to talk about how I'm only a super hero because I happened to be Hank's wife.
But actually, I sought out Hank and insisted on going through the process that got me these powers.
After that, the worst one is that I'm some kind of *team mom.*
Clint called me that once and I stabbed him with one of his own shock arrows.
I've never been the maternal type. I never had kids. I was always doing my own thing.
And yet...this girl gets to me. She's such a little ray of hope. I want her to be *happy.*
Maybe my favorite misconception is that I don't have any useful powers.
That I was somehow redundant on the Avengers. Tony could fly. Hank could shrink and grow.
People who say those sorts of things don't understand the difference between the Avengers and, say...the New Warriors.
Why one team remains the symbol and the other one burns out.
NCY
SHONDA, I'M SORRY TO CALL SO LATE. IS SENATOR BOOKER UP? DO YOU THINK I COULD HAVE A WORD?
That difference, that's my super-power.
CORY! I KNEW YOU'D BE UP. DO YOU EVER SLEEP?
ME? WELL, SUCH IS THE LIFE OF AN AVENGER-SLASH-DESIGNER-SLASH-C.E.O. OF A MAJOR SCIENTIFIC RESEARCH LAB.
I KNOW YOU HAVE ANOTHER CAMPAIGN COMING UP AND I WONDERED IF YOU MIGHT BE INTERESTED IN A PARTNERSHIP THAT WILL LOOK GREAT TO VOTERS.
My secret power is that I get things done.
ONE DOWN, A DOZEN TO GO.
BOOP

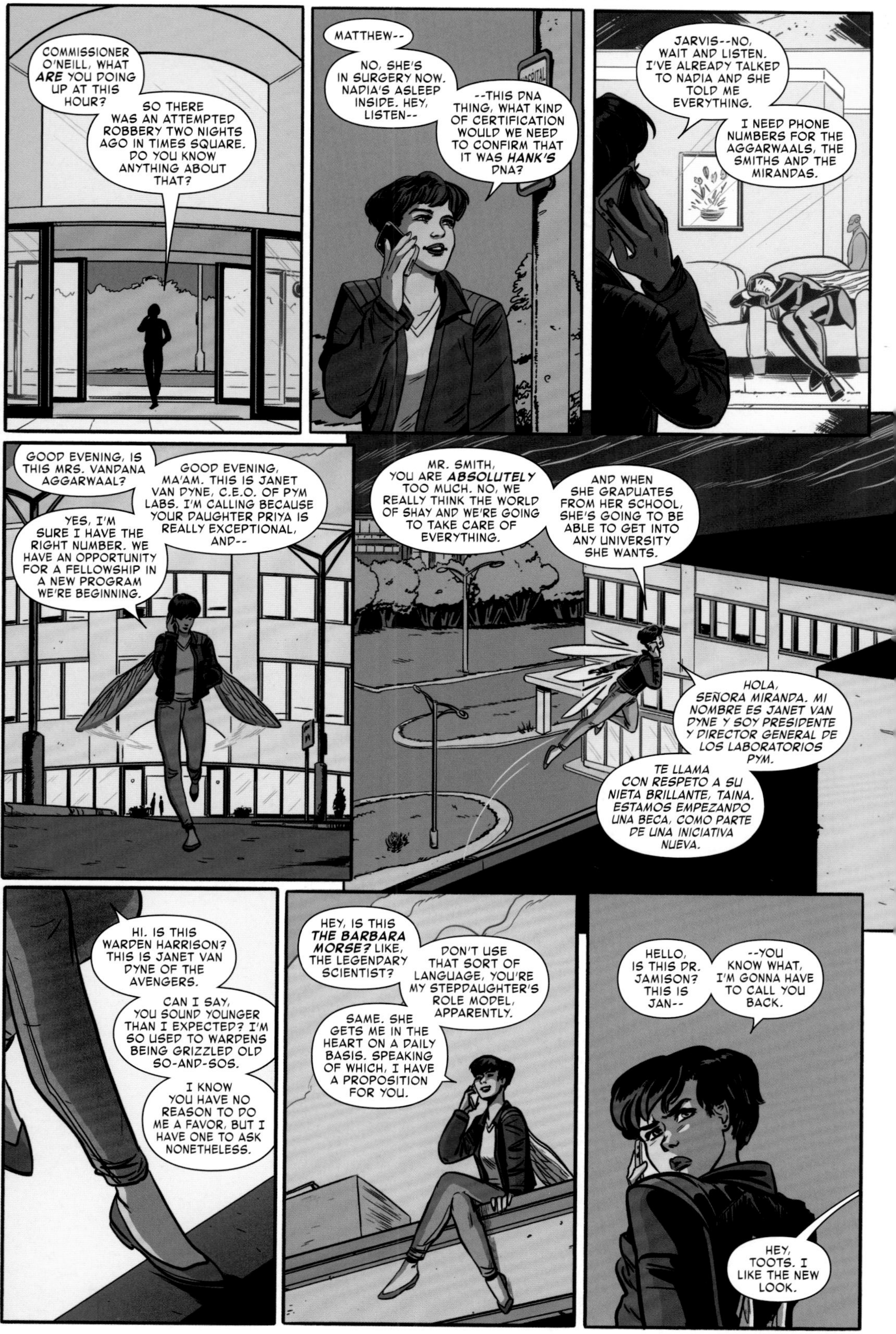
COMMISSIONER O'NEILL, WHAT ARE YOU DOING UP AT THIS HOUR?
SO THERE WAS AN ATTEMPTED ROBBERY TWO NIGHTS AGO IN TIMES SQUARE. DO YOU KNOW ANYTHING ABOUT THAT?
MATTHEW--
NO, SHE'S IN SURGERY NOW. NADIA'S ASLEEP INSIDE. HEY, LISTEN--
--THIS DNA THING, WHAT KIND OF CERTIFICATION WOULD WE NEED TO CONFIRM THAT IT WAS HANK'S DNA?
JARVIS--NO, WAIT AND LISTEN. I'VE ALREADY TALKED TO NADIA AND SHE TOLD ME EVERYTHING.
I NEED PHONE NUMBERS FOR THE AGGARWAALS, THE SMITHS AND THE MIRANDAS.
GOOD EVENING, IS THIS MRS. VANDANA AGGARWAAL?
GOOD EVENING, MA'AM. THIS IS JANET VAN DYNE, C.E.O. OF PYM LABS. I'M CALLING BECAUSE YOUR DAUGHTER PRIYA IS REALLY EXCEPTIONAL, AND--
YES, I'M SURE I HAVE THE RIGHT NUMBER. WE HAVE AN OPPORTUNITY FOR A FELLOWSHIP IN A NEW PROGRAM WE'RE BEGINNING.
MR. SMITH, YOU ARE ABSOLUTELY TOO MUCH. NO, WE REALLY THINK THE WORLD OF SHAY AND WE'RE GOING TO TAKE CARE OF EVERYTHING.
AND WHEN SHE GRADUATES FROM HER SCHOOL, SHE'S GOING TO BE ABLE TO GET INTO ANY UNIVERSITY SHE WANTS.
HOLA, SEÑORA MIRANDA. MI NOMBRE ES JANET VAN DYNE Y SOY PRESIDENTE Y DIRECTOR GENERAL DE LOS LABORATORIOS PYM.
TE LLAMA CON RESPETO A SU NIETA BRILLANTE, TAINA. ESTAMOS EMPEZANDO UNA BECA, COMO PARTE DE UNA INICIATIVA NUEVA.
HI. IS THIS WARDEN HARRISON? THIS IS JANET VAN DYNE OF THE AVENGERS.
CAN I SAY, YOU SOUND YOUNGER THAN I EXPECTED? I'M SO USED TO WARDENS BEING GRIZZLED OLD SO-AND-SOS.
I KNOW YOU HAVE NO REASON TO DO ME A FAVOR, BUT I HAVE ONE TO ASK NONETHELESS.
HEY, IS THIS THE BARBARA MORSE? LIKE, THE LEGENDARY SCIENTIST?
DON'T USE THAT SORT OF LANGUAGE, YOU'RE MY STEPDAUGHTER'S ROLE MODEL, APPARENTLY.
SAME. SHE GETS ME IN THE HEART ON A DAILY BASIS. SPEAKING OF WHICH, I HAVE A PROPOSITION FOR YOU.
HELLO, IS THIS DR. JAMISON? THIS IS JAN--
--YOU KNOW WHAT, I'M GONNA HAVE TO CALL YOU BACK.
HEY, TOOTS. I LIKE THE NEW LOOK.

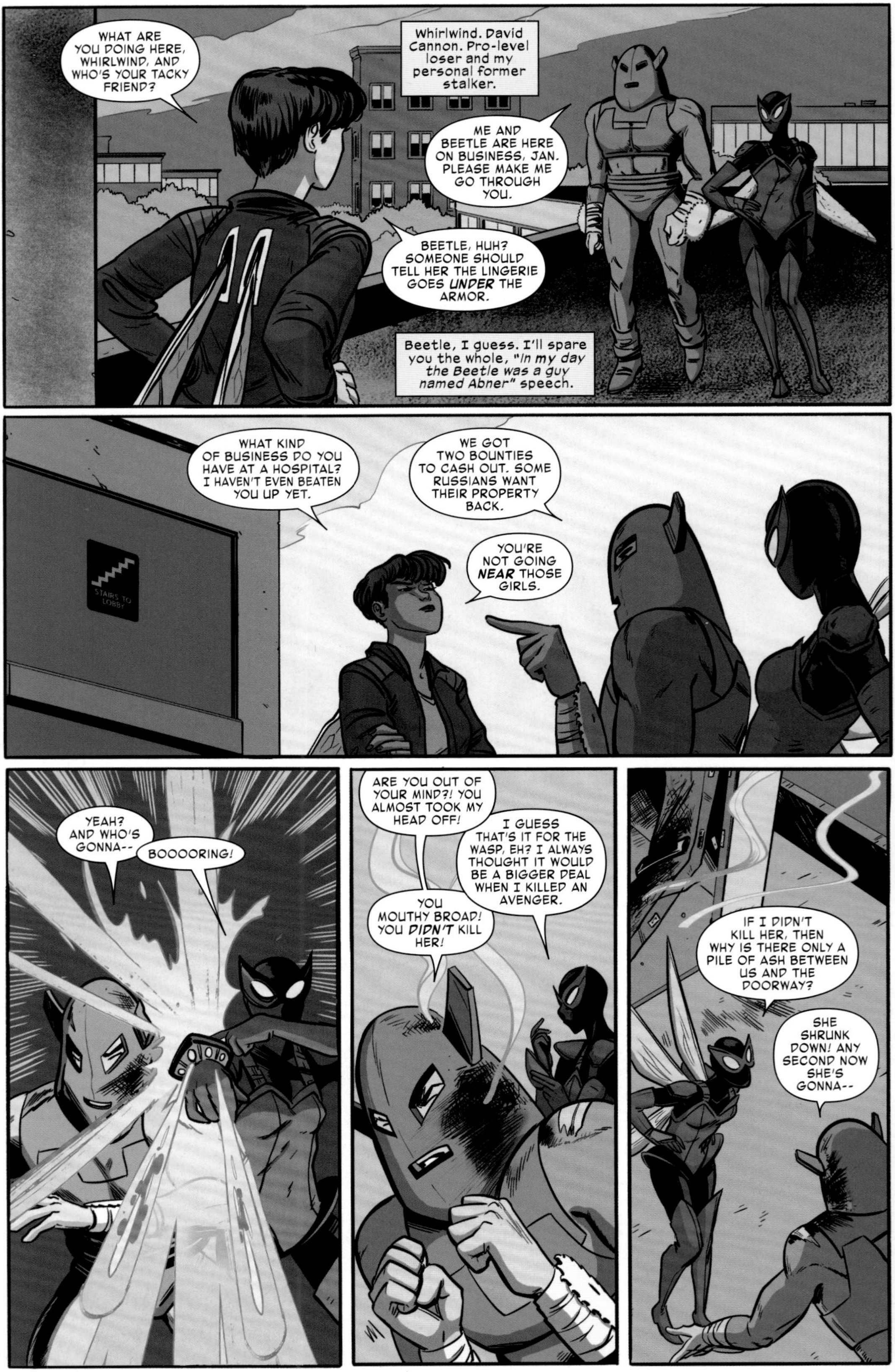

WHAT ARE YOU DOING HERE, WHIRLWIND, AND WHO'S YOUR TACKY FRIEND?
Whirlwind. David Cannon. Pro-level loser and my personal former stalker.
ME AND BEETLE ARE HERE ON BUSINESS, JAN. PLEASE MAKE ME GO THROUGH YOU.
BEETLE, HUH? SOMEONE SHOULD TELL HER THE LINGERIE GOES *UNDER* THE ARMOR.
Beetle, I guess. I'll spare you the whole, "*In my day the Beetle was a guy named Abner*" speech.
WHAT KIND OF BUSINESS DO YOU HAVE AT A HOSPITAL? I HAVEN'T EVEN BEATEN YOU UP YET.
WE GOT TWO BOUNTIES TO CASH OUT. SOME RUSSIANS WANT THEIR PROPERTY BACK.
STAIRS TO LOBBY
YOU'RE NOT GOING *NEAR* THOSE GIRLS.
YEAH? AND WHO'S GONNA--
BOOOORING!
ARE YOU OUT OF YOUR MIND?! YOU ALMOST TOOK MY HEAD OFF!
I GUESS THAT'S IT FOR THE WASP, EH? I ALWAYS THOUGHT IT WOULD BE A BIGGER DEAL WHEN I KILLED AN AVENGER.
YOU MOUTHY BROAD! YOU *DIDN'T* KILL HER!
IF I DIDN'T KILL HER, THEN WHY IS THERE ONLY A PILE OF ASH BETWEEN US AND THE DOORWAY?
SHE SHRUNK DOWN! ANY SECOND NOW SHE'S GONNA--

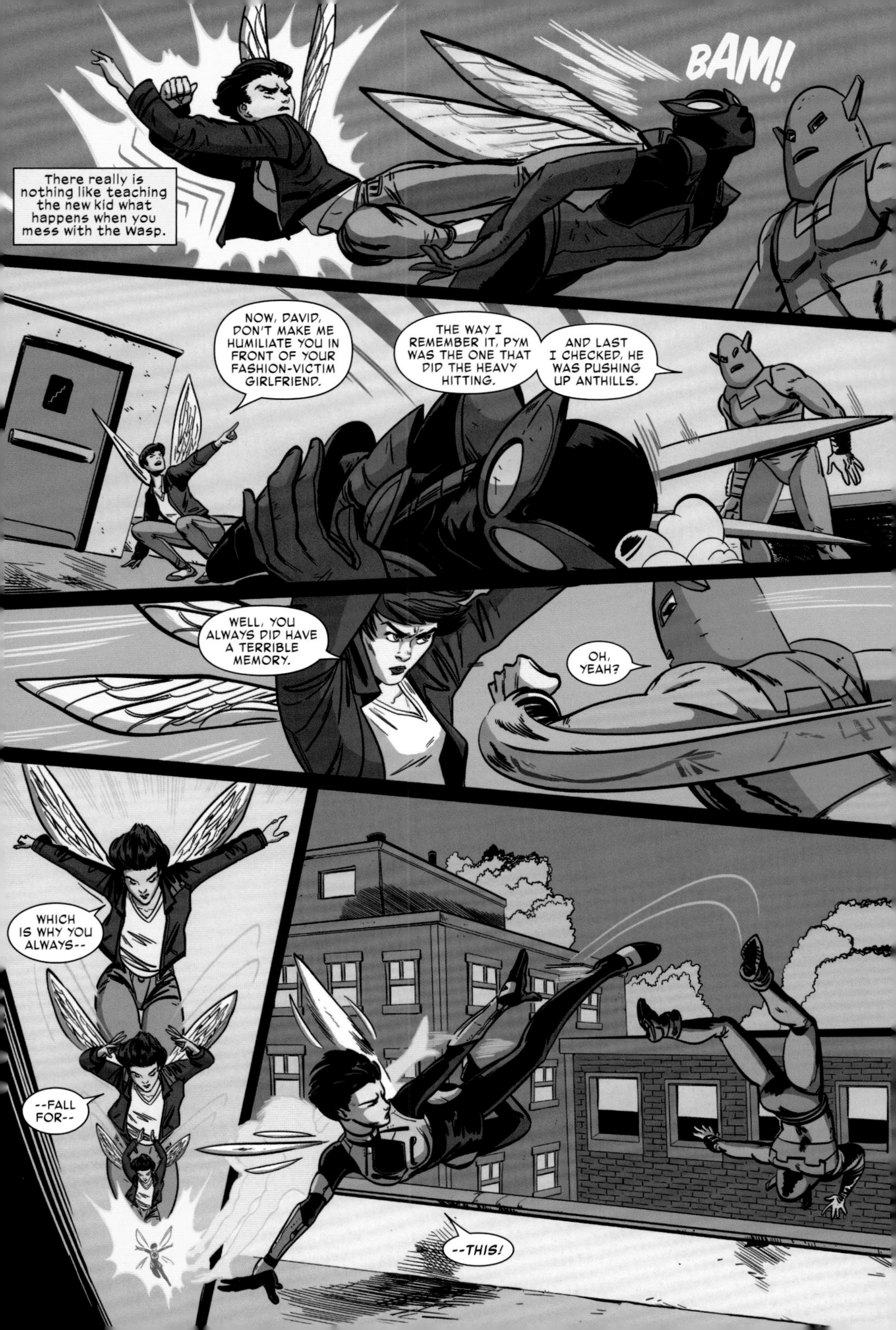
BAM!
There really is nothing like teaching the new kid what happens when you mess with the Wasp.
NOW, DAVID, DON'T MAKE ME HUMILIATE YOU IN FRONT OF YOUR FASHION-VICTIM GIRLFRIEND.
THE WAY I REMEMBER IT, PYM WAS THE ONE THAT DID THE HEAVY HITTING.
AND LAST I CHECKED, HE WAS PUSHING UP ANTHILLS.
WELL, YOU ALWAYS DID HAVE A TERRIBLE MEMORY.
OH, YEAH?
WHICH IS WHY YOU ALWAYS--
--FALL FOR--
--THIS!

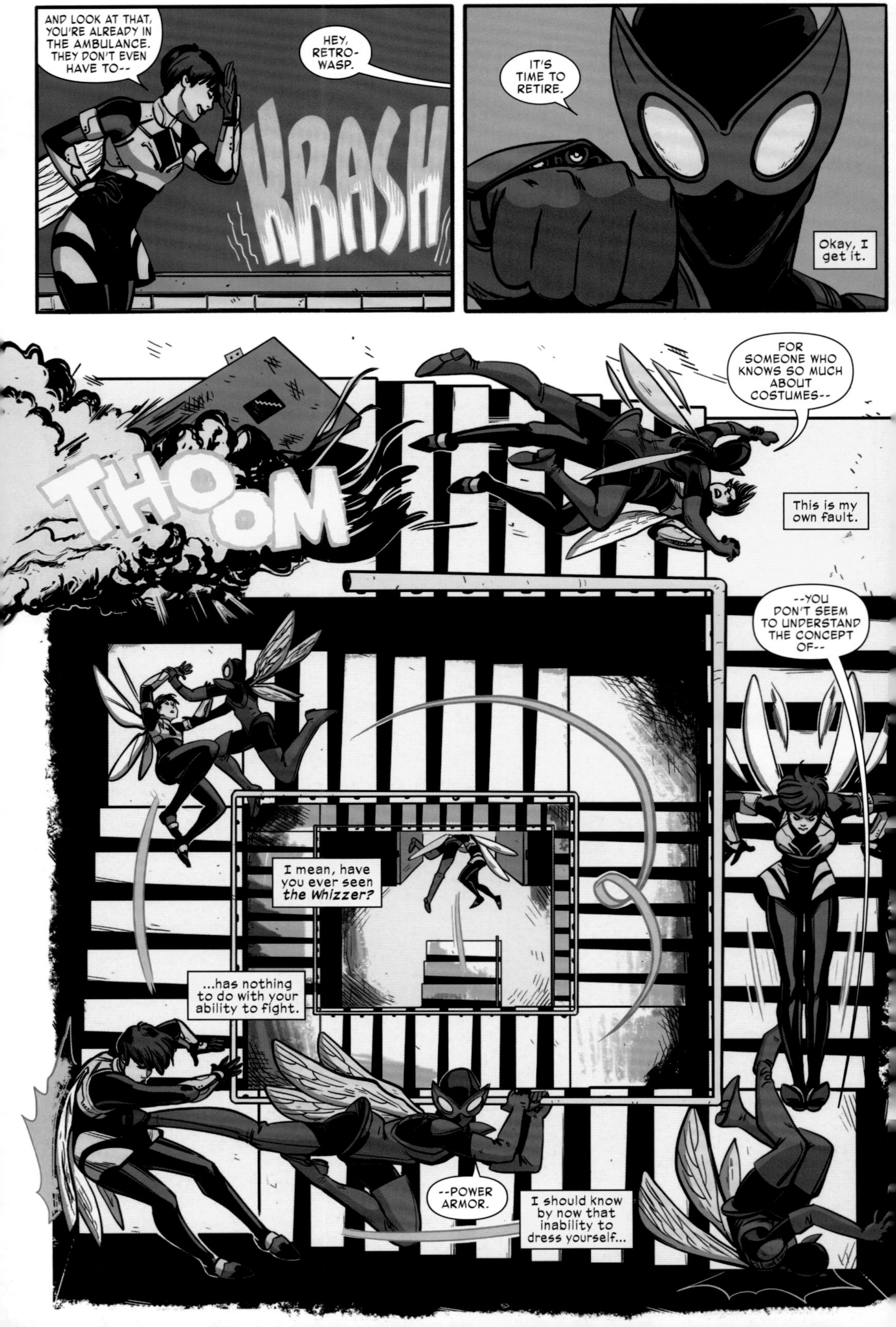
AND LOOK AT THAT, YOU'RE ALREADY IN THE AMBULANCE. THEY DON'T EVEN HAVE TO--
HEY, RETRO-WASP.
KRASH
IT'S TIME TO RETIRE.
Okay, I get it.
THOOM
FOR SOMEONE WHO KNOWS SO MUCH ABOUT COSTUMES--
This is my own fault.
--YOU DON'T SEEM TO UNDERSTAND THE CONCEPT OF--
I mean, have you ever seen the Whizzer?
...has nothing to do with your ability to fight.
--POWER ARMOR.
I should know by now that inability to dress yourself...

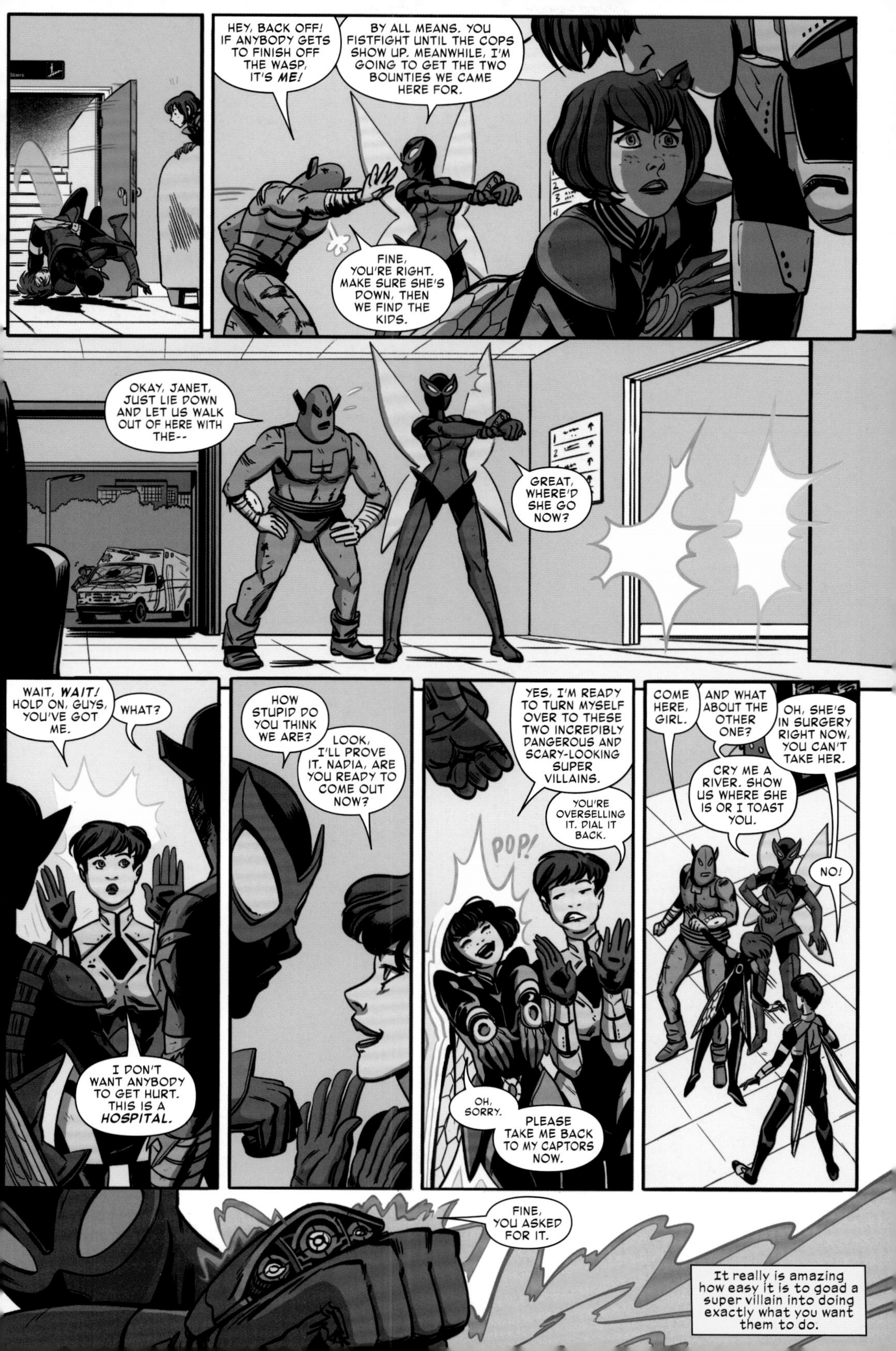

Stairs
HEY, BACK OFF! IF ANYBODY GETS TO FINISH OFF THE WASP, IT'S *ME!*
BY ALL MEANS. YOU FISTFIGHT UNTIL THE COPS SHOW UP. MEANWHILE, I'M GOING TO GET THE TWO BOUNTIES WE CAME HERE FOR.
FINE, YOU'RE RIGHT. MAKE SURE SHE'S DOWN, THEN WE FIND THE KIDS.
OKAY, JANET, JUST LIE DOWN AND LET US WALK OUT OF HERE WITH THE--
GREAT, WHERE'D SHE GO NOW?
WAIT, *WAIT!* HOLD ON, GUYS, YOU'VE GOT ME.
WHAT?
I DON'T WANT ANYBODY TO GET HURT. THIS IS A *HOSPITAL.*
HOW STUPID DO YOU THINK WE ARE?
LOOK, I'LL PROVE IT. NADIA, ARE YOU READY TO COME OUT NOW?
YES, I'M READY TO TURN MYSELF OVER TO THESE TWO INCREDIBLY DANGEROUS AND SCARY-LOOKING SUPER VILLAINS.
POP!
YOU'RE OVERSELLING IT. DIAL IT BACK.
OH, SORRY.
PLEASE TAKE ME BACK TO MY CAPTORS NOW.
COME HERE, GIRL.
AND WHAT ABOUT THE OTHER ONE?
OH, SHE'S IN SURGERY RIGHT NOW, YOU CAN'T TAKE HER.
CRY ME A RIVER. SHOW US WHERE SHE IS OR I TOAST YOU.
NO!
FINE, YOU ASKED FOR IT.
It really is amazing how easy it is to goad a super villain into doing exactly what you want them to do.

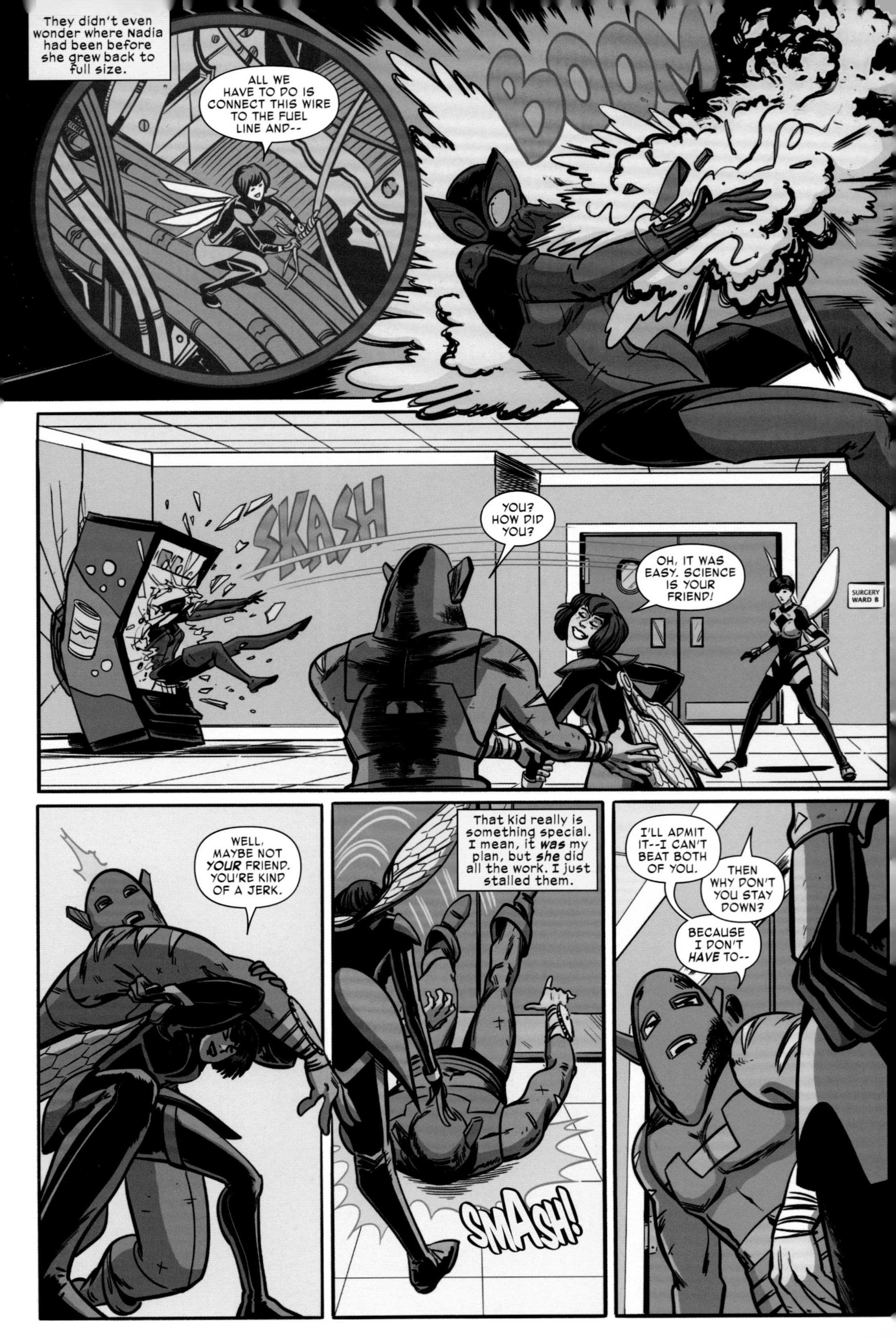

They didn't even wonder where Nadia had been before she grew back to full size.
ALL WE HAVE TO DO IS CONNECT THIS WIRE TO THE FUEL LINE AND--
BOOM
SKASH
YOU? HOW DID YOU?
OH, IT WAS EASY. SCIENCE IS YOUR FRIEND!
SURGERY WARD B
WELL, MAYBE NOT YOUR FRIEND. YOU'RE KIND OF A JERK.
That kid really is something special. I mean, it was my plan, but she did all the work. I just stalled them.
SMASH!
I'LL ADMIT IT--I CAN'T BEAT BOTH OF YOU.
THEN WHY DON'T YOU STAY DOWN?
BECAUSE I DON'T HAVE TO--

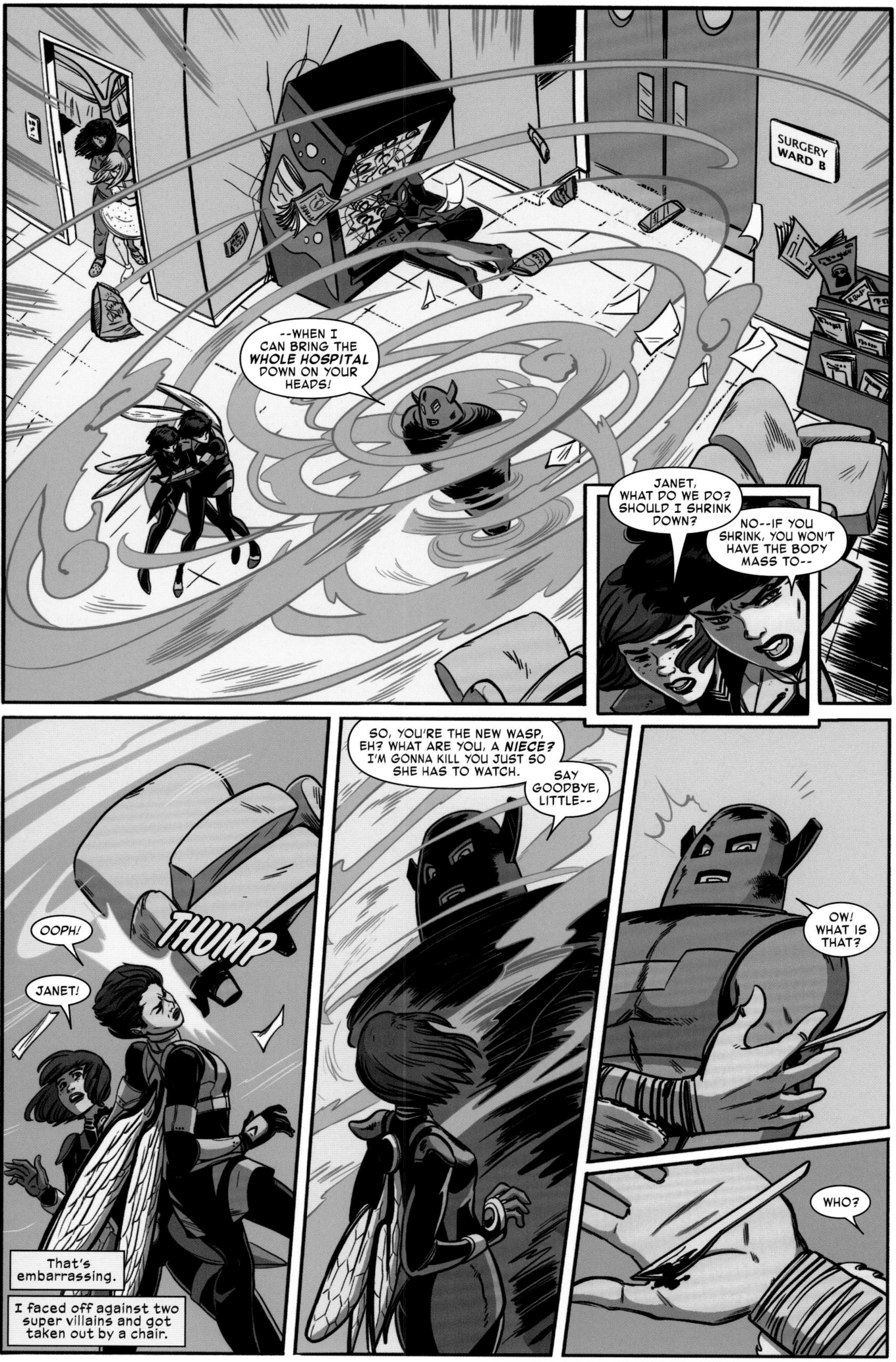
SURGERY WARD B
--WHEN I CAN BRING THE WHOLE HOSPITAL DOWN ON YOUR HEADS!
JANET, WHAT DO WE DO? SHOULD I SHRINK DOWN?
NO--IF YOU SHRINK, YOU WON'T HAVE THE BODY MASS TO--
OOPH!
THUMP
JANET!
That's embarrassing.
I faced off against two super villains and got taken out by a chair.
SO, YOU'RE THE NEW WASP, EH? WHAT ARE YOU, A NIECE? I'M GONNA KILL YOU JUST SO SHE HAS TO WATCH.
SAY GOODBYE, LITTLE--
OW! WHAT IS THAT?
WHO?

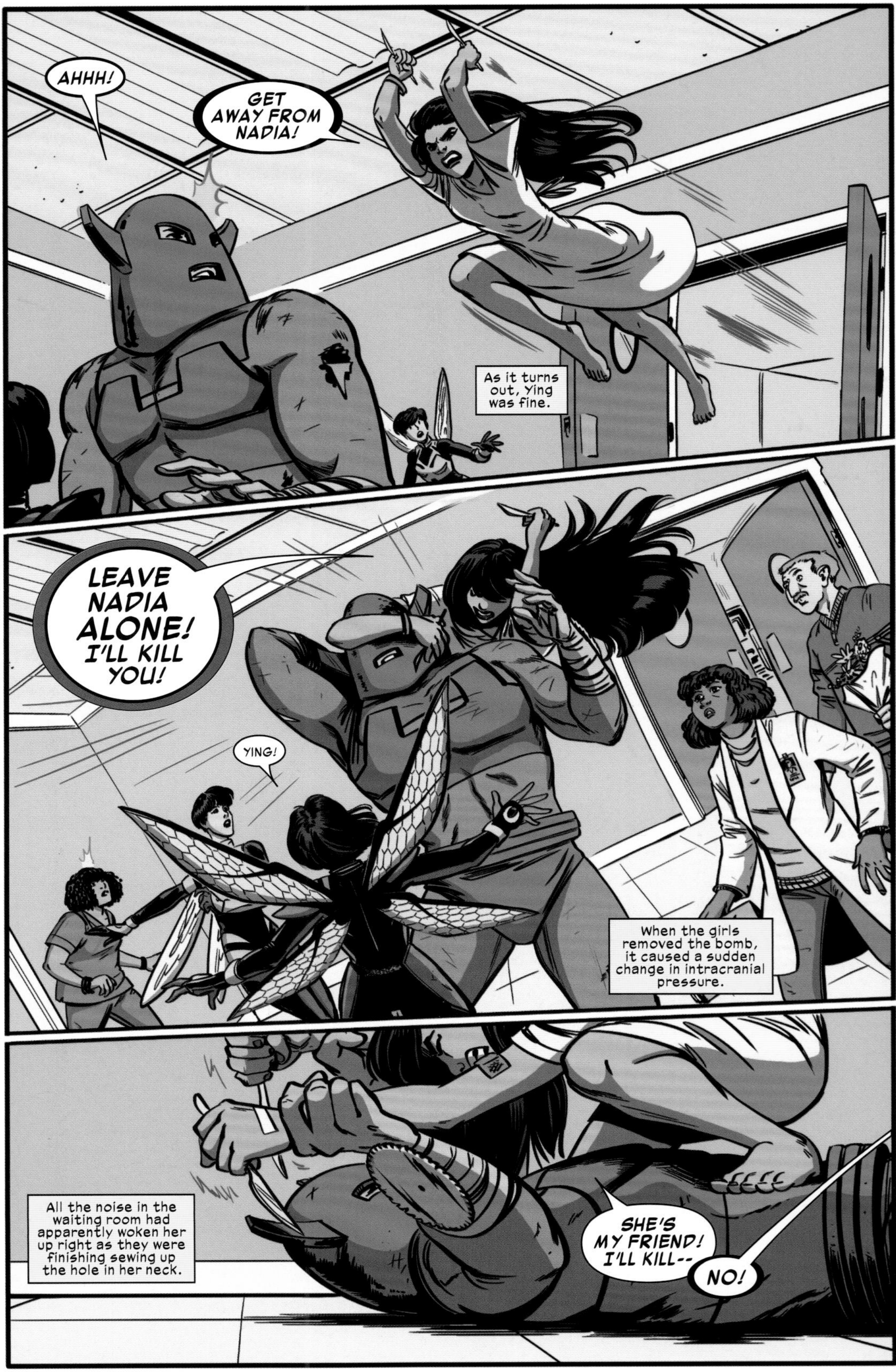
AHHH!
GET AWAY FROM NADIA!
As it turns out, Ying was fine.
LEAVE NADIA ALONE! I'LL KILL YOU!
YING!
When the girls removed the bomb, it caused a sudden change in intracranial pressure.
All the noise in the waiting room had apparently woken her up right as they were finishing sewing up the hole in her neck.
SHE'S MY FRIEND! I'LL KILL--
NO!

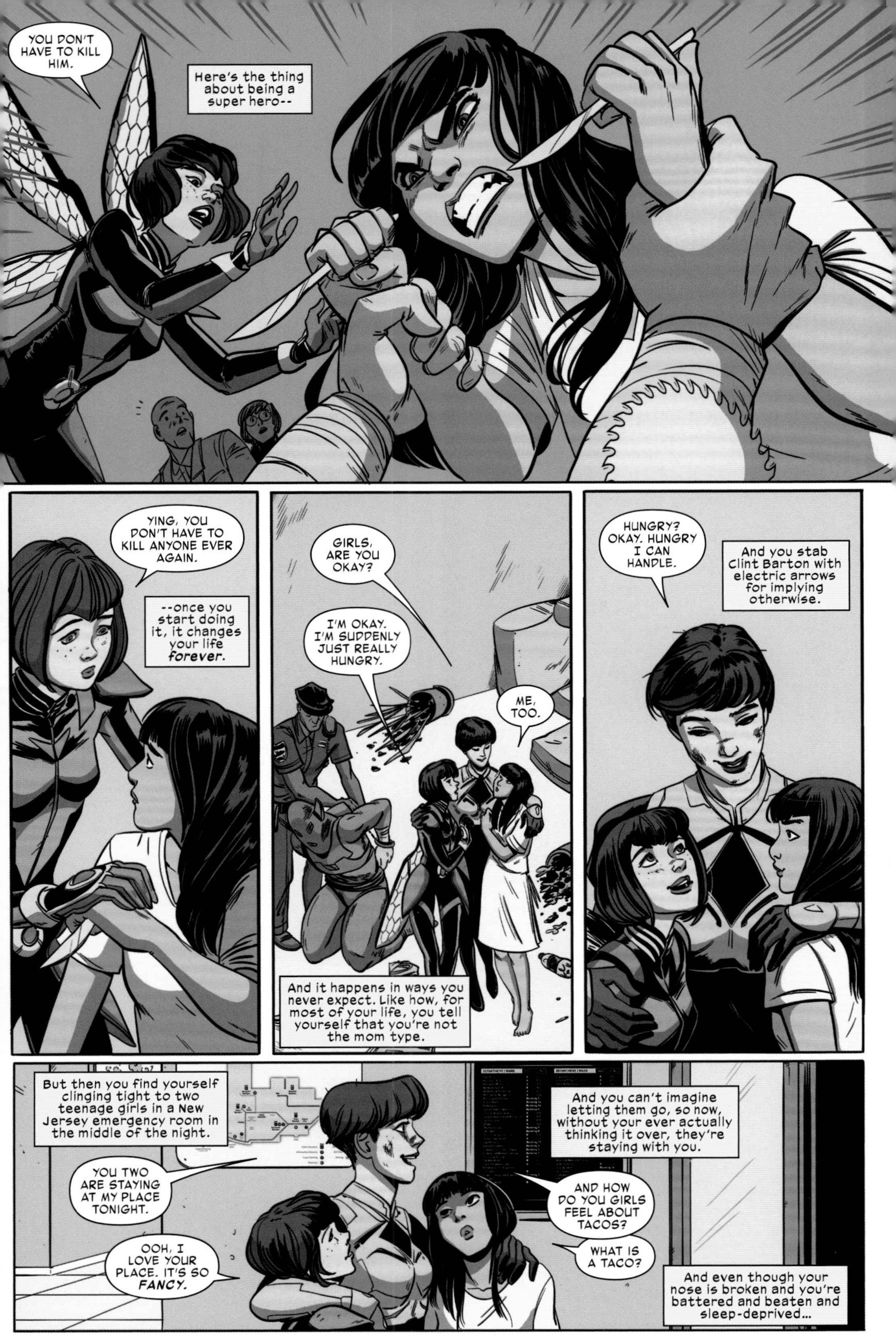

YOU DON'T HAVE TO KILL HIM.
Here's the thing about being a super hero--
YING, YOU DON'T HAVE TO KILL ANYONE EVER AGAIN.
--once you start doing it, it changes your life *forever*.
GIRLS, ARE YOU OKAY?
I'M OKAY. I'M SUDDENLY JUST REALLY HUNGRY.
ME, TOO.
And it happens in ways you never expect. Like how, for most of your life, you tell yourself that you're not the mom type.
HUNGRY? OKAY. HUNGRY I CAN HANDLE.
And you stab Clint Barton with electric arrows for implying otherwise.
But then you find yourself clinging tight to two teenage girls in a New Jersey emergency room in the middle of the night.
YOU TWO ARE STAYING AT MY PLACE TONIGHT.
OOH, I LOVE YOUR PLACE. IT'S SO *FANCY*.
And you can't imagine letting them go, so now, without your ever actually thinking it over, they're staying with you.
AND HOW DO YOU GIRLS FEEL ABOUT TACOS?
WHAT IS A TACO?
And even though your nose is broken and you're battered and beaten and sleep-deprived...

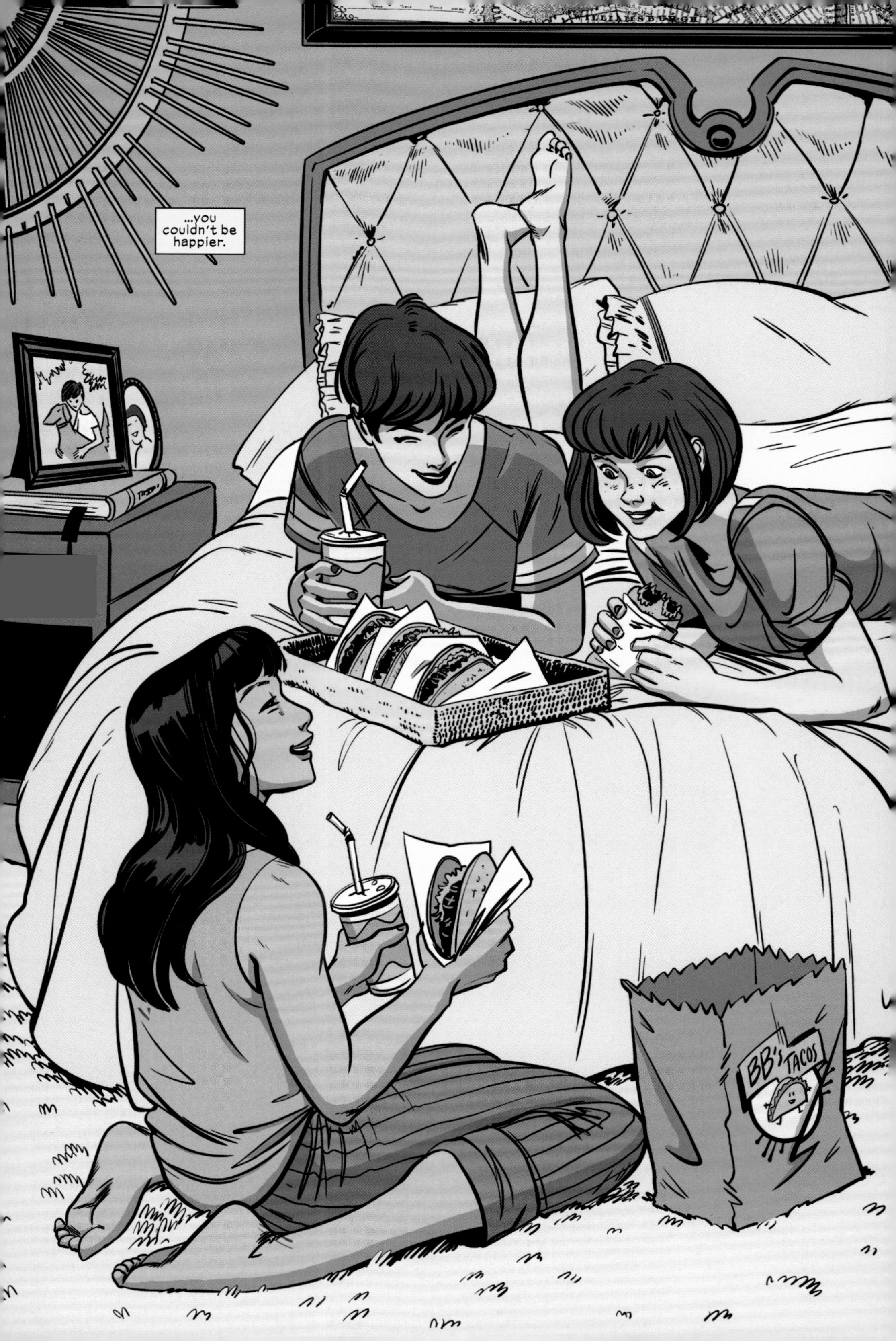
...you couldn't be happier.
BB's TACOS

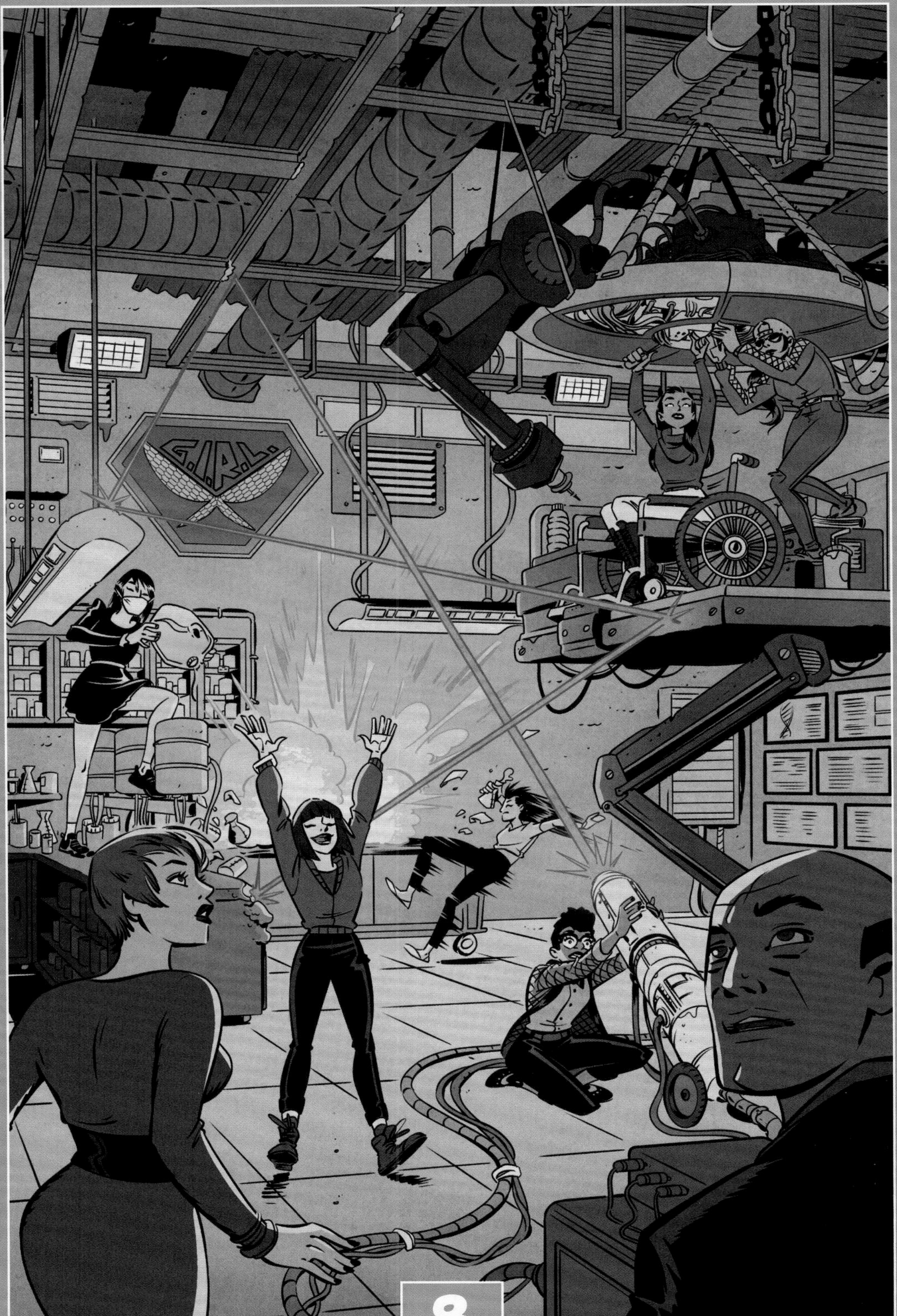
G.I.R.L.

8

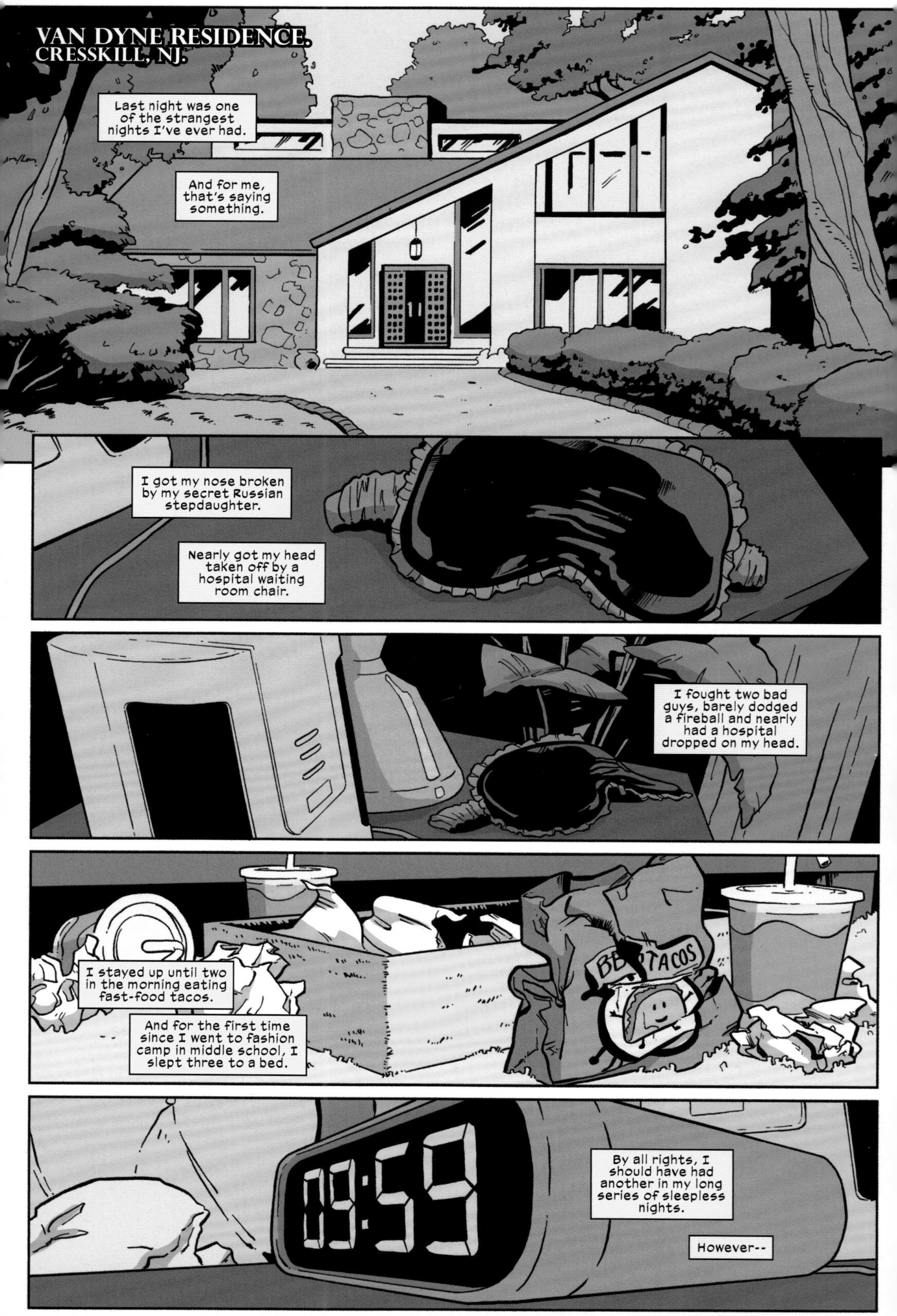
VAN DYNE RESIDENCE.
CRESSKILL, NJ.
Last night was one of the strangest nights I've ever had.
And for me, that's saying something.
I got my nose broken by my secret Russian stepdaughter.
Nearly got my head taken off by a hospital waiting room chair.
I fought two bad guys, barely dodged a fireball and nearly had a hospital dropped on my head.
I stayed up until two in the morning eating fast-food tacos.
And for the first time since I went to fashion camp in middle school, I slept three to a bed.
By all rights, I should have had another in my long series of sleepless nights.
However--

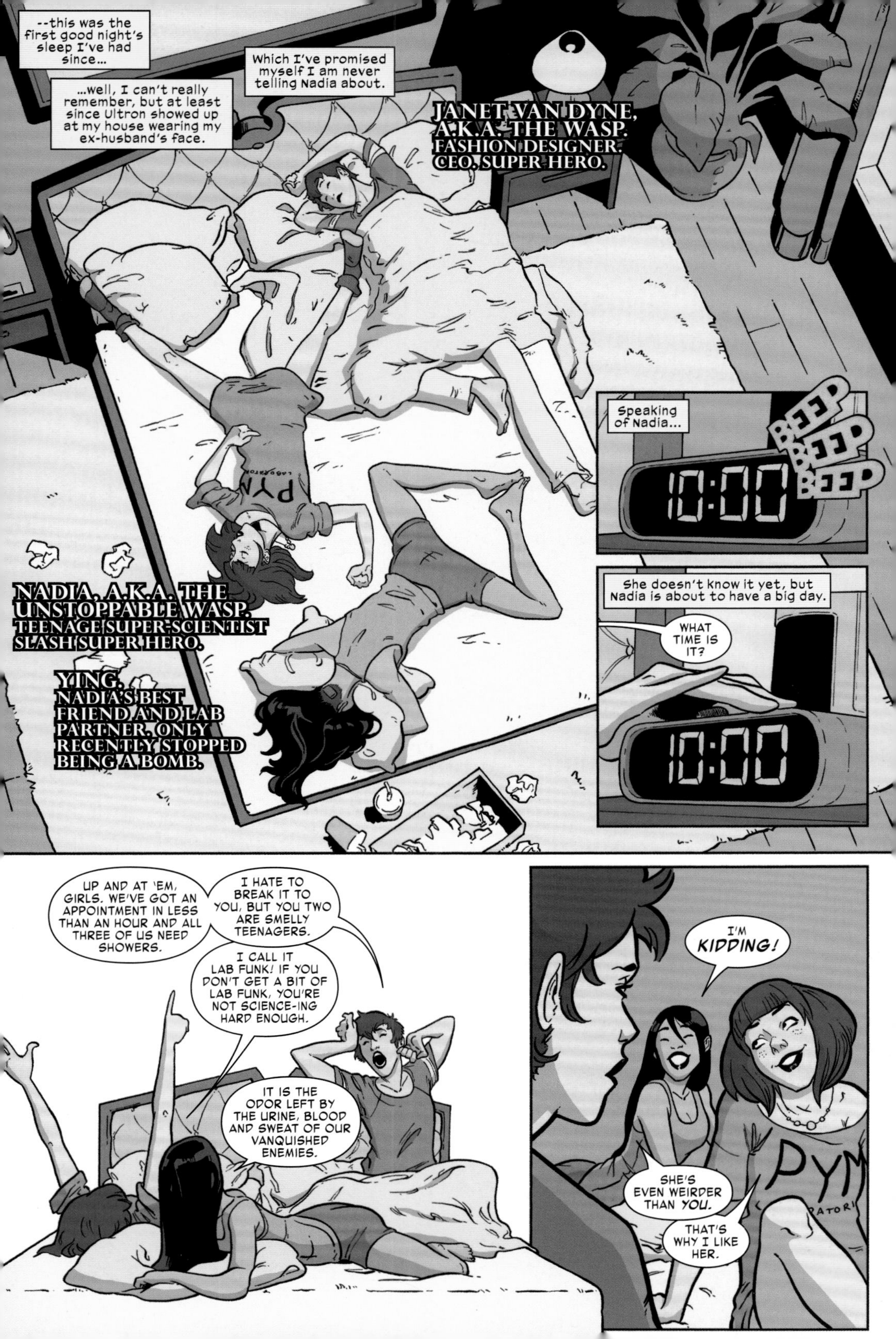
--this was the first good night's sleep I've had since...
...well, I can't really remember, but at least since Ultron showed up at my house wearing my ex-husband's face.
Which I've promised myself I am never telling Nadia about.
JANET VAN DYNE, A.K.A. THE WASP. FASHION DESIGNER. CEO. SUPER HERO.
NADIA, A.K.A. THE UNSTOPPABLE WASP. TEENAGE SUPER-SCIENTIST SLASH SUPER HERO.
YING. NADIA'S BEST FRIEND AND LAB PARTNER. ONLY RECENTLY STOPPED BEING A BOMB.
PYM
Speaking of Nadia...
BEEP BEEP BEEP
10:00
She doesn't know it yet, but Nadia is about to have a big day.
WHAT TIME IS IT?
10:00
UP AND AT 'EM, GIRLS. WE'VE GOT AN APPOINTMENT IN LESS THAN AN HOUR AND ALL THREE OF US NEED SHOWERS.
I HATE TO BREAK IT TO YOU, BUT YOU TWO ARE SMELLY TEENAGERS.
I CALL IT LAB FUNK! IF YOU DON'T GET A BIT OF LAB FUNK, YOU'RE NOT SCIENCE-ING HARD ENOUGH.
IT IS THE ODOR LEFT BY THE URINE, BLOOD AND SWEAT OF OUR VANQUISHED ENEMIES.
I'M *KIDDING!*
SHE'S EVEN WEIRDER THAN *YOU.*
THAT'S WHY I LIKE HER.
PYM

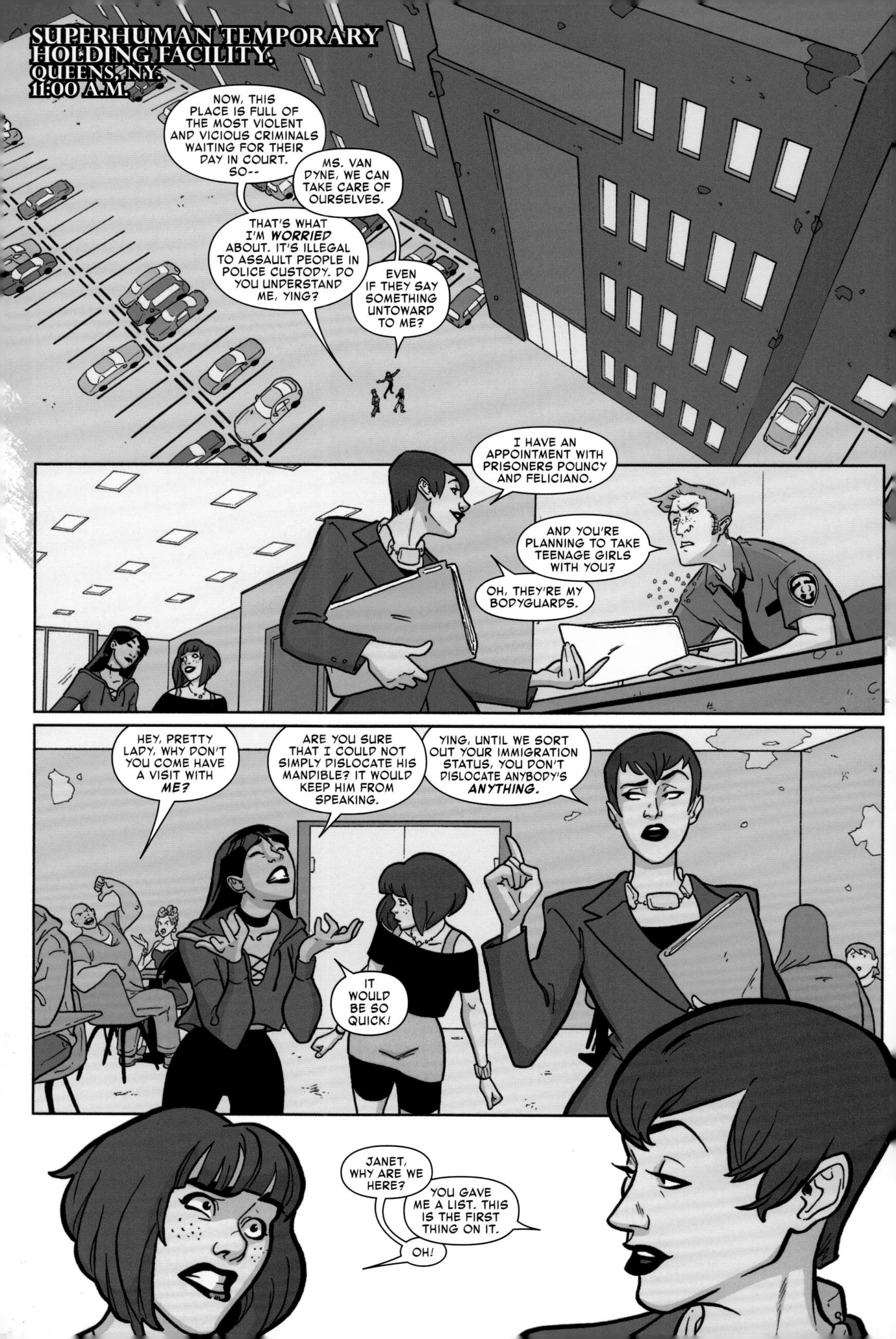
SUPERHUMAN TEMPORARY HOLDING FACILITY. QUEENS, N.Y. 11:00 A.M.
NOW, THIS PLACE IS FULL OF THE MOST VIOLENT AND VICIOUS CRIMINALS WAITING FOR THEIR DAY IN COURT. SO--
MS. VAN DYNE, WE CAN TAKE CARE OF OURSELVES.
THAT'S WHAT I'M ***WORRIED*** ABOUT. IT'S ILLEGAL TO ASSAULT PEOPLE IN POLICE CUSTODY. DO YOU UNDERSTAND ME, YING?
EVEN IF THEY SAY SOMETHING UNTOWARD TO ME?
I HAVE AN APPOINTMENT WITH PRISONERS POUNCY AND FELICIANO.
AND YOU'RE PLANNING TO TAKE TEENAGE GIRLS WITH YOU?
OH, THEY'RE MY BODYGUARDS.
HEY, PRETTY LADY, WHY DON'T YOU COME HAVE A VISIT WITH ***ME?***
ARE YOU SURE THAT I COULD NOT SIMPLY DISLOCATE HIS MANDIBLE? IT WOULD KEEP HIM FROM SPEAKING.
YING, UNTIL WE SORT OUT YOUR IMMIGRATION STATUS, YOU DON'T DISLOCATE ANYBODY'S ***ANYTHING.***
IT WOULD BE SO QUICK!
JANET, WHY ARE WE HERE?
YOU GAVE ME A LIST. THIS IS THE FIRST THING ON IT.
OH!

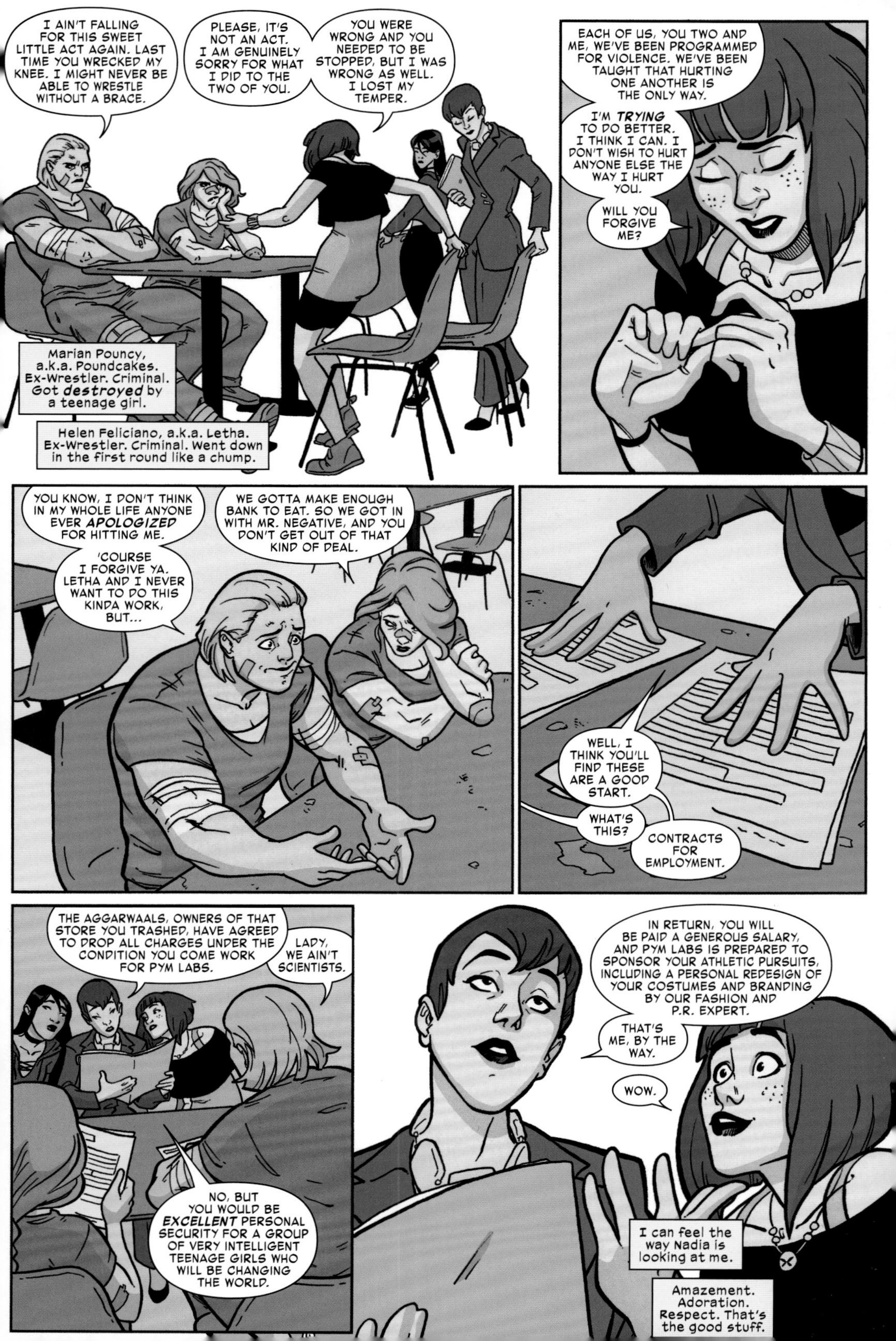
I AIN'T FALLING FOR THIS SWEET LITTLE ACT AGAIN. LAST TIME YOU WRECKED MY KNEE. I MIGHT NEVER BE ABLE TO WRESTLE WITHOUT A BRACE.
PLEASE, IT'S NOT AN ACT. I AM GENUINELY SORRY FOR WHAT I DID TO THE TWO OF YOU.
YOU WERE WRONG AND YOU NEEDED TO BE STOPPED, BUT I WAS WRONG AS WELL. I LOST MY TEMPER.
Marian Pouncy, a.k.a. Poundcakes. Ex-Wrestler. Criminal. Got *destroyed* by a teenage girl.
Helen Feliciano, a.k.a. Letha. Ex-Wrestler. Criminal. Went down in the first round like a chump.
EACH OF US, YOU TWO AND ME, WE'VE BEEN PROGRAMMED FOR VIOLENCE. WE'VE BEEN TAUGHT THAT HURTING ONE ANOTHER IS THE ONLY WAY.
I'M *TRYING* TO DO BETTER. I THINK I CAN. I DON'T WISH TO HURT ANYONE ELSE THE WAY I HURT YOU.
WILL YOU FORGIVE ME?
YOU KNOW, I DON'T THINK IN MY WHOLE LIFE ANYONE EVER *APOLOGIZED* FOR HITTING ME.
'COURSE I FORGIVE YA. LETHA AND I NEVER WANT TO DO THIS KINDA WORK, BUT...
WE GOTTA MAKE ENOUGH BANK TO EAT. SO WE GOT IN WITH MR. NEGATIVE, AND YOU DON'T GET OUT OF THAT KIND OF DEAL.
WELL, I THINK YOU'LL FIND THESE ARE A GOOD START.
WHAT'S THIS?
CONTRACTS FOR EMPLOYMENT.
THE AGGARWAALS, OWNERS OF THAT STORE YOU TRASHED, HAVE AGREED TO DROP ALL CHARGES UNDER THE CONDITION YOU COME WORK FOR PYM LABS.
LADY, WE AIN'T SCIENTISTS.
NO, BUT YOU WOULD BE *EXCELLENT* PERSONAL SECURITY FOR A GROUP OF VERY INTELLIGENT TEENAGE GIRLS WHO WILL BE CHANGING THE WORLD.
IN RETURN, YOU WILL BE PAID A GENEROUS SALARY, AND PYM LABS IS PREPARED TO SPONSOR YOUR ATHLETIC PURSUITS, INCLUDING A PERSONAL REDESIGN OF YOUR COSTUMES AND BRANDING BY OUR FASHION AND P.R. EXPERT.
THAT'S ME, BY THE WAY.
WOW.
I can feel the way Nadia is looking at me.
Amazement. Adoration. Respect. That's the good stuff.

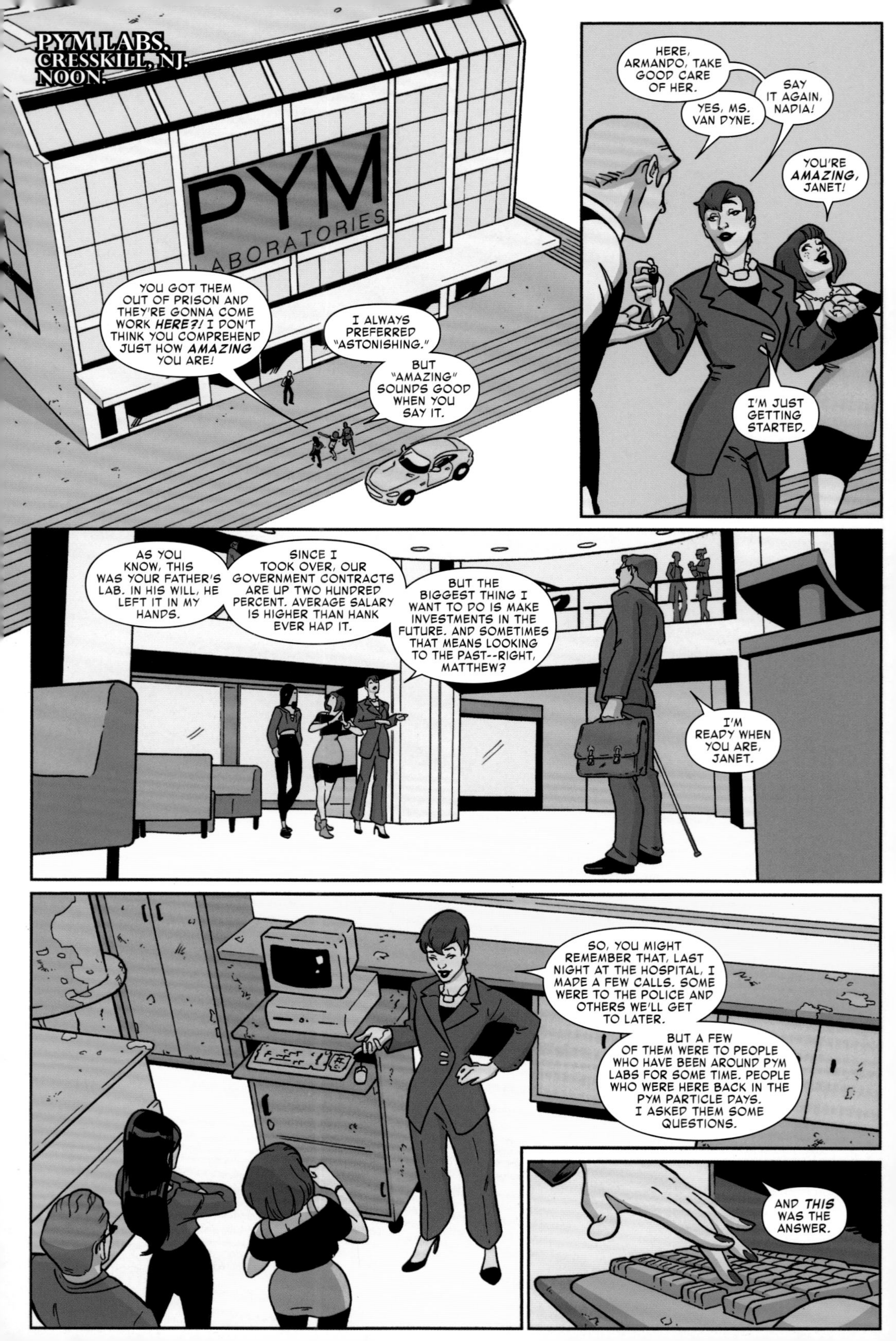
PYM LABS. CRESSKILL, NJ. NOON.
PYM LABORATORIES
YOU GOT THEM OUT OF PRISON AND THEY'RE GONNA COME WORK HERE?! I DON'T THINK YOU COMPREHEND JUST HOW AMAZING YOU ARE!
I ALWAYS PREFERRED "ASTONISHING."
BUT "AMAZING" SOUNDS GOOD WHEN YOU SAY IT.
HERE, ARMANDO, TAKE GOOD CARE OF HER.
YES, MS. VAN DYNE.
SAY IT AGAIN, NADIA!
YOU'RE AMAZING, JANET!
I'M JUST GETTING STARTED.
AS YOU KNOW, THIS WAS YOUR FATHER'S LAB. IN HIS WILL, HE LEFT IT IN MY HANDS.
SINCE I TOOK OVER, OUR GOVERNMENT CONTRACTS ARE UP TWO HUNDRED PERCENT. AVERAGE SALARY IS HIGHER THAN HANK EVER HAD IT.
BUT THE BIGGEST THING I WANT TO DO IS MAKE INVESTMENTS IN THE FUTURE. AND SOMETIMES THAT MEANS LOOKING TO THE PAST--RIGHT, MATTHEW?
I'M READY WHEN YOU ARE, JANET.
SO, YOU MIGHT REMEMBER THAT, LAST NIGHT AT THE HOSPITAL, I MADE A FEW CALLS. SOME WERE TO THE POLICE AND OTHERS WE'LL GET TO LATER.
BUT A FEW OF THEM WERE TO PEOPLE WHO HAVE BEEN AROUND PYM LABS FOR SOME TIME. PEOPLE WHO WERE HERE BACK IN THE PYM PARTICLE DAYS. I ASKED THEM SOME QUESTIONS.
AND THIS WAS THE ANSWER.

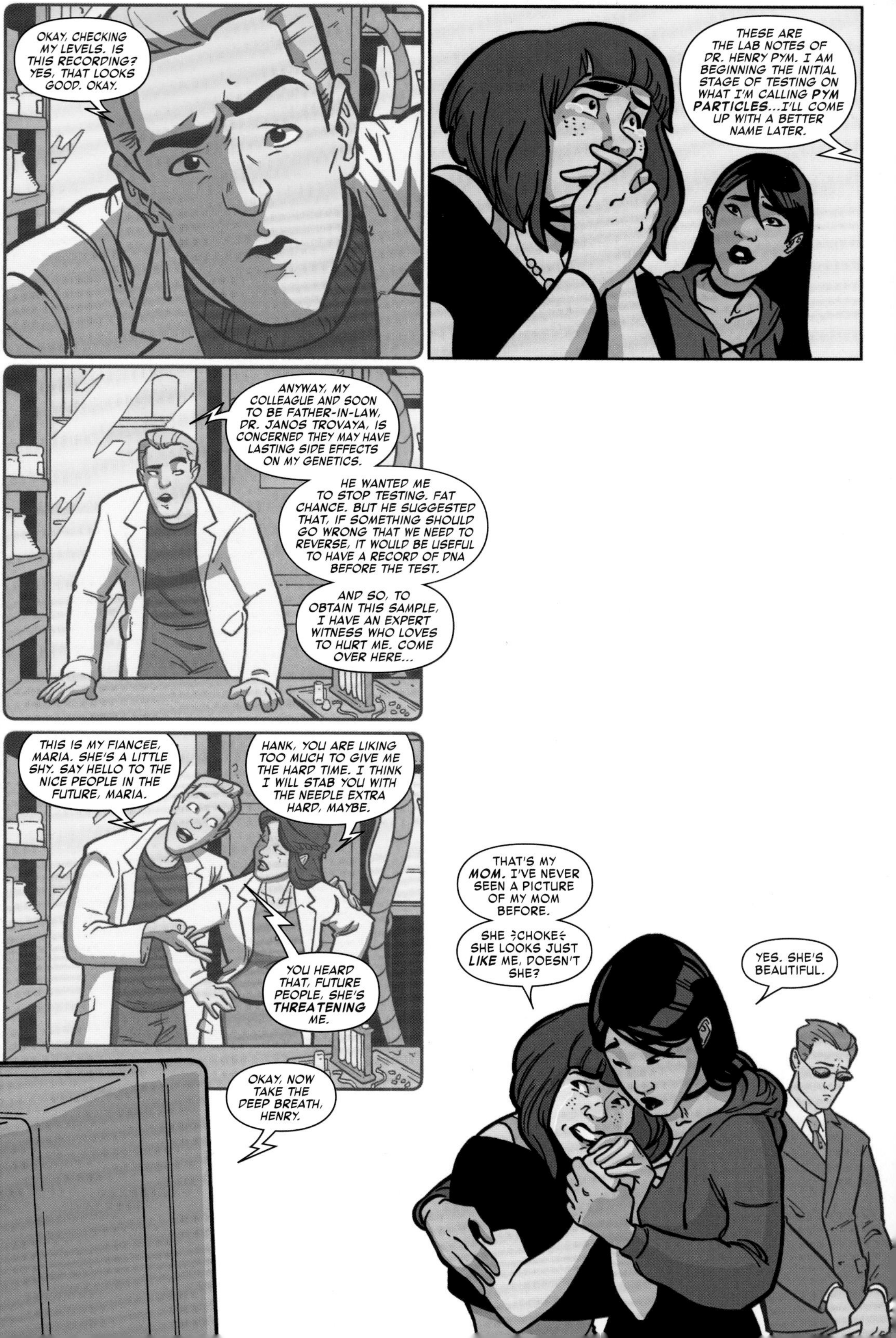
OKAY, CHECKING MY LEVELS. IS THIS RECORDING? YES, THAT LOOKS GOOD. OKAY.
THESE ARE THE LAB NOTES OF DR. HENRY PYM. I AM BEGINNING THE INITIAL STAGE OF TESTING ON WHAT I'M CALLING PYM PARTICLES...I'LL COME UP WITH A BETTER NAME LATER.
ANYWAY, MY COLLEAGUE AND SOON TO BE FATHER-IN-LAW, DR. JANOS TROVAYA, IS CONCERNED THEY MAY HAVE LASTING SIDE EFFECTS ON MY GENETICS.
HE WANTED ME TO STOP TESTING. FAT CHANCE. BUT HE SUGGESTED THAT, IF SOMETHING SHOULD GO WRONG THAT WE NEED TO REVERSE, IT WOULD BE USEFUL TO HAVE A RECORD OF DNA BEFORE THE TEST.
AND SO, TO OBTAIN THIS SAMPLE, I HAVE AN EXPERT WITNESS WHO LOVES TO HURT ME. COME OVER HERE...
THIS IS MY FIANCEE, MARIA. SHE'S A LITTLE SHY. SAY HELLO TO THE NICE PEOPLE IN THE FUTURE, MARIA.
HANK, YOU ARE LIKING TOO MUCH TO GIVE ME THE HARD TIME. I THINK I WILL STAB YOU WITH THE NEEDLE EXTRA HARD, MAYBE.
YOU HEARD THAT, FUTURE PEOPLE, SHE'S THREATENING ME.
OKAY, NOW TAKE THE DEEP BREATH, HENRY.
THAT'S MY MOM. I'VE NEVER SEEN A PICTURE OF MY MOM BEFORE.
SHE ≈CHOKE≈ SHE LOOKS JUST LIKE ME, DOESN'T SHE?
YES. SHE'S BEAUTIFUL.

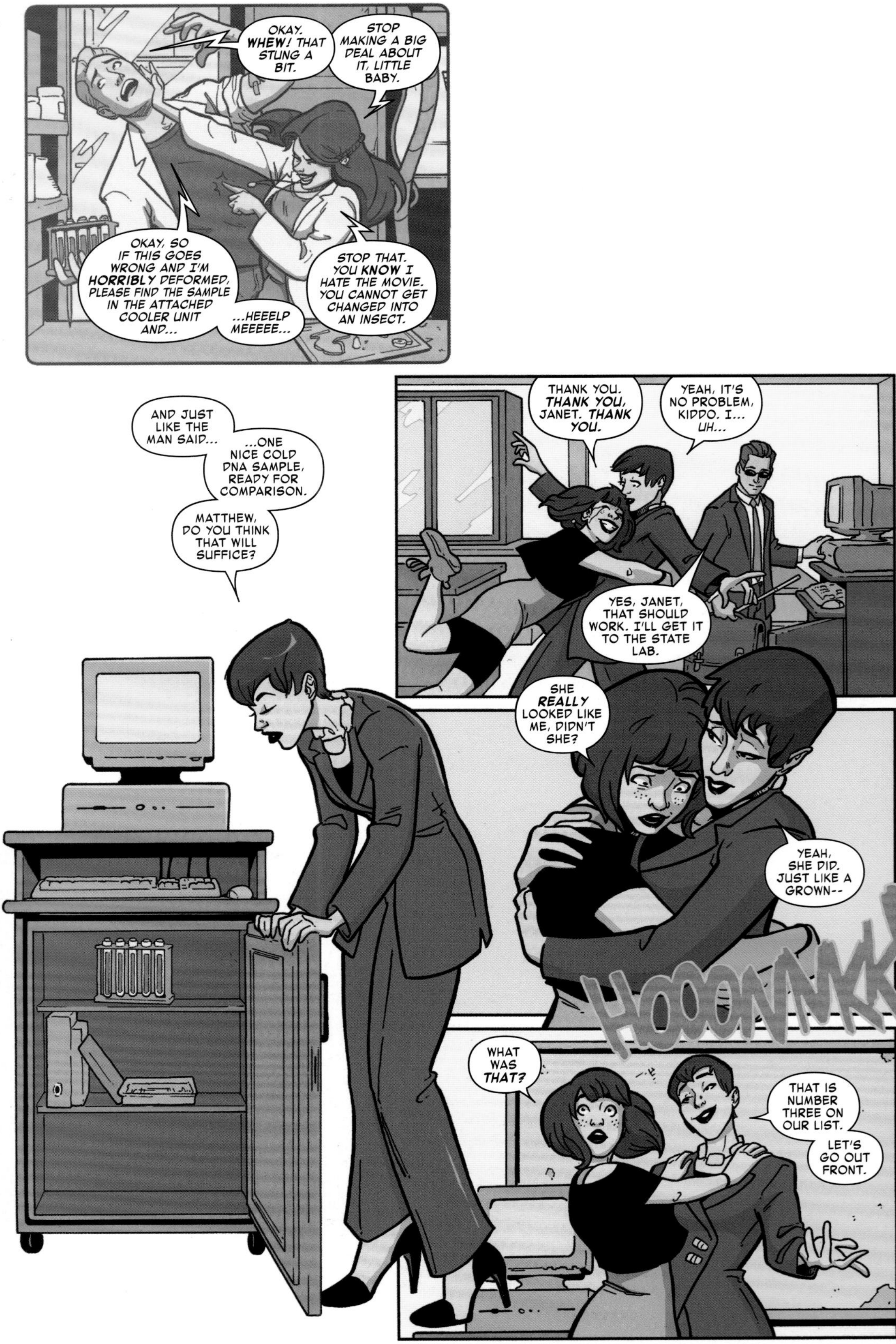

OKAY. **WHEW!** THAT STUNG A BIT.
STOP MAKING A BIG DEAL ABOUT IT, LITTLE BABY.
OKAY, SO IF THIS GOES WRONG AND I'M **HORRIBLY** DEFORMED, PLEASE FIND THE SAMPLE IN THE ATTACHED COOLER UNIT AND...
...HEEELP MEEEEE...
STOP THAT. YOU **KNOW** I HATE THE MOVIE. YOU CANNOT GET CHANGED INTO AN INSECT.
AND JUST LIKE THE MAN SAID...
...ONE NICE COLD DNA SAMPLE, READY FOR COMPARISON.
MATTHEW, DO YOU THINK THAT WILL SUFFICE?
THANK YOU. **THANK YOU,** JANET. **THANK YOU.**
YEAH, IT'S NO PROBLEM, KIDDO. I... UH...
YES, JANET, THAT SHOULD WORK. I'LL GET IT TO THE STATE LAB.
SHE **REALLY** LOOKED LIKE ME, DIDN'T SHE?
YEAH, SHE DID. JUST LIKE A GROWN--
HOOONKK
WHAT WAS **THAT?**
THAT IS NUMBER THREE ON OUR LIST.
LET'S GO OUT FRONT.

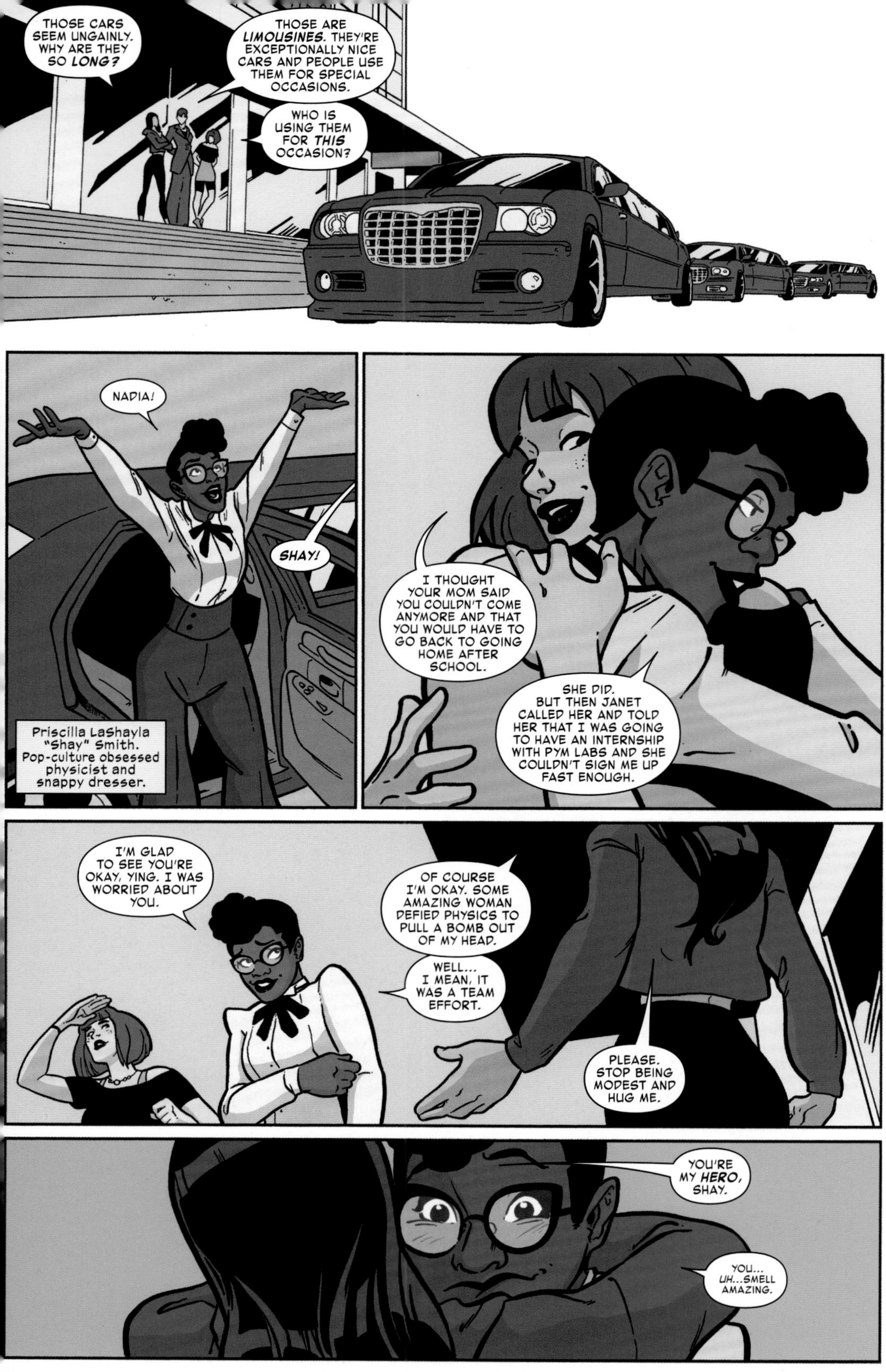
THOSE CARS SEEM UNGAINLY. WHY ARE THEY SO LONG?
THOSE ARE LIMOUSINES. THEY'RE EXCEPTIONALLY NICE CARS AND PEOPLE USE THEM FOR SPECIAL OCCASIONS.
WHO IS USING THEM FOR THIS OCCASION?
NADIA!
SHAY!
Priscilla LaShayla "Shay" Smith. Pop-culture obsessed physicist and snappy dresser.
I THOUGHT YOUR MOM SAID YOU COULDN'T COME ANYMORE AND THAT YOU WOULD HAVE TO GO BACK TO GOING HOME AFTER SCHOOL.
SHE DID. BUT THEN JANET CALLED HER AND TOLD HER THAT I WAS GOING TO HAVE AN INTERNSHIP WITH PYM LABS AND SHE COULDN'T SIGN ME UP FAST ENOUGH.
I'M GLAD TO SEE YOU'RE OKAY, YING. I WAS WORRIED ABOUT YOU.
OF COURSE I'M OKAY. SOME AMAZING WOMAN DEFIED PHYSICS TO PULL A BOMB OUT OF MY HEAD.
WELL... I MEAN, IT WAS A TEAM EFFORT.
PLEASE. STOP BEING MODEST AND HUG ME.
YOU'RE MY HERO, SHAY.
YOU... UH...SMELL AMAZING.

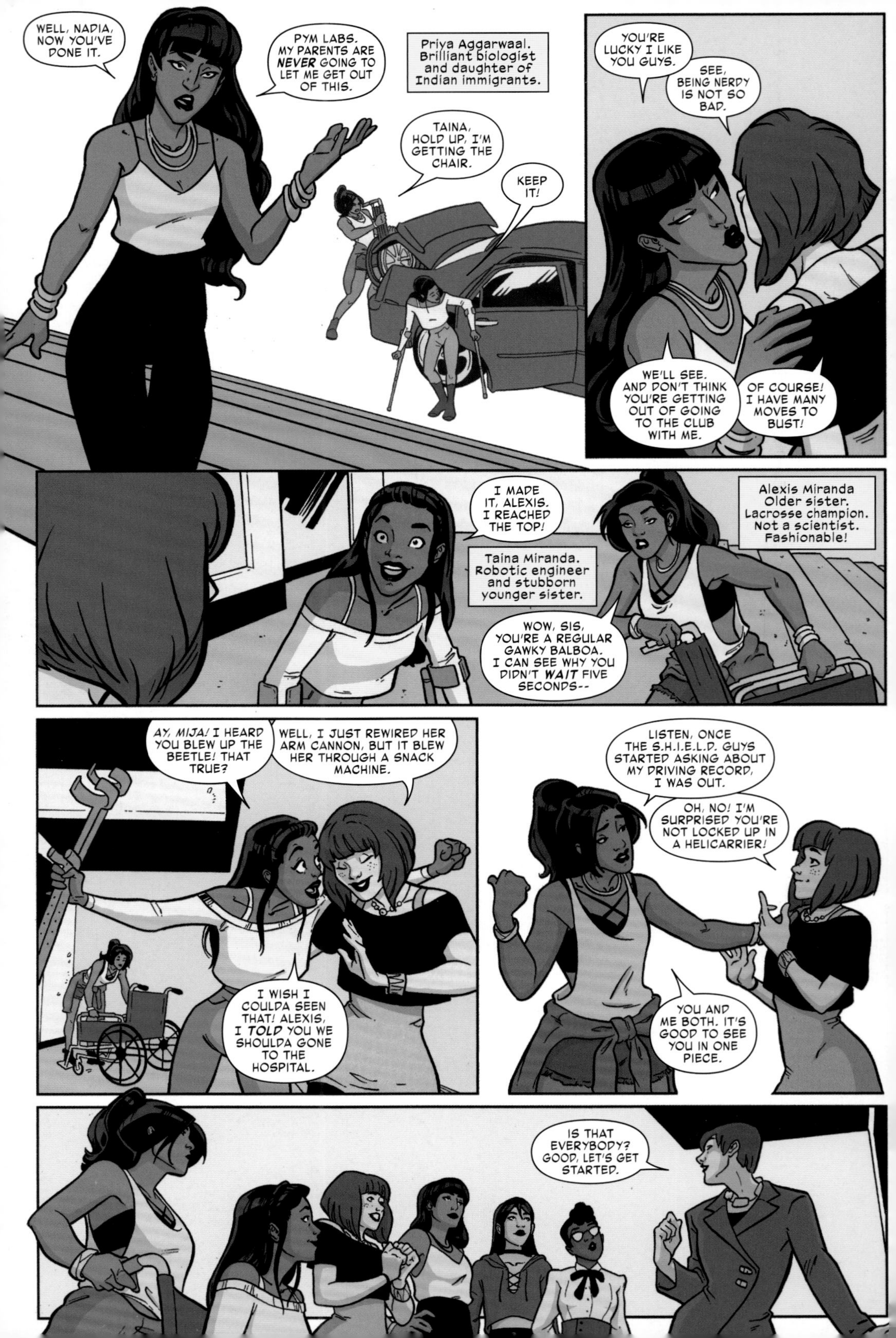
WELL, NADIA, NOW YOU'VE DONE IT.
PYM LABS. MY PARENTS ARE NEVER GOING TO LET ME GET OUT OF THIS.
Priya Aggarwaal. Brilliant biologist and daughter of Indian immigrants.
TAINA, HOLD UP, I'M GETTING THE CHAIR.
KEEP IT!
YOU'RE LUCKY I LIKE YOU GUYS.
SEE, BEING NERDY IS NOT SO BAD.
WE'LL SEE. AND DON'T THINK YOU'RE GETTING OUT OF GOING TO THE CLUB WITH ME.
OF COURSE! I HAVE MANY MOVES TO BUST!
I MADE IT, ALEXIS. I REACHED THE TOP!
Taina Miranda. Robotic engineer and stubborn younger sister.
Alexis Miranda Older sister. Lacrosse champion. Not a scientist. Fashionable!
WOW, SIS, YOU'RE A REGULAR GAWKY BALBOA. I CAN SEE WHY YOU DIDN'T WAIT FIVE SECONDS--
AY, MIJA! I HEARD YOU BLEW UP THE BEETLE! THAT TRUE?
WELL, I JUST REWIRED HER ARM CANNON, BUT IT BLEW HER THROUGH A SNACK MACHINE.
I WISH I COULDA SEEN THAT! ALEXIS, I TOLD YOU WE SHOULDA GONE TO THE HOSPITAL.
LISTEN, ONCE THE S.H.I.E.L.D. GUYS STARTED ASKING ABOUT MY DRIVING RECORD, I WAS OUT.
OH, NO! I'M SURPRISED YOU'RE NOT LOCKED UP IN A HELICARRIER!
YOU AND ME BOTH. IT'S GOOD TO SEE YOU IN ONE PIECE.
IS THAT EVERYBODY? GOOD, LET'S GET STARTED.

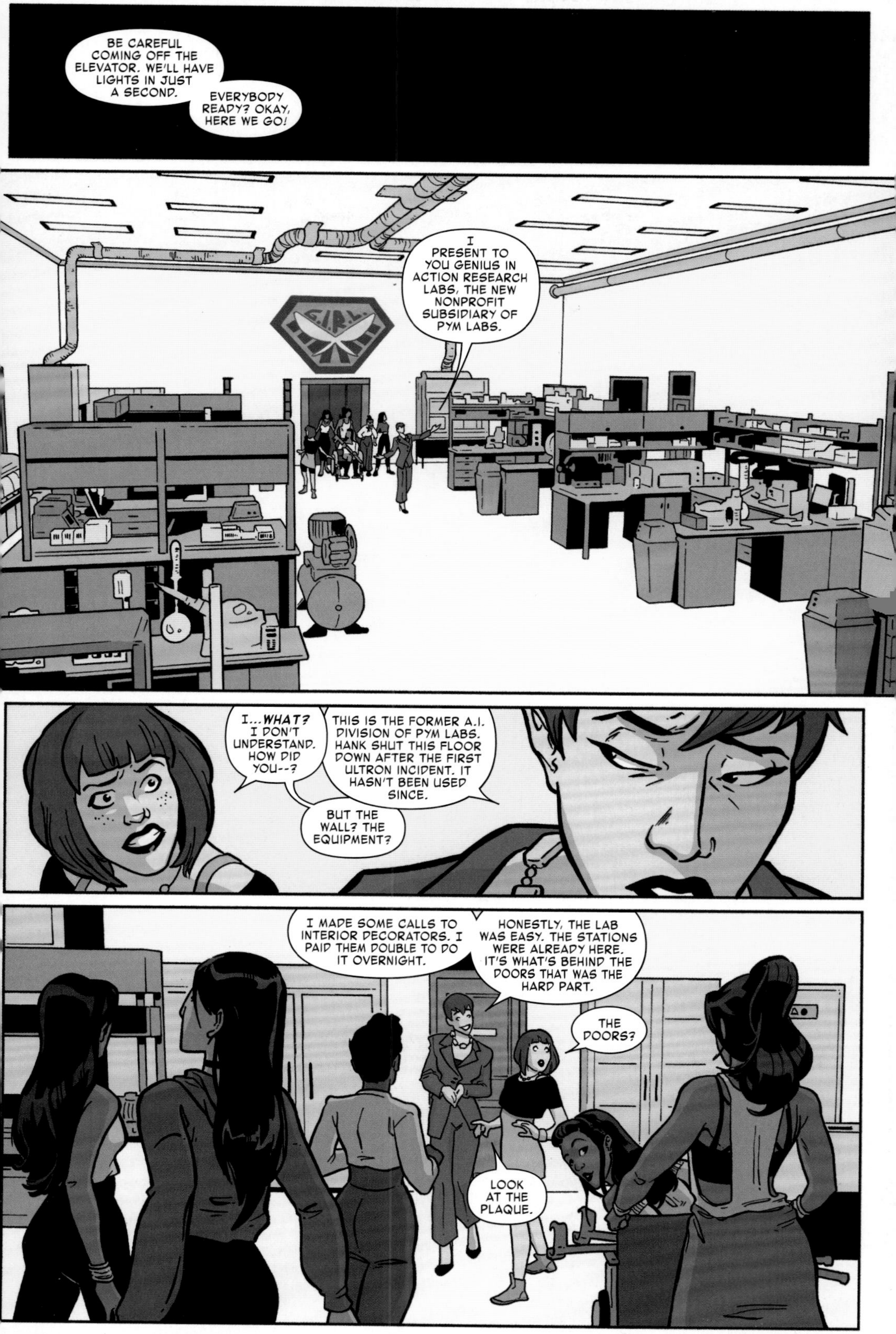

BE CAREFUL COMING OFF THE ELEVATOR. WE'LL HAVE LIGHTS IN JUST A SECOND.
EVERYBODY READY? OKAY, HERE WE GO!
I PRESENT TO YOU GENIUS IN ACTION RESEARCH LABS, THE NEW NONPROFIT SUBSIDIARY OF PYM LABS.
G.I.R.L.
I...WHAT? I DON'T UNDERSTAND. HOW DID YOU--?
THIS IS THE FORMER A.I. DIVISION OF PYM LABS. HANK SHUT THIS FLOOR DOWN AFTER THE FIRST ULTRON INCIDENT. IT HASN'T BEEN USED SINCE.
BUT THE WALL? THE EQUIPMENT?
I MADE SOME CALLS TO INTERIOR DECORATORS. I PAID THEM DOUBLE TO DO IT OVERNIGHT.
HONESTLY, THE LAB WAS EASY. THE STATIONS WERE ALREADY HERE. IT'S WHAT'S BEHIND THE DOORS THAT WAS THE HARD PART.
THE DOORS?
LOOK AT THE PLAQUE.

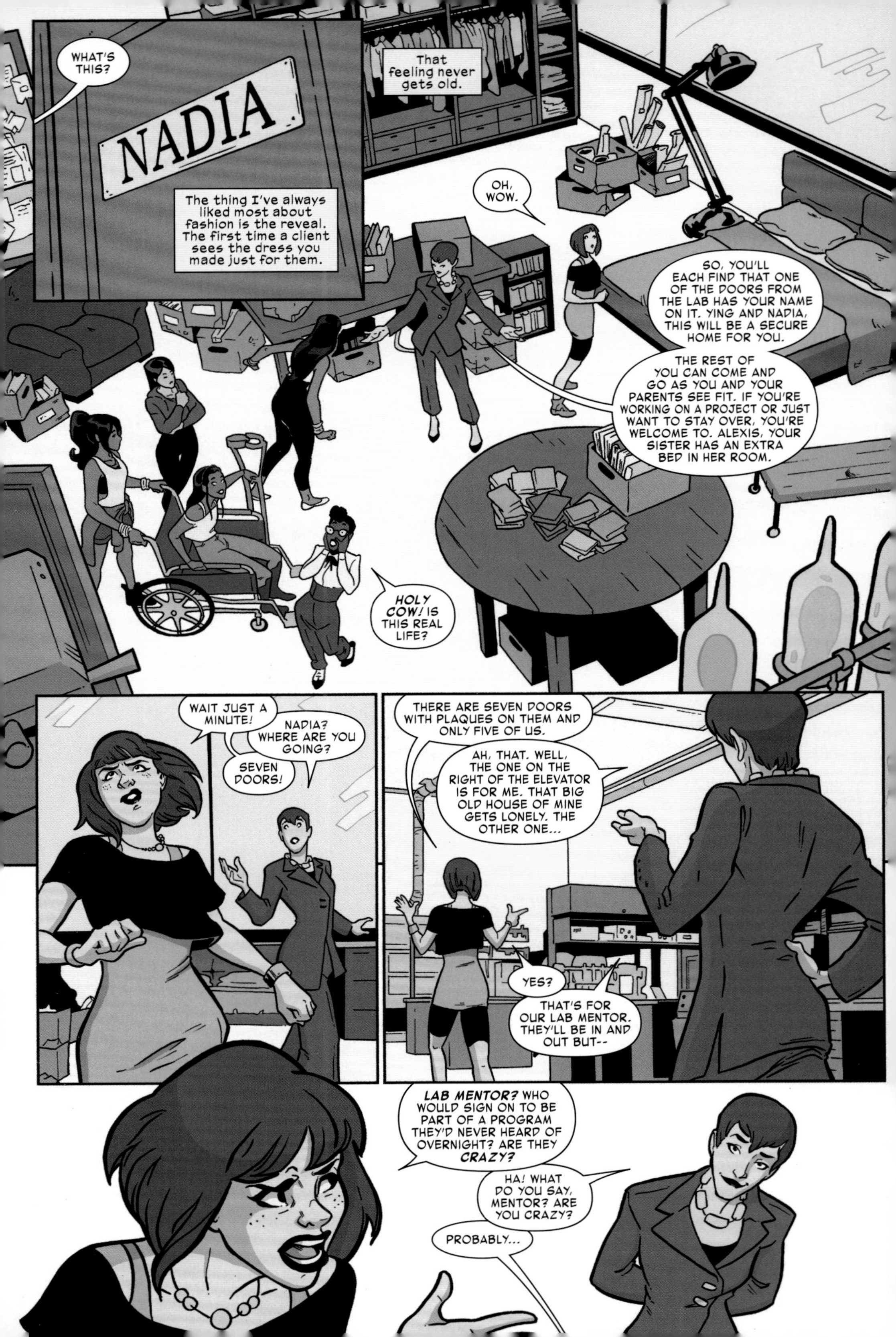

WHAT'S THIS?
NADIA
The thing I've always liked most about fashion is the reveal. The first time a client sees the dress you made just for them.
That feeling never gets old.
OH, WOW.
SO, YOU'LL EACH FIND THAT ONE OF THE DOORS FROM THE LAB HAS YOUR NAME ON IT. YING AND NADIA, THIS WILL BE A SECURE HOME FOR YOU.
THE REST OF YOU CAN COME AND GO AS YOU AND YOUR PARENTS SEE FIT. IF YOU'RE WORKING ON A PROJECT OR JUST WANT TO STAY OVER, YOU'RE WELCOME TO. ALEXIS, YOUR SISTER HAS AN EXTRA BED IN HER ROOM.
HOLY COW! IS THIS REAL LIFE?
WAIT JUST A MINUTE!
SEVEN DOORS!
NADIA? WHERE ARE YOU GOING?
THERE ARE SEVEN DOORS WITH PLAQUES ON THEM AND ONLY FIVE OF US.
AH, THAT. WELL, THE ONE ON THE RIGHT OF THE ELEVATOR IS FOR ME. THAT BIG OLD HOUSE OF MINE GETS LONELY. THE OTHER ONE...
YES?
THAT'S FOR OUR LAB MENTOR. THEY'LL BE IN AND OUT BUT--
LAB MENTOR? WHO WOULD SIGN ON TO BE PART OF A PROGRAM THEY'D NEVER HEARD OF OVERNIGHT? ARE THEY *CRAZY?*
HA! WHAT DO YOU SAY, MENTOR? ARE YOU CRAZY?
PROBABLY...

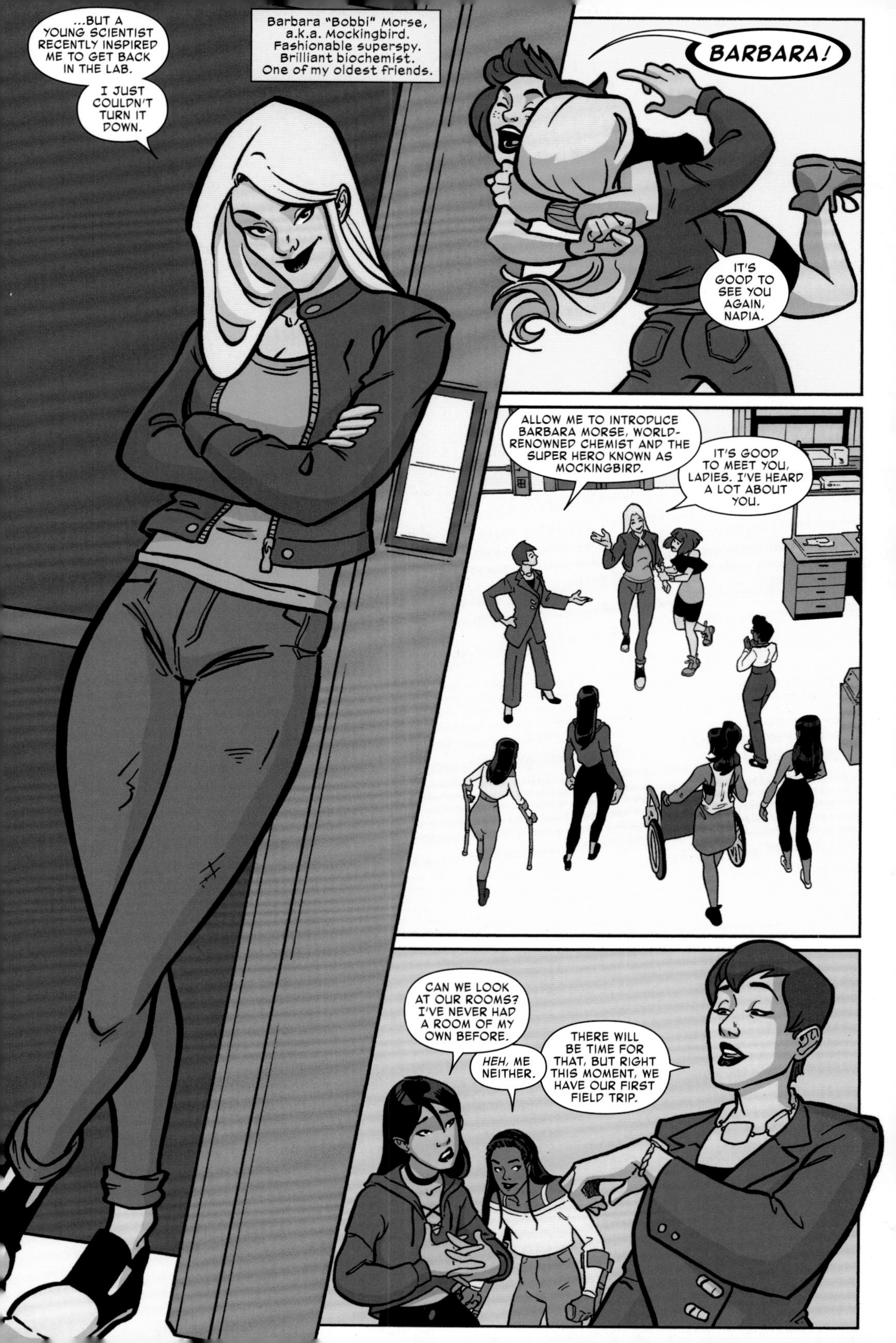

...BUT A YOUNG SCIENTIST RECENTLY INSPIRED ME TO GET BACK IN THE LAB.
I JUST COULDN'T TURN IT DOWN.
Barbara "Bobbi" Morse, a.k.a. Mockingbird. Fashionable superspy. Brilliant biochemist. One of my oldest friends.
BARBARA!
IT'S GOOD TO SEE YOU AGAIN, NADIA.
ALLOW ME TO INTRODUCE BARBARA MORSE, WORLD-RENOWNED CHEMIST AND THE SUPER HERO KNOWN AS MOCKINGBIRD.
IT'S GOOD TO MEET YOU, LADIES. I'VE HEARD A LOT ABOUT YOU.
CAN WE LOOK AT OUR ROOMS? I'VE NEVER HAD A ROOM OF MY OWN BEFORE.
HEH, ME NEITHER.
THERE WILL BE TIME FOR THAT, BUT RIGHT THIS MOMENT, WE HAVE OUR FIRST FIELD TRIP.

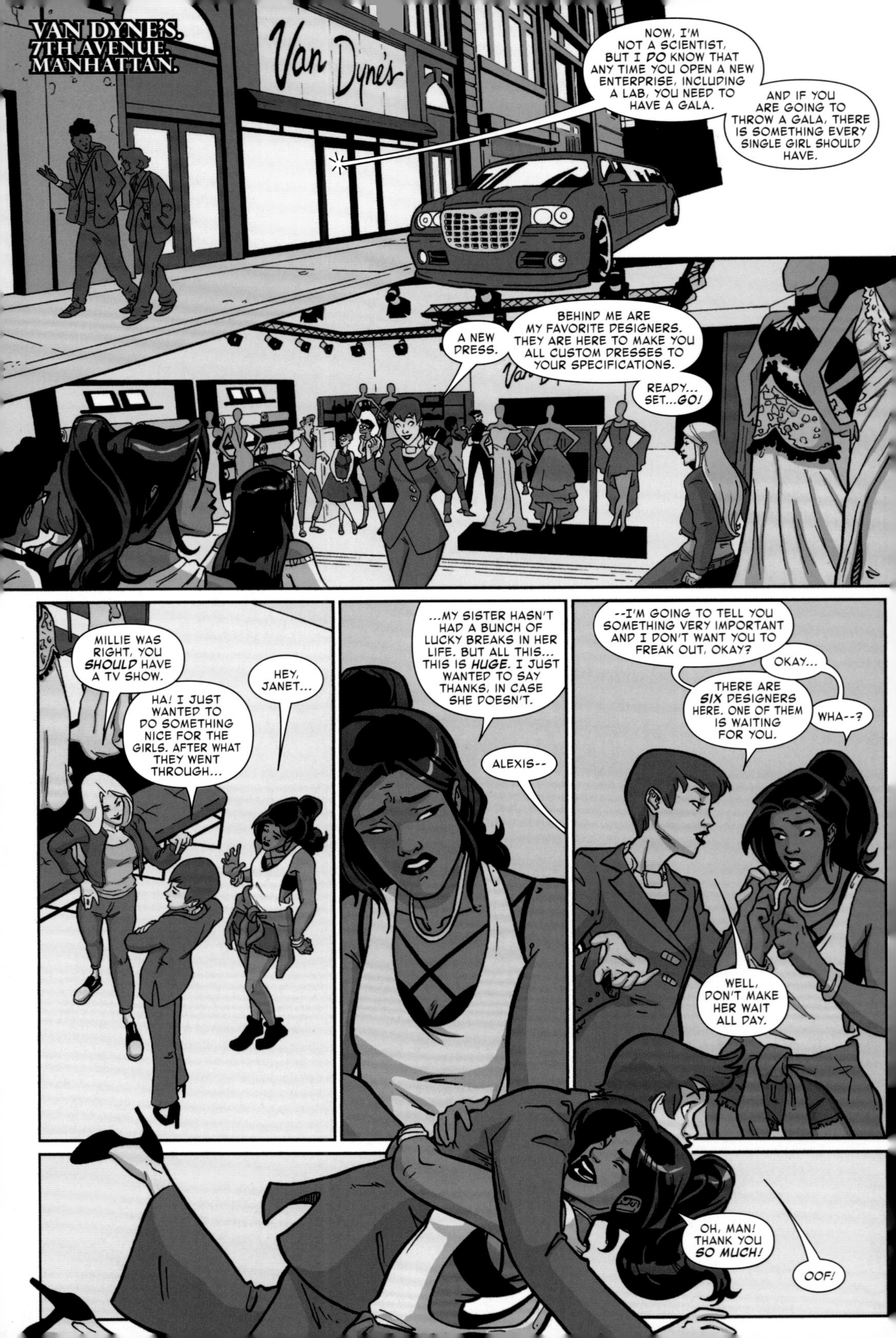
VAN DYNE'S. 7TH AVENUE. MANHATTAN.
Van Dyne's
NOW, I'M NOT A SCIENTIST, BUT I DO KNOW THAT ANY TIME YOU OPEN A NEW ENTERPRISE, INCLUDING A LAB, YOU NEED TO HAVE A GALA.
AND IF YOU ARE GOING TO THROW A GALA, THERE IS SOMETHING EVERY SINGLE GIRL SHOULD HAVE.
A NEW DRESS.
BEHIND ME ARE MY FAVORITE DESIGNERS. THEY ARE HERE TO MAKE YOU ALL CUSTOM DRESSES TO YOUR SPECIFICATIONS.
READY... SET...GO!
MILLIE WAS RIGHT, YOU SHOULD HAVE A TV SHOW.
HA! I JUST WANTED TO DO SOMETHING NICE FOR THE GIRLS. AFTER WHAT THEY WENT THROUGH...
HEY, JANET...
...MY SISTER HASN'T HAD A BUNCH OF LUCKY BREAKS IN HER LIFE. BUT ALL THIS... THIS IS HUGE. I JUST WANTED TO SAY THANKS, IN CASE SHE DOESN'T.
ALEXIS--
--I'M GOING TO TELL YOU SOMETHING VERY IMPORTANT AND I DON'T WANT YOU TO FREAK OUT, OKAY?
OKAY...
THERE ARE SIX DESIGNERS HERE. ONE OF THEM IS WAITING FOR YOU.
WHA--?
WELL, DON'T MAKE HER WAIT ALL DAY.
OH, MAN! THANK YOU SO MUCH!
OOF!

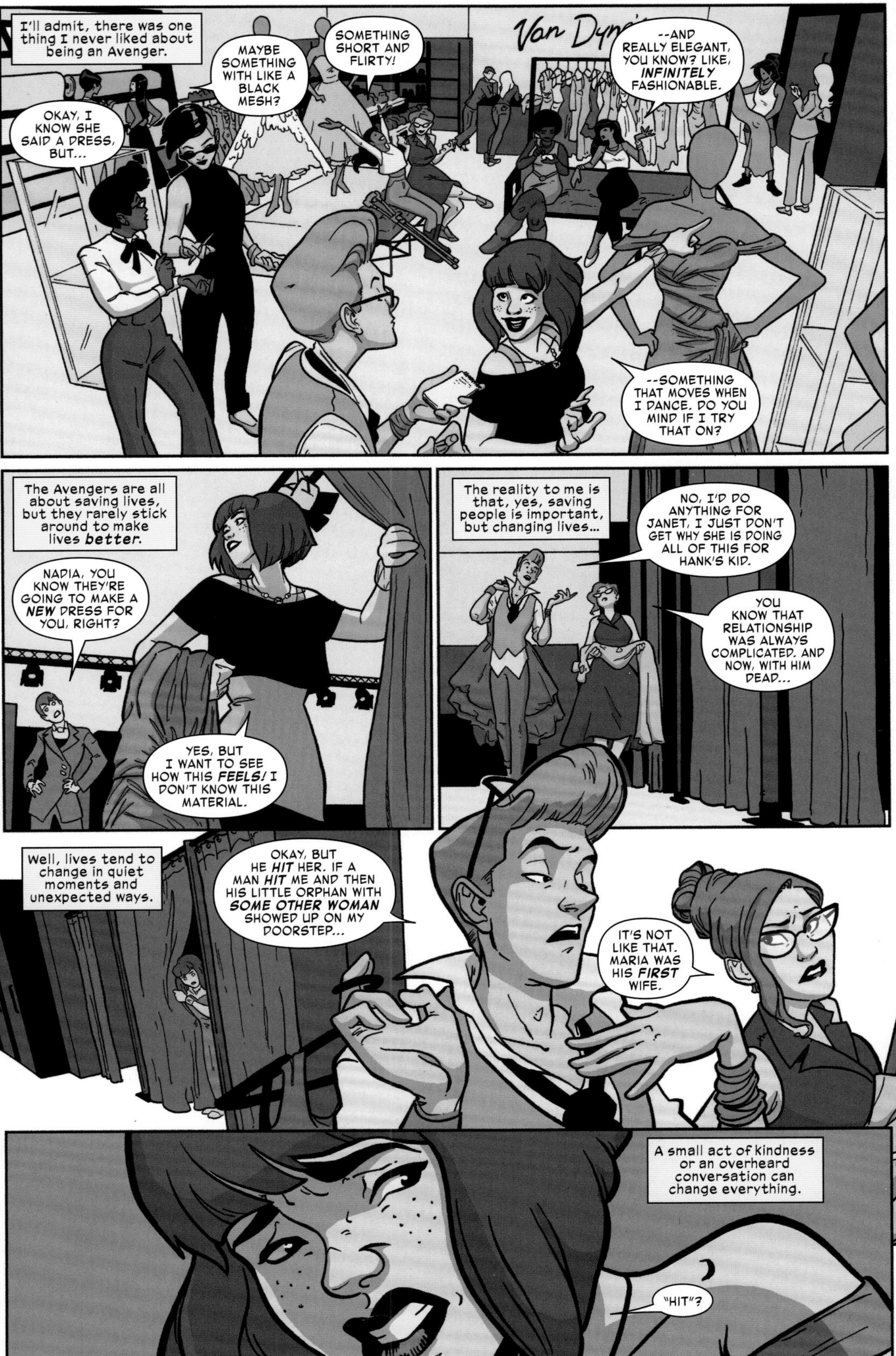

Van Dyne's
I'll admit, there was one thing I never liked about being an Avenger.
OKAY, I KNOW SHE SAID A DRESS, BUT...
MAYBE SOMETHING WITH LIKE A BLACK MESH?
SOMETHING SHORT AND FLIRTY!
--AND REALLY ELEGANT, YOU KNOW? LIKE, *INFINITELY* FASHIONABLE.
--SOMETHING THAT MOVES WHEN I DANCE. DO YOU MIND IF I TRY THAT ON?
The Avengers are all about saving lives, but they rarely stick around to make lives *better*.
NADIA, YOU KNOW THEY'RE GOING TO MAKE A *NEW* DRESS FOR YOU, RIGHT?
YES, BUT I WANT TO SEE HOW THIS *FEELS!* I DON'T KNOW THIS MATERIAL.
The reality to me is that, yes, saving people is important, but changing lives...
NO, I'D DO ANYTHING FOR JANET, I JUST DON'T GET WHY SHE IS DOING ALL OF THIS FOR HANK'S KID.
YOU KNOW THAT RELATIONSHIP WAS ALWAYS COMPLICATED. AND NOW, WITH HIM DEAD...
Well, lives tend to change in quiet moments and unexpected ways.
OKAY, BUT HE *HIT* HER. IF A MAN *HIT* ME AND THEN HIS LITTLE ORPHAN WITH *SOME OTHER WOMAN* SHOWED UP ON MY DOORSTEP...
IT'S NOT LIKE THAT. MARIA WAS HIS *FIRST* WIFE.
A small act of kindness or an overheard conversation can change everything.
"HIT"?

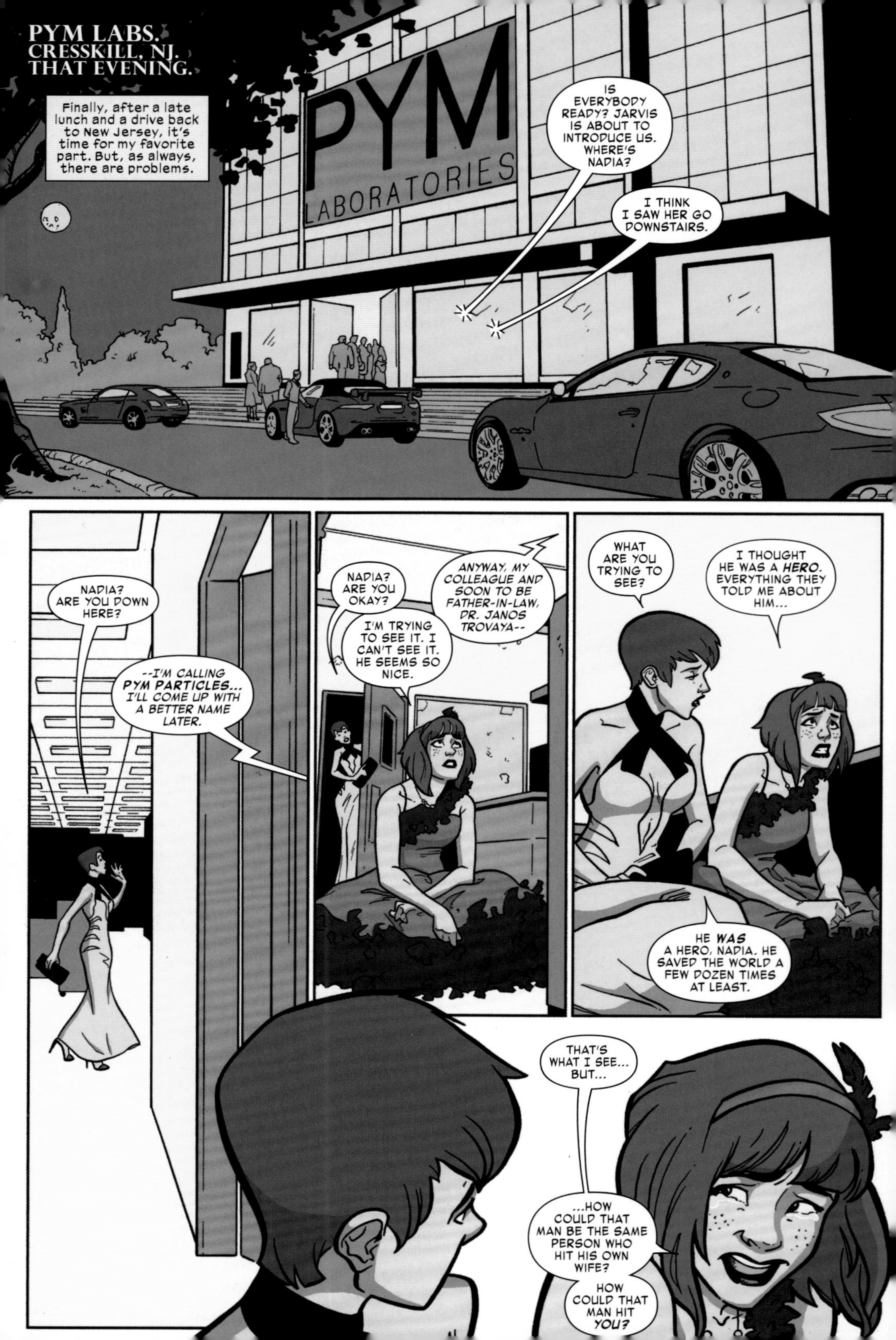
PYM LABS. CRESSKILL, NJ. THAT EVENING.
Finally, after a late lunch and a drive back to New Jersey, it's time for my favorite part. But, as always, there are problems.
PYM LABORATORIES
IS EVERYBODY READY? JARVIS IS ABOUT TO INTRODUCE US. WHERE'S NADIA?
I THINK I SAW HER GO DOWNSTAIRS.
NADIA? ARE YOU DOWN HERE?
--I'M CALLING PYM PARTICLES... I'LL COME UP WITH A BETTER NAME LATER.
NADIA? ARE YOU OKAY?
ANYWAY, MY COLLEAGUE AND SOON TO BE FATHER-IN-LAW, DR. JANOS TROVAYA--
I'M TRYING TO SEE IT. I CAN'T SEE IT. HE SEEMS SO NICE.
WHAT ARE YOU TRYING TO SEE?
I THOUGHT HE WAS A HERO. EVERYTHING THEY TOLD ME ABOUT HIM...
HE WAS A HERO, NADIA. HE SAVED THE WORLD A FEW DOZEN TIMES AT LEAST.
THAT'S WHAT I SEE... BUT...
...HOW COULD THAT MAN BE THE SAME PERSON WHO HIT HIS OWN WIFE?
HOW COULD THAT MAN HIT YOU?

WHO TOLD YOU?

I SAW IT ON THE INTERNET. I DON'T KNOW HOW I DIDN'T FIND OUT BEFORE. IT'S EVERYWHERE.

WHY DIDN'T *YOU* TELL ME HE WAS EVIL?

FIRST, LET'S GET ONE THING STRAIGHT. HANK PYM WAS *NOT* AN EVIL MAN.

HE DID AN EVIL THING AND HE HAD TO LIVE WITH THAT. THERE IS *NO* EXCUSE TO TREAT A PERSON YOU CARE ABOUT THE WAY HE TREATED ME.

HOW COULD YOU *FORGIVE* HIM FOR THAT?

WELL, HONESTLY I DON'T KNOW IF "FORGIVE" IS THE RIGHT WORD. I ACCEPTED WHAT HAPPENED AND MOVED ON.

HANK HAD A LOT OF STRUGGLES WITH MENTAL ILLNESS. HE REFUSED TO HAVE THAT ILLNESS TREATED OUT OF PRIDE. IF HE HAD DEALT WITH IT RESPONSIBLY AT THE TIME, THINGS MIGHT HAVE GONE DIFFERENTLY. BUT HE DIDN'T.

I HELD ON TO THAT ANGER FOR A *LONG* TIME. IT TOOK ME A WHILE TO REALIZE WHAT *YOU* ALREADY KNEW WHEN I MET YOU.

WHAT'S THAT?

YOU CAN'T LET THE THINGS THAT OTHER PEOPLE DO TO YOU DEFINE YOU. YOU HAVE TO TAKE CONTROL OF YOUR OWN LIFE.

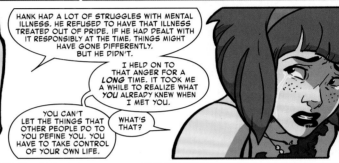

I REALIZED I COULDN'T LET HANK DEFINE MY LIFE. I DIDN'T LEAVE HIM BECAUSE HE WAS ILL, I LEFT BECAUSE HE PUT HIS OWN PRIDE ABOVE MY SAFETY AND THAT'S UNACCEPTABLE.

I'VE BEEN WORSHIPING HIM FOR *YEARS*, YOU KNOW? I THOUGHT HE WAS THE GREATEST PERSON IN THE WORLD.

NOBODY IS GOING TO LIVE UP TO THAT--NOT YOUR FATHER, NOT ME, NOT BOBBI MORSE. IT'S HOW YOU *DEAL* WITH IT THAT COUNTS.

YOU DON'T HAVE TO KEEP BEING SO NICE TO ME. JUST BECAUSE THIS STUFF WAS HIS DOESN'T MEAN IT SHOULD BE MINE.

OH, NADIA. IS THAT WHAT YOU THINK? THAT I'M DOING THIS BECAUSE OF HANK?

WHY ELSE? YOU'RE NOT RELATED TO ME. YOU DON'T HAVE TO DO ANY OF THIS.

LOOK, I'LL ADMIT THAT I SEE HANK IN YOU SOMETIMES AND I WANT TO HELP THAT PIECE, BUT THAT ISN'T IT.

I LOVE YA, KID. YOU MAKE THE WORLD A BETTER PLACE JUST BY WALKING THROUGH IT. YOU CARE ABOUT EVERYTHING AND EVERYBODY. I SEE YOU AND I THINK--

--I WANT TO BE MORE LIKE HER. SHE'S GOT IT ALL FIGURED OUT.

I LOVE YOU TOO, JANET.

YOU KNOW I DON'T REALLY HAVE IT FIGURED OUT THOUGH, RIGHT?

YEAH, KID. ME NEITHER. LET'S GO DANCE.

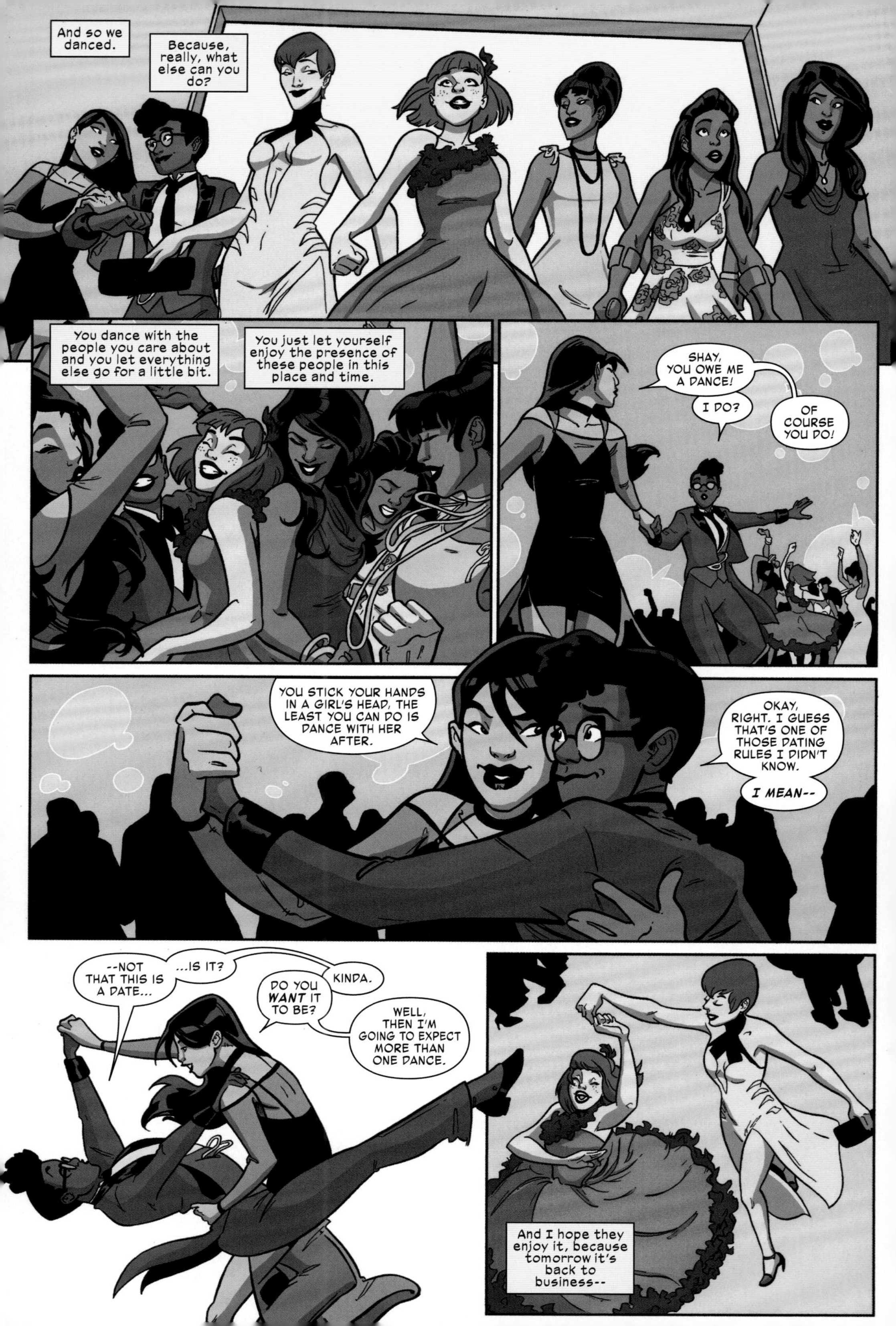
And so we danced.
Because, really, what else can you do?
You dance with the people you care about and you let everything else go for a little bit.
You just let yourself enjoy the presence of these people in this place and time.
SHAY, YOU OWE ME A DANCE!
I DO?
OF COURSE YOU DO!
YOU STICK YOUR HANDS IN A GIRL'S HEAD, THE LEAST YOU CAN DO IS DANCE WITH HER AFTER.
OKAY, RIGHT. I GUESS THAT'S ONE OF THOSE DATING RULES I DIDN'T KNOW.
I MEAN--
--NOT THAT THIS IS A DATE...
...IS IT?
KINDA.
DO YOU WANT IT TO BE?
WELL, THEN I'M GOING TO EXPECT MORE THAN ONE DANCE.
And I hope they enjoy it, because tomorrow it's back to business--

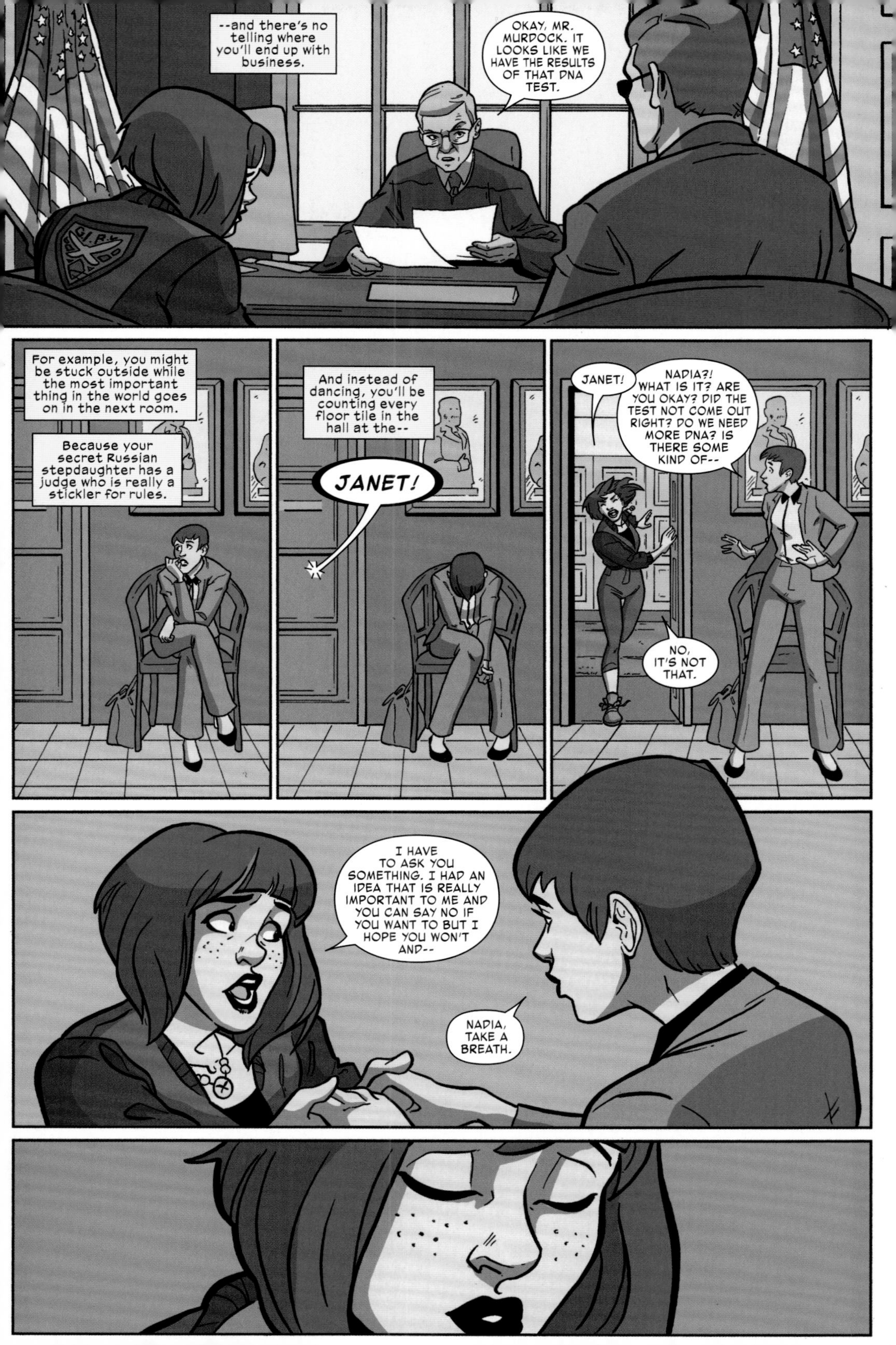
--and there's no telling where you'll end up with business.
OKAY, MR. MURDOCK. IT LOOKS LIKE WE HAVE THE RESULTS OF THAT DNA TEST.
For example, you might be stuck outside while the most important thing in the world goes on in the next room.
Because your secret Russian stepdaughter has a judge who is really a stickler for rules.
And instead of dancing, you'll be counting every floor tile in the hall at the--
JANET!
JANET!
NADIA?! WHAT IS IT? ARE YOU OKAY? DID THE TEST NOT COME OUT RIGHT? DO WE NEED MORE DNA? IS THERE SOME KIND OF--
NO, IT'S NOT THAT.
I HAVE TO ASK YOU SOMETHING. I HAD AN IDEA THAT IS REALLY IMPORTANT TO ME AND YOU CAN SAY NO IF YOU WANT TO BUT I HOPE YOU WON'T AND--
NADIA, TAKE A BREATH.

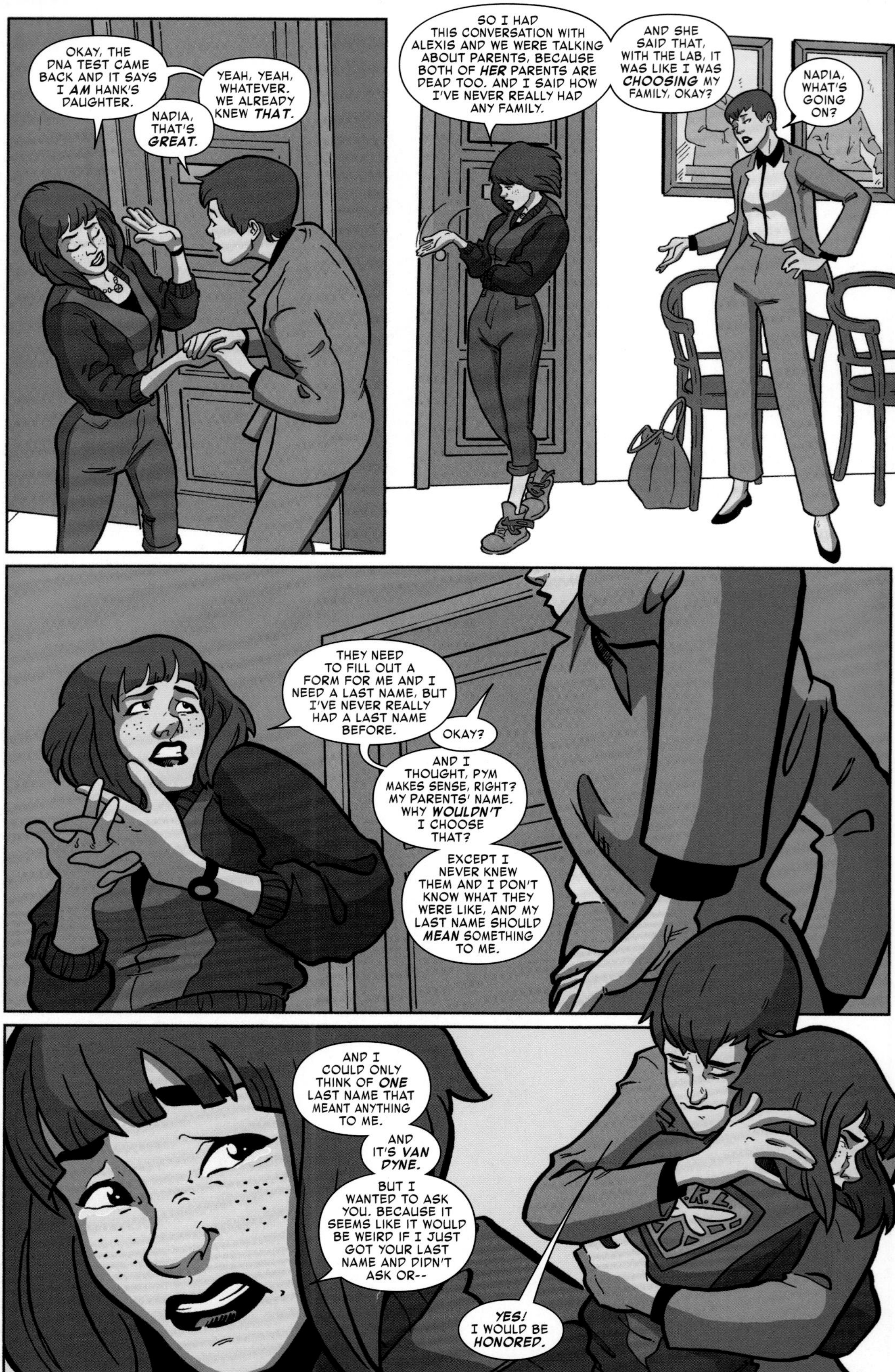
OKAY, THE DNA TEST CAME BACK AND IT SAYS I AM HANK'S DAUGHTER.
NADIA, THAT'S GREAT.
YEAH, YEAH, WHATEVER. WE ALREADY KNEW THAT.
SO I HAD THIS CONVERSATION WITH ALEXIS AND WE WERE TALKING ABOUT PARENTS, BECAUSE BOTH OF HER PARENTS ARE DEAD TOO. AND I SAID HOW I'VE NEVER REALLY HAD ANY FAMILY.
AND SHE SAID THAT, WITH THE LAB, IT WAS LIKE I WAS CHOOSING MY FAMILY, OKAY?
NADIA, WHAT'S GOING ON?
THEY NEED TO FILL OUT A FORM FOR ME AND I NEED A LAST NAME, BUT I'VE NEVER REALLY HAD A LAST NAME BEFORE.
OKAY?
AND I THOUGHT, PYM MAKES SENSE, RIGHT? MY PARENTS' NAME. WHY WOULDN'T I CHOOSE THAT?
EXCEPT I NEVER KNEW THEM AND I DON'T KNOW WHAT THEY WERE LIKE, AND MY LAST NAME SHOULD MEAN SOMETHING TO ME.
AND I COULD ONLY THINK OF ONE LAST NAME THAT MEANT ANYTHING TO ME.
AND IT'S VAN DYNE.
BUT I WANTED TO ASK YOU. BECAUSE IT SEEMS LIKE IT WOULD BE WEIRD IF I JUST GOT YOUR LAST NAME AND DIDN'T ASK OR--
YES! I WOULD BE HONORED.

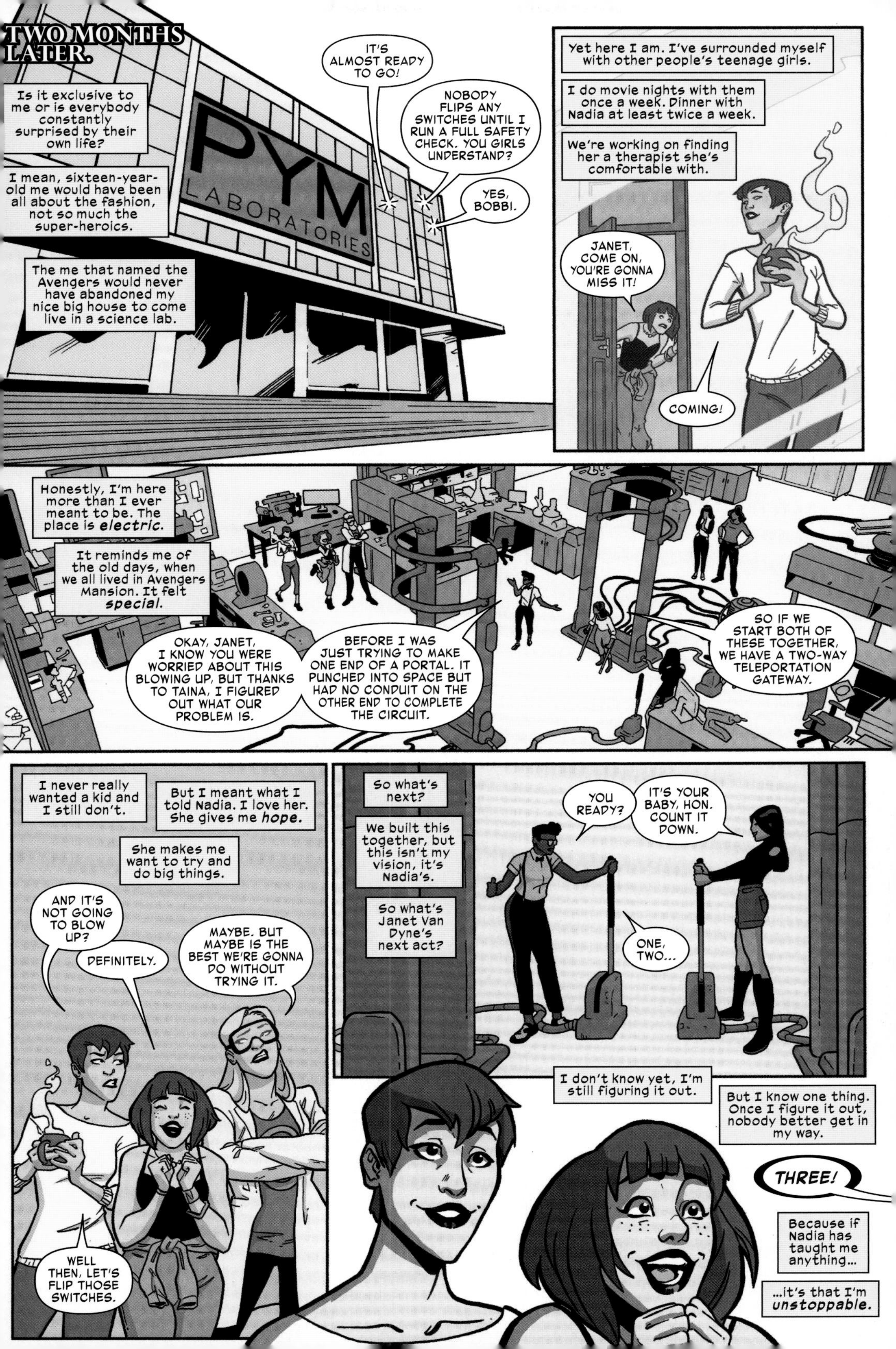
TWO MONTHS LATER.
Is it exclusive to me or is everybody constantly surprised by their own life?
I mean, sixteen-year-old me would have been all about the fashion, not so much the super-heroics.
The me that named the Avengers would never have abandoned my nice big house to come live in a science lab.
PYM LABORATORIES
IT'S ALMOST READY TO GO!
NOBODY FLIPS ANY SWITCHES UNTIL I RUN A FULL SAFETY CHECK. YOU GIRLS UNDERSTAND?
YES, BOBBI.
Yet here I am. I've surrounded myself with other people's teenage girls.
I do movie nights with them once a week. Dinner with Nadia at least twice a week.
We're working on finding her a therapist she's comfortable with.
JANET, COME ON, YOU'RE GONNA MISS IT!
COMING!
Honestly, I'm here more than I ever meant to be. The place is *electric.*
It reminds me of the old days, when we all lived in Avengers Mansion. It felt *special.*
OKAY, JANET, I KNOW YOU WERE WORRIED ABOUT THIS BLOWING UP, BUT THANKS TO TAINA, I FIGURED OUT WHAT OUR PROBLEM IS.
BEFORE I WAS JUST TRYING TO MAKE ONE END OF A PORTAL. IT PUNCHED INTO SPACE BUT HAD NO CONDUIT ON THE OTHER END TO COMPLETE THE CIRCUIT.
SO IF WE START BOTH OF THESE TOGETHER, WE HAVE A TWO-WAY TELEPORTATION GATEWAY.
I never really wanted a kid and I still don't.
But I meant what I told Nadia. I love her. She gives me *hope.*
She makes me want to try and do big things.
AND IT'S NOT GOING TO BLOW UP?
DEFINITELY.
MAYBE. BUT MAYBE IS THE BEST WE'RE GONNA DO WITHOUT TRYING IT.
WELL THEN, LET'S FLIP THOSE SWITCHES.
So what's next?
We built this together, but this isn't my vision, it's Nadia's.
So what's Janet Van Dyne's next act?
YOU READY?
IT'S YOUR BABY, HON. COUNT IT DOWN.
ONE, TWO...
I don't know yet, I'm still figuring it out.
But I know one thing. Once I figure it out, nobody better get in my way.
THREE!
Because if Nadia has taught me anything...
...it's that I'm *unstoppable.*

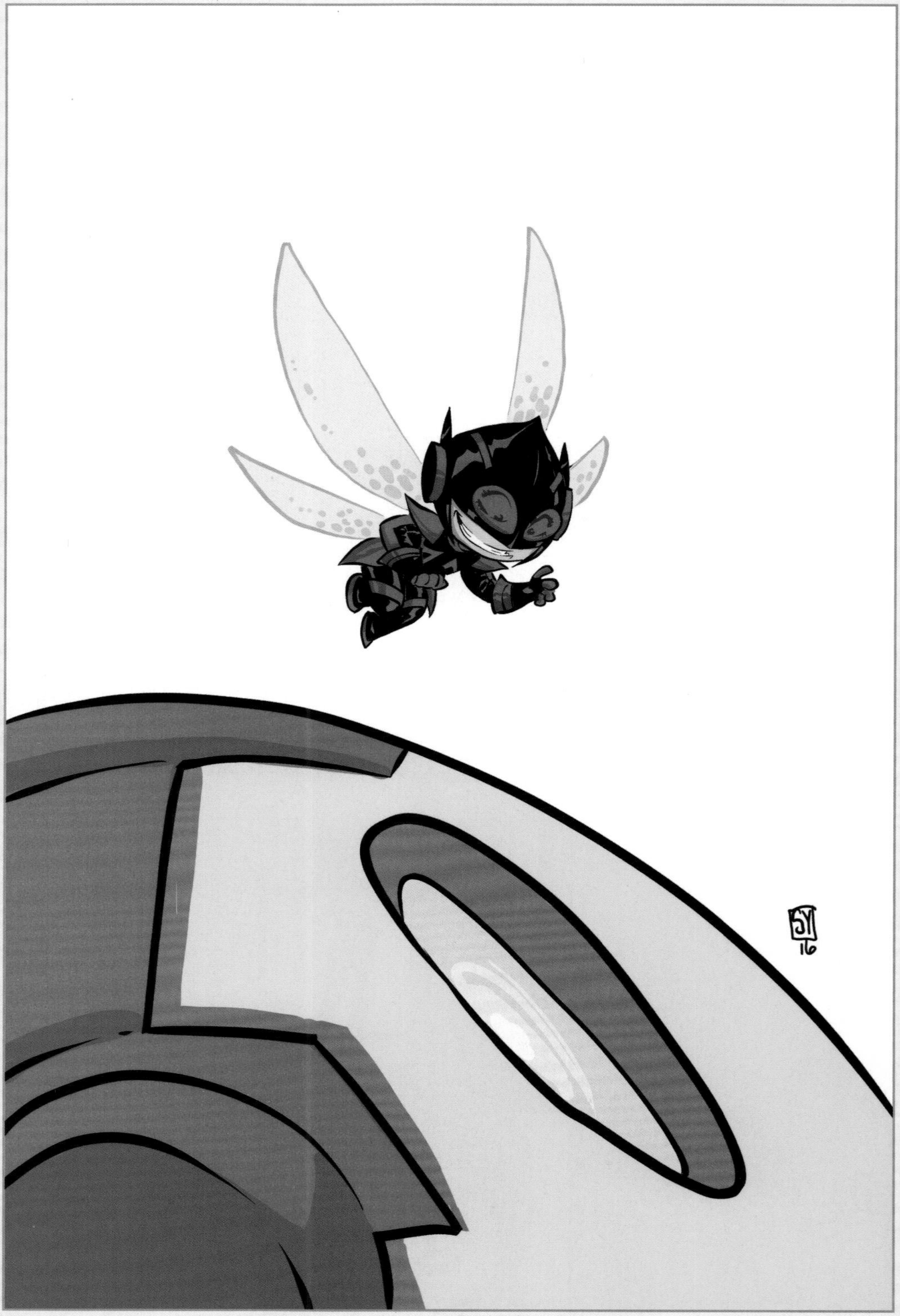
SY
16

#1 VARIANT
BY SKOTTIE YOUNG

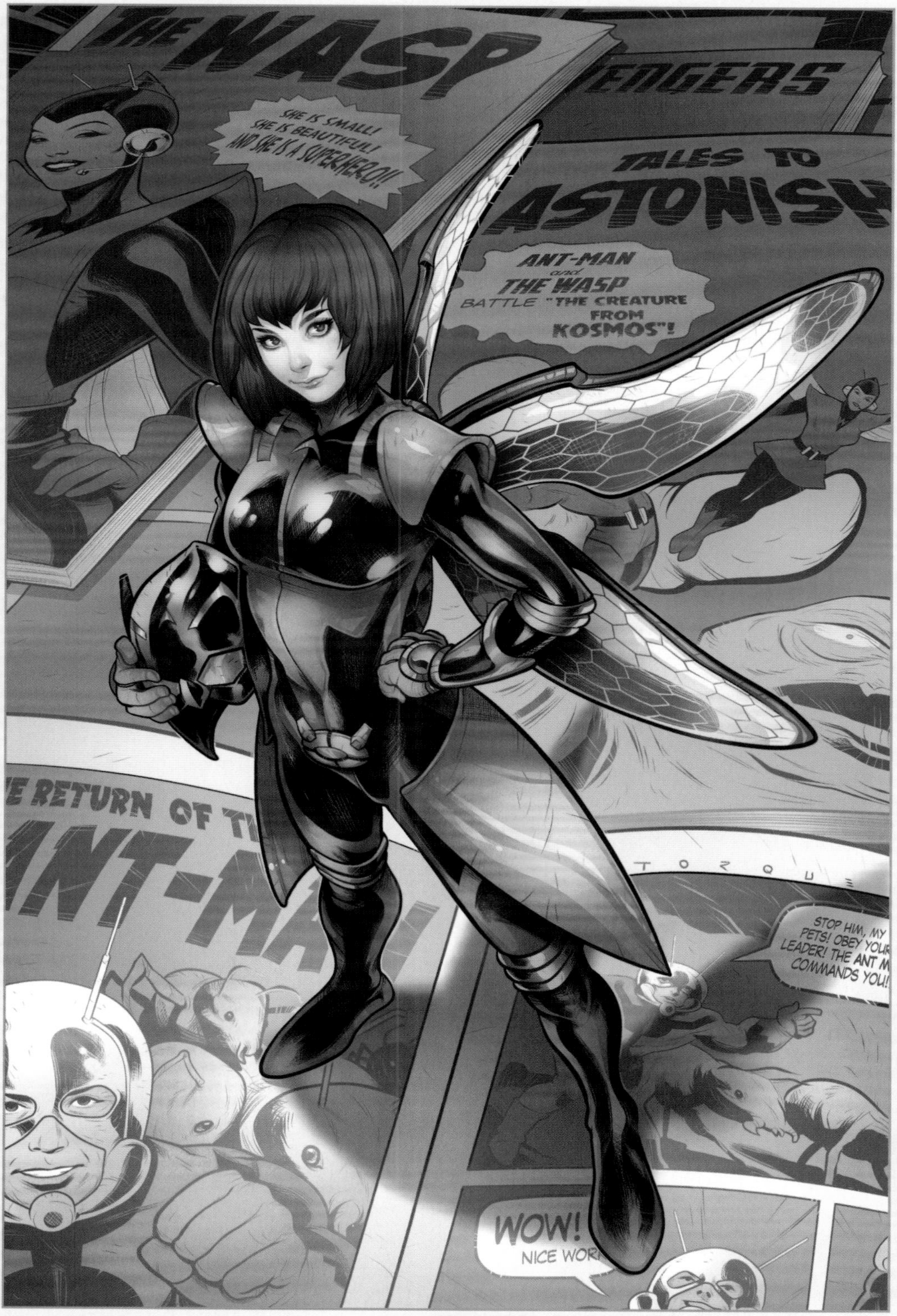
THE WASP
SHE IS SMALL! SHE IS BEAUTIFUL! AND SHE IS A SUPERHERO!!
TALES TO ASTONISH
ANT-MAN and THE WASP BATTLE "THE CREATURE FROM KOSMOS"!
TORQUE
STOP HIM, MY PETS! OBEY YOUR LEADER! THE ANT MAN COMMANDS YOU!
WOW! NICE WOR

#1 VARIANT
BY ELIZABETH TORQUE

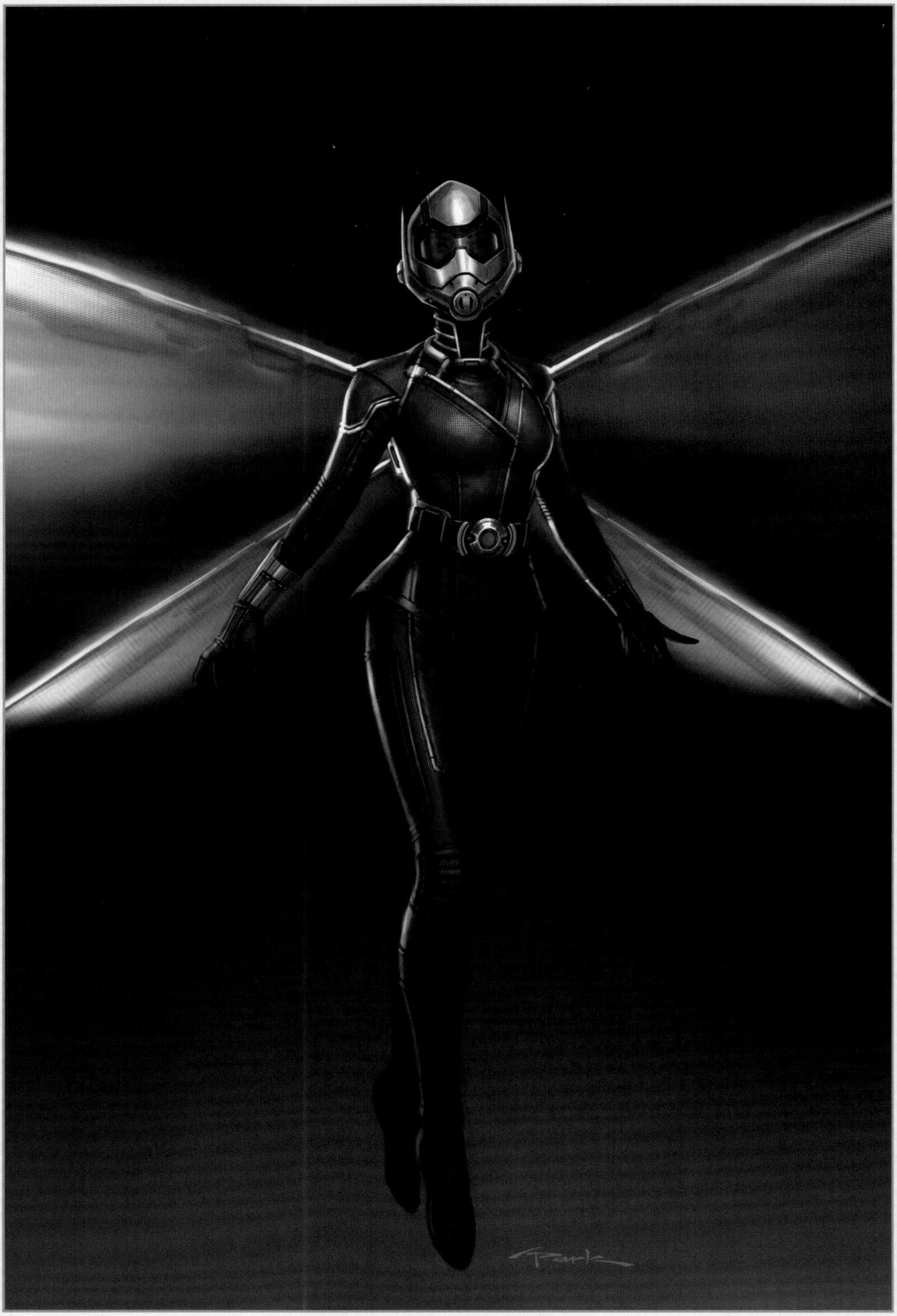

#1 MOVIE VARIANT
BY ANDY PARK

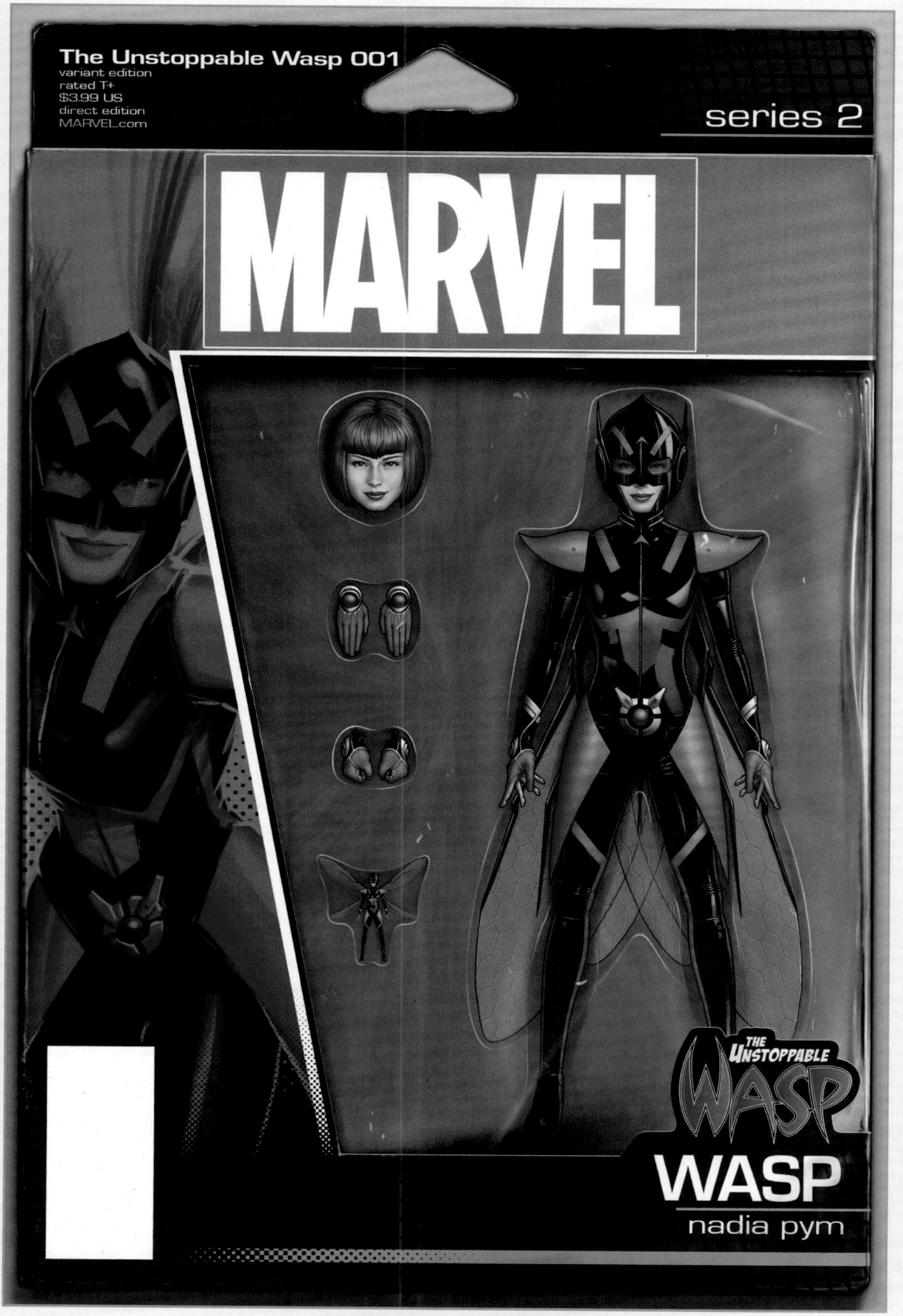
The Unstoppable Wasp 001
variant edition
rated T+
$3.99 US
direct edition
MARVEL.com
series 2
MARVEL
THE UNSTOPPABLE
WASP
WASP
nadia pym

#1 ACTION FIGURE VARIANT
BY JOHN TYLER CHRISTOPHER

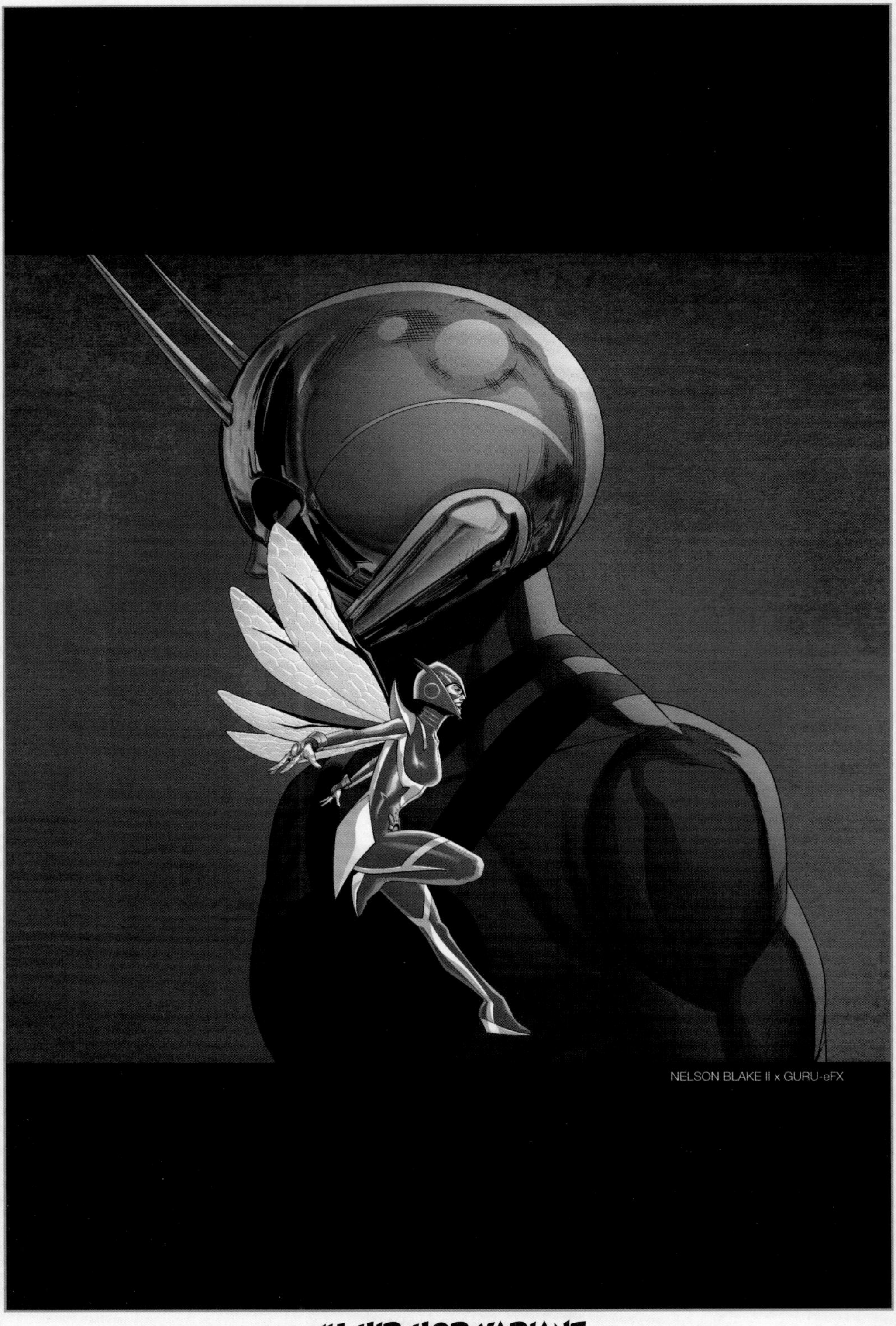
NELSON BLAKE II x GURU-eFX

#1 HIP-HOP VARIANT
BY NELSON BLAKE III & GURU-eFX

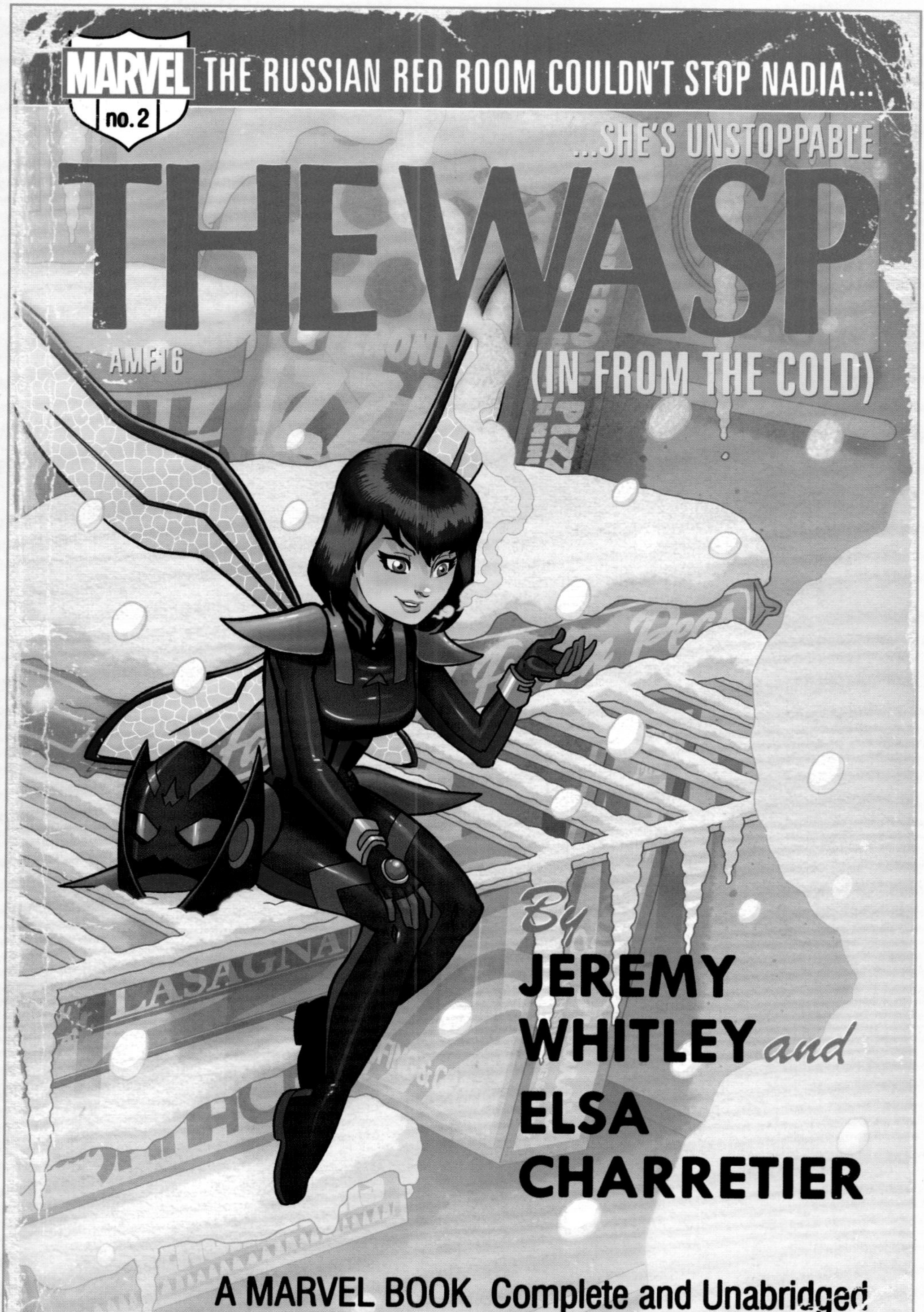
MARVEL
no.2
THE RUSSIAN RED ROOM COULDN'T STOP NADIA...
...SHE'S UNSTOPPABLE
THE WASP
AMF16
(IN FROM THE COLD)
LASAGNA
By
JEREMY WHITLEY and
ELSA CHARRETIER
A MARVEL BOOK Complete and Unabridged

#2 VARIANT
BY TONY FLEECS

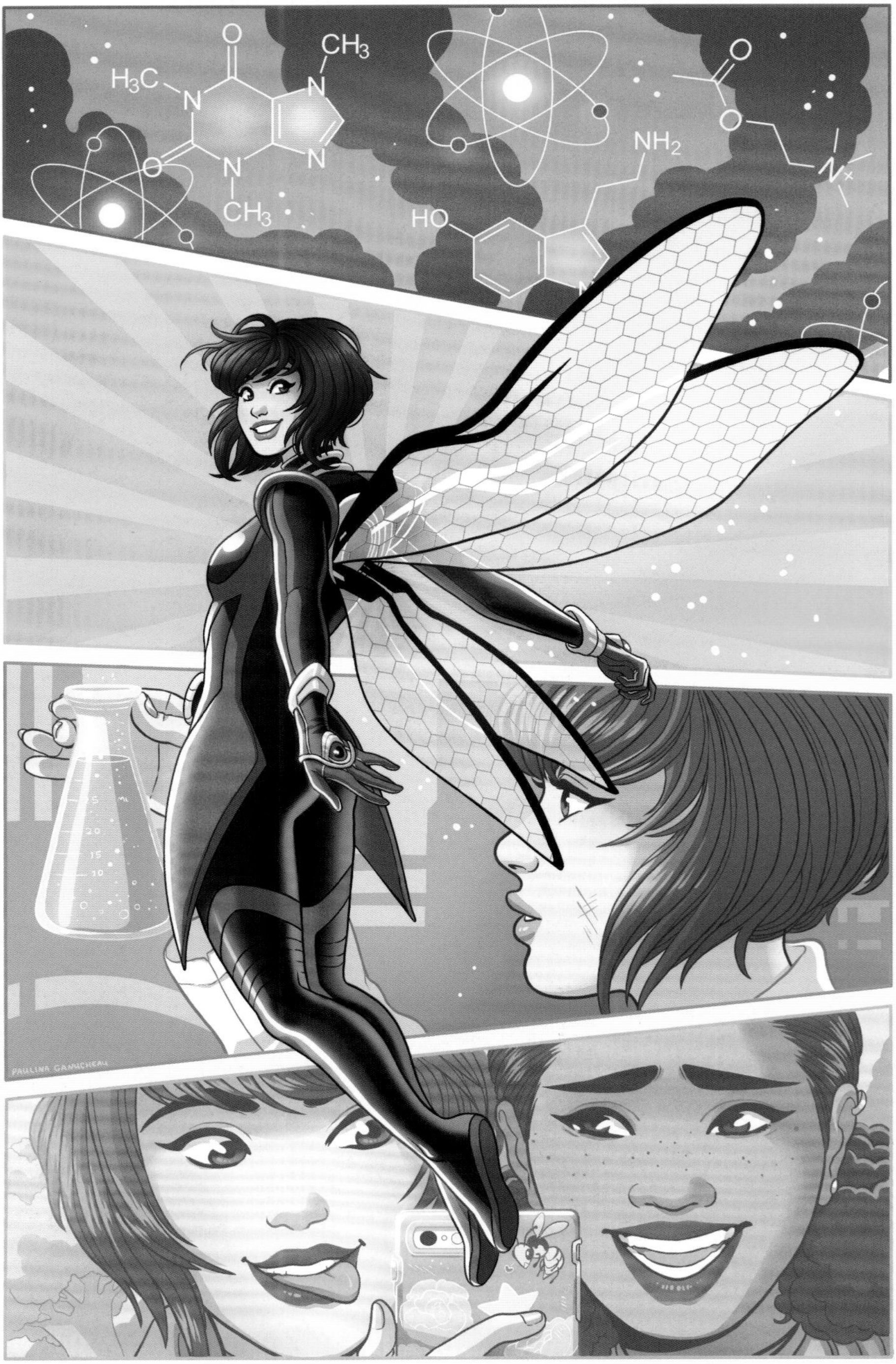
PAULINA GANUCHEAU

#3 VARIANT
BY PAULINA GANUCHEAU

CHARACTER DESIGNS BY ELSA CHARRETIER

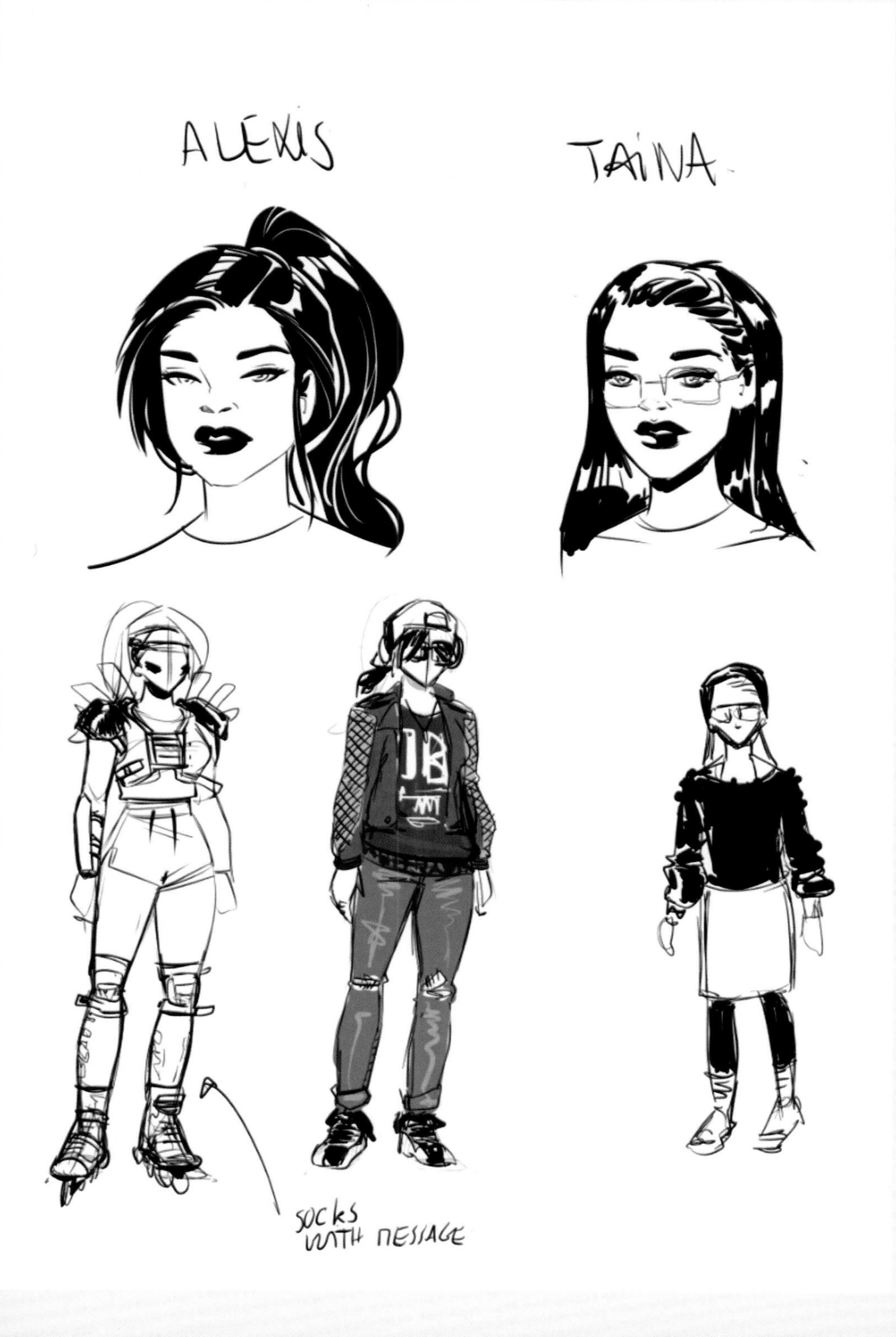
ALEXIS
TAINA
SOCKS
WITH MESSAGE

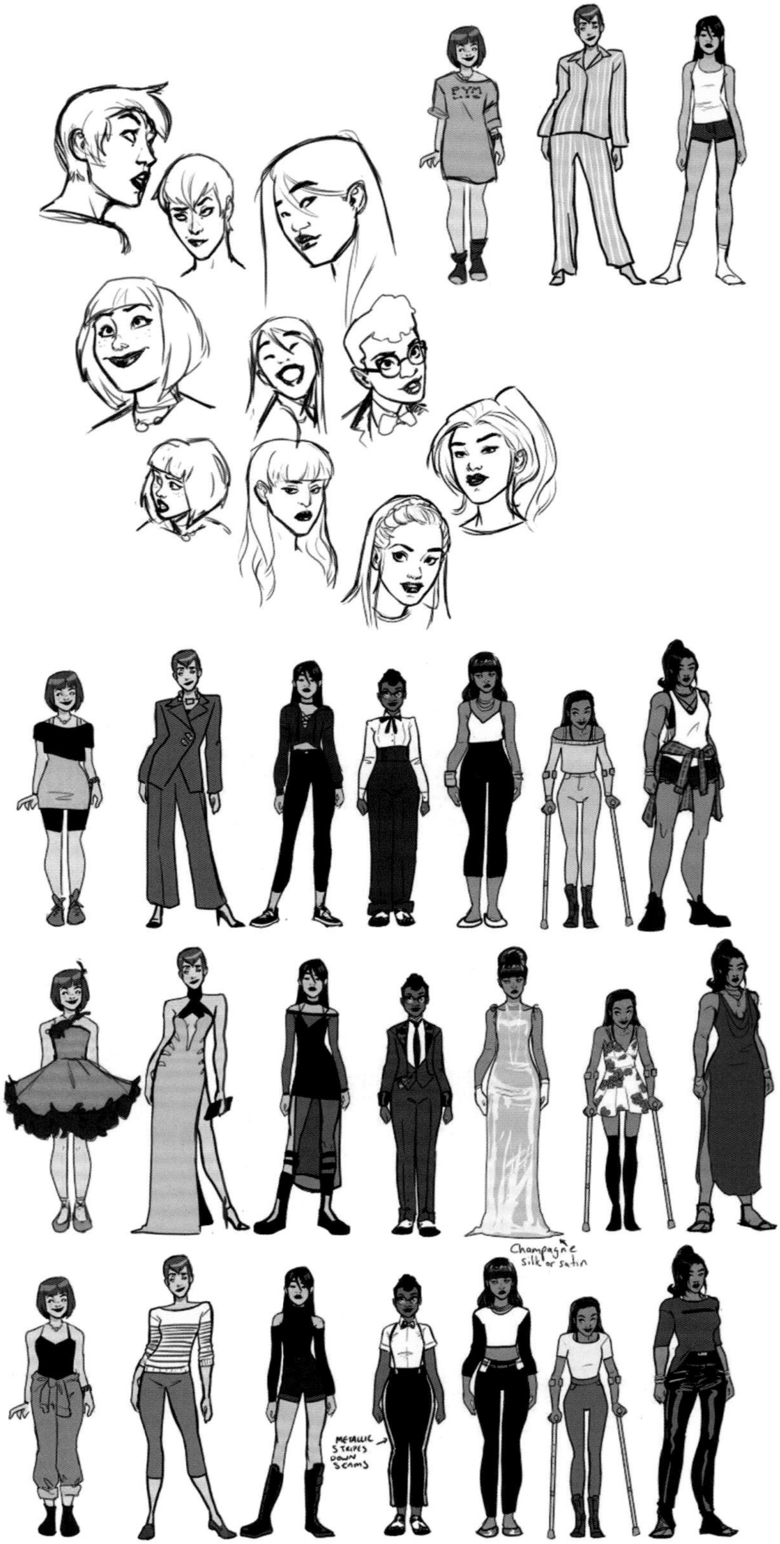
Champagne silk or satin
METALLIC STRIPES DOWN SEAMS

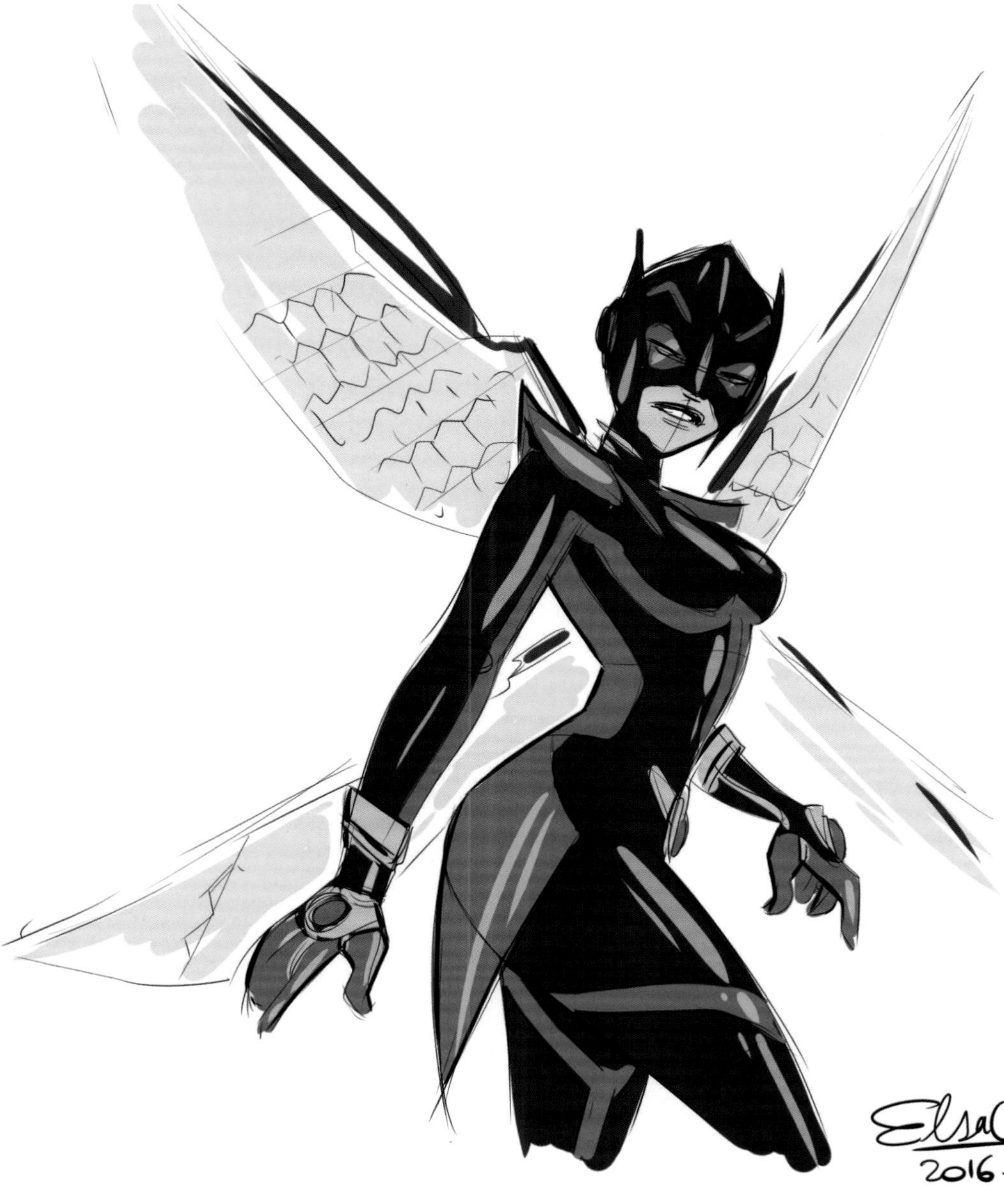
ElsaC
2016.

#8 COVER PROCESS BY ELSA CHARRETIER & NICOLAS BANNISTER

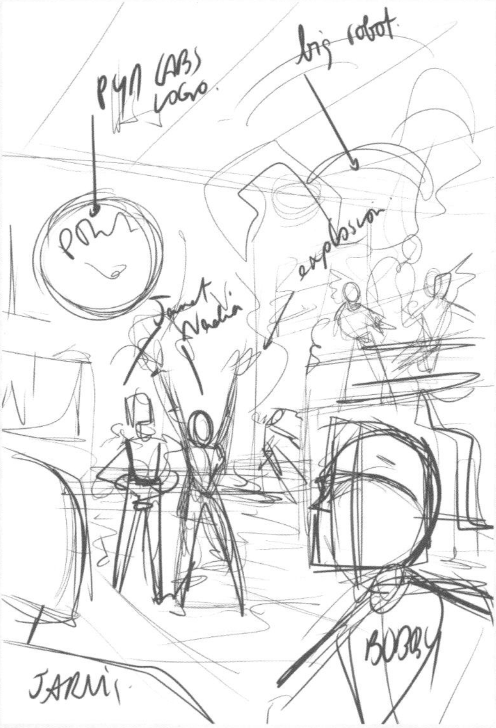
PYM LABS LOGO
big robot
explosion
BOBBY

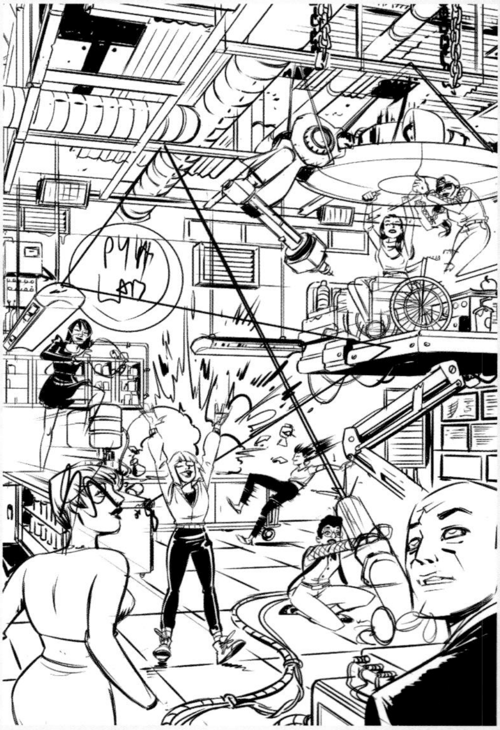
PYM LAB

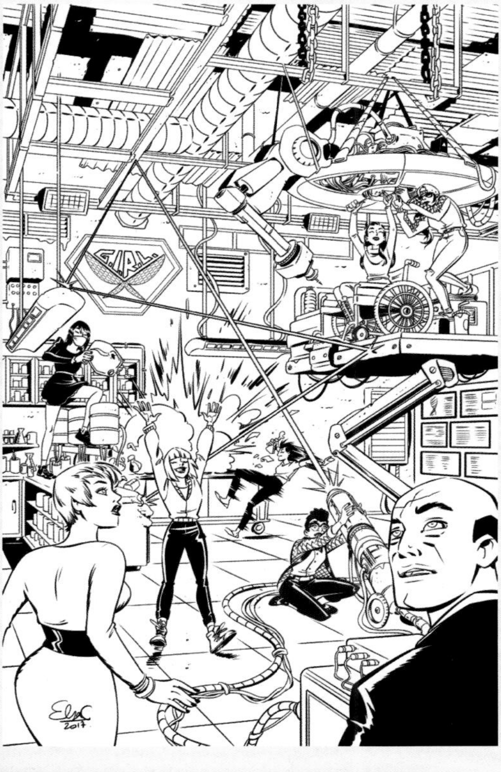
G.I.R.L.
Elsa C 2017

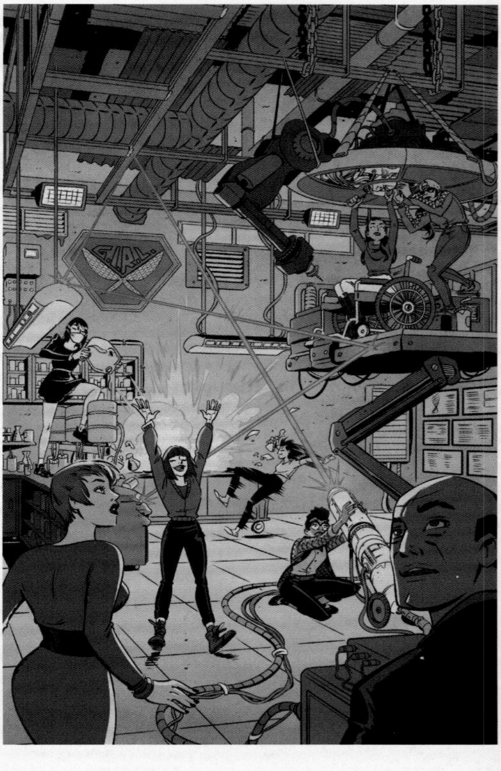
G.I.R.L.

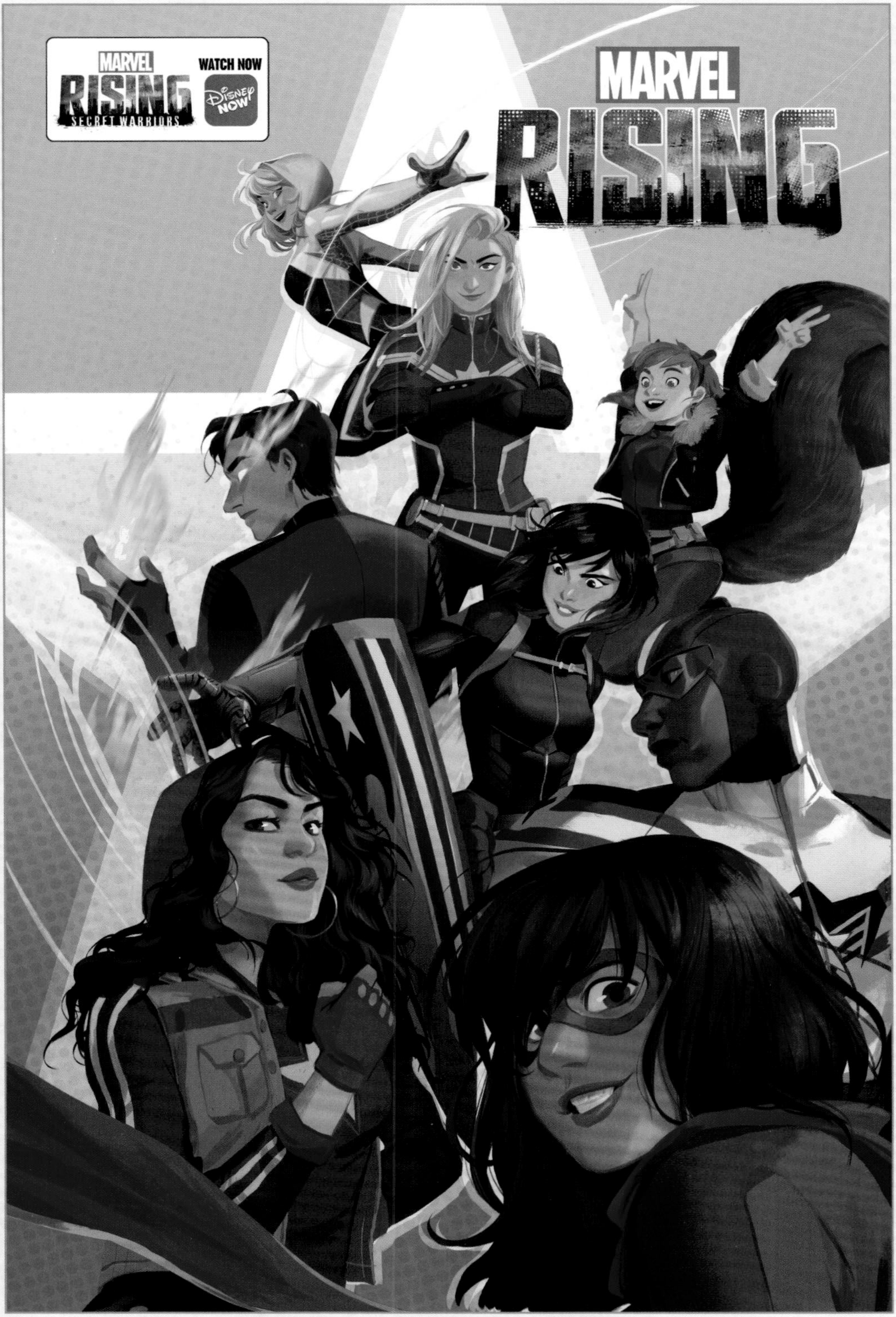
MARVEL
RISING
SECRET WARRIORS
WATCH NOW
DISNEY NOW
MARVEL
RISING

INTRODUCING MARVEL RISING!

MARVEL RISING

THE MARVEL UNIVERSE IS A RICH TREASURE CHEST OF CHARACTERS BORN ACROSS MARVEL'S INCREDIBLE 80-YEAR HISTORY. FROM CAPTAIN AMERICA TO CAPTAIN MARVEL, IRON MAN TO IRONHEART, THIS IS AN EVER-EXPANDING UNIVERSE FULL OF POWERFUL HEROES THAT ALSO REFLECTS THE WORLD WE LIVE IN.

YET DESPITE THAT EXPANSION, OUR STORIES REMAIN TIMELESS. THEY'VE BEEN SHARED ACROSS THE GLOBE AND ACROSS GENERATIONS, LINKING FANS WITH THE ENDURING IDEA THAT ORDINARY PEOPLE CAN DO EXTRAORDINARY THINGS. IT'S THAT SHARED EXPERIENCE OF THE MARVEL STORY THAT HAS ALLOWED US TO EXIST FOR THIS LONG. WHETHER YOUR FIRST MARVEL EXPERIENCE WAS THROUGH A COMIC BOOK, A BEDTIME STORY, A MOVIE OR A CARTOON, WE BELIEVE OUR STORIES STAY WITH AUDIENCES THROUGHOUT THEIR LIVES.

MARVEL RISING IS A CELEBRATION OF THIS TIMELESSNESS. AS OUR STORIES PASS FROM ONE GENERATION TO THE NEXT, SO DOES THE LOVE FOR OUR HEROES. FROM THE CLASSIC TO THE NEWLY IMAGINED, THE PASSION FOR ALL OF THEM IS THE SAME. IF YOU'VE BEEN READING COMICS OVER THE LAST FEW YEARS, YOU'LL KNOW CHARACTERS LIKE MS. MARVEL, SQUIRREL GIRL, AMERICA CHAVEZ, SPIDER-GWEN AND MORE HAVE ASSEMBLED A BEVY OF NEW FANS WHILE CAPTIVATING OUR PERENNIAL FANS. EACH OF THESE HEROES IS UNIQUE AND DISTINCT--JUST LIKE THE READERS THEY'VE BROUGHT IN--AND THEY REMIND US THAT NO MATTER WHAT YOU LOOK LIKE, YOU HAVE THE CAPABILITY TO BE POWERFUL, TOO. WE ARE TAKING THE HEROES FROM MARVEL RISING TO NEW HEIGHTS IN AN ANIMATED FEATURE LATER IN 2018, AS WELL AS A FULL PROGRAM OF CONTENT SWEEPING ACROSS THE COMPANY. BUT FIRST WE'RE GOING BACK TO OUR ROOTS AND TELLING A MARVEL RISING STORY IN COMICS: THE FIRST PLACE YOU MET THESE LOVABLE HEROES.

SO IN THE TRADITION OF EXPANDING THE MARVEL UNIVERSE, WE'RE EXCITED TO INTRODUCE MARVEL RISING--THE NEXT GENERATION OF MARVEL HEROES FOR THE NEXT GENERATION OF MARVEL FANS!

SANA AMANAT

VP, CONTENT & CHARACTER DEVELOPMENT

► **DOREEN GREEN** IS A SECOND-YEAR COMPUTER SCIENCE STUDENT – AND THE CRIMINAL-REDEEMING HERO THE **UNBEATABLE SQUIRREL GIRL!** THE NAME SAYS IT ALL: AN UNBEATABLE GIRL WITH THE POWERS OF AN UNBEATABLE SQUIRREL, TAIL INCLUDED. AND ON TOP OF HER STUDYING, NUT-EATING AND BUTT-KICKING ACTIVITIES, SHE'S JUST TAKEN ON THE JOB OF VOLUNTEER TEACHER FOR AN EXTRA-CURRICULAR HIGH-SCHOOL CODING CAMP! AND WHO SHOULD END UP IN HER CLASS BUT...

► **KAMALA KHAN**, A.K.A. JERSEY CITY HERO AND INHUMAN POLYMORPH **MS. MARVEL!** BUT BETWEEN SAVING THE WORLD WITH THE CHAMPIONS AND PROTECTING JERSEY CITY ON HER OWN, KAMALA'S GOT A LOT ON HER PLATE ALREADY. AND FIELD TRIP DAY MAY NOT BE THE BREAK SHE'S ANTICIPATING...

MARVEL RISING
PART 0

DEVIN GRAYSON
WRITER

MARCO FAILLA
ARTIST

RACHELLE ROSENBERG
COLOR ARTIST

VC's CLAYTON COWLES
LETTERER

HELEN CHEN
COVER

JAY BOWEN
DESIGN

HEATHER ANTOS AND **SARAH BRUNSTAD**
EDITORS

SANA AMANAT
CONSULTING EDITOR

C.B. CEBULSKI
EDITOR IN CHIEF

JOE QUESADA
CHIEF CREATIVE OFFICER

DAN BUCKLEY
PRESIDENT

ALAN FINE
EXECUTIVE PRODUCER

SPECIAL THANKS TO RYAN NORTH AND G. WILLOW WILSON

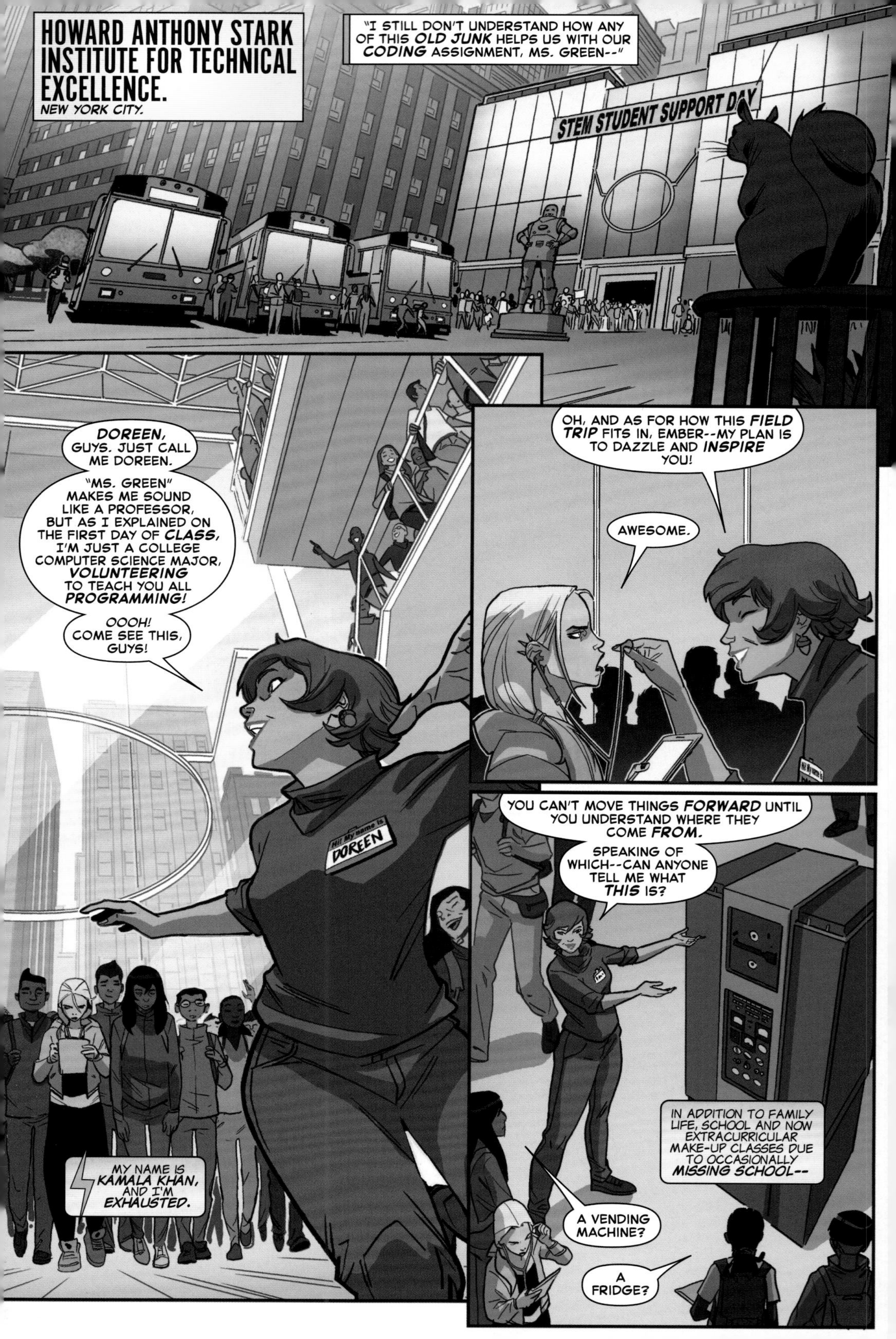
HOWARD ANTHONY STARK INSTITUTE FOR TECHNICAL EXCELLENCE.
NEW YORK CITY.
"I STILL DON'T UNDERSTAND HOW ANY OF THIS OLD JUNK HELPS US WITH OUR CODING ASSIGNMENT, MS. GREEN--"
STEM STUDENT SUPPORT DAY
DOREEN, GUYS. JUST CALL ME DOREEN.
"MS. GREEN" MAKES ME SOUND LIKE A PROFESSOR, BUT AS I EXPLAINED ON THE FIRST DAY OF CLASS, I'M JUST A COLLEGE COMPUTER SCIENCE MAJOR, VOLUNTEERING TO TEACH YOU ALL PROGRAMMING!
OOOH! COME SEE THIS, GUYS!
HI! My name is DOREEN
MY NAME IS KAMALA KHAN, AND I'M EXHAUSTED.
OH, AND AS FOR HOW THIS FIELD TRIP FITS IN, EMBER--MY PLAN IS TO DAZZLE AND INSPIRE YOU!
AWESOME.
YOU CAN'T MOVE THINGS FORWARD UNTIL YOU UNDERSTAND WHERE THEY COME FROM.
SPEAKING OF WHICH--CAN ANYONE TELL ME WHAT THIS IS?
IN ADDITION TO FAMILY LIFE, SCHOOL AND NOW EXTRACURRICULAR MAKE-UP CLASSES DUE TO OCCASIONALLY MISSING SCHOOL--
A VENDING MACHINE?
A FRIDGE?

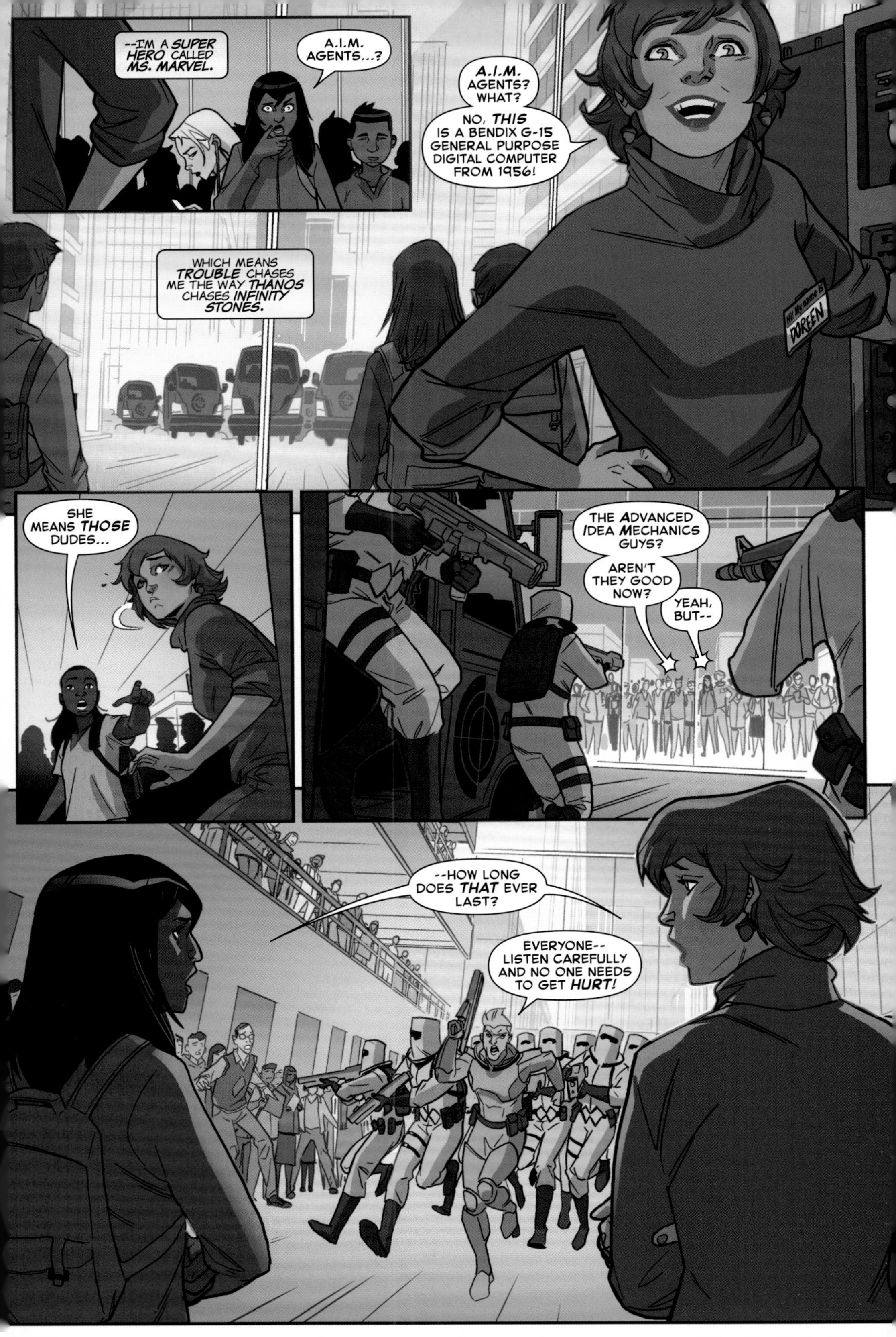
--I'M A SUPER HERO CALLED MS. MARVEL.
A.I.M. AGENTS...?
A.I.M. AGENTS? WHAT?
NO, THIS IS A BENDIX G-15 GENERAL PURPOSE DIGITAL COMPUTER FROM 1956!
WHICH MEANS TROUBLE CHASES ME THE WAY THANOS CHASES INFINITY STONES.
DOREEN
SHE MEANS THOSE DUDES...
THE ADVANCED IDEA MECHANICS GUYS?
AREN'T THEY GOOD NOW?
YEAH, BUT--
--HOW LONG DOES THAT EVER LAST?
EVERYONE-- LISTEN CAREFULLY AND NO ONE NEEDS TO GET HURT!

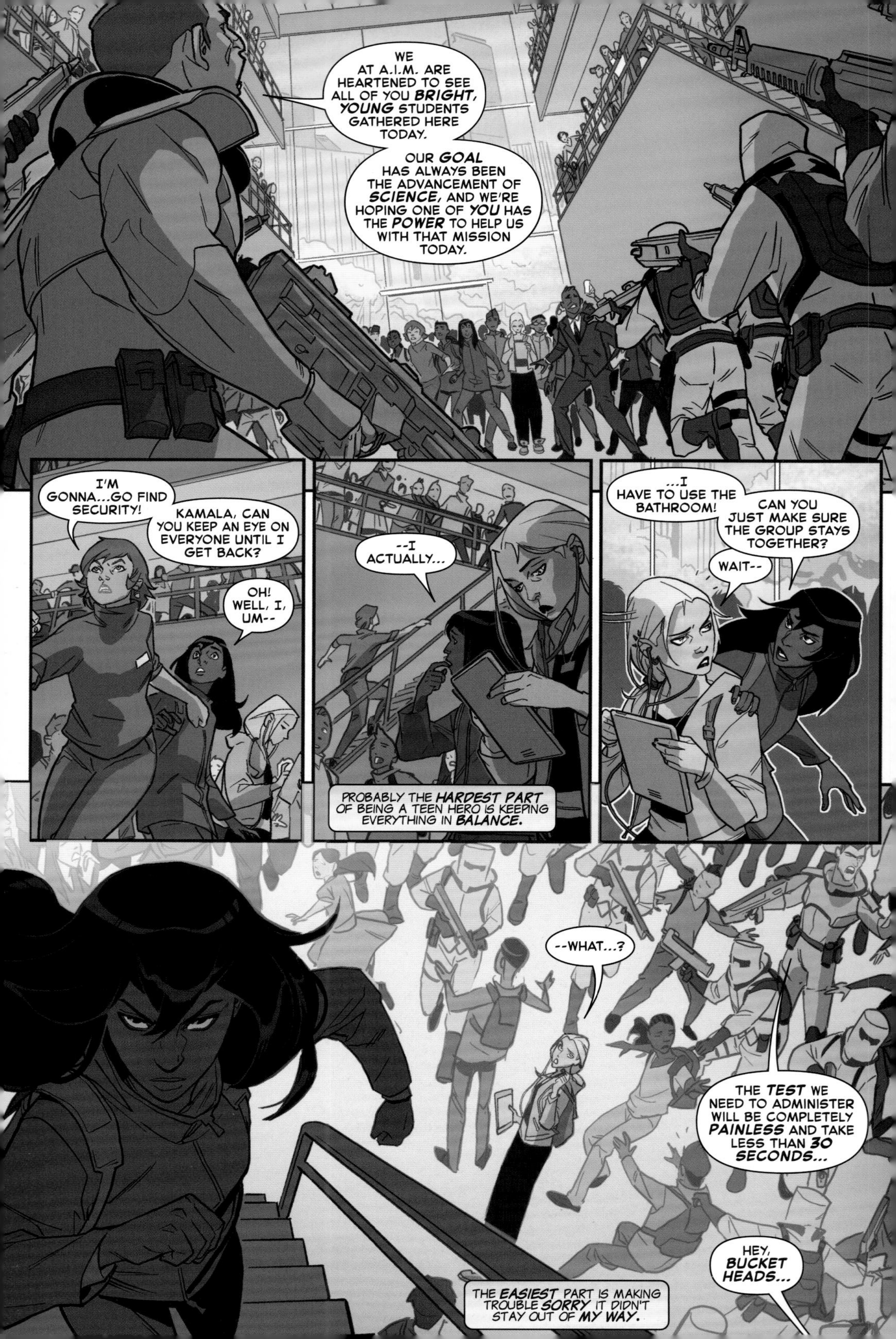
WE AT A.I.M. ARE HEARTENED TO SEE ALL OF YOU BRIGHT, YOUNG STUDENTS GATHERED HERE TODAY.
OUR GOAL HAS ALWAYS BEEN THE ADVANCEMENT OF SCIENCE, AND WE'RE HOPING ONE OF YOU HAS THE POWER TO HELP US WITH THAT MISSION TODAY.
I'M GONNA...GO FIND SECURITY!
KAMALA, CAN YOU KEEP AN EYE ON EVERYONE UNTIL I GET BACK?
OH! WELL, I, UM--
--I ACTUALLY...
PROBABLY THE HARDEST PART OF BEING A TEEN HERO IS KEEPING EVERYTHING IN BALANCE.
...I HAVE TO USE THE BATHROOM!
CAN YOU JUST MAKE SURE THE GROUP STAYS TOGETHER?
WAIT--
--WHAT...?
THE TEST WE NEED TO ADMINISTER WILL BE COMPLETELY PAINLESS AND TAKE LESS THAN 30 SECONDS...
HEY, BUCKET HEADS...
THE EASIEST PART IS MAKING TROUBLE SORRY IT DIDN'T STAY OUT OF MY WAY.

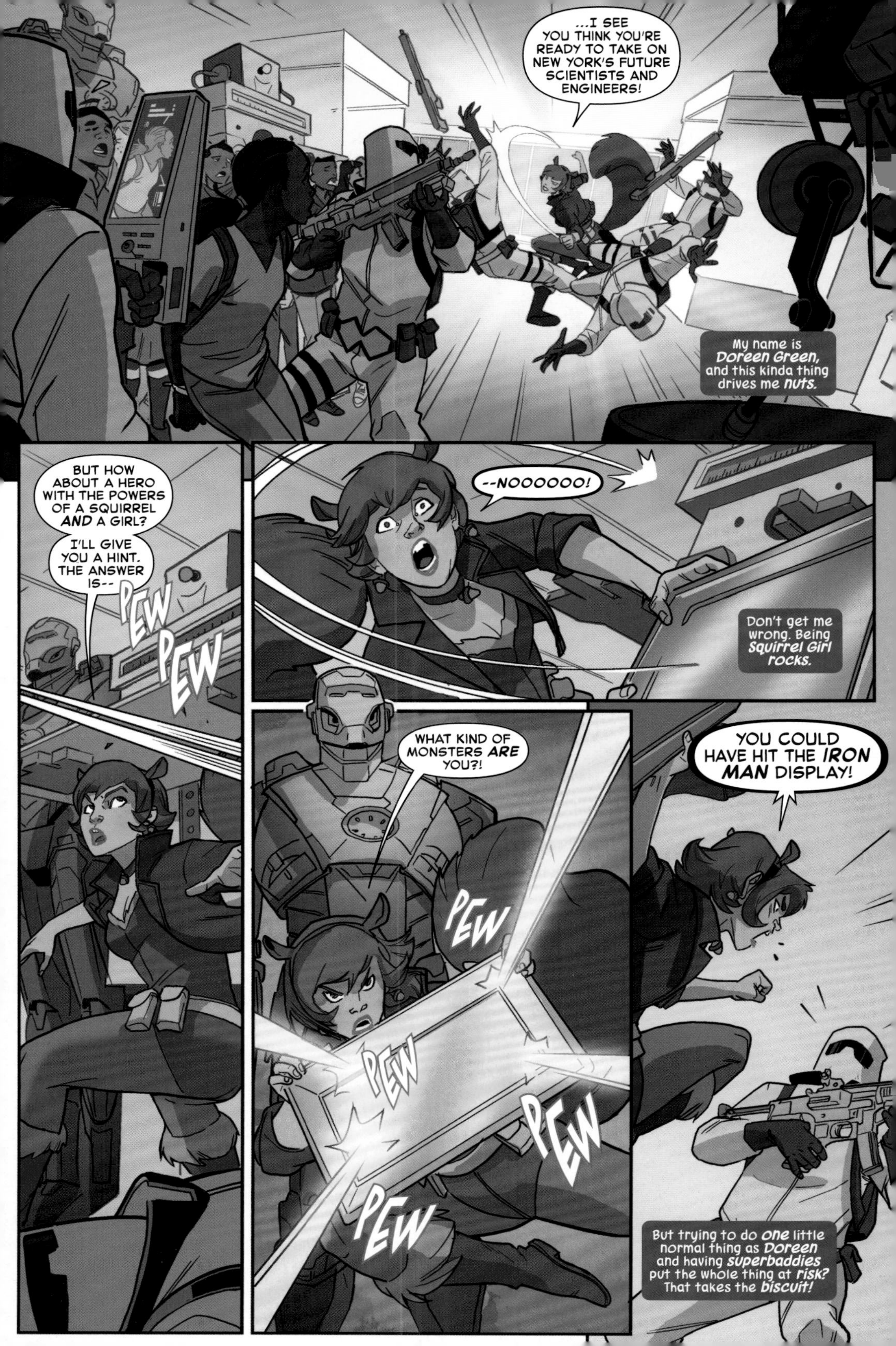
...I SEE YOU THINK YOU'RE READY TO TAKE ON NEW YORK'S FUTURE SCIENTISTS AND ENGINEERS!
My name is Doreen Green, and this kinda thing drives me nuts.
BUT HOW ABOUT A HERO WITH THE POWERS OF A SQUIRREL AND A GIRL?
I'LL GIVE YOU A HINT. THE ANSWER IS--
PEW
PEW
--NOOOOOO!
Don't get me wrong. Being Squirrel Girl rocks.
WHAT KIND OF MONSTERS ARE YOU?!
PEW
PEW
PEW
PEW
YOU COULD HAVE HIT THE IRON MAN DISPLAY!
But trying to do one little normal thing as Doreen and having superbaddies put the whole thing at risk? That takes the biscuit!

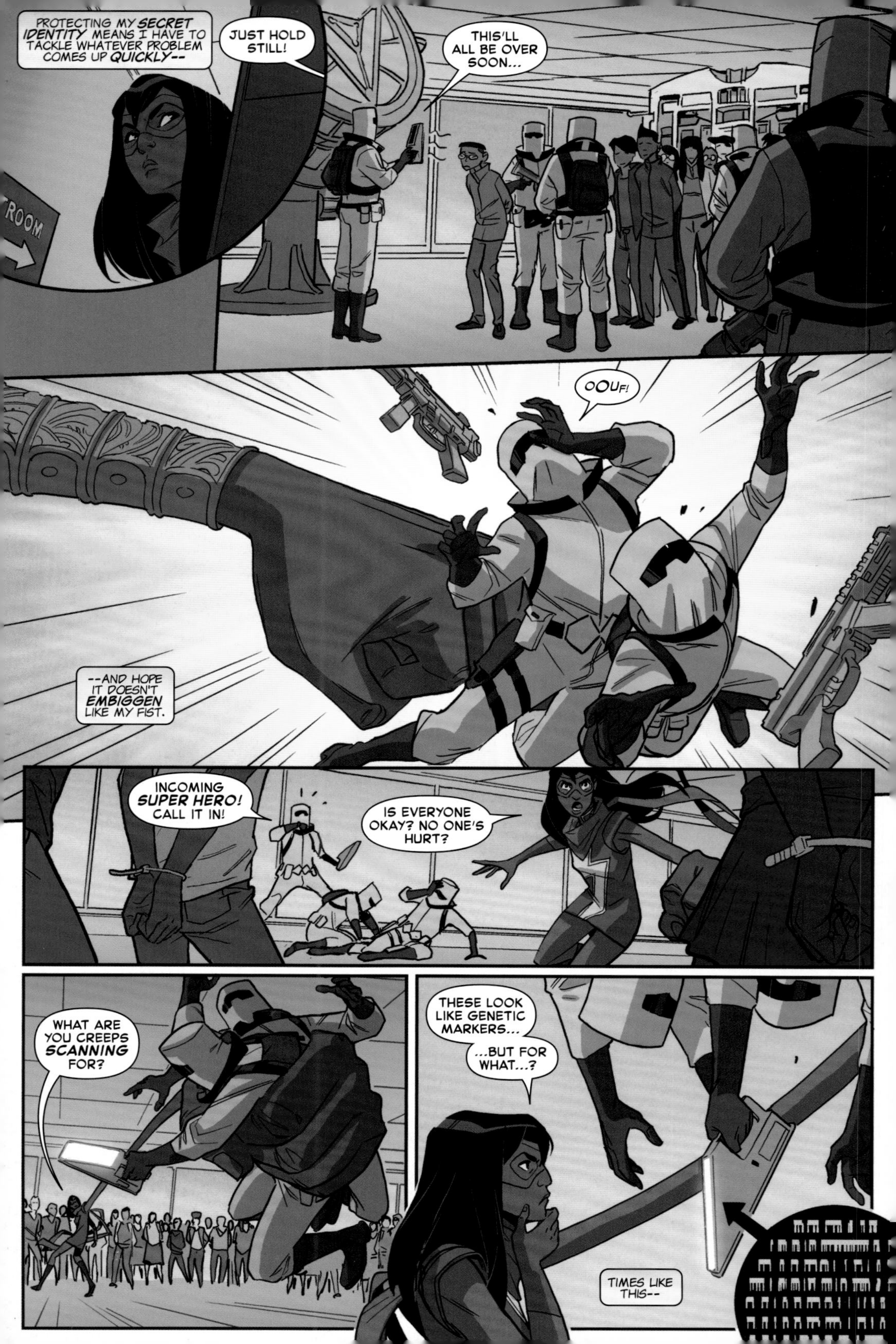
PROTECTING MY SECRET IDENTITY MEANS I HAVE TO TACKLE WHATEVER PROBLEM COMES UP QUICKLY--
JUST HOLD STILL!
THIS'LL ALL BE OVER SOON...
ROOM
OOUF!
--AND HOPE IT DOESN'T EMBIGGEN LIKE MY FIST.
INCOMING SUPER HERO! CALL IT IN!
IS EVERYONE OKAY? NO ONE'S HURT?
WHAT ARE YOU CREEPS SCANNING FOR?
THESE LOOK LIKE GENETIC MARKERS...
...BUT FOR WHAT...?
TIMES LIKE THIS--

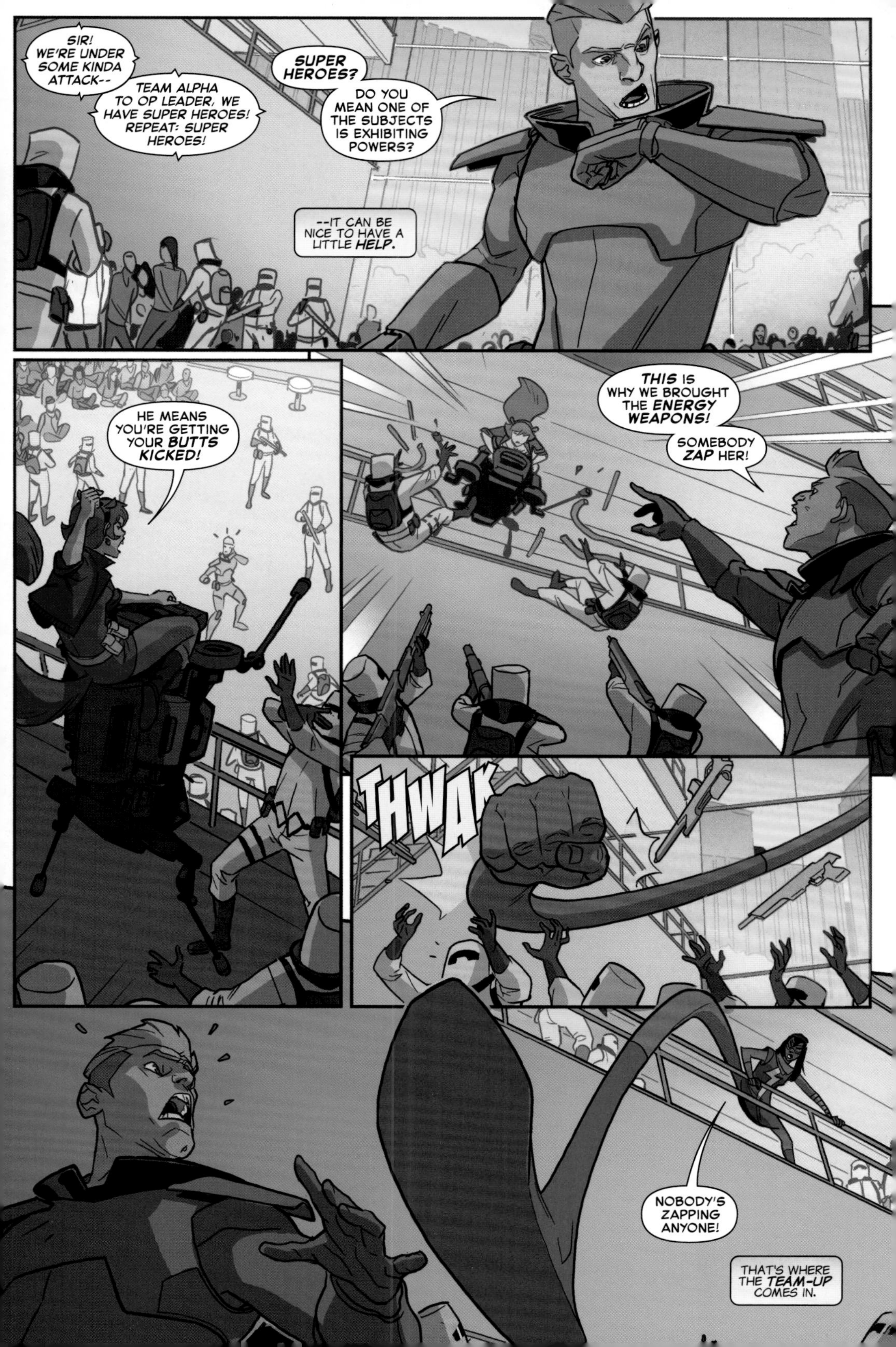
SIR! WE'RE UNDER SOME KINDA ATTACK--
TEAM ALPHA TO OP LEADER, WE HAVE SUPER HEROES! REPEAT: SUPER HEROES!
SUPER HEROES?
DO YOU MEAN ONE OF THE SUBJECTS IS EXHIBITING POWERS?
--IT CAN BE NICE TO HAVE A LITTLE HELP.
HE MEANS YOU'RE GETTING YOUR BUTTS KICKED!
THIS IS WHY WE BROUGHT THE ENERGY WEAPONS!
SOMEBODY ZAP HER!
THWAK
NOBODY'S ZAPPING ANYONE!
THAT'S WHERE THE TEAM-UP COMES IN.

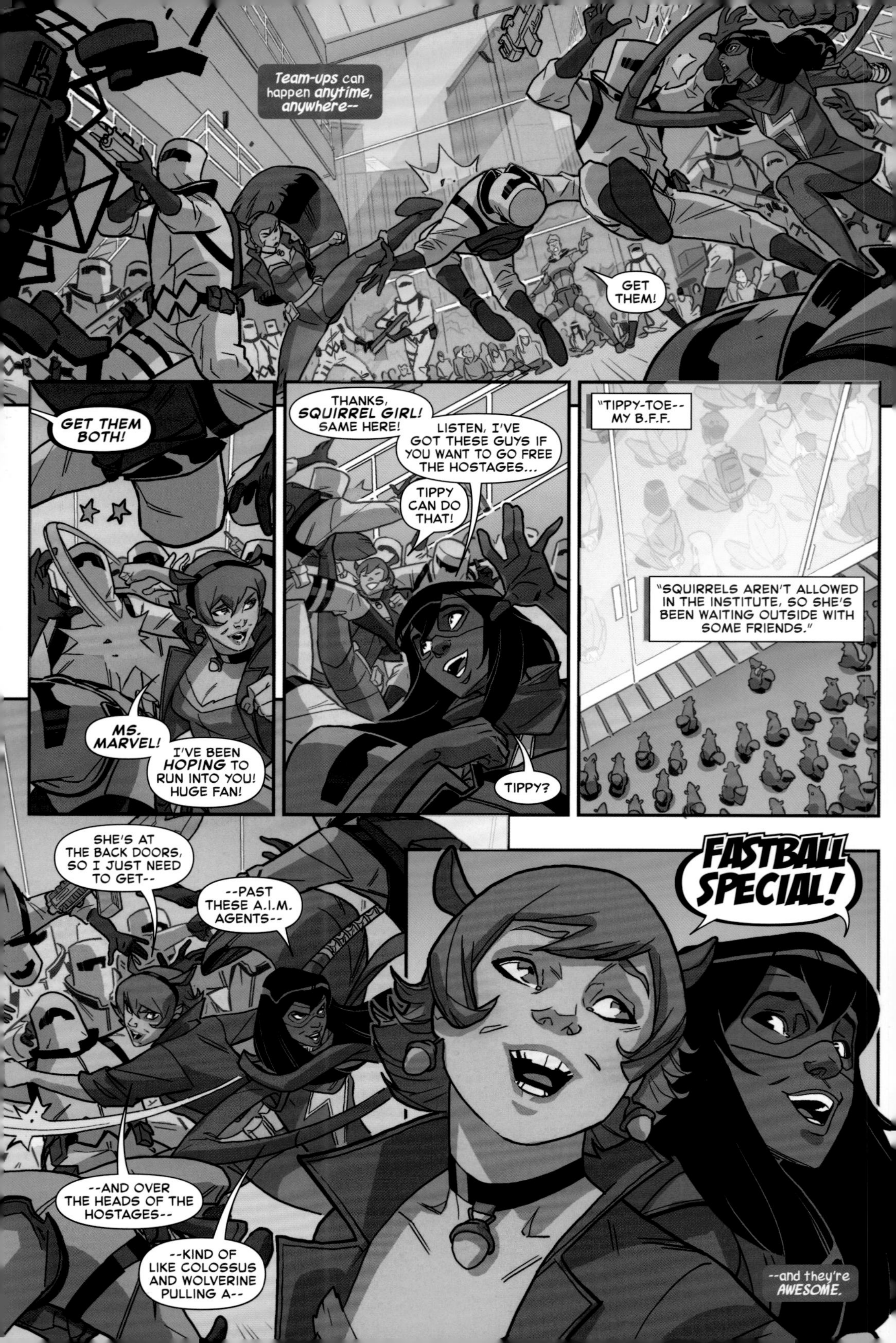

Team-ups can happen anytime, anywhere--
GET THEM!
GET THEM BOTH!
MS. MARVEL!
I'VE BEEN HOPING TO RUN INTO YOU! HUGE FAN!
THANKS, SQUIRREL GIRL! SAME HERE!
LISTEN, I'VE GOT THESE GUYS IF YOU WANT TO GO FREE THE HOSTAGES...
TIPPY CAN DO THAT!
TIPPY?
"TIPPY-TOE-- MY B.F.F.
"SQUIRRELS AREN'T ALLOWED IN THE INSTITUTE, SO SHE'S BEEN WAITING OUTSIDE WITH SOME FRIENDS."
SHE'S AT THE BACK DOORS, SO I JUST NEED TO GET--
--PAST THESE A.I.M. AGENTS--
--AND OVER THE HEADS OF THE HOSTAGES--
--KIND OF LIKE COLOSSUS AND WOLVERINE PULLING A--
FASTBALL SPECIAL!
--and they're AWESOME.

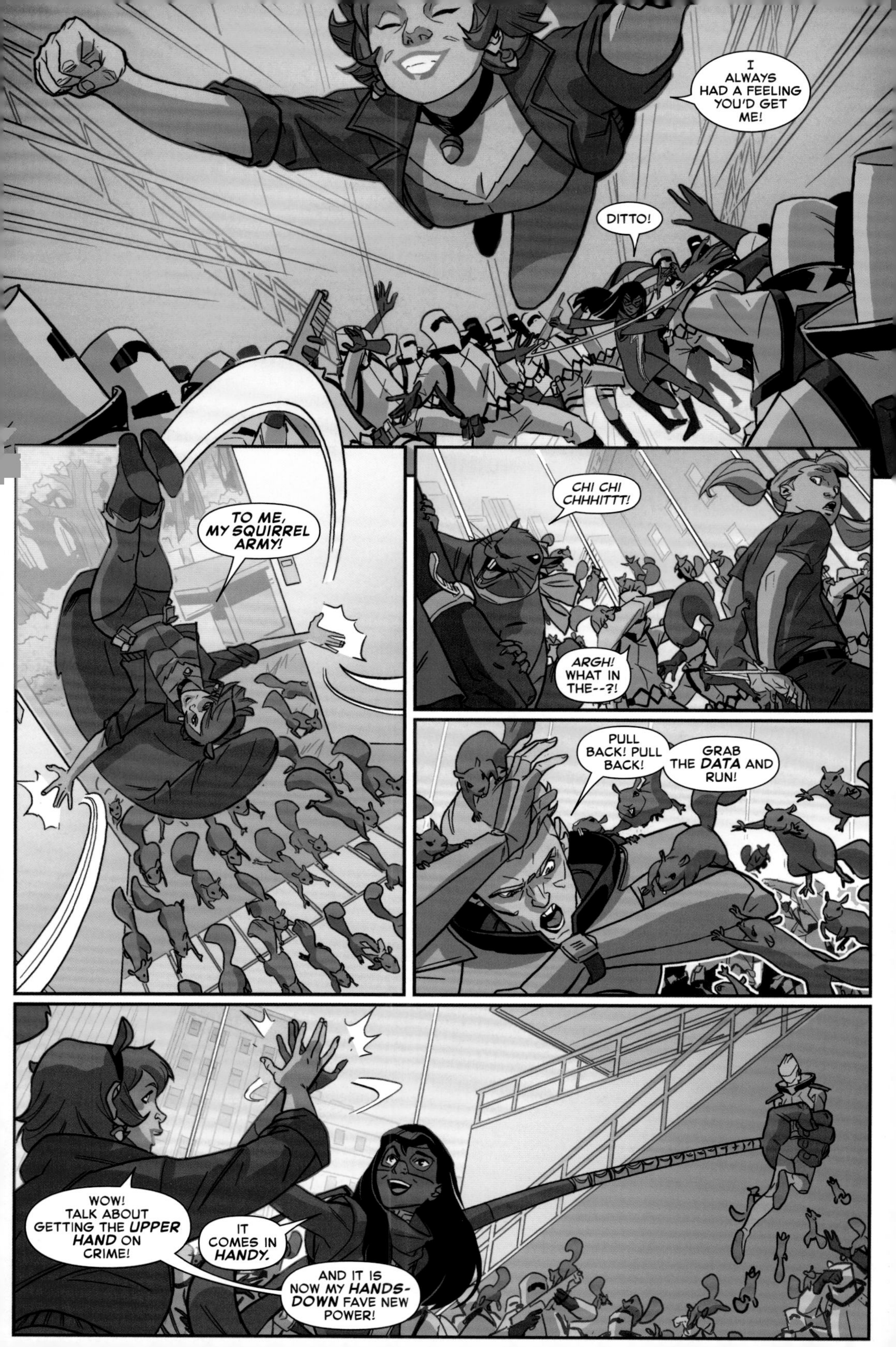
I ALWAYS HAD A FEELING YOU'D GET ME!
DITTO!
TO ME, MY SQUIRREL ARMY!
CHI CHI CHHHITTT!
ARGH! WHAT IN THE--?!
PULL BACK! PULL BACK!
GRAB THE DATA AND RUN!
WOW! TALK ABOUT GETTING THE UPPER HAND ON CRIME!
IT COMES IN HANDY.
AND IT IS NOW MY HANDS-DOWN FAVE NEW POWER!

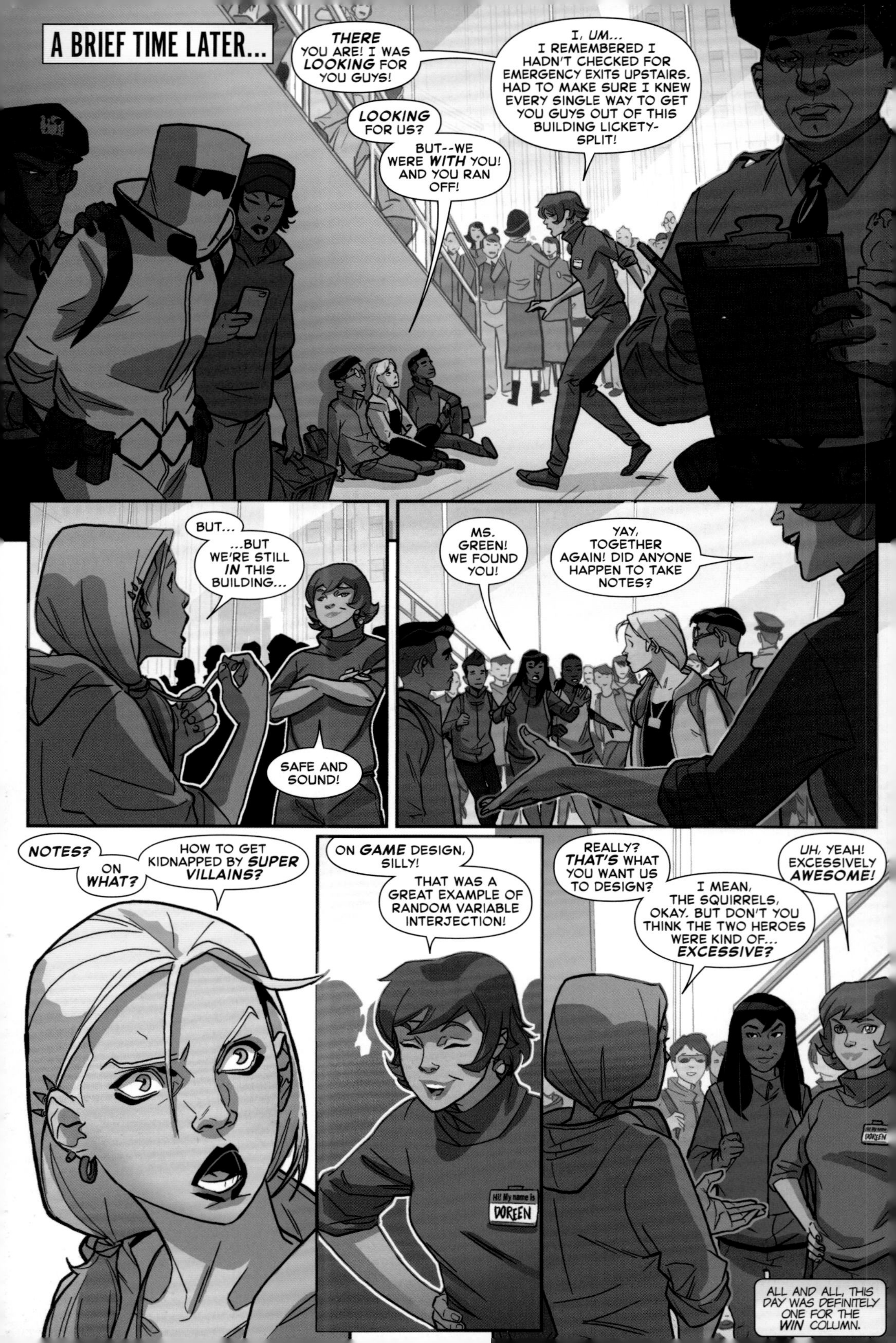
A BRIEF TIME LATER...
THERE YOU ARE! I WAS LOOKING FOR YOU GUYS!
I, UM... I REMEMBERED I HADN'T CHECKED FOR EMERGENCY EXITS UPSTAIRS. HAD TO MAKE SURE I KNEW EVERY SINGLE WAY TO GET YOU GUYS OUT OF THIS BUILDING LICKETY-SPLIT!
LOOKING FOR US?
BUT--WE WERE WITH YOU! AND YOU RAN OFF!
BUT...
...BUT WE'RE STILL IN THIS BUILDING...
SAFE AND SOUND!
MS. GREEN! WE FOUND YOU!
YAY, TOGETHER AGAIN! DID ANYONE HAPPEN TO TAKE NOTES?
NOTES?
ON WHAT?
HOW TO GET KIDNAPPED BY SUPER VILLAINS?
ON GAME DESIGN, SILLY!
THAT WAS A GREAT EXAMPLE OF RANDOM VARIABLE INTERJECTION!
HI! My name is DOREEN
REALLY? THAT'S WHAT YOU WANT US TO DESIGN?
I MEAN, THE SQUIRRELS, OKAY. BUT DON'T YOU THINK THE TWO HEROES WERE KIND OF... EXCESSIVE?
UH, YEAH! EXCESSIVELY AWESOME!
ALL AND ALL, THIS DAY WAS DEFINITELY ONE FOR THE WIN COLUMN.

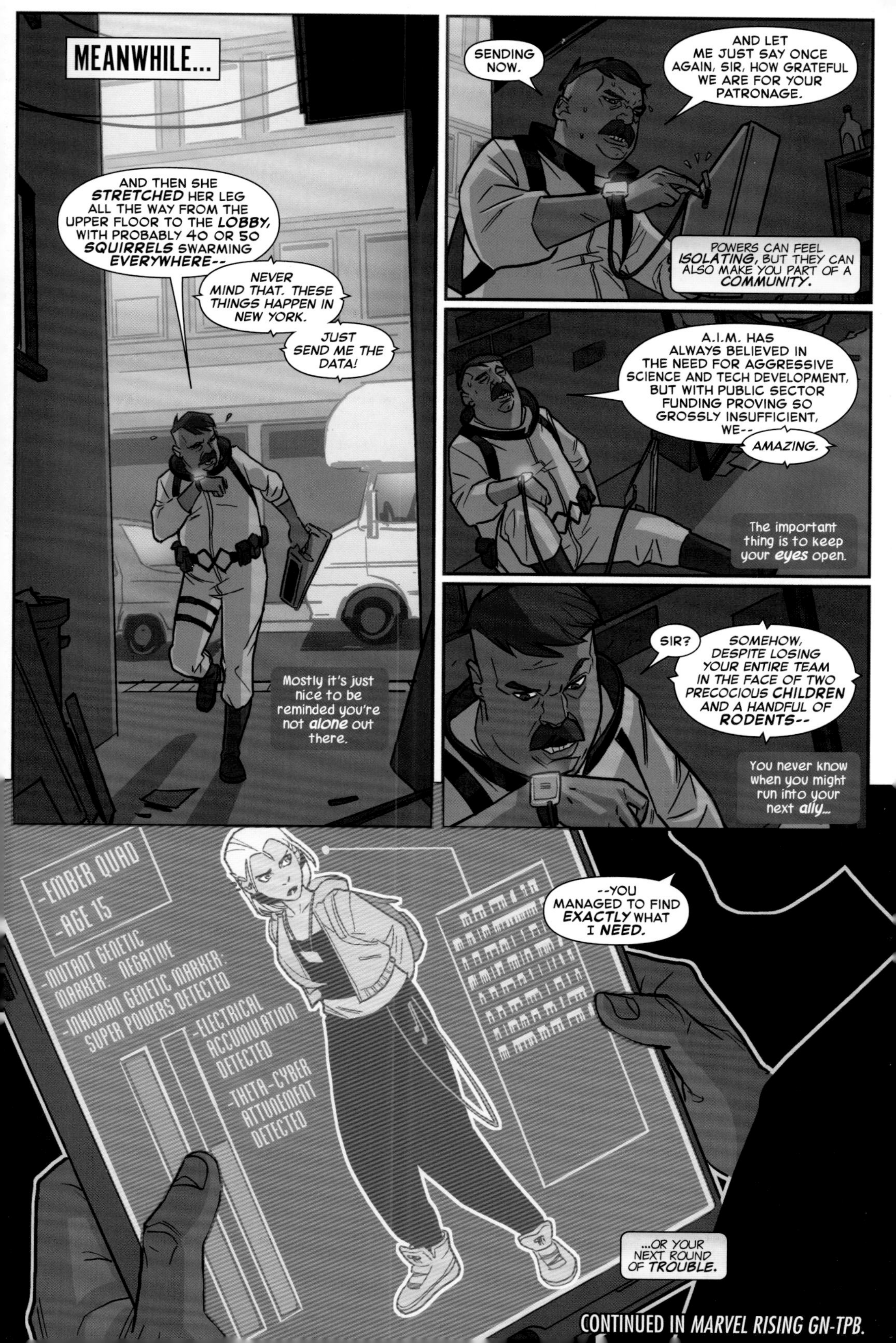
MEANWHILE...
AND THEN SHE STRETCHED HER LEG ALL THE WAY FROM THE UPPER FLOOR TO THE LOBBY, WITH PROBABLY 40 OR 50 SQUIRRELS SWARMING EVERYWHERE--
NEVER MIND THAT. THESE THINGS HAPPEN IN NEW YORK.
JUST SEND ME THE DATA!
Mostly it's just nice to be reminded you're not alone out there.
SENDING NOW.
AND LET ME JUST SAY ONCE AGAIN, SIR, HOW GRATEFUL WE ARE FOR YOUR PATRONAGE.
POWERS CAN FEEL ISOLATING, BUT THEY CAN ALSO MAKE YOU PART OF A COMMUNITY.
A.I.M. HAS ALWAYS BELIEVED IN THE NEED FOR AGGRESSIVE SCIENCE AND TECH DEVELOPMENT, BUT WITH PUBLIC SECTOR FUNDING PROVING SO GROSSLY INSUFFICIENT, WE--
AMAZING.
The important thing is to keep your eyes open.
SIR?
SOMEHOW, DESPITE LOSING YOUR ENTIRE TEAM IN THE FACE OF TWO PRECOCIOUS CHILDREN AND A HANDFUL OF RODENTS--
You never know when you might run into your next ally...
-EMBER QUAD
-AGE 15
-MUTANT GENETIC MARKER: NEGATIVE
-INHUMAN GENETIC MARKER: SUPER POWERS DETECTED
-ELECTRICAL ACCUMULATION DETECTED
-THETA-CYBER ATTUNEMENT DETECTED
--YOU MANAGED TO FIND EXACTLY WHAT I NEED.
...OR YOUR NEXT ROUND OF TROUBLE.
CONTINUED IN MARVEL RISING GN-TPB.

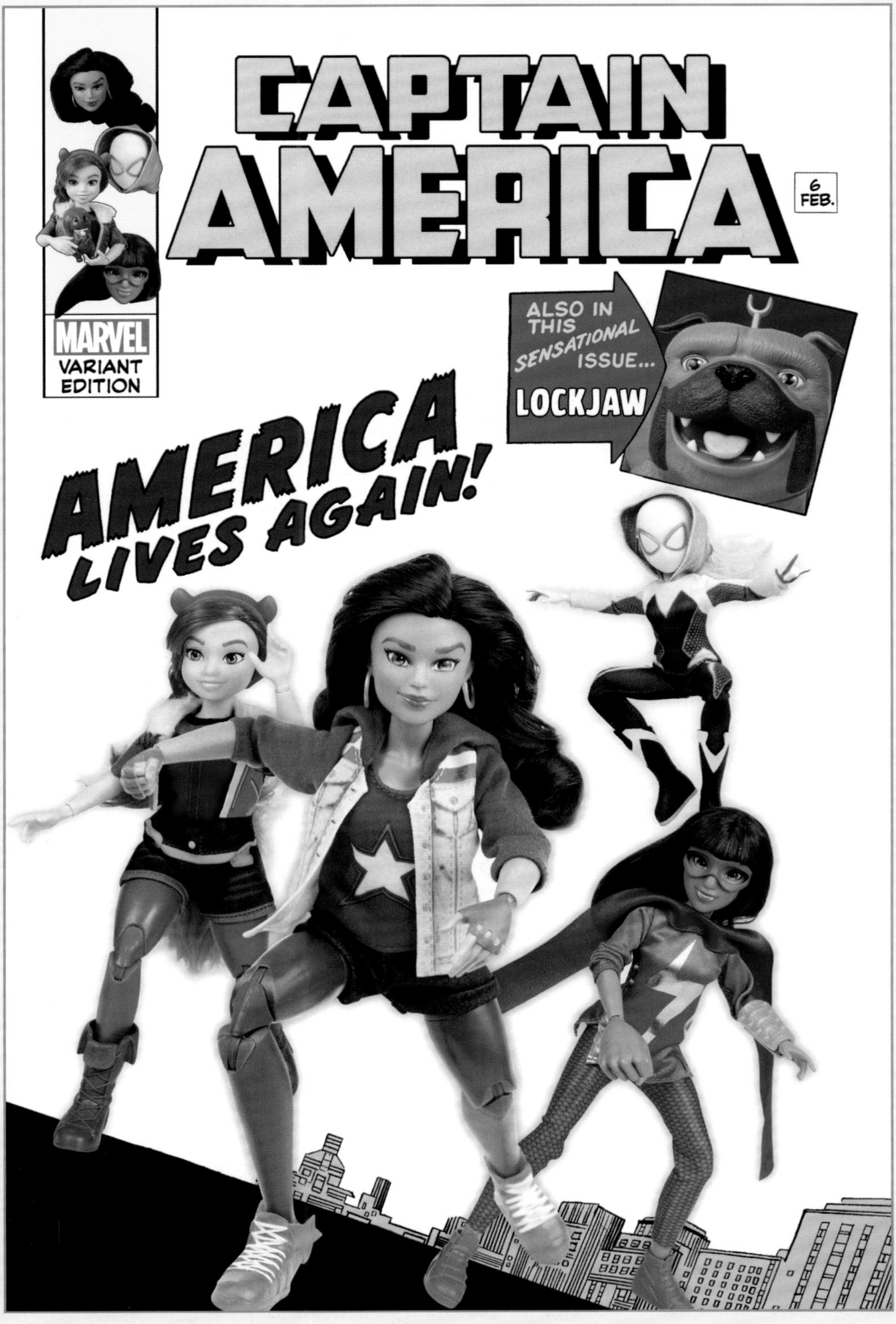
CAPTAIN AMERICA
6 FEB.
MARVEL
VARIANT EDITION
ALSO IN THIS SENSATIONAL ISSUE...
LOCKJAW
AMERICA LIVES AGAIN!

CAPTAIN AMERICA #6 MARVEL RISING ACTION DOLL VARIANT

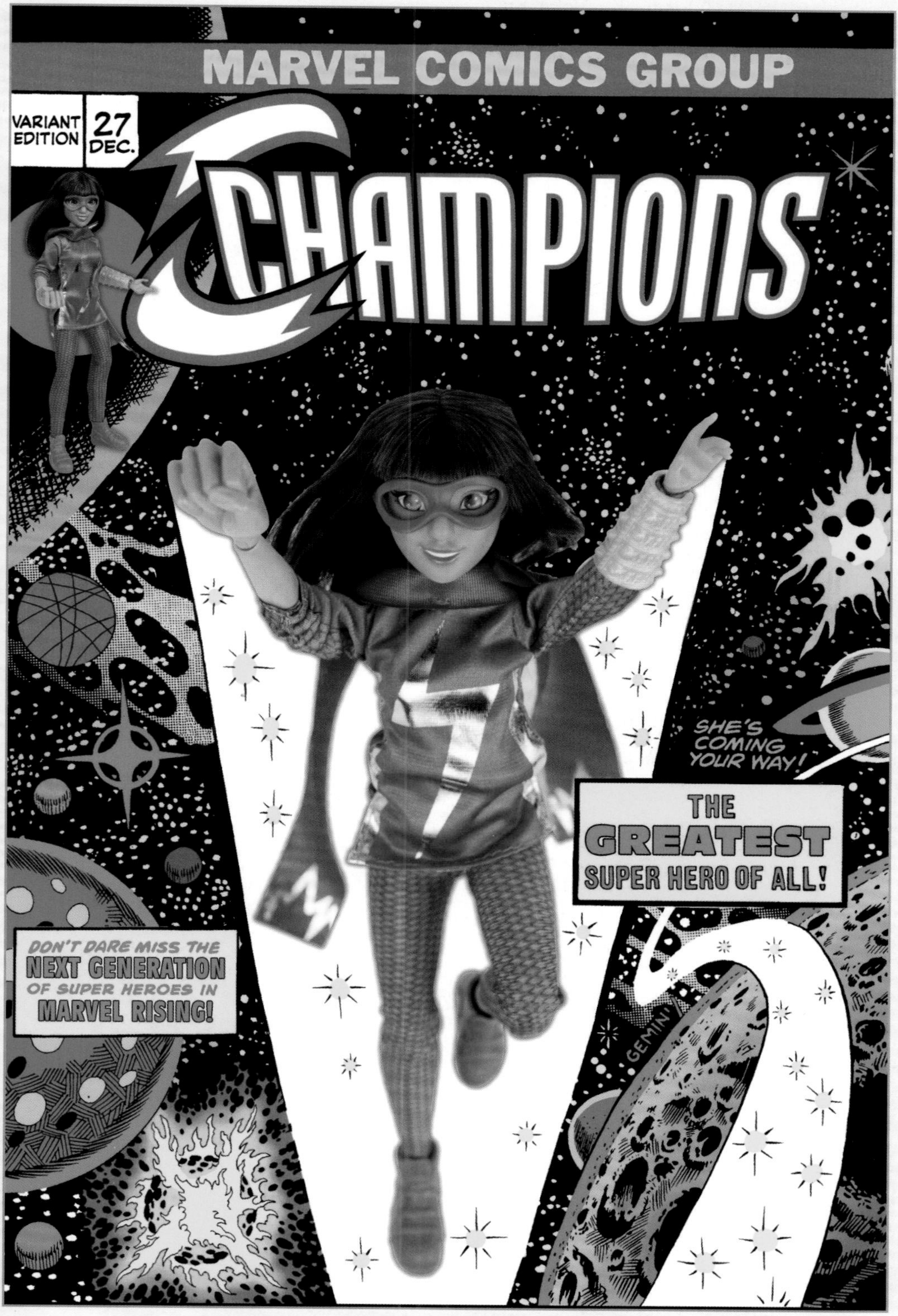
MARVEL COMICS GROUP
VARIANT EDITION
27 DEC.
CHAMPIONS
SHE'S COMING YOUR WAY!
THE GREATEST SUPER HERO OF ALL!
DON'T DARE MISS THE NEXT GENERATION OF SUPER HEROES IN MARVEL RISING!
GEMINI

CHAMPIONS #27 MARVEL RISING ACTION DOLL VARIANT

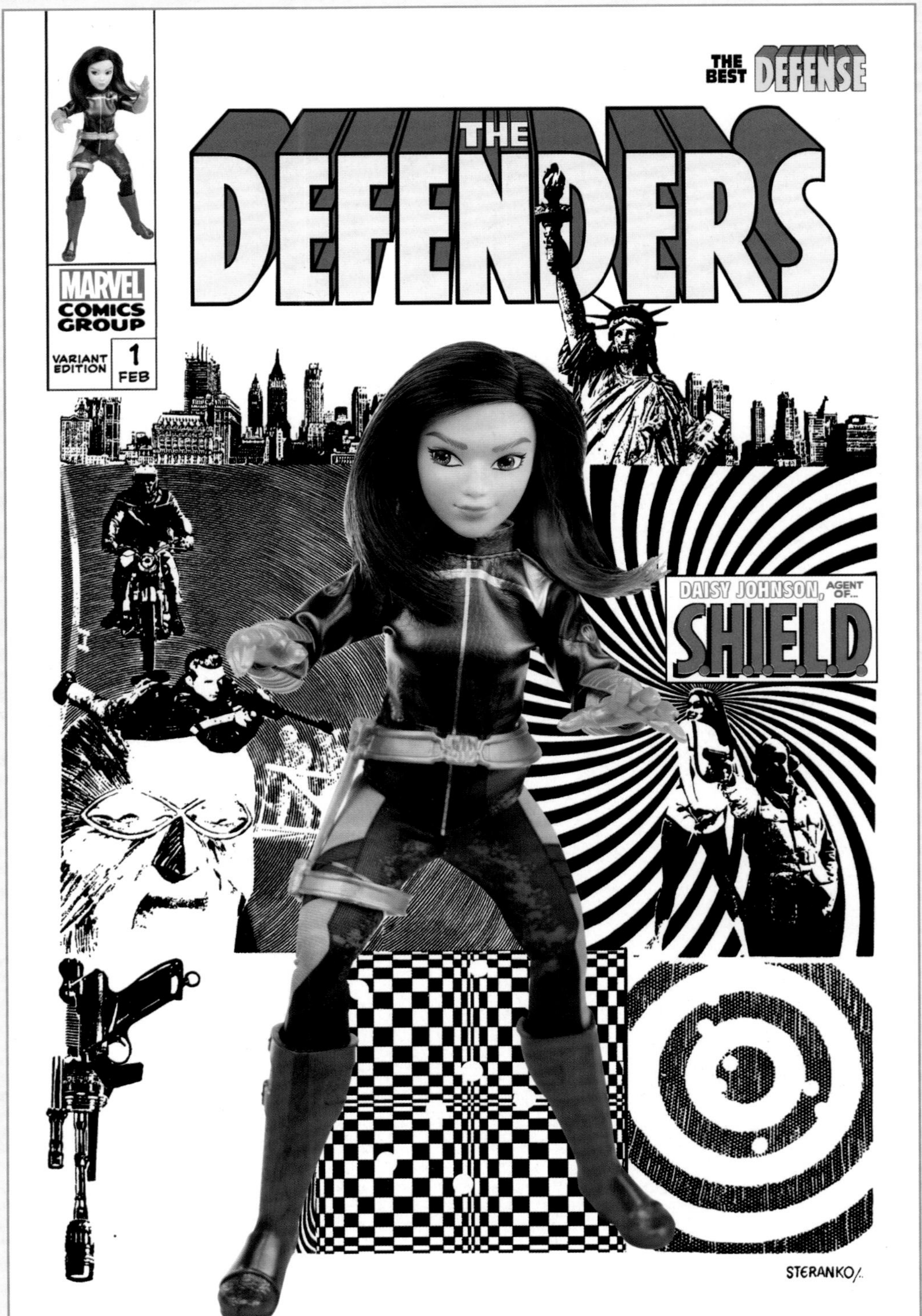
THE BEST DEFENSE
THE DEFENDERS
MARVEL COMICS GROUP
VARIANT EDITION
1
FEB
DAISY JOHNSON, AGENT OF...
S.H.I.E.L.D.
STERANKO/..

DEFENDERS: THE BEST DEFENSE #1 MARVEL RISING ACTION DOLL VARIANT